SelectEditions

SELECTED AND EDITED

SelectEditions

BY READER'S DIGEST

THE READER'S DIGEST ASSOCIATION, INC.
MONTREAL • PLEASANTVILLE, NEW YORK

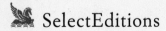 SelectEditions

Vice President, Books & Home Entertainment: Deirdre Gilbert

INTERNATIONAL EDITIONS
Executive Editor: Gary Q. Arpin
Senior Editor: Bonnie Grande

CONTENTS

Sandra Brown

Envy

Envy is a crippling passion.
It can lead to an island of grief...
Or an ocean of deep desire.

Prologue

Envy, Key West, Florida, 1988

Saltines and sardines. Staples of his diet. Add a chunk of rat cheese and a kosher dill spear, and you had yourself the four basic food groups. There simply wasn't any finer fare.

That was the unshakable opinion of Hatch Walker, who had a sunbaked, wind-scoured visage that only a mother gargoyle could love. As he munched his supper, eyes that had blinked against the sting of countless squalls squinted narrowly at the horizon.

He was on the lookout for the lightning flashes that would signal an approaching storm. There was still no sign of it here onshore, but it was out there somewhere. Above the harbor a quarter moon hung in a clear sky. Stars defied the neon glare on the ground. But Hatch wasn't fooled. He could feel impending meteorological change in his bones. There'd be rain before dawn.

His nicotine-stained teeth crunched into his pickle, and he savored the garlicky brine, which he chased with a bite of cheese. It just didn't get any better.

This being a weeknight, the streets were relatively quiet. Tourist season was on the wane. Thank the good Lord for small favors, Hatch thought as he swigged at his can of Pepsi and belched around a harrumph of scorn for tourists in general and those who flocked to Key West in particular. Hatch had nothing but contempt for the fools who worked themselves into early coronaries for fifty weeks a year so that for the remaining two they could work doubly hard at having a good time.

Unfortunately, his livelihood depended on them.

Walker's Marine Charters and Rentals got a share of the money the vacationers spent during their noisy occupation of his town. He equipped them with scuba and snorkeling gear, leased them boats, and took them on deep-sea fishing expeditions so they could return to shore and have their grinning, sunburned mugs photographed with a noble fish.

Business wasn't exactly thriving tonight. The water in the marina was as still as a lake. Shore lights were mirrored on the surface with hardly a waver. Occasionally a mast would creak aboard a sailboat or music would waft from one of the waterfront nightclubs. Otherwise it was quiet, and even though it meant a lean week financially speaking, Hatch preferred it this way.

He might have closed up shop and gone home early, except for that one boat he had out. He'd leased the twenty-five-footer to some kids, if you could rightly call twentysomethings kids. Compared to him, they were. Two men, one woman, which in Hatch's estimation was a volatile combination under any circumstances.

The kids were tan and lean, attractive, and self-assured to the point of cockiness. They were already half lit when they boarded the craft just before sunset, and they'd carried a couple of ice chests on board with them. No fishing gear. They were going offshore strictly for a few hours of drinking and debauchery, or his name wasn't Hatch Walker. He had debated whether or not to lease a craft to them, but his near-empty till served to persuade him that they were not flat-out drunk.

He'd sternly ordered the men not to drink while operating his boat. They flashed him insincere smiles and assured him that such wasn't their intention. One bowed at the waist. The other saluted him crisply and said, "Aye, aye, sir!"

As Hatch helped the young woman into the boat, he hoped she

knew what she was in for. But he figured she did. He'd seen her around. Lots of times. With lots of men. An eye patch would have covered more skin than her bikini bottom, and she might just as well not have bothered wearing the top.

And she didn't for long. Before they were even out of the marina, one of the men snatched off her top and waved it above his head like a victory banner. Her attempts to get it back turned into a game of slap and tickle.

Watching this as the boat chugged out of the marina, Hatch shook his head and counted himself lucky that he'd never had a daughter with a virtue to protect.

FINALLY one last sardine remained in the tin. Hatch pinched it out of the oil, laid it diagonally across a saltine, added the last bite of pickle and sliver of cheese, stacked another cracker on top, and put the whole thing in his mouth. Chewing with contentment, he happened to glance toward the entrance of the harbor. What he saw caused the sandwich to stick in his throat as he forced it down, muttering, "What the hell does he think he's doin'?"

No sooner had Hatch spoken his thought aloud than a long blast from the approaching boat's horn nearly knocked him off his stool. By the time the sardine sandwich hit his stomach, he was out the door of the weather-beaten shack that housed his charter service and angrily lumbering down the quay, shouting at the boat's pilot that he was coming into the marina way too fast.

Then Hatch recognized the boat as his. His! The fool was abusing his boat—the finest and biggest in his fleet!

Hatch fired a volley of expletives, wicked holdovers from his years as a merchant marine. When he got his hands on those kids, they'd regret the day their daddies spawned them. He might be old and ugly, but he could hold his own with a couple of pretty beachboys.

Even after the boat cleared the buoys, it didn't slow down. It kept coming. It missed a forty-two-foot sailboat by inches and set it rocking. A dinghy slammed into the side of a multimillion-dollar yacht, and the folks sipping nightcaps on the yacht's polished deck rushed to the rail and shouted down at the careless mariner.

Hatch shook his fist at the young man at the wheel. The drunken fool was steering straight for the pier, kamikaze-like, when he suddenly cut the engine and spun the wheel sharply to port. The outboard sent up a rooster tail of spume.

Hatch had barely a second to leap out of the way before the boat crashed into the quay. The young man clambered down the steps of the cockpit and across the slippery deck, leaped onto the pier, tripped over a cleat, then crawled a few feet forward on all fours.

Hatch bore down on him, grabbed him by the shoulder, and flipped him over, as he would a fish he was about to gut. Luckily, he was armed only with a litany of curses and threats.

But they sputtered and died, now that he saw the boy's face was bloody. His left eye was swollen practically shut. His T-shirt was in shreds, clinging to his lean torso like a wet rag.

"Help me. Oh, God." He threw Hatch's hand off his shoulder and scrambled to his feet. "They're out there," he said, frantically motioning toward the open sea. "They're in the ocean. I couldn't find them. They . . . they . . ."

Hatch recognized the wild panic in the young man's eyes. This was no prank, no drunken escapade. The kid—the one who'd smartly saluted him earlier—was in distress to the point of hysteria.

"Calm down, sonny." Hatch took him by the shoulders and shook him. "What happened? Where are your friends at?"

The young man covered his face with hands that, Hatch noticed, were bruised. He sobbed uncontrollably. "In the water."

"Overboard?"

"Yeah. Oh, God."

A man wearing flip-flops came slapping up. "That kid nearly wrecked my yacht! What the hell was he doing?" He was wearing only a Speedo swimsuit beneath an overhanging belly covered with black, curly hair. He had a thick gold bracelet on his right wrist and spoke with a nasally northeastern accent.

"The boy's hurt. There's been an accident."

"Accident, my ass. He put a big dent in the *Dinky Doo*." They'd been joined by the man's female companion, who was dressed in a bikini and a pair of high heels. Her tan was store-bought. Under each arm she was holding a toy poodle.

"Call 911," Hatch said.

"I want to know what this—"

"Call 911!"

THE interior of Hatch's "office" smelled of sardines, damp hemp, dead fish, and motor oil. The kid who'd crashed his boat had heaved twice into his toilet, but Hatch figured the nausea was more from nerves and fear than from the shot of brandy he'd sneaked him when no one was looking.

Of course, the kid had had a lot to drink prior to the brandy. He'd admitted as much to the coast guard officer who was currently questioning him. Key West police had had their turn at interrogating him about crashing the boat into the marina. He was then turned over to the coast guard officer, who wanted to know what had happened on board that had caused his two companions to wind up in the Atlantic. The coast guard had organized a search-and-rescue party.

It was clear that the kid was on the brink of total breakdown. He was still wearing wet swim trunks and sneakers that leaked seawater onto the rough plank flooring. Hatch had thrown a blanket over him, but the kid had since discarded it, along with his tattered T-shirt. He looked hopefully toward the door.

The coast guard officer, helping himself to Hatch's coffeepot, correctly read the kid's expression. "You'll know something as soon as we do, son."

"They've got to be alive." His voice sounded like someone who'd been outyelling a storm: Every now and then, it would crack over a word. "I just couldn't find them in the dark." His eyes bounced back and forth between Hatch and the officer. "I called and called, but . . . Why weren't they answering? Unless they . . ." He was unable to say out loud what they all feared.

The officer cradled his coffee mug between his palms and swirled the contents. "How come you didn't use the radio to call for help?"

"I did. I mean, I tried. I couldn't get it to work."

"Coupla other boats heard your SOS. Tried to tell you to stay right where you were at. You didn't."

"I didn't hear them." He glanced across at Hatch. "I guess I didn't pay much attention when he was showing us how to operate the radio."

"Costly mistake. Tell me about the fight."

"Fight?"

This drew a frown from the officer. "Son, your eye's all but swollen shut. You've got a bloody nose and busted lip. Your knuckles are scraped and bruised. I know what a fistfight looks like, okay? So don't play games with me."

The young man's shoulders began to shake. His eyes streamed, but he didn't even bother trying to stem the tears.

"Was it over the girl?" the officer asked in a gentler voice. "You and your buddy fight over her favors?"

"No, sir. Not . . . not exactly. She wasn't the reason it started."

"Then what was?"

"We were drunk. And . . . and . . ." The kid looked over at Hatch, then back at the officer, and said earnestly, "He's my best friend." He licked his upper lip. "He got mad. Mad as hell. I've never seen him like that. Like he snapped or something."

"What'd you do to cause him to snap?"

"Nothing! One minute he's down below with her. Next minute he's back up on deck, coming at me."

"For no reason? Just like that?"

The kid's head wobbled up and down. "It was supposed to be a party. A celebration. I swear to God, I don't understand how it went to hell so quick." He lowered his battered face into his hands and began to sob.

The officer looked at Hatch as though for consultation, then turned back to the young man. "Best friends don't fight for no reason. Not even when they've had too much to drink. So tell me, what caused your friend to get mad enough to start beating up on you?"

Silence stretched out for about twenty seconds; then the kid mumbled a single word.

Hatch wasn't sure he'd heard correctly, mainly because the first clap of thunder from his predicted storm rattled the small square window in the shack just as the boy spoke.

The officer leaned forward to hear better. "Speak up, son."

The young man raised his head. He cleared his throat. He blinked the officer into focus with his one functioning eye. "Envy," he said gruffly. "That's what this is all about. Envy."

P.M.E.

St. Anne Island, Georgia

Chapter One

"BUT there's got to be." Maris Matherly-Reed impatiently tapped her pencil against the notepad on which she had doodled a chain of loops. Below those she'd rough-sketched an idea for a book jacket.

"I'm sorry, ma'am," the operator replied. "There's no such listing. I double-checked."

"You don't have a listing for P.M.E. in this area code?"

"In any area code. I've accessed the entire U.S."

"Maybe it's a business listing, not residential."

"I checked both. I don't have anything under those initials, period. If you had a last name—"

"But I don't. Thank you for trying."

Frustrated, Maris thought about the prologue of *Envy* she had read that afternoon. She had discovered it among a stack of unsolicited manuscripts collecting dust until that unspecified day when her schedule permitted her to scan them. Before sending the anxious authors the standard rejection letter, she felt that each writer deserved at least a few minutes of her time. And there was always that one-in-a-million chance that the next Steinbeck or Faulkner or

Hemingway would be mined from the slush pile. That, of course, was every book editor's pipe dream.

Maris would settle for finding a bestseller. These fifteen pages of prologue had definite promise. They had excited Maris more than anything she had read recently, even material from her portfolio of published authors.

It had piqued her curiosity, as a prologue or first chapter should. She was hooked, eager to know more. Had the rest of the story been written? she wondered. Or at least outlined? Was this the author's first attempt at fiction writing? What were his/her credentials?

There was nothing to indicate the writer's gender, although her gut feeling said male. Hatch Walker's internal dialogue rang true and read like the language in which a man would think. But the pages had been sent by someone untutored in how to submit a manuscript to a prospective publisher. It lacked a cover letter. There was no phone number, street address, or e-mail address—only those three initials and the name of an island Maris had never heard of. How did the writer hope to sell his manuscript if he couldn't be contacted?

She noticed that the postmark on the mailing envelope was four months old. If the author had submitted the prologue to several publishers simultaneously, it might have already been bought. All the more reason to locate the writer as soon as possible.

"You're not ready?"

Noah appeared in her open office door wearing his Armani tuxedo. Maris said, "My, don't you look handsome." Glancing at her desk clock, she realized that she had lost all track of time and that she was indeed running late. Raking her fingers through her wheat-colored hair, she gave a short, self-deprecating laugh. "I, on the other hand, am going to require some major renovation."

Her husband of twenty-two months closed the door behind him and advanced into her corner office. He tossed a trade magazine onto her desk, then moved behind her chair and began massaging her neck and shoulders. "Tough day?"

"Not bad, actually. Mostly I've used today to clear some space in here." She gestured toward the pile of rejected manuscripts.

"You've been reading the stuff in your slush pile? Maris, really," he chided lightly. "Why bother? It's a Matherly Press policy not to buy anything that isn't submitted by an agent."

"But since I'm a Matherly, I can bend the rules."

"I'm married to an anarchist," he teased, bending down to kiss the side of her neck. "But if you're planning an insurrection, couldn't your cause be something that streamlines our operation instead of one that consumes the valuable time of our publisher and senior vice president? Why bother with the slush pile when even our most junior editors don't?"

"Because my father taught me to honor anyone who attempted to write. The effort alone deserves some consideration."

"Far be it from me to dispute the venerable Daniel Matherly."

Despite Noah's mild reproof, Maris intended to continue the practice of going through the slush pile. Even if it was a time-consuming and unproductive task, it was one of the principles upon which a Matherly had founded the publishing house over a century ago. Maris firmly believed that her family's respect for the written word and for writers had been fundamental to the house's success.

"I got an advance copy of the article," Noah said.

She picked up the magazine he'd carried in with him. A Post-it marked a specific page. Turning to it, she said, "Ah, great photo." Then she read aloud: " 'Noah Reed is forty but could pass for much younger. Daily workouts in the Matherly Press gym—one of Reed's innovations when he joined the firm three years ago—keep all six feet of him lean and supple.' Well, this writer is certainly enamored. Did you ever have a thing with her?"

He chuckled. "Absolutely not."

"She's one of the few."

On their wedding day Maris had teasingly remarked to him that so many single women were mourning the loss of one of the city's most eligible bachelors, she was surprised that the doors of St. Patrick's Cathedral weren't draped in black crepe. "Does she get around to mentioning your business acumen and the contributions you've made to Matherly Press?"

"Farther down."

"Let's see. 'Graying at the temples, which adds to his distinguished good looks.' And so on and so forth. Oh, here's something. 'He shares the helm at Matherly Press with his father-in-law, publishing legend Daniel Matherly, who serves as chairman and CEO, and with his wife, Maris Matherly-Reed, who, he claims, has perfect selection and editorial skills. He modestly credits her with the company's reputation for publishing bestsellers.' " Pleased, she smiled up at him. "Did you say that?"

"And more that she didn't include."

Maris read the remainder of the flattering article, then set the magazine aside. "Very nice. But for all her gaga-ness, she overlooked two major biographical points."

"And they are?"

"That you're also an excellent writer."

"*The Vanquished* is old news," he said in the brusque tone he used whenever she brought up his one and only published novel. "What's the second thing?"

"She said nothing about your marvelous massage techniques." Closing her eyes, Maris tilted her head to one side. "A little lower on your . . . Ahh. There." The tension began to dissolve.

"You're in knots," he said. "Serves you right for scavenging through that heap of garbage all day."

"As it turns out, it might not have been time wasted. I actually found something that sparked my interest."

"I want to hear all about it, darling. But you really should shake a leg if we're going to get there in time." He dropped a kiss on the top of her head, then tried to withdraw.

But Maris reached for his hands and pulled them over her shoulders, holding them flattened against her chest. "Is tonight mandatory?" she asked. "We could miss one function, couldn't we? Dad begged off tonight."

"That's why we should be there. Matherly Press bought a table. Two more empty seats would be noticeable. One of our authors is receiving an award."

"His agent and editor are attending with him. Let's call in sick. Go home and shut out the world. Open a bottle of wine. Make love in some room other than the bedroom. Maybe even two rooms."

Laughing, he pulled his hands from beneath hers and headed for the door.

Maris groaned with disappointment. "I thought I was making you an offer you couldn't refuse."

"Tempting. Very. But if we're not at this dinner, it'll arouse suspicion. We have professional responsibilities."

"And that's why we attend nearly every publishing event held in New York," she said.

"Precisely." Noah believed it was extremely important, virtually compulsory, that they be seen as active participants within literary circles, especially since her father could no longer be involved to the extent he once had been.

Recently Daniel Matherly had slowed down. For more than four decades he had been a force to be reckoned with. His name had become synonymous with book publishing. He had been a juggernaut who, over a period of months, had voluntarily been decreasing his momentum.

Noah checked his watch. "How much time do you need?"

Maris sighed with resignation. "Give me twenty minutes."

"I'll be generous. Take thirty." He blew her a kiss before leaving.

But Maris didn't plunge into her overhaul right away. Instead she asked her assistant to place a call. She'd had another idea on how she might track down the author of *Envy*.

While waiting for the call, she gazed out her floor-to-ceiling office windows. Midtown Manhattan was experiencing a mild summer evening. The sun had slipped behind the skyscrapers, casting a premature twilight on the streets below. Lights were coming on inside buildings, making the brick and granite structures appear to twinkle.

The telephone beeped. Maris depressed the blinking button. "Hello?"

"Yeah. Deputy Dwight Harris here."

"Hello, Deputy Harris. Thank you for taking my call. My name is Maris Matherly-Reed." She went straight to the reason for the call. "I'm trying to reach an individual who I believe lives on St. Anne Island."

"That's in our county."

"Is St. Anne actually an island?"

"Not much o' one, ma'am. What I mean is, it's small. About two miles out from the mainland. Who're you looking for?"

"Someone with the initials P.M.E. Have you ever heard of anyone who goes by those initials?"

"Can't say that I have, ma'am. A man or a woman?"

"Unfortunately, I don't know."

"What do you want with 'em?"

"It's business."

"Business, huh."

Dead end. This was going nowhere, and her allotted time was running out. "Well, thank you for your time, Deputy Harris. Would you mind taking down my name and numbers? Then if you think of someone with these initials, I would appreciate being notified."

"Okay," he said. "Sorry I couldn't he'p you."

After she gave him her telephone numbers, she thanked him again, then closed her office and hurried down the hallway to the ladies' room, where her cocktail dress had been hanging since she'd arrived for work early that morning and where she kept a full complement of toiletries and cosmetics in a locker. She changed from business to evening attire. When she joined Noah at the elevator fifteen minutes later, he gave a long wolf whistle. "You look fantastic."

As they descended to street level, she assessed her reflection in the metal elevator door. She'd chosen to wear a cranberry-colored silk sheath with narrow straps and a scooped neckline. Her nod toward evening glitter came in the form of diamond studs in her ears and a crystal-encrusted Judith Leiber handbag in the shape of a butterfly. She was carrying a pashmina shawl purchased in Paris during a side trip there following the international book fair in Frankfurt, Germany.

She had gathered her shoulder-length hair into a sleek, low ponytail. The hairdo looked chic and sophisticated rather than desperate, which had been the case. She had retouched her eye makeup, outlined her lips with a pencil, and filled them in with gloss. To give color to her fluorescent-light pallor, she had applied powdered bronzer to her cheeks, chin, forehead, and décolletage. Her push-up bra, an engineering marvel, had created a flattering cleavage that filled up the neckline of her dress.

" 'Her tan was store-bought.' "

The elevator doors opened onto the ground floor. Noah looked at her curiously as he stepped aside to let her exit ahead of him. "I beg your pardon?"

She laughed. "Nothing. Just quoting something I read today."

ALTHOUGH it had stopped raining a half hour earlier, the air was so moisture-laden, the rainwater couldn't evaporate. It collected in puddles and beaded on flowers' petals. Deputy Dwight Harris alighted from the golf cart he had borrowed at the St. Anne landing. Before starting up the pathway to the house, he paused, telling himself he needed to get his bearings, when what he was actually doing was second-guessing his decision to come here alone after sundown. He didn't quite know what to expect.

He'd never been here before, although he knew about this house. Anybody who was ever on St. Anne Island had heard stories about the plantation house at the easternmost tip of the island. Some of the tales he'd heard stretched credibility, but the descriptions of the house were accurate.

Typical of colonial low-country architecture, the two-story white frame house was sitting on top of an aged brick basement. Six broad steps led to the deep veranda that extended across the front and wrapped around both sides. The front door had been painted a glossy black, as had the hurricane shutters. Six smooth columns supported the second-floor balcony. Twin chimneys acted like bookends against the steeply pitched roof. The house looked pretty much like Deputy Harris had imagined it would. He hadn't counted on it looking so spooky, is all.

Dodging puddles, he made his way up the crushed-shell path, which was lined by twin rows of live oaks. Spanish moss hung from the branches. The roots of the ancient trees snaked along the ground, some of them as thick as a fat man's thigh.

Altogether, it was an impressive front entry. Majestic, you might say. The back of the house, Harris knew, overlooked the Atlantic.

The house hadn't started out this grand. The four original rooms had been built more than two centuries before by the planter who'd bought the island. The house had expanded with the plantation's success, first with indigo and sugarcane, then with cotton.

Around the beginning of the twentieth century the boll weevil ruined the cotton crop and crushed the local economy. A descendant of the plantation's original owner had correctly forecast his economic doom and hanged himself from the dining-room chandelier. The rest of the family stole off the island in the middle of the night, leaving debts and unpaid taxes.

Decades passed. The house remained in ruin until a little over a year ago, when an outsider bought it and commenced a massive renovation. But in Harris's opinion there was still a lot to be done. Legend had it that the hanged man's ghost still resided in the old house and that the dining-room chandelier swung from the ceiling for no reason that anybody could detect. Harris didn't put much stock in ghost stories. Even so, he would have welcomed a little more illumination as he mounted the steps, crossed the veranda, and approached the front door.

He tapped the brass knocker tentatively, then harder. Seconds ticked by as ponderously as the rain dripping from the eaves. Harris considered leaving, but then the front door was pulled open from the inside, though not by much.

The voice sounded pleasant enough. "Yes?"

Harris peered into the shadows. "Evenin', sir. I'm Deputy Dwight Harris. From the sheriff's office over in Savannah."

The man leaned forward and glanced past him toward the golf cart parked at the end of the path. To discourage tourism to the island, there wasn't a ferry to St. Anne from the mainland. Visitors came by a boat they either owned or chartered. When they arrived, they rented a golf cart to get around the island's nine thousand acres.

The man behind the door asked, "How can I help you?"

"First off, I apologize for disturbing you. But I got a call earlier this evening from a gal up in New York. Said she was trying to track down somebody who goes by the initials P.M.E." A long silence ensued. Harris cleared his throat nervously. "So anyhow, I thought I should oblige this lady. Came over in the department's motor launch. Asked around at the landing and was directed here."

"What did this lady from New York want?"

"Well, sir, I don't rightly know. Just that she had business with P.M.E. I thought you might be a big winner in one of those sweepstakes." Harris tipped his hat forward so he could scratch the back of his head. Then he bluntly asked, "You P.M.E., or what?"

"Did she leave her name?"

"Yeah." Harris fished a piece of notepaper from the breast pocket of his uniform shirt. "Those're her phone numbers. All of 'em. So I figured this business of hers must be pretty important. That's why I came on out tonight."

The man took the sheet. "Thank you very much for your trouble."

Then, before Harris could blink, the door closed in his face. "Good evenin' to you, too," he mouthed as he turned away.

Chapter Two

"JUST one more picture please, Mr. and Mrs. Reed?"

Maris and Noah smiled for the photographer who was covering the literary-awards banquet for *Publishers Weekly*. The event had concluded. As promised, the photographer snapped one last picture, then scuttled off. As Maris and Noah crossed the elegant lobby of the Palace Hotel, she sighed. "At last. I can't wait to get into my jammies."

"One drink at Le Cirque, and we'll say our good-nights. Nadia invited us to join her and one of the award recipients for a drink."

Maris disliked Nadia Schuller intensely. The book critic was meddlesome and pushy, always roping Noah into a commitment from which there was no graceful way out. Her Book Chat column was syndicated in major newspapers and carried a lot of weight. Authors and publishers couldn't afford to offend her, or they risked their next book being slammed in her column.

"Please, Noah. Can't we just go home?" Maris took a step closer. "Those jammies I mentioned? They can be dispensed with."

"Tell you what. Let's compromise. I think this might be an important meeting. I'll tell Nadia you have a headache or an early breakfast appointment tomorrow. Have the driver take you home. After one drink I'll follow you. Half an hour, max. I promise."

"Noah? We're waiting." Nadia Schuller approached them, her phony smile in place. Her arm was linked with that of a best-selling novelist, who looked dazed. Or stoned, if the gossip about him was true. Or maybe he was only dizzy from being propelled by the turbo engines of Nadia's personality.

"They won't hold our table forever, Noah. Coming?"

"Well . . ." He hesitated and glanced down at Maris.

"What's the matter?" Nadia asked in a voice as piercing as a dentist's drill. She addressed the question to Maris, automatically assuming that she was the source of the problem.

"Nothing's the matter, Nadia. Noah and I were having a private conversation."

"Oh, my. Have I interrupted one of those husband-wife things?"

The critic could have been pretty if not for her edge. She was always impeccably dressed, but even arrayed in fine silk and finer jewelry, there was nothing feminine about her. It was rumored that she went through men like a box of Godivas, spitting out the ones who didn't challenge her or who could do nothing to further her career—the ones with soft centers. Maris had no problem believing the gossip about Nadia's promiscuity. What surprised her was the number of men who found Nadia sexually appealing.

"Yes, we were having a husband and wife *thing*. I was telling Noah that the last thing I want to do is join you for a round of drinks," Maris said, smiling sweetly.

"You do look tired," Nadia returned, her smile just as sweet.

Noah intervened. "I'm sorry, Nadia. We must decline tonight. I'm going to take my wife home and tuck her in."

"No, darling," Maris said. She wouldn't play the wounded wife in front of Nadia Schuller. "You stay. I'll see myself home."

"Then it's settled. You two say your good-byes while we go claim the table." Nadia gave the writer's arm a sharp tug. To Maris she called back airily, "Get some rest, dear."

PARKER Evans stared out the window into nothingness. He couldn't see the shoreline from this vantage point, but if he concentrated, he could hear the surf. Rain clouds obscured the moon. From this first-floor window overlooking the rear of his property, Parker could see across a breast of lawn to the point where it sharply dropped off, before sloping gradually toward the beach—a black void that melded with the ocean farther out.

His six months of waiting had finally paid off. Maris Matherly-Reed was trying to contact him. As recently as yesterday, Parker had come close to scratching his plan. After months of not hearing from her, he figured that she had read the prologue of *Envy*, hated it, and tossed it.

It had also occurred to him that the partial manuscript had never reached her desk. Manuscripts usually got in through literary agents, or they didn't get in at all. In any case, he'd almost convinced himself that this plan was a bust and that it would be necessary to plot another.

That was yesterday. Apparently, the pages *had* made it to her desk and she *had* read them, because today she *had* tried to track him down. From that he deduced her response must be favorable.

But it wasn't yet time to ice down the champagne. Success or failure hinged on what he did next.

So instead of celebrating this milestone, he had stared for hours out this window into the rainy night. While the calm surf swept the shoreline, Parker Evans plotted. It helped that he already knew the ending to this story. Not once did he consider changing the outcome from his original plot. He was committed to seeing it all the way through the denouement. But between here and there he couldn't make a single misstep. Each chapter had to be carefully thought out, with no mistakes allowed. It had to be the perfect plot.

And if his resolve to finish it ever faltered, he had only to remember how long it had taken him to reach this point in the saga: six months. Well . . . six months and fourteen years.

MARIS groped for the ringing telephone. She squinted at the lighted clock on her nightstand: five twenty. In the morning. Who— Then panic brought her wide-awake. Was this that dreaded, inevitable phone call notifying her that her father had suffered a coronary or stroke? Anxiously she clutched the receiver. "Hello?"

"Maris Matherly-Reed?"

"Speaking."

"Where do you get off screwing around with my life?"

"I beg your pardon? Who is this?" She sat up, switched on the lamp, and reached out to rouse Noah. But his side of the bed was empty.

"I don't appreciate you calling the sheriff," the caller said hotly.

Where is Noah? "I'm sorry, I was— Did you say sheriff?"

"Sheriff, *sheriff*. Ring any bells?"

She sucked in a quick breath. "P.M.E.?"

"A deputy came to my house, snooping around."

Maris sensed waves of resentment pushing through the line. After taking a couple of calming breaths, she said, "I read your prologue and liked it. I wanted to talk to you about it, but I had no way of contacting you. You *left* me no way to contact you. So I called the sheriff's office—"

"Send it back. The prologue. Send it back."

"Why?"

"It's crap."

"Far from it, Mr.—"

"I shouldn't have sent it."

"I'm glad you did. These pages intrigue me. If the rest of your book is as good, I'll consider buying it for publication."

"It's not for sale."

"What do you mean?"

"Look, I've got a southern accent, but I'm still speaking English. Which part didn't you understand?"

His voice was geographically distinctive. Usually she found the soft *r*'s and slow drawl of southern regions engaging. But his manner was abrasive. If she hadn't seen real potential in his writing, she would have ended the conversation long before now. Patiently she asked, "If you didn't want your book published, why did you submit the prologue to a book publisher?"

"Because I suffered a mental lapse," he answered, imitating her precise enunciation. "I've since changed my mind."

Maris took another tack. "Did you multiple-submit?"

"Send it to other publishers, you mean? No."

"Why did you send it to me?"

"You know what? Forget sending it back. Toss it in the nearest trash can or line your birdcage with it. I don't care."

Sensing he was about to hang up, she said quickly, "Before you decide against selling your book—a decision I think you'll regret—I'd welcome the chance to give you my professional opinion of it. I promise to be brutally honest. Let me decide if it's good or not. Please send me the entire manuscript."

"You have it. The rest of the story is in my head."

"Oh." That was disappointing. "I urge you to finish it. In the meantime—"

"In the meantime you're running up my long-distance bill. If you don't want to spend any money on return postage, then shred the damn thing. Good-bye. Oh, and don't send any more deputy sheriffs to my door."

Maris held the dead phone to her ear for several seconds before hanging up. The conversation had been surreal; perhaps she had dreamed it. But she wasn't dreaming. She was wide-awake—and her husband wasn't in bed with her.

Throwing off the covers, she got out of bed and was reaching for her robe when Noah strolled into the bedroom, his shirttail hanging out of his tuxedo trousers. He was carrying his shoes.

He said, "Did I hear the telephone ring?"

"Yes."

"Was it Daniel? There's nothing wrong, I hope."

She was greatly relieved to see him but dumbfounded by his nonchalance. "Noah, where have you been all night?"

Her tone stopped him in his tracks. "On the sofa in the den. You were asleep when I came in. I hated to disturb you."

"What time did you get home?"

"About one, I think."

His calm manner only fueled her irritation. "You said—you promised—you'd be half an hour behind me."

"We had two drinks instead of one. What's the big deal?"

"The big deal is that I was awakened at five twenty in the morning, and I was alone in bed!" she exclaimed. "Call me irrational, but unless I know the reason why not, I expect my husband to be sleeping beside me." Her voice had gone shrill—the voice of a ranting wife. She took a moment to get her temper under control. "If you'll recall, Noah, I tried to seduce you into coming home with me straight from the office. But you elected for us to go to that interminably long banquet instead. Following that, I tried to talk you into salvaging at least part of the evening just for us, but you chose to have drinks with Vampira and that dopehead."

He dropped his shoes to the floor, then removed his shirt. "Each book that 'dopehead' writes sells over a half-million copies. He's unhappy with his present publisher and is considering us. 'Vampira' set up the date for drinks, thinking that it would be a beneficial meeting for both parties. Indeed it was. I had hoped to surprise you and Daniel with this good news tomorrow, but . . ." He shrugged eloquently, then sat down on the edge of the bed.

"You could have called, Noah."

"I could have. But knowing how exhausted you were, I didn't want to disturb you."

"I don't like being obligated to Nadia."

"I don't like being obligated to anyone. On the other hand, it's not very smart to intentionally alienate Nadia. If she likes you, she bestows favors. If she dislikes you, she can inflict serious damage."

"And either way—if you're a man—you get screwed."

That caused him to smile. "Why is it that a woman, and especially you, is never more beautiful than when she's angry? Don't be. I'm sorry I worried you." He looked at her and said gently, "You have no reason to be jealous, you know."

Reluctantly she moved toward him. He tucked a strand of her hair behind her ear and kissed her cheek. She put up token resistance but not for long.

DANIEL Matherly laid aside the manuscript pages and thoughtfully pinched his lower lip between his thumb and fingers.

"What do you think?" Maris asked. "Is it my imagination, or is it good?"

Taking advantage of the mild morning, they were having breakfast on the patio of Daniel's East Side town house. Terra-cotta pots of flowers provided patches of color within the brick enclosure. A sycamore tree shaded the area.

While Daniel was reading the *Envy* prologue, Maris had helped Maxine put together their meal. Maxine, the Matherlys' housekeeper, had been practically a member of the family a full decade before Maris was born. This morning she was her cantankerous self, criticizing the way Maris squeezed the orange juice. In truth, the woman loved her like a daughter and had acted as a surrogate since the death of Maris's mother when she was still in grade school. Maris took the housekeeper's bossiness for what it was—an expression of her affection.

Maris and Daniel had eaten their egg-white omelets and grilled tomatoes in silence while he finished reading the prologue. "Yes, dear," he said now. "It's good. New writer?"

"I don't know. This wasn't a typical submission by any stretch."
She explained how she had come to read the prologue, then
recounted her predawn telephone conversation.

Daniel chuckled as he stirred cream substitute into his cup of coffee. "I think it adds a dash of mystery."

As he contemplated the enigmatic author, Maris studied her
father. When did he get so old? she thought with alarm. His hair
had been white for almost as long as she could remember, but it had
only begun to thin. Her mother had been fifteen years his junior,
and by the time Maris was born, he was well into middle age.

Recently the years seemed to catch up with him. He sometimes
used a cane for support. The liver spots on his hands had increased
in number and grown darker. But his eyes were as bright and
cogent as ever when he turned to her and asked, "I wonder what all
that was about? Failing to provide a return address or telephone
number. Then the phone call this morning."

Maris left her chair and moved to a potted geranium to pluck off
a dead leaf. She considered her father's question. "He wanted to be
sought and found, didn't he?"

"He couldn't resist the temptation to establish contact with you
and hear what you had to say about his work."

She returned to her wrought-iron chair. "Which I think is compelling. That prologue has me wondering about the young man in
the boat. Who is he? What's his story? What caused the fight
between him and his friend?"

"Envy," Daniel supplied.

"Which is provocative, don't you think? Envy of what?"

"I can see the prologue served its purpose. The writer has got
you thinking about it and asking questions. What are you going
to do?"

"Try and establish some kind of professional dialogue. If that's
possible to do with such a jerk."

"Do you even know his telephone number?"

"I do now. Thanks to caller ID."

"Ah, the miracles of advanced technology. In my day—"

"In your day?" she repeated with a laugh. "It's still your day."

Reaching for his speckled hand, she patted it fondly. One day he would be gone, and she didn't know how she was going to survive that loss. "So you think I should pursue *Envy?*" she asked.

"Absolutely. The author has challenged you, and you, Maris Matherly-Reed, can't resist a challenge. And you certainly can't resist a good book."

"I think that's why I'm so excited about this, Dad," she said. "My gut instinct—"

"Which I trust implicitly."

"Tells me that it's going to be good. It's got texture, and it's heavy on the southern overtones, which you know I love."

"Like *The Vanquished.*"

Suddenly her balloon of enthusiasm burst. "Yes."

After a beat or two Daniel asked, "How is Noah?"

As a reader, as well as his wife, she'd been massively disappointed that Noah hadn't followed his first novel with a second. "You know how he is, Dad. You talk to him several times a day."

"I was asking as a father-in-law, not as a colleague."

Maris remained quiet for a time, tracing the pattern of her linen place mat with her index finger. "Noah came home very late last night," she began. She gave him the gist of their argument. "We ended up lovers and friends, but I'm still upset about it."

"It sounds to me as though Noah had a logical explanation." He frowned thoughtfully. "Are you thinking that Noah has reverted to the habits he had while living a bachelor's life?"

Knowing the admiration and respect her father had for Noah, she was reluctant to recite a litany of complaints against him. Daniel had brought Noah into their publishing house a little over three years before because he had proved himself to be a smart, shrewd publisher. When Maris and Noah's relationship became more social than professional, Daniel had cautioned her against an office romance. But he had given his approval when Noah, after being with Matherly Press for a year and a half, confided in Daniel his plans to marry his daughter. He had even offered to resign in exchange for her hand. Daniel had embraced Noah as his son-in-law with the same level of enthusiasm as when he had hired him as business manager of his publishing house.

But Maris needed to vent, and her father had always been her most trusted confidant. "In answer to your question, Dad, I don't believe that Noah's having an affair."

"Something's bothering you. What?"

"I just hope he isn't getting tired of me. Over the last few months I've had very little of his attention. We're coming up on our two-year anniversary. That's got to be a record for him."

"You knew his record when you married him," he reminded her gently. "He had a solid reputation as a ladies' man."

"Which I accepted because I loved him. Because I had been in love with him since I read *The Vanquished* as a college student."

"And out of all those women, Noah chose to marry you."

She smiled wistfully, then shook her head with self-deprecation. "You're right, Dad. He did. I'm feeling neglected. That's all."

"And I must assume some of the blame for that. I've vested Noah with an enormous amount of responsibility. He's doing not only his job, he's begun taking up the slack for me as well. I think it would be a good idea for the two of you to go away together for a few days. Bermuda perhaps. Get some sun. Spend a lot of time in bed."

She smiled at his candor, but she didn't share his confidence that time in bed would solve the problem. Their disagreement this morning had ended with sex, but she wouldn't call it intimacy. To her it had felt that they were doing what was most expedient to end the quarrel, but their hearts weren't in it.

For Daniel's benefit she pretended to think over his suggestion, then said, "Actually, I was thinking of going away by myself for a while."

"Another good option. To the country?"

Frequently, when the city became too claustrophobic, she went to their house in Massachusetts. It was natural for Daniel to assume that she would choose their house in the Berkshires for her retreat.

But she shook her head. "I think I'll go to Georgia."

Chapter Three

. . . Members of the fraternity thought it brilliant of their chapter founders to have designed and built their residence house to correlate with the diamond shape of the fraternity crest. Its location at a key intersection gave the fraternity a commanding presence on campus. The three-story building's façade was imposing, and the path leading up to the entry was lined with Bradford pear trees, which blossomed snowy white each year. In autumn their leaves turned the vibrant ruby red they were on this particular Saturday afternoon.

The weather was rainy and dreary. Students were using the day to catch up on sleep, study, or laundry. The halls of the fraternity house, smelling dankly of beer, were dim and hushed. The quiet was punctured by "Roark!" followed immediately by a slamming door.

Roark dodged the wet towel hurled at his head and started laughing. "You found it?"

"Whose is it?" Todd Grayson brandished a Styrofoam cup that contained his toothbrush. Which wouldn't have been remarkable, except that the cup had been used as a spittoon. The bristles of the brush were steeping in viscous brown fluid in the bottom of the cup.

Roark was reclined on the sofa beneath their sleeping lofts, which were suspended from the ceiling by short chains.

Todd was angry. "Tell me. Whose spit cup is this?"

Roark was still laughing. "You don't want to know."

Todd tossed the offensive cup into their trash can. He'd been showering in the communal bathroom down the hall when Roark sneaked in and put Todd's toothbrush in tobacco-laced sputum.

"Don't be pissed," Roark said. "It was a good joke and worth the expense of a new toothbrush."

"Are you going to tell me whose it was?"

"Don't know. Found it on a windowsill on the third floor."

"I'll get you back," Todd threatened as he pulled on a T-shirt.

Roark merely laughed.

"Didn't you have anything better to do? You've been lying on your butt all day."

"Gotta finish this over the weekend." Roark held up a paperback copy of *The Great Gatsby*.

Todd snorted scornfully. "Want to go get something to eat?"

"Sure." Roark rolled off the sofa and shoved his feet into a pair of sneakers.

T.R.'s wasn't much of a place, but it was an institution. It provided two basic needs of the male collegian: cold beer and hot pizza. By midterm, T.R., the owner, could call every customer by name and knew how he liked his pizza. Todd's and Roark's never varied—thick crust, pepperoni, extra mozzarella.

As they ate, Todd and Roark discussed the merits of *Gatsby,* then of F. Scott Fitzgerald's work in general, which brought them around to their own literary aspirations.

Roark asked, "How're you coming on your manuscript?"

A novel of seventy thousand words was their senior project, their capstone prior to receiving a B.A. The one obstacle standing between them and graduation was Professor Hadley.

Todd frowned. "Hadley's on me about characterization."

"Specifically?"

"They're cardboard cutouts. No originality, depth, blah, blah."

"He says that about everybody's characters."

"Yours included?"

"I haven't had my critique yet," Roark replied. "Next Tuesday, bright and early, eight o'clock. I'll be lucky to escape with my life."

The two young men had met in a composition class their first semester as freshmen. The instructor was a grad student. The first week, he assigned a five-page essay based on John Donne's *Devotions.* Taking himself far too seriously, the instructor had assumed a professorial stance and tone. "You may not be familiar with the text, but surely you'll recognize the phrase 'for whom the bells toll.' "

"Excuse me, sir." Todd raised his hand and innocently corrected him. "Is that the same as 'for whom the bell tolls'?"

Recognizing a kindred spirit, Roark introduced himself to Todd after class. Their friendship was established that afternoon.

They received the two highest grades in the class on that first writing assignment. "The jerk wouldn't dare award an A," Roark sourly observed. Scrawled on his blue book was a large B plus.

"At least you got the plus sign," Todd remarked of his B.

"You would have if you hadn't been a smart-ass that first day."

"When I write the great American novel, he'll still be grading freshmen writing assignments."

"Ain't gonna happen," Roark deadpanned. He flashed a wide smile. "Because *I'm* going to write the great American novel."

Love of books and the desire to write them were the foundation on which their friendship was built. It was a few years before cracks were discovered in that foundation.

They were good-looking, so there was never a shortage of girls. When they weren't talking about books, chances were good the subject was women. They talked about women tirelessly and shamelessly. Only Roark came close to having a serious relationship, and only once.

He met her during a campus-wide food drive he had organized to benefit a homeless shelter. She was beautiful, intelligent, and had a good sense of humor. Passionate kissing was as far as she would go. She clung to a strict moral code, founded on her religion, and didn't intend to break it. She hadn't in high school with her longtime sweetheart, and she wasn't going to until she knew she was with the man she would marry. Roark admired her for it, but it was frustrating.

Then she called him one night and said she had just finished reading *The Grapes of Wrath* and would like to see him. He picked her up. They went for a drive, then parked.

She had loved the classic Steinbeck novel and thanked him for sharing it with her. Her kisses that night were more passionate than ever. He wondered if he was falling in love.

A week later she dumped him. He was tearfully informed that she was resuming the relationship with her high school sweetheart. Roark was dumbfounded. "Do I at least get to ask why?"

"You're going to be somebody great, Roark Slade. Famous. But I'm just a simple girl from small-town Tennessee. I'll teach elementary school maybe, then become a mother."

"There's nothing wrong with that."

"Oh, I'm not apologizing for it. It's the life I choose, the life I want. But it's not the life for you."

"Why do we have to plan the rest of our lives now?" he argued. "Why can't we spend time together and see what happens?"

"Because if I continue seeing you, I'll sleep with you."

"Would that be so terrible?"

"Not at all terrible. It would be . . ." She kissed him deeply. "I want to," she whispered against his lips. "I want to so bad. But I made a pledge of abstinence, so I can't see you anymore."

To his mind that was totally irrational. He was depressed and testy for weeks. Todd, sensing that the romance had suddenly withered and died, walked on eggshells around him.

But women continued to consume their thoughts and fuel their lusts, and on that rainy Saturday evening it was a girl that brought to a close their conversation about Professor Hadley.

Roark left Todd at T.R.'s with a coed named Christie. It was hours later before he returned to his and Todd's room. After listening at the door for several moments, he knocked tentatively. "Okay if I come in?"

"Yeah."

Todd was alone in his loft, lying on his back, one bare leg dangling over the side. He looked completely done in but managed to mumble, "Thanks for keeping your distance. Where've you been?"

"The library. When did Christie leave?"

"About ten minutes ago. Your timing was perfect."

"Happy to oblige."

"Oh, before I forget. Our favorite professor called and left you a message."

"Hadley?"

"Said he has a conflict at eight, so he bumped your appointment up to nine o'clock Tuesday morning."

"Fine by me. I won't have to get up so early."

Todd yawned and turned toward the wall. "G'night."

❧

FOLLOWING a meeting that she and Noah had been required to attend, Maris went home from the office alone. She checked her calendar one final time. She had blocked out the remainder of the week for her trip to Georgia, which might be a tad optimistic considering that the author hadn't been notified of her pending visit.

Having put off for as long as possible the unpleasant chore of alerting him to her arrival, she dialed the number that had appeared on her caller ID machine that morning.

The telephone rang four times before it was answered. "Yeah?"

"This is Maris Matherly-Reed. I'm coming to St. Anne Island to see you," she declared.

"I beg your pardon?"

"I was speaking English. Which part didn't you understand?"

He made a gruff sound that could have passed for a laugh.

"I'm coming to talk to you."

"What about? The flora and fauna of Georgia's sea islands?"

"Your book."

"I've already told you that my book isn't for sale."

"You also told me that there is no book. Which is it?" She had trapped him. His stony silence indicated that he knew it. "I'll be arriving tomorrow evening."

"It's your money."

"Could you recommend a—" She was talking to a dead line. He'd hung up on her. Stubbornly she dialed him back.

"Yeah?"

"I was asking if you could recommend a hotel in Savannah?"

When he hung up on her again, Maris laughed. The more he balked, the more determined she became.

She had just begun packing when the telephone rang. She expected it to be the author. To her surprise a man with a broad Brooklyn accent asked to speak with Noah.

"I'm sorry. He isn't here."

"Well, I gotta know what to do with this key. We don't make house calls after hours. Only, Mr. Reed give me twenty extra bucks to get it here tonight. You his ol' lady?"

"Are you sure you have the right Noah Reed?"

"Deals with books or something?"

"Yes, that's my husband."

"Well, he give me this address in Chelsea, said—"

"What address?"

He recited an address on West Twenty-second Street. "Apartment three B. He axed me to change the lock yesterday, on account of he'd already moved some stuff in there and didn't want old keys floating round, ya know? Only, I didn't bring an extra key yesterday, and he said he needed at least one extra. So I tole him he'd have it tonight. I'm here with the key."

"You said some stuff had already been moved into the apartment. What kind of stuff?"

"Stuff. Furniture. You know, the kinda nice stuff rich folks have in their places. All I know is, I'm ready to get home on account of the Mets game. Only, Mr. Reed, he give me twenty extra—"

"I'll be there in fifteen minutes."

Maris left her building and practically ran the two blocks to the subway station at Seventy-second and Broadway. A taxi would take too long. She wanted to see the nice stuff that Noah had moved into an apartment in Chelsea that she knew nothing about. And she wanted to know for whom he was having an extra key made.

IVY clung to the old brick, contributing charm to the building's exterior. The locksmith was waiting for Maris in the foyer. "Who buzzed you in?" she asked him after introducing herself.

"I ain't a locksmith for nothin'," he said with a snort.

She asked for the key.

"I gotta check it out first," he told her. "There ain't no elevator. We gotta climb."

She nodded for him to precede her up the staircase. He was huffing and puffing by the time they reached the third level. As he approached the door, he withdrew the spare key from his pocket and slipped it into the lock. "Pouyfect," he said as he swung open the door. Then he stood aside and motioned for Maris to go in. "The light switch is there on your right."

She felt for the switch and flipped it on.

"Surprise!" The shout went up from fifty or so people, all of whom she recognized. Her mouth dropped open. Everyone was laughing over her dumbfounded expression.

Noah came toward her, grinning. He embraced her tightly, then soundly kissed her mouth. "Happy anniversary, darling."

"B-but our anniversary isn't until—"

"I know when it is. But you always catch on to my attempted surprises. This year I thought I'd get the jump on you." He looked beyond her shoulder at the locksmith. "You were terrific."

As it turned out, he was an actor hired to play the role. "Happy anniversary, Mrs. Reed," he said in a voice that resonated with the Queen's English.

After seeing to it that she had a flute of bubbly, Noah maneuvered her to greet their guests, which included most of the editorial staff of Matherly Press. Then the crowd parted to reveal Daniel. He was seated with one hand resting on the engraved silver head of his cane, while the other was saluting her with a glass of champagne. "Anniversary wishes a few weeks early, sweetheart."

"Dad! I can't believe you were in on this!" She bent down to kiss his cheek. "You gave nothing away this morning."

"Which was hard, considering the topic of our conversation."

Feeling her cheeks grow warm with embarrassment, she said softly, "This explains why Noah has been distracted lately. I feel like a fool now."

"Don't," Daniel ordered, his brows lowering sternly. "A fool is someone who ignores warning signs."

She kissed him again, before being pulled away to mingle. Noah had planned a wonderful party. Although it was a weeknight, guests stayed late. Eventually, however, they said their good-nights.

Daniel was the last to leave. As Noah guided him down the stairs and to the car waiting at the curb, he called to Maris, "I'll be right back, darling. I haven't given you your present yet. Just wait. And no snooping!"

Now that the apartment was empty of guests, she could see it well for the first time. The "stuff" was nice, but not pricey. The emphasis was on functionality and comfort. Off the living room, a closed door led to what she assumed was a bedroom. She was making her way toward that door, when hands seized her around the waist.

"I thought I told you not to snoop," Noah said, nuzzling her ear.

"Is my present behind door number one?"

"Let's take a look." He walked her toward the door. "You may open it now."

The room was a small cubicle, but a generous window made it appear larger. It was furnished with a desk, a leather swivel chair, a telephone, a computer, and a printer. Maris looked at Noah.

He laid his hands on her shoulders and massaged them gently. "I know you've wondered about the late hours I've been keeping."

"I confess."

"I apologize for causing you worry. I wanted this place to be completely set up before you saw it. It's taken me weeks to get it ready."

"For what?"

"Well, not for conducting the illicit affair you thought I was having."

She lowered her eyes. "Again I confess. But if this apartment wasn't designated as a love nest, what did you lease it for?"

"That's your anniversary present. I've begun writing again."

For several moments she was too stunned to speak. Then she threw herself against him. "Noah! That's wonderful. When? What made you— Oh, I'm thrilled!"

She rained kisses over his face. He laughed and indulged her enthusiasm. "Don't get carried away. I'll probably fail miserably."

"You won't. I don't believe for a moment that you're the one-book wonder you fear you are. *The Vanquished*—"

"Which I wrote years ago, Maris, when I was full of passion."

"And *talent*. Talent like yours isn't depleted by one book."

"We'll see." He glanced at the computer dubiously. "In any case, I'm willing to test your theory. I'm going to give it a shot."

"You're not just doing it for me, are you?"

"I couldn't do it just for you. Writing is damn hard work." He rubbed his knuckles against her jaw. "This is something I want to do. Very much. And if it pleases you, that's a bonus."

"It pleases me very much." She kissed him with more heat than she could remember feeling for a long time.

As their lips clung, Noah slipped off his jacket. Her heart quickened. It would feel a shade illicit if they made love in this new apartment—on the sofa, on the rug . . . on the desk. Why not? They were grown-ups.

She slid her hands up his chest and began working on the knot of his necktie. But he moved her aside, sat down at the keyboard, and booted up the computer. "I'm so anxious to get started."

"Now?"

He swiveled his chair around and looked up at her, grinning sheepishly. "Do you mind if I work awhile? I've been toying with an idea. I'm afraid if I don't commit it to paper, it'll vanish."

She forced herself to smile. "Of course not. Not at all."

There wasn't to be a romantic conclusion to the evening, and that was disappointing. But fairly, she couldn't complain. This is what she had been encouraging him to do for years. "I'll say good-bye and leave you to your work," she said. "I don't want to be a distraction. Besides, I need to go home and pack for my trip."

He took her hand and kissed the palm. "Will you be all right hailing a cab?"

"Don't be silly. Of course." She leaned on the arms of his desk chair, bringing her face down to the level of his. "It was a lovely surprise party, Noah. Thank you for everything but especially for this.

I can't wait to read your next novel. Look what happened after I read the first one."

As they kissed, his hand followed the curve of her hip down to her thigh. When she withdrew, he continued to stroke her leg. "On second thought, maybe I'll postpone starting until tomorrow."

She aimed her finger at the computer keyboard. "Plot!"

FIFTEEN minutes later Noah let himself into another apartment. It was half a block away from the one where he had set up an office he planned never to use. He dropped his key onto the table in the short entry hall and moved into the living area.

Nadia was lying on the sofa, naked except for a royal-blue silk robe that lay open. He sauntered over to the sofa. "You're shameless, Nadia."

"I know." She stretched. "Isn't it delicious?"

He began undressing. "The surprise party was a stroke of genius. Maris is now completely defused."

"Ooh, tell me."

"She admitted to harboring a suspicion that I was having an extramarital affair. But now that she has seen my writer's retreat, which made her positively misty, I can use it as an excuse to get away at any time of day or night."

"For this."

"Definitely for this. Along with the other business in which we're involved."

"Maris is only half the problem, though. What about Daniel?"

"He's an old man, Nadia. In his dotage."

"He'll never sell Matherly Press. He's gone on record."

Nonchalantly Noah pulled his belt through the loops of his trousers. "Not to worry, my dear. I'll have Matherly Press sold before either of them knows what's what. Maris is hot for a new author she's discovered in her slush pile. That'll keep her distracted. Daniel has virtually retired, entrusting the company's business dealings almost entirely to me. The first they hear of the pending sale will probably be when they read about it in *Publishers Weekly,* and then it'll be too late to stop it. I'll have Daniel's position, along with ten thousand shares of WorldView stock in my portfolio and a cool ten million in my bank account."

"And the Matherlys will be left with only each other."

"I suppose. I really couldn't care less."

Chapter Four

THE roads on St. Anne Island were banked on either side by woods that were deeper and darker than any Maris had seen anywhere. She had arrived later than anticipated. Stormy weather in Atlanta had delayed her connecting flight to Savannah. By the time she checked into a hotel and made arrangements for transportation to the island, the sun was setting. The sea island would have been alien territory to her in broad daylight, but the gloaming exaggerated its strangeness and lent it a sinister quality.

As she chugged along in her rented golf cart, she felt extremely vulnerable. The woods intimidated her. They were as unfriendly as the man at the landing from whom she had rented the golf cart. When she asked him for directions to the home of the local writer, he had responded with a question of his own. "Whada ya want with 'im?"

"He's expecting me." She'd unfolded a map of the island, given to her by the pilot of the boat she had hired to bring her over. "I'm here, right?" She indicated on the map the landing where the boatman had docked for her to disembark. "Which way do I go from here?"

The man had spit tobacco juice into the dirt; then a stained, chipped fingernail traced the fork she should take.

She had thanked him curtly and set out on the final leg of her trip. The landing's "commercial district" was limited to two places of business: the cart rental and Terry's Bar and Grill.

Terry's was a circular structure with a corrugated tin roof. Out front, a man, presumably Terry, was cooking meat on a large grill. Even after she drove past, she could feel his eyes boring holes in her back until she rounded a bend in the road and was no longer in sight.

She had the road all to herself. Eventually she detected salt air over the dominant scent of evergreens. The cart jounced over potholes. Tree branches formed an opaque canopy—thick, silent, and foreboding.

She was beginning to think that she should be sensible and retreat to the safety of her hotel room in gracious Savannah. But then she caught her first glimpse of the house and was instantly enchanted. It was beautiful. Beautiful in a way that evokes sadness.

Maris stepped out of the cart and followed a pathway marked by twin rows of spectacular moss-shrouded live oaks. She climbed the steps. Now she wished she had at least changed clothes. Her traveling suit had been seasonably lightweight for New York but was too heavy for this climate. It looked citified and grossly out of place.

When she reached the veranda, she bolstered herself with a deep breath and walked boldly to the front door and reached for the brass knocker.

"Maris Matherly-Reed?"

Startled, she jumped. A man was peering at her through one of the tall, screened front windows. He continued to stare at her. Finally he said, "Come on in."

She pushed open the glossy black front door and stepped into a wide foyer. He emerged from one of the rooms opening off it. He was dressed in khaki shorts and an ordinary chambray work shirt, the sleeves rolled up to his elbows. He wasn't as intimidating as she had anticipated. He was older than his telephone voice had suggested. The drawl was there but not the brusqueness. However, he wasn't being overly friendly. His blue eyes were regarding her warily. "You're a long way from Manhattan, Mrs. Matherly-Reed."

Feeling self-conscious and wanting to divert attention away from herself, she said, "The house is extraordinary. How long have you lived here?"

"A little over a year. It was in total disrepair. Like to see it?"

"Very much."

He smiled at her and turned back into the room from which he'd come. The crystal chandelier in the center of the ceiling was swinging slightly. He motioned toward the fireplace. The ornately carved mantel had been stripped down to the naked wood and was being prepared for refinishing. "It's become more of a project than I had counted on," he admitted.

"I'm sure it will be lovely when you're finished."

"Parker's expecting it to be. He's a perfectionist."

"Parker?"

"The owner."

"Oh. I assumed you owned the house."

He shook his head in amusement. "I only work here. Obviously, you've mistaken me for Parker, the man you've come to see. Parker Evans." He smiled and extended his hand. "I'm Mike Strother. Forgive me for not making that clear when you arrived."

She smiled and shook his hand, liking the older gentleman and wondering how she could have mistaken him for the abrasive individual on the phone.

"I'm the chief cook and bottle washer, housekeeper, gardener, valet," he explained.

Her preconceptions of Parker M. Evans were being dispelled. He hadn't sounded like a man who would have a manservant. "I'm looking forward to meeting him."

Mike avoided looking at her. "He's not here. He didn't want to be sitting around here when you arrived. So he went out."

"Out? Where?"

MARIS angrily marched up to the man who'd rented her the golf cart. "Why did you send me all the way out to Mr. Evans's house?"

He smirked. "Knew you's lying 'bout him expecting you."

"Why didn't you tell me he was here?"

"Don't recollect you askin'."

She was seething, but he was too coarse and stupid to waste her anger on. She would save her anger for Mr. Parker Evans. He had probably known about the wild-goose chase she'd been sent on. Terry, the cook, surely had. His charcoal grill had gone cold, but he was tending bar when she pulled open the squeaky screen door to his establishment and went inside.

She crossed a bare concrete floor and strode past the pool tables straight to the bar at the back of the room. The man who had rented her the cart followed her inside.

Billiard balls stopped clacking. Conversations died. The floor show was about to begin, and the angry New Yorker was the featured act. Terry was grinning at her sardonically.

"Give me a beer."

His grin slipped a notch. He hadn't expected that. But he reached into an ice chest and pulled out a longneck. He uncapped it and passed it to her.

"I'm here to see Parker Evans," she announced.

Terry planted his hairy forearms on the bar and leaned across it toward her. "Who should I say is calling?"

His customers guffawed. Maris spun around and confronted the room at large. The interior was thick with tobacco smoke despite the overhead fans. A dozen pairs of eyes were focused on her. Maris drew a deep breath. "Isn't this rather juvenile, Mr. Evans?"

No one said a word.

"To say nothing of rude," she continued. "I've come an awfully long way to see you."

"You can go back the same way." The voice issued from a shadowed corner and elicited more chuckles.

"Mr. Evans, the least you could do is give me ten minutes of your time."

"Come on over here, honey," a nasally voice invited. "I'll give you the best ten minutes you've ever had."

"In your dreams, Dwayne," a tattooed woman drawled.

Laughter erupted, louder than before.

The vulgarity got to Maris, but not in the way they expected. It didn't frighten her; it made her mad. Not even attempting to disguise her contempt, she said, "Whoever you are, Mr. Evans, you're a damn coward."

The snickering ceased abruptly. Any other insult was pardonable, but apparently, cowardice wasn't. Name-calling couldn't get more serious than that. Using it as her exit line, Maris made a beeline for the door. As she passed a billiards table, a pool cue arced down in front of her like the arm of a tollgate. She took hold of it in a tight grip and tried to shove it out of her way, but it was unyielding. She turned her head toward the man holding it.

"I'm Parker Evans."

Maris was astonished. Not by his audacity or the hostile eyes that glared up at her.

What astonished her was the wheelchair in which he sat.

THE contraption was green—a cross between a golf cart and a pickup truck. Maris learned later that it was called a Gator, but she had never seen one before. Parker Evans nodded her toward the one parked outside Terry's Bar and Grill. He invited her to get in. She climbed into the passenger seat and kept her head averted as he used his arms to lift himself onto the driver's seat. Then he leaned down, folded his chair, and swung it up into the shallow trailer.

The Gator had been reconfigured for him. The brake and accelerator were hand-controlled. He handled the vehicle with an ease that comes from practice as he steered it away from Terry's, toward the dock. "I can take you only as far as the ramp," he said.

Maris was at a complete loss. "Ramp?"

"Down to the dock. Where you left your boat."

"I don't have a boat. I paid someone to bring me over."

"He didn't wait to ferry you back?"

"I didn't know how long I'd be here. I told him I'd call."

He brought the Gator to a stop, looking displeased. His shirt was chambray, like Mike's, except that the sleeves had been cut out, revealing muscled arms that compensated for the limitations his legs imposed. "Shouldn't take a boat long to get over here. Terry will call for one."

"Couldn't we talk awhile, Mr. Evans? I've come a long way—"

"Without an invitation."

"You invited me when you sent me that prologue."

He registered mild surprise over her snappishness and raised his hands in mock surrender.

Doggedly she continued. "You sent me your work. Despite your claims to the contrary, you want this book to be published. I publish books. So could we please have that conversation?"

His expression was inscrutable. Then, before she could prepare herself, he reached across the space separating them, hooked his hand around the back of her neck, and yanked her forward, bringing her mouth up to his. It was more an assault than a kiss. His tongue forced her lips apart.

Making angry sounds of protest, she pushed against his chest, but he didn't stop. Her anger shifted to distress.

When he ended the deep kiss, Maris turned her head away. She stared out across the water. The lights on the shore of the mainland seemed a world away. "It won't work, Mr. Evans," she said quietly. "I'm not going to flee in terror of you. I'm calling your bluff. You kissed me to scare me off."

"All right. You can think that if you want to." He put the Gator into motion. "Did Mike happen to mention what's for supper?"

IT TURNED out to be smoked-ham sandwiches, served in a casual room at the back of the house, overlooking the beach. Mike referred to it as the solarium.

"Fancy name for a glassed-in porch," Parker commented wryly.

Maris noticed the computer set up in one corner of the room, which otherwise was furnished with rattan pieces. Stacked around the computer—on the stone tiled floor, in shelves, on every conceivable surface—were books, every kind imaginable. Some, she was pleased to see, bore the Matherly Press imprint on the spine. Gauging by their worn appearance, Parker Evans was well read.

"Whatever you call this room, I like it," she told them. "It's a wonderful place to read. And write."

After serving them, Mike sat down across the table from her, confirming what she had guessed—that he was as much a friend as a valet, the need for which was now sadly apparent.

"You went to far too much trouble, Mike," said Maris.

"No trouble. We planned to have a late supper anyway, and I'm glad to have a guest in the house. Parker isn't always the best company. In fact, when he's writing, he can be a real grouch."

Parker shot him a sour glance. "And you're a perpetual pain in the ass."

Maris laughed. Despite the swapped insults, the affection between them was obvious. "I've experienced Mr. Evans's grouchiness firsthand, Mike, but I don't take it personally. I work with writers every day. A gloomy bunch, for the most part."

She and the author had spoken little on the drive to his home. She had kept her eyes trained on the twin beams the Gator's headlights cast onto the road, although at one point she couldn't resist taking one furtive glance into the trees. "Oh!" she exclaimed. "Fireflies. There in the woods."

"Down here we call them lightning bugs," he said.

"When I was little, I'd catch them around our house in the country, put them in a glass, and keep it on my nightstand overnight."

"I did that, too."

So he had been able to chase fireflies. He hadn't always been confined to a wheelchair. She was curious about his disability, but she was too polite to ask.

Parker Evans was undeniably attractive, although years of pain or unhappiness had etched lines into his face. His rare smiles were tainted by bitterness. His brown hair was thick and threaded with gray. He was wearing two days' worth of stubble. His eyes were best described as hazel and would have been unremarkable except for the occasional amber spots that flecked the irises. That unique feature made his eyes compelling.

Staring at her now, he seemed to know what she was thinking. *Go ahead,* his eyes seemed to say. *You're dying to know why I'm in this chair, so why don't you ask?*

"Have you written any more for me to read, Mr. Evans?"

Parker looked pointedly at Mike, who took the hint and got up. "Excuse me. I need to put some things away." He left the room.

As soon as Mike was out of earshot, he said, "You're a very determined woman." He backed away from the table, turned his chair, and stared through the glass window as though he could penetrate the darkness and see the surf. After a time he turned back. "Do you really think it's good?"

"Yes, Mr. Evans, it's good."

He looked at her with exasperation. "Call me Parker."

"Okay. And you can call me Maris."

"I planned to." For several long moments he seemed to wage a battle with himself. Then he whipped his chair about and rolled it to the worktable. He booted up the computer, saying to her over his shoulder, "This means nothing, understand?"

She nodded, although she was certain it meant *something*.

"I've written a first chapter. If you want to read it, I'll let you. With the understanding that I'm under no obligation to you."

Maris moved beside his chair and watched the pages roll out of the printer. "Does the chapter start where the prologue left off?"

"No. The prologue scene comes toward the end of the story."

"So you go back and bring the reader forward?"

"Right."

"How far back?"

"Three years. Chapter one takes place when Roark and Todd are college roommates."

"Roark and Todd," she repeated. "Which is which? Which one do we see in Hatch Walker's office in the prologue?"

This time his grin was free of bitterness.

"You're not going to tell me, are you?" she asked.

His grin slipped. "If I did, why read the rest of the book?"

"The rest? So you *are* planning to finish it?"

"Let's see what you think first." He removed the pages from the tray on the printer. "When I kissed you? It didn't have a damn thing to do with trying to scare you off."

Before she could respond, he passed her the pages and shouted for Mike. "Bring her a phone so she can call for a boat," Parker told the older man when he appeared in the doorway.

"But it's after eleven o'clock!" Mike exclaimed. "You can't send her back at this time of night."

Maris, flustered, said, "It's fine, Mike. I'll be fine."

"I won't hear of it." Ignoring Parker's warning look, Mike declared, "You'll stay here tonight. In the guesthouse."

THE luncheon meeting was held in a private dining room on the thirty-first floor of WorldView Center. The paneled room was expensively furnished, and the expansive window provided a magnificent view of the midtown skyline.

The host, seated at the head of the dining table, asked politely, "More coffee, Nadia? Mr. Reed?"

Nadia Schuller indicated to the white-gloved waiter that she would like her cup refilled. Noah declined, then thanked their host for the sumptuous meal.

"I'm glad you enjoyed it," Morris Blume said.

In addition to Blume, five other representatives from WorldView were seated around the table. Six months earlier, Nadia had arranged an introductory meeting between Blume and Noah. Blume hadn't been coy at that initial meeting. Rather, he had stated plainly that he wished to acquire Matherly Press for WorldView.

Immediately after that meeting, his corporate lawyers had begun working feverishly on an acquisition proposal. The final rendition had been delivered to Noah in an enormous three-ring binder. This meeting was set up for the purpose of hearing his response.

"You've had a month to study our proposal, Mr. Reed," Blume said. "I'm eager to hear your impressions."

Morris Blume was whipcord-thin and strikingly pale, a feature emphasized by his prematurely bald head. He wore eyeglasses with silver wire frames and always dressed in conservative gray.

He had been at the helm of the international media conglomerate since his hostile takeover four years before, at age thirty-six.

Under his leadership WorldView had expanded from its base entertainment and broadcast entities into Internet commerce, satellite
communications, and fiber-optics technology.

So what did a mammoth like WorldView want with a gnat like
Matherly Press? That was the question Noah now posed to Blume.

"Because it's there?" the pale CEO glibly replied. Everyone at the
table laughed, including Noah. Blume let the laughter wane before
he resumed. "You publish books with mass appeal. But you also
publish literary works. Without question yours is a profitable house
that has a cachet of respectability. We like that."

"I've studied the proposal thoroughly," Noah said. "You did your
homework. The research was impressive. However, before we move
forward, there are a couple of points that must be addressed. First,
what about antitrust laws? I don't want to become embroiled in a
protracted legal dispute with the federal government."

"I assure you we've taken every precaution to avoid it. What's
your second point?" Blume asked.

Noah plucked an invisible piece of lint off the sleeve of his suit
jacket and said blandly, "Matherly Press isn't for sale."

"TO WHICH he said?" Daniel Matherly asked.

"Nothing that bears repeating," his son-in-law replied.

"Something about stubborn old men, I'd bet."

"Nothing that blatant but definitely along those lines."

They were having drinks together in Daniel's home study.

"The mongrels are closing in on us, Noah. They're mean, and
they have sharp teeth."

Noah made a negligent gesture. "I don't know how I could have
stated it any more plainly: Matherly Press isn't for sale."

"They'll persist."

"Let them come. We can stave them off."

Daniel smiled at his son-in-law's confidence. Everyone in the
industry had become acquainted with Noah Reed a decade earlier,
following the publication of *The Vanquished.* The novel, set during
the Reconstruction, had taken the nation by storm. But to every-

one's surprise and his new fans' dismay, Noah's ambitions lay not in writing, but in publishing. He had followed every step of the publishing process on *The Vanquished*. Some of his ideas on how to market his book had been implemented by his publisher. The house reasoned that Noah would be equally successful publishing other books and had hired him. He had been a quick study editorially, but the business side of the industry was where he truly distinguished himself. He was a fearless negotiator, whom literary agents admired but dreaded facing across the bargaining table. He was a born leader.

"You still agree with the company philosophy, don't you?" Daniel asked him.

Noah gave his father-in-law a retiring look. "From the beginning of our association I've known how you felt about mergers, Daniel. Unquestionably, there would be benefits. We would have more funds at our disposal, more venues for marketing and promotion."

"But we'd no longer be autonomous."

"Which was the point I was about to make," Noah said. "Autonomy was the basis on which Matherly Press was founded. I knew the family mantra even before I married into it."

Daniel said, "The next time someone approaches you with an offer to buy my publishing house, tell him to go to hell."

Noah laughed. "Shall I quote you?"

"Absolutely. In fact, I would prefer it."

Two vodka martinis hadn't dulled the edges of Nadia's nerves. They seemed to be on red alert and had been since Noah had recounted for her his conversation with Daniel. For half an hour she'd been pacing the hardwood floor of her Chelsea apartment, which was used strictly for romantic trysts.

"No matter how blasé he seems, I don't trust the old codger," she said. "How do you know he can't see through your act?"

"Because he isn't looking."

"I don't mean to question your perception, Noah. I'm just afraid that something might go wrong. I want this deal so badly for you."

"I want it for *us*."

Her anxiety dissolving, she stopped pacing and moved to where he stood. Coming close, she rested her hands on his shoulders. Their kiss was passionate and deep. She unbuttoned his shirt and slipped her hand inside. "It's just that Daniel Matherly has been overseeing that publishing house for . . . how long?"

"He's seventy-eight. His father died when Daniel was twenty-nine. He's been in control since then."

"So almost fifty years. He hasn't made himself into a living legend by being a dimwit. He's savvy. He's—"

"Not as sharp as he used to be." Noah disliked being second-guessed. Pushing her away, he moved into the kitchen, where he refilled his highball glass with ice cubes and splashed Scotch over them. "Your job is to keep Blume and company pacified."

"I'm having dinner with Morris tomorrow night."

"Good. Be a knockout. Eat, drink, and dance. Blow in his ear. Keep him happy. Let me handle the Matherlys."

His timetable had been in place for years. The first step had been accomplished when Daniel Matherly hired him. By toeing the company line, he had earned the old man's trust. A major hurdle had been cleared when he married Maris, further solidifying his position. Then, when the time was right, he had subtly, through Nadia, telegraphed to Blume his interest in a merger.

"I don't know why you're being testy with me," Nadia said. "Morris issued the deadline today, not I."

That had been the one crimp in Noah's plan that he hadn't seen coming. Throughout his cocktail hour with Daniel he'd been only half listening to the old man. Instead he'd been remembering Blume, with his lizardlike smile, imposing on him a two-week deadline to either fish or cut bait.

"I'm well aware of Blume's deadline," Noah said. "I'll see that it's met."

"What about Maris?"

"She'll go the way Daniel goes."

"That wasn't what I was talking about."

Sighing wearily, Noah closed his eyes and pinched the bridge of his nose. "I know what you were talking about, Nadia." Lowering his hand and opening his eyes, he looked at her. "Think about it. Does it make sense for me to ask Maris for a divorce now? I can't do that until I have that WorldView contract signed, sealed, and delivered." He expelled a breath of exasperation. "Do you think I've enjoyed being married to her? I won't miss my wife, but I'll regret losing a good editor. However, with the operating budget Blume has promised me, I'll be able to hire three of her. And even if none prove to be as good as she, I'll have my ten million to console me."

PARKER was at his computer. He'd been up for hours, his mind skipping like a stone over water. He couldn't focus on the last few sentences he'd written. Then he realized that he was nervous. Which was odd, considering that everything had fallen into place more or less as he had planned. Maris Matherly-Reed was responding even better than he had dared hope. Getting her here had been almost too easy. He had pulled the strings, and she had made the correct moves, but ultimately, she was in control. Everything depended on how well she liked *Envy* or if she liked it at all. What if she thought it stank? Then his plot would be screwed.

Agitated, he turned his wheelchair and saw her picking her way along the path between the main house and the cottage. Originally, the cottage had been the detached kitchen of the plantation house. Parker had converted it into a guesthouse with only one guest in mind—the one presently occupying it.

Maris glanced up and saw him watching her from behind the glass panels of the solarium. She smiled and waved. Waved? He couldn't remember the last time someone had waved at him. Feeling rather goofy, he raised his hand and waved back.

She let herself in through the sliding door. "Good morning." Her skin looked dewy. She smelled like floral-scented soap. Magnolia maybe. She had his manuscript pages with her. "It's gorgeous here, Parker!" she exclaimed breathlessly. "Last night it was too dark for me to fully appreciate the property. But seeing it in daylight, I understand why you fell in love with this place." She tucked a strand of damp blond hair behind her ear. "I couldn't find a hair dryer. That's all the cottage lacked, however. You did an excellent job on it."

Mike appeared in the doorway, pushing a wheeled cart with a carafe of coffee and platters of scrambled eggs, bacon, biscuits, and wedges of melon.

Maris and Mike took their time, chatting as they ate, but Parker cleaned his plate in record time. Then Mike collected their used dishes, loaded them onto the service cart, and went back out.

Parker took a deep breath and, turning to Maris where she had sat down on the rattan sofa, said, "Okay, let's get this over with."

"It's not an execution, Parker." She laughed lightly. "What you've written is good. Very good."

"Why do I feel that there's a 'however' in my near future?"

She smiled, then said quietly, "You've written a terrific outline."

"I see." Turning his chair around, he rolled it close to the wall of windows and watched the shallow waves break against the sand.

Maris, who had come to her feet, pushed an armchair close to him and sat down. "Do you understand what I'm getting at?"

"The characters need to be fleshed out."

"Precisely. Where do they come from? What were their families like? We know they want to be writers, but you haven't told us why." Maris was in high gear. "Life in the fraternity house—"

"There's more of that in the next chapter."

"There's a next chapter?"

"I worked on it this morning."

"Great. I liked that part. It's vivid. I could smell the gym socks." She shuddered. "And the bit with the toothbrush—it's almost too outrageous to be fiction. Personal experience?"

"What else needs work?" he asked.

"Ah. I get it. Personal questions are disallowed." Maris thumbed through the manuscript to refresh her memory on the notes she had jotted in the margins. "I'd like to see you expand, well, just about all of it." She glanced up at him to gauge his reaction, then sighed. "You expected this, didn't you? You knew what I was going to say."

He nodded. "I skimmed the surface, just as you said."

"To test my competence. You auditioned me."

"Something like that."

Her smile was self-deprecating. Her bluish gray eyes darkened to the hue of a storm cloud, but she was being a good sport. Actually, he would prefer that she rant and rave. What he had to do would be easier if she were as much of a bitch as he was a bastard. They were unequally matched opponents. She was out of her league and didn't even know it.

Consulting her notes again, she resumed. "There's no page limit, Parker. Leave the trimming and editing to me." She evened up the edges of the sheets, then laid them in her lap. "I'm glad I passed that silly test of yours," she said candidly. "I've missed being involved in this stage of the process. I didn't realize how much until I began making these notes last night. I love brainstorming with the writer, especially a talented writer."

Her gaze, so candid and earnest, made him uncomfortable. He looked out toward the ocean so he wouldn't have to see her sincerity, wouldn't have to feel . . . So he wouldn't have to feel, period.

Maybe he was the one playing out of his league.

Chapter Five

Envy, continued—1985

. . . That Tuesday morning before Thanksgiving was cloudy and cold. Checking his wristwatch, Roark saw that he had fifteen minutes to reach Hadley's office—more than enough time. He drained his coffee, stuffed his manuscript into his backpack, and left the dining hall. Not until he got outside did he realize the drastic change in the weather that had occurred overnight. He wished he had grabbed a heavier coat before setting out.

As soon as Roark was in sight of the language-arts building, he picked up his pace. He offered up an obscure little prayer as he crossed the portico and entered the building. He was assailed by the burning-dust smell of old furnaces. He shrugged off his jacket as he jogged up the stairs to the second floor, then continued down the hallway. The coffee had left a sour taste in his mouth. When he arrived at office number 207, the door was standing slightly ajar. He wiped his damp palm on the leg of his jeans and knocked softly.

"Come in."

Professor Hadley was seated behind his desk. His feet, laced into a pair of brown suede Hush Puppies, were propped on the open top drawer. A stack of reading matter was in his lap.

"Good morning, Professor."

"Mr. Slade."

Was it just his imagination, or did Hadley's greeting sound peremptory? As Roark stepped into the cramped office, he reassured himself that curtness was a habit with Hadley and that he shouldn't take it personally.

"No, don't close the door," Hadley told him.

"Oh. Sorry." Roark reached back to catch the door, which he had been about to close.

"You should be."

"Sir?"

"I said you should be sorry. You are"—he glanced at something beyond Roark's left shoulder—"fifty-six and one half minutes late."

Roark turned. On the wall behind him was a clock: White face. Stark black numerals. The short hand was already on the nine. The minute hand was three dashes away from the twelve. *The old man's lost it,* Roark thought. He cleared his throat. "Excuse me, sir, but I'm right on time. Our meeting was scheduled for nine."

"Eight."

"Originally, yes. But don't you remember calling and changing it to nine?"

"I assure you that my memory is in perfect working order, Mr. Slade. I made no such call. Our meeting was at eight."

HE WAS AN OLD MAN. UNTIL recently, Daniel Matherly had refused to acknowledge his elderly status. Lately, however, the reflection in his mirror was tough to dispute, and his joints made an even better argument.

Today, as he sat at his desk in his home study, Daniel was reflecting on his life and his mortality. He didn't fear dying. He did fear dying a fool. That was the worry that had robbed him of sleep the previous night. Morning had brought no relief from this pervasive uneasiness. He couldn't shake the feeling that he was missing something—a revealing word or deed or demeanor. His instincts were telling him something wasn't right. Perhaps he was just overly troubled by Maris's unhappiness. He'd picked up signals of marital disharmony. And then there was Noah. He wanted to trust the man both as a protégé and as a son-in-law, but only if Noah deserved his trust.

Grunting with the effort, Daniel brought his leather chair upright and opened a desk drawer. He withdrew his day planner and unzipped it, then removed a business card.

WILLIAM SUTHERLAND, the card read.

Daniel thoughtfully fingered the card, as he often had since obtaining it several weeks before. He hadn't called the number. He hadn't yet spoken to Mr. Sutherland personally, but after this morning's ruminations he felt that the time was right to do so.

As he reached for the telephone, he resolved to be more watchful, more attuned to what was going on around him. He didn't want to be the last to know . . . anything.

MARIS had spent all day indoors, reading until her eyes felt strained. It was good to get outside, although the heat was impossible, the humidity worse. The island was exotically beautiful. The live oaks had an ancient dignity that was enhanced by the curly Spanish moss draping their limbs. The dense air smelled of salt water and mingled with the intoxicating perfumes of the flowering plants that bloomed in profusion.

As she walked, Maris passed a house that was set well back from the road. She met no cars on the road. Her only company were the cicadas that buzzed loudly but lazily under cover of the thick foliage.

The abandoned cotton gin was located right where Mike had said it would be when she had asked for directions to Parker's solitary retreat. The forest had virtually reclaimed the structure.

To reach it from the road, one had to take a crushed-shell path. She made it up the path without encountering any local fauna. She dropped the stick she had picked up for protection, dusted off her hands, and took a good look at the hulking building. It was, as Mike had described, a structure on the brink of collapse. The wood was gray and weathered. The tin roof had been corroded by rust. Large patches of the exterior were covered by an impenetrable carpet of vines.

With misgiving Maris approached the wide door that was standing open. The interior was cavernous and dark, with only an occasional stripe of sunlight shining through a separation in the vertical wooden slats that formed the walls. The rear half of the lower story was covered by a loft. A large wheel about ten feet in diameter was situated just beneath this loft and was connected to the dirt floor by a wood column as big around as a barrel. Maris had never seen anything like it.

She blinked to adjust her eyes to the gloom. "Hello?" She stepped inside. "Parker?"

"Here."

She jumped and flattened her hand against her heart. He was in a corner behind her, invisible except for one ray of sunlight coming through the roof and reflecting off the chrome of his chair.

Recovering, she asked crossly, "Didn't you hear me?"

"How'd you get here?"

"Walked. How'd you get here?"

"How do I get everywhere?"

"You can roll your chair along that path?"

"I manage. Where'd you get the clothes?"

She wore a casual skirt, shirt, and sandals. Her blond hair had been gathered into a makeshift ponytail. Her white shirt was tied in a knot at her waist. Her khaki skirt was short enough to show a couple inches of thigh. It was an outfit she usually took to the country house for a summer weekend.

"Mike arranged for my suitcase to be picked up at the hotel and sent over. He went to the dock and met the boat."

"He's gone dotty. He's got a crush on you."

"He's just being nice."

A silence ensued. Her eyes had adjusted to the dimness, but she could still barely see him in the deep shadows of the corner. To fill the awkward silence, she said, "This is a picturesque building. What's its history?"

"Do you know anything about cotton?"

Cheekily she quoted a popular TV commercial. " 'It's the fabric of our lives.' "

To her surprise Parker laughed. A real laugh. "When this gin was first built," he said, "three sides of it were left open. The machinery was animal-powered. Follow me." He wheeled toward the back of the building, then pointed to the faint ring in the hard-packed earth. "If you look closely, you can see a circular depression there in the dirt. That's the path worn by the mules that turned the drive wheel that powered the gin stand."

"Was this the only gin on the island?"

"Right. One planter, one gin, one family—the family that built my house. They had a monopoly that made them rich until the whole market collapsed."

He swept his arm toward the front part of the building, and she preceded him. Her attention was drawn to a circle of bricks in the dirt floor. They were stacked two-deep, forming an enclosure roughly five feet in diameter. "What's that?"

"Careful," Parker warned as he quickly rolled his chair to her side. "That's an abandoned well."

"Why in here?"

"One of the more innovative patriarchs of the cotton dynasty decided to convert the gin to steam power. He began digging this well for the water supply but died before the project was completed."

She peered over the rim of bricks. "How deep is it?"

"Deep enough." He backed up, then wheeled past her. He hitched his chin toward an upended crate. "That'll do for a perch if you want to sit down."

After testing the crate's sturdiness, she gingerly sat down on the rough wood. "Was that thunder?" she asked.

He glanced over his shoulder toward the open door. It had grown noticeably darker outside. "Afternoon thunderstorms frequently boil up during the summer." Overhead the first raindrops struck the roof with fat-sounding slaps.

She inhaled deeply. "You can smell the rain."

"Smells good, doesn't it?"

The rain didn't cool the air much, but it had a definite effect on the atmosphere. It became closer, denser. He was aware of it. And so was Maris. Her eyes moved away from watching the rain through the open door and found his. They stared at each other through the deepening gloom. Oddly, it wasn't an uncomfortable exchange. He felt her gaze drawing him closer, and he was looking at her with the same level of intensity. Given the electricity arcing between them, he was curious to know what she would say.

She played it safe by commenting on *Envy*. "That was a rotten trick that Todd played on Roark."

"Rigging it so he missed his appointment with Hadley."

"You set me up perfectly. I didn't see it coming. Now what is Roark going to do about it?"

"What do you think he should do?"

"Beat the hell out of Todd. Isn't that what a guy would do?"

"Probably," he replied. "But remember, Todd was only paying Roark back for the toothbrush stunt."

"But that was a prank!" she exclaimed. "Gross and disgusting, granted. But college boys do stuff like that, don't they?"

"Did you know college boys who did stuff like that?"

"I attended a girls school."

"So it's safe to assume that you have no experience of college boys and how they act."

"No. It's safe to assume my experience is limited to how they act on dates, which is different from how they act with each other."

"Is that how you met your husband? On a date during college?"

"Much later than that. When he came to work at Matherly Press."

"Smart move on his part. He married the boss's daughter."

That irked her. So much so that Parker knew he wasn't the first to connect those two dots. It had crossed her mind, too.

Her expression turned professional. "Can we get back to your book, please?"

"Sure. Sorry for the digression."

While taking a moment to collect her thoughts, she absently fiddled with a button on her blouse. Parker wondered when this insignificant, subconsciously feminine gesture had become so sexy.

"A prank is one thing," she said. "But Todd's joke had a meanness about it. It wasn't harmless. It couldn't be undone as easily as buying a new toothbrush. He was tinkering with Roark's future."

"True. Roark won't easily forgive the experience, but it'll sure as hell motivate him."

"Yes," she said. "This will fuel his determination to succeed."

"To reach a level of success that Todd will—"

"Envy," she said, finishing the thought for him.

He grinned. "Per your suggestion, I'll let him blow off steam, land a few punches, which Todd will concede he deserved."

"So they remain friends?"

"Wait and see, Maris. Give me time."

Her eyes widened. "You've got it plotted already, don't you?"

"For the most part," he confessed with a negligent shrug.

"May I make another suggestion? Could we see Roark in love?"

"With the girl who went back to her boyfriend?"

"Yes. You told the reader that he fell in love, but we didn't get to see it. We didn't experience it along with him."

"I repeat, Maris, give me time."

She leaned forward eagerly. "You've already changed it, haven't you? There's more, isn't there? Same girl?"

"Why don't you have your navel pierced?"

"I beg your pardon?"

"If you're going to wear hip-riding skirts and shirts that tie at the waist, why don't you have—"

"I heard you."

"Then why? A tiny diamond stud. It'd be sexy. Er, *sexier*. Those glimpses of your belly button are already a major turn-on."

She squared her shoulders. "Parker, if we're going to have a professional relationship, you cannot talk to me like that."

"You're free to go."

But she stayed seated on the crate, as he'd known she would. As he'd hoped she would.

Thunder rumbled, and rain pelted the roof, but the racket only emphasized the strained silence between them. Parker rolled his chair closer to her. "What did you tell your husband?"

"About what?"

"Being here. I assume you called him."

"I did. I left word with his secretary that things were going well."

"He doesn't have a cell phone? He strikes me as the kind of guy who'd have one of those things glued to his ear."

"He was having lunch with the editor of our electronic publishing division. I didn't want to interrupt them. I'll call him later."

"What'll you talk about?"

"None of your business."

"That good, huh? Or that bad?"

She drew a deep breath and said tightly, "I'll tell him that I've discovered an extremely talented writer who—"

"Please, I'm blushing."

"Who is also the crudest, most obnoxious man I've ever met."

He grinned. "Well, that would be the truth." Then his smile gradually faded. Giving the wheels of his chair a small push, he rolled another inch or two nearer to her. "I bet you won't tell him I kissed you," he said in a low voice.

She stood up hastily, knocking the crate over backward. She tried going around him, but he used his chair to block her path. "Get out of my way, Parker. I'm going back to the house now."

"It's raining."

"I won't melt."

"Melt down, maybe. You're angry. Or afraid."

"I'm not afraid of you."

"Then sit back down." When she failed to move, he motioned toward the door. "Fine. Go. Get drenched."

She glanced outside at the downpour, then reluctantly upturned the crate and resumed her seat on it.

"Tell me how you met your husband, Maris."

Gauging her expression, he expected her to clam up, but she folded her arms across her middle—no doubt to hide her navel—and said, "Noah came to work at Matherly Press. But long before that, I knew him by reputation as the brains behind a rival publishing house. When he joined us, I was thrilled to be working with him. Over time, however, I realized that my feelings ran much deeper than admiration for a colleague. I was in love with him."

"How long have you been married?"

"Almost two years."

"Children?"

"No."

"How come?"

She glared at him, and he held up a hand in conciliation. "Okay, okay, the topic of children is taboo." He paused as though realigning his thoughts. "So you were seeing Noah every day at work and fell head over heels."

"Actually, I had had a mad crush on him even before I met him. I had read his book, *The Vanquished.* I loved it. The main character, Sawyer Bennington, became the man in my fantasies."

"You have fantasies?"

"Doesn't everyone? It's nothing to be ashamed of."

After a moment Parker leaned forward in his chair and spoke only loudly enough to be heard above the pounding rain. "Maris, is it remotely possible that you fell in love with the character and not the author?"

Her expression turned angry. "Don't be ridiculous. I fell in love with my husband. His talent first and then the man himself."

Becoming aware of loose strands of hair on her neck, Maris raised her hand to them, but repair seemed beyond her. She lowered her hand back to her lap, but not before it made a brief stop at that button she had fiddled with before. Parker's gaze fastened on it.

Suddenly she stood up in the narrow space separating them. "I'm going back now. The rain has stopped."

That wasn't altogether true. It was still raining lightly. Parker didn't argue, however. He let her pass.

Almost. Before she could take a step, he reached out and stopped her. His hands clasped her just below her waist, the heels of them pressing her hipbones. He was eye level with that alluring strip of bare skin between blouse and skirt. Slowly his eyes moved up. "We know why I kissed you last night, Maris."

"To frighten me off."

He frowned. "I kissed you because you braved Terry's and showed up everybody in the place, including me. I kissed you because just looking at you made me ache. I kissed you because your mouth looked so damn kissable. Simply put, I kissed you because I wanted to. It's something I admit and you damn well know. But there is one question that's driving me crazy." His eyes focused harder on hers and, by doing so, penetrated. "Why did you kiss me back?"

Chapter Six

MARIS'S call came at an inopportune time, but Noah figured he'd better take it to avoid her becoming suspicious. "Darling! I'm so glad to hear from you."

"It's nice to finally talk to you, too," she said. "It's been so long, your voice sounds strange. My ears have become attuned to a southern drawl."

Noah checked the clock on his desk, wondering when he could gracefully break this off. "How's the book coming along?"

"The author is talented, Noah. He's also difficult at times and impossible at others. But he's a challenge I can't resist."

"So the trip has been productive?"

"Yes. I'm going to stay here through the weekend and spoon-feed him constructive criticism and encouragement. There's no reason for me to rush back, is there?"

"Besides my missing you, no."

"Your missing me is no small thing."

"I wouldn't selfishly have you return strictly on my account. I can tell that you're enjoying being a hands-on editor again."

"Very much. Are you writing?"

"When I can. I've managed to put in a couple of hours' writing each evening. Remember, it's a part-time job, Maris. It can't take precedence over my responsibilities here."

"I understand. It's just that I'm eager to read something new by my favorite author. Anyway," she said with a laugh, "I've got my hands full with this project, in addition to the other manuscripts coming in the next few months. I'll be editing in my sleep."

He liked the sound of that. If she was distracted by work, he'd be freer to devote more time to finalizing his deal with WorldView. He was feeling the pressure of the deadline unexpectedly set by Morris Blume. Meanwhile, this was a perfect time for Maris to be out of town. Her absence made it more convenient for him to manipulate Daniel. The old man had to be carefully finessed, subtly stroked to whittle down his objections to a merger.

"I can't wait for you to read this book, Noah," Maris said, drawing him back into their conversation. "I think it's going to be good."

"If you think it's going to be good, then it will be. Listen, darling, I hate to cut this short, but I have a meeting with Howard in two minutes. If I'm a nanosecond late, he'll stay miffed for days." Howard Bancroft was Matherly Press's chief counsel and head of the legal department.

"Apologize to Howard for me. Tell him it's all my fault that you're late."

"Don't worry. I will." He chuckled. "Bye, now."

"Noah," she added just before he disconnected, "I love you."

"I love you, too, darling."

Professions of love meant nothing to him, but her declaration gave him pause. It wasn't the words, but the manner in which she'd spoken them, as though she were trying to reestablish, either in his mind or her own, that she loved him.

As Noah breezed past Bancroft's assistant and entered the chief counsel's office, the exchange with Maris lingered in his mind. One thing was certain: She would not be proclaiming her love if she knew the contents of the folder he carried into the lawyer's office.

"Hello, Howard. Sorry I'm late." Without invitation he sat down on an upholstered love seat and spread his arms along the back of it—a study in nonchalance. Looking through the windows behind the attorney's desk, he continued talking to prevent Bancroft from commenting on his tardiness. "I was on the telephone with Maris, informing her she'd be receiving this document tomorrow. She's in the boonies, but she assured me that the parcel carriers deliver."

His cavalier attitude was calculated to distract Bancroft from the business at hand. But Noah knew from experience that the lawyer was no pushover. His wizened appearance added a decade to his age. He stood five feet five inches tall in elevator shoes. He had a bald, pointed head with a distinct knob on the crown. On his nose were perched small, round reading glasses. Howard Bancroft looked like a gnome. Or exactly what he was—a shrewd legal mind.

"Is the document ready?" Noah asked.

"It's ready," Bancroft replied. "I drew up the document as you requested, but . . . May I be candid?"

"That would save time."

"Its content is troubling." The lawyer removed his glasses and began polishing them with a white handkerchief. It looked to Noah as though he were waving a flag of surrender, which he might just as well do. Howard Bancroft could not win this fight.

"Oh? How is it troubling?" Noah asked.

"You're certain that Maris approves of this?"

"I made the request on her behalf, Howard."

"Why does she feel that such a document is necessary?"

"That document," Noah said, pointing to where it lay in plain view on the lawyer's desk, "is our safety net. Publishing is changing constantly and swiftly. Matherly Press must be able to operate with fluidity, so that if an opportunity arises, it can be immediately seized."

"Without Daniel's consent."

Noah assumed a sad expression. "Ah, Howard, that's the hitch. It breaks Maris's heart, as it does mine, that Daniel is getting on in years. If he should take a sudden downward turn, say a stroke that renders him incapable of making business decisions, this power of attorney guarantees a smooth transition."

"But similar documents are already in place. Daniel's personal lawyer, Mr. Stern, drew them up when Maris turned twenty-one. She has power of attorney to make all his decisions."

"I'm aware of the previous documents. This one's different."

"Indeed. It supersedes others and grants *you* power of attorney."

Noah took umbrage. "Are you suggesting—"

"No." Bancroft raised his hands, palms out. "Daniel and Maris have both mentioned the need to amend their power-of-attorney documents to include you. But that should fall to Mr. Stern, not to me."

"You're more convenient." Noah glared at him. "What else do you find *troubling,* Howard?"

The lawyer hesitated. "I get the impression that this is being done behind Daniel's back."

"He's authorized it. You said so yourself not thirty seconds ago."

Obviously frustrated, Bancroft ran a hand over his knobby head. "It also bothers me to release such an important document when it hasn't been signed and witnessed in my presence."

"I told Maris that I refuse to sign it until she has," Noah said. "She'll have her signature notarized in Georgia. When the document is returned, I'll sign it. As soon as she gets back, we'll meet with Daniel. Frankly, I think he'll be glad that we relieved him of this responsibility."

"But why not wait until Maris's return and do it all at one time? Explain the urgency."

"Her being away is one reason Maris wanted this done with dispatch. She's working with a reclusive author. She'll be out of town for extended periods of time. Things happen, Howard. Plane crashes. Car accidents. She wants Matherly Press protected."

"Is that why the document becomes valid with your signature alone?"

Noah said tightly, "I told Maris, and I'm telling you, I will not sign it until her signature is in place."

Bancroft shook his head. "I'm sorry, Noah. I need Maris's verification that this is the document she wants."

"All right. Call her." He gestured toward the phone. "Better yet, Daniel's at home today. Ask him to come in and review this."

"I'd like to reacquaint myself with their original documents before wasting their time." Bancroft folded his hands. "I cannot release this document to you today."

Noah leveled a hard look on him. "Well, Howard," he said with soft menace, "it seems as though you suspect me of subterfuge."

"I suspect you of no such thing," the lawyer returned blandly.

"That's good. Because I find duplicity despicable, don't you? Duplicity. Betrayal. Disloyalty to one's family. One's race."

Noah picked up the folder that he'd brought in with him. Gently he set it on the desk and slid it toward Bancroft. After a minute of palpable silence and dread, the attorney opened the cover.

"Who would have thought it?" Noah said. "Your mother slept with Nazis."

Bancroft's narrow shoulders sagged forward.

"See, Howard, knowledge equates to power. I make it a point to learn all I can about the people around me. Investigating your background yielded more than I bargained for. I paid your mother a visit in the nursing home where you had sequestered her. After a little arm-twisting she confessed her shameful secret to me, and for a nominal fee an attendant wrote it all down. Your mother signed it. At that point she was so weak, she could barely hold the pen. Frankly, I wasn't surprised that she died just a few days later.

"You know the story well, Howard, but I was fascinated. She was twenty-three when she was dragged from her home in Poland. The rest of her family—her brothers, sister, parents—were backed against a wall and shot. She was lucky enough to be transported to a concentration camp. There she made merry with Nazis. She was the camp whore, trading sex for comfortable quarters and food. Now, is it any wonder she changed her name and created a fictitious history for herself when she emigrated to America? That story she told about the Jewish freedom fighter who had sacrificed his life for her and his unborn child was sweet, but it was completely untrue, as you yourself discovered years ago."

Bancroft's hands were trembling so badly that when he removed his eyeglasses, he dropped them onto his desk.

"She couldn't be sure which of the camp guards was your father. But she suspected it was an officer who shot himself in the head hours before the Allied troops liberated the camp. You were born four months later.

"Howard, Howard, what a nasty secret you've kept. I don't think the Jewish community would look too kindly on you if they knew that your mother happily serviced the men who marched them into the gas chambers and that your father ordered thousands to be exterminated, do you? Considering the advocate you've been for Holocaust survivors, they might regard your crusade as hypocritical. Now, you might say to me, 'You can't prove this.' But the rumor alone would effectively destroy your reputation as a good Jew. Your family would be shattered, because even your wife and children believe the fabrication that your mother concocted."

Bancroft was weeping into his hands.

"No one need ever know, of course," Noah said. He stood up and retrieved both his folder and the power-of-attorney document. "But should it become necessary, your mother's signed statement will be mailed to all the synagogues in and around the five boroughs. It would make for interesting reading, don't you think?"

Noah crossed to the door. Although the lawyer had made no effort to move but continued to cry into his hands, Noah said, "No, no, Howard, don't bother seeing me out. Have a nice day."

"YOU'RE LEAVING TOMORROW?"

"In the morning," Maris replied. Her gaze moved around the solarium, never stopping on Parker. "Mike arranged for a boat."

If Parker's scowl was any indication, she'd been smart to keep her distance all day. He looked ill-tempered, spoiling for a fight.

Mike appeared with a tray. "Fresh peach cobbler," he announced. He deposited the tray on the table, then left.

Parker attacked his helping of the cobbler as though angry at it. When he finished, he rolled his chair to the computer. "Want to read the latest?"

"Of course I want to read it."

While the new pages were printing out, Maris ate her cobbler. Carrying the bowl with her, she moved slowly along the crammed bookcase, surveying the titles. "You like mysteries."

His head came around. "If they're well written."

"You must think Mackensie Roone writes well."

"He's okay."

"Just okay? You have the entire Deck Cayton detective series."

"Ever read one?"

"A few, not all." She pulled one of the books from the shelf and thumbed through it. "I wish we were publishing them. They sell like hotcakes. The Deck Cayton character appeals to both men and women, and why not? He's charming, witty, good-looking. He's—"

"A jerk."

"Sometimes. But he's been so engagingly written that a reader forgives his flaws. Even though he's tough-talking, Deck has an underlying vulnerability."

"Because of his wife's death."

"Right. It's referred to, but I haven't read that particular book."

"First of the series," he explained. "Skiing accident. He challenged her to a downhill race, and she crashed into a tree. Autopsy revealed she was several weeks pregnant. They hadn't known. You should read it."

"I definitely will." She polished off her cobbler. "I'm a fan. Deck is your basic larger-than-life hero that every man fantasizes being."

"Did he live up to your fantasy?"

"Deck Cayton?"

"Your husband. His book sparked your fantasy life. Did his performance in bed—*does* it—live up to expectations?"

She faced him squarely. "Your curiosity about my private life is out of line. Which is why I avoided being alone with you today. What happened in the cotton gin made me uncomfortable."

"I don't remember anything happening in the gin that would compromise you as a married woman."

His feigned innocence infuriated her. "You asked why I allowed that kiss. I allowed it because a wrestling match would have been undignified. And don't delude yourself into thinking I was afraid of you." She shot him an arch look. "I could've outrun you."

"Ouch! That one hurt, Maris. Now you're fighting dirty."

"Which is the only kind of fighting I think you understand."

"It's the only kind of fighting, period," he said tightly. "Win at all costs. I learned—or rather was taught—that lesson."

Although his intensity on the topic intrigued her, there was a dangerous glint in his eyes that warned her against probing any further.

"I wanted to work with you on *Envy*. If one meaningless kiss bought me that opportunity, it was a small price to pay. Can't we concentrate on your book and my desire to buy it?"

"For how much?"

She was caught off guard. "I haven't thought about it."

"Well, do."

The recently printed sheets were neatly stacked in his lap. She was itching to read them. "I would be willing to offer you a moderate advance once I see a detailed outline."

"No sale. I'd rather channel my energy into the story than into writing a stupid outline." They stared at each other until he finally asked, "Do you want to hear what I wrote today?"

"Of course I want to— Did you say *hear* it?"

"Have a seat."

Maris sank into the deep cushions in one of the wicker armchairs, slipped off her sandals, and tucked her legs beneath her.

He rolled his chair near hers. "I took your advice and enhanced the girl's role. This scene between her and Roark takes place on the night following his snafu with Professor Hadley. The professor rescheduled their appointment for after the Thanksgiving holiday. Roark returns to the frat house, pulls Todd off his sleeping loft, and, as you suggested, commences to beat the hell out of him. Some frat brothers break up the fight. Todd apologizes."

"He does? Is he sincere?"

"We have no reason to believe otherwise, do we? Todd says he hadn't counted on Hadley being so severe when Roark turned up late. Anyway, Roark has accepted his apology, but he's still mad. He calls up the girl and makes a date with her for that evening."

"He's in need of some TLC."

"Exactly." Parker flipped through the top several pages. "Oh, I've named the girl Leslie."

"I like it."

"To paraphrase, Roark drives to the lake. He parks. Leslie asks him what's put him in such a funk, and he vents for ten solid minutes. I'll pick up with Leslie's response." He began to read from the text.

> "She spoke quietly, as one would to a temperamental animal who was momentarily docile. 'What happened today is a good thing, Roark.'
>
> "He snorted. 'Good? How is it good?'
>
> " 'The reason you're taking this so hard is because your writing means so much to you. The misunderstanding with Professor Hadley hit you where it hurts most, which affirms that you're doing what you were born to do.' She smiled. 'I didn't need it affirmed. But perhaps you did. And if you did, then this experience was worth all the anxiety it's caused.'

"Well, they kiss, and it gets predictably slippery. Roark opens her coat, cuddles up to her chest. She gives him access to some skin. 'Velvety, warm, fragrant woman skin.' He caresses her."

Maris's heart bumped inside her chest.

He looked across at her. "Roark tells her he loves her."

"How does Leslie respond?"

"Ah," he said, frowning. "As it turns out, she still dumps him."

"Then and there?"

"It's right here in black and white."

"For the reasons stated in the first draft?"

"Yeah."

"Then she's being kind, isn't she? And smart. As much as it hurts her, she's doing what she realizes is best for both of them."

"Maybe. But in Roark's mind she's being heartless."

Maris was about to protest, when Parker raised a finger to halt her. "At least initially." He picked up the remaining pages.

"As much as he wanted to lay blame on Leslie, on Hadley, on Todd for today's miseries, Roark acknowledged that most of the blame lay squarely with him.

"Leslie was wise beyond her experience. Their dreams were too disparate for them to have a future together. The wisdom of her choice to return to her small-town aspirations and long-standing sweetheart didn't make it any easier to lose her now, but ending the relationship before it actually started would spare them future heartache. At least they had parted while all the memories were still sweet. Today had been the first day of Roark Slade's life as an adult. Without ceremony or sacrament he had undergone a rite of passage.

"Roark wasn't aware of this transition until years later, when he had hours, days, months in which to leaf back through the pages of his personal history, searching for the moment when his life had ceased being charmed and became cursed. His search always ended on this day."

Parker stared at the last sentence for a time, then let the sheet slip from his fingers. By now the floor was littered with pages of manuscript. Quietly, without looking at Maris, he said, "That's it so far."

She slowly unfolded her legs and lowered her feet to the floor. "All right, Parker. It goes against company policy as well as my own, but I'll give you a ten-thousand-dollar advance just to finish the manuscript. When it's completed, we'll negotiate the terms of the contract. I suggest you get an agent."

"I suggest you get a grip on reality."

"That's a no?"

"Twenty-five thousand. Which barely covers my expenses."

"Fifteen."

He mulled it over for several seconds. "Fifteen, and it's not applicable to the advance finally agreed upon. In other words, the fifteen's mine no matter what. If Matherly Press can't afford to gamble fifteen grand, you should padlock the doors tomorrow."

"Deal. As soon as I return to New York, I'll have our legal department draw up a letter of agreement. For now, we have a gentleman's agreement." She stuck out her hand.

He took her hand and used it to draw her closer to him. "By no stretch of the imagination are you a gentleman."

She leaned even closer, whispering, "Neither are you."

Laughing, he released her hand. "Got that right. Want to take these with you?" He indicated the pages scattered over the floor.

Parker wheeled his chair backward so she could kneel down and gather the pages. She gathered them with quick motions. Then she noticed the scar. He wasn't wearing socks, so his feet were bare inside a pair of docksiders. The scar crossed the vamp of his right foot and crawled up his ankle to disappear inside the leg of his trousers.

"It only gets worse from there."

She looked up at him. "I'm sorry, Parker."

"No need to apologize. It's human nature to be curious over something that grotesque. I'm accustomed to stares."

"No. I meant I'm sorry for whatever happened to you."

Affecting indifference she knew was false, he wheeled his chair around. "I'm going to get more cobbler. Want some?"

With all the sheets now in hand, she came to her feet. "No, thanks. I need to get to bed. I left an early wake-up call with Mike."

"Right. Good-bye, Maris." His attitude frosty, he wheeled into the kitchen, never looking back.

She'd seen his scars, internal ones as well as those on his legs, and he couldn't tolerate that. He equated the scars to weakness, a limitation to his masculinity, which was ridiculous. Because with the exception of those scarred legs, Parker defined masculinity. His arms were heavily muscled; even his legs were muscular. He wasn't as classically handsome as Noah. There was a distinct asymmetry to Parker's features, but the irregularities made his face arresting and interesting.

Left standing alone, Maris felt awkward and deflated. She was sad to be leaving. The island had captivated her. It was otherworldly, entrancing, and seductive.

And so was Parker Evans. But she shoved that thought aside.

Before she left the solarium, she borrowed a Mackensie Roone novel from Parker's library. The mystery would be a pleasant diversion. Deck Cayton could keep her company.

WHEN Parker entered the gin the following morning, he startled a raccoon. "It's almost daybreak, pal. Better haul ass." The animal scuttled out between broken boards in the wall.

He liked coming to the cotton gin before the sun came up, when it was still reasonably cool and there was a light breeze coming off the ocean. He came here to the emptiness of this ruin to rethink his plot and look for holes in it. He came to anticipate how sweet it was going to be to have his revenge, to see an end to it, to bring it to closure after fourteen years.

This morning he'd come here to think specifically about Maris. Within these weathered walls he had hatched the plan to get her to St. Anne Island, under his roof, and under his influence.

He hadn't planned on her getting under his skin. He couldn't go feeling sorry for her, though. So what if she looked at him with woeful eyes and felt compassion for his scars. He didn't want her pity. And she wouldn't be pitying him if she knew what was in store for—

"You son of a bitch!"

Parker spun his chair around barely in time to duck the hardcover book hurled at his head. He batted the book away just before it could connect with his temple. It landed in the dirt beside his chair, sending up a puff of dust. He recognized the cover. It was the first volume of the Deck Cayton series. Maris was standing just inside the open doorway, her aura glowing red-hot.

Unflappably he asked, "You didn't like the book?"

She walked toward him, quoting as she came, " 'At least they had parted while all the memories were still sweet.' " She came to a stop within a yard of his chair. "You're either a plagiarist or a consummate liar, and either way you're a son of a bitch."

"I believe you quoted from chapter seventeen, when Deck is at his late wife's grave." He feigned puzzlement. "I'm not sure if one can plagiarize oneself. Can one?"

She was too angry to speak.

"Deck is grief-stricken but grateful that he'd had her in his life for even a short time," he continued. "It was rather good, I thought."

"Good enough to use again. In *Envy*. After Leslie broke up with Roark. Why did you lie to me, Parker?"

"I never lied about it," he countered calmly. "You never asked me if I was Mackensie Roone. You never asked me if I wrote a mystery series featuring Deck Cayton."

"Don't be obtuse, Parker! You lied by omission."

"If I hadn't wanted to be found out, I wouldn't have deliberately used that sentence in *Envy* and then recommended that you read the first Deck Cayton book."

"Which was another of your games to test how sharp I am," she shouted. Her hair was tousled, and her cheeks were pink, as though she had run all the way from the house. "Why did you play this ridiculous game with me, Parker? Or Mackensie, or whatever your name is."

"Parker Mackensie Evans. Mackensie was my mother's maiden name. When I was deciding on a pseudonym, it seemed a logical choice. Has a nice ring. It's androgynous, safe."

"From what?"

"Discovery. When I sold the Deck Cayton series, I wished to remain anonymous. I still do."

"Why hide behind a pseudonym?"

He gave her a pointed look. "Why do you suppose, Maris?"

Her lips parted as though to speak, but then realization dawned, and her lips closed. She looked away, embarrassed.

"Right. Deck Cayton is every man's fantasy. Every woman's, too, according to you. Why would I want to dispel his dashing image by showing up at personal appearances in a wheelchair?"

"No book signings or personal appearances. I often questioned your publisher's marketing strategy. They were protecting you."

"Wrong. I was protecting me. Even my publisher doesn't know who Mackensie Roone is. No one knows anything about Mackensie Roone's true identity except my agent."

"I know Mackensie Roone's agent," Maris interrupted. "You didn't go through her when you submitted *Envy*. Why?"

"She doesn't know about it."

"Why?"

"Because I wanted to write a different book. Totally different from the Deck Cayton books. I sent the prologue to you because I wanted you to approach it without preconceptions, not as the work of a best-selling author. I wanted it to be good."

"It would have been just as good without the charade, Parker. My reaction to it would have been the same."

"But I would never have known for sure, would I?"

"Why did you send *Envy* to me, Parker? What set me apart?"

"A magazine article." He hoped she wouldn't detect that he was lying. "The things you were quoted as saying convinced me you were the editor for *Envy*. I liked what you said about commerce versus quality. I'm not writing this book for the money. I've got more money than I'll ever need. Deck Cayton has seen to that. I'm writing *Envy* for me."

"It'll find an audience," she said. "I'll see to that. I have too much invested in it not to."

"A measly fifteen grand?"

"I wasn't referring to the advance."

Suddenly he was consumed with the desire to touch her. "I don't want you to leave." He hadn't known he was going to say that until he heard his own gruff voice filling the silence.

"Write your book, Parker."

"Stay."

"I'll be in touch." She walked away and didn't look back, not even when he called her name.

Chapter Seven

"THIS visit is long overdue. I'm glad you were free." Nadia Schuller sent a smile across the table to her luncheon guest.

As the setting for this intimate get-together, Nadia had chosen a small, cozy restaurant on Park Avenue. It had a friendly ambience, and that was the note she was trying to strike with this lunch— friendliness. Which was somewhat of a challenge when you were sleeping with your guest's husband.

"Thank you for the invitation." Maris offered a strained smile.

A waiter approached their table and took their orders. As Nadia passed Maris a basket of bread, she remarked, "Tragic news about Howard Bancroft."

Maris's eyes turned sad. "Very tragic. I didn't learn of it until I returned late yesterday afternoon."

"How long had he been at the helm of your legal department?"

"Since before I was born. We were all shocked."

"Has anyone speculated on why he killed himself?"

"Nadia, I—"

"Oh, this isn't for Book Chat. The facts were in the newspaper."

Howard Bancroft had been discovered in his car, half a block from his house on Long Island, with a pistol in his hand.

"No one at Matherly Press picked up warning signals?"

"No," Maris replied. "In fact, Noah had a meeting with him just that afternoon. He said Howard was being typically Howard." She shook her head. "He was such a well-loved man. I can't imagine what drove him to commit such a desperate act."

Their main courses arrived. As they ate, they switched to a brighter topic—the books Matherly Press had scheduled for its fall lineup. After jotting the titles and authors down, Nadia laid aside her pen. "When I called to ask you to lunch, your secretary said you were working in Georgia. Tell me about it."

"I can't. It's not open to discussion. The author chooses to remain anonymous."

"How positively fabulous. I love projects swathed in mystery. Give me something," Nadia cajoled. "Friend to friend."

"You're not my friend, Nadia. We will never be friends."

Nadia was taken aback. "Why do you say that?"

"Because you want to sleep with my husband."

In spite of herself, Nadia was impressed. Miss Goody Two Shoes had more grit than the girls school polish suggested. Dropping all pretense, she met Maris's level gaze. "You can't wonder why. Noah *is* an attractive man."

"An attractive *married* man."

Maris remained stubbornly mute about her secret project. Not that Nadia cared. The purpose of this lunch was to keep Maris derailed, unaware, and blissfully ignorant of what Nadia and Noah were doing behind her back with WorldView. As their lunch concluded, Nadia graciously asked, "Anything else, Maris? A cappuccino?"

"No, thank you. I should get back to the office. I'm playing catch-up after being away, as I knew I would be."

"Then why'd you come?" The question was out before Nadia realized she was going to ask it.

"For a long time now, we've detested the sight of one another. But we always played polite. I hate phoniness, especially in myself. It was time to tell you that I'm onto you."

Nadia smiled wryly. "Fair enough." As they left their table, she said, "You'll still feed me industry news items, won't you?"

"News. Not gossip."

"When you're ready to reveal this mysterious author—"

"Nadia, what a nice surprise."

Nadia turned at the greeting and found herself looking into the colorless countenance of Morris Blume, the last person on earth she would choose to bump into when Maris was standing beside her.

An introduction was unavoidable. As the two shook hands, Blume said, "I've long been an admirer of your publishing house."

"And a suitor," Maris remarked.

He grinned disarmingly. "So you've read the letters I've written to your esteemed father and agree with his replies?"

"Wholeheartedly. While we're flattered that WorldView is interested in merging with us, we like ourselves the way we are."

"So your husband told me during our last meeting."

NOAH was reviewing the company's financial statements when his wife stormed into his office and slammed the door behind her. She tossed her handbag onto the nearest chair and strode to his desk.

"Hello, Maris. How was your lunch?"

"I was just introduced to WorldView's whiz kid—Morris Blume. He told me to give you his regards."

Damn Nadia! he thought. Why hadn't she called to warn him? Then he remembered he had given his assistant instructions to hold his calls. "How nice of Mr. Blume to remember me," he said.

"Apparently, it wasn't that much of a stretch, given you had a recent meeting with him." Her eyes flashed. "*What* meeting, Noah? And why wasn't I informed of it?"

He stood up. "Maris, kindly calm down."

"You actually met with those jackals behind my back?"

Noah sighed. "Yes, I met with them. Blume's flunkies had been hounding me for months. The most expedient way to handle the situation was to attend a meeting and tell Blume to his face that we were not interested. I didn't tell you about it, because you were busy."

"I'm always busy."

"The meeting was inconsequential, and frankly, I hoped to avoid a scene such as this."

"This isn't a *scene,* Noah. This is a private conversation between husband and wife, between business partners. Two relationships that should come with an implied trust."

"Exactly," he said, raising his voice to match hers. "Which is why I'm amazed by your apparent lack of trust in me."

A knock on the door brought them around. Daniel was standing on the threshold, leaning heavily on his cane. "I'm exercising one privilege of old age, which is to intrude when uninvited."

"Of course you're welcome," Noah said. "We were having a discussion about—"

"I heard. From way down the hall." Daniel came in. "Maris is upset about the meeting you had with WorldView."

She reacted with a start. "You knew about it?"

"Noah told me of his decision to meet with them. I thought it was a sound idea and was glad he was going instead of me."

"Why wasn't I informed?"

She addressed the question to both of them, but Noah answered. "You were leaving for Georgia. Daniel and I could see how excited you were about this project and were afraid that if you knew about WorldView, you'd change your plans."

"I'm not a child." She glowered at him, then at Daniel. "I'm an officer of this corporation."

"We made a mistake in judgment," Daniel said. "I apologize."

"So do I," Noah echoed.

Daniel took her silence as a tacit pardon. "Are we still on for dinner tonight? Maxine's making pot roast."

"We'll see you at seven," Noah confirmed.

Daniel split an uneasy glance between them, then left them alone.

Maris went to the window and turned her back to the room. Several minutes passed before she spoke. "I'm sorry I lost my temper."

"Have I told you how beautiful you are when you're angry?" Noah said.

She came around quickly and angrily. "Don't patronize me."

It was a little alarming that his charm seemed to have lost some of its effectiveness. "What's with you, Maris? Since you got back, you've been as prickly as a porcupine."

"Did Nadia know about your meeting with Blume?"

He covered his discomfiture with a short laugh. "What? You think I called up our local gossip columnist and leaked the story?"

Maris turned back to the window. "You're lying."

"I beg your pardon?"

"She knew, Noah. Nadia's the most conniving woman I've ever met. When Blume mentioned his meeting with you, she blanched. Then she couldn't hustle me away from him fast enough."

Only an act of will kept his voice calm. "If Nadia knew, she heard it from Blume. I've seen them with their heads together on several occasions. They probably stroke each other for inside information."

Maris came around slowly. "She confessed."

His heart knocked against his chest. "Confessed what?"

"I told Nadia that I knew she had designs on you."

"Designs?" he repeated with amusement. "Quaint phraseology."

"I didn't use it to be cute," she said testily. "I had lunch with a woman who told me to my face that she wants to sleep with you."

He rolled his eyes toward the ceiling. "Nadia wants to sleep with every man. Do you think I'm that easily flattered?"

"A lot of men find her attractive."

"Is that what all this has been about? You let Nadia upset you?"

"No. I was more upset over the WorldView thing than I was about Nadia. If you want Nadia, then you deserve her."

He sighed. "I'm glad you gave me an opportunity to explain both misunderstandings. These things shouldn't fester." He smiled the tentative smile of a scolded puppy. "If that's the end of the interrogation, I'd like to hug my interrogator."

Since she didn't raise any barriers, he put his arms around her and pressed his face into her hair. Then he bent his head and kissed her. She returned the kiss. Not with the fervor he sought, but when he pulled back, she smiled up at him, assuaging his concern.

She retrieved her handbag. "I may stay late and try to clear my desk, so I probably won't change before dinner with Dad."

"Then we'll leave straight from here and ride over together. I'll have a car waiting downstairs at six forty-five."

"See you then."

He blew her a kiss as she went out, then returned to his desk, confident that he had dodged a bullet. His phone rang. Before he could speak, his assistant apologized for the interruption. "I'm sorry, Mr. Reed, but Ms. Schuller has called five times and insists on being put through."

"Fine." Noah depressed the blinking button. "Hello, Nadia," he said breezily. "I understand you had quite an exciting lunch."

Envy, continued—Key West, Florida, 1986

. . . Todd Grayson's first impression of Key West was a crushing disappointment. He likened the place to an old whore. It looked used, seedy, a little unhealthy, and a lot tired.

His and Roark's plan had been to depart for Florida the afternoon of their college graduation, but a family obligation prevented Todd from leaving. Roark offered to postpone leaving, too, but they agreed that he should go ahead and start looking for housing.

"I'll be the scout. By the time you get there, I'll have camp set up," Roark had said as they exchanged their dejected good-byes.

"This sucks," Todd muttered about the change in plans.

"Big time. But hey, it's only a minor setback."

As Roark wedged himself into the driver's seat of his packed Toyota, he tried to lift Todd's spirits. "I know this seems like a big deal now, but one day we'll barely remember it."

As agreed, he had called Todd immediately upon his arrival in Key West. A few days later he phoned again to report that he had rented an apartment. It was six weeks before Todd was able to set out for his relocation to the tip of the continent. He drove almost twenty hours that first day and crossed the state line into Florida before pulling off at a roadside park and napping in the car. He arrived in Key West at midafternoon the second day.

Todd navigated the tourist-clogged streets, following the rudimentary directions Roark had given him, until he located their newly leased domicile. Dismayed, he checked the address twice, hoping he'd made a wrong turn.

Surely this was one of Roark's practical jokes. Tall oleander bushes formed an unkempt hedge between the street and the weedy lawn in front of the building. Todd expected Roark to leap from between the shrubs, grinning and saying, "Man, you oughta see your expression. Looks like you've been hit with a sack of buzzard waste." They would have a good laugh, and then Roark would guide him to their actual address. Later they would retell the story, as they retold all their good stories.

Except the one about the incident with Professor Hadley. That was one story that neither retold.

Todd parked his car at the crumbling curb, got out, and followed the sidewalk up to the door of the three-story building. It had been painted a flamingo pink, as though the lurid hue would conceal the cinder blocks. Hurricane shutters, the color of pea soup, seemed to be clinging to the building only out of fear of falling into the stagnant water that had collected around the foundation.

Todd opened the front door and stepped into a dank vestibule. Two green lizards were lounging on the interior wall, where six mailboxes had been secured. Their apartment was on the third floor. By the time he reached it, he was sweating. He knocked on the door of 3A—three times in all, before Roark answered. His suntanned face broke into a wide grin. "Hey, you made it!"

"No air-conditioning?" The apartment was a rathole. The heat inside was more stifling than on the staircase. Todd was so angry he could barely suck the stifling oxygen into his lungs. His deposit money had been squandered. If Roark had signed a lease on this place, then he could eat it, for all Todd cared. He would flatly refuse to be responsible.

"Come on, you gotta see this." Roark turned and headed toward an open door that led into another room.

It was a small cubicle with twin beds. Next to one was a computer terminal, the tower and printer on the floor beside it.

"A computer!" Todd exclaimed. "You got a *PC?* When?" They had wanted word processors the way most collegians covet TransAms. "Is that what you spent our money on?"

"My uncle gave it to me for graduation," Roark said in a stage whisper. He was staring out an open window. "Now get over here. Hurry, before they go inside."

In spite of everything, Todd was intrigued. Pushing Roark away from the window, he peered through the rusty screen.

On the second-floor roof of the neighboring building three naked girls were sunbathing. All they had on was a glistening layer of suntan oil. One of the girls was languidly spreading the oil over her torso.

"That one's name is Amber," Roark whispered.

Todd gulped. "You know them?"

"Yeah. To speak to and call by name. Our buildings share a parking lot. They dance at a strip joint."

Which explained why this was no trio of ordinary-looking women. They were spectacular.

"Oh, man," Todd groaned. "This is fantastic. I can't think of any-place I'd rather live."

~

MIKE Strother laid the manuscript aside. He was never quick to comment, whether his review was good or bad. But when he was piqued at Parker for one reason or another, he deliberately withheld his remarks until Parker asked for them. Today, making noncommittal harrumphing sounds, he was taking even more time than usual.

"Could you please translate those grunts?"

Mike scowled. "You didn't go to the cotton gin today, did you?"

"What's that got to do with the manuscript?" Parker asked impatiently. "You're being awfully contrary this afternoon."

"You're changing the subject, Parker. After months of preoccupation with that place, you haven't been back to it since Maris left. What happened there between you and Maris the other morning?"

"Nothing happened. You're as nosy as an old woman."

"Maris is my business, too, Parker. I could have told her you were Mackensie Roone. Instead I went along with the whole charade, and I'm ashamed of myself for it."

"Don't be, Mike. You're blameless. This is all my doing."

They lapsed into silence. Parker turned away and stared out over the ocean. A small flock of pelicans flew in formation just above the treetops. Parker wondered if it was constraining or comforting to be part of such a closely knit group. He had been a loner for so many years, he couldn't remember what it was like to be a member of a family or community of individuals. But that had been his choice. Recently, however, he had begun to realize the tremendous price he had paid for his years of being alone.

Eventually Mike picked up his reading glasses. "These young men seem to have reconciled completely," he remarked as he thumbed through the manuscript pages again.

"Following the incident with Hadley, Roark made a conscious decision not to let it affect their friendship," Parker explained.

"Noble of him. Nevertheless, it's still—"

"There," Parker interrupted, completing the other man's thought. "Neither wants to acknowledge the blemish on their friendship."

"You didn't specify or explain the family obligation that prevented Todd from leaving with Roark."

"It's discussed in the next scene. Roark extends condolences to Todd for his mother's death. She had been diagnosed with a rampant cancer. Not wanting to worry him, she didn't tell him until graduation. So rather than leaving for Florida, Todd accompanied her home. He stayed with her until she died."

"Quite a sacrifice, especially when you consider what moving to Key West represented to him."

Parker smiled sardonically. "Save the kudos. I have him saying— Wait, let me read it to you." He shuffled the sheets of handwritten notes scattered across his worktable until he found the one he was looking for. "Todd thanks Roark for his expression of sympathy, then says, 'Actually, her death was very convenient.' Roark reacts with appropriate shock. Then Todd adds, 'I'm only being honest.'

" 'Cruelly honest,' says Roark.

"Todd shrugs indifferently. 'Maybe, but at least I'm not a hypocrite. Her dying left me free.' "

Mike assimilated that. "So the white gloves are coming off."

"If by that you mean that Todd's true character will be revealed, no. We do, however, begin to detect chinks in the façade."

"The same way Noah Reed's true character was revealed to you once you moved to Key West. Bit by bit."

Parker felt his facial muscles stiffen. "It takes Roark only a few chapters to see his so-called friend for what he really is. It took me a couple of years. By then it was too late." He stared hard at his legs.

Mike seemed about to remark on something but changed his mind. A minute passed. Finally Parker asked Mike what was on his mind. "The pacing? The dialogue?"

"The strippers on the roof. Is the girl—"

"Who accompanies the boys on the boat in the prologue one of them? Yes. Remember, one of the boys removes her bikini top and waves it above his head before they're even out of the harbor. So it's important that I establish in the reader's mind that she's a friendly, playful sort. There's more about her in an upcoming scene. She has a miscarriage, and the reader suspects that Todd got her pregnant, but never knows for sure."

"She's a nice girl, Parker."

"The stripper?"

Mike gave him a sour look. "Maris."

Parker cursed beneath his breath. Mike was determined to talk about her. Parker returned his notes to the worktable. "First of all, Maris is a woman, not a girl. And whoever said she wasn't nice?"

Mike fixed an admonishing glare at him. "Admit it. She's not the spoiled rich girl you expected. She made an impact, didn't she?"

"Don't get misty, Mike," Parker said more harshly than he had intended. "She plays sensitive because she wants a book from me."

"A book. Not income. I don't think she cares if *Envy* makes her company a red cent. She loves your writing."

Parker shrugged indifferently, but secretly he agreed.

"I guess there's no need mentioning she's beautiful," Mike added.

"Then why'd you mention it?"

"So you noticed?"

"What, you think I'm blind as well as lame? I expected her to be attractive. Noah never dated an ugly girl. I'm glad she's attractive. It'll make what I'm going to do all the more enjoyable. Now, I've work to do."

Mike riffled through the manuscript pages again. He stood and passed the sheets to Parker. "It's coming along."

"Don't go overboard with the praise," Parker said drolly.

On his way out, Mike said, "You may want to rethink your motivation."

"My characters' motivations are perfectly clear."

Mike didn't even deign to turn and address Parker face to face when he said, "I wasn't referring to your characters."

Chapter Eight

"THIS is my favorite room." Maris basked in the familiar comfort of her father's home study, where they were having cocktails.

At the last minute Noah had needed to consult with the contracts manager over a disputed clause, so he had urged her to go to Daniel's house ahead of him.

"I'm rather partial to this room myself," Daniel said. "I like it even more when you're sharing it with me."

Maris sensed a melancholia in him tonight. "Dad, aren't you feeling well?"

"It's just that I'm going to miss Howard. For the life of me, I can't understand what drove him to do such a terrible thing."

Maris nodded sympathetically. He was grieving his loss, naturally, but she wasn't exactly a barrel of laughs tonight either. She was feeling a huge sense of loss herself. She'd been reluctant to pinpoint the source of it and assign it a name, but in her heart of hearts she knew its name: Parker Evans.

As she let her gaze wander around the room, she couldn't help contrasting the expensive furnishings of this study to the wicker chairs in Parker's solarium. And she realized that as much as she loved this room and the fond memories of childhood it evoked, she was homesick for St. Anne Island and Parker's house. She missed the oddly harmonious racket of the cicadas, the distant swish of the surf breaking on the beach, and . . . Parker. She missed Parker.

"Maris?"

She smiled at Daniel with chagrin. "Did I drift, Dad?"

"No farther than a million miles. Are you thinking about him? Is he what has made you sad?"

"Made me sad? Hardly," she said. "Would I like to throttle him? Definitely. He stays hidden away on that island, a recluse because of his disability. Oh, have I told you, Dad? He's wheelchair-bound. At first I was shocked, but after a while . . . I don't know, it's strange. When I look at him now, I don't even see the wheelchair."

She paused, wondering at what point that had happened. "He's not handsome exactly, but he's got an . . . an animal magnetism. He's got a sly sense of humor, and when he speaks to you, you're drawn right into his eyes." She took a sip of wine.

Daniel studied her for a long moment as he packed tobacco into his pipe. "Actually, Maris, my question referred to Noah."

She flushed hotly. "Oh—oh, well," she stammered, "I wouldn't say Noah made me *sad,* but I was upset that he didn't tell me about his meeting with WorldView."

Daniel set the pipe aside and picked up his tumbler. As he contemplated the amber contents, he asked, "Did Noah tell you that he had a meeting with Howard the afternoon he killed himself?"

The manner in which he posed the question indicated this wasn't a casual inquiry. "He mentioned it," she said.

"It took place a couple of hours before Howard ended his life."

"What was the nature of their meeting?"

"According to Noah, Howard needed him to sign off on a contract with one of our foreign licensees."

"Do you . . ." She cleared her throat. "Do you doubt that?"

"I have no reason to." He took a sip of whiskey. "Although Howard's secretary told me that his meeting with Noah was his last for the day and that when he left the office, he seemed distressed."

"Dad, do you think—"

"Good. I see you started without me." Noah pushed open the double door and breezed in. He bent down and kissed Maris, then smacked his lips as though tasting them. "Good wine."

"It is. I'll pour you one." She got up and moved to the wet bar.

"Thanks, but I'd rather have what Daniel is having. Rocks only. It's been that kind of day."

Noah crossed the room to shake hands with his father-in-law, then joined Maris on the love seat and placed his arm around her as she handed him a highball glass. "Cheers." After taking a sip of his drink, he said, "Maxine sent me in with the message that dinner is ready."

The dinner was delicious. But by the time the lemon tarts were served, Daniel was yawning. As soon as Maxine removed the dessert dishes, he asked to be excused. "Stay and enjoy another cup of coffee," he told his guests as he stood up. "But I should retire."

"I need to say good night, too, Dad. Today was long."

As they left the dining room, Maris held back and detained Noah. "Could I ask a favor? Would you please stay and help Dad get upstairs to bed? I know it's not your place—"

"I don't mind at all. Daniel's looking a little down in the mouth tonight," he whispered. "Once he's tucked in, I think I'll offer to have a bedtime brandy with him."

"Do. But make it a short one. I'll be home waiting."

MARIS didn't go straight home. She had never intended to. Using her father as a pawn to delay Noah made her feel guilty, but only a little. She would never have deceived them if she weren't desperate to rid herself of nagging doubts. She took a taxi downtown to the apartment in Chelsea.

By the time she reached the door of the apartment, her heart was beating hard, and not because of the steep staircase. She unlocked the door with the key she'd had in her possession since the night of her surprise party and, remembering where the light switch was, flipped it on. The apartment was silent. She moved toward the room designated as Noah's office.

It looked exactly as they'd left it that night. There were no paper balls in the trash can, no reference books with pages marked, no notes scrawled on legal tablets. Noah's writing space was immaculate, although upon closer inspection, Maris saw that his computer keyboard sported a fine layer of dust.

Her heart wasn't beating fast now. It felt like a stone inside her chest as she turned off the lights and left the apartment. She exited the building and descended the front steps, weighted down with dread for the inevitable confrontation with Noah. When he returned from her father's house, he would be expecting his docile wife to be waiting for him at home. Meek, malleable Maris. Stupid Maris. That's what he thought of her. But he thought wrong.

As she reached street level, she noticed a passenger alighting from a taxi half a block away. She raised her hand to signal the driver. As soon as he received his fare, he drove to where Maris stood at the curb. But she was no longer looking at the taxi. Instead she was watching the man who had alighted from the cab as he jogged up the steps of another brownstone, entering it with an air of familiarity.

She motioned the taxi driver to go on. Walking briskly, she quickly covered the distance to the other apartment building. She entered the vestibule and checked the mailboxes. All except one were labeled with a name. Either the apartment was vacant, or the tenant in 2A received mail at another location.

Again she climbed stairs. But it was with amazing calm that she approached the door of apartment 2A and rapped smartly.

Nadia Schuller opened the door. She was dressed for romance, wearing only a silk wrapper, hastily tied at her waist. She didn't even have the decency to look alarmed or shamefaced.

Maris's gaze slid past her to Noah, who was coming from a connecting room, presumably a kitchen, with a drink in each hand. He was in shirtsleeves. Upon seeing her, he stopped. "Maris."

"Don't bother explaining, Noah. You're a liar and an adulterer, and I want you out of my life. Immediately. I'll have Maxine pack up your things, because I can't bear the thought of touching them myself. I don't want to see you again, Noah. Ever."

Then she turned and jogged down the stairs, across the small lobby, and out onto the sidewalk. She wasn't crying. In fact, she felt surprisingly unshackled and lighthearted. She had no sense of leaving something, but rather of going toward something.

She didn't get far. Noah gripped her arm from behind and roughly jerked her around. He grinned down at her, but it was a cold and frightening grin. "Well, well, Maris. Clever you."

"Let go of me!" She struggled to pull her arm free, but his fingers closed more tightly around her biceps.

"I heard what you had to say, Maris. Brave speech. But now let *me* tell *you* how it's going to be. Our marriage has been and will remain on my terms. You don't order me out of your life. You don't order me to leave. I leave you only when I'm damn good and ready. I hope you understand that. Your life will be so much easier if you do." His eyes glinted with an evil light.

"You're hurting me, Noah."

He laughed. "I haven't begun to hurt you yet." He squeezed her arm tightly, cruelly, his fingers mashing muscle against bone. Tears of pain sprang to her eyes. Then he released her so suddenly, she fell against an iron fence, painfully banging her shoulder.

As he turned away and started back toward the brownstone he shared with Nadia, he called cheerfully, "Don't wait up."

Too stunned to move, Maris watched him go. Tonight, for the first time, she had been introduced to the real Noah Reed.

NOAH decided to give Maris a week to simmer down. He concluded that a woman who catches her husband in adultery deserves a seven-day grace period in which to lick her wounds. It was more than an adequate amount of time for an ego to be restored. In the meantime he had a suite at The Plaza. Since they had never been overtly affectionate at work, no one at Matherly Press noticed the chill between them.

He let Maris brood for the full seven days before approaching her. Geared up for his showdown with her, he stepped off the elevator and pushed through the glass doors leading into the executive offices of Matherly Press. He went into Maris's office straightaway, but she wasn't there. On his way out, he bumped into her assistant. "Can I help you, Mr. Reed?"

"I'm looking for Maris."

She looked at him quizzically. "She's not coming in today, Mr. Reed. Remember, she's going back to Georgia."

It required all his acting skills not to give his ignorance away. This was the worst possible time for her to play the betrayed wife and run away. Her pouting could ruin this whole thing.

On second thought, he had the document that Howard Bancroft had drawn up for him. He would rather not use it. From a legal standpoint, that document could make things sticky. But it was there in his safe-deposit box—an insurance policy, an emergency measure to be used if it became necessary.

DANIEL Matherly finished reading the last page of the manuscript. "That's all you've got so far?"

Maris nodded. "I haven't received anything from him since I returned. So I'm going back. I'm on my way to the airport now. I only stopped by to hear your opinion of what you've read so far."

She had postponed her departure for a week. After catching Noah in Nadia Schuller's apartment, it was a foregone conclusion that she would return to Georgia and see Parker again. Her husband's affair had given her a green light to examine her conflicting feelings about Parker. For the past seven days she had thought of little else.

But even if she hadn't caught Noah with Nadia, she would be leaving him. That night on the sidewalk in Chelsea, Noah had revealed an aspect of himself that appalled and frightened her. Their marriage was over. Noah Reed was her past.

What she needed to determine was if Parker Evans was her future. She could no longer deny her attraction to him. It wasn't strictly his intellect and talent that appealed to her. She was attracted to him, the man. Countless times she had fantasized kissing him again, having his hands on her. She didn't even know if he was capable of making love in the traditional sense, but it didn't matter.

As for informing Daniel of the split, she would postpone it for as long as possible. It would come as a double blow to him. He would be losing not only his son-in-law but his protégé.

Daniel was watching her now with his unsettling intuitiveness.

"So what do you think, Dad?"

"About the book? I think it's very good. Speaking as a publisher, I would prod the author to complete it."

"Then I guess I'm off." She stood up.

"What does Noah think of your going away to spend more time with this writer? I remember well when you fell in love with a book and then with the author."

She gave him a faint smile. "Is that what you're thinking? That I've got a schoolgirl's crush on this writer?"

He reached for her hand. "It wouldn't be the first time."

"I'm older and wiser now. This book, this author have nothing to do with Noah and our marriage. Nothing whatsoever."

That was the truth. Had she never heard of Parker or *Envy,* her marriage would have ended.

"So Noah's agreeable to your going?"

She looked her father straight in the eye and for the first time in her life lied to him. "Yes, he's agreeable."

Daniel took her face between his hands and kissed her on both cheeks. "What time is your flight?"

"I've barely got time to make it." Plagued by guilt for lying to him, she embraced him tightly. "You're my best friend, Dad. I love you very much."

"And I love you, Maris." He set her away from him so he could look into her face. "More than you could ever know."

PARKER answered the door. For several moments he looked at Maris blankly. Finally he said, "Did you forget something?"

"Very cute. Are you going to ask me in?"

He hesitated, then pushed his chair backward into the foyer, giving her room to step inside.

"Where's Mike?" she asked.

"He went to the mainland for groceries."

"And left you here alone?"

"I'm not helpless," he said in what amounted to a snarl. "I lived by myself before Mike came on board. Besides, I'm not alone."

He was with a woman. Maris realized now that all the signs were there. Mike was away. Parker's shirt was unbuttoned, and his hair was more disheveled than usual. "I'm sorry. I . . . I should have called before I came."

"Yeah, you should have," he said crossly. "But since you've made the trip, come on in. We're in here." He wheeled his chair around and rolled it into the dining room.

Reluctantly Maris stood her suitcase in the foyer, then followed, wishing she didn't have to meet his lady friend. Fortifying herself with a deep breath, she stepped through the arched opening between the hallway and dining room.

Except for Parker, the dining room was empty. She looked at him inquisitively. "Up there," he said, motioning with his chin.

"I've noticed it swaying before," she told him, looking at the chandelier. "It catches the current from the air-conditioning vent."

"Reasonable explanation. But wrong. It's the hanged man's ghost."

She expelled a short laugh. "Ghost?"

He proceeded to tell her a tale about a planter who'd fallen on hard times. "He hanged himself right here in the dining room."

"You really believe that his ghost is . . . up there?"

"Yes. Ordinarily, we ignore him. Today he's kept me company."

Maris peered at Parker suspiciously. Then her eyes strayed to the open decanter on the sideboard. "You're drunk."

"Not yet."

"Is this what you do now instead of write? You drink?"

"You must've been talking to Mike."

"When you refused to take my calls. Why are you doing this?"

"Why'd you come back?" he snapped in return.

"I asked you first."

"Because I don't have any of the narcotics I used to take, and I'd have a hard time hanging myself from the chandelier."

"That's not funny."

"It wasn't meant to be."

"Your mention of suicide is tasteless. Particularly today, since a good friend of mine blew his brains out last week."

The exchange ended there, and for a time neither of them spoke. Finally Parker asked, "Who was your friend?"

"Our corporate lawyer. I'd known him all my life."

"I'm sorry."

He glanced down at her high-heeled shoes. "You're dressed for New York. Why don't you change. Then you can read the segment I've been working on since you left."

She smiled in surprise. "So you have been writing?"

"Mike only *thinks* he knows everything."

"THIS couldn't have worked out more perfectly. We can speak freely." Noah was pretending a nonchalance he didn't feel. He idly twirled the olive in his martini glass. "Maris went out of town again."

Morris Blume had arrived at the Reeds' West Side co-op wearing his condescending attitude like a fashion accessory. They were seated on facing sofas, martini glasses in hand.

"She goes away frequently, doesn't she?" Blume asked.

"Not until recently, when she began working on a project with an author who lives on an island off the coast of Georgia."

"You're sure it's all work?"

Noah chuckled. "This writer is shriveled and disabled, wheelchair-bound. Passion hasn't drawn Maris to Georgia."

"I assume she'll be surprised when Matherly Press becomes part of WorldView."

"We'll know soon."

"I like the confident ring of that."

Smiling, Noah set his glass on the coffee table and reached for his briefcase. With a flourish he clicked open the latches. "Delivered on time, as promised."

He passed Blume the document prepared by Howard Bancroft, and Blume scanned it, rapidly flipping through the pages. Noah waited to be congratulated.

But when Blume finished glancing over the last page, he said, "Very nice. Now all that's needed is their signatures."

"Not necessary, Morris. Didn't you read—"

"That it's valid with your signature alone?" He stood up. "A problematic clause, Noah. I'm already dodging antitrust laws and myriad other trade regulations." He waved his hand in a dismissive gesture. "This document, as it is now, would flag the feds. Even if it didn't, the Matherlys could raise a hue and cry, and then we'd all be screwed. Now if you'll excuse me, I have a dinner date."

He turned and headed for the door. Noah blinked the pulsing red lights out of his vision and followed. "Not to worry, Morris. I'll get the signatures."

Blume said, "I never worry." He opened the door, then paused and turned back to Noah. "One of their signatures would probably be sufficient. Either your father-in-law's or your wife's." He mulled it over, then nodded. "Yes. I'd feel protected with only one in addition to yours."

An hour later Noah entered Daniel's home study. An open book was resting on Daniel's lap, but his head was bowed low over his chest, and for a second Noah feared the old man had died. "Daniel?"

He raised his head. "Hello, Noah. I was just reading."

"Do you always snore when you read?"

"Tell me I wasn't drooling, too."

"Not that I saw."

"Good. Have a seat."

On the way over, an unpleasant thought had crossed Noah's mind: What if Maris had told her father about his affair with Nadia? But the old man was behaving normally. Noah sat down on the love seat. "I'm sorry to disturb you. But Maris will call later, and I'll be required to give her a full report, right down to what you ate for dinner."

"Grilled sole, brown rice, and steamed vegetables."

"A menu she'll approve. She also put me in charge of keeping you company while she's away."

Daniel snorted. "I don't need a baby-sitter."

"I agree. But please go along with me, or I'll catch hell when she returns." He leaned forward. "How about going to the country tomorrow for the weekend? Get in some fishing?"

Daniel pondered it for a moment. Noah said no more. He couldn't push too hard, or the old man would become suspicious.

"What time tomorrow?"

Noah's tension eased, and he smiled. "I have a breakfast meeting that would be difficult to reschedule. We could leave right after."

"That doesn't give Maxine much time to—"

"Actually, Daniel, I was thinking that we could go alone. Really bach it." Lowering his voice, he said, "If Maxine goes, she'll fuss over you like a mother hen."

"And everything I do will be reported straight to Maris."

"Sometimes we men must take a stand."

"Hear, hear."

"I'll be over in the morning around ten."

WHILE Maris studied his manuscript, Parker studied her. She had taken a full hour at the guest cottage and had returned wearing a casual skirt that came almost to her ankles, along with the shirt that tied at her waist and allowed a glimpse of bare midriff. She had kicked off her sandals when she settled into the easy chair, and tucked her feet beneath her.

Her hair had been shampooed. A fresh application of lip gloss had left her mouth with a peachy shine, and there was more color in her cheeks than when she arrived. She looked and smelled delectable.

As it had been since she left, he could think of little else today— Maris smiling at Noah, kissing Noah, sleeping beside Noah. The revolving mental images had been enough to drive him to drink. He'd been steeping in his misery, stewing in—

"Was it Todd's?" she asked, looking up. "The baby that the stripper Mary Catherine miscarried in this chapter. Was it Todd's?"

He shook off his reverie. "What do you think?"

"It's suggested. Do we ever know?"

He shook his head. "I think it's better to leave it with just a suggestion. Let the reader come to his own conclusion."

"I agree." She thumbed through the pages again. "He's a remarkable character. Roark, I mean. He's so . . . well, heroic. As Mary Catherine says, he's nice."

Parker grimaced. "He's not *too* nice, is he? I don't want him coming across as a saint."

"He doesn't." She smiled reassurance.

"Women readers aren't turned on by nice heroes. There should be at least a hint, maybe even a promise, of corruptibility."

"You don't have to worry about Roark. Women will love him. He's very male, but at the same time he's sensitive. He helps Mary Catherine after her miscarriage, but he declines her invitation to have sex, demonstrating that he knows where the lines of decency are drawn. Without hitting the reader over the head, you imply that he has a strong conscience. He upholds a code of honor, a . . ." She glanced up and caught him silently laughing at her. "What?"

"You really get worked up over this stuff, don't you?"

"That's my job."

"I understand your need to get excited over it. But at the end of the day it's still only a book, Maris."

"Not to me it isn't." She spoke softly and a bit shyly. "When I really love a book, the characters become real to me."

"You're dedicated."

"Yes, I am."

"So is that why you came back? Am I a job you left unfinished?"

"I came back to deliver the letter of agreement, along with your signing check for fifteen thousand. I wanted to make sure you were writing, Parker, and, if you weren't, to prod you along." She looked at him, opened her mouth to speak, reconsidered, and began again. "We had quarreled before I left. I wanted to clear the air between us. Otherwise—"

He held up his hand to stop her next argument. "You hopped that plane because you wanted to see me again. Admit it, Maris."

Her chin went up defiantly, and he thought she might deny it. But she surprised him. "Yes, I did. I wanted to see you."

He leaned toward her. "Why? Not because of my natural charm. We established early on that I have none." He stroked his chin. "So I'm wondering, did you and your hubby have a spat? Afterward you thought, 'I'll show him. I'll trot myself down to Hicksville and have a fling with a gimp.' Is that why you came back?"

He figured she would storm from the room, retrieve her things from the guest cottage, then hightail it to her golf cart. But again he guessed wrong. She remained where she was.

"Tell me, Parker, why do you insist on being cruel? To cancel out the wheelchair? Or do you hurt people before they have a chance to hurt you? If that's the case, then I'm truly sorry for you."

When she stood up, her posture was dignified, her head high. As Parker watched her disappear through the door, he felt like the lowest life-form on earth. He had accused her of using him to get to Noah, when precisely the opposite was at play—he was using her to get to Noah.

Afraid she would leave before he could apologize, he rolled his chair out of the kitchen, down the hallway, and through the front door. He was relieved to find her on the veranda, leaning into one of the columns, staring out at the giant live oaks that stood sentinel on both sides of the front path.

"Maris."

"I'll leave in the morning."

"I don't want you to go."

She laughed softly but without humor. "You don't know what you want, Parker. To write. Not to write. To be famous. To be a recluse. To have me here. To send me away. You don't even know whether or not you want to go on living. Whatever the case, I shouldn't have come back. I should have left you alone to luxuriate in your bitterness and to keep boozy company with a ghost."

He rolled his chair directly behind her and placed his hands on either side of her waist. "Don't leave." Leaning forward, he pressed his forehead into the small of her back. "I don't give a damn why you came back, Maris. You're here, and I want you to be."

He moved his hands around to her front, where he rested them on the knot of her shirt before slipping them beneath it and touching her skin. He gradually drew her backward.

She spoke his name plaintively—part statement, part query, part sigh of resignation.

He continued to draw her backward until her knees bent and he settled her onto his lap. He turned her, draping her legs over an armrest of his chair, so that he was cradling her like an infant.

She looked up at him with concern. "Is this all right?"

He sifted her hair through his fingers, then stroked her cheek with his thumb. "This is perfect." It required all his willpower not to kiss her then. "Want to go for a ride?" he asked.

"A ride?"

"Down to the beach."

"I can walk."

"You can ride."

He disengaged the brake and navigated the wheelchair down the ramp off the veranda onto a paved path that led through the woods. The path went as far as the sand dunes, where it connected to an elevated path constructed of weathered wood planks. Sea oats brushed against Maris's legs as they went over the dunes. Beyond them the path expanded into a platform. Parker stopped and set the brake on the wheelchair.

The deserted beach spread out before them. The moon was obscured by a dense cloud cover, but it shed enough light to see the surf as it broke. It left a silvery residue that sparkled briefly before dissolving into the sand.

"This is an amazing place." Maris spoke in a reverential whisper. "Dense forest growing right up to the beach."

"And no high-rise hotels to spoil the view." He was rubbing a strand of Maris's hair between his fingers.

She turned her head to look at him. "What kind of narcotics?"

"Ah. I should've known you'd catch that slip of the tongue." He let go of her hair. "Painkillers. Heaping handfuls."

"Because of your legs?"

"It was a long recovery."

"From what, Parker?"

"My own stupidity." After a short pause he continued. "I underwent several operations. First to reconstruct the bones. Then the muscles and tendons had to be reattached. After that the skin. Hell, Maris, you don't want to hear all that. Bottom line, I was in the hospital for over a year, then in . . . other facilities. I went through years of physical therapy and got hooked on prescription painkillers. When the doctors refused to prescribe any more, I bought the pills off the street."

"But you pulled yourself out of it."

"No. I got yanked out of it."

"Mike."

"Mike," he repeated, shaking his head over the miracle of it. "For reasons I will never understand, he befriended me. He appeared one day out of nowhere and slapped me into detox. When I got out, he cleaned me up, enrolled me in therapy, asked what I intended to do with the rest of my life. When I told him I had an itch to write, he set me up with a computer. He put it in the form of a dare."

"Can I ask a very personal question, Parker? Is Roark you?"

He'd known she would get around to it sooner or later. Naturally, she would see the parallel and ask. "Not entirely."

"Loosely based upon?"

"Fair to say."

She nodded solemnly but pried no further. Raindrops began to fall. They felt as warm and soft as tears. "Parker, remember that first day I came to the cotton gin, you suggested that Noah had married the boss's daughter to further his career?"

"That yanked your chain."

"Yes. But only because you hit the nail on the head. Deep down I knew it." She turned and looked into his face. "I caught him this week with another woman."

His expression was neutral. "He's a fool."

She gave him a smile for the indirect compliment, but it turned rueful. "So am I. I'm a fool for not acknowledging sooner that our marriage wasn't what I wanted it to be. Nor was Noah the man I wanted him to be. He wasn't the hero of his book." She reached for Parker's hand. "My marriage, such as it was, is over. Behind me. I don't want to talk about Noah anymore."

"Fine by me." He gathered a handful of her hair and drew her closer, until their faces were inches apart. He hesitated for several heartbeats, then settled his lips against hers. They kissed long and deeply.

THE following morning in New York, Daniel got up early. He dressed quickly, then packed for the country before going downstairs to ask Maxine if it would be too much trouble to have his breakfast on the patio.

"No trouble at all, Mr. Matherly. It'll take me just a few minutes to get the tray ready."

"Perfect. I can use the time to make a couple of calls." He went into his study and placed the first call to a number he now had memorized. He said little during the five-minute call. The majority of the time was spent listening.

Mr. William Sutherland finally said everything he had to say and asked, "Do you want me to proceed, Mr. Matherly?"

"By all means."

Daniel placed the second call of the morning to Becker-Howe. He wasn't surprised that it was answered by Oliver Howe himself. Apparently, his schedule was as arduous as it had always been despite his advanced age. Howe's publishing career had been launched at approximately the same time as Daniel's and in a similar fashion. Howe was bequeathed his company by his grandfather within months of his graduation from his university. He and Daniel had remained friendly rivals through the years, and they held each other in the highest esteem.

"Ollie, it's Daniel Matherly."

As expected, his old colleague was delighted to hear from him. After exchanging pleasantries, Howe said, "I thought you had retired."

"That's the rumor, but the fact is, I've run across an exciting proposition I thought might interest you. . . ."

Daniel emerged from his study a few minutes later without the benefit of his cane. He felt invigorated. He was even rubbing his palms together as he approached Maxine. "Would you please go out and buy some bread at that kosher bakery I like?"

"They don't have bread in Massachusetts?"

"But I'm hungry for the kind with the seeds on it."

"I know the kind. That bakery is across town. I'll go after you've had breakfast."

"Noah will be picking me up after breakfast. Better go now. I can serve myself breakfast."

She eyed him suspiciously but eventually left. She'd only been gone a few minutes when Daniel answered the front doorbell and invited his guest inside. "My housekeeper is out on an errand," he explained as he led the way to the patio. He indicated a chair at the round wrought-iron table. "Please sit. Coffee?"

"Yes, thank you."

Daniel poured. As he passed the cream and sugar, he said, "Thank you for coming on such short notice."

"It wasn't so much an invitation as an edict, Mr. Matherly."

"Then why did you come?"

"Curiosity."

Daniel acknowledged the candor with an appreciative nod. "So you were surprised to hear from me?"

"Shocked, actually."

"I'm glad that we can speak frankly, because I know your time is valuable, and I'm on a tight schedule myself this morning. My son-in-law is picking me up at ten o'clock and driving me to our house in the country. He invited me to spend some quality time alone with him while my daughter is away." He lifted a napkin-lined silver basket toward his guest. "Muffin?"

"No, thanks."

He returned the basket to the tabletop. Clasping his hands together, Daniel looked at his guest from beneath his white eyebrows. "I would stake my fortune on the probability that when Noah and I arrive at our country place, he will have in his possession a document that empowers him to conduct business for my publishing house." He spoke with brusque efficacy. "Over the course of the weekend I will be pressed into signing this document." He raised his hand to stop his guest from speaking. "No. Say nothing. You would do well only to listen."

Chapter Nine

Envy, continued—Key West, Florida, 1988
. . . Todd hadn't counted on its taking this long. He was impatient to attain wealth and achieve fame—in that order.

The cost of living was higher than he and Roark had estimated. Todd earned good tips parking cars, but the cash was quickly consumed by rent, gas, food, and his monthly installments on a PC. Unlike his roommate, he wasn't fortunate enough to have been given one as a graduation gift. Roark's advantage had rankled. Todd had wasted no time in leveling the playing field and acquiring a computer on a lease-purchase plan.

He was bummed over his chronic shortage of legal tender. He was even more bummed over his chronic shortage of creativity.

Writing fiction was hard, labor-intensive work. Talent was something you were born with, but hours of tedious effort were required to exercise that talent. There were days when he couldn't find a grain of genius in his work. Nor could anyone else, it seemed.

He balled up the written critique he had received from Professor Hadley and hurled it toward the corner of the room.

Roark walked in just as the paper ball landed several inches short of the trash can. "Hadley was a hard-ass? He raked me over the coals, too."

"Seriously?"

"Then left me there to smolder. So what I thought is, tonight being our night off, we should get drunk."

Todd rolled off his bed. "You don't have to ask me twice."

On the beach, they passed a bottle of cheap whiskey back and forth, toasting the sunset, then the twilight, finally the stars that began to blur and bob. Roark stretched out on the sand, his hands beneath his head. "Which manuscript did you send him?"

"The Vanquished."

"What'd he say?"

"He said my dialogue stinks."

"He said my dialogue was crisp and well paced, but my plot is predictable and needs punch." Roark looked at Todd. "Maybe we should collaborate."

"No way. I've put in a two-year apprenticeship without any remuneration."

"You sold a short story," Roark reminded him.

"One lousy short story to a local magazine for twenty-five bucks." Todd pitched a seashell into the surf. "I'm living in an apartment where the roaches are carnivorous and the tenants are armed and dangerous. When all this hardship pays off, I want the glory to me, myself, and I. No offense."

"None taken. I don't want to collaborate either. I was joking."

"Oh." Todd flopped down onto his back in the sand. "So what did Hadley really say in his notes to you?"

"I told you."

"Was it the truth?"

"Why would I lie?"

"To make me feel better."

Roark snorted. "I'm not that charitable."

"Right. So maybe you would lie for another reason."

Roark sat up. "Something on your mind, Todd?"

"You always downplay Hadley. Maybe to throw me off track."

Roark shook his head. "What are you talking about? First you accused me of lying, and then you provided me with a petty motivation for it. I take exception to both."

"And I take exception to your thinking you're a better writer than me."

"Than I," Roark corrected.

"Damn you!" Todd surged to his feet, but the earth tilted drastically. He landed back in the sand.

"Why would I deliberately mislead you about Hadley's critiques?"

"To get the jump on me. You can't stand the idea of me getting—of *my* getting—published before you."

"Oh, like you'd be thrilled if I sold a manuscript ahead of you."

"I'd rather have my guts ripped out up through my throat."

For several moments the narrow distance between them was volatile, teeming with molecules of hostility ready to spark. Then, to Todd's surprise, Roark started to laugh. "You'd rather have your guts ripped out up through your throat?"

Todd tried not to smile, but he lost the battle, and soon he was laughing, too. "That's all I could think of to say."

"I don't recommend it for your book." Then Roark stood and said, "I'm done for the night. Think we can make it to the car?" He helped Todd to his feet.

"You know, a little rivalry could be good for us—make us work harder."

"Don't start that again. I don't consider you a rival, Todd."

"Okay, okay, I'll drop it. Anyway, the point's moot. I'll be offered megabucks for my book before you even complete your book. Then we'll see who's green with envy."

"That is *not* going to happen."

Todd laughed. "Oh, man, I wish you could see the malicious glint in your eye. You just won my argument for me."

MARIS COULDN'T ACCOUNT FOR the mood in the house, mainly because she couldn't define the mood. It had started the previous night when she and Parker returned from the beach. Mike, who had arrived in their absence, had been on the veranda watching for them, looking perturbed. He'd admonished them for getting soaked to the skin, then hustled Parker to his bedroom at the back of the house. Maris knew which room it was, but she'd never been invited to see it.

When she returned to the guest cottage, she'd discovered that she hadn't buttoned her shirt correctly, that in her haste she'd skipped a button—a dead giveaway to hanky-panky. Still, she was more mystified than embarrassed. She and Parker were well beyond the age of accountability. Mike was more concerned than the situation had warranted.

In any case, their return to the house had quelled any plans either she or Parker had for continuing what had been started on the beach. She prudently remained in the guest cottage until morning, and although she'd lain awake for a long time half expecting him to come to her, he hadn't. This morning at breakfast he'd been testy and irritable. More so than usual. He'd been working on a difficult passage, and he had made it plain that Maris and Mike should make themselves scarce. And he'd acted as though her time with him on the beach had never happened.

All this was weighing heavily on her mind as she now entered the kitchen, where Parker and Mike were drinking coffee. Despite the tenderness the previous night, her relationship with Parker was still unspecified and tenuous. She'd been made a fool of by one man. She didn't want to repeat that mistake. Ever. But certainly not within the same week.

Feeling awkward, she asked if Parker was happy with what he'd written that morning.

"It's all right, I guess," he mumbled into his coffee mug, keeping his head down. He handed the pages of manuscript to Maris, then said suddenly, "I need to get back to it." He wheeled his chair toward the solarium. "Don't talk about me while I'm gone."

"We've got better things to talk about," Mike retorted.

Parker slammed the door shut behind him.

Maris laughed. "You two are like quarreling siblings. Or an old married couple."

"Heaven forbid."

"Were you ever married, Mike?"

"A confirmed bachelor."

"Was Parker?"

"Married? No." He indicated the manuscript pages she had carried in with her from the guesthouse. "Do you like the latest installment?"

"I've been rereading the chapter about Mary Catherine's miscarriage. Todd is beginning to reveal himself as the villain."

"Interesting," Mike murmured. "That you think of him as the villain." Then he asked if any of her associates at Matherly Press had read the manuscript.

"To honor Parker's request for anonymity, I'm keeping it under wraps. I did share it with my father, though. He's as positive about it as I am." Switching gears, she said, "Speaking of Dad, I haven't been able to get an answer at his house this morning, and that's unusual. Will you excuse me?" Collecting the new pages of manuscript, she headed for the back door. "I'm eager to curl up with the next chapter."

THE Matherlys' country house was a bit fussy and cluttered to suit Noah's taste. But for what it was, the restored colonial had been nicely done. Here in the living room the easy chairs were wide and deep, and each had a requisite footstool. Scattered about on end tables and on shelves were photographs of Daniel with luminaries, including two Presidents. Pictures of Maris chronicled her childhood, adolescence, and emergence into young womanhood.

Daniel entered the room, settled into one of the easy chairs, and propped his cane beside it. "I worked up quite a thirst during my nap."

Noah laughed easily. "Double Scotch?"

"On the rocks, please."

"I called the deli in town. They'll soon be delivering double-thick Reuben sandwiches, potato salad, chocolate cake and vanilla ice cream for dessert."

"I love the bachelor life," Daniel said as he accepted the drink from his son-in-law. "What a good idea this was."

DANIEL was holding the power-of-attorney document. Noah had waited until after dinner to produce it. They were relaxing in the living room, now lighted only by the soft glow of table lamps.

Daniel peered at Noah over his reading glasses. "So, there was an ulterior motive behind this weekend."

Noah expelled a puff of cigar smoke. "Not at all, Daniel. I could have presented this to you in the city at any time. But here in the country we can talk uninterrupted, son-in-law to father-in-law."

"If this is a family meeting, why conduct it when one family member is noticeably absent?"

Noah took his time answering. He wistfully studied a photograph of Maris and smiled fondly. "Your daughter thinks first with her heart, then with her head. She can't bring herself to accept some of life's inescapable certainties."

"Like my mortality."

Noah nodded solemnly. "Or even the possibility of reduced capacity. She might even feel that by executing a power-of-attorney document like this, we're tempting fate." He paused strategically and pretended to consider his wife's behavior. "In all honesty I doubt Maris would sign it at all unless you had signed it first."

Daniel tugged thoughtfully at his lower lip. "I'm not a moron, Noah. I see the validity of such a document."

Noah tried to sound perfectly composed as he said, "Apparently, so did Howard. He authorized it."

"Which puzzles me. Howard knew that a similar document is already in place. Mr. Stern drew it up years ago."

"As Howard explained it to me, that document is outdated." And now came the tricky part. With calculated casualness Noah rolled the ash off the tip of his cigar into a pewter ashtray. "I think

Howard brought it to my attention first instead of Maris's because he didn't want to upset her."

"Why didn't he bring it to my attention?"

"For the same reason, Daniel." Noah averted his gaze as though it pained him to say what he was compelled to say. "Howard didn't want you to think that he thought you were no longer capable of making these kinds of decisions for yourself."

"We were better friends than that," Daniel snapped.

"I'm only telling you what he told me. He thought it might be better if someone in the family were to bring it to your attention."

Daniel took a sip of port and flipped through the document again. Even before he said anything, Noah knew which clause had snagged his attention. "Until Maris signs this—"

"I would have full power of attorney. I spotted that flaw, too."

"Why would Howard construct the document this way?"

"When I pointed the loophole out to him, he was mortified and acknowledged that it was an oversight." Noah chuckled. "I think his old-world heritage sneaked in while he wasn't looking. He was thinking of Maris as the sweet little girl in pigtails he used to bounce on his knee, not as a senior executive of a multimillion-dollar company. Anyhow, I insisted that he add the codicil on the last page, which stipulates that the document is invalid until signed by all of us."

He hoped Daniel wouldn't notice that the last page could be detached without it appearing that the document had been tampered with or altered. He'd hired an unscrupulous lawyer to write the codicil. After this was settled, Noah would have to deal with him or risk being blackmailed. But that was a problem for another day.

Noah took one final draw on his cigar. "Speaking for myself, I'm bushed. Obviously, you need to sleep on this."

"I don't need to sleep on it," Daniel said abruptly. "Let me sign the damn thing and get it over with."

Noah hesitated. "Don't decide anything this weekend, Daniel. Take the document back to the city. Have Mr. Stern review it."

"And by doing so, question the judgment of my late friend? No. Howard's suicide has already generated nasty speculation. I won't have people saying his competence had slipped. Where's a pen?"

"Signing won't make it legal. It has to be notarized."

"We'll make it official once we get to the city," Daniel grumbled. He yanked the pen from his son-in-law's hand and scrawled his signature on the appropriate line.

MARIS was glad she had changed for dinner, because for the first time since her arrival, it was being served in the formal dining room. She was wearing a gray silk dress whose lightweight fabric, slip-style bodice, and flared skirt seemed perfect for dinner in an antebellum plantation house. Parker had changed for dinner, too. He was wearing his customary casual pants, but his shirt was tucked in. The sleeves were rolled back, revealing his strong forearms.

Mike had laid a beautiful table. Fragrant magnolia blossoms had been arranged in a crystal bowl in the center of the table, flanked by silver candlesticks with white tapers. The candlelight softened the hardness that resentment had stamped on Parker's face. He seemed relaxed and enjoying himself as they ate Mike's delicious crab au gratin.

After dinner Maris suggested that they take their desserts onto the veranda, which should be comfortably cool if they turned on the ceiling fans. Mike served their strawberry sorbets in frosted compotes garnished with sprigs of mint, while Maris poured the coffee. The overhead fans blew gently on them.

"It was a good meal, Mike," Parker said. "Thanks."

"You're welcome." Mike idly stirred a sugar cube into his coffee. "What we need to round out the evening is a good story."

"Hmm. If only we knew a good storyteller," Maris said. Being deliberately coy, she looked at Parker from beneath her eyelashes.

He grimaced, but he was pleased by their curiosity. "Okay, I can't fight both of you. Where'd you leave off?"

"They'd gone to the beach and killed a bottle of whiskey," Maris said, the scene still fresh in her mind. "Todd accused Roark of being less than straightforward about the critiques he had received from the professor."

"Have you read the part where Roark got pissed?" Parker asked.

"Yes, and his anger was justified. He's never given Todd any reason to mistrust him."

"Not so fast," Parker said quietly. "Didn't it strike you that he protested too much when Todd accused him of being dishonest?"

Slowly she nodded. "Now that I think about it . . . Have Hadley's critiques been more favorable than Roark let on?"

Parker withdrew several sheets of folded paper from the pocket of his shirt. "I dashed this off before I quit for the day."

Maris suggested that Parker read them out loud.

Parker unfolded the sheets of manuscript and held them up to the light. " 'Dear Mr. Slade,' " he read. " 'According to your last letter, you wish me to send future correspondence to your recently acquired post-office box instead of to the street address. I can only assume that the request arises out of an unspecified desire to convenience yourself.' "

Parker cringed. "Verbose old guy, isn't he?"

Maris smothered a laugh. "You might consider trimming some of the fat, Parker. Just a little."

"Okay. No problem." He continued reading: " 'Your writing has surpassed my ability to critique it. It deserves an appraisal more distinguished than mine. It far surpasses that of any other student, past or present, including your friend Todd Grayson. He has written an engaging story, but his writing lacks the emotional depth, the *heart,* with which yours resonates. I have no doubt that he will publish. That does not necessarily mean that he writes well.

" 'Thank the god to whom you pray, Mr. Slade, for you were blessed with a rare and wonderful talent. Your friend was not. I fear that eventually this lopsided appropriation of talent will cause a breach between you, since he is governed by greed and envy.

" 'I look forward to reading the next draft of your manuscript. In your cover letters you never fail to apologize for taking up my time. Mr. Slade, be clear on this: It is a privilege. Sincerely yours, Professor Hadley.' "

Parker refolded the pages and returned them to his shirt pocket.

No one spoke for a moment. Maris had been lulled by his words and the cadence with which he'd read them. She shook off the mild daze. "So Todd's gut instincts were right. Roark's reviews from Hadley *were* better than the ones he received."

Parker nodded. "And Roark was dishonest about it."

"He was trying to spare Todd's feelings. He sensed that Todd lacked—" Maris snapped her fingers. "No. He *knew* he was better. He had to. Why else did he get a post-office box? He was afraid that Todd would intercept one of his glowing critiques from Hadley. Todd intercepts one of the letters, right?" she guessed. "Maybe even this letter. Todd, uh—let's see—borrows a pair of jeans or something and finds the letter in a pocket."

"Thanks. I hadn't figured out yet how he was going to get his hands on it. That's pretty good."

She beamed. "Todd reads this letter. He can't believe what he's reading. His secret fear is realized: Roark is superior to him. He reacts by . . . doing what?" She concentrated hard. "I think he would be furious. Livid."

"How does he channel that rage, Maris?"

"He confronts Roark with the letter."

"No, he doesn't."

"Parker," Mike cut in softly.

"He's not honest enough to take that approach. He—"

"Parker," Mike repeated.

"He waits. He—"

"Parker!"

"*Dammit, Mike!* What?"

The air was electrically charged, as it had been in the kitchen this morning. Thoughts were telegraphed that Maris couldn't interpret.

Parker was the first to relent. "I'm sorry, Mike. Forgive me. I was following a train of thought."

"It's okay. I know you hate distractions when you're on a roll." Mike stood. "Before the mosquitoes carry me off, I think I'll go in."

"Good idea. Good night."

"Good night, Mike," Maris echoed.

Once they were alone, Maris raised her hands in a helpless shrug. "Explain to me what just happened."

"Nothing."

"Parker," she cried softly. She got up.

"It's this . . . this *thing* between Mike and me. Sometimes he sees a darkness creeping over me. Like I was when he found me. He's afraid I'll drop back into that abyss. He yanks me out of it before I can sink too far." They looked at each other for several moments. Then he smiled crookedly. "It's been a roller-coaster evening."

"Yes, it has. But I wouldn't trade a minute of it."

He reached out. She moved nearer. Hooking his hand around the back of her neck, he drew her down for a kiss.

When at last they pulled apart, he pressed his face into the softness of her middle. "I've been craving this all day."

"There were times I thought you'd forgotten about last night."

He gave a soft, harsh laugh. "Not hardly."

His head nudged her breasts through the silk cloth of her dress. Threading her fingers through his hair, she sighed. "Parker, please. I can't do this." She stepped out of his reach.

He gulped a breath. "Why not?"

She licked her lips. "I'm worried about my father."

"Your father? You're afraid he wouldn't approve? Come after me with a shotgun? What?"

She smiled. "No, nothing like that. I've been trying to reach him all day." She gave him a summary of her attempts. "Finally, just before dinner, I tracked our housekeeper to her sister's house. She told me that Dad and Noah had gone to our country house in western Massachusetts for the weekend. They insisted she stay behind."

"So? They're big boys. What does their leaving New York for the weekend have to do with us necking here on the veranda?"

"Nothing. Directly."

"Then I don't get it."

What she didn't tell Parker was that Noah had assured Maxine that Maris was aware of their plans. Maxine had been distraught to learn that Maris hadn't known. "Why did Mr. Reed mislead me?"

Why indeed? Maxine had then told her that Daniel had entertained a guest for breakfast. She explained about the errand he'd sent her on. "When I got back, he was washing dishes. He didn't want me to know that two place settings had been used."

"Did he seem upset?" Maris had asked.

"No. In fact, he seemed very upbeat and eager to be off."

"Then I'm sure we're worrying over nothing." Maris hoped her assurances sounded sincere to the anxious housekeeper. To her own ears they rang hollow as she repeated them to Parker. "I've called the country house. The line has been busy for hours. I also tried Noah's cell phone. It was busy, too, so I left a voice-mail message and the phone number here."

"Sorta weird, actually—that your dad would spend a weekend with your estranged husband."

"Dad doesn't know we're separated. He knows I've been unhappy. He just doesn't know the extent of my unhappiness." Lowering her voice, she said, "Until I came to St. Anne Island and met you, *I* didn't know how unhappy I'd been."

THERE were no messages on Maris's phone. Terribly worried now, she dialed the number for the country-house telephone.

Daniel answered on the second ring. Her greeting sounded like a reprimand. "Dad, where have you been? I've been trying to reach you all day. I didn't know you'd gone to the country until I talked to Maxine. Since then I've called repeatedly."

"This is the first time the telephone has rung. I just noticed that the receiver in the kitchen was askew. Apparently, Noah didn't hang it up properly when he called in a food delivery."

"Are you all right, Dad? I've imagined all sorts of things."

"Rest assured that I've had a very pleasant day."

Starting with a mystery guest for breakfast. She wanted to ask him about that but couldn't without giving away that Maxine had tattled on him. "What did you do that made it so pleasant?"

"Nothing much, and that was the beauty of it. How's the book coming?"

"Great, actually. The story is really percolating now."

"And the author? Still the curmudgeon?"

"Either he's mellowing, or I'm becoming accustomed to him."

Maris sensed him hesitating. Then he said, "I'm glad you heeded your instincts and went back to work with him."

"So am I, Dad. It was the right decision."

"You're happy there? With the work? With everything?"

"Yes. Very," she said quietly.

"You deserve to be, Maris. Don't deny yourself that happiness."

She knew that her father was conveying more than he was saying. It wouldn't surprise her if he knew about Noah's infidelity. She swallowed a knot of emotion. "I needed to hear your voice. I'll call you again tomorrow. No, wait, Dad. I'd like to send Maxine up there tomorrow. She's been dying to go to the country. Would you mind?"

He sighed. "If it would make you feel better."

"It would. I'll call her first thing in the morning."

"All right. And Maris? Don't worry. Everything is going to work out well. Will you trust me on that, sweetheart?"

"I always have." She leaned her cheek into the small telephone, wishing it were his spotted, wrinkled hand. "Good night, Dad. I love you."

"I love you, too."

PARKER'S bed was king-size. The headboard was tall and carved, the wood aged to a saddle-brown patina that reflected the glow from the light on the nightstand. Parker was bare-chested, propped against the headboard reading, when Maris slipped through the door. He slowly lowered the book to his lap. "Hello. Are you lost?"

She laughed nervously. "Nice try, but I think I was expected."

"I hoped."

"Then it's all right if I come in?"

"Are you joking?"

Since coming into the room, she'd kept her hands behind her. Her short silk nightgown was no weightier than air against her skin.

As she approached the bed, she brought her hands from behind her back. "I brought you presents. Two, to be exact."

The first was a drinking glass from the guesthouse. She extended it to him. He held it up, then laughed when he saw the winking phosphorescent lights inside. "Lightning bugs."

"I caught them myself," she said proudly. She'd sealed them inside the glass by stretching a piece of plastic wrap over the top, then puncturing it to ensure the fireflies a longer life.

"It's a great present. Thank you." He set the glass on the nightstand. "What's the other?" He indicated the book she was now hugging to her chest. "Are you going to read me a bedtime story?"

Nodding toward the empty side of his bed, she asked, "May I?"

"Be my guest." He placed one hand behind his head.

She rounded the end of the bed and crawled onto it, then folded her legs beneath her and sat back on her heels, facing him. She turned the book toward him.

" '*Grass Widow,*' " he read, smiling. "A novel by my favorite author. What do you like about this book, Ms. Matherly?"

She opened the book. "Well, in particular, I like the scene between the sexy, roguish Deck Cayton and the bimbo, Frenchy."

"The fans liked it."

She pursed her lips and frowned. "However—"

"Uh-oh. Here it comes. It's too explicit?"

"To the extreme. But my problem is with its accuracy. I'm not sure that the, uh, positions you've described are anatomically possible."

He snuffled a laugh, then stroked his chin somberly. "I see." He remained still for several moments, gazing at her. Then slowly he removed his hand from behind his head. "As I recall, our sexy, roguish hero begins by placing his hand on Frenchy's thigh. It's a comforting gesture to reassure her that he poses no threat."

He placed his hand on her thigh just above her bent knee.

"Debatable," she murmured. "The part about him posing no threat, but we'll give him the benefit of the doubt."

"In exchange for that gesture of kindness, Frenchy gives him a valuable piece of information about the murder," Parker said. "Our hero thanks her with a kiss."

Parker framed her face between his hands, then kissed her softly, sensually. He kept the kisses gentle. They teased and tantalized and left her feeling drugged. Slowly her hand moved toward the sheet. But Parker reached down and stopped her. "This is where the fantasy ends, Maris. This isn't fiction. It's reality."

"I know."

"You don't have a clue," he said harshly. "You pull that sheet back, and you'll get a jolt of reality you never bargained for."

She shook her head. "Do you think I care about your scars?"

"I think you will, yeah."

"You're wrong." She gazed into his face and, near tears, said, "Parker, you can't possibly comprehend what you've done for me."

He looked more vulnerable than she would have believed possible. "I'm not pretty, Maris."

"You're beautiful."

Tentatively she leaned toward him. He didn't stop her. She could feel the rugged terrain of his scarred legs. But she couldn't, wouldn't, think about that now. She had scars, too. Less visible than his, but there nonetheless. Later, there would be time to ask questions, to listen, and then to return their previous unhappiness to the past, where it belonged.

DANIEL stood at the kitchen window eating a sandwich and staring out at the rainy night, periodically illuminated by lightning. His telephone conversation with Maris had thrust his mind into overdrive. After the call he'd tried to fall asleep. Finally surrendering to his insomnia, he had come downstairs for a midnight snack.

He was glad Maris was in Georgia, away from New York, where things were about to get ugly. It didn't take a rocket scientist to conclude that the allure of Georgia wasn't strictly the book, but the author Parker Evans, a.k.a. Mackensie Roone.

Oh, yes. He had discovered the name of Maris's elusive author, as well as his successful pen name. Years earlier, when the Deck Cayton mystery series had started appearing on bestseller lists, he had wanted to lure the writer to Matherly Press but had been unable to coax the author's real name out of his agent. He knew it now. For several weeks he'd had a private investigator on retainer. Hoping that his misgivings about Noah would be proved wrong, he had hired the investigator to probe into his son-in-law's past, including his life prior to the publication of *The Vanquished.*

When William Sutherland had arrived for their discreet appointment, he contradicted the stereotype of the sleazy private investigator. A retired Secret Service agent, he had a firm handshake, an authoritative bearing, and a distinguished record. The last thing Daniel had expected to learn from Sutherland's initial report was novelist Mackensie Roone's true identity. Unexpectedly, one of publishing's best-kept secrets had landed in his lap in a sealed folder.

But the staggering revelation was yet to come: Parker Evans and Noah Reed had a history. They had been roommates at a university in Tennessee, and then after graduation they had lived together in Key West. There they'd had some sort of falling-out, the particulars of which were still being investigated.

While waiting for the facts to be disclosed, Daniel had gambled that Maris, and her heart, would be safe with the writer. If Evans's friendship with Noah had ended over a matter of honor, then Daniel must assume that Evans was an honorable man. Indisputably, Noah Reed was not. Regardless of what else transpired, Noah's affiliation with the Matherlys was about to come to an end. Unbeknownst to the self-assured and insufferably smug Mr. Reed, his head was on the chopping block and the axe was about to fall.

In a symbolic gesture Daniel dusted breadcrumbs off his hands. He switched off the kitchen light and then made his way through the dark house. As he climbed the staircase, he leaned heavily upon the balustrade. Damn, he hated getting old! No sooner had the thought flashed through his mind than a voice came out of the darkness at the top of the stairs. "You forgot your cane."

Daniel raised his hand to his lurching heart. In a brief flash of lightning, he saw Noah on the landing. "You startled me."

By now Daniel was only two steps below the landing, but Noah made no attempt to step aside. Indeed, he seemed to be blocking his path. Noah was holding sheets of paper at his side.

"Reviewing the document I signed earlier?" Daniel asked.

"No," Noah replied calmly. "This is the report on me from your private investigator—Mr. William Sutherland."

More than being alarmed, Daniel was angry that his privacy had been invaded. "That was locked in my desk at home."

"Yes, I know. It took some riffling, but eventually I found it. Did you really think I wouldn't know I was being investigated? Your bloodhound asked questions of one friend too many." Noah smiled. "I'm curious to know when the surveillance began."

There was no reason now to play dumb or to equivocate. "Shortly after your premature anniversary party."

"Why then?"

"Because that was the night I became convinced that you are a seasoned deceiver and liar. I caught you in several lies. And while some could be explained as necessary for surprising Maris, others bothered me. So I began observing you carefully, looking beyond the man you show to the world."

Noah leaned indolently against the newel post. He looked at the sheets in his hand. "I'll admit that some of this is less than flattering. I assume you're most upset over my alliance with WorldView."

"I can forgive that before your mistreatment of Maris."

"She told you about the affair with Nadia?"

"No, but her unhappiness has been apparent for some time."

"She's been happy enough. She loves her work more than ever, now that she's working with this new author."

So he didn't know about Parker Evans! Daniel happily clung to that secret knowledge.

"Maybe I didn't cater to the nurturing aspect of Maris's personality," Noah continued, "but your precious daughter wasn't too dissatisfied with her life. Not until she caught me with Nadia."

"She was happy in spite of you, Noah, not because of you. You even sabotaged her chance of being truly happy."

Noah snapped his fingers. "You're referring to the vasectomy."

"Yes," Daniel said bitterly. That had been one of the most disheartening discoveries to come from Sutherland's report. "The secret vasectomy. I was puzzled when I first read about it. Wouldn't a child have secured your ties to us and the Matherly fortune? And therein lay the answer." He looked Noah full in the face. "You didn't want a child competing with you for a share."

"That's the first thing you've said that's incorrect, Daniel. I'd never settle for a measly *share*."

Daniel snorted with contempt. "Don't count your chickens yet, Noah. That document I signed tonight is worthless."

"You think so?" Noah asked smoothly.

"I was only playing along, seeing how far you would go. What I really find galling is that you attached Howard Bancroft's name to that document. He would never have drawn up a—"

"Oh, but he would," Noah said, interrupting. "He did rather than let it be circulated that his father was a Nazi officer."

Daniel received that news like a punch to the gut. "You used that to coerce him?"

"So," Noah said, "you knew about his whoring mother?"

"Howard was my friend." Daniel practically strained the words through his clenched teeth. "He confided in me years ago. I admired him for making his life into what it was instead of letting what he couldn't change defeat him."

"Well, it did, didn't it? He couldn't live with the truth."

"A truth you threatened to spread," Daniel said.

Noah shrugged and smiled beatifically. "See, that's the difference between you and me, Daniel. You go after what you want, but you fall short of total commitment. Your conscience has drawn a line, and you never step across it. I, on the other hand, am willing to do whatever it takes. My credo is 'Find a man's weakness, and you own him.' To achieve the goal I've set for myself, I'll go to any lengths."

Daniel realized he was looking into the face of pure, unrepentant depravity. "You are despicable," he growled, and charged up the last two steps.

Chapter Ten

PARKER was the first thing Maris saw when she opened her eyes, and nothing could have pleased her more. He was sitting in his wheelchair beside the bed, watching her while she slept. She smiled and stretched luxuriously. "What time is it?"

"Time for you to clear out. Unless you want Mike to catch you."

He was wearing only a pair of boxer shorts. The previous night she had made a point to show no interest in his legs because of his self-consciousness. Apparently, their lovemaking had convinced him that his apprehension was unnecessary.

So she looked. And it was impossible to conceal her reaction. She stopped just short of gasping out loud.

His voice sliced like a razor. "I warned you it wasn't pretty."

"Oh, my darling, you were terribly, horribly hurt."

She slid from the bed to kneel in front of him. Shark attack was the first thing that came to mind. His scars could be compared only to something that vicious. The worst of them was a hollow as large as her fist where a section of his quadriceps had been gouged out. On his lower legs was a network of crisscrossing scars—some raised and bumpy, others like flat, shiny ribbons of plastic.

She looked up at him sorrowfully, then leaned forward and kissed one of the worst of the scars that snaked up his shin.

He said, "Now that your morbid curiosity has been satisfied, can we get in one quick lay before breakfast?"

She yanked her head back. "What?"

"I think you heard me."

As shocked as if he'd struck her, she stood up, clutched her nightgown. "Why are you acting like this?"

"This is what I'm like, Maris."

"No, you're not."

He gave a dismissive shrug. "Okay, whatever." He pushed his chair backward, then turned it away from her and headed across the room toward a chifforobe. "I've got something for you."

"Parker?" she called in exasperation. "I don't understand. What happened between last night and this morning?"

"You don't remember?" He opened the door of the chifforobe and removed a box from one of the interior drawers. He spun around and faced her, grinning cruelly as he looked her up and down. "Well, I'll say this for you, Mrs. Matherly-Reed. You're very nice. I wonder why your husband went out for it."

Tears of mortification filled her eyes. "I don't know what's the matter with you, but I won't continue this. I can't match your vulgarity."

"Sure you can. You'll come up with something suitable. Maybe on your plane ride back to New York. I assume you're leaving."

Not even deigning to answer, she headed for the door.

"Wait!" He rolled his chair over to her. "*Envy*. The final draft."

He practically thrust the box into her hands, so she had no choice but to take it. She looked at him. "It's finished?"

"Has been all along. I never submit a partial manuscript."

She gaped at him. "Why, Parker? Why?"

Deliberately mistaking her meaning, he shrugged. "Personal policy. That's just the way I work."

Maris felt as though the spot on which she stood were eroding rapidly. But she wasn't going to sink without a fight. "That's just the way you work?" she repeated, raising her voice. "What the hell was all this for, Parker? Or is that even your name? Why the lies, the games?"

"They seemed like fun at the time."

For several beats she just stared at him. Then she hurled the box as far as she could throw it, sending some four hundred manuscript pages across the polished hardwood floor.

Maris stalked to the door and jerked it open.

Mike was standing on the other side, one hand raised, about to knock. The other was holding a cordless telephone. He extended the telephone toward Maris. "For you. I hated to disturb you, but the gentleman said it was an emergency."

She took the telephone from him with a shaking hand and stepped out into the hallway. Blinking away tears, she leaned against the wall and took several seconds to compose herself. Then, clearing her throat, she said, "Hello?"

"Maris?"

"Noah?" His voice was strangely muffled and subdued. She barely recognized it.

"It's imperative that you return to New York immediately. A ticket is waiting for you at the Savannah airport. Your flight departs at eleven. So you haven't got much time."

Her dread was so absolute, she felt suddenly very cold. She closed her eyes, but tears leaked through. "It's Dad, isn't it?"

"I'm afraid so, yes. He . . . You shouldn't have to hear this news over the telephone, Maris, but . . . he's dead."

She cried out. Her knees buckled, and she sank to the floor.

PARKER was in the solarium, staring out at the ocean in abject despair and self-loathing. He was replaying in his head his last words to Maris. His stomach knotted when he recalled the horrible things he'd said. Her stricken expression haunted him.

As soon as Maris could pack her things, she and Mike had departed for the mainland. She left without a word to Parker. He'd expected that. What he hadn't expected was that it would hurt so much.

"I stayed with Maris until they boarded her flight."

Until Mike spoke, Parker hadn't heard him come into the solarium. He kept his stinging eyes on the surf. His back still to Mike, he said, "Maris was worried about her father last night. Maybe she had a premonition."

"I wouldn't be surprised. They were very close."

After Noah's call she was able to tell Mike that her father had fallen down the stairs of their country house. She'd been told that he had died instantly of a broken neck. It had happened during the middle of the night. The noise had awakened Noah. He had rushed to Daniel's aid, then called 911. The paramedics reached the house in minutes, but Daniel was already dead.

"How was she when she left?"

"How do you think she was, Parker?"

"She probably felt like she'd been run through a thrasher."

"You certainly did your part."

Parker turned around. "Getting Maris into bed was part of the plot. You probably guessed that."

"I guessed it. That doesn't mean I liked it."

"Nobody asked you to," Parker snapped. He wheeled his chair to his keyboard. "Excuse me. I'm trying to write."

"Fine," Mike said. "Turn your back on me. But I'm going to tell you something you need to hear. You resurrected yourself when, for all practical purposes, your life was over. It was a heroic effort. Your body has healed, but not your soul. It's more twisted than your legs ever were."

"That's what I've been trying to tell you for years, Mike. I'm a lost cause."

"You're not a lost cause. You're a coward. It takes far less courage to cling to the past than it does to face the future."

"Very good, Mike. I should write that down. 'It takes far less—' "

Mike's lined features turned earnest. "Parker, consign Noah Reed to God. Or to the devil. Let them haggle over what his punishment is to be. Then go to Maris. Explain everything. She may forgive you. She may not. Either way, you'll be rid of it. For the first time in fourteen years you'll be free of what happened in Key West."

Parker's heart was pounding, but he kept his expression passive. "Good sermon. Very moving. But I'm going to stick to plan A."

"Perhaps you're right, Parker. Perhaps you are a lost cause. Your cruelty to Maris goes beyond reprehensible. All you care about is this revenge plot of yours."

"That's right. Now you're catching on."

"What's the next chapter?"

"Well, since Maris threw the manuscript at me, I don't think I can count on her to get it to Noah. So I guess I'll have to send it to him myself, along with a cover letter saying that *Envy* is being simultaneously submitted to every publishing house in New York. If that doesn't get his attention, then perhaps a postscript about his wife's talent in bed will."

Mike shook his head with disgust. "And then what, Parker?"

"The gripping climax, of course."

Mike subjected him to a long, hard stare, then walked to the kitchen, where he'd left two suitcases. "I won't be a party to this."

A few moments later Parker heard Mike leaving through the back door. And he was truly alone.

MARIS could barely remember her return trip to New York. She had operated in a dreamlike state. Parker's inexplicable behavior and her father's death had been a double-barreled assault.

Noah was at La Guardia Airport to meet her. As the limo wended its way through heavy traffic into Manhattan, he somberly filled in the details that he hadn't told her over the telephone. Daniel's body was still in Massachusetts, where the autopsy and police investigation would be conducted. Noah had made preliminary funeral arrangements but was awaiting her approval before finalizing them. "I wanted to spare you as much unpleasantness as possible." He was solicitous, soft-spoken, obsequious.

She couldn't bear to be near him. She instructed the chauffeur to take her to her father's East Side town house. Accepting a friend's offer to help, Maris sent her to the apartment with a list of clothing she wanted. If she could help it, she would never return to the residence she had shared with Noah.

She moved back into her childhood bedroom. For the next three days, when she and Maxine weren't receiving people who came to offer condolences, they comforted each other.

Maris endured the daylong funeral with a steely determination not to crack under pressure. Dressed head to toe in black, she was photographed exiting the cathedral, standing at the gravesite with her head bowed in prayer, receiving the mayor's condolences.

Nadia Schuller sidled up to Maris after the gravesite observance and gripped her hand. "I'm sorry, Maris. Terribly terribly sorry."

Maris was struck not only by Nadia's audacity in attending the service but also by her convincing portrayal of shocked bereavement. Maris pulled back, but Nadia wouldn't be shaken off. "We need to talk soon. Call me." As she walked away, she had the decency not to lock eyes with Noah.

Noah was the worst part of Maris's endurance test. He was never far from her side, demonstrating a loving affection that was false. Dusk had fallen before the house cleared of guests. That's when Maris approached Noah. "I want to talk to you."

"Certainly, darling."

"You can drop the pretense, Noah. No one's around except Maxine, and she already knows that I've left you."

She led him into her father's study. The room smelled of him, his pipe tobacco, and the books he had loved. She sat down in the leather chair behind his desk. It was the closest she came to being hugged by him. She had spent the past four nights curled up in this chair, weeping.

Noah lowered himself into an easy chair. "I had hoped your second visit south had mellowed you, Maris. You're as prickly as you were before you left."

"Dad's death didn't change anything between us. Nor did it change your character. You're a liar and an adulterer." She paused a beat before adding, "And possibly those are the least of your sins." She opened a drawer of Daniel's desk and took out a business card. "I came across this in Dad's day planner while I was looking up addresses for acknowledgment cards. Only a name and telephone number. Curious, I called. Imagine my surprise."

He indolently raised his shoulders in silent inquiry.

"I spoke personally to the man Dad had retained to investigate you," she told him. "Mr. Sutherland was extremely professional. Ethically, he couldn't discuss another client's business, even a late client's. However, he said, if I had access to Dad's files, he was sure I'd find his report among them." She spread her arms across the top of the desk. "I've searched for it, Noah. It's not here or at the office.

"Coincidentally, you spent time in here the morning before you left for the country. While Dad was upstairs packing, you told Maxine that you had calls to make, and came in here. She thought it odd at the time, since you typically use your cell phone."

He shook his head. "Maris, I have no idea what you're talking about. If this is about Nadia—"

"It isn't," she said tersely. "I don't give a damn about Nadia." She wanted to pound the conceit out of his expression. "I also spoke to the authorities in Massachusetts, questioning their ruling that Dad's death was accidental. They've agreed to reinvestigate." Looking at him evenly, she said, "I'm convinced beyond a shadow of doubt that you had something to do with his fall."

Noah's narrow lips stretched into a smile that raised the hair on the back of her neck. "There's absolutely nothing to substantiate these nasty suspicions of yours."

"I think Dad was onto you. I think he knew you were dirty-dealing. Maybe he even had proof. When he confronted you with it, you killed him. I hope you haven't committed murder in the hope of securing a deal with WorldView. Because if you have, you're going to be sorely disappointed."

"Be very careful, Maris." Noah's voice was low, but it vibrated with menace. He stood up, reached over, and took a strand of her hair, winding it tightly around his index finger. "Nobody is going to prevent me from having everything I want."

She laughed softly. "What are you going to do, Noah? Push me down a staircase, too?"

"Daniel alone was responsible for his death. He lost his temper and recklessly forgot his physical limitations. But," he continued silkily, "I'll admit that his death was very convenient."

She recoiled, and because he still had hold of her hair, the sudden movement caused a painful yank on her scalp. But the yank on her memory had been even sharper: *Actually, her death was very convenient.* She'd read that line a dozen times. It was a key piece of dialogue, so she had dwelled on it, on its deliberate cold candor. Parker had used that simple sentence to provide a revealing sneak peek into the dark soul of the character. Realization slammed into her. "You're Todd."

Noah's chin went back. "Who?"

Thoughts were snapping in her mind like a sail in a high wind, but one thought became jarringly clear: This could not be a coincidence. "Noah, let go of me."

"Of course, darling." He uncoiled her hair from around his finger. "You're free to go. Now that we understand one another."

"You have no idea how well I understand you."

Envy, continued—Key West, Florida, 1988

. . . It was one of those days when the words simply would not come. Roark pressed his skull between his hands, trying to force the words out. To no avail. For the past three hours his computer cursor had been stuck in the same spot, winking at him.

"Roark!" Todd's running footsteps echoed in the stairwell. Then he barged through their door, yelling, "I sold it."

"Your car?"

"My book! I sold my book!" His cheeks were flushed.

Roark just looked at him, dumbfounded. Unsteadily he came to his feet. "I . . . That's great. When did you submit it?"

Todd somehow managed to look abashed while maintaining his wide grin. "I didn't tell you. I sent it on a whim about two months ago. I didn't want to make a big deal of it, because I was positive I'd get another rejection letter. Then today I got this call at work. In my cover letter I listed every conceivable way they could contact me. Just in case, you know? Anyway, this editor goes on and on, raving about my book. Says he's willing to offer in the neighborhood of high five figures."

Roark, forcing elation into his expression, crossed the room and gave Todd a mighty hug. "Congratulations, man. You've worked hard. You deserve it."

Within seconds Todd was bouncing around the apartment. "I don't know what to do first," he said, laughing. "Yes, I do. A celebration. Blowout party. On me."

Roark, feeling less like celebrating than he ever had in his life, was already shaking his head. "You don't have to—"

"But I want to. Tonight. I'll make the arrangements."

"I've got to work."

"Screw work."

"Easy for you to say. You've sold a book. For high five figures."

Todd treated Roark to several minutes of hard scrutiny. "Oh. Now I get it. You're pissed because I sold before you did."

"No, I'm not." But it was true. He was acting like a jackass, ruining the happiest day of his best friend's life. Roark plastered on a fake grin. "What time's the party start?"

Todd flew out to run his errands. He returned within an hour, bringing two bottles of champagne, insisting that they drink them before moving to phase two of the celebration.

Phase two included Mary Catherine. Wearing three postage stamp–size patches of electric-blue fabric that passed for a bikini, she arrived ready to party. She got there just in time to help them polish off the champagne.

Todd gave her a gentle push toward Roark. "She's all yours tonight, pal. Don't say I never gave you anything."

Mary Catherine looped her arms around Roark's neck. "Fine by me. I've had a lech for you for a long time."

Courtesy of the champagne, Roark had a lively buzz going. He had sustained a blow to his ego, and Todd was trying to make it up to him. He'd be a jerk to decline. He applied himself to kissing her.

"Hey," Todd said after a few moments, "am I gonna have to turn the water hose on you two?"

Laughing, they clomped downstairs and piled into Todd's car. He drove them to a marina, where he had chartered a boat from an old salt named Hatch Walker.

It was just before sunset. As soon as the rental agreement was signed, Todd jumped aboard and climbed the steps to the pilot's chair. Roark staggered aboard after him. Mary Catherine stumbled against Roark as Walker helped her onto the deck. "Oopsy-daisy."

She giggled as she squirmed against Roark. She gave old Hatch a wave as he untied the ropes from the cleats and tossed them onto the deck.

"Crazy kids," Walker muttered.

"I don't think he likes us," Mary Catherine whined.

"What I think is, you have on too many clothes." Roark reached around to untie her top. She shrieked and slapped at his hands, but the protests were all for show. Roark came away with her bikini top and waved it like a banner above his head as Todd slowly guided the boat out of the marina and into the Atlantic.

Todd had proclaimed this would be a celebration none of them would ever forget, and Roark was surprised by his extravagance. The coolers were stocked with brand-name liquors. The food came from a deli that had the self-confidence to call itself Delectables.

"This is a mean shrimp salad." Roark licked spiced mayonnaise from the corner of his lips.

"Let me do that," Mary Catherine said as she sponged away the mayo with her tongue.

Roark was sick to death of being such a boy scout. Nose to the grindstone all the time. For what? For *nothing,* that's what.

He was going to have a good time tonight if it killed him.

ROARK woke up with Mary Catherine draped across him. Thirsty, he wiggled out from under her, pulled on his trunks, and stumbled up the steps to the deck. Todd had a bottle of rum cradled in his arm and was staring at the constellations. Hearing Roark, he turned and smiled. "You survived?" Then he chuckled and motioned toward one of the ice chests. "Help yourself to a fresh bottle."

"Thanks, but I'm still too wasted to stand."

"And jealous."

Roark used an arm to brace himself against the exterior wall of the cabin. "Huh?"

"You're jealous."

Roark shrugged. "Maybe." He gave a weak grin. "Okay, a little."

"More than a little, Roark." Todd raised the rum bottle to his eye like a telescope and peered down the length of it at Roark. "Admit it. You thought you'd be the first to sell."

Roark's stomach was queasy. The horizon was seesawing. "Todd, I couldn't be happier."

"Oh, yeah, you could. If you'd sold your book today, you'd be a lot happier. So would Hadley. What was that he said about it being an honor and privilege to review your work?" Todd took a swig of rum. "Something like that."

"You read his letter to me?"

"Clever of you to get that post-office box, but careless of you to leave his letter in the pocket of your jeans. I was short the cash to pay for a pizza delivery, so I raided the pockets of your jeans looking for money and . . . pulled out a plum."

"You shouldn't have read my mail."

"You shouldn't have lied to me about Hadley's enthusiasm for your work and his lack of it for mine."

Todd stood up. He was steady on his feet, leaving Roark to question if he had drunk as much as he had pretended to. He moved along the deck with a predatory, malevolent tread.

"What's eating you, Todd? You won. Hadley was wrong."

Todd lunged at him and took a vicious swing at his head with the liquor bottle. Roark caught it on the temple and roared in pain and outrage. The bottle shattered, showering them with broken glass and rum. Todd attacked with a fury then, throwing blows at Roark's face and head. Dazed but fueled by anger, Roark struck back. He landed a fist against Todd's mouth and felt the scrape of teeth against his knuckles.

Mary Catherine appeared in the open doorway of the cabin. "Wha'sgoin'on?" She drunkenly staggered onto the deck and stepped on a piece of broken glass. "Ow!"

"Shut up!" Todd rounded on her and struck a blow that caught her at waist level. Favoring her bleeding foot and already off-balance, she reeled backward. The chrome side railing caught her in the back of her knees. Arms windmilling, she went overboard with a scream that died as soon as she hit the water.

Roark sobered instantly. "She's too drunk to swim!"

He executed a shallow dive into the water. The salt water seared the open wounds on his face, and he came up gasping. "Do you see her?" he yelled up at Todd, who was standing on the deck, looking down at him, blood dripping from his chin.

"No."

"Turn on the lights."

But Todd just stood there, staring into the water.

"Call the coast guard!" Roark shouted.

Heart pounding, head bursting, he jackknifed beneath the surface. Again and again he went down, coming up only long enough to take a breath. He struggled to the surface one last time. Greedily he sucked air into his lungs. He couldn't survive another submersion. Weakly he treaded water. "Todd," he called hoarsely, "I can't find her. I can't look anymore. Throw me the preserver."

Todd left to get the life preserver, and Roark wondered vaguely why Todd hadn't had it ready. Exhausted, he longed to close his burning eyes. He must have been only a heartbeat away from losing consciousness, because he was startled awake when the boat's motor roared to life.

Todd shouldn't be starting the motor. He should be throwing him a preserver. "Todd, what are you doing?"

Todd was bringing the boat to him too fast for safety.

"Hey!" It was a nightmare's yell, when you open your mouth and try to scream but can't utter a sound. Roark tried to wave his arms, but he couldn't even lift them out of the water. "Todd," he croaked, "turn to port. Can't you see me?"

Todd could see him. He was looking straight at him through the plastic windshield that protected the cockpit. Control-panel lights were making a Halloween mask of his bruised and swelling face. His eyes glowed red. Torches of hell.

Roark screamed one last time before fear sent him plunging beneath the surface. Then came the pain. Excruciating and immeasurable. Pain that splinters the body but slays the soul.

⌒

Chapter Eleven

NADIA arrived at the martini bar wearing a snug black dress and a cocktail hat, one of those saucy numbers with a veil that covered half her face. Very fetching. Very femme fatale.

Heads turned as she made her way through the bar. Noah was inflated with pride that the most exquisite woman in the room was joining him. When she reached his table, he embraced her warmly as she slid into the banquette beside him.

He placed their order with the waiter, then said, "You look sensational. I like the veil. It lends a mysterious air."

"Thank you."

When their martinis arrived, they clinked glasses, sipped.

"You've been busy laying your father-in-law to rest. I thought the eulogies were rather moving."

"A lot of folderol. But actually, it wasn't all that bad, except for having to keep Maris's hysteria at bay."

"Wasn't it natural for her to be upset?"

"Her behavior went beyond normal grief. My wife got the harebrained notion that I was responsible for her father's fall. She coerced the local police in Massachusetts to reinvestigate. Naturally, they found nothing to substantiate her suspicions."

"How lucky for you."

"Luck had nothing to do with it, Nadia."

"I'm sure that's true." She stared out over the crowd. "If you had pushed the old gentleman down the staircase, you would be shrewd enough not to get caught."

"I didn't. But you're right. I would be shrewd enough not to get caught. And that's why you like me so well."

She turned back to him. "True. I would never be involved with a loser."

"We're so much alike, it's frightening." Leaning closer to her, he added, "Daniel's death was the final nail in the coffin of my marriage. It is now beyond repair. But before his accidental fall I persuaded Daniel to sign a power-of-attorney document that enables me to sell Matherly Press to WorldView, and Maris can't do a thing about it."

Nadia's eyes went wide. "But Matherly Press isn't yours to sell."

"Nadia! There you are!" Morris Blume suddenly materialized on the other side of the table.

Noah hadn't noticed his approach, and he didn't welcome the intrusion. His plan for this evening had been to wine, dine, and romance Nadia. He needed good press, and no one could provide that better than Nadia.

WorldView's CEO looked colorless, as he often did in his gray suit, gray shirt, silver tie. "I didn't see you at first and thought there'd been a mix-up about the time," Blume was saying to Nadia.

"Your timing couldn't be more perfect." She scooted from behind the table and walked into Blume's embrace. They locked lips.

Blume appraised her from hat to heels. "You look gorgeous."

"I'm glad you think so. I bought the ensemble with you in mind."

Nadia signaled the waiter, who scurried over and took Blume's order. She didn't return to sit beside Noah, but took the chair Blume was holding for her. They now faced him across the table.

Noah was certain that their public display of affection was for his benefit. Okay. If she wanted to flaunt her new boyfriend in front of him, fine. It didn't change anything, except that her sex life would take a severe downward plunge.

After thanking the waiter for his drink, Blume turned to Noah. "My secretary told me that you called today requesting a meeting."

"That's right. In light of my recent family tragedy—"

"My condolences, by the way."

"Thank you." Noah brushed an invisible speck off the cuff of his shirt. "Daniel's death imposed a temporary postponement of our schedule. Now we're able to pick up where we left off."

"I really don't see the need for a meeting now."

"Now" was a troubling adverb. "Now" indicated that circumstances had undergone a change. "Why is that?" Noah asked.

"Noah and I were getting to this when you joined us, Morris," Nadia said to Blume. "Apparently, there's been some confusion."

"Well," said Noah, "since I seem to be the only one in the dark here, perhaps you'll enlighten me."

She looked at Noah. "I thought someone would have told you by now. Out of respect for Daniel, I've been sitting on this story for a week."

Noah was growing uncomfortably warm. "What story?"

Taking center stage, Nadia readjusted herself closer to Blume. "Out of the blue, Daniel Matherly invited me to his house for breakfast. It was the same morning you left for the country. He gave me a scoop but asked me to sit on it for a few days, at least until Maris returned from Georgia."

Noah forced himself to smile. "You still haven't told me the nature of this exclusive story."

"Daniel appointed Maris chairman and CEO of Matherly Press. I thought perhaps Daniel would tell you while you were away together in the country. No? Well, he probably thought it only fair that Maris be informed first."

Noah could feel the increased pressure of his pulse. "Daniel didn't think too highly of you, Nadia. I think he played a cruel practical joke on you."

"The possibility crossed my mind. So I had the story corroborated by a Mr. Stern, the Matherlys' personal attorney. He verified it. Maris's appointment is irrevocable and incontestable."

"Why didn't you mention this to me earlier, Nadia?"

"It wasn't my place."

"But now it is?"

"I'm sparing you having to read it in my column tomorrow." She gave him a sympathetic smile. "Honestly, Noah, I thought that by now you would have been officially informed. I suppose that since your marriage is over, you're no longer in the inner circle. You're only hired help."

"Would you like another drink, Noah?"

"No, thank you, Morris. I'm late for another appointment." If he didn't get out of here, he was either going to kill Nadia or explode.

"Oh, please stay," Nadia said in a cajoling voice. "We've got so much to celebrate. One of Morris's fondest desires has been fulfilled. WorldView has acquired Becker-Howe. You know Oliver Howe, I'm sure, because he and Daniel were old friends. In fact, it was Daniel who put Morris in contact with him."

"I had my heart set on Matherly Press," Blume said. "But since Maris will be at the helm—"

"I felt it only fair to tell him," Nadia interjected.

"And Maris has made absolutely clear her intention never to sell it, so I decided to acquire another company."

Noah was clenching his jaw so tightly, it ached. "How nice for you. I really hate to break up the party, but I must get on my way."

"Wait! That's not the only good news." Nadia thrust her left hand across the table. "You failed to notice that I'm wearing an obscenely enormous diamond ring. Morris and I are getting married next Sunday at The Plaza." She beamed at Morris, then turned back to Noah. "Three o'clock. We'll be crushed if you're not there."

EIGHT-O'CLOCK classes were just about to convene when Maris parked her rental car in a lot reserved for campus visitors. It was the summer session, so there weren't many students. Although she had never been here before, she didn't need to ask directions. The university campus wasn't similar to the one described in *Envy*. It *was* the one described in *Envy*.

Less than twenty-four hours before, with Noah's words replaying inside her head—*his death was convenient*—she'd reserved an airline ticket to Nashville. She had planned to go to the office only long enough to check her mail before returning to Daniel's town house to pack, then dash to the airport for the late evening flight.

It didn't quite go according to plan.

Her appearance in the office had galvanized her assistant. "Thank heavens you're here. Mr. Stern has been calling all morning and made me swear to notify him the moment I spoke to you. He'll be on line two."

Maris went into her office and sat down behind her desk. It was fortunate that she was seated, because the news Stern had imparted was staggering. "Mr. Matherly had in mind to announce his decision when you returned from Georgia. I think he wanted it to be a ceremonious occasion. Unhappily, he didn't have that opportunity."

Maris was deeply touched to know that her father had placed so much confidence in her and had entrusted her with Matherly Press.

Stern had coughed delicately. "It's at your discretion whether or not to keep Mr. Reed on staff. Mr. Matherly intimated that having him there might be awkward, considering your pending divorce."

So he had known.

"Frankly, your father no longer trusted Mr. Reed to perform in the best interest of the publishing house," the lawyer had told her. "But, as I said, his continuance with the company is up to you."

Following that conversation, she had taken a cab to Daniel's house, where another shock awaited her.

As she was jogging up the steps of the brownstone, a limousine had pulled up to the curb. Nadia Schuller alighted, dressed in a black dress and a cocktail hat that on anyone else would have looked ridiculous. "I understand why you don't want to talk to me, Maris. But I need one minute of your time."

"I don't have one minute. I'm in a hurry."

"Please. I fortified myself with two martinis before I came."

Maris had listened with dismay as Nadia told her about her breakfast meeting with Daniel.

"I was told he'd had a mystery guest," Maris said. "You would have been the last person I would have guessed."

"Me, too. I was floored by the invitation. But the real shocker came when he told me about this bogus document Noah was going to press him to sign. He then offered me an exclusive on your promotion. The story about the transfer of power will run tomorrow. I agreed to hold it for a week. Of course, when I did, I had no idea that . . . that he wouldn't be here to read it."

Maris had been further surprised to see tears in Nadia's eyes. "Your father was a gentleman, Maris. Even toward me. I wish I had warned him not to go with Noah, but I never thought he'd go so far as to commit murder. Now I wonder."

"So do I. If he did push Dad down the stairs, he got away with it. I guess all of us underestimated Noah." Maris turned toward the steps, then turned back. "Why do you suppose Dad gave you the story?" she asked.

"I've asked myself that a thousand times. I have an idea. Speculation, of course. He knew Noah had cheated on you, so he wanted to use my column to publicly humiliate him."

Maris smiled. It was her aged father they'd all underestimated.

Now, reviewing yesterday's startling events, she followed the path on the college campus that Roark had taken that blustery November morning. Parker's vivid narrative led her to the classroom building where Professor Hadley had his office. She ascended the stairs and walked down the hallway to the office numbered 207. The door was slightly ajar, as it had been that morning Roark approached it with his capstone manuscript inside his backpack. Her heart was thumping hard as she gave the door a gentle push.

A man was seated at a desk, his back to her. "Professor Hadley?"

He turned around. "Hello, Maris."

She sagged against the doorjamb. "Mike."

"Have a seat." He smiled at her. "I knew you'd eventually figure it out. What was the breakthrough?"

Maris lowered herself into the only available chair. "I guessed days ago that Roark was Parker. Yesterday Noah said something that was almost a direct quote from the book—about how convenient my father's death was to him."

"As his mother's death was. It enabled him to move to Florida without further delay."

"I should have realized sooner that you were Hadley."

"Frankly, I'm glad you didn't. Parker's descriptions weren't always flattering."

Her eyes roved the cluttered office. "What's your position here?"

"Professor emeritus. I get to keep the office till I die. In exchange, once each semester I give a lecture to a couple hundred bored young people who attend only because they're required to."

Quietly she said, "I'll bet Parker wasn't bored by your lectures."

"He was exceptional. In his book he hasn't exaggerated how I felt about 'Roark' and his talent. If anything, he's minimized it."

"Too bad he's not as fine a human being as he is a writer."

Mike studied her for a moment, then reached across his desk and pulled forward a manuscript. He passed it to her. She looked down at the cover sheet with bitterness. "I've read it."

"Most of it," he corrected. "Not all. There's some you haven't read. Read it before you judge Parker too harshly." He stood up and made his way to the door. "I'm going for coffee. Can I bring you back something?"

ONE of Noah's strongest personality traits was his ability to deny that anything was wrong. On the Richter scale of complications, his disastrous martini date with Nadia was a blip. WorldView had bought itself a white elephant. Becker-Howe had been hanging on by its fingernails for years. The merger would be an abysmal failure, and Morris Blume would become a laughingstock.

As for Nadia's exclusive story, he would deny it. Daniel wasn't around to corroborate it, and Nadia was probably lying about Stern's corroboration. The hubbub would die down, and soon no one would remember the details.

Maris, however, was the hitch in this plan.

What was he to do if Daniel had, in fact, given Maris control of Matherly Press? Say, the attorney—Stern—had the documentation to prove it. What then? All right. He would go along. He would say that Daniel had informed him of it. They'd discussed it at length, and Noah had agreed that Maris should have the title. But Daniel had asked him to serve as her adviser. To steer her around pitfalls. Yes, that was very good. And who could contradict him?

Now, what about their personal relationship? Tricky to resolve, but not impossible. She was so easily pacified.

With a jaunty air Noah stepped off the elevator and walked briskly down the hallway toward his office. He sailed past his assistant, Cindy, and entered the office, where he came to an abrupt standstill. "Stern? What the hell are you doing behind my desk?"

Stern gestured toward the two men with him. "These gentlemen from my law firm have agreed to help you box up your personal items—a project I will closely monitor. You have one hour to complete the task, at which time I will relieve you of your keys to this office and your security pass into the building. I will then escort you out through the Fifty-first Street exit. When stipulating to me the terms of your immediate dismissal, Ms. Matherly was very specific about that. She did not want to cause you any embarrassment by conducting you outside through the main entrance."

Cindy squeezed in through the door behind him. "Excuse me, Mr. Reed? The deliveryman won't release this package until you personally sign the return receipt." She thrust the package at him. "It's from a Mr. Parker Evans."

MARIS had just completed her read-through. She was sitting motionless, staring at the last line until the letters blurred.

Pain that splinters the body but slays the soul.

"This isn't the ending, is it?" she asked.

Mike frowned into his coffee. "He hasn't shown the last chapter to me. I'm not sure he's written it. It may be too painful for him."

"More painful than this? What happened afterward, Mike?"

"Noah returned to the marina. As related in the prologue, he faked hysteria. Claimed that Parker had gone crazy on the boat. Abused the girl. Attacked him. They fought. The girl went overboard, and so did Parker. Noah tried to save them."

"He blamed Parker's violent outburst on envy."

"A lie, of course. But a good one. Believable. The coast guard organized a search-and-rescue effort."

"Mary Catherine?"

"Her body was never recovered."

"What about Parker?"

Mike sipped his coffee before answering. "Parker was found that night by sheer accident. A fisherman spotted him. His legs had been chewed to pieces by the blades of the outboard motor. When the fisherman first saw him, he mistook him for an animal carcass that had been used for chum."

With a shaky hand Maris set aside the Styrofoam cup of tea that Mike had brought back for her.

"For over a week his condition was listed as critical," Mike continued. "Somehow he lived."

"He told me he underwent several operations. What was Noah doing all this time? Surely he was afraid that Parker would give his version of the story and convince the authorities of the truth."

"While Parker was fighting for his life, Noah was putting on quite a show for the authorities. Mary Catherine wasn't there to dispute his version of what had happened. He painted Parker as a jealous hothead who had gotten drunk, snapped, and turned violent. He attacked Noah. When Mary Catherine tried to break them apart, Parker lashed out and knocked her over the railing. His momentum caused him to fall overboard, too.

"By the time the doctors granted the investigators permission to question him, Parker had already been cast in the defensive role. Confronted with these false accusations, he played right into Noah's hands. He reacted like a maniac. His ranted denials made him appear guilty rather than innocent. From his hospital bed he threatened to kill his lying friend.

"In any case, Noah was believed. Parker wasn't. He was charged with involuntary manslaughter for Mary Catherine's drowning. When he was well enough to leave the hospital, he was taken to court for his arraignment. He pleaded no contest."

"Why?" Maris exclaimed. "He wasn't guilty."

"But he felt responsible. Parker blamed himself for being unable to save her. Noah didn't attend Parker's sentencing, but he sent a videotaped deposition. He said that he and Parker had been closer than any two brothers. But when Noah succeeded ahead of him, it did something to Parker. Noah looked into the camera and sobbed,

'I don't understand what happened to Parker that day. He turned devious, lecherous, and murderous.' I think I'm quoting correctly."

Maris took a deep breath and expelled it slowly. "So Noah went to New York in a blaze of glory because of *The Vanquished*."

"And Parker went to prison."

"Prison?" She ground her palm against her forehead. "He told me once that he had spent years in rehab hospitals and 'other facilities.' I would never have imagined he was referring to prison."

"Because of his physical condition, he was sent to a minimum-security prison and allowed to continue with his physical therapy. He was released after serving twenty-two months of an eight-year sentence." He looked at her. "I believe you know that he'd sunk pretty low by the time I heard what had happened to my star pupil and went looking for him."

"Parker's not evil, like Noah. But he's cruel." She looked down at the pages still lying in her lap. "Why did he do this, Mike?"

"Revenge."

"Why did he involve me?"

"I apologize for my part, Maris. I was uncomfortable with it from the start." He eased back in his chair. "You see, in that video deposition Noah accused Parker of lechery with Mary Catherine."

"So he made the accusation a reality. With Noah's wife. I was the element that made the plot work. What's the ending to be?"

"He wouldn't tell me."

"Maybe deceiving me, bedding me, is vengeance enough for him."

Mike responded to the bitterness she couldn't conceal. "I'm not justifying what he's done, Maris. But I can understand it. He wanted Noah to experience the pain he had suffered. He wanted Noah to know what it felt like to be betrayed and—"

"Oh, my God!" She gripped Mike's sleeve. "I've just figured out his plot. His ending. In Noah's videotaped deposition he claimed that Parker had turned devious, lecherous, and—"

"Murderous," Mike finished, slapping his forehead. "Damn me for being so old and stupid. That's why he hasn't shared the last chapter with me."

Maris rattled off her racing thoughts. "Parker's done everything Noah accused him of. Except—" She looked at Mike with alarm. "He wouldn't," she said huskily. "I know he wouldn't."

"I don't believe so either."

But neither sounded convinced. An eye for an eye. Noah's life in exchange for Mary Catherine's. Parker might not kill for revenge, but he might for justice.

She surged to her feet. "We've got to stop him." But at the door she drew herself up short. "Thank heavens." Turning back around, she said to Mike, "We're not too late. Noah doesn't know that the writer I've been working with is Parker. He hasn't read *Envy*."

Mike dragged his hands down his face, groaning, "Oh, no."

Chapter Twelve

NOAH, fresh off a chartered boat from the mainland, entered Terry's Bar and Grill with a condescending attitude that immediately catapulted him to the top of the endangered species list. The locals disliked non-islanders in general, but they particularly disliked any who looked down their noses at them. They despised Noah Reed on sight. In fact, he might not have been allowed to tie up his boat at the dock if Parker hadn't spread word that he was expecting a citified visitor from up north. If anybody spotted such a person, he was to be directed to Terry's, where Parker would be waiting.

Noah approached the bar and addressed Terry. "Hey!"

Terry ignored Noah.

"Didn't you hear me?"

Terry shifted a gnawed matchstick from one corner of his mouth to the other. "I heard ya. Now get outta my place."

"I think you've already worn out your welcome, Noah." At the sound of his voice Noah spun around. Parker grinned up at him. "Record time, too."

Noah gave Parker and his wheelchair a long, slow once-over. "She told me you were a cripple."

Terry produced a baseball bat from beneath the bar.

"She told me you were a bastard," Parker returned, keeping his smile in place. "But then, I already knew that." He motioned with his head for Noah to follow him outside. Every eye in the bar was on them as they left through the screen door.

"You've got nerve, Noah. I'll give you that."

Noah scoffed. "Coming to see you?"

"No. Going into Terry's bar wearing those loafers." He looked down at Noah's Gucci shoes with the gold trademark.

Noah ignored the dig.

Parker led him to the Gator. "Climb in." As Noah settled in, Parker raised himself into the driver's seat. He reached down for his wheelchair, folded it, and placed it in the trailer, then clicked on the ignition. For the next five minutes they rode in silence. Parker returned the waves of people they passed along the way.

Noah turned to him. "What are you? The local celebrity?"

"The only professional writer they know."

"You haven't sold this book of yours yet."

"No, but the Mackensie Roone books sell." He laughed at Noah's stunned expression. "You didn't know? Well . . . surprise!"

With aplomb Noah recovered quickly. "So that's how you afford the lovely home and loyal valet that my wife mentioned."

"The home still needs a lot of work. And my loyal valet up and quit on me this week. He thinks I'm a rotten person."

The sun had sunk below the tree line by the time they reached the derelict cotton gin. Noah assessed the dilapidated building. "I can see what you mean by the place still needing a lot of work."

Parker reached back and swung his wheelchair to the ground. "It's not the homestead, but it's an interesting building. As long as you're here, you should get a taste of local history."

He wheeled his chair into the gin, leaving Noah no choice except to follow. Inside, waning sunlight squeezed through the cracks in the walls. The interior was gloomy, with deep shadows. Like a tour

guide, Parker pointed out aspects of the gin. Tired of the mono-
logue, Noah interrupted him. "I read your book."

Parker slowly brought his wheelchair around to face him. "Of
course you did, Noah. You wouldn't be here if you hadn't."

"It'll never see print."

Parker shrugged. "Here I was thinking that maybe, after all these
years, you'd be ready to relieve your conscience."

"Cut the bull, Parker." Noah's voice cracked across the stillness
like a whip. "I assume this *Envy* is the manuscript that Maris has
been raving about?"

"The very one. She's read every word. Likes the story."

"She's easily impressed by melodrama."

"Wrong. She's a good editor and a classy lady."

Noah snickered. "You've slept with her, haven't you?"

Parker clenched his jaw and refused to answer.

Noah shook his head with amusement. "Ah, Parker, Parker.
Some things haven't changed. You're still the chivalrous lover who
never kisses and tells." He continued nonchalantly. "You must
know, Parker, that this book of yours will never be published."

"Actually, Noah, I didn't write it for publication. I wrote it to get
you here so I could watch you die, the way you watched me that
night."

Noah snorted. "What? You're going to run me down with your
wheelchair?"

Parker merely smiled and withdrew a small transistor from his
shirt pocket.

"Oh, you're going to beat me to death with a remote control."

"I own this building," Parker said conversationally. "Some folks
think it's a hazard—that abandoned well and all." He hitched his
thumb in that direction. "So I've decided to do my fellow islanders
a favor and destroy it."

He depressed one of the buttons on the transistor. Out of the
shadows in a far corner came a loud pop, followed by a spark. Startled, Noah spun around and watched as a flame leaped up against
the weathered wood. Parker gave his chair a hard push toward

him. Noah, sensing the motion, turned and lunged at him. Noah's reflexes were good. He landed a couple of good punches.

But Parker staved off his slugs. When Noah began pushing him backward toward the open well, Parker wasn't surprised. Noah came on ferociously, blindly—the predator moving in for the kill. Then, at precisely the right instant, Parker jammed down the brake lever of his wheelchair. It brought the chair to a jarring stop Noah hadn't expected. Inertia propelled him forward. His Gucci shoes caught the low rim of the well, tripping him. He groped at air. Then he stepped into nothingness with a startled cry.

Parker wiped his bloody nose on his shirtsleeve.

"You son of a bitch!" Noah shouted up at him.

"The cripple outsmarted you, Noah. Isn't that what you had in mind for me? To push me down that well?"

"Get me out of here."

"Ah, don't be such a baby, Noah. It's not nearly as deep as the Atlantic." Parker set off another of the charges. "There are twelve more like that. But long before I've set all of them off, you'll already be choking. Smoke inhalation doesn't have the drama of water flooding your lungs, but it's pretty effective, wouldn't you say?"

"You expect me to believe you'd let me die down here?"

"Why not? I'm a killer. You said so yourself. Remember? I turned devious, lecherous, and murderous."

"I was . . . I was—"

"You were sentencing me to prison. Since I did the time, I think it's only fair that I commit the crime."

Noah was silent for a moment, then said, "My ankle's broken."

"You're breaking my heart."

"Okay, what I did . . . was wrong. I got scared. Ran away. Once I realized what I'd done, there was no way out. I can understand your carrying a grudge. But you've made your point."

"Like you could have made yours by leaving me to die. Wasn't that enough? Did you have to let Mary Catherine die, too?"

"You won't get away with this," Noah said in a new tone of voice.

"Oh, I think I will. All I have to do is tell the truth. We had words. You attacked me, and I've got the bloody nose to prove it. You lost your balance and fell into the well. Unfortunately, I had already set off the charges and couldn't stop the inevitable. I tried to save you, but it was no use. I'm a cripple, remember?" He peered over the rim and smiled down at Noah, whose face was a pale oval looking up at him from the bottom of the dry well. "It's as plausible as the story you told the coast guard."

"Parker! Parker, listen to me."

"Excuse me just a moment." Parker depressed a button, and another charge sparked. By now flames were working their way up the loft.

"Stop this, Parker," Noah cried.

"No."

"Okay, you want me to beg. I'm begging. Get me out of here."

Parker coughed on smoke. "Sorry, Noah. Even if I wanted to, it's too late. I've got to save myself."

"Parker! Don't do this," Noah sobbed. "Please. What can I say?"

Parker stared down at him. "Say you're sorry. Admit that you knocked Mary Catherine overboard and did *nothing* to save her."

Noah hesitated. Parker placed his hand on the wheels of his chair and started to turn it around. "See ya."

"Wait! What happened to Mary Catherine was my fault."

"And me. You deliberately ran that boat over me."

"Yes."

"Why?"

"I . . . I was trying to kill you and make it look like an accident. I wanted you out of the way of my career."

"Was that also why you killed Daniel Matherly? How'd you arrange that fall, Noah?"

"I provoked him. He got angry, came at me. I deflected—"

"You pushed him."

"All right, I pushed him."

Parker coughed on smoke. It was stinging his eyes. "You are an abomination, Noah. A miserable human being. A murderer." He shook his head regretfully. "But you're not worth killing."

Parker wheeled his chair backward to retrieve the rope he had stashed earlier in preparation for this moment. He threaded the rope down to Noah, who grasped it frantically. "Make a few loops around your chest and tie it tightly," Parker instructed.

"Okay," Noah called when he was done. "Pull me up."

Parker backed away, pulling the rope taut. "Ready? If you can get some footholds, walk the wall."

"I can't. My ankle."

"Okay, but easy does it. Don't—"

He was about to say "yank." But it was too late.

In his panic to be rescued, Noah had pulled sharply on the rope. Parker wasn't braced for it. He was jerked forward out of the wheelchair, landing on the packed dirt floor. "Dammit!"

"What? What's happening? Parker?"

For several seconds Parker lay there with his forehead resting on the floor. Then, using his forearms to pull himself along, he inched his way over to the rim of the well and peered down into it. "You pulled me out of my chair."

"Well, do something." Noah's voice was now ragged with desperation. He could hear the crackle of old wood burning. The smoke grew thicker by the second.

"Can't help you, buddy. I'm a cripple, remember?" Parker shook his head ruefully. "I'll admit this isn't the way I had the ending plotted. I never intended for you to die. I wanted to scare you into confessing your sins." He laughed. "I hope you grasp the irony of this situation. I'm your only hope of salvation. But I'm powerless to save you because of the injuries you inflicted on me. That's rich, isn't it? It's the kind of built-in irony that Professor Mike Strother loved." Parker suddenly spoke softly. "You have one more sin to confess, don't you, Noah?"

"I had to be first, Parker. I had to be."

"Professor Strother hadn't heard from either of us for more than a year. He didn't realize you'd sold *The Vanquished* until he saw it in his local bookstore. He recognized the title and your name immediately, of course."

"Parker—"

"Imagine Professor Strother's surprise when he opened his copy of *The Vanquished* by Noah Reed. And read the first page of my book. *My* book, Noah!"

"It was that letter! Strother always favoring you. He thought your manuscript was so fine. I thought I'd test it, get a second opinion. One day while you were out, I went into your computer and printed out a copy. I put my title on it and submitted it under my name."

"And when it sold, you had to get rid of me. Immediately."

"That was the plan."

"Bet you freaked when I turned up alive."

"I didn't panic. I hurriedly put your book into my computer and mine into yours. You couldn't have proved your claims, because by then I had painted you as unstable and violent."

"Strother always gave you credit for clever plotting."

"Our dear professor was another concern, but I figured that if he ever came forward and tried to expose me, I'd—"

"You'd think of a way to worm your way out."

"I always have."

"Until now."

"At least I'll die knowing that you're right behind me. You can't crawl on your belly fast enough to get out of here now, Parker."

"No. But I can walk fast enough." Then, as Noah watched with mounting disbelief, Parker struggled to his knees and then stood up. "It's a Mackensie Roone trademark, Noah," Parker said, smiling down at him. "Save one final plot twist for the very end."

"I'll kill you, Parker. I'll see you in hell! I'll—"

"You all right, Mr. Evans?" Deputy Sheriff Dwight Harris rushed through the door, accompanied by two other deputies.

"Exhausted," Parker told him. "Otherwise okay." He depressed a button on the remote control, and the flames immediately died.

"Fire truck's outside. We were getting worried." Just then the spray from the fire hose struck the exterior wall with a hard whomp.

"I was getting a little worried myself," Parker said. "Those smoke machines are killers."

Deputy Harris glanced at the scorched walls. "Those smudge pots did some damage to your building."

"It's survived worse. Besides, it was worth it."

"So you got it?"

"Every incriminating word." Parker pulled out his shirttail and removed a cassette tape recorder clipped to the waistband of his pants. He disconnected it from the microphone wire taped to his chest and passed them both to the sheriff. "Thanks for setting this up, Deputy Harris."

"No thanks necessary. I appreciate your calling me. It'll probably be the only sting of my career." The two shook hands.

Noah had been shouting obscenities, but the deputy acknowledged him only now. "How you doin' down there, Mr. Reed? The police chief up in Mass'chusitts sure is anxious to hear what you had to say about your daddy-in-law's fall. My department's talking to the folks down in Florida, too."

Parker turned away as the deputies hauled Noah out with a rope. He was taken aback to see Mike, his old friend, standing just beyond the gin's wide door. Maris was beside him.

Deputy Harris noticed his hesitation. "They were tearing up the road in a golf cart. Intercepted them before they could barge in here and ruin the whole thing. They were worried about you."

"Afraid Noah would kill me?"

"No, sir. Afraid *you* would kill *him*."

Parker smiled. "Wonder where they got that idea."

"The old man said Ms. Matherly figured out your plot."

"That doesn't surprise me." Shuffling across the dirt floor in a stiff-legged, awkward gait, his legacy of Noah's treachery, Parker slowly made his way outside. Mike went to fetch his chair. Maris continued to stand stone-still, staring at him. "You thought I was paralyzed?" he asked.

She nodded.

"I figured. For this to work, I needed Noah to think that, too. I ride whenever I can. This is about the best I can do. Will ever do."

A tear rolled down her cheek. "It doesn't matter. It never did."

"THE SWEETEST GIFT I EVER received was that glass of fireflies."
Parker was stroking her back in the aftermath of lovemaking.

"Lightning bugs."

He chuckled. "You're learning."

"That was a sweet night all round. The sweetest. Until tonight."

"Maris, that next morning—"

"Shh. I understand now why you had to be so wretched. You had
to get rid of me before you could bring Noah here."

He tipped her chin up so he could see her face. "But you know
I used you to get to him."

"Your original plan was probably to have him catch us like this."

He glanced down the length of their entwined bodies. "Yeah."

"But that changed when you fell in love with me. You couldn't
bring yourself to subject me to an ugly scene like that. So you hurt
me in order to protect me. You made certain I would leave."

He stroked her cheek. "You're so smart, you amaze me."

"So I'm right?"

"As rain. Especially about my falling in love with you." He lifted
her face toward his and kissed her in a way that left no room for
doubt.

"There is one thing I can't figure out," she said when the kiss
finally ended. "I know we promised not to talk about this tonight,
but I'd like to have one point clarified. Mike discovered that *The
Vanquished* was actually your book with Noah's title on it. And he
tried to contact you for an explanation."

"It took him almost a year to track me down. By then the paperback edition had already come out."

"Why didn't Mike expose Noah then?"

"Because I threatened his life if he did. I was in poor condition,
Maris—an ex-con who looked like a beggar and was living like one.
Wheelchair-bound. Addicted to pills." He shook his head stubbornly. "Before confronting the book world's crown prince, I chose
to wait until I was strong and confident."

"And successful."

"That, too. I wanted to challenge Noah as an equal, when I

had the credentials to back up my claim that he'd stolen my book."

"I'm surprised you got Mike to agree."

"He didn't agree. He just gave in."

"Or?"

"Or I swore that I would never write another word."

"Ahh. That would have cinched it."

They lay facing each other, their heads sharing the pillow. He was tracing her collarbone when she said, "I recognized you the first time you kissed me. The night we met."

His finger fell still. He raised his eyes to hers. "What?"

"That's why that kiss alarmed me. Because I knew you. Intimately. I had spent so many nights with you, poring over every word. Your book was like a personal love letter. When you kissed me, it was so familiar." Adoringly she touched every feature of his face. "I have loved you for so long, Parker. For years. From the day I first read *The Vanquished*."

He swallowed hard. "Can you imagine how hard it was for me not to tell you that I was the author? That it was me, not Noah, you'd fallen in love with?"

"Why didn't you tell me?"

"I couldn't. Not then. Not yet. Besides, I was afraid I wouldn't live up to your expectations."

She ran her fingers through his hair. "You surpassed them, Parker. You created my fantasies. Now you're fulfilling them."

They kissed long and deeply, and when they finally pulled apart, she asked him what his original title had been.

And he told her.

And she told him that she liked it much better.

Soccer mom Sandra Brown has close to 60 million books in print.

Fiction is her trade, but it's the facts that are truly amazing. Sandra Brown—former actress, model, cosmetics-store manager, and TV reporter—has published more than sixty books, forty-four of which have scored as bestsellers on the feverishly competitive *New York Times* bestseller list. Close to sixty million copies of her books are in print, and her work has been translated into thirty languages.

For all this global acclaim, however, Brown is a homegrown Texas spirit, born in Waco, raised in Fort Worth, and, today, most at home on her ranch in Arlington with her husband of thirty-three years, Michael (her college sweetheart), and their pet longhorn steers Boudreaux, Bowie, and Bubba.

Brown is also a devoted family woman. She forged her writing credentials as a skilled romance novelist with an early pseudonym based on the names of her two children, now adults: Rachel and Ryan. Of that comically hectic era when the children were young, the award-winning author says, "At three thirty every afternoon I switched from professional writer to Mom, driving someone to ballet, someone else to soccer." And percolating ideas all the while: She once plotted a novel during a school field trip to the Barnum & Bailey Circus.

"**BRIAN HAIG** is John Grisham
in an army uniform, and
Secret Sanction is marvelous."

—*Jack Higgins*

SECRET
SANCTION
BRIAN HAIG

IN THE ARMY

YOU LEARN TO REVERE DUTY,

HONOR, AND COUNTRY.

IN KOSOVO YOU LEARN TO CHOOSE

TWO OUT OF THREE.

ONE

FORT Bragg in August is so hellish you can smell the sulfur in the air. Actually, though, it's not sulfur; it's 98 percent humidity, mixed with North Carolina dust, mixed with the raunchy bouquet of about thirty thousand men and women who spend half their lives scurrying about in the woods. Without showers.

The moment I stepped off the plane, I had this fierce urge to call my bosses back in the Pentagon and beg them to reconsider. It wouldn't work, though.

So I hefted up my duffel bag and oversize legal briefcase and headed for the taxi stand. Of course, this was Pope Air Force Base, which adjoins Fort Bragg, which makes it all one big happy military installation. No taxi stand, and shame on me for not knowing that. I therefore marched straight to a pay phone and called the duty sergeant at the headquarters of the 82nd Airborne Division.

"Headquarters, Sergeant Mercor," a stern voice answered.

"Major Sean Drummond here," I barked, doing my finest impersonation of a bitchy, obnoxious bully, which, by the by, I always do pretty well.

"How can I help you, sir?"

"That's pretty obvious, isn't it? Why wasn't the duty jeep waiting for me at the airport?"

"We don't send jeeps out to the airport to pick up personnel. Not even officers, sir."

"Hey, Sergeant, think I'm stupid?"

I let that question linger a moment. Then, much friendlier, I said, "Look, the general who works upstairs in that building of yours promised a jeep would be waiting when I arrived. Now, if it were to get here inside twenty minutes, then we'll just write this off as an inconvenience. Otherwise . . ."

There was this fairly long pause on the other end. "Sir, I . . . Well, uh, this is really irregular. No one told me to have a jeep there to meet you. I swear."

Of course nobody told him. I knew that. And he knew that.

"Listen, Sergeant. Sergeant Mercor, right? It's ten thirty at night, and my patience wanes with each passing minute."

"All right, Major. The duty driver will be there in twenty minutes."

I sat on my duffel bag and waited. I should've felt bad about fibbing, but my conscience just wasn't up to it. I was tired, for one thing. Besides, I had a set of orders in my pocket that assigned me to perform a special investigation. In my book, that entitled me to a special privilege or two.

Private Rodriguez and the duty jeep showed up exactly twenty minutes later. I threw my duffel into the back of the humvee and climbed in. "Where to?" Rodriguez asked, staring straight ahead.

"Visiting officers quarters. Know where they are?"

"Sure. You assigned here, sir?"

"Nope."

"Reporting in?"

"Nope."

"Passing through?"

"You're getting warmer."

"You're a lawyer, right?" Rodriguez asked, glancing at the brass on my uniform that identified me as a member of the Judge Advocate General's Corps, or JAG for short.

"Rodriguez, it's late and I'm tired. I appreciate your need to make conversation, but I'm not in the mood. Just drive."

"Hey, no problem, sir." Rodriguez whistled for two minutes. Then, "I see you got a Combat Infantryman's Badge."

Private Rodriguez, annoyingly clever fellow that he was, kept adjusting the rearview mirror to study the items on my uniform.

"I used to be infantry," I admitted.

"And you went to combat."

"Only because they shipped me off before I could figure out how to go AWOL."

"No offense, sir, but why would a guy wanta stop being an infantry officer just to become a lawyer?"

"Someone gave me a test, and wouldn't you know it, I was too smart to be an infantry officer anymore. You know the army. Rules are rules. You done asking questions?"

"No, sir. Only a few more. Why you here?"

"Passing through, Private. Heading to Europe."

"Would that be . . . uh, Bosnia?"

"That's where it would be. I'm supposed to catch a C-130 that leaves Pope Field at seven o'clock in the morning, and as a result, I have to sleep here."

A more truthful reply would have included the fact that I had an appointment in the morning with a four-star general named Partridge, and only after he was through with me was I allowed to head for Bosnia. But Private Rodriguez did not need to know all that. In fact, nobody but the general, myself, and a few select people back in Washington needed to know all that.

"VOQ just ahead," Private Rodriguez announced.

"Thanks," I said as we pulled into the parking lot of the visiting officers quarters.

I retrieved my duffel, checked in, and found my room. In less than a minute I was undressed, in bed, and asleep.

It didn't seem like a full five hours later when the phone beside my bed rang and the desk clerk informed me that General Partridge's military sedan was waiting in the parking lot. I showered and shaved with dazzling speed, then rummaged through my duffel for my battle dress and combat boots.

The drive out to the John F. Kennedy Special Warfare Center, which is, among other things, the headquarters for the United States Army Special Forces Command, took thirty minutes.

A sour-faced major met me outside Partridge's office and told me to wait. Twenty minutes later Partridge's office door opened, and I marched briskly to the general's desk. I stopped, saluted crisply, and introduced myself in that strange way army guys do.

"Major Drummond reporting as ordered, sir."

The general looked up from some papers, nodded slightly, popped a cigarette between his lips, and calmly lit it. My right hand was still foolishly stuck to my forehead. "Put down that hand," he grunted, and I did. He sucked in a roomful of smoke, then leaned back in his chair. "You happy about this assignment?"

"No, sir."

"You studied the case already?"

"A bit, sir."

He sucked on the cigarette again. He had thin lips, a thin face, and a thin body, all of which looked nicely weathered and almost impossibly devoid of both body fat and compassion. "Drummond, every now and again there's a military court case that captures the attention of the American public. When I was a lieutenant, the big one was the My Lai court-martial. Then came Tailhook, which the navy botched beyond redemption. Then the air force had that Kelly Flynn thing. Now it's your turn. You screw this one up, and generations of future JAG officers are gonna wonder just how this guy Drummond managed to mangle things so bad. You thought of that?"

"It has crossed my mind, General."

"You decide there's not enough grounds for a court-martial, and you'll be accused of shoving the army's dirt under a rug. You decide there *are* sufficient grounds, then we'll have us a nice little brawl in a courtroom, with the whole world watching." He stopped and studied my face. "You got any idea why we picked you?"

"Only a few vague suspicions," I cautiously admitted.

He lifted three fingers and began ticking off points. "First, we figured that since you used to be an infantry officer and you actually saw a few shots fired, you might have a little better understanding of what these men went through than your ordinary run-of-the-mill attorney in uniform. Second, your boss assured me that you come equipped with a brilliant legal mind and are independent by nature. Finally, because I knew your father, served under him, hated his guts—but he just happened to be the best I ever saw. If you got even a fraction of his gene pool, then there's an outside chance of your being pretty damned good, too."

"That's very kind, sir. Thank you very much."

Partridge took another mighty drag on his cigarette. "Look, Drummond, I'm treading on quicksand here. I'm the commander of the Special Operations Command and am therefore responsible for those men and for what they did. And when you're done with your investigation, your recommendation on whether to proceed with a court-martial will come to me. I'll have to decide which way to go."

"That is the correct protocol, sir."

"And you and I both know that if I say anything to you that indicates anything but a neutral predisposition on my part, I can be accused of exerting command influence into a legal proceeding. That would get all our butts in a wringer. So the reason I had you fly down here," he said, pointing toward a tiny tape recorder on the corner of his desk, "is to ask you two questions."

"Fire away, sir."

"Do you believe that I, or anyone in your chain of command, has a predisposition, or have any of us, in any way, tried to influence you prior to the start of your investigation?"

"No and no, sir."

"Do you believe you are being given adequate resources to perform your duties?"

"I have ample resources, sir."

"Then this interview is hereby terminated," he said, reaching down and turning off the tape recorder.

My right hand was just coming back up to my forehead when those thin lips bristled with a nasty little smile. "Now, Drummond, it's time for some real guidance. This case is an embarrassment for the army—but there are several types of embarrassment. There's the kind where some soldiers did a bad thing and the public wonders just what this barbaric army did to these fine young boys to transform them into such monsters. Then there's the kind where the army gets accused of covering up. Finally, there's the kind where everyone believes that the army is too heavy-handed to handle such delicate situations."

"Sounds accurate to me, sir."

His eyes fixed my eyes with an uncompromising stare. "This time it's gonna be up to you to decide which of those embarrassments we have on our hands. Don't be naïve and think there's any way you can win. Got my drift?"

I did get his drift, although I was naïve and arrogant enough to believe I could pull this out and walk off into the sunset looking good. "I believe I have a firm grasp of the situation, General."

"You're wrong, Drummond. You think you do, but you don't."

"Begging the general's pardon, but is there a point to this?"

The general's eyes blinked a few times, and I was instantly reminded of a lizard contemplating a fly and considering whether to lash out with his long tongue and have himself a Happy Meal with wings. Then he smiled, and I'd be lying if I said it was a friendly smile. "All right, Drummond, you're on your own."

Now, the general might've thought he was making some kind of theatrical point here, but the truth is, he was the fifth high-ranking official in three days to use one of those damned tape recorders as he offered me a little on- and off-the-record guidance.

In the old army a man who was about to be executed was marched down a line of his peers, and a slow drumroll was sounded to accompany him to the gallows. The modern version of this death march, I was learning, was to stand in front of a bunch of powerful desks listening to lots of windy lectures, all timed to the beat of tape recorders being flicked on and off.

As a burly air force tech sergeant ushered me through the aircraft doorway, I spotted Captain James Delbert and Captain Lisa Morrow waiting for me in the cavernous rear of the C-130. The first thing I noticed, though, was that the C-130, which is a cargo plane, was indeed packed to the gills with cargo. So much for my putative sense of importance. It was worse than that, though. The aircraft was stuffed with feminine hygiene products in green boxes.

The second thing I noticed was that both Delbert and Morrow had sour faces. Whether that was because of me or the fact that, without warning, they'd both been ordered to drop everything and meet me on this airplane was as yet unclear.

Neither had been told why they had to be here, but both were ridiculously clever and probably had some strong suspicions. For three days headlines and talk shows around the world had focused on nothing but this case. It wasn't hard to deduce that a gathering of the army's top lawyers on an airplane headed to Europe had something to do with the massacre. They both stood as I worked my way past four massive cartons marked TAMPON, 1 EACH.

"Delbert, Morrow, good to meet you," I said, thrusting my hand forward and awarding them my most winsome smile.

"Good to meet you, too," said Delbert, a fine-looking soldier who smiled as he pumped hands with holy fury.

"No it's not," complained Morrow.

"You're not happy to be here?" I asked.

"Not in the least. I was right in the middle of an armed-theft trial. You pulled me away from my client."

In that instant it was easy to understand why this woman was such a successful attorney. She played for keeps. After eight years of trying cases, she still took it personally.

"That's exactly what I did," I told her. "I pulled you out of a trial that concerned one soldier to put you on the biggest, most important army case in three or four decades."

The general in charge of the army's JAG Corps had told me I could have as many of the army's top lawyers on my investigating board as my heart desired. Being one myself, I know that the more lawyers you gather under one roof, the more the situation gets to be like a barroom donnybrook. I therefore informed him that I only wanted two lawyers: one prosecutor and one defender.

I decided that because there are two ways to look at any case: from the standpoint of guilt and from the standpoint of innocence. Prosecutors are the spoiled stepchildren of the law. They get to decide which cases they'll try. If the facts don't favor them or they detect any infringements on the rights of the accused, they simply take a pass. Defense attorneys, on the other hand, are eternally cursed. They get appointed only *after* a prosecutor has decided there's at least a 99 percent chance of a conviction. There are plenty of prosecutors who win almost all of the time. There is only a small handful of defense attorneys who win even half the time.

Lisa Morrow was the exception. After eight years as a defense attorney she had won 69 percent of her cases. Still, she had never defended anyone accused of violating a rule of the Geneva Convention.

James Delbert had a 97 percent conviction rate, and even though the law is stacked in a prosecutor's favor, that's striking.

Before this moment I had never met either of them. They were handpicked because I told Major General Clapper that I didn't want just any attorneys. I wanted the prosecutor and defense counsel with the best win-loss records in the army. He picked them, then gave me copies of their military files. And I must admit I spent more time studying Morrow's packet than Delbert's. There was this great picture of her in there, standing stiffly at attention in her dress greens.

It did not take more than a quick glance to see why so many juries and boards had fallen under her sway. I don't know that I'd describe her as beautiful, although she certainly was that. She just had the most sympathetic eyes I ever saw. Sympathy, I should mention, is not a real popular emotion in the army, unless it happens to be pasted on a gorgeous female face. Then exceptions get made.

Delbert, on the other hand, looked every bit the soldier. Trim, fit, handsome, with straight dark hair that sat perfectly in place. He had a razor-sharp face, and eyes that looked ready to pounce.

I would have liked to have talked with them, but the thing about riding in the rear of a C-130 is that once the engines kick in, the racket gets simply awful. Furthermore, the thing about a transatlantic plane ride is that it gives you plenty of time to read. And while I had assured General Partridge that I'd already familiarized myself with the particulars of this case, the truth is that in the past two days, between meetings with lots of very important army officials, a meeting with a very antsy aide from the personal staff of the President, and assorted others, I barely had time to breathe.

I knew little more than had been described to me by these Washington people, and the interesting thing about that was that all of them seemed to be convinced these nine men had done nothing wrong. Nobody had said that outright, but I'm a careful listener. I can sniff a subtlety or a nuance from ten miles away.

My legal briefcase was stuffed with a number of news articles as well as a long-winded statement by a Lieutenant Colonel Will Smothers, who was the direct commander of the accused.

The facts were these: A Special Forces A Team—comprising nine men from the 10th Special Forces Group—had been assigned to train a group of Kosovar Albanians who had been driven from their homeland by the Serbian militia. It was part of the effort to build up the Kosovar Liberation Army, or KLA. The A Team spent seven or eight weeks training their recruits, then were given secret orders to accompany the unit they trained back into Kosovo.

A week later the Kosovar unit attempted a raid on a village, and the entire unit was killed. The A Team, against orders—make that *supposedly* against orders—took it on their own to seek vengeance. They set an ambush on a Serbian supply route and unleashed blistering fury on a Serb column containing thirty-five men.

The next Serb column to come down that route discovered their slaughtered brethren, found lots of expended American munitions, informed their superiors, and after several very dramatic press conferences the international media became persuaded that some American troops must've done a terrifically bad thing.

The army arrested the entire A Team, who were currently being held in detention at an air base in northern Italy.

Now, here's where the case gets both real interesting and real mawkish. The United States and NATO were bombing the hell out of the Serbs in a desperate attempt to coerce them into changing their stance toward Kosovo. As much as this sounded like war, and I'd bet it sure as hell felt like war—at least to the folks being bombed—the legal nicety of a state of war had not been declared. The rules of the Geneva Convention are written to cover a state of war, so exactly what laws were supposed to govern the behavior of these soldiers? Some lawyers love those kinds of questions. Others loathe them. I, for instance, fall squarely into the loathing category. I happen to be pretty simpleminded. Black and white are my favorite colors. Gray just doesn't suit my mental complexion.

The second thing was that there were no survivors from that Serb column. Thirty-five men and not one survivor. Now, those who know a little about land warfare know that for every man who gets killed in battle, there nearly always are one or two wounded. There was a very nasty implication here.

Finally, the talk show pundits around the Beltway were in high dudgeon. The big question was, What orders had that A Team been given? Every time the Pentagon spokesman got asked that question, or what limits had been set on their behavior, he got deliciously vague. All he'd admit was that the name of the mission was Guardian Angel and that it was some kind of humanitarian thing.

I read the documents, then passed them on to Delbert. He read them, then passed them on to Morrow. We were becoming a smoothly oiled team. By the time we landed at Tuzla Air Base, a nice tidy pile of papers was stacked on the seat next to Captain Morrow and all three of the army's top legal guns were snoring loudly.

THIS time there actually was a vehicle waiting by the ramp to transport us. In fact, there were two humvees—except that one was already filled with this huge brigadier general in battle dress, with a natty little green beret tucked neatly on top of his head.

He was about six feet five, and anybody in uniform would recognize him instantly. He'd been an all-America tackle at West Point, first in his class, a Rhodes scholar, and was the youngest brigadier general in the United States Army. His name was Charles "Chuck"

Murphy, and he was the army's most dazzling boy wonder. At that moment, though, his face was clouded with anxiety because the A Team that was in detention worked for him, which meant his fabulous career was now up for grabs.

I gave him the same kind of snappy salute I'd given General Partridge, his four-star boss. "Major Drummond, sir."

He actually returned the salute. "Welcome to Bosnia, Drummond. How many lawyers are with you?"

"Three of us, sir."

"Okay. Stow your gear in the other humvee and follow me."

We did, and we peeled out of the airfield about thirty seconds later. We drove past about a mile of large tents built on concrete slabs, large metal containers, and a bunch of prefabricated wooden buildings. Tuzla Air Base had been the supply and operations center for the Bosnian mission, and when the situation in Kosovo boiled over, the military decided to use it for that purpose as well. And if there's one thing the military is good at, it's creating large sprawling cities out of thin air. Tuzla was a case in point.

We finally came to a two-floored wooden building with a couple of flags out front. Our humvees stopped, and we all piled out and walked inside, where lots of soldiers were scurrying about.

We ended up in a meeting room in the back of the building, with a large conference table. General Murphy told us to sit, so we did.

His eyes marched across our faces, and I guessed he was wrestling with how to approach us. Friendly or cold? Informal or stiff? One way or another his future might well rest in our hands. He finally broke into a charmingly disarming smile. "Well, I can't exactly say I'm happy to meet you, but welcome anyway."

This struck me as a pretty ingenious compromise. "Thank you, General," I said on behalf of the group.

"I've been told to offer you whatever assistance you need. We've arranged a private tent for each of you. I've also had a building cleared for your use. Five legal clerks arrived last night from Heidelberg, and they're busy preparing your facility as we speak. Is there anything else you need at this moment?"

"Nothing I can think of," I answered. "Although if anything comes to mind, I'll be sure to contact you."

That was a wiseass crack, but I'd made my choice on how to approach him. Friendly just wasn't in the cards.

His lips tensed ever so slightly. He studied my face, made an assessment, then got up and walked to the door. He opened it, and in marched a lieutenant colonel—a tall, lean, handsome sort with a nice little green beret perched on his head as well.

General Murphy said, "Let me introduce Lieutenant Colonel Will Smothers, commander of the First Battalion of the Tenth Special Forces Group. Will's going to handle your day-to-day needs."

This was Murphy's way of saying that he wasn't going to fetch for me. It was masterfully done. It almost worked, too.

I said, "Excuse me, General. That won't be acceptable. As battalion commander of the accused A Team, Colonel Smothers is a possible suspect in this case. Please arrange another liaison."

Now, here's where it gets important to understand that army lawyers aren't held in particularly high esteem by *real soldiers,* especially Green Berets. Warfare is the business of soldiers, and lawyers talk a lot but don't shoot a lot, so we're seen as an inconvenience or an annoyance or an evil, but certainly not as part of the brotherhood.

A silly oversize frown instantly erupted on Murphy's big-jawed, handsome face. He said, "You think that's necessary?"

"In my legal opinion, absolutely."

"Then I'll appoint a new man."

"Thank you," I said.

"You're welcome," he said. It didn't sound real sincere, though. In fact, by the time he said it, he had turned and was halfway through the door.

My two legal colleagues wore befuddled expressions as a result of this swift display of one-upmanship, but this was neither the time nor the place to make my explanations. We got up and left the building and, after a short humvee ride, were deposited at another wooden building.

We strolled in, and there were indeed five clerks buzzing about, setting up computer workstations and hefting large boxes of legal-sized paper to be positioned at strategic locations throughout the four rooms that constituted the interior of the building.

A female soldier wearing the stripes of a specialist seven, a very high rank in the specialist field, immediately dropped two boxes of paper and rushed over to greet us.

Her name was Imelda Pepperfield, which is a pretty odd name for a black female noncommissioned officer who was short and squat, had tough, squinty eyes that peered out from a pair of gold wire-rimmed glasses, and who made it clear from the opening shot exactly who was in charge of this legal compound.

Her finger popped up and began waving. "Keep them duffel bags out of my entry. Store them in your offices or carry them back out to that humvee. Just don't trash up my entry."

"Good day to you, too," I said. "You might find this hard to believe, but I'm supposed to be in charge of this investigation."

The finger instantly shifted to my face. "Nope! You're in charge of doing the legal work of this investigation. I'm in charge of the investigating team and the building and every damn bit of work's gotta get done. And don't any of you forget that."

"Perish the thought," I said. "You wouldn't happen to have allocated a little space for us useless officers, would you?"

Captains Delbert and Morrow were standing with their jaws hung a bit loosely, so I figured it was time to do a little explaining. I gestured for them to follow me. Specialist Seven Pepperfield interpreted that to mean her, too, so she trailed along as we filed into one of the offices. A desk had been set up, with five chairs arrayed around the front, and we all picked our seats. I took the chair behind the desk, of course. Rank doth have its privileges.

"Imelda," I said, "I'd like you to meet Captain James Delbert and Captain Lisa Morrow."

She stared fiercely at both of them.

I turned to the other two. "Imelda and I have worked together about a dozen times the past few years. She's the best. She runs a tight ship and demands that we all be at work every morning at six o'clock sharp. She'll make sure we're fed and bathed and coffee'd and carried out to our cots at midnight. Her only requirement is that we work our asses off and do everything she tells us to do."

Imelda straightened her glasses and announced, "You got that right." She then got up and stomped out of the room.

Captain Delbert was staring at me like I was getting things all wrong. You're not supposed to be rude to generals and take guff off of sergeants. As for the expression on Morrow's beautiful face, well, as a highly polished defense attorney, she was used to being around scoundrels.

Now that we had our own office, with a little privacy, I figured the time had come for us to get better acquainted.

I leaned back in my chair, folded my hands behind my ears, and plopped my feet on my desk. "Congratulations to you both. You've been selected to make legal history. What we have here are nine good clean-cut wholesome American soldiers accused of murdering thirty-five men. Against orders, no less. They were led by an army captain with a chief warrant officer as his assistant, and the rest were all noncommissioned officers. This was no group of youngsters, but a team of hardened professionals. Now, most Americans want to believe that this was just a mistake or that these were just some group of green, frightened soldiers who simply broke under pressure. That ain't so. What we have here is mass murder."

"You're talking like they definitely did it," Morrow said, instinctively jumping to the defense.

"They did," Delbert politely corrected her.

"The odds are they did," I corrected them both.

"Why us?" Morrow logically asked.

"Well, that's an interesting question. I was selected because I'm very good at what I do, but I don't exactly fit into the system real well, if you hadn't already guessed. I think the powers that be said, Hey, this guy Drummond. Pick him. He's expendable."

"Then why us?" Delbert asked. He obviously believed the handsome piece of meat stuffed inside his combat boots was not the least bit expendable.

"Well, Delbert, in your case, because your record says you're maybe the best prosecutor in the army. And Morrow, you just might be the best defense attorney. It's a yin-and-yang kinda thing."

"There's lots of good defense attorneys," Morrow said, which was true and, no doubt, left her suspecting that her sex and looks had something to do with her being picked.

"Okay. Let me elaborate a bit more. Aside from your sterling case records, you two got the second- and third-highest grades ever awarded by the JAG School. Colonel Winston, who taught you both, described you as the two best minds he ever saw. Next to the guy who scored first, of course."

"And was that you?" Morrow asked.

I shrugged and gave them my aw-shucks grin, and they both appeared suitably awed. But no, it wasn't me. Not by a long shot. Still, why discourage my troops before we even got our feet wet? Besides, another thing about lawyers is that they are eternally competitive creatures. Delbert was a grad of Yale and Yale Law, and Morrow went to U.V.A., then Harvard Law.

Morrow's eyes flicked nervously in Delbert's direction before she coughed a little, then said, "By any chance, would you happen to remember which of us was second?"

See what I mean?

"Perhaps I should make one other point," I said, and they both fidgeted with frustration because they really did want to know who was second. "At the moment, we are surrounded by the enemy. All these soldiers and airmen running around here, they're wearing our uniform, but they're different from us. They're gonna be real nice, but don't be fooled. They don't like us. Those nine men in that prison are their brethren. We're outsiders who're here to decide whether they should be tried and lynched. Also, there may be more men in this compound who might be implicated in this thing."

"I think you're overstating it," Morrow said.

"Actually, I'm not. There are men on this base who wouldn't mind if we got lost in the woods and gave them a chance to shoot us in the back of the head."

Morrow was looking at me incredulously.

"The point is," I continued, "we're on our own. There's not a soul we can trust except one another, so carry yourselves accordingly. We've been given twenty-one days to get to the truth of what happened here, and more likely than not, it's an ugly tale."

TWO

I HAD fourteen years in the army—the first five in the infantry, then three years at law school, six months at the JAG School, then the rest practicing military law. I'd prosecuted and I'd defended, and I'd developed the opinion that the best place to begin a murder investigation is at the morgue.

I'd told them before I left Washington that my investigating team would be visiting the morgue on the outskirts of Belgrade, where the bodies were stored. The problem was that the morgue was in Serbia, and we were still dropping lots of large metal canisters filled with explosives on that country's villages and cities. So there were a few understandable complications.

Back in Washington I'd met with two stiff-necked Foreign Service officers who lectured me like I was some kind of idiotic novice in international affairs. Well, I am a novice, but I am also a lawyer—and a stubborn one. There were a lot of peevish faces, but finally a U.N. diplomat got on the phone and asked Bad Boy Billy Milosevic if we could come, and he did not even hesitate.

He said yes. Of course he said yes. See, Milosevic wanted more than anything for my team to verify that there were in fact thirty-five slaughtered bodies in that morgue. Still, his assent had its worrisome aspects. If he was willing to let us come see the bodies, then he must've been pretty damned sure that our boys killed them.

We all got a good night's rest, and at five in the morning on day two of our investigation Delbert, Morrow, myself, and a pathologist all climbed aboard a snazzy Blackhawk helicopter. The pathologist was an odd-looking duck with pale skin and hyper-looking bulgy eyes. I'd been assured he was one of the best.

The flight took about three hours. Two sedans with Serb military drivers were waiting for us at the Belgrade International Airport. No one said a word as we drove through the city, going straight to the morgue. It was not the fancy-type morgue you so often see back in the United States. In fact, it was a pretty grim, dilapidated old building. A Serbian doctor met us at the entry and escorted us down some stairs and into a gloomy cellar.

The basement was cold and dank and had the kind of dim hanging lamps that tall people bang their heads against. We went along a dark hallway, took a left at its end, and entered a very large room. The doctor flipped a switch. Ten long fluorescent bulbs flickered and crackled, then finally illuminated everything.

Thirty-five nude bodies were neatly arrayed in four long columns. Somebody had gone to the trouble of placing props behind the backs of the corpses, so that they all sat up, perfectly erect. It looked ghastly. We all froze in our tracks. The first of us to recover was Dr. Simon McAbee, our pathologist, who rushed forward with his doctor's bag and a savory gleam in his eyes.

Delbert and Morrow fell in behind me as I began walking the columns, pausing at each body for only a few seconds to determine what specific trauma caused the death. The bodies had been cleansed, which made it fairly easy to interpret the wounds. What I saw generally met my most dismal expectations.

Some of the corpses were horribly mangled, but it seemed every single one had been shot in the head. One corpse, though, had no head at all, just an ugly stump at the bottom of the neck. Some of the head entry wounds were from the back or the front, but most were from the side. The entry holes were small, about the size made by a 5.56-mm round, which just happens to be the size bullet fired by an M-16 rifle, which just happens to be the standard issue weapon for American troops.

At least half the bodies were so seriously mangled that they had obviously been hit by mines. It was the kind of mine that intrigued me. American troops are issued something called a claymore—an upright mine that sits above the surface, planted on a pair of tiny metal tripods. The claymore has a rectangular, curved shape, and the explosives are packed into its concave hollow, while the outward half is packed with thousands of tiny pellets that are propelled forward with great force. It's a highly favored weapon in ambushes. The mines are triggered by an electric pulse, and the technique of choice is to connect several of these nasty little things together with commo wire into what is called a daisy chain. That way, once the electric charge is triggered, all the mines appear to go off at once.

The badly mangled bodies had lots of little pellet holes. Mysteriously, though, all of the wounds seemed to be somewhere in the back, which implied several possibilities, most of which were ugly.

After the first pass Delbert, Morrow, and I gathered in a small knot in the back corner and whispered among ourselves. Dr. McAbee and the Serbian doctor continued to traipse around and examine pieces of wounded flesh.

"What do you think?" I asked Delbert and Morrow.

Morrow quickly said, "It's sobering."

"*Very* sobering," Delbert quickly one-upped her. "It doesn't look good, does it?"

"No," I grimly admitted. "We won't know for sure till McAbee's done, but I'd guess most of the damage was done with M-16s and claymores. There was a machine gun or two involved as well."

"Some of them were little more than boys," Morrow said.

On my first sweep through I had deliberately ignored the faces because I didn't want my reason clouded by emotion. Now it was time to go back and look at each corpse anew. Perhaps some of them had done very nasty things to the Albanians they were herding out of Kosovo. Still, I had to remind myself that they were also human beings. So I spent another twenty minutes wandering through and trying to order my ever pliant conscience.

Dr. McAbee was now taking photographs of each corpse. He worked efficiently and completed his task before I was done. Then he walked over to me. "It doesn't look good, Counselor. Our host gave me a collection of projectiles removed from the corpses."

"Did you personally remove any?"

"A few. The bullets are 5.56. The pellets appear to be claymore."

"So all the wounds were made by American weapons?"

"With thirty-five bodies I would need three X-ray machines and a full week to prove that beyond any shadow of doubt."

"But that is your general impression?" I asked him.

His bulgy eyes fixed mine, and he seemed to sigh. "Every wound I saw appeared to come from an American weapon."

"What about the head wounds?"

"Most of these men were shot from a distance of less than two feet."

"And how would you guess that happened?"

"That's obvious, isn't it? Someone walked through and made sure there were no survivors."

"Nothing's obvious," I chided. "Did you tell that Serb doctor to maintain these bodies until we're done?"

"I did. But he said he can't. Milosevic has ordered a large state procession where the families of the dead are to be honored for their sacrifices. After the ceremony the bodies are to be returned to their families for funerals."

"That will create a vast problem for us and the Serbs," I said. "If I were the defense attorney for the accused, I would insist on equal right to examine the corpses."

"Well, the corpses have now been examined by me."

I gave him my best cross-examining look. "And could you tell me, Doctor, with complete certainty, exactly how many of these men were killed with American weapons? If the members of that A Team are charged with murder, how many counts do we charge them with? You have to list those things. Then you have to be able to prove that was exactly how many people they murdered."

"Of course," he sheepishly said. "I'm sorry. I've never handled a situation of this magnitude."

"None of us has. What I want you to do is classify each corpse. I want to know how many died immediately and how many were initially wounded and then dispatched. Can you do that for me?"

He nodded. "I'll do my best."

"Good. Is there anything else you need?"

"I'd love to have a couple of these bodies to carry back, so I can determine the exact circumstances of death."

"All right. The first thing you do when we get back is file an official request for just that. I'll file one, too."

WE ARRIVED back at Tuzla shortly after three p.m. Our stomachs had gone from queasy to growling, so I asked Imelda to scramble us up a meal. Sounds easy, but you have to remember that this was the army, and the army has mess halls. Of course, you also have to remember that this was Imelda Pepperfield, who can make rocks cry.

She came huffing back into my office, followed by two of her female legal clerks. They plunked down several trays loaded with meat-loaf sandwiches and mashed potatoes larded with gravy.

"Any trouble?" I asked.

"Nope. That mess sergeant tried to say no, so I kicked his butt a little, and he snapped to."

The thing about Imelda is that she was raised in the rural back-country of Alabama and has all the inflections and manners of a poor, uneducated southern black girl. And if you are too stupid for words, you buy into that act. But the truth was, she'd earned two master's degrees, one in criminal justice and the other in literature. She never went anywhere without a few thick books in her duffel.

Delbert and Morrow were eyeing the meat-loaf sandwiches with pure disgust, while I launched in with gusto.

Imelda gave them a speculative glance, then flapped her arms once or twice. "You got some kinda problem with that meal?"

Delbert very foolishly said, "Actually, I do. I like to eat healthier."

Imelda bent toward him. "This is army-issued food. If Uncle Sam says it's good for you, it's good for you."

Morrow was watching this exchange, and I saw her quickly grab a sandwich and start chomping. Smart girl, that one.

Imelda straightened back up and stared at Delbert. "Okay, fancy pants. You either eat that food or you're gonna get bone-ass skinny these next few weeks."

"I like salad," he said with almost pitiful politeness. "Could you get me a salad?"

"Salad?" she roared. "I don't fetch rabbit food."

"I'll get it myself," he announced, then stood up and left.

Imelda grumbled something and stomped from the room.

Visibly relieved, Morrow placed her half-eaten meat-loaf sandwich back on the plate. "You run a loose ship," she complained. "She was very disrespectful. I would have thought a former infantry officer would instill a little more discipline in the ranks."

Did I mention before that Morrow is an astonishingly beautiful woman? Well, if I didn't, she is. And there's nothing like having a great-looking woman challenging your manhood. The average guy would choose just that moment to flex his muscles and mutter something tough and virile.

I said, "That's why stereotypes don't come with guarantees."

I finished my third sandwich and glanced at my watch. Unless I missed my guess, there should've been a witness waiting outside our door. That morning I'd asked Imelda to contact Lieutenant Colonel Will Smothers to request his presence at 1530 hours.

I walked over and opened the door. In fact, Smothers was standing there. And surprise, surprise, a bespectacled, slightly overweight bookish-looking captain wearing JAG insignia stood behind him.

"Please come in," I told Smothers, then quickly stretched my arm across the doorway, blocking his lawyer, whose nametag read SMITH. "You won't be needed," I told him.

Smothers spun back around. "I want him here."

"No," I said. "This is just an interrogatory. I won't be reading you your rights, and therefore nothing you say can be used against you. This is merely a background session."

"If he wants me along, I'm coming in," Captain Smith screeched.

"Wrong," I said. "I'm the chief investigating officer. And if I say no lawyers, there'll be no lawyers." I grabbed the door and closed it in Smith's stricken face. "Please have a seat," I said as I turned around and faced Smothers.

The thing about interrogatories with potential suspects is that you lose if you don't have the upper hand. Smothers outranked me, so I had to make up some lost ground.

I sat behind the desk, and Morrow and I stayed perfectly still. Smothers was trying to compose himself. I withdrew a tape recorder from the desk drawer and turned it on.

"Colonel, could you please state your full name and describe your relationship to the accused men?"

"My name is Will Smothers. I'm the commander of the First Battalion of the Tenth Special Forces Group. The A Team commanded by Captain Terry Sanchez was assigned to my battalion."

"How long have you been in command?"

"Nearly two years."

"How long was Captain Sanchez one of your team leaders?"

"Maybe half a year."

"So you've only known him half a year?"

"No. He was on my staff before that, in operations."

"So you've known him two years?"

"Yes, two years. That's about right."

All of this was just a warm-up. Always start an interrogation by asking for simple, noncontroversial facts, to get the subject into the mode of answering quickly, almost automatically.

"Who made the decision to appoint him as team leader?"

"Me. It had to be approved by the group commander, but I recommended him."

"The group commander would be—"

"Brigadier General Murphy."

"Is Sanchez a good officer?"

"Uh . . . yes. A—uh—well, a very good officer," Smothers said, appearing eminently thoughtful. "In fact, outstanding in every way."

"What ways? Was he a strong leader? Did he compel his men to follow him? Was he smart? Did he have backbone?"

"All the above."

"How old is he?" I asked.

"I don't know exactly. About thirty."

"How many years does he have in?"

"Ten, I think. Maybe eleven, maybe twelve. He's a senior captain. He should be up for major this year."

"He needed the team leader job to get promoted, right?"

"He's an outstanding officer. I've never looked at his record, but I'm sure it reflects that."

By this time Smothers had caught on to where I was going and was parsing his words very carefully. If the team led by Terry Sanchez slaughtered thirty-five men in cold blood, then, de facto, Terry Sanchez was not up to the job he'd been given. That meant Will Smothers had made a mistake.

He'd worked closely with Sanchez for two years, yet could not tell me his precise age, could not describe his command style. He knew the answers; he just wasn't going to tell me.

"So," I said, changing tack, "exactly what were Sanchez's orders when he was sent into Kosovo?"

"Well, he and his team had spent two months training a ninety-five-man Kosovar guerrilla unit. Since the Kosovars were still very green, Sanchez's team was ordered to accompany them back in and continue their training."

"Isn't that an odd mission?"

"No. It's a very common mission for Special Forces. Training indigent forces is exactly what we're organized to do."

"I'm not talking about the training part, Colonel. I'm talking about Sanchez's team following them back into Kosovo."

"I wouldn't call it unusual, no."

"Really? What exactly were his instructions?"

"To continue training the Kosovars."

"Was he supposed to become involved in the fighting?"

"Absolutely not. Everybody here knows the rules, Major. There's no ground war."

"Were Sanchez and his people allowed to assist the Kosovars in planning their operations?"

"Yes and no. We're not combatants. So, no, Sanchez and his people were not supposed to help plan their operations. But if the Kosovar commander asked for advice, they could offer it."

"Pretty sketchy line, that one. Tell me, Colonel. Say Sanchez and his people were attacked by a Serb unit. Were they authorized to shoot back?"

"Yes. Self-defense is authorized. If they were detected, they were supposed to extricate. If that required them to fight their way out, that was acceptable."

"Who wrote these rules?" I asked.

"I don't know—some staff officer somewhere, I guess. But I believe they were approved by the Joint Chiefs of Staff."

"Thank you, Colonel," I said. "You can go now."

He regarded me for a moment with a kind of slack-jawed look, like what the hell happened to the hard part. I just stared back. The hard part would come. Just not yet.

As Smothers walked out, Delbert walked back in.

"Enjoy your lunch?" I asked.

"Uh, yeah, sure." He rubbernecked around and watched Smothers's retreating back. "What was that about?"

"Colonel Smothers stopped by for a little interrogatory."

"Why didn't you wait for me?"

"Because you decided to run off and eat."

"I had no idea this was scheduled. Why didn't you say anything?"

"I don't think I heard you ask me."

I'd be a liar if I didn't admit I was enjoying Delbert's discomfort. He might be the best prosecutor in the army, but he was still a prig. "Don't sweat it," I said reassuringly. "It's all on tape. Listen to it tonight after we close shop."

The door suddenly crashed open, and Imelda bustled back in with three legal clerks in tow, all carrying heavy boxes.

"What's all that crap?" I asked.

"All the operations orders, and the duty communications log, and the personnel files of the accused."

"I don't remember asking for that."

"And what are you gonna do without it? You're not going to get any further on this case unless you go over all this." Imelda mumbled some unintelligible curse. Then she marched back out, shooing her three assistants ahead of her.

We each took a box, then spent the next eight hours trading files back and forth, reading furiously, saying little, and making our first real acquaintance with the nine American soldiers who were accused of mass murder across the border in a land called Kosovo.

I HAD two phone calls that night. The first came from a general in the Pentagon and went something like this:

"Drummond, that you?"

I squeezed and pinched myself. "It's me, Drummond."

"General Clapper here."

"Morning, sir."

"It's not morning here. It's eight o'clock in the evening."

"That right? So that's why it's two o'clock in the morning here." A mighty chuckle. "How's it going?"

"Well, we went to the morgue at Belgrade yesterday and spent some time with thirty-five corpses. The pathologist is still doing his report, but the preliminary isn't good. All the perforations in the bodies appear to have been made by American weapons."

"We expected that."

"Yeah, but I'll bet you didn't expect this. Somebody shot each corpse in the head."

"All of them?"

"Well, a few didn't have much left for heads, and one didn't have any head at all, but yeah, about all of them."

"Why didn't Milosevic and his people make hay of that in the press conferences?"

"You'll really have to ask him, General. I do recommend, however, that you wait until it's morning over here. From what I hear, he's not as nice a guy as I am."

"That's debatable. Are you getting sufficient cooperation?"

"Sure. They love us. We got the best tents in the compound."

"We got your request for Milosevic to postpone his state funeral and hold on to the bodies."

"Good. The coroner's sending a request through his channels, too."

"Won't make any difference. I took yours over to the State Department and got laughed out of the building. How damaging will it be if the request is denied?"

"It creates an opening for a good defense attorney to poke a few holes."

"Well, nothing to be done about that. Need anything else, Sean?"

"No, sir. But thanks for asking."

He hung up, and I hung up, and it took a few minutes before I dozed off again. Major General Thomas Clapper was the closest thing to a friend I had in this case. He had taught me military law way back when he was a major and I was a brand-new lieutenant going through my basic officer's training. If I wasn't the worst student he ever had, the other guy must have been a stone-cold putz. One can only imagine his dismay when, four or five years later, I approached him to ask if he would sponsor my application to law school and the JAG Corps. I've never understood what went through his brain, but he said yes, and the rest is legal history.

Unlike me, Thomas Clapper was always on a fast track. He was now the two-star general who headed up the corps of army lawyers. This is the largest law firm in the world, with thousands of lawyers, judges, and legal specialists.

The next call came about an hour later, and the caller identified himself as Jeremy Berkowitz. Even at three a.m. I recognized the name. Berkowitz was a reporter for the Washington *Herald* who had earned a handsome reputation by exposing lots of embarrassing military scandals. That call went something like this:

"You're Major Sean Drummond?"

"Says so on my nametag."

"Heh, heh, that's a good one. My name's Jeremy Berkowitz. A common friend gave me your number."

"Name that friend, would you? I'd like to choke him."

This resulted in another nice chuckle. "Hey, you know the rules. A good reporter never discloses his sources."

"What do you want?"

"I've been assigned to cover the Kosovo massacre. I thought it would be a good idea for us to get to know each other."

"I don't."

"You ever dealt with the working press before?"

"A few times."

"Then you know it's always a good idea to cooperate."

"And in turn you'll cooperate with me, right?"

"Exactly. I'll make sure your side of things gets printed, and I'll make sure you're well treated in our stories."

Click! Oops, my receiver accidentally fell into the cradle.

Actually it landed in the cradle because I don't like being threatened, and if you read between the lines, that was exactly what he was trying to convey. Of course, it was a dumb, petulant thing to do. On my part, that is. But like I said, I was tired.

My mood had not improved when at six a.m. I entered our wooden building, where Captains Delbert and Morrow were hovering over a couple of steaming cups of coffee and awaiting my arrival. Both looked bright-eyed and bushy-tailed, and I resented that.

"Morning," I said, or barked or growled. Whatever.

"Ouch," said Morrow. And wouldn't you know that at just that moment the phone rang.

"Hello," I said, lifting it up.

"Major Drummond, this is Captain Smith. Remember me?"

"Yeah. You're the chubby guy with the screechy voice, right?"

"I called Colonel Masterson, the military judge with jurisdiction over this command. I told him you blocked me from representing my client. He said that if you ever do that again, he will seek to have you disbarred."

"I'm deeply ashamed of myself," I boldly admitted.

"You should be. Now, my client told me you taped the interrogatory. I would like a copy delivered to my office."

"Did the judge say I had to do that?"

"I didn't ask him. I will, if you insist."

"I insist."

"Have it your way," he said, almost choking with anger, and then hung up.

Now it might sound perverse, but Smith's call really brightened my mood. The thing about big investigations like this one is that you have to get people's attention. You have to show people you're a rampaging barbarian, and then anybody with any inkling of guilt immediately starts racing for the nearest lawyer and looking for protection. Lieutenant Colonel Will Smothers had done exactly that.

"What was that about?" Delbert asked.

"Wrong number," I said.

The door crashed open, and in came the hurricane known as Imelda, followed by two assistants carrying trays piled high with eggs and bacon and dried-out muffins covered with greasy gravy and chunks of ground beef.

Imelda gave Delbert and Morrow a dreadful look and had her assistants carry the trays to the conference table. I walked to the table and launched voraciously into my army-prepared breakfast.

Imelda turned to Morrow and Delbert and said, "Are you two gonna eat those damned breakfasts?"

The good defense attorney acted as though she were speaking to nobody in particular. "I usually have yogurt, oat-bran muffins, and juice for breakfast."

Imelda said back to her, "You want me to tell that mess sergeant to whip you up a cup of that latte crap, too?"

Delbert started to open his lips, wisely thought better of it, and just stood there shuffling his feet.

Morrow's eyes darted down in time to see Delbert's feet do their little retreat dance, and then she covered her own defeat with a half-hearted, "But there was a time when I loved eggs and bacon."

"Then you learn to love it again."

Not two seconds later Delbert and Morrow were beside me, taking mighty bites and silently praying Imelda would go away.

"What's on for today?" Delbert asked.

I said, "I thought we'd spend our morning talking with the group chaplain, then the group commander."

"The chaplain?" Morrow asked. "When are we going to talk to Sanchez and his men?"

"Soon enough."

They both nodded. They didn't agree, but they nodded. That's one of the things I love about Imelda. She sucked all the feistiness right out of them.

The chapel was located in a large tent, long and broad enough to hold about forty chairs. The group chaplain, Major Kevin O'Reilly, walked to the rear of the tent, where we were gathered.

As one might anticipate from a Special Forces chaplain, he didn't look much like a priest. He had a broad face, a pugilist's nose, and big, strong hands that squeezed painfully when we shook and introduced ourselves.

"Father, thanks for agreeing to meet with us," I said. "How long have you been with the unit?"

"Four years."

"That's a long time. You must like it."

"Sure. These are good boys, Major. There's an image out there of Special Forces troops being wild and rowdy that's completely out of character. Most of these men are good family people."

"I guess Captain Sanchez is Catholic, isn't he?"

"Yes, he is. A good one, too."

"You know his family?"

"Very well. His wife, Stacy, and both kids. Three other members of that team are Catholic also, so I've been busy with their families."

"Of course. Now, Father, if you don't mind, I'm going to ask a few questions. If you feel they're too sensitive or I'm infringing on your clerical confidences, please feel free to tell me."

"Okay. That's fair," he said.

"How would you describe the command environment here?"

He contemplated that a moment. "On the whole, pretty good. Special Forces soldiers are older than you find in regular units, and the men are rigorously tested before they get to wear the beret."

"And if you could only use one word?"

"Gung ho."

I smiled. "How about another word?"

"Okay, troubled. These are can-do men with strong consciences. It's very taxing to be around all these Kosovar refugees. It's very rending on the nerves to have to witness firsthand what's happening on the other side of that border."

"Of course. I imagine that has a dampening effect on morale."

"Dampening? Major, some of these men can't sleep."

"Have you had to do a lot of counseling?"

"We've had one suicide and one attempted suicide since we've been here. My days are filled with counseling."

"Did you have to counsel Terry Sanchez or any of his men?"

O'Reilly hesitated. Finally he said, "I'm afraid I'd be uncomfortable answering that."

"Father, I'm asking off the record, one soldier to another."

"Okay. I don't believe Terry's boys did it. However, the pressures are certainly there."

Like hell, he wasn't saying they did it. That was exactly what he *was* saying, although I couldn't tell if he knew that for a fact. "What can you tell me about Smothers's battalion?"

"It's a great unit. It should be, though. He's a first-rate commander, and there's a lot of veterans in his unit. A lot of his men saw duty in the Gulf, Somalia, Haiti, Bosnia."

"Why so many veterans in his battalion?"

"The men call it the old-timers' club. There's sort of an unwritten tradition in the Tenth Group that after five or ten years in another battalion a lot of the sergeants put in for transfer to Smothers's unit."

"Why would they do that?" I asked.

"Camaraderie, I suppose."

By now several soldiers had gathered in the chapel and were anxiously waiting. I'd heard everything I wanted to hear, so I thanked Father O'Reilly, and we parted. As soon as we had left, Delbert said, "That was really helpful. He was trying to offer us their motive."

"Maybe," I said, looking over at Morrow.

"Is there something we didn't hear?" she asked.

I pulled on my nose a bit. "That old-timers' club thing. That bothers me. A battlefield veteran is a very different breed from a green buck sergeant who might be highly trained but has never been truly tested. It's the green guys who can get you killed."

"I don't get it," Delbert said.

"The old-timers' club sounds like a survivors' union. A guy spends five or ten years, and he becomes eligible. He gets to spend the rest of his career with seasoned, battle-tested pros, the kind of guys who don't make mistakes or break under pressure."

"And something's wrong with that?" Morrow asked.

"Maybe not. Your chances of survival go way up, since I'd suspect the First Battalion is very choosy about who it takes and who it turns down."

The two of them nodded, and I decided not to expose everything else I suspected. I'd done time in the infantry, whereas Delbert and Morrow put on their JAG shields straight out of law school. Some things you just gotta be there to learn.

We arrived at General Charles "Chuck" Murphy's wooden building about ten minutes later. He met us at the door and led us to his office. It was fairly spartan for a man of his rank, containing a long field table that was being used as a desk, two smaller tables, and two metal file cabinets.

A group of chairs had been arranged in the middle of the floor, and he directed us to have seats. With some difficulty he lowered his six-foot five-inch frame into a chair, crossed his legs, and folded his arms across his chest. "I apologize," he said. "I can only give you ten minutes this morning. We have an important operation going on."

"No problem, General. We'll make this quick." I paused briefly, then asked, "How long have you known Captain Sanchez?"

"I've commanded the group the past eighteen months. Terry was here when I arrived."

"You approved his appointment as a team commander?"

"Yes, but it was a pro forma thing."

"Why pro forma?"

"There are four battalions in Tenth Group. It's hard enough to know all the colonels, lieutenant colonels, and majors. I recognize the names of most of the captains, but I don't know them well."

I gave him a dubious look. "But was Sanchez maybe one of the ones you know well?"

"Not really. I'd recognize him on a street, but not much more than that."

Frankly, this didn't wash. And he apparently sensed my doubts.

"Look, if you'd like," he swiftly added, trying to sound and appear gracious, "I'll ask my adjutant to go through my log and see how many times I've met with Sanchez over the past six months."

I wasn't nearly as gracious. "That would be very kind, General, but why don't you tell your adjutant to provide us the log, and we'll do the checking?"

He said, "That log is classified and can't be released."

"General, we all have top secret clearances."

His strong jaw pushed forward an inch or two. "If you don't mind, Major, I'd like to talk to legal counsel before I comply."

"Okay, do that, sir. But do it quickly, because I'd like to have that log before close of business today."

His eyes got like little round ice cubes. "Any other questions?"

Morrow inched forward in her chair. "Could you tell us why the First Battalion is called the old-timers' club?"

The general's right eyebrow sort of notched up. "That? Well, it's an old tradition with some of the sergeants in the group. It's kind of a natural evolution to want to move up to a unit that has higher standards. And I can tell you that from my perspective it's a good thing to have one unit that's totally reliable, that you can put in to handle the really tough missions."

Delbert, the prosecutor, took his shot. "Sir, could you tell us who ordered the arrests of Terry Sanchez and his men?"

"I did."

"What chain of events led to that decision?"

"When Milosevic and his people began holding daily press conferences, we realized that something had happened."

"But how did you narrow it down to Sanchez's team?"

"Simple, really. The corpses were found inside what we call Zone Three. That's where Sanchez's team was operating."

"Did you order his team out?"

"I didn't have to. They had extricated three or four days before I ordered their arrests."

"Why did they extricate?"

"Because the Kosovar unit they were training were all dead."

"How long had they been dead?"

"Three or four days."

"When their Kosovars were killed, didn't they report that immediately?"

"I believe they did."

"Then why weren't they ordered to extricate at that point?"

"Because I decided to leave them in place. After their Kosovars were ambushed, Terry relocated his team to a new base camp, one known only to his team. Their safety wasn't at issue. We're training more Kosovar guerrilla units, and when we infiltrate those units into Kosovo, we might have wanted to use Sanchez's team to perform the same Guardian Angel function with a new team."

I said, "How is morale in the unit, General?"

"Great. In fact, as high as I've ever seen."

"I heard you've had a suicide and an attempted suicide."

"Every unit has suicides."

"True, but you've had one successful and one attempt in only a few months."

Murphy's eyes got real narrow. "Look, Major, the group hadn't had a suicide for three years. Our number came up. Study any unit, and you'll see we're way below average." He then looked at his watch. "Listen, I've got to get down to the operations center. We're doing two insertions today, and I have to be on hand."

"Of course, General," I said. "Sorry to take so much of your time." I was lying, of course. I would love to have had this guy in a room for about twelve hours, with a few hot klieg lights and some small pointy objects to jam under his fingernails. Sometimes you can just smell a lie. If anything he said was true, it was an accident.

What I found intriguing was the gap between the time when Sanchez's team reported that their Kosovars were all dead, and when they extricated. Murphy really didn't seem to have a good explanation for that. Though I was sure he'd think one up.

Right after we got out of the building, I turned to Morrow and Delbert. "So what do we know?" I asked.

Delbert rubbed his chin and said, "We know Sanchez's team was the pick of the litter."

Morrow said, "We know that all of a sudden nobody seems to know Terry Sanchez very well. All of a sudden he's a leper."

We all thought about that. Then Delbert said, "So what's on for this afternoon?"

"We're going to Albania to visit a refugee camp."

"Why? When are we going to see Sanchez and his men?"

"Look, Delbert, consider it's a near certainty that Sanchez and his team killed thirty-five men. Worse, somebody went around afterward and did the *coup de grâce*. We've got corpses, and we've got weapons, and we've got suspects. What don't we have?"

"Motive," Delbert said.

THE flight to Albania took about two hours. We had to wind down the coastline of Bosnia, then veer sharply to the left. Albania itself is a small place, very poor, filled with lots of shabbily dressed people and dilapidated Stalinist architecture.

Albanians are a fairly tough and hardy folk. They don't mess with others, and they don't expect to be messed with in return. The shaky history of the Balkans being what it is, lots of Albanians ended up living in other places, like Macedonia and Kosovo.

Kosovo is kind of a Serb's Jerusalem, filled with old Orthodox shrines and historically significant places, and although only some 10 percent of the people who live there could claim even a drop of Serbian blood, selfish old Billy Milosevic had decided to rid the land of Albanians either by killing them or driving them over the mountains into neighboring Macedonia or Albania.

We landed with a series of whumps on a roughed-in airstrip about fifteen miles south of the Kosovar border. Once again a humvee was standing by when we climbed off the plane, and a Special Forces major named Willis was waiting in the front seat to escort us to a refugee camp inelegantly named Camp Alpha.

This wasn't my first introduction to refugee misery. I'd seen similar sights after the Gulf war, when thousands of Kurds and Shiites fled south into Kuwait. Delbert and Morrow, however, developed an instant case of the wide eyes, as the troops call it. The wide eyes are about 30 percent horror, 30 percent pity, and the rest pure guilt.

"You get used to it," Major Willis said as we drove past row after row of hastily constructed tents crammed with mostly old men, old women, mothers, and young children.

"How many are in here?" Delbert asked.

"We're not sure. It kind of shifts from day to day. Sometimes it goes up by a few hundred, sometimes a few thousand."

"How do you know how many to feed?" Morrow asked.

"The U.N. caregivers handle all that. You'll meet the lady who's in charge of it. Later."

We pulled into a small compound surrounded by barbed wire, with two armed guards at the front gate.

We clambered out and walked into a large tent, where a mixture of Green Berets and Albanians in makeshift uniforms were running what appeared to be an operations center.

"This is one of three centers we've set up for training the Kosovo Liberation Army," Willis said. "The KLA was already fighting the Serbs before NATO started its bombing campaign, but the Serbs rolled right over them."

"How large is the KLA?" Delbert asked.

"Maybe five or six thousand, all told."

"Only five or six thousand? That's not even a pinprick."

"Right. Well, the Serbs have been real selective in the way they've done their cleansing. About any Albanian male who looks old enough to hump a gun, they take 'em into the woods, shoot 'em, and bury 'em. We try to recruit whatever survivors make it out."

"Did Sanchez's team operate out of this camp?" I asked.

"Nope. Sanchez and his guys worked out of Camp Charlie, maybe forty clicks east of here. All the camps are pretty much alike, though." Willis looked at his watch. "If you wanta spend a little time with the U.N. folks, we'd better get moving."

We left the operations center and got back into the humvee. We drove by more tents to another fenced compound, where a wiry, birdlike woman of about fifty was waiting for us. She climbed in beside us, then directed the driver to take us to the middle of the camp. She spoke English with a French accent. Her name was Marie.

We finally came to a bunch of tents encircled by wire, with a big red cross in front. We got out of the crowded humvee.

Marie said, "New refugees are brought first to this station for medical processing. To get across the border and reach this camp, they must complete a very dangerous trek across the mountains. Many arrive with frostbite and wounds inflicted by the Serbs."

We entered one of the tents. As we walked in, we saw five or six stations where doctors were inspecting people. Marie led us over to a little girl lying on a cot. The child was filthy, her clothes ragged. A woman was huddled over her while a doctor made notes.

Marie and the doctor exchanged words in French for a minute or so while all of us stared at the little girl, who seemed to be in a waking coma, wide-eyed but unseeing.

"The girl is twelve," Marie finally explained to us. "Her mother says a Serb militia unit came to their house late one night. They broke down the door and dragged her little girl and her two sisters from the house out into the yard. They raped them; then they shot her sisters. The mother does not know why they spared the little one, but they left her there with her mother and gave them two days to be gone, or they promised they would come back."

We then moved to the next doctor. He had a stethoscope on the chest of an old man whose feet were wrapped in rags. The man was sitting on a metal table, stoically enduring his checkup. Again Marie and the doctor exchanged words.

Marie turned to us. "This man was swept up by the Serb police about three weeks ago. They beat him with heavy metal truncheons. The doctor says it's a miracle he made it out alive."

When we left the tent, she said, "The old man won't last another two days. He has severe internal bleeding."

And so it went for the next hour as we wandered through tent after tent, dropping in on one awful case after another.

I have to confess that after seeing that little girl and that old man, I wasn't feeling real sympathetic to the Serbs. During the whole flight back to Tuzla the three of us hardly said a word.

THREE

IMELDA and her assistants waltzed in carrying trays of eggs and bacon. Again she looked primed for battle, awaiting a challenge from Delbert or Morrow or both. Neither said a word. They picked up their knives and forks and began eating breakfast, listless and indifferent. Imelda watched them through narrowed, distrustful eyes, just sure this was some kind of slick new tactic cooked up by the pair. She didn't get it. After a visit to Camp Alpha even the most chauvinistic health nut knew it would be cosmically wrong to complain about a little too much cholesterol.

I had lain awake nearly the whole night, unable to sleep while an old man was dying from the wounds of a brutally senseless beating and a little girl was reliving nightmares and dying in her own silent, tortured way. From the dark circles under Delbert's and Morrow's eyes I guessed they'd had the same nocturnal visitors.

Delbert, Morrow, and I at least now had some kind of moral compass with which to begin this investigation. "I think it's time to take a trip to Italy to visit our suspects," I announced.

The ever efficient Imelda had already arranged our transportation. A fresh C-130 was at the airstrip, this one packed with boisterous soldiers and airmen waiting to go to Italy for a little R and R.

Mercifully, the flight was brief. It took only an hour and a half before we found ourselves at a modern airfield in northern Italy. Imelda had also lined up a military sedan, and the driver was waiting for us at the flight building.

He drove us to a small hotel located on a hilltop. It offered a stunning view of long, stretched-out plains dotted by tiny hills, with castles or palaces mounted atop nearly every one. This being Italy, it was a wildly romantic setting. Aviano Air Base, where the prisoners were being held, was three miles away.

Delbert and Morrow immediately broke out their running togs and loped off down the road. Now that they were back in civilization, they meant to make amends for all the cholesterol they'd sucked down as a result of Imelda. I put on a bathing suit and went to sit by the pool. This was the kind of place where I normally did my best thinking.

We had decided to start our interrogation with Captain Terry Sanchez, the team leader. I had studied his file and was curious to meet him. What I had learned was that his mother and father were Cuban immigrants, part of the vast tidal wave who fled from Fidel Castro and settled in southern Florida. Sanchez himself was thirty-two years old and a graduate of Florida State University. He had earned his way through on an ROTC scholarship. His file contained an official photo that showed him standing at attention in dress greens. He was medium height, medium weight, with dark hair, and eyes that struck me as sorrowful.

Lieutenant Colonel Smothers had described Sanchez as an outstanding officer. But like the rest of the performance reports in Sanchez's packet, the two signed by Smothers put Sanchez in the middle of the pack. So much for open disclosure.

After I'd been sitting beside the pool for an hour, I saw Morrow and Delbert steaming up the road. Morrow was in the lead, and both were heaving like draft horses by the time they made it to my lounge chair. Morrow had on a pair of those skin-hugging nylon runner's pants, and I have to be honest, she fit into them like they were meant to be fit into.

I checked my watch. "We've got about thirty minutes before we're supposed to meet our first suspect."

The two of them headed up to their rooms while I loitered beside the pool for another fifteen minutes before I went upstairs to climb back into my uniform.

The air force detention center at the air base put the army to shame. It was close to being a luxury hotel, with cable TVs in the cells, separate showers and toilets, and a nice modern eating hall.

The warden, a chubby air force major, met with us before we were permitted to interview his prisoners. I told him I was sure he had been keeping the team separated. He said something evasive, so I got real close to his face and asked him. "These prisoners have been quarantined from one another, haven't they?" He said no, that the team members were allowed to commingle. I asked him what idiot had allowed them to commingle. He blushed deeply and said that privilege had been authorized by the 10th Group commander, General Murphy.

Sanchez's team was being investigated for conspiracy, among other charges, and any penologist would know that standard procedure called for co-conspirators to be kept strictly separate so they can't connive on their alibis. The air force major asked me if I wanted to see a copy of the authorization order from General Murphy. I said that I sure as hell did and that I was hereby countermanding the order.

We were then led to a room where we were asked to wait. About three minutes later Captain Terry Sanchez was led in. He wore battle dress, without manacles or restraints. The air force sergeant who led him in discreetly disappeared.

Sanchez looked thinner than he had in his photo, and his eyes were harder, less sorrowful, almost tight. Being accused of mass murder can have that effect.

"Captain Sanchez, I'm Sean Drummond, chief of the investigating team, and these are the other two members, James Delbert and Lisa Morrow. Please have a seat," I said, indicating for him to sit across the table from us.

He walked wordlessly across the floor and fell into the chair.

"This is just a preliminary interview," I said. "We've been told you waived the right to have counsel present. Is that correct?"

"That's right," he answered, and his voice broke a little.

"We have just a few opening questions," I said, placing the tape recorder on the table. "Please start with the mission of your team when you went into Kosovo."

He leaned forward and cupped his hands tightly in front of his lips, which any professional interrogator will tell you is exactly the kind of gesture a man might make when he's preparing to tell a few whoppers. "We were part of an operation called Guardian Angel. The KLA company we'd trained was being put into operation. Our job was to accompany them and provide assistance."

"Weren't they well trained enough to handle themselves?"

"No."

I withdrew a piece of paper from my bulging legal case. "I have here a copy of the evaluation you gave that team when their training ended. You said here they were ready."

He stared at the paper. "I said that they met the minimal standards each KLA company had to attain before they were certified."

"Was something wrong with those standards?"

"Yes. Those standards are slightly below what a basic trainee gets in our army. We taught them just enough to get them killed."

"How was your relationship with your KLA company?"

"Professional."

"Did you feel responsible for them?"

"No, I didn't. It's not our war; it's theirs."

"Good point," I said. "Still, I'd think it would be awfully hard not to develop some feelings for them."

"Major, we both know where you're trying to go with this."

"Where am I trying to go?"

"That when the KLA company got slaughtered, we went on some kind of rampage and took revenge. That's not what happened."

"No?" I said, interested that he chose the word slaughtered. "Then tell me what happened."

"After our KLA company got, uh, wiped out, we reported that back to Tenth Group headquarters. We were told to relocate our base camp and await instructions. So we did. We'd been there about two days when we suspected our new base camp was compromised, so we—"

"Why did you suspect that?" I interrupted.

"Because Sergeant Perrite and Sergeant Machusco detected a Serbian patrol that appeared to be surveilling us."

"When was that?" I asked.

"The afternoon of the seventeenth."

"I don't remember seeing that in the communications log at the Tenth Group ops center."

"I didn't report it."

"Why? I'd think you'd report that immediately."

"Maybe that's because you're a lawyer and you've never been in that kind of situation before."

I had most definitely been in that kind of situation before, but I wasn't about to tell him that. Sanchez was giving me the cover he and the rest of his team had concocted, and for the time being, the best path was to hear the entire tale.

"What did you do, then?" I asked.

"We could have been attacked at any moment, so we reverted to an escape and evasion plan we'd planned two days before."

"And were you followed?" I asked.

"Yes."

"How did you know?"

"Because we laid trip flares on our trail."

"How many went off?" I asked.

"I don't remember exactly. Maybe one, maybe two."

"What kind of trip flares were they?"

"Star clusters with a string on the pin."

"How many did you set?"

"I don't know exactly. The trailman was laying the flare traps."

One of the tricks when you're investigating a conspiracy is to ask for more details, because usually the conspirators have only agreed on a broad cover, and it's the details that get them in trouble.

"Then what happened?"

"Our E and E plan called for us to move south and cross the border into Macedonia. I became worried that the Serb team tracking us would call their headquarters and have an ambush set up ahead. I decided to shift our direction to the east."

"Did you discuss that with anyone in the team?"

"Not that I remember. Things were happening fast."

"How far behind you was the Serbian unit?" I asked.

"They were behind us—that's all I knew."

"But you said several trip flares went off. If the flares went up into the sky, you must've been able to judge the distance they were behind you."

He looked at me a moment before he answered. "I didn't see them go off. I was busy leading the unit. The word was passed up the file, I guess. I don't remember exactly who told me."

Now it was my turn to stay quiet, but he decided not to embellish any further. "Okay," I said. "What did you do then?"

"We walked the rest of the day, zigzagging so our route wasn't predictable. We could see dust columns over the treetops, and occasionally we heard the sounds of vehicles off in the distance."

"And what did you interpret that to mean?" I asked.

"The Serbs were moving forces around to try to trap us."

"But you still didn't radio back to Tenth Group headquarters?"

"No. We were moving fast. Things were happening quickly. Besides, what could they do about it?"

"Provided an aerial recon to let you know your situation. Offered you air cover. Maybe even mounted an aerial extraction to get you out of there."

He appeared nettled for a moment. Then he shrugged. "Look, I'll admit I wasn't thinking that clearly. I was just trying to get my team out alive. Besides, I was worried about the Serbs intercepting a radio transmission. They would've vectored in and known exactly where we were."

"I thought they already knew exactly where you were."

"No. I said I assumed they knew. I was told trip flares had gone off, but that didn't mean they knew exactly where we were."

Sanchez was becoming flustered. All of these questions were beginning to unhinge him. Which was exactly what I wanted.

"Okay, go on," I told him.

He took a moment to compose himself, then said, "We kept running all day. I hoped that after it grew dark, we could turn south again and try and head for the border. Around midnight we drew into a perimeter. We could still hear vehicles moving on the roads around us, so we knew the Serbs were intensifying their search. Then, at around two, another trip flare went off about a mile away. That's when I decided we had to ambush a Serb column."

"And why did you decide that?"

"Because we had to get the Serbs' attention. We couldn't outrun them. They were building a noose around us. If I didn't find some way to make them slow down, they were going to get us."

"And you figured an ambush would make that happen?"

"Sure. They had to know we were dangerous."

"Didn't your orders say you were only allowed to kill in self-defense?"

"This was self-defense," he insisted. "I decided to hit them at first light. I used the map to pick a spot on the road where there was a double curve with hills on both sides. We were in position by around four in the morning. Then we set up the ambush and waited. Every now and again a vehicle passed by, but we let them go through. Then, around six thirty, a column with about six vehicles came into the kill zone, and we unleashed."

"Why did you pick that particular column?"

"Because it was larger. I wanted the Serbs to think we were bigger than an A Team."

"But if they were following you, don't you think they already had some idea of the size of your unit?"

"That's exactly the point. I believed they did, and I figured that if we took on a large column, they might think there were more of us than they'd originally thought."

"And how long did the ambush take?"

"Five minutes. We planted two command-detonated antiarmor mines in the road to blow the lead vehicle and stop the column. We set up a daisy chain of claymore mines along the opposite side of the road that we blew after the troops emptied out of the trucks and were taking cover behind their vehicles. We raked the column with M-16s and machine guns for a few minutes. Then we left."

That answered why so many of the corpses back in Belgrade had their backs shredded with claymore pellets. It was a relief to hear, because the alternative was that Sanchez and his men cruelly blew off a bunch of claymores at the backs of a retreating enemy.

"Were there any survivors?"

"Yes."

"How do you know?"

"Because they were still shooting when we left."

"How many survivors would you say there were?"

"There were probably four or five who were still firing. And there had to be a fair number of wounded."

"You know the Serbs are claiming there were no survivors?"

"That's a lie!" he shouted with evident outrage. "There were men still alive on that road when we left."

"I've examined the corpses," I said. "Thirty-five of them."

At that point our eyes met, and we just sat and stared at each other for a moment. I finally asked, "What did you do next?"

"I led the team south again. We were about fifty clicks from the border. I figured we could make it that night if we moved fast."

"Did you report to headquarters?" I asked, knowing he had, because his report was noted in the communications log.

"Yes."

"Did you report the ambush?"

"No."

"Why not?"

"Because I didn't want anyone second-guessing me. I knew they weren't gonna be too happy about what we'd done."

"So what did you report?"

"That we were extricating."

"Did you explain that you felt your team was at risk?"

"No."

"Why didn't you?"

"I figured the ambush bought us enough time to get out."

"And you still didn't report the ambush after you returned. Why was that?"

"Look, I made a mistake there," he said, looking suddenly repentant. "I admit that. I figured that no harm had been done, and I really didn't see any reason to have to report it."

The underlying concept of the cover story was good. You could split hairs over what constituted self-defense, but the notion of a desperate team trapped behind enemy lines, surrounded by bloodthirsty Serbs—that was likely to elicit a sympathetic response from anyone.

"Do you have any questions?" I asked Delbert and Morrow.

They both shook their heads.

Sanchez was still sitting with his hands folded in front of his mouth. I guessed he was feeling tremendous anxiety over how his performance had gone over with us.

"Thank you for your time, Captain Sanchez," I said, turning off the tape recorder and putting some papers back in my legal case.

He stood up and pushed his chair back into the table. He waited there, looking awkward. "Hey, Major," he finally said.

"What?" I answered, standing and preparing to leave.

"We didn't murder those Serbs. I swear we didn't. When we left, there were still some of them alive."

AN ENVELOPE had been slid beneath the door to my room when we returned to the hotel, and that irritating little red message light was blinking on the phone.

The envelope contained a fax that had been forwarded by Imelda. The fax was a copy of a Washington *Herald* story from the day before. It was written by none other than Jeremy Berkowitz, the same fella I'd hung up on, and it exposed the shocking revelation that the army had turned over the investigation of perhaps the most serious criminal case in its history to a lowly army major and two captains. My name was even mentioned a few times. If that's the best Berkowitz could do, then bring him on.

There were two phone messages. One was from the same pushy, antsy special assistant to the President I had met before I left Washington, and the second was from General Clapper, the chief of the JAG Corps. I was not about to call the White House operative. The way those guys are, you call them once, and they never get off your back. Like a bad date that just won't go away.

I asked the operator to connect me to General Clapper's number immediately. A moment later I heard his voice.

"How's it feel to be famous?" He chuckled.

"I liked it better yesterday, when nobody ever heard of me."

"What did you do to piss Berkowitz off?" he asked.

"Does hanging up on him count?"

"It's not the way I would've recommended you handle him."

It wasn't the way I wished I'd handled him, either, but I wasn't going to say that. "So how's the weather in Washington?" I asked.

"Hot as hell. Some folks are having second thoughts about having you head up this investigation. Nothing against you personally, Sean, but Berkowitz's article struck home in certain quarters."

"Anybody in particular having second thoughts?" I asked.

"I haven't talked with him directly, but I'm told the President read the article and had to be peeled off the ceiling."

"Oh, him," I said with as much phony sangfroid as I could muster. "Anybody else? I mean, anyone important?"

"The Chairman of the Joint Chiefs doesn't sound too happy, either. And him I did talk to."

Apparently Berkowitz had fired a much better-aimed shot than I'd thought. The phone went silent, and there was one of those long pauses that could only be termed as strained. I figured out that it was Clapper's subtly polite way of allowing me to make the choice of voluntarily turning over the reins of the investigation to someone else. Finally I blurted out, "Look, General, I've started this thing, and I'd like to see it through."

Without hesitation he said, "All right. We'll try it that way. One thing, though, Sean. You work on how you deal with the press."

"That's fair," I said, and hung up.

I hadn't had a good strong drink in over a week, and things being what they were, I very badly wanted that rectified. *Tout de suite,* as they say. I lifted the phone and asked first Delbert, then Morrow if they wished to join me downstairs in the bar.

Delbert begged off, saying he wanted to prepare his questions for tomorrow.

Morrow said, "Sure. Be down in ten minutes."

I'd be lying if I said this was a disappointing outcome.

I was on my first Scotch on the rocks when Morrow arrived in tight jeans and a loose-fitting shirt. I decided on the spot that if this woman ever wanted to get out of the legal field, she could make a pretty good go as a model.

"So what will you have?" I asked as she slipped into the chair across from me.

"Scotch on the rocks," she said, which nearly threw me off my chair. I halfway expected her to order Evian with a twist of lemon.

I stuck my finger up for the bartender to send over one of the same. "That your normal drink?" I asked.

She sort of smiled. "No. Usually I'd just order an Evian with a twist of lemon, but I wanted to surprise you."

I guess I blinked once or twice. "Yeah, I usually drink Evian, too," I finally said, thinking I was being witty.

"No, you usually drink Scotch. In fact, I'd be willing to bet that you've never taken a sip from a bottle of Evian in your life."

"And why would you bet that?"

"Because. Want to play a little truth or consequences?"

If I weren't such an overconfident guy, I would've said no right then and there. Instead, I stupidly said, "Sure. What's the stake?"

"Point-by-point loser chugs a shot of Scotch. Overall loser pays the tab."

"All right," I said.

She smiled. "What's your father do?"

"He's a hairdresser," I said. "Lives in San Francisco."

"Drink!" she ordered me. "If I were to guess, I'd say your father was career army."

I wiped a few drops of Scotch off my lips, stuck my hand up for the bartender to send over another, and did my best to hide my shock. "Why'd you guess that?" I finally asked.

"I wasn't guessing. I was making a reasoned deduction. Sons of strong-willed men often become rebellious and act like wiseasses."

"Okay," I said. "Where are you from?"

"Ames, Iowa. I grew up on a farm and spent my childhood milking cows and plucking eggs from underneath hens."

"That's true," I declared. "Drink! And don't forget the part about how you were crowned homecoming queen and almost married the captain of the football team."

"You drink," she ordered. "I've never been to Ames, Iowa, in my life. I'm from the Northeast, born and raised in a city, and the closest I've come to a cow is digging into its broiled carcass on my plate."

My mouth fell open. "Really?" I asked, dumbfounded.

"Really," she said with a vague smile.

I gulped the Scotch and considered the proposition that she had schemed on playing this game before she ever came down here.

She grinned, then said, "Okay. Why'd you leave the infantry and become a lawyer?"

I thought about that. Finally I shrugged. "I guess I got tired of killing people. I went to war a couple of times and decided I really didn't like it all that much."

She studied me a moment, and her face suddenly became very soft. "Drink," she said almost remorsefully.

"Nah, you drink!" I shot back. "I had a great time at war. In fact, I nearly cried when they were over."

Which actually was true. And which actually was why I became a lawyer. I developed this huge phobia that I would end up like my father, in love with combat.

"All right," I asked, relishing my victory. "Were you ever married?"

She seemed suddenly very sad. "I was. My husband was also an army lawyer. One day I came home early, and there he was, in bed with a twenty-year-old paralegal." Her eyes seemed fixated on something inside her glass. "I guess I blame myself. I've always worked too hard, and I . . . well . . . I, uh, I guess he felt neglected."

"Drink!" I barked.

She looked at me in shock. "What?"

"You heard me! Drink!"

She gulped it down, then gave me this really cute, really spiteful look. "How did you know?"

"You said too much. You're the type who likes to keep everything private."

"All right. Were you ever married?" she asked.

"No."

"Were you ever in love?"

"Once."

"And why didn't you marry her?"

"Because you can't marry your dog, no matter how much you love her," I said, giving her a perfectly evil smile. "Now drink."

She frowned. "That sucked."

"By the way," I said, "it's three to two, my favor. You pay for the drinks."

She drained the last of her Scotch, and she looked a little tipsy, and her lips looked kind of moist. I felt kind of frisky, and our eyes met. Then came this long, awkward moment, which ended with her telling me to get my big shoe off her sandaled foot.

She paid the bill, and we parted ways at the elevator, since she wanted to limp the two flights upstairs to her room, while I insisted on ascending in comfort. The last I saw of her, she was stumbling occasionally on the stairs and trying to appear graceful.

THE next morning, my head throbbed ever so lightly on the car ride to the air force holding facility, although poor Miss Morrow obviously got the full, vituperative brunt of the Scotch. Only Delbert seemed in a remarkably chipper and garrulous mood.

This was the day when we would split up and each take different team members to interrogate. If we limited ourselves to two hours with each of the remaining eight team members, then by midafternoon we'd be done. I decided to handle Chief Warrant Officer Michael Persico, Sergeant First Class Andy Caldwell, and Sergeant First Class François Perrite.

Persico was forty-six years old. He was a former staff sergeant who'd applied for warrant officer training and been accepted. Every A Team has a chief warrant officer. They are the technical experts of the teams, the masters of every function of the other members— from weapons to communications to medical. Persico had been with the same team the past eighteen years. He had earned a Bronze Star for valor in Somalia and a Silver Star for valor in the Gulf.

I studied him closely when he was led into the room. He was of average height and build. He looked leathery and tough, with mostly gray hair, and harshly weathered skin that had left deep creases on his face. He moved confidently, like a man who'd gotten most of what he wanted out of life.

He brought a lawyer into the play, a female captain named Jackie Caruthers, who resembled a middle linebacker, only a little bigger.

"Please have a seat," I said to both of them.

Persico's eyes were gray, like a wolf's. Those eyes were now taking my measure, as he would a foe on a battlefield.

I said, "Chief, could you explain the series of events that led to the destruction of the KLA unit you trained?"

He glanced at his lawyer, who nodded.

"All right. The KLA company commander was named Captain Kalid Akhan. He came to us on the afternoon of the thirteenth and said he planned to do a raid on a Serb police compound at dawn the next morning—"

"Did he plan the raid?" I interrupted.

"Yes, sir, he did. He said he had heard from some locals that the police compound was poorly guarded."

"And did he have any help from you or your team?"

"No. He pretty much decided what he wanted to do on his own."

"Did you like his plan?"

"Looked okay to us. Based on what he said about the Serbs, it sounded like kid's play."

"Could you describe that plan for me?"

"Sure. The police station was located in the middle of a village named Piluca. Captain Akhan had ninety-five men. He planned to break 'em into three elements and hit at first light. One element was to go into the village and isolate the police station from the other houses. The second was to build a security screen along the main road that led into the village from the north. The third was the assault element. It would take down the police station."

"And what did they plan to do once they took the station?"

"Well, you gotta understand a few things about that Piluca station. The Serb captain who commanded it—he was regarded as an expert on ethnic cleansing. He even had a nickname: the Hammer. He always carried a hammer in his belt. He liked to use it to bash fingers and toes and testicles. He was a real sadist."

"Did he have a large force?"

"About thirty Serbs were under him, give or take a few. They'd pretty well terrorized that little town for a whole year."

"So Akhan's team wanted revenge?" I asked.

"There was probably some of that, but what Captain Akhan figured was that the Piluca station was a symbol. Knocking it off would show every Albanian Kosovar in our sector that the Liberation army had balls and could actually accomplish something."

"What do you mean by knocking it off?" I asked.

"They'd take it over for an hour or two. Take the Serb captain prisoner and as many other Serbs as they could get."

"What did you assume they were going to do with the prisoners?" I asked.

"I assumed Captain Akhan planned to turn 'em over to U.N. authority so they could be tried for crimes against humanity."

"And how did he plan to do that, given that you were behind enemy lines, at least a two-day march from Macedonia?"

"I just trusted they would," he said very simply. "Captain Akhan wasn't the type to commit murder."

"Did you report the planned KLA attack to headquarters?"

"No. We didn't have to. We had authority to approve Captain Akhan's operations."

"Authority? I thought you were there in an advisory capacity."

He never blinked. "That's right. I misspoke. The truth was, Captain Akhan had the authority to decide on the attack himself."

"And what happened?" I asked.

"They left about two in the morning, figuring to hit the station at first light. We don't really know what happened after that. Maybe the Serbs expected them, or maybe it was just bad luck."

"Could there have been a security leak?"

He appeared thoughtful for a few moments. Finally he said, "Probably a pretty good chance that's what happened."

"Were you in radio contact with Akhan's company?"

"No. The SOP was to maintain radio silence."

"So what happened?"

"What happened? Well, it went to hell, and they were all wiped out."

"How did you find that out?"

"Around ten or so, when they still weren't back, we sent Perrite and Machusco to check on 'em. They snuck into the village."

"And how did the members of your team react to that news?"

"It's war. Guys get killed."

"Weren't you disappointed?"

"Not enough to go out and kill a bunch of Serbs. Look, Captain Akhan and his company were pretty good guys, but we weren't real close. We kept to ourselves; they kept to themselves. Most of them didn't speak English, and only two of our guys speak Albanian."

Persico was making what I regarded to be a very enlightening mistake. Warrant officers are notoriously disrespectful. They occupy an awkward position in the army, caught in a netherworld between the enlisted ranks and the officer ranks, accepted by neither. Persico's constant referrals to Akhan as *Captain* Akhan was a sign of respect, if not reverence. I didn't buy the breezy indifference.

"How was your relationship with Captain Sanchez?"

"Great."

"Was he a good team leader?"

"Yeah, fantastic."

"Could you please describe what you did for him?"

"I was his deputy. I was responsible for the training and professional competence of the team. He led, and I made sure the men who followed knew their jobs."

"Was there any friction between you?"

"None. We got along real well. Look, Major, what are you angling at? I've known Sanchez two and a half years. We ain't drinking buddies, but we get along. I *liked* the way he ran the team."

"Could you please describe the events of the seventeenth, the day you believed your team had been discovered by the Serbs?"

"Okay, sure. We were in our base camp, and Sergeants Perrite and Machusco were pulling perimeter security. Perrite came running back from his outpost and reported that he and Machusco had seen some Serbs up on a hilltop observing us. Then—"

"How many Serbs did they spot?"

"A few. He said they didn't get a real good look at 'em. Then Sanchez gave the order for everyone to get their gear together and book. We'd built an E and E plan the day before that called for us to move almost straight south."

"Is that what you did?"

"For a while. Perrite was laying trip flares every mile or so, and a few of 'em went off, so Sanchez decided to deviate."

"How many went off?"

"I dunno. Maybe two, maybe three."

"How far away were the Serbs when they went off?"

"I'd guess about two miles."

"Where were you in the column?"

"The middle. We've got a movement SOP. Perrite and Machusco handle rear security, Sanchez handles the map and compass stuff, while I make sure the team's following good procedures."

"If you were in the middle, then I assume you and Captain Sanchez weren't discussing his decisions?"

"Not all the time, but we talked once or twice."

"What did you talk about?"

"We talked when we knew the Serbs were following us. I recommended we change course to a zigzag and start moving eastward, since I figured the Serbs would deduce that we'd move south, straight for the Macedonian border."

"And when was the next time you talked?"

"That night. We took a halt about midnight and formed a perimeter. We could hear convoys and see dust columns all day, so we figured the Serbs were trying to box us in. We knew we had to do something. We decided the best idea was to hit the Serbs with an ambush to make 'em slow down."

"Whose idea was that?"

He paused for a moment. Then he said, "Might've been mine. Or maybe Machusco or Perrite. We all thought it was a good idea."

"So it wasn't Captain Sanchez's idea."

"No, but he bought into it right away. Why not? Wasn't like we had another option."

"At the ambush site, did the Serbs return fire?"

"At first, no. The lead vehicle blew, and they were unloading out the back of the trucks and scrambling for cover. Then we blew the chain of claymores, and that set 'em back a bit, too. Took 'em two to three minutes before they began returning fire."

"How many people would you estimate were returning fire?"

"At first maybe ten or so. By the end, maybe four or five."

I stared at him hard. "So how many Serbs do you think were still alive when you and the team departed?"

"I don't know. At least the four or five who were shooting at us. Probably a fair number of wounded, too."

"How do you think they all died?"

"My guess would be that the Serbs killed their own people."

"Why would they do that?"

"Maybe to punish 'em for being caught like that. Maybe just to make it look worse than it was. Seems to have worked, too. The army and the press all believe we massacred those guys."

"Did you?" I asked.

"No. We were just trying to escape."

I reached over and turned off the tape recorder, placed my note page back in my briefcase, and stood up as though I were ready to leave. Persico and his attorney coolly watched all this.

I walked to the door, then turned. "One other question, Chief. After the ambush, when you all were heading back to the Macedonian border, do you remember how many trip flares went off?"

He stroked his chin a few times. "Yeah. Two, I think."

FOUR

WE BROKE at noon, right after I'd finished with Sergeant First Class Andy Caldwell, who was definitely not one of the leaders of the team. Everything he said closely mimicked everything Persico had said.

We ate in an air force dining facility that had a well-stocked salad bar, and Delbert and Morrow made three trips each, apparently having experienced withdrawal from the leafy stuff as a result of Imelda. Delbert had spent his morning with Staff Sergeant George Butler and Sergeant Ezekial Graves, the team medic. Morrow had interrogated Sergeants Brian and James Moore, twin brothers who had been with the team for six years.

"Did you hear anything exciting?" I asked Delbert.

"I spent two hours with Butler and one hour with Graves. Their testimonies corresponded. However, neither Butler nor Graves were involved in any of the key decisions."

"Did they contradict anything Sanchez said?" I asked.

"Not in any significant way. Graves said he didn't see the ambush. Because he was the medic, he was positioned about a mile south of the ambush site."

"That would make sense," I said. According to the laws of war, medics have to act as noncombatants unless they are killing in self-defense. "How about you?" I asked Morrow. "What did you get from the Moore twins?"

She said, "Like Butler and Graves, neither was involved with the decisions. All they could do was describe the events."

"All right," I said. "Here's what we're gonna do. This afternoon I'm gonna take Perrite while you two double-team Machusco. Perrite and Machusco were the eyes and ears of the team. They seem to have been involved in everything."

We then quickly finished our meals, dashed off, and got ourselves repositioned in the interview rooms.

Sometimes you look at a man and just know he's a killer. That was François Perrite, a lean, swarthy Cajun with the most frigid eyes I ever saw attached to any breathing thing. Added to that, there was no break between his eyebrows, which stretched across his narrow forehead, running almost perfectly perpendicular to the thick black mustache above his lips. He came without a lawyer.

"You know the rules of this session?" I asked.

"No. Tell me," he ordered, as though he were talking to a waiter.

I didn't answer, but stared at him coldly, hoping to make him uncomfortable. I didn't. He just stared back.

I very politely said, "Let's start over, Sergeant Perrite. I'm Major Drummond, the investigating officer. I'm used to being addressed by my title or as sir."

"And I guess that's rule one, right?"

"You're catching on. Now, rule two stipulates that anything you say can be used against you in a court of law. Are you sure you don't want an attorney present?"

"I'm sure. I don't really like lawyers . . . sir."

I leaned toward him and smiled. "Now rule three. Don't screw with me, Perrite. You're implicated in the possible murder of thirty-five men, so park your macho horsecrap in a box."

I'd like to say Perrite turned red or blinked a few times. He didn't. He gave me this look I'd seen somewhere before. It was that squinty tightness a sniper gets just before he pulls the trigger.

I continued. "Let's start with the seventeenth, when you and

Sergeant Machusco reported that you saw Serbs watching your team. Could you describe that event?"

He leaned back with an amused expression, but his lips stayed tightly shut.

I leaned toward him again. "Oh, did I forget to mention rule four? This is an official investigation, and I am ordering you to answer. So far you've been convicted of nothing, but if you refuse to answer my questions, I'll convene a summary court-martial tomorrow and convict your ass for refusing a lawful order."

He casually scratched his chin, then leaned forward and planted his elbows on the table. "Machusco and I was on security, and we saw a bunch of Serbs on a hill staring down at our patrol base."

"How many Serbs did you see?"

"Maybe three."

"How far away were you?"

" 'Bout half a mile. Maybe a little more."

"Were they wearing uniforms?"

"Yes. Camouflage."

"Who did you report that to?"

"Chief Persico."

"Why him? Why didn't you report it to Captain Sanchez?"

"Because I couldn't find Sanchez."

"Wasn't he in the base camp?"

"I just told you I couldn't find him," he said, grinning like I was a simpleminded idiot. "How the hell do I know where he was?"

I grinned back. "Persico testified that when you told him about the Serbs, you admitted you didn't get a good look at them. Are you sure they were watching your base camp?"

"I didn't walk up to them and say, 'Yo, you wouldn't happen to be staring at my base camp, would you?' But that was sure as hell the direction they was looking at."

"Okay. Now, while your team was escaping and evading, what were you doing?"

"Machusco and I handled rear security, like always. We hung back 'bout half a mile behind the team, puttin' down trip wires."

"How many did you set?"

"I don't know. A lot. About ten or fifteen each."

"How did you happen to have so many flares with you?"

"Because we're the security team. We always bring lots of 'em wherever we go."

"While your team was moving, were you being followed?"

"Yeah."

"How do you know that?"

"Because the Serbs kept setting off trip flares."

"How many times did that happen?"

He seemed to hesitate a moment, then gave me what I'd call a screw-off grin. "I don't rightly remember."

"Captain Sanchez said it happened five times," I lied.

"Okay. Sounds about right to me."

"Persico said it happened eight times," I lied again.

"Well, Persico's miles smarter than Sanchez, so make it eight. Yeah, it was eight," he said, obviously lying right back at me.

"I'm sorry. Persico's smarter than Sanchez? Smarter how?"

"Smarter like he's been in lotsa tight situations and knows what he's about."

I decided I wasn't going to delve into that at the moment. "How was the decision made to execute the ambush?"

"I dunno. I wasn't involved. I guess it happened sometime after we drew into a perimeter that night. Sanchez and Chief huddled together for a while; then the word got passed around that we was gonna ambush some Serbs. That's all I know."

"Did more flares go off that night?"

"I don't remember."

I acted like I was reviewing some notes. After about twenty pensive seconds I said, "Captain Sanchez reported that three more flares went off, and Persico agreed with that number."

"Okay, that's right," he said. "Now that you've refreshed my memory, it happened three times."

And now that we'd confirmed he was still lying, we continued. "Who provided the security element for the ambush?"

"I did. I put myself about half a mile east of the ambush site. I picked a hillside where I had visibility for about a mile."

"Was it your job to notify the team which column to hit?"

He nodded.

"Did you have any instructions to follow?"

"Yeah. They wanted me to pick a nice big fat column without any armored vehicles in it. I let three or four minnows pass through before I found one that was just right," he said. His eyes were lit up, as if he were remembering the taste of a thick, cold milk shake on a hot summer's day.

"Did you participate in the ambush itself?"

"No. I stayed in my position, watching to see if any more Serb columns or vehicles was coming. When the ambush was over, I rejoined the rest of the team at the designated rally point."

"And then you continued your E and E?"

"That's right."

I turned off the tape recorder and shoved my papers back inside the briefcase. "Thank you, Sergeant Perrite," I said in my most civil tone. "You've been extremely helpful."

For the first time, he appeared to lose his composure, and I departed with a smug sense of self-satisfaction. The truth was, he hadn't been the least bit helpful.

IMELDA and two of her assistants flew into Aviano late that afternoon to prepare written transcripts of the taped interviews. She booked a room at our hotel, which she and her crew turned into a makeshift office.

Delbert, Morrow, and I got together at seven and spent three hours reviewing what we'd heard—as well as what we'd learned, which, from my viewpoint anyway, wasn't the same thing.

Delbert and Morrow's session with Sergeant Machusco apparently went a lot like my session with Perrite, which is to say that Machusco also proved to be about as charming as a rattlesnake.

"Those two're scary," Delbert said.

I nodded. "Every army, from the beginning of time, has attracted men like them. It's a good thing, too. If there wasn't an army for them to join, they'd be out on the streets looking for blood. This way, at least, they kill for the good of their country."

"How reassuring," Delbert said with a priggish twang.

"Did any of us hear anything today that contradicted their main defense?" Morrow asked, trying to steer us back on course.

"That depends," I replied. "They're all vomiting out the same general concept, but they're walking all over each other on the details."

Delbert gave me a speculative look. "Maybe, but I sure wouldn't want to try to prosecute them." He began ticking down fingers. "One, they have a splendid justification for what they did. Two, they were the only witnesses. Three, they're all telling the same story. Four, and most ominously, it's an incredibly believable story."

I said, "Then you think they've got a good defense?"

Delbert nodded, while Morrow said, "No, Major, not a good defense. They've got a great defense."

"Aha. Haven't you overlooked one inconvenient little fact? What about those little holes in the heads of the Serbs?"

Morrow said, "Maybe Persico was right. Maybe the Serbs did it themselves to fabricate an atrocity—just in case we conclude that Sanchez's ambush was justified."

"Like blackmail?" I asked.

"Sure. It's brilliant if you think about it," Delbert said. "We recommend against charging Sanchez's team; then the Serbs convene another big press conference. They hand out the close-ups of the holes in the head, and they announce what our troops did to their people. We'd be stuck looking like we tried to cover it up."

"So you think that's it? A setup?" I asked.

Delbert stood up and began pacing. "Who knows?" he said, gesturing with his arms as though this were a courtroom. "Maybe they were polished off by a roving band of Albanians who heard the shots and made it to the ambush site before the Serbs. The corpses were shot with M-16s. The Kosovars are armed with U.S. weapons."

"I suppose that's another possibility," I admitted.

"The problem is that all the possibilities are just conjecture."

"And the inconsistencies don't bother you?" I asked.

"You mean that flare thing you keep bringing up? It's completely irrelevant. Also, under similar circumstances I doubt I could recall how many flares were set and how many went off. I think those men were scared witless, running for their lives."

"He's right," Morrow said. "Any defense attorney would turn you into hamburger if you tried to bring that up in a courtroom."

"So you believe they're innocent?" I asked them.

Delbert said, "I've seen nothing that indicates otherwise."

I looked at Morrow.

"Let's just say I'm a lot less convinced they murdered those men than I was two days ago, before I heard their side. Don't tell me you aren't, too."

I looked from her to Delbert. So far I had not agreed with either of them on anything. "What I believe is that every man I've talked to so far has lied to me. Some in small ways, others in large ways. Men lie for a reason. They had a week together to cook up a common defense. Something doesn't smell right."

EARLY the next morning we all trundled back out to the airfield and climbed into another of those ubiquitous C-130s. We stuffed in our earplugs, grateful to be relieved of the obligation to converse.

As soon as we landed in Tuzla, we went back to our little wooden building. There was a message for me to call General Clapper, so I went into my office and rang up the Pentagon.

Clapper's ever efficient secretary put me right through.

"How was Aviano?" the general asked.

"Nice place. Next time I do a crime, promise to lock me up in an air force facility. I smelled lobster and champagne on the prisoners' breaths. By the way, I see you're working early," I mentioned, since it was six a.m. his time.

"Just trying to catch up," he groused. "Spent nearly the whole damned evening over at the White House."

"They're not still talking about me over there?"

"Your name popped up a few times, but you're passé, no longer the topic du jour. They wanted me to help brainstorm the options."

"Options? What options?"

"Option one is you recommend a court-martial. Option two is you don't."

"Don't they have better things to do, like feed the homeless, fix the interest rates, check out the new crop of interns?"

"It's not so simple, Sean. The President's policy on Kosovo does not enjoy wide national support. They're scared. This thing's been presented as the first war fought solely on moral grounds—on principle. That's how they're justifying it. So let's say you go with option one and recommend a court-martial. See any problem there?"

"No. The actions of a few men shouldn't undermine the moral underpinnings of the President's policy."

"That's because you and I don't live, breathe, and eat politics the way those guys over in the White House do. They're catching hell from some of our allies. Some of the Republicans up on the Hill are threatening to cut off all funding and hold hearings."

"So this is a battle for the high ground."

"You might call it that. Now, the other alternative is you recommending that there's insufficient grounds for a court-martial."

"And what's wrong with that one?"

"Nothing, unless it's due to insufficient evidence. Here we are dropping bombs on a bunch of Serbs we publicly vilify as war criminals, and it turns out we have some of our own war criminals. Only thing is, we let them go scot-free. God forbid we ever eventually capture Milosevic and his bloodthirsty henchmen. The moment we attempt to try them for war crimes, we'll be branded the biggest hypocrites there ever were."

"Rules of evidence are rules of evidence."

"You know that, and I know that, because we're lawyers. Joe Six-pack doesn't understand it, though. As for the rest of the world, they haven't got a clue what our legal system's all about."

"So the only thing that works for them is if I say Sanchez's team acted responsibly and innocently?"

"Did they?" he asked a little too quickly.

"I still don't know. They've got a good tale to tell. It just doesn't all add up."

"But their stories coincide?"

"Except for some details."

"Then maybe they're telling the truth."

"I don't think they are."

There was a moment of awkward quiet before Clapper said, "Sean, do you know my one reservation when I recommended you for this? Your infantry background. I was worried that you'd start trying to second-guess what Sanchez and his men did out there."

"What makes you think I'm doing that?"

"I'm not saying you are. I'm just warning you not to get caught up in details, like who held whose rucksack during the ambush."

"Thanks, General, I'll bear that in mind."

"Uh . . . there's another thing. A decision was made to shorten the time line. It's no longer twenty-one days."

I said, "You're kidding, right?"

"No. The White House thinks this is dragging out too long. They want it wrapped up in ten days."

"Ten? That's ten days from today, right?" I asked.

"That's ten from when you started. Four days from today. I know you're doing a great job, Sean. Just stay with it."

I hung up the phone and took three deep breaths.

Either Delbert or Morrow had ratted me out. Hell, maybe they'd both ratted me out. I could just hear their two voices on the phone, competing to see who could out-rat whom.

And why did I get this feeling that Clapper had just pressured me to declare these men innocent of all charges? I wanted to vomit— and I might have—except I'm too cool for that.

There was a knock on my office door. It slowly opened, and one of Imelda's assistants stuck her face in. "Uh, Major . . . excuse me," she said. "There's a man here to see you. A civilian."

"Does he have a name?"

"I asked him, sir, but he wouldn't tell me. If you'd like, I'll tell him you're busy."

"Show him in."

For some reason or other, nearly all reporters, when they're in the field, like to wear those silly-looking tan vests that have a dozen or so pockets, like bird shooters use. This man wore one of those vests, only it was a really big one, more like a tent with pockets. He looked to be about three hundred pounds. He was a little shorter than I and about thrice as wide.

"Hi," he said, real friendlylike, as his beady little eyes did a quick inspection. "You must be Major Drummond. Know who I am?"

"Mr. Berkowitz, right?"

"Hey, no hard feelings."

"Hard feelings?" I asked with an inquisitive frown. "I'm sorry, Mr. Berkowitz, we don't get the Washington *Herald* out here. Is there something I should know about?"

This sly grin crossed his lips. "Nah. It's just that some military guys don't like my writing slant. I worry about it."

"Well, don't. I never read the papers."

He edged over and planted himself on the corner of my desk. "Call me Jeremy." He stuck out his hand.

"Nice to meet you, Jeremy. Call me Major Drummond."

"Okay, if that's what you're comfortable with," he said, becoming more amiable by the second now that he thought I didn't know he'd raped me on the front page of his paper.

"So what're you doing out this way, Jeremy?"

"I'm doing a story on how the operation's going. Of course, I'm also working on the ambush story, and I thought I'd stop by and see if you changed your mind. About talking with me."

"Geesh, this is tough, Jeremy. I'd really love to. But there's a certain amount of risk in it for me. I mean, what do I get out of it?"

Jeremy stared at my desktop for a moment, contemplating this new twist. Then he tentatively said, "Perhaps a small emolument would be in order?"

"Jeremy!" I yelled.

"Sorry," he declared quite insincerely. "I didn't mean to insult you, but lots of you military guys insist on being paid."

"Was that how you got my name? Did you pay someone?"

"I didn't pay anyone, but that's as much as I'm gonna say."

I grinned. "Yeah, sure. More power to you. In fact, confidentiality was gonna be one of my requirements."

He gave me this real righteous look and sketched a cross on his heart. "I'd never divulge anything." Then he said, "What other requirements you got?"

"I want a two-way street. I give you info; you give me info."

He actually looked relieved. "Just info? Hey, no problem."

"Okay, me first. What nasty rumors are you hearing back in Washington about the investigation?"

He bent toward me very conspiratorially. "Well, did you know, for instance, that the President starts every day with a fifteen-minute update on your investigation?"

I tried my best not to look surprised. "Of course he does," I said, as though where else could the briefer be getting his information if not from me? Except that I hadn't given out fifteen minutes of information on the investigation since we started. Not to anyone, not even Clapper. So where the hell was the information coming from?

"They say this thing has him tied up in knots," Berkowitz added. "The press secretary says that his conscience is eating him alive, that the thought that our soldiers—American soldiers—would massacre a bunch of Serbs has him begging the Lord's forgiveness every night."

"Maybe he's worried that this thing might erode support for the whole operation."

Berkowitz jumped off the desk, and his body shook like a bag of Jell-O that had been tossed out of an airplane. "What's there to erode? There is no support for this thing. Okay. My turn, right?"

"Shoot."

"What'd you do before you became a JAG officer?"

"I was an infantry officer with the Eighty-second Airborne."

His arms reached out, and his hands landed on my desk. "Well, that's the interesting thing, Major. See, I got a copy of your personnel file from one of my buddies. And that's what it says in your file, so I called a buncha friends of mine who were in the Eighty-second at the same time. Now here's a coincidence. One of my buddies was actually a captain in the same battalion your file says you were in."

"So?"

"So he never heard of you before."

"Odd," I said. "I mean, there's only forty officers in a battalion. Either he was in a different battalion or you must've misread my file."

"So why do you think you were picked to be the chief investigating officer? I mean, no offense, but wouldn't you think the army would pick someone more senior?"

"Gee, I don't know," I said. "Must be because I'm hot and have ethics like a rock."

"I've got a more interesting theory." He took his hands off my desk. "There's this very special unit down at Bragg that's so outrageously secret that nobody's ever supposed to have heard of it. Anyone assigned to that unit, their files are separated from the rest of the army's and are administered by a special cell. Of course, once these guys leave that unit . . . well, then they gotta have regular files like everyone else. So what happens is their files are filled in with units they never really served in."

"They really do that?" I asked.

"They really do," he said, grinning. "Of course, those guys are never allowed to disclose they've been in that outfit or even that it exists. But it does. Kind of like Delta, that other unit that doesn't really exist—only the boys in this outfit are tougher, more deadly, and do more dangerous stuff."

"Isn't that something. Here I've been in the army all these years and never heard of any such thing."

"Really something," he said. "Now, just for the sake of argument, let's say a Special Forces A Team went out and did a very bad thing while they were performing a very secret mission. Then let's say that the army actually had a lawyer who used to belong to that special unit that doesn't exist."

"First there would have to be such a guy. Personally, I did my time in an infantry battalion in the Eighty-second—"

"Of course you did, Major. But what would worry me is that the army might pick just such a guy because he'd be most likely to feel some sympathy for that A Team. He might even be more inclined to help build a cover for that team."

I grinned at him, and he grinned back at me. Then he added, "Of course, like I said, all of this was just for the sake of argument."

"That's good, because it's all wrong," I said.

We both chuckled at the irony of that. There's nothing like starting a relationship of trust based on what we both knew was a lie.

"So," he said, "what's their story?"

"Their story is that they were detected by the Serbs and had to fight their way out. The team leader felt the Serbs were boxing his team in. He decided that ambushing a large column was the best way to make the Serbs believe his unit was larger than it was and to make the Serbs slow down."

Berkowitz let out a loud whistle. "No kidding. You believe 'em?"

"So far, sure. And all nine men are telling the same tale."

His eyes kind of lit up, and the letters PULITZER seemed to emerge on his forehead. "What a great story line. Here these poor bastards were—trapped behind enemy lines, doing a secret mission this administration ordered them to do. They fight their way out, and instead of getting the medals they deserve, they get stuffed behind bars and investigated like common criminals."

"That about sums it up," I said. "Frankly, these guys are genuine heroes. Left to me, I'd wrap this whole thing up in two days. Only problem is, one of the other investigating team members seems dead set on proving they did something wrong. He keeps nitpicking details. The rest of us are convinced these men are innocent."

I could see he was itching to race out of my office and file a story. The international press were all convinced these guys had committed a heinous crime, and now Jeremy Berkowitz was about to break the *real* story, that these men were not only innocent but heroes to boot. He walked toward the door, then turned around. "You know I have to refer to you in the story?"

"Uh, actually, no," I lied. "I hadn't thought about that."

"I'd like to call you a source on the investigating team."

"I don't know. . . . There's only a few of us . . . and, uh—"

"Hey, Major, I've never had a source caught. Trust me."

I let out a heavy sigh. "If it's absolutely necessary, okay."

I felt pretty smug when Berkowitz walked out the door. It isn't often when you get two vindictive retaliations for the price of one. Berkowitz would print his story, make a big splash. Then, as soon as I proved that Sanchez and his team had cold-bloodedly murdered the Serbs, he'd look like a worldwide horse's ass.

The White House and Clapper would have no reason to suspect me of being the leaker. I had pooh-poohed myself in the story. Now Delbert or Morrow or whoever was leaking on me was going to be suspected of leaking to the press also. Pretty slick, that.

FIVE

HENRY Kissinger once said that just because you're paranoid doesn't mean they really aren't trying to get you. Suddenly I was beginning to think it was true, and he'd been talking about me.

Someone inside my organization was leaking things to somebody who worked for the President—who for some inexplicable reason spent his early mornings listening to someone talking about me. One, or maybe both, of my coinvestigators was spilling their guts to the chief of the army's JAG Corps about how incompetent I am. A ruthlessly ambitious reporter knew something very dangerous about my background, and to top everything off, the very same general who got me this assignment had suddenly developed a severe case of character deficiency.

That's a fairly long list of crappy things to discover in only one day. The problem was, like most paranoids, I wanted someone to lash out at. But who? There were Delbert and Morrow, neither of whom I knew anything about. Then there was Imelda's chorus of four legal assistants, any of whom could be passing information along.

I kind of wanted the mole to be Delbert, since I didn't like him all that much. I was praying it wasn't Morrow. She was gorgeous and had those sympathetic eyes. I'd already built myself this nice little scenario where I cracked the case, got the pretty girl, and rode off into the sunset. The problem was that Morrow was every bit as scheming and ambitious as Delbert.

Then just as I was about to nod off, a new hallucination slowly interrupted my progress. If these guys in Washington were going to all this trouble, they must know something. Something really awful. Like maybe this was one of those sinister White House conspiracies they always make such great movies about.

No, I decided, I was going way too far. Now that I thought about it, Clapper never actually came out and asked me to give Sanchez and his crew a clean slate. He just hinted how convenient that would be. What the hell. That was nothing more than a harmless restatement of the obvious.

I awoke the next morning feeling game and fresh. By the time I reached our little office building, I was actually thinking about being nice to Delbert for a change.

I noticed when I walked in that everybody was sitting somberly at their desks. Somberly, like something was terribly wrong. I also noticed two big, burly military policemen sipping coffee and lounging by the entrance to my office.

"Excuse me, Major Drummond?" the bigger of the two asked, shoving himself off the wall. He wore captain's bars, and his nametag read WOLKOWITZ.

I said, "How can I help you, Captain?"

"We need to talk to you. Alone, if you don't mind."

We walked into my office, and I politely offered him and his sergeant seats, which they both declined. I sat behind my desk and tried to look relaxed.

Captain Wolkowitz said, "Could you tell us where you were between 2400 and 0500 hours this morning?"

"I could, but you haven't given me any reason."

"Do you know a man named Jeremy Berkowitz?" he asked.

"Again, Captain, why are you asking?"

"I'm asking because Berkowitz was murdered last night."

I stared at him, and he stared at me.

"Now, I'll ask you again. Did you know Mr. Berkowitz?"

"I met him here yesterday."

"And where were you last night?"

"I was on my cot, in my tent, trying to fall asleep."

"You share that tent with anyone?"

"No."

"Then there are no witnesses to corroborate your story?"

"Captain . . . uh, Wolkowitz," I said, "do you have some reason to suspect me of murdering Mr. Berkowitz?"

He paused, and that was his first serious mistake.

I stood up and pounded a fist on my desk. "I asked you a question, Captain! You've got two seconds to answer, or I'll press charges against you for refusing a lawful order."

He backed up a bit. "Sir, I—"

"Are you gonna answer my question," I barked, "or do I need to pick up the phone and call your commanding officer?"

By this time he had backed up all the way to the wall. "Sir, I—"

"You nothing, Captain! Obviously you've already questioned my office staff?"

Like most people do when they get flustered, his eyes quickly darted toward the floor. Mistake number two.

I pounded the desk again. "I can't believe this! You know why I'm here at Tuzla? The secretary of the army personally appointed me an investigating officer. And you come in here without my permission and interview my people?"

"Sir, you're not a suspect," he said. "At least not yet."

"Then why are you asking me these questions?"

"We found your name in Mr. Berkowitz's notebook."

"How did he die?" I demanded.

"Sir, he was strangled. With a garrote. His arteries were cut, but the actual cause of death was asphyxiation."

"And where did this happen?"

"He was staying at the press quarters inside the information officers compound. He apparently got up in the middle of the night to go to the latrine. He was murdered right at the urinal."

"With a garrote, you said? Homemade or professional quality?"

"It looked store-bought. A metal wire attached to two wooden handles."

"Who found him?"

"An AP reporter named Wolf."

I studied the two military police for a moment. Then I said, "Sergeant, please step out of my office."

The sergeant did as he was told. Then I stood up. I walked around the desk and leaned against it. The time had come to restore relations with Captain Wolkowitz.

"You've already called the Washington *Herald?*" I asked in a much calmer, much friendlier tone.

"Yes, sir. They're real unhappy. This isn't going down well."

"Are you aware what Berkowitz was doing here?"

"The information officer told us he was working on a story about the bombing operation."

"He was also working on a story about my investigation."

Wolkowitz scratched his head, then said, "The *Herald* told us he filed a dispatch at about 2330 hours last night. They didn't say what it was about, though."

This was where it was going to get tricky. I had to appear forthcoming without actually being all that forthcoming.

I said, "He came here yesterday to interview me. I had the impression he had an inside source and was ready to break something big. He was obviously excited, like he was onto something."

"And what did he want from you?"

"I think it was just routine journalistic courtesy. He wanted to give me the chance to confirm some details."

"He gave you no hints or clues who his source was?"

I looked disgusted. "His exact words were that he's never had a source uncovered. He seemed very proud of that."

"Was this your only interaction with him?"

"No. He called me from Washington the other day."

"And what was that about?"

"I don't know. I hung up on him before he could get into it. I think he wanted me to leak, and frankly, I found the idea repugnant." So far I'd managed to be completely truthful without being the least bit truthful. But if this conversation continued, then this big captain was liable to ask me a question or two I couldn't contort into a wholly wrong context. I quickly said, "So . . . hey, what's your first name anyway?"

"Paul. My friends call me Wolky, though."

I smiled warmly, like I was one of those friends. "Okay, Wolky. First, I apologize for my blowup. It's just that, well, I've been under a lot of pressure. Coming in here as the investigating officer, you know, folks haven't been real friendly."

"Hey, I understand," Wolky said, and I was sure he did. I mentioned that lawyers aren't real popular in the army. Well, military policemen are about ten notches down from that.

"Good," I said. "Now, I imagine you're bringing the Criminal Investigation Division into this?"

"A team's flying in from Heidelberg right now."

"That's good. It's not that I suspect there's any connection between Berkowitz's murder and my investigation, but I'd like to play it safe. When CID gets here, I want them to stop by. I want to know everything you learn about this murder."

"You think there might be a connection?"

"Wolky, there are a million plausible reasons Berkowitz was murdered. This guy made his living writing derogatory stories about the military. He's hated by about everyone who's ever worn a uniform."

Wolkowitz was listening intently. A nice guy, but he sure wasn't the brightest bulb in the hardware store. Of course Berkowitz's murder was connected with my investigation. I was sure of it.

The garrote is no weapon for amateurs. You have to sneak up behind someone, then fling that little wire just right so it forms a perfect lasso around the neck. At the same instant, you have to whip the two handles in opposing directions with lightning speed.

A killer who is untrained gets the wires caught on the victim's nose or chin, or the victim's hand shoots up and gets in the way.

Regular Army troops wouldn't know a garrote from a carrot. However, garrotes are highly favored among Special Forces, who sometimes need to kill silently. Whoever murdered Jeremy Berkowitz chose his weapon deliberately. He meant to leave a signature.

I ASKED Delbert and Morrow to join me in my office at noon. Delbert came in first, then Morrow, who gave me a full dose of those sympathetic eyes. "Are you in any trouble?" she asked.

"Nope, no trouble," I assured her. "The MPs heard I was the smartest guy on the compound, and they just wanted to stop by and see what I thought about that dead journalist."

Delbert had this perplexed look on his face, like why hadn't the MPs dropped in to have a chat with him, too? He was the one who went to Yale. Morrow, on the other hand, gave me the look all mothers award to their naughty three-year-olds.

"I've got some terribly good news," I said to get the subject changed. "Because of the outstanding progress we've made, the army has decided to shorten the time line of the investigation."

"To when?" Morrow asked.

"Four days, starting this morning."

"Wow, that *is* short," Delbert said, restating the obvious.

I said, "If we had to vote today, where would we be?"

They stared at each other for a moment. Then, at the same time, they both said, "No grounds for prosecution."

"Okay. So is that no grounds because you think they're innocent or because you think there's insufficient evidence?"

"The former," Delbert said.

"The former," Morrow echoed. "What about you?"

I said, "If I had to vote today, I would vote no, because there's insufficient evidence, but I don't feel this team has had time to make a proper recommendation."

We all knew that if I did such a thing, it would invalidate the entire investigation.

Morrow said, "Then we have four days to change your mind or change our own. What would it take for you to change your mind?"

"I'd have to see some positive confirmation that Sanchez and his men aren't lying."

"There is no confirmation," Morrow said quite painfully. "These nine men are the only living witnesses."

A strange expression suddenly came over Delbert's face. "Maybe there's an alternative to a living witness," he said. "The National Security Agency or somebody must have satellites orbiting over Kosovo. I've never personally seen a satellite photo, but from what I hear, they can read the print on a dime."

I could have kicked myself. If anybody should have thought of this, it was the guy who spent five years in the world of supersecret operations, where we used up satellite photos like toilet paper.

"Delbert, you genius," I declared. "You're absolutely right."

I checked my watch. If I called right now, I could catch Clapper just as he arrived at the office. I dialed the number and waited. It took three rings before Clapper's secretary picked up. She put me right through. A moment later Clapper said, "Hello, Sean."

"Hi, General. Having a nice day?"

"I haven't had a nice day since I took this job. You've heard about this dead reporter?"

"You mean the guy who called me the other day?"

"Right. Did you actually meet with him?"

"He stopped by yesterday. We had some words."

"The editor of the *Herald* called the Chairman of the Joint Chiefs. He says he'll raise hell until we catch whoever did this."

"I don't blame him. Listen, the reason I called is we might have a breakthrough. We'd like to see if NSA or any of those other agencies might have any surveillance tapes or pictures of Zone Three that were collected between the fourteenth and the eighteenth."

"Good idea," he said. "I'll make the calls."

"Thanks, General," I said; then we both hung up.

I suppose I could've shared my suspicions of the Berkowitz murder with General Clapper, just like I should've shared them with

Wolky. But the truth was, the moment Wolky said that Berkowitz was dead, I instantly lost trust in everyone I knew. All that dark paranoia I'd managed to bury the night before came rushing back like a tidal wave.

There was a knock on the door, and I looked up to see Imelda enter. "There's two men in civvies waiting to see you," she said.

"CID?"

"Uh-huh." She nodded.

"Could you two please wait outside the office?" I asked Morrow and Delbert.

They left with Imelda and were immediately replaced by two young crew-cutted investigators who, like most military men, wore cheap civilian suits. Their ties were something out of the *Twilight Zone*, and their shirts were polyester blend, no-iron specials.

A pair of badges were flashed, and they quickly muttered their names. David something and Martie whatever.

"Sir, we were told by Captain Wolkowitz that you wanted to meet with us," said Martie whatever.

"He must have mentioned that Berkowitz was writing about my investigation?"

"He did," said Martie. "We understand Berkowitz did an article about you on the front page of his paper three or four days back."

"Yes," I admitted. "And that's why I killed him."

Their heads snapped up in surprise.

"Just kidding," I said. "He misspelled my name, but otherwise the article wasn't objectionable. He expressed the view that the army should've picked a more senior officer to head my investigation."

"Did that make you angry?"

"You're kidding, right? I wished I wrote it. Gentlemen, how would you like to be the one who has to decide what to do with those nine men at Aviano Air Base?"

"That bad, huh?" David asked.

"David, I'll be honest. It's a no-win situation." I shook my head in pure misery. "So, anything new turn up in the investigation?"

Martie said, "There's not much to go on."

I said, "Captain Wolkowitz mentioned the garrote. I assume there are no fingerprints on the handles?"

"Right."

"You ran traces for shoeprints?" I asked.

"We're still collecting molds."

"I think you can narrow it down to rubber-soled shoes. The killer had to sneak up behind Berkowitz without being heard."

"Good point," said David, who had withdrawn a little notebook and was scribbling in it.

"Was there a lot of blood around the body?" I asked.

"All over the wall, the urinals, and the floor," Martie said.

"Yeah, cut arteries are messy things. If you're lucky, the killer got some on himself, too."

David added this to the list in his tiny notebook. Then they both stood up.

"Listen," said Martie, obviously the leader of the two, "we gotta get runnin', Major. Mind if we call on you again?"

"On the contrary, I'd appreciate it. Maybe I can help."

I doubted, though, that my new friends were going to get very far with their investigation. I had this sense that the man who murdered Berkowitz was highly trained and had killed a number of times before. If we were in Topeka, Kansas, knowing that much would be a lucky breakthrough. It would allow the police to trim their list of suspects down to a nice workable number. At Tuzla Air Base, with the 10th Special Forces Group in residence, you could throw a rock in any direction and hit a suspect.

THE 10th Group commander, Brigadier General Chuck Murphy, looked profoundly pissed off, and I guess I didn't blame him. Nobody likes to start their day inspecting a purple-faced corpse in a blood-soaked latrine.

"Good afternoon, General," I said, falling into the seat across from his desk. "I'm sorry to bother you, sir, but I have a few questions I really have to get answered."

"My time is your time," he said, glancing at his watch.

"Okay, here's the thing. We've interviewed Sanchez and all his men. We've been through the operations logs. We've viewed the Serb corpses. I guess what I still don't get is what Sanchez and his guys were doing inside Kosovo in the first place. Whose idea was it—the whole operation, I mean. Who gave you the orders?"

"My orders were signed by General Partridge."

"So then where does General Partridge get his orders from?"

"From the Joint Chiefs."

"Does Partridge deal straight with the White House?"

Murphy gave me a hard, discerning look. "Has this got something to do with your investigation?"

"Well, yes. See, Sanchez and his men are saying their ambush was an act of self-defense. You see the problem there? An ambush is a form of attack, right? I'm just trying to determine what constituted self-defense. To do that, I might have to interview the people who crafted this operation in the first place."

"It wasn't anybody at the White House, I can tell you that. I mean, of course General Partridge works for the Commander in Chief, who happens to be the President, but everything is channeled through the Chairman of the Joint Chiefs."

"So maybe the idea for this operation originated with someone in the Pentagon or maybe from someone on Partridge's staff?"

"That would be my guess."

"Do you have time for one more question?" I asked.

"One more, Drummond. That's it," he said, shaking his head.

"According to the operations order, Sanchez was supposed to provide a situation report twice a day. Once at dawn and once at dusk. Sanchez missed making his reports three times between the fourteenth and the eighteenth. What do you make of that?"

"Maybe he didn't miss making his reports. Maybe the ops center forgot to log it in. The ops center is run by soldiers, and soldiers are not perfect."

"Yes, sir, but these teams are operating behind enemy lines. Wouldn't some major alarm bells go off if they failed to report?"

"No. Not necessarily," the general said. "In most cases I think the ops staff would wait before pushing the panic button. Certainly, if a team missed making two sitreps in a row, then flags would go up."

"What would happen if a team stopped reporting?"

"We'd increase the aerial recon over their sector. If that didn't get us anywhere, we might insert a recon team."

"But none of that happened when Sanchez's team missed its reports. Should it have happened, General?"

"Look, the team still made it out okay, all right? We haven't lost a team yet, so I guess we're doing something right."

I could see I'd worn out my welcome. Nobody likes being second-guessed, but General Chuck Murphy obviously liked it less than most people. That's the problem with being told all your life that you're something special. You might eventually start to believe it.

I looked at my watch. "Oops. Hey, sir, I really gotta run. I'm supposed to be taking another deposition." I just couldn't resist giving him the bum's rush for a change.

I left Murphy's office and hurried to the Operations Center, five buildings down from Murphy's headquarters. The guard spent about thirty seconds trying to tell me why I wasn't allowed to enter this supersecret facility before I finally whipped out the set of orders the secretary of the army had provided me. According to these, I could enter the White House situation room if I so desired. No kidding.

I followed a trail of stenciled signs that took me down a long hallway, then down a dimly lit stairway. In the basement, there was another guard standing before a metal door, but all I had to do was whip out my identification card.

The metal door was flung open, and I instantly entered the next century. A whole wall was covered with a massive electronic map of Kosovo. It was peppered with lots of tiny blinking dots, some red, some green, and some blue. Another wall was lined with high-tech communications consoles, where about ten communicators sat very alertly with special headphones on their ears. It looked like AT&T's global nerve center, only all the workers in this room wore battle dress and natty little green berets.

I stood and watched and listened to the bustling activity. Like nearly all the ops centers I'd been in, most of the business was conducted in low decibels. There was this constant, low hum of voices and computer keys being mashed and radio messages being received. A hulking monster wearing sergeant major's stripes sat at a big wooden desk in the middle of the floor. It was clear that he was the big boss of this machine and its many parts.

After a while he glanced over and saw me standing observantly in the corner. He got up from his desk, fixed a fresh cup of coffee, then walked toward me. That's when I noticed he'd fixed two cups of coffee. I also noticed his hands. They were so big and beefy that the coffee cups looked like a couple of thimbles.

His hands matched the rest of him. He was a big, rough-looking man who obviously had had his nose broken at least a few times. He had an enormous ugly head that seemed to be connected directly to his shoulders, because his neck was the size of a tree stump. He had the standard Special Forces crew cut. A tall man, too, maybe six feet three, with broad, ponderous shoulders.

He squinted at my nametag and the JAG emblem on my collar. "You the same guy doing the investigation?" he asked.

"Yeah. Thanks," I said, quickly grabbing a coffee cup from his hand before he could decide he didn't want to talk with me.

His nametag read WILLIAMS, and I said, "I take it you're the ops sergeant."

"Yup. Welcome to my kingdom."

"My compliments, Sergeant Major. Looks like a tight ship."

"We try. Gets a little kinky when you're running U.S. teams, KLA teams, and trying to keep watch on the bad guys."

"How many teams are there?"

"Right now there are nine KLA teams operatin' with our guys and another seven KLA units without A Teams."

"I didn't know there were KLA units operating without Guardian Angels."

"We call 'em GTs . . . uh, graduate teams. Every KLA unit that goes in starts with baby-sitters—till they've done three or four successful missions. Then they operate more or less independently."

He took my arm and ushered me over to the huge electronic map on the wall. He looked it over for a moment, then pointed toward a blue dot located in the northeastern corner of Kosovo.

"Red dots are Serbs; green dots are our guys; blue dots are KLA. That's GT seven. One of the first teams we formed."

I stared up at the team-seven dot. "That a good team?"

"Very good. They're the exception. Most of these KLA teams haven't done a damn thing since we put 'em in."

He kept studying my face as we talked. He had that perplexed look some people get when they're trying to remember something.

I said, "So tell me, Sergeant Major, how well do you remember Akhan's company?"

"Damned shame, that one," he said. "Great scores in training, but they got wiped out before they had a chance to strut their stuff."

"Yeah. I heard they ran into a real butcher's mart at that police station."

"A nasty business," he issued forth without the slightest hint of genuine remorse. Then the corners of his mouth twisted up, and his head canted to the side. "Hey, you ever been to Bragg?"

"Years ago, back when I was in the infantry."

"Yeah. I knew I seen you before." He lowered his voice. "You don't remember me, do ya?"

"Nope, I'm afraid I don't."

He winked. "Course you don't. I didn't recognize your name, 'cause the outfit didn't use names when we screened. We just gave you all numbers. But I never forget a face."

I looked at Williams and tried to place him. The voice was disturbingly familiar, as were the eyes. "Sorry, Sergeant Major, you've got the wrong guy. I never heard of the outfit."

His smile broadened. "Remember the POW camp? Remember that big guy wearing a hood that kept kickin' the crap outta you?"

This I remembered all too well. One of the tests the outfit expected all recruits to endure was two weeks in a simulated POW camp that was about as brutally realistic as they could make it. For some reason this huge interrogator developed a very nasty affection for me. He liked me so much he made sure I got one-hour personal workouts with him every day. When he was done, I had two fractured ribs and a broken nose to remember him by.

"You were that bastard?" I asked.

"Hey, no hard feelings." He chuckled. "That was my job. And it didn't help that you were a wiseass all the time."

"A job, huh? Well, you certainly seemed to enjoy it."

That brought another chuckle. "So you left the outfit and became a lawyer?" he asked.

"Yeah. After five years I decided I needed to preserve my mental health."

"Hey, got that. I was there six years. That POW training thing was my final fling. They let me go after that."

"You've been here ever since?"

"Yeah. It's not a bad unit."

I walked over to the wall of communications consoles, and he followed me. I said, "I guess all the teams in the zone make daily sitreps, don't they?"

"Twice a day. One at first light, one at dusk."

"Anybody ever miss?" I asked.

"Once in a blue moon. Not our guys, though. They never miss."

"What do you do when you don't get a timely sitrep?"

"Try to initiate contact. We've never had to go beyond that, but if we couldn't get contact, we'd get a bird up immediately."

"Why wouldn't you just wait till the next sitrep time?"

He looked at me like that was a spectacularly stupid question. "Those sitreps are their only lifeline. Miss even one, and we start moving heaven and earth to find out what happened."

"Were you on duty when Sanchez's team was in the zone?"

"Part of the time, but I gotta tell you, Major, *paesan* to *paesan,* we've been told to watch what we say to you about that."

"Who told you that?"

The smile had left his face, and he began shaking his head. "Can't really say. But you better play this real smart. Don't go actin' stubborn like I remember. Might not have seemed like it, but that POW camp was kid's play. What's goin' down around here's for keeps."

Just at that moment a fella with a full bird on his collar walked over to join us. He looked like he'd just bit into a lemon.

The colonel grabbed Williams by the sleeve. "Excuse me, Sergeant Major," he said, then dragged Williams over to a corner. I could see the colonel's forefinger doing a tap dance on Williams's chest. I guessed Williams was getting his ears cleaned out pretty good, and I can't really say that bothered me all that much. I mean, the guy once spent two weeks beating the doo-doo out of me.

Clearly the watchdogs were onto me, so I knew I wasn't going to get any more help here. I retreated quietly and thought about Williams's warning.

SIX

THE fellow waiting for me back at my office looked like a spook. Maybe it was all those spymaster novels that were the rage during the cold war, but sunglasses and trench coats had become the shibboleths for anybody connected with intelligence collection. Now, just how an NSA guy expected to be perceived as a daring spy was beyond me. I mean, give me a break. NSA guys and gals don't do secret missions. They rely on satellites and fancy airplanes with lots of odd gizmos to do all their work.

At any rate, this guy was sitting in a chair beside my office door, trench coat slung across his lap, Washington *Post* splayed open. He was handsome, with slicked-back blond hair grayed nicely at the temples, and by his build I'd say he and the NSA gymnasium were fairly well acquainted.

"Hi," I said as I walked past him.

The newspaper was instantly closed; then he popped out of his chair and followed me. "You're Major Drummond?"

"Last time I checked," I said.

He trailed me into my lair, where I got myself situated behind my desk. Digging his wallet out of his trench coat, he flung it open to show me some kind of ID. I caught a glimpse of the letters NSA before he slammed it shut.

I said, "I guess you got my request."

"The home office back in Maryland got it. They asked me to make contact with you. You're in luck, Major. We did have a satellite focused on Zone Three."

"Great. When can I have the pictures?"

"Well, I'm afraid that's going to take a while. Zone Three is a large area—nearly two hundred square miles. We've requested Tenth Group to provide us the coordinates of the base camp and the exact location of the ambush. Once we have those, our analysts should be able to do the cutouts. You want film or stills?"

"Both. You've got a facility here at Tuzla?"

"Located right beside the air force's C3I facility. You can view the shots there."

"What if I want to take pictures out?"

He broke into a knavish smile. "Uh-uh. That's not gonna happen. They're too highly classified."

"Look, Mr. . . . uh, I didn't really catch your name."

The smile changed to a half-assed smirk. "That's because you weren't meant to. Just call me Mr. Jones."

I said, "That's real original. So what happens if I decide I have to include some of your satellite shots in my investigation packet?"

"That's your problem. They're not leaving my facility."

I brooded over that a moment. "How do I get hold of you?"

"You don't. I'll get hold of you when we're ready."

"You're stationed here?"

"Yep. They called me from home station this morning and told me to assist you. Just be a good boy, and we'll make this as painless as possible for both of us."

"Gee, thanks. I'm really looking forward to working with you," I said as he walked out the door.

This guy really bothered me. His eyes bothered me. His manners bothered me. But you know what bothered me more than anything? The Washington *Post* tucked under his arm. And that silly trench coat. It hadn't rained in Tuzla in days.

I walked out and found Imelda. "Hey, Imelda, do me a favor. Call Washington and find out what the weather's been like the past twenty-four hours. Oh . . . one other thing."

"What's that?"

"Where are you storing our case materials at night?"

"Those cabinets over there," she said, pointing at three large gray military-issue file cabinets.

"Requisition a safe immediately. You—or one of your assistants—sleep next to those cabinets till it gets here."

Her eyebrows went up a notch or two, but she didn't ask why.

I went back into my office and called my big new buddy Wolky. I very nicely told him I was hereby requisitioning the services of two of his strapping military policemen to stand guard outside my building's doorway every night.

A moment later Imelda came in to inform me that it had been raining torrentially in Washington the past twenty-four hours. Mr. Jones didn't walk down the street to see me; he took off from Andrews Air Force Base. But why did he fly all this way? And why was he so secretive about his name? I pondered this until there was a knock on the door, and I looked up to see my two CID buddies, Martie and David, anxiously waiting to be invited in.

"Please," I said, standing up and walking over to shake hands.

Martie said, "Hi, Major. Hope we're not bothering you."

"No, no bother at all."

They threw themselves into a pair of seats. Their moods had changed since earlier this afternoon. Martie said, "Have you seen the two articles on the front page of this morning's *Herald?*"

I admitted I hadn't, so he handed me a couple of pages that had obviously been faxed to him. The first was a headline banner about Jeremy Berkowitz and his murder. It was a nice piece, exalting him as one of the nation's foremost military experts, a courageous, dedicated journalist, and an all-around saint of a guy.

The second piece was the final story Berkowitz filed, the one about my investigation. Only it wasn't even remotely the story he told me he was going to write. This was a very shallow, vague thing about how the investigation was slowly unfolding. I tried not to show my surprise.

Martie was now angled back in his chair with this real ambiguous expression. "That the same piece he told you he was going to write?" he inquired, and not in a friendly way.

I calmly said, "He never told me what he was going to write."

"But you told Captain Wolkowitz—"

"I said he seemed excited. I said he alluded to an inside source."

"Your office staff says Berkowitz spent over ten minutes in your office. This afternoon you gave us the impression that he barely stopped by, only briefly, to confirm a few details."

"And I stand by that. We also engaged in a little harmless chit-chat about how the investigation is being perceived in Washington. He mentioned that the White House is very interested."

"That took ten minutes, huh?" he said very skeptically. "Well, we've gone through his notebook more thoroughly. Your name was mentioned a lot. A few of the notations are very curious."

I said, "Was it curious like 'I think Major Drummond is going to strangle me tonight?' Or was it more like 'Drummond is in charge of the investigation, and he seems like a real swell guy'?"

Martie said, "Somewhere between those two."

I got up and walked to the door. I got it open and was halfway out when Martie said, "Where do you think you're going?"

"I'm going to find an attorney. I'm sure there are one or two around here somewhere."

"Wait a minute," he said, trying to put some iron in his voice. "I'd advise you to sit down and hash this out."

And I said, "Fat chance. We both know what's happening here. You are in a vise until you come up with a suspect. I'm sorry for you—I truly am—but I don't want to be your suspect. What will it be? Will you two leave, or should I go find an attorney?"

Martie pondered that; then he and David got up to leave.

THAT NIGHT I LAY IN MY BUNK trying to fit all these little pieces together, but everything I came up with was too moth-eaten for even me to believe. Clapper's call came at two o'clock in the morning, and I was still fully awake. He started the conversation with, "Damn it, Drummond, what the hell's happening out there?"

I said, "Things are proceeding well. Some NSA guy stopped by today and said we're in luck. Thanks for your help."

"I'm not talking about that. I just got off the phone with General Murphy. He says you're harassing him and other members of his command. He faxed me a long list of official complaints. Being disrespectful to senior officers. Threatening senior officers with indictments. Blocking an officer from his defense counsel."

"Look, sir—"

"He attached a stack of witness statements. Let's see, here's a set from Lieutenant Colonel Smothers and his attorney, Captain Smith. Here's another from Sergeant Major Williams. Now, I'm going to ask you once again, what the hell are you doing out there?"

It suddenly struck me that what I was apparently doing out here was being outwitted at every turn. I'd underestimated the opposition. I very weakly said, "I'm sure we can clear this up."

"You're right. When this is over, there'll be an official inquiry into your conduct. I hope I don't need to remind you that Chuck Murphy might well be the most respected officer in the armed forces. His integrity is unblemished and unquestioned."

I stammered, "I understand that; b—"

"And another thing. The head of the Criminal Investigation Division was in here a few minutes ago. He asked me for your military file. What exactly is your involvement with Berkowitz's murder?"

"None that I know of, General. Two CID investigators have been to see me twice. They said they were bothered by some curious notes in Berkowitz's journal."

There was this long, tense pause; then, "I'm not happy with your performance, Drummond."

"I'm not happy with it, either," I admitted, although for very different reasons than his.

"We'll have an inquiry when this is done," Clapper threatened again before his phone came down hard in the cradle.

It was no use trying to fall asleep. I got out of my bunk, got dressed, then walked over to our little wooden office building. Two of Wolky's MPs stood beside the door. I showed them my ID, and they let me in. Imelda was inside, sitting on her bunk, flashlight in hand, reading one of those big thick books she likes so much.

"Who's there?" She blinked into the darkness.

"It's me, Imelda."

"Oh," she said. "What are you doin' here at this hour?"

"I couldn't sleep. I thought I'd review some law books."

"This gig's not goin' too good, huh?"

"No, it really isn't," I mournfully admitted.

She pondered that for a moment. "You think they're guilty?"

"To tell you the truth, I don't know. I suspect they're guilty, but I seem to be the only one who holds that opinion."

"I think they're guilty," she said.

"Why?" I asked.

" 'Cause I read all your statements. They're lying. That Captain Sanchez? That warrant and those sergeants ran all over his weak ass. Read those statements. Those men were dissin' him bad."

"Maybe," I said, "but what if the army doesn't really want me to find out what happened out there?"

"The army doesn't always know what's best for itself."

She was sitting there on top of her sleeping bag, hair messed up, wearing a wrinkled army-green T-shirt, old gym shorts, and white socks. Frankly, she looked like a pretty shabby font of wisdom.

I said, "Thanks, Imelda."

"No problem. Now quit snivlin' and get your ass in gear."

"Yes, ma'am." I went into my office and shut the door.

I could hear the sounds of Imelda pulling open drawers and riffling through files. After a few minutes she walked in with her arms piled high with folders. She dropped them onto my desk in a large heap. Without saying another word, she left.

I looked down at the stack. She had gathered all the transcripts of the statements we'd collected in Italy. I rummaged through, found Chief Persico's, and started reading. Then I worked my way through each of the other statements. By six a.m. I was done. Imelda was right. There was a common theme that ran through all the statements. It was a lack of respect for Terry Sanchez.

Several times during the interrogatories I'd asked Persico and Perrite how various decisions got made. Their responses had been vague. Persico had assured me that all the operational responsibility was on Sanchez's shoulders, but as I read through the statements, there was barely a hint that Sanchez was even present.

The same with the others. Here were the Moore brothers, the twins, saying that Persico told them where to place themselves in the ambush. Graves, the medic, saying it was Persico who'd put him in his safe position half a mile behind the ambush. Butler, one of the two heavy-weapons men, saying it was Persico who checked his aiming stakes, who supervised the laying of the claymores. More of the same from Sergeant Caldwell.

Delbert and Morrow came in at six thirty. I decided not to mention a word about this to either of them. The entire progress of the investigation now rested on what NSA's satellite photos indicated.

At eight a woman called on behalf of Mr. Jones. She had a sweet singsongy voice, and she invited us to the NSA field station for a private showing in one hour.

I didn't want Sanchez and his men to be guilty, but my whole career rested on my being right. If the tapes showed that Sanchez's team was innocent, I'd have to pack my bags and be back in Washington. Any official inquiry would be stacked completely against me, and Delbert and Morrow would say I seemed obsessed with finding Sanchez's team guilty despite a screaming lack of evidence.

At a quarter till nine I went and collected Delbert and Morrow. We found our way to the air force's C3I facility, and a guard directed us to a small metal building off to the left. Two guards stood at the entry. They obviously expected us, so we flashed our identity cards, and they ushered us right in.

A woman was waiting for us. "Hi. I'm Miss Smith," she said with a wooden smile. She had precisely aligned gleaming white teeth.

It struck me that everybody who worked at NSA was named Jones or Smith or some other monosyllabic name. I said, "Nice to meet you, Miss Smith. I assume you work with Mr. Jones?"

"That's correct. I'm his administrative assistant."

She led us down a set of steep stairs to an underground compound. Like a good tour guide, she talked as we walked. "We had this constructed underground because we had to shield the walls with lead lining. Modern microwave listening devices allow a sophisticated eavesdropper to read everything that passes through a computer."

"And what do you all do in this special facility?"

I was staring at the back of her blond head and couldn't see her expression, but she didn't answer for a very long moment. "Mostly target analysis for bombing," she finally informed me, although she didn't sound all that sure.

We had now reached a large metal door, and Miss Smith deftly flicked a plastic card through a door lock, then pushed open the door. Mr. Jones was seated at the end of a long table, coffee cup in hand. He had traded in his dark suit and tie for more casual garb. In fact, he was dressed much like Berkowitz had been, duck-shooting vest and all. He stood up and walked around the conference table while I introduced Delbert and Morrow.

Jones did a quick, automatic handshake with Delbert, then a long, lingering smiley one with Morrow.

Then he looked over at me. "You mentioned you wanted to see the raw footage, Major. What we've got are thermals taken from seven hundred and fifty miles up. Because they're thermals, the shots are grainy. You can't identify the figures."

"You didn't have any photographic satellites over Zone Three?"

"Turns out we didn't. But don't worry. I'm sure you'll be very satisfied with what we have."

Jones invited us all to have seats, and I noticed that he positioned himself right beside Morrow. The lights were dimmed, and then the film started. What we saw was all green, with a few tiny dots in brighter, almost translucent green. The particular group of dots we were looking at were gathered in a fairly small clot. There were seven dots collected together, and two more some distance away.

Jones had a notepad in front of him, and he did the narrating. "This film was taken at one o'clock in the afternoon of the fourteenth. The grid coordinates correspond with the position Tenth Group gave us for Sanchez's base camp. We assume that what you're seeing here are the usual afternoon activities in a base camp."

We watched for two minutes before Jones said, "This tape runs for another fifty-two minutes. If you'd like, Major, we'll run the whole thing, but all it contains is more of the same."

"No. This is good enough. What have you got next?"

"The next film was taken on the seventeenth." A silent moment passed as the projectionist changed tapes. Then a new flash of green tones appeared on the screen. There were a lot more of the small bright green dots, all of which were moving. As I watched, I felt my heart land somewhere in the pit of my stomach.

Finally Mr. Jones stood up and walked over to the screen. He began using his hands to point as he said, "For those who are unfamiliar with our technology, these smaller green dots are personnel. The larger, brighter dots, like this one right here, are from stronger heat sources. In this case they correspond to automobile engines."

Delbert asked, "Where is Sanchez's team in all that mess?"

"Good question." He turned around and whipped a laser pointer out of his field vest, flicked it on, then flashed its tiny red beam at a small line of slowly moving green dots. "Count here, and you'll recognize there are seven dots. They're moving in a single file."

Jones's little red pointer shifted position to show a pair of dots located some distance behind the bulk of Sanchez's team. "We think this might be Sanchez's rear security element."

Morrow said, "That must be Sergeants Perrite and Machusco."

"If you say so," Jones remarked. "Now, if you'd like, I can explain what you're looking at."

"Explain," I said, feeling sick.

"Oh, before I do, one other piece of good news," he announced with a lofty smile. "We also have audiotapes taken the same day from some of our other assets. They were sent in code, and the language is Serbian, but our analysts decoded and transcribed them for us."

He paused for a moment to let the drama of that sink in.

"What we have here is a massive manhunt in progress. All told, nearly seven hundred Serb troops were involved. A Serb recon unit reported the sighting of an American A Team at two fifty-eight in the afternoon. Immediately afterward Serb militia radio traffic got very busy. Mobilization orders went out to various units in what we call Zone Three, but it took the Serb militia a while to get all these units in place."

He paused again and looked down at his yellow pad. "This tape we're watching was actually taken around ten p.m. I guess that's about eight hours before the ambush. As you can see, Sanchez's team was pretty well hemmed in. It's actually a miracle they made it out. Right here are two intersecting roads where Serb vehicles appear to be moving to establish a block."

I said, "Can you show us where the ambush took place?"

"Be happy to, pal." His little red dot moved to a position along one of the lines where he had indicated there were roads. Then he said, "No satellites were overhead at the time of the ambush, but we did get another pass the next day, when Sanchez's team was nearly to the Macedonian border. Wanta see it?"

"No, not really," I sourly replied.

The light flipped back on, and Morrow and Delbert were both beaming like children under a Christmas tree.

Morrow turned to Jones. "Did you get any audio transcriptions of the Serb response to the ambush?"

"Actually, we did. We've got a transcript of a unit reporting the discovery of the bodies. Then there's another transcript of the Serb headquarters ordering all units to halt in place. That's all we got, though. When the Serbs want to hide things from us, they stop transmitting and start using messengers."

Morrow said, "But you have a copy of the transcription when the ambush site was discovered?"

Jones riffled through a stack of computer printouts, then culled one out. "Okay, here we are. The sender's call sign was Alfa 36, and the receiving station was Foxtrot 90, the Serb headquarters." He looked down at the page. "It was a series of four transmissions. First transmission went, 'Foxtrot 90, this is Alfa 36. Report that there has been an ambush at grid 23445590.' Now second transmission: 'Alfa 36, this is Foxtrot 90. Describe condition.' Now the third transmission: 'Foxtrot 90, this is Alfa 36. Seventeen dead, thirteen wounded, five living.' Now the fourth transmission: 'Alfa 36, this is Foxtrot 90. Hold in place and await further instructions.' "

You could almost hear Delbert and Morrow gasp. There were still eighteen living Serbs when the ambush site was discovered. Ergo, Sanchez and his men must not have killed the survivors. *K-chunk!* The two of them had just won the daily double.

Morrow asked, "You said it's common for the Serbs to go to radio silence when they have sensitive orders to pass?"

"Right. Why? Is there something here I should know about?"

"There sure as hell is," Morrow said. "Somebody went around that ambush site and put bullets into the heads of the survivors."

Jones took a heavy breath, then looked down at the table. "Their own men? Why would the Serbs kill their own men?"

Delbert said, "To create an atrocity to pin on American troops."

Jones nodded, as though everything just fell into perfect place. After that, there really wasn't anything left for me to say. The daily double had become the trifecta. Jones began quietly murmuring with Morrow, and Miss Smith decided I was no longer good company, so she got up and walked around the table and initiated a similarly low-key conversation with Delbert. It was as if they were having a winners' convention while I stewed in loser's melancholy. Finally I got up and showed myself out of the NSA facility, wondering what I was going to do after Clapper banned me from ever practicing military law again.

BY THE time I got back to my little office building, I must've looked pretty doleful, because Imelda's girls all started offering me coffee and asking if there was anything they could do for me. The truth was, the only thing left to be done was to finish the report. Then I'd climb on an airplane and go face Clapper's tribunal.

Suddenly it struck me. The coroner's report. I asked Imelda to put me through to Dr. Simon McAbee, and about a minute later she stuck her head in and told me to pick up the phone.

"Hey, Doc. Sean Drummond here. Listen, I owe you an apology. Our due date got moved up. We need your results tomorrow."

"Oh, that's no problem," he assured me. "I finished three days ago anyway. If you don't mind my asking, what's the outcome?"

"We're recommending against court-martial."

"Ah, that's a great relief, isn't it? How did you account for the bullets in the head?"

"The Serbs did it themselves. We found definite proof that there were still survivors when the first Serbs arrived at the ambush site." I was preparing to wrap up our conversation when some impulse made me ask, "Hey, Doc, one thing. Remember I asked you to see if you could estimate how many of the Serbs would've died from wounds other than head shots? Were you able to do that?"

"I made an estimate. Let me see . . ." he said, and I could hear the sound of papers being shuffled around. "Ah yes, here. Perhaps twenty-five of them would have died as a result of the wounds received previous to the head wounds."

"Twenty-five?" I asked.

"Well, I wouldn't want to be held to that number. I mean, I didn't have the bodies here to examine them properly."

"Does that mean twenty-five who would've died eventually?"

"Oh, goodness. Maybe I misunderstood what you wanted. Twenty-five of those men would have died almost instantly. Certainly others would've died afterward."

I felt this sudden heavy pounding in my heart. "Doc, listen. I need you to be perfectly clear. Are you saying that twenty-five of those men were killed instantly?"

He paused, and I nearly bent the corner of my desk.

"Instantly, no," he finally said, and my heart rate started to settle back down.

Then he clarified. "I would state it like this. Twenty-five of the Serb bodies were inflicted with such catastrophic trauma that they would have expired within three minutes of receiving their wounds. There were four others who would be borderline. With proper first aid a few of them might've lingered longer."

"Doc, you're sure of your numbers?"

"Of course. I even erred toward the safe side. It's very likely that twenty-seven or twenty-eight died almost immediately. Judging by the wounds, it was a hideously violent ambush."

"Again, Doc, tell me you are positive of your numbers."

"Major Drummond, I'm a graduate of Johns Hopkins School of Medicine. I think I can recognize when tissue damage is severe enough to cause imminent mortality."

"Thanks," I said. I hung up the phone and sat there, mystified. Jones had said that when Alfa 36 arrived at the ambush site, it reported that there were seventeen dead and still eighteen survivors. Yet according to McAbee, twenty-five of the thirty-five Serbs should most definitely have been dead. That would've left, at most, only ten survivors.

So what was going on here? Either McAbee was incompetent, or I'd been duped. The transcripts of the Serb radio transmissions had to be fakes. And if those were faked, well, then maybe—no, definitely—the satellite films were fakes as well. Mr. Jones had somehow managed to orchestrate a bit of high-tech chicanery.

There was a very unsettling problem with that scenario, though. Mr. Jones wasn't a freelancer. Mr. Jones was here because General Clapper had officially requested NSA to assist my investigation. And Mr. Jones had the authority to waltz in and sequester the use of a fully functioning NSA field facility. And Mr. Jones had the resources to create false satellite images. I mean, I'd seen my share of satellite images, and the ones I just saw sure looked genuine.

I wanted to kick myself. I should have seen it. The con job was too perfect by half. Of course, Jones could not have done it without help from someone inside my team. He knew every pressure point of our investigation. Well, all of them except one—the body count.

But then no one knew that I'd asked McAbee to prepare that particular article. Back at the morgue, McAbee and I had been alone when we spoke about that. Delbert and Morrow were off in another corner together, comparing notes. Therefore Jones and his people had probably applied that old tried-and-true well-studied maxim that for every man killed in battle, there are usually one or two wounded. Jones just split it right down the middle and made it one survivor for every corpse.

But where did knowing all this get me? I had no proof. Yet I now knew there really was a conspiracy. I hadn't been imagining things. The problem with this being a conspiracy was that there was no one I could trust. I'd already convicted Delbert and Morrow in my mind. Well, I'd convicted one of them. Which one, though?

Was it Delbert, who came up with the bright idea to start checking around for satellite shots in the first place? I mean, how did he think of that? His specialty was criminal law, not strategic intelligence. Or was it Morrow, who'd asked all the right questions for Jones to unfold his spiel?

Then, of course, back to the basic question I was supposedly sent here to answer. What had really happened out there with Sanchez and his men? The one thing Jones's charade accomplished was to confirm that it was something terribly rotten. Where there's smoke, there's fire, and where there's a cover-up, there's a sin. Usually a really big, really smelly sin.

SEVEN

DELBERT and Morrow waltzed into the office at quarter past one. They were chattering happily, all too pleased to have spent the rest of the morning with Mr. Jones and Miss Smith—their new, or old, NSA chums. Whichever.

Imelda was smoldering. She had this stern notion of duty, and long, unaccounted-for absences were close to mortal sin. I heard her demand to know where they'd been all morning.

I walked out of my office in time to hear Delbert say, "I'm sorry. We were with Harry and Alice."

"Harry and Alice? Just who the hell are they?" I demanded.

Morrow, who looked baffled, said, "Mr. Jones and Miss Smith."

"You spent half the day with those two. Get your asses in my office," I coldly ordered.

They traded quick, fearful glances, then scurried away like chastened children. Imelda was checking me out, and I gave her a wink. She smiled and winked back. She never did like those two.

I waited a moment, then walked slowly back into the office and sat in my chair. I stared icily. "Think this investigation's over?"

Delbert gulped and said, "Sir, well, yes, after this morning . . ."

"So everything's wrapped up?" I said. "Captain Morrow, what was the exact chronology of events between the fourteenth and the eighteenth of June?"

"Chronology, sir?"

"You didn't think we'd turn in our report without a chronology. And Delbert," I yapped, "isn't something else missing?"

He blushed. "Perhaps a few more interviews wouldn't hurt."

"You're grabbing at straws, Delbert. What about the rules of engagement? Shouldn't someone fly to Bragg and find out what the inventors of this operation intended? See if an ambush was a permissible act of self-defense."

"Why, yes, I see what you mean," he said.

"Good. We're all in agreement," I announced. "Morrow, get back to Aviano. Build a chronology. Delbert, your butt better be on an airplane to Bragg tonight. Don't come back without an answer to my question. Only three days left."

"What are you going to do?" Morrow asked.

"I'm writing the closing summary," I announced.

"And what position are you going to take?" she asked.

"Isn't that obvious? Now move it, damn it! Both of you!"

They were gone in less than two seconds. Whichever of the two was the mole would report back to Mr. Jones or General Clapper that I'd caved in, that we were wrapping things up. Then both of them would climb on airplanes and be out of my hair for at least a day or two. I felt pretty proud of myself.

I picked up the phone and called my old MP buddy Wolky. I thanked him for lending me his guards. I told him they were no longer needed. He was profusely happy. Ever since Berkowitz's murder he was being required to provide guards for every journalist in the guest quarters. To make matters worse, the murder of one of their brethren had drawn them like flies. A whole flock of fresh, inquisitive reporters were now in Tuzla, which, Wolky complained, was stretching his meager resources to the breaking point.

I walked out of my office and nodded at Imelda. She left her desk and followed me out into the street. I looked around a few times, then indicated for her to walk with me awhile.

"What do you want?" she asked.

"I'm over my head, Imelda. I need your help. I'd like you to go to my tent and get one of my uniforms. Remove all the patches and sew on sergeant's stripes. Then get a nametag from one of your assistants and sew that on."

Imelda's tiny brown eyes got tinier, and I laid it all out. She listened attentively but did not seem the least bit surprised.

"One of those two legal aces has been rattin' on you, huh?"

"At least one. Maybe one or two of your girls as well. I'd guess our phones are bugged. Maybe the office also."

She considered that a moment. "I can get that checked."

"Please don't. Let whoever's listening think everything's normal. They have to believe they won."

She agreed, and I headed over to the mess hall for a belated lunch. As I walked, I began thinking about marble-eyed Mr. Jones and the lovely Miss Smith. The army teaches that before you go into battle, you must know your enemy. Right now the enemy knew me, whereas I knew next to nothing about them. Well, I knew their lousy aliases. And I knew that they supposedly worked for NSA.

As things stood at that moment, those two were my best leads. If

I could find out who they were, then maybe I could find out who sent them and exactly what the hell was going on here.

AT SIX o'clock I was in position across the road from the NSA facility. I was hiding behind another wooden building and watching the entrance. Miss Smith walked out and smiled brightly at the two guards, then moseyed down the street. I hoped Mr. Jones was still at his desk. Finally, about a minute before seven, Jones emerged. He ignored the guards and headed off in the opposite direction from Miss Smith. We walked about five minutes before he hooked a left into a wooden building. This one had a big sign that read VISITING GENERAL OFFICERS QUARTERS.

If our Mr. Jones was a government employee, he was a hefty one. I waited around for three minutes and watched to see if I could tell which lights went on inside which room. I saw nothing. Jones's room had to be on the back side of the building.

Among the many useful skills we were taught in the outfit was breaking and entering. They even brought in some ex-cons to put us through the paces. I could break into and hot-wire a car in one minute flat. I could do a reasonable second-story job on a well-protected home and get past most any safe.

I went back to my tent and set my alarm for one a.m., then fell asleep. When the alarm went off, I dressed in running shoes and a pair of army sweats. I grabbed my black gloves, a knife, a penlight, and a poncho, all of which I tucked into my waistband.

It was dark, and very few people were out and about. I jogged as though I were a late-night fitness addict. Since this was an army base and lots of folks pulled night shifts, late-night runners were a common sight. Nobody paid me any attention. I got to the visiting general officers quarters and quietly went through the front entrance and into a hallway. There were four doors, two on the left and two on the right. I immediately ruled out the two nearest doors because both had windows that faced the front of the building. This left the last two. I had a 50 percent chance of hitting the right one.

I walked down and stood by the doorway on the left. I let two minutes go by to give my eyes a chance to adjust to the darkness. Then I bent down and studied the lock. It was a simple two-way tumbler. I took out a straightened paper clip and went to work, hitting it on the first try.

Then I stayed where I was for a full minute. Picking a lock makes noise, so I waited to see if I could hear anyone stirring inside the room. Finally I twisted the knob and entered, quietly pulling the door shut behind me. The room reeked of men's cologne, which meant it was almost certainly Jones's lair. Soldiers in the field, even general officers, don't wear cologne. But civilians do.

I stood for a moment and listened to Jones's breathing. He was a quiet sleeper. I worked my way over to his desk. Then my hand pawed softly around on the floor until it hit his briefcase. I squeezed it and felt it. It was smooth leather. I lifted it up and left the way I came in, making sure to leave the door unlocked.

I walked out the entrance, ran across the street, and dodged between two buildings. I pulled the poncho from inside my waistband, whipped it open, then got inside it, using it like a little tent. I got on my knees and placed Jones's briefcase on the ground. Then I pulled out my penlight and inspected my haul.

The briefcase was locked. I took out my knife and cut a long slit along the bottom edge of the case. That done, I reached in and felt around. I finally found a tiny booklet, which I pulled out and opened. There was Jones's handsome face inside his passport. The name wasn't Jones, though. It was Tretorne. Jack Tretorne, to be exact.

Since I'd already had to break into his briefcase, I decided to keep his passport. It might come in handy. Then I began rummaging around inside the briefcase again. It took a while, but I finally felt a hard plastic card. I pulled it out and flashed my penlight on it. There was Jack Tretorne's handsome face again. Only this card did not show his name, just a long number. Oh, and of course, it also proudly displayed the shield of the Central Intelligence Agency.

I decided to keep his ID also, before I put everything away and walked back across the street to the visiting general officers quarters. I went back down the hallway to Tretorne's room, entered quietly, and gently set the briefcase back down on the floor, right where I found it, with the edge I'd cut open flat against the floor.

I made my way back out the door, raced over to my tent, and changed into battle dress. Then I went to General Murphy's headquarters building. I whipped out my fancy orders and told the sergeant who was pulling night duty that I needed a private office with a secure phone. He let me into the office of the operations officer. Then he used a key to open up a special metal cabinet that contained another special key that would convert the phone to secure. He handed the key to me and left me alone.

Colonel Bill Tingle was a living legend in the Special Operations community. It was widely rumored he was the real-life guy John Wayne portrayed in that sappy 1968 movie *The Green Berets*. Tingle was long past mandatory retirement age, but a special committee of Congress just automatically extended him on military duty every year. He'd been a full colonel during the Vietnam War. After the war ended, it was Tingle's idea to form the outfit, and he'd remained on board ever since as the official adviser.

I dialed a special number that all outfit vets were required to carry in our wallets. A male voice answered and said, "Ling Hai's Chinese Takeout." This was the outfit's screening service, and I said, "I'd like to talk with the bull, please." The bull was Bill Tingle.

I heard some switching noises in the background; then this deep, gravelly voice said, "Tingle."

I said, "Hey, sir. Sean Drummond here."

"Drummond? Drummond? Ah yeah, the dumb-ass who quit and went to law school."

"Right, sir. If you don't mind, sir, we have to go secure."

Tingle grunted. We used the special keys to change our phones to secure. Then I said, "Listen, I think I need some help."

"All right, spill it, Drummond."

And I did. I spilled everything that had happened, right down to breaking into Jones's room and stealing his passport and ID. Tingle listened to it all and said nothing for a moment.

Finally he broke the silence. "Don't know nothin' about it."

"I didn't think you did. That's not why I called. I need to find out more about this Jack Tretorne guy."

"And you figure I can do that?"

"Yes, sir. You've got all kinds of contacts. Maybe you can find who I'm up against."

There was another long silence. He finally said, "All right, Drummond. By the way, you ever hear of Operation Phoenix?"

I said, "Vaguely. One of those Vietnam things, wasn't it?"

"Right. Look it up," he ordered me. "I'll get back to you."

"Colonel," I said, "if you don't mind, I think my phones are bugged. I'll call you. By the way, I ran into another outfit vet out here. A Sergeant Major Williams. Remember him? He worked the POW hard sell when I went through screening."

"You stay away from him. He's a bad egg. One of them white supremacist nuts. We booted him out because he was helping train some group of goombahs in the backwoods."

"How'd you find that out?" I asked.

"Ah, we tapped all of your phones. Bet you never knew that, did ya? Okay, Drummond, get back to it. And watch your ass, boy."

I hung up, returned the secure key to the duty sergeant, and walked back to my tent. Then I lay down and got three more hours of sleep before I showered and shaved, got dressed again, and went to our little wooden building.

Imelda was still asleep on her cot by the file cabinets when I came in. I tiptoed over to the coffeemaker and prepared a pot. Imelda awoke while I was pouring a cup. "Fix two," she growled.

"Yes, ma'am."

While Imelda crawled out of her sleeping bag, I carried the two cups over, politely turning around to give the lady some privacy. After a minute I heard her stomping her combat boots on the floor, and I turned back and handed her the coffee. Then I hooked a finger and indicated for her to follow me.

I sat at my desk and began writing on a legal pad while asking, "So how'd you sleep?"

"Good as can be. You?"

"Like a baby," I said, holding up what I'd written on the page. It read, "Research this: Operation Phoenix."

She shrugged her shoulders. "Good. Maybe you won't be such a grump to my girls anymore."

I wrote out, "Vietnam era. Might find it on Internet."

I said, "Today what I'd like to do is work on the summary statement. I told Delbert and Morrow I'd write it."

"Yeah, okay," she said, also nodding her head at what I wrote on the paper. "No problem." She wandered back out of my office.

In the interest of authenticity, since I couldn't be sure whether one or more of Imelda's girls was informing on me, I quickly began scribbling out a long, rambling statement about how Sanchez and his men were innocent of all charges.

I scribbled for two hours; then there was a knock on the door. When I looked up, Martie whoever and David the wimp, my two favorite CID agents, were standing there.

"Could you spare a moment, Major?" Martie asked.

I decided to be politic. "Sure. Can I get you coffee?"

"No thanks," he said as the two of them entered and sank into the chairs across from my desk. "Just thought I should inform you that I've got two agents in your tent right now. I've got a military judge's order to search your personal possessions and to borrow your running shoes."

I gave him a hard stare. "And may I ask why?"

"Just some lingering concerns about a few notes Berkowitz left. Don't get all bothered, though. We're just borrowing your shoes to compare them with some molds back at the lab."

"But I shouldn't be concerned?"

"No. It's just standard procedure. We're collecting lots of molds. You never set foot in that latrine, right?"

"That's right," I said.

"Then you'll be cleared faster than you can say Jack the Ripper."

ONE thing you learn when you practice criminal law is that the moment a police officer tells you not to be concerned, start gnawing on your nails. Fortunately, or unfortunately, I didn't have time to worry. I kept writing my opus summary while I waited for Imelda to bring me some materials on Operation Phoenix.

She waltzed back in at quarter after eleven and dropped a bunch of printouts on my desk. She bent over and began writing on my yellow legal pad: "Found on Internet. To be safe, used supply-room terminal." Then she collected my stack of yellow pages for the clerks to type, and departed.

I grabbed the printouts she left behind and dug in. Operation Phoenix was a secret operation run jointly between the CIA and the Green Berets during the Vietnam War. It actually bypassed the military chain of command, and neither the Joint Chiefs nor General Westmoreland even knew it was happening.

It was a classic counterinsurgency operation, where the CIA penetrated a number of communist cells in South Vietnam; then the Special Forces did the nasty work of eliminating the suspects. Killed them without trial—just knocked off whoever the CIA told them to take out. The sterile euphemism they used was "sanctioned." The operation got exposed sometime in the early or mid-'70s.

I saw immediately why Bill Tingle wanted me to research this. Here was Jack Tretorne, a.k.a. Mr. Jones, masquerading as an NSA employee while he helped cover up a possible massacre committed by a Green Beret team. You couldn't escape the parallels.

I decided I needed to be cheered up. All morning I'd been working out a scheme, and I decided its time had come. I left the office and walked back over to the NSA facility. The guards passed me through to the inner sanctum. I pushed the doorbell and looked up and stuck out my tongue at the camera in the corner. Sometimes I wonder how I ever made major.

A moment later the door made that humming sound, and I pushed it open. Miss Smith was waiting. I gave her a shy grin and asked to see Mr. Jones. She led me back through the building, then down the stairs to the conference room. There were five men sitting around the table, with Jack Tretorne at the head. Aside from Tretorne, it looked like a nerds' convention. There were lots of thick bifocals and pocket penholders and short-sleeve white shirts. NSA employees, no doubt about it. They had that certain charisma.

Tretorne had on his duck-murdering vest again. He studied me. Then he looked around the table and said, "If you all can please excuse us for a few moments."

The nerds all got up and began filing out of the room. Finally it was just the three of us, and Miss Smith closed the door.

Tretorne got right to the point. "What do you want?"

I collapsed into a chair. "Remember yesterday when we looked at those films and you read those radio transcriptions? I'll need some kind of verification that all that was authentic."

"I can get you that," he said.

"That's great. One other thing. I'm gonna need your full name, Social Security number, and where you work at NSA."

"Why?"

"Well, since you wouldn't let me have the films or transcripts, I have to cite you as a material witness in my exhibit."

Tretorne's jaw, I noticed, became very tight. He leaned across the table and, in a tellingly reasonable tone, said, "Listen close, Drummond. I'm not going to be listed in your report. My job requires me to do sensitive work, and I cannot risk being exposed. Just use the name of the NSA chief, Lieutenant General Foster."

I grinned. "Hey, don't sweat it, Jonesy, old pal. My report's going to have 'Top Secret Special Category' stamped all over it. If it'll make you more comfortable, I'll list your name and employment data in a special annex that's eyes only to the Secretary of Defense and Chairman of the Joint Chiefs."

"No."

"Suit yourself," I said, getting up and preparing to leave.

"Where are you going?" Tretorne demanded.

"I'm going to call a military judge. I'm gonna tell him to write me a court order addressed to the director of the NSA that gives him six hours to release your name and job data."

"That wouldn't be a very good idea," Tretorne muttered.

"Why, Mr. Jones, you're not threatening me, are you? There is another way I can handle this. I'm pretty damned sure I can also talk that judge into issuing a writ against you and your agency for withholding evidence critical to a criminal investigation."

Tretorne was sputtering something when I closed the door behind me. I was sure he would immediately get on the phone to the lawyers back at the CIA to ask them if I could accomplish everything I'd just threatened. What he would eventually learn was that I could get the writ for his name, but no military judge can compel another government agency to hand over classified information. Regardless, it was going to be a while before he got this confirmed, and I wanted to see if I could force his hand.

I went back to the office and returned to working on my phony screed. At four o'clock I went back over to General Murphy's headquarters building and asked an eager-looking captain if he could find me a secure phone in a private room.

I called the Chinese take-out again and was put right through to Colonel Bill Tingle. We did the shift to secure mode thing; then Tingle said, "Found him. Tretorne's a GS-seventeen in Operations."

A GS-17 is like the equivalent civilian rank of someone between a two- and three-star general, and Operations is the half of the CIA that does fieldwork.

He added, "He's in charge of field operations for the Balkans. Career man, too. Not one of them political Pudleys."

I had no idea what a Pudley was, but that was the word Tingle commonly used to describe anyone he didn't like. Most often I'd heard him use it to describe lawyers.

I said, "Did you learn anything else about him?"

"He's got a good rep. Also, he went to West Point."

I said, "By the way, I read about Operation Phoenix."

"Don't believe the half of it. Believe the other half, though. That really happened."

I said, "Any chance that's what's going on here?"

"How do I know, Drummond? I'm here, and you're there."

"There must be some reason you wanted me to look it up."

"Look, son, I've been in the army since 1950. You have no idea how stupid we can be. One more thing. Think before you act, boy. Sometimes what looks bad is really good."

I WENT back to the office and exchanged my battle dress for the uniform onto which Imelda had sewn the new insignia. My new nametag and rank declared me to be Sergeant Hufnagel. Harold, I decided. I would be Sergeant Harold Hufnagel, although the tag had been borrowed from one of Imelda's girls.

I left and walked over to the supply room Imelda had staked out as her unofficial communications center. I asked if I could borrow the phone. The private on duty said sure. I called the 10th Group's information office. A sergeant named Jarvis answered.

I said, "Sergeant, this is Barry McCloud at the day desk of the Washington *Herald*. You got any of my reporters out there?"

"Right, sir," he very politely said. "Two to be exact."

"I'm trying to get hold of them. We had their numbers here, but the night shift misplaced them. Would you do me the kindness of telling me where they're staying?"

"Sure," he said. I heard him tapping computer keys. "Clyde Sterner's in room 201. You can reach him at 232-6440. Janice Warner's in room 106, same number, only put a three at the end."

"Great. Thanks," I said, then hung up.

Let's see, which one should I call? Sterner or Warner? I flipped a coin, and it came down heads. Clyde Sterner it was. Then I dialed the number for Janice Warner's room. Like I was going to call a Clyde over a Janice.

An intriguingly soft voice answered, "Janice Warner."

"Hi, Miss . . . Uh, is that Miss or Mrs. Warner?" I asked.

"It's Miss. What can I do for you?"

"Name's Sergeant Hufnagel. I knew Jeremy Berkowitz. He was a swell guy. Damn shame what happened."

"No, Jeremy was not a swell guy. He was rotten, but you're right about it being a shame. Is there some reason you called?"

"Yeah. I might know something about what got him killed."

"Then it sounds like you and I should get together."

"Yeah, I'd like to," I said, "but there's complications. We'd have to meet in secret. Meet me tonight. Nine o'clock, by the entrance of the mess hall. And come alone, or you'll never see me."

She said, "Okay. Oh, and Sergeant Hufnagel, I'll be armed. I'm a really good shot, too. Get my drift?"

"Yes, ma'am. Farthest thing from my mind."

There were two more hours before we were supposed to meet. For want of anything better to do, I returned to my hiding place across from the NSA building. I stood there and watched for over an hour, but there was no sign of Mr. Tretorne or Miss Smith.

I was just getting ready to call it quits when who should walk out of the entrance but General Murphy. Now, what would draw him to this facility? Maybe he was in there meeting with Tretorne. Maybe he was there picking up new lists of people to be sanctioned. Maybe I was on the list to be sanctioned.

But that would really be stupid. I mean, how would the army and CIA explain the murder of the chief investigating officer of the Kosovo massacre? Were they that stupid? Worse, were they that desperate? No, I decided. Right now they thought they had me right where they wanted me. Anyway, there was no more time to ponder those lofty questions, because it was time to go meet Janice.

I jogged and got there twenty minutes before nine. I found a spot about three buildings away, where I could safely observe. At nine o'clock exactly I saw a slender woman dressed in civilian attire stroll toward the entrance of the mess hall. Her hair looked long and black. She wore jeans with a short black leather jacket.

I walked to the corner of a building located about forty yards from the mess hall. "Miss Warner!" I yelled.

She glanced over, and I meandered slowly to the nearest street. She followed me. When she finally caught up, I started walking, and she fell in beside me. "Where are we going?" she asked.

"I thought we'd just walk," I said, inspecting her face for the first time. Sharp, perceptive eyes. Pronounced cheekbones. Wide lips. "This your first time at Tuzla?"

"Yes. This isn't my beat."

"What is your beat?" I asked.

"West European politics. Clyde Sterner and I have been thrown into the breach to cover what Berkowitz was working on."

"Do I take it you and Jeremy weren't friends?"

"Let's just say we had different philosophies on reporting. I don't believe in paying my sources. If that's your game, you've got the wrong reporter. Try Sterner. He's got an expense account."

"Actually, that's not what I'm asking for. I'd like the same deal I had with Berkowitz. We traded information."

She stopped walking. "Why would a sergeant be interested in information? Who do you work for, Hufnagel?"

I gave her a big broad smile. "Look, we're not at that point yet. Are you ready to talk the deal or not?"

She considered that a moment. "Okay, continue," she said.

"The way this works is you're going to give me a little information. Then I'm gonna give you a little information. Play me right, and I'll give you a story that stops hearts."

"All right, we'll try it," she said. "You give me one piece of information, and I'll give you one piece. Right?"

"Nope, you first," I insisted. "I happen to know that Berkowitz was onto something big. Why wasn't there any hint of that in his final story?"

"I'm not sure what you're talking about. Berkowitz was working several different story lines."

"Come on. Don't be cute. The Kosovo massacre."

She seemed genuinely bewildered. "He sent a dispatch back to the paper the night he died."

"That's right," I said. "But the next day's story was a puff piece."

She canted her head sideways. "I don't know what happened. Let me check with the paper on Berkowitz's last dispatch."

"Okay, you do that," I said. "But do it quickly. Now my turn. Berkowitz believed there was some kind of conspiracy here. I'm gonna give you a name. Jack Tretorne. Ever hear of him?"

She shook her head. "Can't say I have."

"He's a big muckety-muck with the CIA. He's here at Tuzla."

"And this has something to do with Berkowitz's murder?"

"It's related," I assured her.

"And what am I supposed to do?"

"Maybe shake the trees to find out a little more about Tretorne."

"That it?" she asked, eyeing me speculatively.

"For now, yes. I'll get hold of you again tomorrow. When I call, I'll say I'm Mike Jackson and your order is ready."

We were only a block from the reporters compound, so I left her there and headed back to my tent.

The only thing that confused me was that Janice Warner sounded clueless about the Kosovo massacre. Maybe Tretorne had succeeded in throwing her paper off track. Since Berkowitz never got his real dispatch filed, the *Herald* had no idea what he'd discovered.

When I got back to my tent, I noticed that my possessions had been rifled through. The CID guys had put everything back where they found it, but my running shoes were gone. Such are the terrific inconveniences I had to work with.

GENERAL Clapper called at two that night. I began to suspect something insidious in these late-night calls.

Clapper said, "I had a call from General Foster over at NSA. He's furious. He said you're making trouble for one of his employees, a Mr. Jones. What's this one about?"

I should have expected this. I said, "I'm just trying to get his name and section so I can refer to him in my report."

Clapper said, "You should be able to get by perfectly fine without them. General Foster offered to let us use his own name. Besides, if you're going to recommend against court-martial, it's irrelevant."

I said, "Sir, I'm the investigating officer. I don't do shoddy work. You can advise me on this, but you can't order me."

"You're already facing an inquiry into your professional conduct, Sean. Let's not make this any worse."

"Sorry, General, but I have to do what I think is right."

"Have it your way," he said before he hung up.

I hung up myself, then pushed the STOP button on the tape

recorder I'd turned on the moment he identified himself. I knew the editors at the Washington *Herald* would love listening to the tape, if things came to that. Besides, they—whoever they were—weren't playing fair with me. So why should I?

On that note, I slept soundly until I felt a rough hand shaking my shoulder. I blinked a few times, until I could squint and just make out vague shapes. The CID guy Martie whatever was hunched over beside my cot. Behind him were two military policemen.

"Please get dressed and come with me," Martie said.

I sat up. "Are you going to explain what this is about?" I asked. "Are you arresting me?"

"I'm taking you into custody."

I felt very groggy. I got dressed quickly, then staggered along behind Martie. A military policeman walked on each of my flanks.

The time was three in the morning, so the streets were still dark and empty. This seemed like a perfect pretense to perform one of those nasty "sanction" things on me. It wasn't until we got to the MP station that I relaxed. I shouldn't have, though.

"Sit down, please," Martie ordered once we were gathered around a table in an interview room. He read me my rights; then he asked, "Do you wish to retain counsel at this time?"

This is always the critical question. I had no idea what I was charged with. I had no idea if I was even going to be charged. I decided that a lawyer probably wasn't going to do me any more good than I could do for myself. I mean, I'm a lawyer, right?

I said, "Not at this time."

Martie looked at the two military policemen and nodded for them to leave. They closed the door behind them. Martie then spent a moment just staring at me. "You have a serious problem," he finally said. "Your running shoe matches a print we took from the latrine where Jeremy Berkowitz was murdered."

"That's impossible. I didn't go near the latrine that night."

"You don't expect me to believe that somebody borrowed your running shoes, murdered Berkowitz, then put them back?"

"I don't expect you to believe anything."

He leaned back and began playing with his pen. "There's more," he said. "Among the notes we found in Berkowitz's room was one where you asked him to meet you in the latrine at one o'clock."

My coolness suddenly dribbled away. I now knew I was in very serious trouble. The running-shoe prints could be challenged in a courtroom. The note, though—that was a slam dunk. Again I blurted out, "That's impossible."

"We've had two experts examine the handwriting. It's yours, Major. You're an attorney. Do I have to spell it out for you?"

No, he didn't have to spell it out for me. I was being framed.

I said, "Martie, I'm done talking without counsel."

He stared at me a few seconds, then stood up, walked over to the door, and knocked. The two MPs came back in, and he ordered them to book me and put me in a cell. They did.

In the cell, I collapsed onto the bunk. For thirty minutes I lay there thinking how terrifically stupid I'd been. Worse, I'd once again underestimated who I was dealing with.

I suddenly heard the sound of a lock being opened down the hall. Then footsteps. No lights were turned on, so the hallway and my cell remained dark. The footsteps stopped in front of the cell. I could smell the cologne. "Tretorne, you bastard," I said.

"You look good in there, Drummond," he said.

I said, "Yeah? Why don't you come on in and join me?"

He chuckled. "I knew it was you who burgled my room. You have no idea what that briefcase cost. And I really would like to get my passport and ID back."

"Let me out of here."

"I'm afraid it's no longer that easy."

"Sure it is, Jack. If I go to jail, I won't take my secrets with me."

"You don't have any secrets. You only think you do."

"Hah," I said. "I know all about what you and Murphy are up to. You frame me, and I'll get the word to every reporter I know."

"You think they'll listen to you? No one listens when an accused murderer starts mumbling about conspiracies."

He was right, of course. He moved back, and I saw him lean

against the wall. When he spoke again, he sounded suspiciously reasonable. "Regardless, I'm here to make a deal. Want to hear it?"

I said, "I've got nothing better to do for the moment."

"Okay. You do what you're supposed to do on this investigation, and we'll call this thing even. I'll even convince Clapper to cancel that inquiry, and you can get on with your career."

"And I'm supposed to just overlook this little thing you've got going with the Green Berets?"

"In a nutshell, yes."

"What about Berkowitz?"

"We didn't do Berkowitz's murder."

Now it was my turn to chuckle. "Horsecrap."

"It's the truth. I don't know who murdered him."

"But you're framing me for it."

"Sure. You've put us in a difficult corner. But if you're the leading suspect in a murder investigation, well, you can hardly remain the chief of the investigating team. Nor can you leak to the press like you tried with Berkowitz. Very cute, that."

So that confirmed it. My office was bugged.

I said, "Come on, Tretorne. What was it? Was Berkowitz getting too close? Why'd you have him killed?"

"I'll say it again. I don't know who killed Berkowitz. We didn't do it. However, his death gives me the opportunity to get you out of the way. I'm not proud of this, but I'm doing it for my country."

I almost guffawed. Instead, I said, "How'd you work the frame?"

"Easy, really. Everything today is electronic, even police lab work. You'd be surprised to know how easy it is to hack in and change the image of a shoeprint stored in a lab computer. These NSA people can do miracles."

"And the note they found in Berkowitz's room?"

"The right technology can also produce flawless forgeries."

I didn't say anything, so he added, "Look, Sean, don't force us to do this. I admire you. I really do. I know all about your time in the outfit. You did some very courageous things. But I can't let you damage your country. Don't make this personal."

Back when I was dancing with Sergeant Major Williams in the hard-sell interrogation room, every time he hit me, something nasty took control of my brain. I kept mouthing off at Williams, and he kept hitting me harder, doing more serious damage to my frail body. Now I was twelve years older, but was I twelve years wiser? All I had to do was give Tretorne what he wanted. I could get on with my life. I said, "Okay, Tretorne, I'll do it."

He pulled away from the wall and approached my cell. "Give me your word as an officer," he demanded. He was a West Pointer, so he'd been trained to believe that an officer's word was a sacred bond. It was kind of funny, really. He looked right past the irony of forcing me to swear I'd lie in an official report.

"You have my word," I said.

"Okay. In a few hours General Murphy will come in here and swear you were with him the night Berkowitz was murdered. That'll get you released. But you try to screw me, and I'll have you right back in this cell. There won't be any second chance, either."

Then I heard his footsteps echoing down the hallway again. I was lying, of course. The second I got out of here, I was going to do every damned thing I could to screw Tretorne and Murphy. These guys had framed me and blackmailed me, and I was mad enough to spit. Only I'd settle for a little revenge.

EIGHT

AT EIGHT o'clock they came to get me. I went back to my tent, showered, shaved, and put on a fresh uniform. Delbert and Morrow were both back when I walked into the office. Nobody knew I'd been arrested and released. At least nobody acted as if they knew.

I invited Delbert and Morrow into my private office. Then we spent an hour or so reviewing what they'd accomplished. The folks back at Bragg had told Delbert that a preemptive ambush wasn't exactly what they'd envisioned when they wrote their rules of engagement. However, the parameters certainly fit as long as the team was under genuine duress.

Morrow had built a lengthy, intricate, color-coded chronology of events. When we were done, they both stood up and started to leave. Morrow paused at the door and asked if she could speak to me. In private, she stressed. I nodded, and she shut the door and returned to her seat.

She looked deeply troubled. She said, "I'm having second thoughts. I no longer think they're innocent."

I shook my head. "You're kidding, right?"

She looked me dead in the eye. "No." She stood up and began pacing. "Look, I make my living dealing with guilty clients. Nine men don't remember events with the kind of coordinated accuracy I heard over the past two days. It's like they've been drilled."

I stared at her incredulously.

She stopped pacing. "There's a clincher, too. Every man now knows exactly how many flares went off. Both before and after they were detected. I couldn't find a single point of disagreement."

This really was ironic. Here I'd suspected Sanchez and his men because they'd walked all over one another on the details, and now Morrow thought them guilty because their stories were so mysteriously identical.

That's when it hit me. Morrow was the mole. Tretorne had put her up to coming in here with this last-minute change of heart just to flush me out and see if I was going to keep our Faustian pact.

Well, I knew how to handle this. I said, "Look, Morrow, you can't do this. It's . . . Well, it's too late."

She wheeled around, and her eyes got kind of pointy and narrow. "It's not too late until the packet's signed."

I tried my damnedest not to smile. She was such a charming schemer, but I now had her number. "And how are you going to explain it?" I asked derisively. "You gonna vote for court-martial on the basis of your sixth sense? Or are you gonna try to explain that the witnesses were too good to be believed?"

"I'll vote whatever my conscience tells me. I've got two more days to decide, and I will not be pressured."

"Hey," I said, "I'm just trying to save you from embarrassing yourself. Delbert and I believe they're innocent. I'm totally convinced of it. In fact, they're heroes."

She scrutinized my face, and I guessed she was trying to decide if I was being genuine. Finally she pounced angrily from the room.

I, on the other hand, now had a vital phone call to make. I returned to my tent, put on my Hufnagel disguise, then went back to the supply room. The same private was there. I asked him if I could use the phone again; then I dialed Janice Warner's number.

"Hello," she answered.

"Hi, Mike Jackson here," I said, employing my password.

"Oh, you," she replied. "Is my delivery ready?"

"Yeah. Can you come pick it up in fifteen minutes?"

"All right," she said. "I'll be right there."

I then positioned myself midway between the mess hall and the visiting journalists quarters. After about five minutes I saw her heading my way, and I walked out and intercepted her. I took her arm, and we started walking through the streets again.

She wore khaki trousers, a blue button-down shirt, and the same black leather jacket. Her eyes, I now noticed, were nearly black, like her hair. And she had these thinly arched eyebrows, like curved scimitars. Very alluring.

"So did you get hold of your home office?" I asked.

"I did. They have no idea what you're talking about. Berkowitz never mentioned anything about a breakthrough in his dispatch."

"That's curious. He went off like a whirling dervish the last time we spoke. I can't believe he wasn't gonna write about it."

"I also did some checking on Jack Tretorne. Our reporter who covers the Agency knows him. He's in charge of the Balkans. He's even got a nickname. Jack of Serbia. He's been working Serbian affairs since 1990. He's got a great reputation. They say he's the behind-the-scenes mastermind on nearly everything."

"Makes you wonder why he's here, huh?" I asked.

She said, "Why wouldn't he be here? There's a war raging just across the border. In fact, if he wasn't here, I might wonder."

I got this sense she was losing patience with me. I said, "So you're telling me nobody heard Berkowitz mention anything interesting about this investigation?"

"No. But then, the Kosovo massacre wasn't really the main attraction that brought him here. Look, Sergeant Stupnagel, I have to admit that I'm having a little trouble taking you seriously."

"Like I told you, my name's Hufnagel."

She said, "Well, that's part of our problem here. I had the information office run down your name. There's only one Hufnagel in Tuzla. She's a legal specialist. Who are you?"

My first impulse was to lie again. But why not tell her who I really was? It wasn't like I could get in any deeper trouble than I was already in. "Okay, I'm Major Sean Drummond. I'm the chief investigating officer for the Kosovo massacre."

She looked at me curiously. "Why this masquerade?"

"Because I believe Berkowitz's murder was somehow connected to my investigation."

"And you wanted me to fill in some blanks for you?"

"Actually, yes. That's exactly what I wanted."

She seemed very disappointed in me. Those scimitar-like eyebrows sliced downward in a deeply disapproving frown. "And you have no solid information about Berkowitz's murder? Do you?"

"I can tell you he was murdered by a pro. I can tell you it had something to do with the story he was covering. And I'll repeat, I believe it was connected to my investigation."

She said, "All right. I just don't think I can help you. If we had any idea what got Berkowitz murdered, you'd be reading about it on the front page of the *Herald*. He was covering your investigation. And he was doing the occasional routine piece on the operation in Kosovo. We just don't see any angles there that got him killed."

"Was there anything else?" I asked.

"Well, he was also running some silly investigation on neo-Nazis and white supremacists in the army. It was a personal passion of his.

A crazy thing he'd been working on for years. Berkowitz was Jewish, you know. His grandparents died in the Nazi death camps."

"What kind of investigation?" I asked.

"This time he was following a trail he had picked up at Fort Bragg. Some group of soldiers helping train a bunch of hicks to blow up and burn synagogues and black churches."

"And that's why he was here?"

"According to his editor, it's one of the things he was checking on. Remember that string of church arsons about a year back? Berkowitz thought the man behind it might be here."

My mind suddenly got very busy. It would be an incredible coincidence, but fate owed me a break. Sergeant Major Williams was an expert with a garrote, since all of us in the outfit were taught how to use that ghoulish thing. He'd been thrown out of the outfit for mucking around with a bunch of backwoods racists. And he had a bent toward cruelty. I could testify to that.

Then one more piece of the puzzle suddenly went *kerplunk!* Maybe this was how Berkowitz knew about the existence of the outfit. Maybe he had a source somewhere who told him about Williams, and maybe that same source put him onto me. My thoughts were interrupted by Janice Warner, who grabbed my arm. "Do you know something about this?"

I summoned every ounce of innocence I could. "No. Probably just some crazy idea Berkowitz had that didn't pan out."

She looked disappointed. As much as I didn't want to arouse her suspicions, I glanced down at my watch and said, "Geez, look what time it is! Listen, I've got to take another interrogatory. Why don't I give you a call if I find something."

She was no dummy. Her eyes got narrower. "Yeah, why don't you do that," she said as I dashed away.

I really couldn't tell her about my old buddy Sergeant Major Williams. She was a reporter, and all I had was a suspicion. Besides, I had other plans for my newest revelation. The neat box Tretorne and Murphy had built around me had suddenly developed a fatal flaw. They'd lose all their leverage over me if I could prove Williams murdered Berkowitz. I rather looked forward to that. I'd rewrite my investigation summary and blow them all to pieces.

LISA Morrow was still in a sulky funk when I got back to the office. Give the girl credit. She was very tenacious.

I drafted a note to Sergeant Major Williams, then asked Imelda to please have one of her aides deliver it to him in the ops center. Then I went back to the MP station. Martie and David had been given a conference room in the rear, right next to Captain Wolkowitz's office.

I knocked, and someone called for me to come in. All three of them—Martie, David, and Wolky—were seated at a conference table. About two dozen empty white foam coffee cups were strewn around, and both Martie and David had loosened their ties.

I said, "Hi, guys," and gave them my cheeriest smile. At least somebody here was getting less sleep than I was. "Any new suspects?"

"We're making headway," Martie said.

I fell into a chair. "Oh, good," I said. "Then I won't waste your time by telling you who the killer is."

Wolky was the first to recover and open his mouth. "Is this some kind of a joke, Major?"

"Actually, no. Did you ever get around to asking the *Herald* what stories Berkowitz was working on?"

"Of course," Martie said. "All they said, though, was that he was writing about the Kosovo operation. We knew your investigation was also one of his subjects, because of the article he wrote."

"Well, turns out he was working on a third story, too. He was trying to uncover some neo-Nazi white supremacist ring."

All three of them were now bent forward.

I added, "It seems a source told Berkowitz that a soldier stationed here might have been implicated in the black church burnings that happened about a year back."

Martie said, "How do you know this?"

"I have my sources, too."

Martie turned to Wolky. "You aware of any white supremacist activity here?"

Wolky shrugged his big shoulders and said, "Nope."

This was no surprise, because Tuzla was a temporary operational base. Units floated in and out on a rotational basis, and their troublemakers passed in and out with them. Still, I was glad Martie asked. Now they knew they needed me.

I said, "Are you ready to hear my deal?"

"Deal? What do you mean, deal?" David asked.

I leaned back in my chair. "Well, for various reasons your chief suspect is going to require special handling. You can make the arrest. You will then lock him up in a quarantined cell, and nobody will be allowed to go near him. Someone will be here within a day to take him into custody. He'll be whisked out of here, and your relationship with this case will be over. You'll forget all about it."

All three of them were looking at me like I was nuts.

Martie said, "I never heard anything so weird."

I said, "Take it or leave it. If you can't live with it, I'll get someone else to handle it."

"What's so special about this guy?" Wolky asked.

"I'm sorry, Wolky. I can't tell you."

"Who's gonna take him into custody?"

"Guys in dark suits. They'll have special orders signed by the Secretary of Defense. That's all you need to know."

You see, the truth was that the real reason Clapper had once been so agreeable about sending me to law school was because it solved a delicate problem for the army. The outfit was only one of several "black units" on the army's rolls. Altogether there are several thousand secret warriors roaming around out there. As you might imagine, that kind of duty attracts some real rogues. When they did a crime and were apprehended, your standard-fare open court-martial would have exposed not only them but also the existence of their units. The army's answer to this ticklish conundrum was to convene a permanent "black court," located at a tiny secret base in northern Virginia. There was even a special "black review court" to handle appeals. That, of course, was my unit, where I worked until I was yanked out to conduct this investigation.

Sergeant Major Williams was going to have to be tried by us.

It did not take Martie and David and Wolky long to realize their hands were tied. In the end, they caved in.

Only we now had to prove Williams did it. I explained as much about Sergeant Major Williams as they needed to know and nothing more. I asked Martie to call the lab in Heidelberg and have them immediately transmit the largest shoeprint that had been collected at the crime scene. Williams was big, about six feet three, and oddly enough, I had once spent about two weeks staring at his feet. One of his interrogation techniques was to order me to keep my eyes focused on the floor, like a repentant monk. I remembered that he had very big feet.

The shoeprint came across the wire. The size was thirteen double E. It was an Adidas running shoe. Martie told me there was a reporter from the Los Angeles *Times* staying at the visiting journalists quarters the night of the murder who also wore size thirteen shoes, and they had all assumed this was his shoeprint. They had wired the LAPD and asked for background on the reporter. They were still awaiting a response.

I told him to get on the phone and ask the jurisdictional military judge to issue us a search order to get into Sergeant Major Williams's room so we could get a pair of his shoes.

This led naturally to trying to figure out how Williams knew that Berkowitz was onto him. I turned to David. "Find out if Williams was on duty at the ops center that night."

David ran out, then returned. "He was on day shift," he said a little breathlessly. "He was in the ops center from six in the morning till six at night."

So he was off-duty when Berkowitz was murdered. That much fit. There was a knock at the door; then an MP entered carrying a pair of real big running shoes. Thirteen double E's. They looked brand-new. We all nodded sagely. Now we were getting somewhere.

How would Berkowitz have learned where Williams worked? I wondered. I went to the phone and called the information office. That same friendly sergeant named Jarvis answered again.

I said, "Hey, Sergeant Jarvis. Major Sean Drummond here. Who handles press inquiries in your office?"

"They come to me first, sir."

"Do you remember if Jeremy Berkowitz asked you to track anyone down?"

"Just a second. I keep a record of every request. It's SOP here." I heard Jarvis tapping his computer keys. Then, "Yeah, I've got the list. Uh, let's see. . . . Major Sean Drummond. Captain Dean Walters. Sergeant Major Luther Williams—"

"Stop there," I said. "Did you tell Berkowitz how to get hold of Williams?"

"I did. But he asked me to get hold of him and have Williams call him back. I've got it all logged right here. Let's see. . . . I called the sergeant major at 1030 hours on the morning of the second."

"Very good. Now, I'd like you to put a copy of that file you're reading on a disk and bring it down to the MP station."

He said, "Be right there. Only take ten minutes."

We finally had a motive, and the makings of a very good circumstantial case. What we didn't have was tangible proof. And time to build a better case.

It was nearly noon. I turned to Martie. "I need you to provide me a wire, and I need you to call your judge and get me permission to tape a conversation with Williams. You've got proximate cause."

He called the judge, and it took about ten minutes before the judge wrote out an order.

The note I had earlier sent to Williams asked him to meet me at 1230 hours at my office. I'd also told Imelda to make sure everyone was gone and that the building was empty.

I asked Wolky to position a few of his best MPs in the nearby vicinity, without their identifying brassards, just in case Williams got violent. I then returned to my office to meet him.

Imelda had done her job, and the building was empty. She'd also brewed me a fresh pot of coffee. I love that woman.

Sergeant Major Williams swaggered in two minutes late. I went out to meet him, offered him some coffee. He nodded, and I went over and poured us each a cup. He followed me back into the office and sat in a chair across from my desk.

"So what you doin'?" he asked, grinning. He had a cocky manner anyway, but in my case, since he'd once spent two weeks pounding me like Silly Putty, he felt a bit superior.

I said, "I'm leaving tomorrow. My investigation's complete, so I gave the rest of my staff the day off. Us being old comrades, I just thought you and I should get together."

He looked at me curiously and took a sip of coffee.

"Ever get to thinking about the outfit days?" I asked.

"Sure do. Great days. We did some wild-assed stuff."

"Sure did, didn't we? If it wasn't for getting accepted to law school, I'd probably still . . . So why exactly did you leave?"

"Ah, y'know, you get burned out."

I said, "That's funny. I heard different. I heard you got in some kinda trouble back there."

He became noticeably tighter. "Yeah? Where'd you hear that?"

"Here and there. Something about you working with a bunch of bigots down in North Carolina."

I had his undivided attention. He was staring at me hard. "You must be listenin' to the wrong people," he said.

"Did you know the outfit tapped all of our phones?"

"Uh-huh," he said. "But that was a long time ago."

I took a sip from my coffee, and he took a sip from his coffee. He knew now this was no idle chat.

"Hey," I said, "ever meet that reporter who got murdered? What's his name? Jeremy Berkowitz."

His eyes were now very narrow. "Can't say I ever did."

"That's odd. I met with him the day he got killed. In the morning. He told me he was gonna see you around lunchtime," I lied.

"Well, he never told me. I never heard of him till he was dead."

"Well, there's this sergeant who works for the information officer. He says he helped line up a meeting between you two."

"He must be lying," Williams growled.

"Actually, he's got an official log to prove it. Oh, and another thing. CID lifted the footprints of whoever killed Berkowitz. He wore running shoes so he could sneak up behind him. You know, we're talking about a real gutless coward. Never gave Berkowitz a fair chance. Same kind of low-life scum who'd burn a church." I added, "Killer used a garrote, too. Back in the outfit we always figured that was a real sicko's weapon. You know, like something maybe an angry faggot might use. Or maybe a sexual deviant. I mean, what kind of guy you figure would kill a man that way?"

"I never thought about it." His knuckles were very white.

"Another thing. From the footprints, turned out the murderer was some big goofy bastard with splayed feet. Size thirteen double E. You've got big wide feet. I didn't mention it to CID yet, but I remember staring at 'em all the time while you were beating the crap out of me. What size you figure you wear?"

"I never went near that latrine," he said.

I said, "Hey, you know, after you left Bragg, that rash of child molesting that had been happening in the housing area stopped."

He was now glaring at me with a very nasty scowl. One thing I'd learned about him in the hard sell was that he'd get real touchy when it came to sexual perversions. He'd be slapping me around, and I tried calling him all kinds of names. Wasn't long before I learned that faggots or variants thereof really hit his funny bone.

He said in this very menacing tone, "I don't have to sit here and listen to you."

I stared at him hard. "Yeah, you do. I'm a major now, and you're a noncommissioned officer, and I'm ordering you to stay right where you are. Besides, you leave here, and I'll walk right over to CID and tell 'em what I suspect about you."

A murderous look crept into his eyes.

"Anyway," I continued, "only reason I haven't mentioned anything yet to CID was because I wanted to be sure. But I got to thinking about your feet, and what Sergeant Jarvis told me, and why you were thrown out of the outfit, and the cowardly way Berkowitz was killed, and it all kinda makes sense."

I knew the signs. Because he always wore a mask when he was

kicking the crap out of me back at Bragg, I got to know his eyes real well. Right at that moment they were scrunched with a calculating shrewdness because he now knew I was the only man on this base who could put all that together.

"Know what else, Williams?" I chuckled. "I think you probably screwed Berkowitz before you killed him."

He leaped out of his chair and came across the desk. I saw the punch, but I couldn't dodge it. Williams hadn't lost his touch, either. I went flying backward, right over my chair, and ended up sprawled on the floor, hearing a loud ringing in my ears.

He shoved the desk aside and came after me. He lifted me right off the ground by my collar. I'd forgotten how incredibly strong he was when he got mad. He threw me across the room, and I bounced off a wall. Then he ran over and jerked me up by the hair and started punching my head back and forth while I screamed, "You pervert! You sick bastard."

He was now completely out of control. He pulled my face right up to his and hissed, "I didn't screw him. I used that garrote so I didn't have to touch the filthy Jewboy."

He threw me across the room and sent me crashing into another wall. I felt something snap, maybe a rib. Everything hurt.

He moved across the room for me. "We're all alone here, Drummond. I'm gonna kill you, and I'm gonna make it hurt."

He made only one mistake. His feet were spread apart when he bent over to jerk me up again. I aimed and felt the wonderfully satisfying sensation of my left heel burying itself in his groin. He doubled over completely, incapacitated by the pain.

I am not one to kick a man when he's down. However, I was bent on revenge. I got to my feet, and my left knee came straight up and ended up in Williams's face. Crunch. I heard his nose break. My right hand flew into his solar plexus. That blow doubled him over again. Then my right knee came up, and there was another snap, only this time it was Williams's jaw, or maybe a few teeth.

The door flew open. Three big MPs came diving through the air and jumped on Williams. That's about the point where I stopped paying attention. When you're in your twenties, you can take a beating like the one he'd just inflicted on me. When you're thirty-nine, you feel like a steamroller just mashed you into the road. I slumped to the floor and lapsed into a remarkably deep trench of self-pity.

THE doctor spent two hours inspecting and repairing the carnage Williams had administered to my body. There were two fractured ribs, not one. And I now sported eighteen stitches, about evenly divided between three different gashes.

While the doctor taped and sewed and X-rayed, I spent the entire time thinking about how I was going to handle Tretorne, Murphy, and Clapper. I couldn't afford to underestimate them again. They weren't as dangerous as I had thought, since they hadn't murdered Berkowitz, but framing and blackmail and obstructing justice weren't likely to get them on anybody's list for sainthood, either.

The first thing I did when the doc released me was make a call to that little base in Arlington, Virginia. I talked to that special judge they had there. I explained everything we had on Williams and told him we needed a team dispatched to collect our prisoner. The judge said they'd have someone here within ten hours. Then I made sure Williams was locked away in a cell.

I went to Imelda's tent, instructed her on what we were going to do, and we walked together back to our office building. It took nearly three hours before we were done making our preparations.

I left her there and walked over to the NSA facility. Miss Smith greeted me and led me down the stairs to the conference room. Tretorne and General Murphy were seated together. Tretorne, I noticed, wasn't wearing his duck-murdering vest. In fact, he looked quite natty in a tailored dark blue serge suit and a starched white shirt with French cuffs. A pair of big presidential cuff links were poking out of his sleeves, where they were meant to show.

Murphy said, "What do you want, Major?"

I said, "A little wrinkle has developed in your plan, guys. CID just arrested Berkowitz's real killer."

Tretorne did not look happy to hear this. He toyed with one of those cuff links, then looked up. "It's irrelevant, Drummond. You gave your word. There were no conditions."

"You're right," I said. "No conditions. Just like when I took my oath to become an officer. No conditions then, either. Or when I took my oath to become an officer of the court. That's two unconditional oaths to one. You lose."

Tretorne said, "Don't do this, Drummond. Force my hand, and I'll just come up with something else. You can't win."

I said, "I've just written a long statement that exposes everything. Both of you are mentioned prominently. So is Clapper. If I don't make a call in forty minutes, that statement will be in the hands of the *Herald,* the *Post,* the *Times,* and *Newsweek.*"

Tretorne shook his head. "You have no idea what you're doing, how serious this is, what's at stake."

"But I do," I assured him. "You and your big buddy here are assassinating Serbs, and it don't get much more serious than that."

The two of them looked at each other in shock.

"Sit down. Please," Tretorne said.

He waited till I was seated and comfortable, then asked, "What do you *think's* going on here? What we're doing."

I said, "I *know* what you're doing. You're using Green Berets to murder Serbs. Sort of a modern version of Operation Phoenix. 'Sanction' was the euphemism then, wasn't it?"

"You're wrong," Murphy said. "Dead wrong. To start with, Operation Phoenix was the result of an informal handshake between the Special Forces and the CIA. It was done without official knowledge or permission. This operation is fully approved by the President. It's also known within a select committee of Congress. Also, we're not assassinating Serbs."

I said, "Sorry, I'm not buying it."

Murphy studied me for a moment, then said, "Please step out of the room. Just for a moment. Jack and I need to speak."

I didn't like it, but I did it. I mean, what the hell, I had nothing to lose. Imelda and all four of her assistants were positioned at various locations around Tuzla, each poised over a fax machine, each ready to push a button. Each had a sealed envelope in her hand that contained a copy of the statement I'd written earlier. In less than forty minutes the cat would leap out of the bag. There was nothing Tretorne or Murphy or NSA could do to stop it.

About five minutes passed. When the conference-room door opened, Murphy waved his hand for me to reenter. I walked back in and took the same seat.

Murphy said, "We are going to clear you for this operation."

I said, "Don't think I'm falling for that. I'm not taking any vows of secrecy."

Murphy nodded at Tretorne, and I had the impression they'd guessed I'd say that. Then Tretorne said, "What's happening here is we're losing a war. We're losing because it's a NATO operation and the President has his hands tied. Our allies are dead set against ground forces. All we're allowed to do is bomb."

Like a member of a tag team, Murphy said, "You can't win a war with bombs. That's why we came up with the idea of building the KLA. We hoped to use them as our ground element, only they've been a terrible disappointment. Six or seven KLA units have done good work, but the rest are completely outmatched."

"That's not a justification," I said. "Assassination's illegal."

"We're not assassinating anyone," Tretorne said, sounding tired. "Guardian Angel is a ruse for an operation we call Avenging Angel. Some of the Special Forces teams we're sending into Kosovo with the KLA are selectively performing the missions their KLA units are supposed to be doing."

"What kind of missions?" I asked.

"Raids, ambushes, interdicting supply lines. Several times we've learned the Serbs were planning another massacre, and we had the SF teams go in and free the Kosovar prisoners. We're very careful, believe me. No assassinations, no vigilante stuff."

"Then what happened with Sanchez's team?"

They exchanged more looks. Then Murphy said, "We don't know. The KLA company they were with, Akhan's team, all of them were killed. We're still not certain how it happened."

"But Sanchez's team wasn't detected by the Serbs, was it? And they weren't responding in self-defense, right?"

Tretorne said, "We have no way of knowing. The satellite tapes and transcripts we showed you were forgeries. Our real images for those days showed no unusual activity for Sanchez's team. We've got nothing that shows them being detected or chased."

"Then why—"

"We couldn't allow Avenging Angel to be exposed," Murphy said.

Tretorne was drumming a finger on the table. "When Sanchez's team extricated, they didn't report anything about the ambush. We didn't learn of it until three days later when Milosevic started holding press conferences."

"So you arrested Sanchez's team?"

"Right," Murphy said. "And they gave us the story about being detected and chased. Jack had NSA check their files, and there was nothing that substantiated their story. Nothing contradicted it either, though."

"Then why was I brought in?"

"The massacre suddenly had international attention. We all felt that the easiest solution for all concerned was to conduct a genuine investigation. Sanchez's team was sticking with their story, and we were ordered to make it a more convincing tale."

"And where was this decided?" I asked.

Tretorne didn't answer, at least verbally. He simply held up a hand and pointed at his cuff link.

With as much disdain as I could, I said, "So you cooked up a deal with Sanchez and his men. They work with you on the cover-up, and they walk away scot-free."

Murphy did not appear the least bit ashamed to admit it. "That's right," he said. "Except you're forgetting one thing. We have no proof they're guilty. Maybe it happened exactly the way they said."

"Really?" I said. "I went to the morgue. I saw the Serb corpses. How do you explain the holes in their heads?"

Tretorne stopped tapping the table. "Please believe me—we didn't know about that until you reported it to Clapper."

"But you kept right on with the cover-up."

"We had our reasons," Murphy said. "But we're prepared to make a deal with you now."

I looked down at my watch. In another twenty-seven minutes Imelda and her crew were going to unleash an army of hungry reporters on these two. They'd probably guessed what I had in store for them. I chuckled and shook my head. "I'm listening."

Murphy said, "We're willing to let you complete your investigation. We won't hinder you in any way. No more games. We'll tell you everything we know, and you see if you can find the truth."

I said, "How kind of you."

Tretorne ignored my sarcasm. "There're only two conditions."

"And what are those?" I snarled.

"Hold off on going to the press. And when you're done, come back and talk with us. After we talk, if you want to go public, that'll be your option. We won't try to stop you."

"No more phone taps? No more bugs in my office?"

Tretorne grinned. "Done."

"Oh, and your mole goes. Morrow climbs on the next plane."

Tretorne's grin became a smile. "She's not working for us."

I cocked my head a little, and he actually chuckled.

"Delbert?" I asked.

"Floyd Collins, actually. Floyd's a real army lawyer, too, although his trial record nowhere near matches the one you were provided."

Sometimes you just outsmart yourself. I had thought Delbert—or Floyd—had just seemed too obvious to be the mole.

"Okay. He goes," I said.

"Done," Tretorne said.

"And I'll have to tell Morrow what's going on."

"Okay."

I got up and started to leave. I made it to the door before Murphy said, "One more thing, Major."

I turned and faced him. He was staring up at me. He said, "Sometimes those principles they teach at West Point about duty and honor and country—sometimes they clash against one another.

Sometimes you have to decide which of those three is most important, which principle you need to sacrifice."

I stared back at him. "I didn't go to West Point, so I don't know about all that. I'll tell you what I do know. I know what makes us different from the Serbs. We don't coddle our murderers. We don't lie to the world when our troops commit a massacre. We wash our laundry in the open. That's duty and honor and country, all in one."

He shook his head in a condescending way, like I just didn't get it. Only he was wrong. He was the one who didn't get it. At least that's what I thought.

NINE

A GOOD night's sleep did a lot for my disposition, but I couldn't say the same for my body. My bruises and broken ribs sort of calcified, and the pain seeped down through another few layers of tissue. I awoke feeling terrifically stiff and sore.

Delbert was gone when I walked into the office. He left a note in my message box. It read, "Sorry," and it was signed, "Floyd G. Collins, Captain, JAG."

Morrow was back at her desk, rabidly scribbling something in longhand. She coldly ignored me as I walked by. I went to the coffee urn and began making a cup. She kept right on giving me the bone-chilling indifference routine.

I walked over and irritatingly peered across her shoulder at what she was doing. She kept writing. I finally said, "Guess you don't want to know what happened to Delbert. Why he isn't with us anymore. Or how I got us a five-day extension."

Then I turned and walked back into my office, closing the door behind me. I stared at my watch. Thirty-six seconds passed before she knocked. I told her to come in and have a seat, then spent thirty minutes explaining what had really been going on around here.

That gorgeous face of hers traveled through a range of emotions from surprise to hostility, then indignation, then eventually full circle right back to curiosity again.

"Why didn't you tell me about all this?" she asked. "You thought I was Tretorne's stooge, didn't you?"

I winced. "I wasn't sure. Besides, what does it matter? We have a green light now."

This was an awful lot of disturbing news to learn in a few minutes. She was mad as hell—at them and at me for not trusting her. But she was also a lawyer and thus was trained to keep her emotions in tight rein. "Why don't we just hold a press conference and blow the whistle?" she finally asked.

The truth was, there was no good answer to that. If we were smart, that's exactly what we'd do.

I said, "We always have that option. Anyway, aren't you curious? Don't you want to know if Sanchez and his men did it?"

"I guess," she said, sounding as if she really didn't.

"Well then, that settles it," I quickly announced before she could change her mind. Or I could change my mind.

I walked to the door and called Imelda. She came steaming in, and I said, "We've got five more days. Get us a flight to Aviano for this afternoon. Also, call Lieutenant Colonel Smothers's office and tell him Captain Morrow and I will be there in an hour."

"Got it," she said.

After packing our bags and loading up several boxes with documents, Morrow and I went to see Lieutenant Colonel Will Smothers, Sanchez's battalion commander. He had his lawyer there, the same Captain Smith who had filed a complaint against me.

I looked at Smothers. "No need for him," I said, pointing a digit in Smith's direction.

Smith's face showed his outraged surprise. "I'm gonna call the jurisdictional judge again," he threatened.

"Do that!" I barked. "And tell him I'll cite him, and you as well, as an accomplice in an obstruction of justice charge if he makes a move against me."

Smith quickly got up and departed the office.

I gave Smothers an only slightly milder version of my I'd-also-like-to-rip-your-guts-out look. "Party's over, Colonel. Lie or mislead us once, and I'll indict you as a co-conspirator to murder. Got it?"

He nodded.

"Okay. Let's go back to the beginning. Tell me about your role in this Operation Avenging Angel."

He looked over at Morrow, and she somehow managed to hide those sympathetic eyes. In fact, she looked positively fierce.

"Okay," he said. "My battalion, the First Battalion, we're the avenging angels. I've got one or two teams in every zone. We do the dirty work."

"Why just your battalion?" Morrow asked.

"Because we obviously can't afford any mistakes in this thing, and my teams are the most experienced."

"Tell us about Sanchez," I demanded.

Smothers looked at me. "I probably made a mistake. Terry's a good guy, and he needed the job to get promoted. I thought that if I gave him the strongest team in the battalion, things would work out. Persico's probably the best warrant in all of Tenth Group."

"And Sanchez's performance since then?"

"I guess I'd have to say that on good days he's fairly mediocre. Not for lack of trying, though."

"So it's a matter of talent?"

"Some guys just do it naturally. Terry has to work at it every minute. Guys like that run scared, and his people smell it."

Morrow said, "When Akhan's team were killed, what happened?"

Smothers became very focused. "That happened on the four-teenth. In the morning, I think. Sanchez called on the radio some-time around noon. All he said was Whiskey 66—that was Akhan's call sign—was at black. You understand that?" he asked.

Morrow shook her head.

"It's a color code we use to describe unit strengths. Green means the unit's at one hundred percent. Red is fifty percent. Black is zero percent. Some of our KLA units have gotten shot up pretty bad, but we've never had a whole company, ninety-five men, go from green to black in only a few hours."

"Did he explain what happened?" Morrow asked.

"Only that they were performing an operation. But that bothered us because we hadn't approved an operation for Akhan's team."

"According to the statement Sanchez gave us, they were attacking a police station in a town named Piluca," I said.

"Well, that's what he said. We had a problem with that, though. Piluca wasn't on our approved target list—"

"Excuse me," I interrupted. "What approved target list?"

"We get a list of what to hit. It's screened all the way up the line to the Joint Staff in the Pentagon. No targets of opportunity are permitted in Avenging Angel. Everything's run tight, you know?"

I guess I did know. If the Avenging Angels made a mistake, like the air force hitting the Chinese embassy, the ensuing furor would blow the lid right off their secret war.

"Okay," I said. "Then what?"

"I ordered him to extricate."

"General Murphy told us he was ordered to stay in place."

"That's not right. We considered it, but I was worried."

"What specifically worried you?" Morrow asked.

"Sanchez, I guess. Every time one of our teams trains a KLA company, you get this big brother mentality. They're just so damned helpless and needy and eager. American soldiers can't resist it."

"So you were worried Sanchez couldn't control the situation?"

"Two of our other A Teams had their Kosovars get beat up pretty good, and we actually had to stand them down and let the group psychiatrist and chaplain help them sort through it. Yeah, I guess I was worried that Terry couldn't do it."

"But Sanchez and his team, they didn't extricate?" I asked.

"No. Not when I told them to. For two days they kept reporting heavy Serb activity in their sector. Sanchez said he felt it was too risky to move south."

"And how did you respond to that?"

"What could I do? He was the guy on the ground. I did ask the

NSA station here to increase surveillance over Zone Three. They put a thermal up for an hour or two each day. The films showed Sanchez's team in their base camp, but there were no signs of unusual Serb activity. Basically, though, we had to believe him."

I said, "So his team finally extricated four days later?"

"Right. But you had to figure it would've taken nearly two days to make it out on foot. So there were only two days unaccounted for."

"When they got back, did they report the ambush?"

"No," Smothers said, and you could hear a note of anger in his voice. "They never mentioned it."

I said, "Then three days later Milosevic started holding his press conferences, and what did you do?"

"I went to General Murphy. I told him I thought Sanchez's team might've done it."

Morrow said, "Back to what happened to Akhan and his unit. Did Sanchez and his men clarify what occurred?"

"They all said Akhan made the decision to attack the station himself. They couldn't stop him. Zone Three was where most of Akhan's men lived. The commander of Piluca's police station supposedly murdered or tortured some of their family members."

I said, "Have one of your people run a copy of the debriefing notes over to my office as soon as we're done."

"Okay."

"Doesn't it feel better to tell the truth?" I asked.

"No, not really," Smothers said. "None of us liked lying to you. But we believe in what we're doing out here."

Well, so much for truth and justice being the American way. We left him there and headed to the airfield, where a C-130 was already revved up and waiting.

In Aviano we pulled up to the marble entrance of the same hotel on the hill. Morrow and I got side-by-side rooms, stowed our gear, then went back downstairs to the lobby.

Imelda and two of her girls took rooms a floor below us and rented a full suite to use for our office. When Morrow and I got outside to take the van to the air base, Imelda and her assistants were still lugging computers and boxes of paper up the entry stairs.

It took fifteen minutes to get to the air force holding facility. The same pudgy air force major was there to greet us. He was real deferential and courteous, but I treated him coldly, and Morrow followed my lead. Let him sweat.

Morrow and I had spent a lot of time considering our next move. Our first inclination was to start the reinterrogation with Sanchez. We needed one of the nine to break, and he was the team member carrying the most baggage. But the more we talked about it, the more we persuaded ourselves that Sanchez probably wasn't the right man. He was ultimately responsible for whatever went wrong out there and therefore had the most to lose. It is a prosecutor's maxim: Most to lose very often equals last to confess.

It was Morrow's notion to bring in Persico first. In every organization there's the leader appointed by the system—that was Sanchez. Then there's the leader appointed by the men themselves—that was Persico. Get him to talk, and the rest would follow.

But there was another reason, too. At some point while in Kosovo the formal chain of command in Sanchez's team simply disintegrated. Quite possibly there'd been a mutiny. I was guessing it occurred around the fourteenth. That's when Akhan's company got wiped out. That's when Sanchez got on the radio and claimed they couldn't extricate. It was just a guess, but I was pretty sure that was the day Persico took over command of that team.

Morrow and I positioned ourselves in the interview room and began arranging tables and chairs into a rough-and-tumble resemblance of a courtroom. Imelda showed up a few minutes later with both her girls. They began setting up a desktop computer and a court transcription device. Morrow and I had decided to make the room look as much like an actual courtroom as we could. It would get the witnesses thinking about what lay ahead.

We were finally ready, and I sent Imelda to bring in the first witness. She formally announced Chief Persico, as though she were a court bailiff.

"Please sit down, Chief," I said, indicating a chair we had positioned in the middle of the floor.

He sat down, folded his legs, and spent a brief moment studying Morrow, who was holding a tape recorder. Then his gray eyes shifted to me. "Mind if I smoke?"

"If you'd like," I told him.

He reached into his pocket and pulled out a pack of Camels, knocked out a fag, then stuffed it between his lips and lit it.

I said, "The purpose of this session is to take your full formal statement concerning the events that transpired between 14 June and 18 June 1999. Are you sure you want to waive your right to have an attorney present?"

"I'm sure," he said.

"At your interrogatory you stated that you and your team were in Kosovo participating in Operation Guardian Angel. You were lying, weren't you? You were participating in Avenging Angel, which involved the performance of combat missions against Serbian forces in Kosovo. Isn't this correct?"

Morrow and I had decided the best way to handle Persico was to shock him with our best punch. We knew now why he and his team had been such confident liars. They had the U.S. government behind them. Who couldn't tell a great whopper when NSA was building evidence to support you, when the CIA was fronting for you, when the United States Army was tying the hands of your listeners?

Persico took a long draw from his cigarette. Finally he said, "I ain't got the slightest idea what you're talking about."

I said, "Jack Tretorne and General Murphy cleared Captain Morrow and me on the details of Avenging Angel. Now, please answer my question."

"Okay," he said. "We were part of Avenging Angel."

"Let's deal with another lie," I said. "When Captain Akhan's unit raided the police station in Piluca, was this an approved and authorized operation?"

"No."

"Why did you lie to Colonel Smothers about what happened?"

"We didn't lie," he calmly said.

I withdrew the notes of the team's debrief and pretended to study the sheet. "On the nineteenth you informed Major Grenfeld, your battalion operations officer, that throughout the day of the thirteenth you and Captain Sanchez attempted to stop Captain Akhan from raiding the police station at Piluca."

He took another heavy drag, looked around for an ashtray, then flicked his ashes on the floor. Then he said, "I tried damned hard to keep Captain Akhan from going after that station."

"You tried hard? What about Captain Sanchez?"

"Well . . . he, uh . . . he tried, too. It was a risky operation."

"Why was it risky? Why were you so opposed to that raid?"

"For starters, never go into an operation that ain't well planned. That one was hardly planned at all. Hardly any recon. No rehearsal. Captain Akhan and his guys just wanted to march down there and kick some ass."

"When Akhan insisted on doing it anyway, why didn't you call group and report that?"

He said, "That was Sanchez's call. Ask him."

I made an instinctive guess. "Was it because Sanchez wanted them to do the raid? Was that the reason you didn't call group?"

"You're asking the wrong man. I ain't no mind reader."

There was nothing to do but make another guess. "My point is that Sanchez wanted Akhan to do the raid, whereas you didn't. When they were all killed, you blamed Sanchez."

I was right. I could see it in his eyes. But what he said was, "That ain't the way it went down, Counselor. You ain't got a clue."

I said, "Colonel Smothers ordered your team to extricate. That was around noon on the fourteenth. Sanchez spoke to the ops center at 1800 hours. He said the area was thick with Serbs."

"That's right," Persico said. "I remember that call."

"Then the next morning, at the 0600 sitrep, he repeated the same message. Then again at the 1800 hours sitrep on the evening of the fifteenth. Who was detecting all this Serb activity?"

"Perrite and Machusco were on security. We figured that after

Akhan's raid the Serbs must've guessed there was a base camp, so they were out looking for it."

"What kind of activity did Perrite and Machusco report?"

"Patrols. They heard heavy vehicle activity nearby."

"Then, on the morning of the seventeenth, they spotted the Serb recon unit that was supposedly surveilling your base camp?"

"That's right. Only it wasn't supposedly. If Perrite tol' me we were being observed, we were being observed."

"Why did Perrite report that to you, Chief? Why didn't he tell Captain Sanchez?"

"I ain't got a clue."

"Then you gave the order for the team to move out?"

"That's right," he replied, making another telling mistake. If Sanchez had been in charge, he would've given the order.

"Then you moved throughout the day until around midnight, when you decided to ambush a Serb column. The other members all testified that you were in charge at the scene of the ambush itself. You gave the order to fire. You gave the order to cease fire. Yet you told me yourself that Sanchez was the operational leader."

Persico appeared confused as he tried to think up a response. Then he said, "Sanchez wasn't feeling all that well. He hadn't got any sleep for two days, so I offered to help him out."

I almost smiled. "That was very good of you," I said. Even better was that he just gave us the hook we needed. I turned to Morrow, and she nodded. She had picked up on it, too.

"SERGEANT First Class François Perrite," Imelda announced with great formality.

Perrite had the same cocky, self-assured walk I remembered from before. It was my idea to do him next. He was the hothead of the team. He had also been at the center of nearly everything that happened. More important, though, he was very clearly Chief Persico's boy. There was a powerful bond between them.

I indicated for him to take the same seat Persico had vacated. I repeated the explanation of our purpose and invited him to smoke.

He pulled from his pocket a pack of Camels. Among other loyalties, he and Persico preferred the same brand. Smoking buddies.

I stared down at some papers in front of me till he had a cigarette lit and was seated in a relaxed posture.

Then I looked up. "Sergeant Perrite, we've already determined that you and other members of this team have perjured yourselves. We know Captain Sanchez supported Captain Akhan's desire to raid the Piluca station. We know that afterward there was a general loss of confidence in his abilities, and Chief Persico virtually took charge of your team. We know your location was never detected by the Serbs. We also know the ambush was not an act of self-defense. It was a deliberate act of retribution."

Perrite stared up at me, scratched his face, and smiled. "Then what the hell do you need me for?"

"We need to question you about your role in these events. Start with when you and Machusco went into Piluca on the morning of the fourteenth. What did you encounter?"

He bent over and stubbed out his cigarette on the floor. When he came back up, he said, "I got no reason to answer your questions."

"But you do," I said. "Once you've been charged with a single court-martial offense, I can add as many charges as I deem fit. Even if you're found innocent of everything that happened in Kosovo, the additional charges I might bring against you—for refusing an order, for disrespect, for obstructing justice, for perjury—will all be weighed and sentenced separately. Is this clear to you?"

He nodded. It was a flinty, reluctant nod, but it was a nod.

"Sergeant, what exactly did you encounter when you and Machusco entered Piluca?"

"You really wanta know, huh? Okay, then I'll tell ya. For starters, it wasn't just me and Machusco. Brian Moore came with us, too, 'cause he speaks the local patois. We went in around ten. The place was real quiet, but there was this heavy odor in the air. Blood and cordite. The reason it was real quiet was because everybody left. There was lots of smoke, and some of the buildings was still burnin'. There was lots of pockmarked buildings, like you'd see after a real nasty fight. It sure didn't look like Akhan won."

He paused to take out another Camel. "Then what happened," he continued, "was we snuck down some side streets. Moore kept cover for me and Machusco, and we worked our way close to the town square. That's where the police station was located. Machusco and I got as near as we thought was smart, then dodged into this three-story building. We worked our way to the top. We climbed out a window and got up on the roof."

His hands and arms did a panoramic sweep through the air. "We could see the whole square and the police station. It was crawling with Serb militia. We could see about ten tanks, all lined up, and the crews was climbing all over 'em, doing post-op chores. We could also see this huge stack of bodies. We had binos with us, so we pulled 'em out, and we studied those bodies. We recognized most of the faces we saw. Then Machusco elbowed me and pointed at something by the police station. There was this tall pole that'd been stuck in the ground right by the front door. On top of that pole was this black, dripping thing. It was Captain Akhan's head. They'd chopped it off and stuck it there like a trophy."

He paused to look at us. He wanted us to know it was a terrible, gruesome scene. "After that," he said, "we climbed back down and got out. We found some tracks just outside of town and followed them. After about three miles we found some villagers hiding in the woods. They said the Serbs had brought in a real big unit— maybe six hundred men—late the day before. They parked tanks inside barns and hid most of the men inside buildings around town. They spent all night stacking ammunition. Then around six in the morning, the villagers told us, the town just kinda exploded. The fight lasted about two hours."

I asked, "And what did you judge had happened?"

His face was red, and his anger was beginning to boil over.

"What happened? Pretty obvious, ain't it? The Serbs knew Akhan and his team was coming. Poor bastards never had a chance. They was all butchered. One of the villagers told us that the last thirty minutes of the fight was just Serb troops roaming around hunting down survivors. They butchered 'em to death with bayonets."

The way Perrite told the story made it enormously affecting. His jaw was tight, and his eyes were gleaming with anger.

I said, "Do you blame Captain Sanchez for that?"

"Of course!" he exploded. "Bastard was desperate to get something good on his record so he could get promoted. Chief Persico told him not to let Akhan go. Sanchez wouldn't listen to him. He kept sayin' it would be a real coup if Akhan and his guys knocked off that police station. Dumb bastard."

"When you, Machusco, and Moore rejoined the team, what happened?"

"Well, uh, we went to see Chief first. I wasn't in no mood to talk to Sanchez."

"And what did Chief Persico do?"

"He got real upset. I mean, he felt guilty. That's the kind of guy Chief is. He done everything he could to stop it, but he still felt responsible."

"And did he confront Captain Sanchez?"

"Not that I know of. Chief can swallow a lot and keep goin'."

I said, "What can you tell us about the ambush?"

"Nothing really. I was half a mile away performing security. I never saw what happened."

I turned to Morrow, but she shook her head, indicating she didn't want to ask any questions. I told Perrite to return to his cell and nodded for Imelda to escort him.

When he left the room, you could almost feel the decompression.

Morrow went, "Whew!" Then she and I tried to figure out what to do next. She said, "I think we ought to bring Brian Moore back in."

I thought about that but wasn't sure what he could add. "Give me another name," I told her.

"Okay. Ezekial Graves, the medic."

"Why him?"

"He's got the least to lose. He didn't participate in the ambush."

She was right, of course.

Ten minutes later Imelda announced Sergeant Ezekial Graves.

He was thin, mulatto-skinned, and handsome, with large brown eyes, clean-cut features, and a long, narrow chin.

I told Graves how much we already knew about what had happened out there, adding the new details we had just learned from Perrite. I then said, "Could you please tell us what happened after Perrite, Machusco, and Moore returned from Piluca with their report about the fate of Akhan's team? Was there a blowup?"

"No, sir, there was no blowup. It took a while for the word to get around about what happened in Piluca. Sergeant Machusco and Sergeant Perrite sort of circulated around and let us know."

"Did they blame Captain Sanchez?"

"Yes, sir. They didn't need to, though. We all knew. A team that small gets to be like a family."

I nodded but didn't say anything.

Finally he said, "It wasn't like a mutiny, sir. I swear it wasn't."

"What was it like?" I asked.

"Well, you have to understand, sir, we all liked Captain Akhan. He was different. He was a doctor. A heart surgeon, in fact. Graduated from Harvard Medical School. That's how I got to know him real well. At night after the training he'd take me over to the U.N. medical tents. They were swamped with all these wounded, sick people pouring out of Kosovo, and we'd work there about seven or eight hours every night. I don't know how he did it. He'd get up every morning at five thirty for the military training and work till one, sometimes two or three in the morning. You had to see him with those people in those tents. He wasn't just a doctor. He was like a saint. You'd get some little kid, with maybe a broken leg and maybe some shrapnel wounds, and the kid would be wailing with pain till Akhan got there. He'd talk to the kid in this incredibly soothing voice while he was operating on him, and the kid would stop crying and just let him do it. None of the other doctors had that touch."

Graves stopped for a moment, and you could see he was in some kind of private reverie. Then he said, "I mean, Captain Akhan, he didn't even have to be here. His parents had immigrated to the U.S.

a long time before. Did you know he was a U.S. citizen? He had a wife and three little kids, a house in Boston, and he worked in some big hospital there. When this thing blew up, he parked his life, paid his own fare, and got over here."

Graves's face had by this point become a study in human agony. It was evident that he, like Persico, had developed a very deep affection for Captain Akhan.

Then Graves said, "I'm sorry. It's hard to describe sitting here in a room with you all, but he was . . . Well, people didn't just like him. People sort of loved him. Even Chief, I think. I mean, whenever he and Akhan were together, there was some kind of a special bond there."

"So what happened?" I asked. "If it wasn't a mutiny, what did happen?"

"Uh . . . I guess we all just decided we weren't going to follow Captain Sanchez anymore. Nobody said anything. It was just a feeling. We didn't mutiny, though, sir, I swear. Even Captain Sanchez seemed to be part of it. He just sort of faded out. He was there, but he stopped giving orders. Chief just sort of filled in the gap."

"Then you spent a day and a half in your base camp, right?"

"That's right, sir."

"What was the team doing during all that time?"

"Waiting. Perrite and Machusco and the Moores kept going out on their patrols, while I guess they were all trying to think about what to do next. I mean, after what happened to Captain Akhan and his company, none of us wanted to slink back home with our tails between our legs."

"Was your camp detected by the Serbs?"

"Not that I know of."

"How did the ambush come about?"

"I don't know, sir. I just remember that on that night, word went around to start checking ammo and cleaning weapons for a fight. Sergeant Caldwell woke me when it was time to move."

I looked at my watch. It was seven o'clock, and none of us had eaten since breakfast. I wasn't particularly hungry, but the golden rule of the army is that you have to feed your troops. I thanked Sergeant Graves for his insights and asked Imelda to please escort him back to his cell.

Morrow and I then walked out together. We didn't say much until the van delivered us back to the hotel. Until this point we'd been handling a legal case with all the cold, rational pieces of evidence that lawyers are trained to delve into. Now the fragments of an immensely human tragedy were coming together before our eyes, and that has a tendency to leave one disturbed.

"Dinner?" I asked.

"Who's buying?" she parried.

"That depends. If we treat this like a date, I'll buy. If it's a business meeting, my hands are tied, and we go dutch."

"Dutch it is," she said, leaving me thoroughly dispirited as she headed up the stairs.

I got changed faster than she did, and rushed downstairs and got us a table right beside a big picture window that looked out over the plains below. There were twinkling lights as far as the eye could see.

I guiltily and swiftly knocked down two tall glasses of Scotch and decided not to mention that I'd started before her. My ribs hurt, though, and I owed them a nice surprise. I even had the waiter carry off the evidence before she joined me.

He was just escaping with the glasses when she glided through the entrance. If this wasn't a date, she was a little overdressed. She had on this short, clingy blue skirt that stopped about five inches above her knees, and a perfectly lovely blouse with what is politely termed a plunging neckline. Suddenly you could see just about everything she'd been hiding under those BDUs these past few weeks. I almost gasped, but I'm too cool for that. I limited myself to some heavy panting and a long, filthy ogling stare.

Her walk across the dining room attracted a flock of attention.

I said, "Nothing like making an unobtrusive entrance."

She smiled politely and blushed a little. "I had nothing else to wear. Should we get a bottle of Chianti?"

"Go ahead," I said. "I've got two broken ribs and a body that's screaming for medication." I looked up and winked at the waiter. "I'd like to start with two Scotches, straight up."

She said, "A glass of Chianti, please."

Then there was this long, awkward silence. Finally she said, "Who do you want to start with tomorrow?"

"Why not Sanchez? We have enough to get him to open up."

The glasses were deposited on the table, and I tried not to appear desperate as I grabbed one. Before I knew it, the glass was empty.

Morrow was twirling her glass of wine with her slender fingers. "It's a terrible story, isn't it? It really touches your soul."

"Yep," I said, feeling the effects of that third Scotch.

"I've never handled a case like this. It's confusing. Not very black and white."

"But it is. You're wrong. Because they were wrong," I said, starting on the next glass and hoisting up two fingers at the waiter to rush over with reinforcements. "One of the reasons the army insists on iron discipline is situations just like this. Officers are human, too. They screw up, and when they do, their men see it. The structure, the discipline—they have to remain. Persico's an old soldier. He knew that. Hell, they all knew that."

My glass was now empty, and the waiter was there with the two fresh ones. I smiled at him quite happily.

Morrow said, "Are you all right?"

"I'll be fine," I assured her. "Just administering a little painkiller. Look, there's going to be plenty enough blame to go around for everyone. Smothers never should've given Sanchez the job," I said, taking another huge swallow. "Sanchez should've gutted it out when things went south. His men should've supported him. The system has rules, and everybody has to obey them."

"Strange words coming out of you," she said.

"What? Because I act like a wiseass? Because I don't seem to have a lot of respect for the system? Don't kid yourself, Morrow. I was an army brat. I saw my father go off to war three times. I believe in the army and its silly rules. Doesn't mean I like them, but we've won a lot of wars. We must be doing something right."

Morrow was wearing a look of surprise, and I realized that I was drinking too much and letting my mouth get carried away.

She took a sip from her wine and studied the bruises on my face. "Do your ribs still hurt?"

"I think sho," I admitted.

She giggled a little.

"What?" I asked. "Wassshh so funny?"

"We'd better order dinner quickly and get some food in your stomach," she said, flashing those wonderfully sympathetic eyes.

This was also about the same moment when I looked down at my silverware and there were at least ten forks. I said, "Mmmnydnod-mebok," or something like that.

Morrow stood up and came around the table. She took my arm, and she was really strong, because she hoisted me out of that chair like I was a fluffy pancake. She wrapped my left arm around her shoulder and led me out of the dining room.

She leaned me against the wall in the elevator, and I stood happily humming some song as we sped up to the third floor. Once we got to my room, she actually dug around inside my pants pocket until she found my key. Then she led me over to the bed. This was the moment I was waiting for. She thought I was intoxicated. She thought I was a harmless, incapacitated, drunken eunuch, too Scotched out to raise ye olde noodle. Heh-heh-heh. I lunged toward the bed, tugging her along.

I said, "Youydod a jummbock," and it was a real good thing she couldn't understand a word I said, because what I'd just invited her to do was something nice girls don't usually do.

The next thing I knew, the alarm on the nightstand next to my bed was howling at me, and I could hear someone pounding on my door. I rolled out of the bed and stumbled over and opened it. Morrow had changed out of that fetching skirt and was back inside her battle dress uniform again. Now, how had she done that so fast?

She brushed past me and headed for my bathroom while I stood there feeling stupid. I looked at the alarm clock. It read 7:40. I had set it to go off at six. I heard the shower go on, and Morrow went over to the phone and called room service. She told them to send up two American-style breakfasts.

She put the receiver down and said, "You've got five minutes to shower and shave. Don't walk out of the bathroom naked, either. Army rules dictate that higher officers shall not display their Pudleys to lower officers. And you're the one who loves army rules."

So that's what a Pudley is, I thought as I lurched toward the bathroom. The shower felt great, and my ribs only ached a little. I emerged from the bathroom fully dressed about seven minutes later. Morrow was at the door paying the bellhop for our breakfasts.

I couldn't help myself. "Where'd you learn about Pudleys?" I demanded. "Where'd you learn that word?"

That made her giggle. "At the private girls' school I went to. That was the word we used for . . . well, you know. Only for little ones, though. Big ones we called Humongos."

I thought about that a moment. I took a bite of eggs and wetted it down with a little coffee. "I don't have a Pudley," I insisted.

"Be that as it may," she said, smiling, "we're going to be late, so eat quickly."

"Okay," I grumbled. "Just remember. I don't have a Pudley. Maybe I'm not a Humongo, but damn it, I'm no Pudley."

"Eat," she ordered.

We finished breakfast, then went out and caught a sedan to the air base.

TEN

TERRY Sanchez looked thinner. And more gaunt. There were dark, hollow pockets around his eyes, and he shambled when he walked. I had the sense of a man who was rapidly deteriorating.

I pointed at the chair in the middle of the floor and asked him to be seated. He slumped into it and stared at me with a blank expression. I repeated the explanation I had used the day before, taking care to update our understanding of what had happened in Kosovo.

His eyes were wandering around the room as I spoke, and he appeared too listless to be fazed that we had learned so much about the terrible events that occurred out there.

I paused, but before I could continue, Morrow said, "Terry."

He looked at her. Her voice was very soft, mellow.

"Terry, we know now what happened out there. We want to hear your side, though. Things like this are never black and white."

He was staring into her eyes as though they were a life raft he wanted to climb into.

She continued, taking over the interrogation. "The other members of your team have all been truthful. It's your turn, Terry."

He nodded, but his eyes stayed glued to hers. I knew that I could never do what she was doing.

"Good, Terry. Why don't we start with the decision that led Captain Akhan to raid the police station in Piluca?"

He licked his lips, and I thought of a man who was stuck in a desert. He said, "I know what you've been hearing from the others about that. They're wrong, though. It's not the way it happened. Akhan begged me to let him hit that station. A lot of his men lived near Piluca, and they were begging him. There was a Serb captain named Pajocovic. He'd terrorized that town for a year."

"But," Morrow said, "it wasn't on the approved target list, was it?"

"I told Akhan that. I swear I did, but he said the target list didn't apply to him and his men. He said that list only applied to my team. He was right about that, you know."

"Yes, Terry. According to the rules, he was right. Did you want him to raid that station at Piluca?"

"Sure. I understood what his men were feeling."

Morrow said, "Was Akhan's operation properly planned?"

"Yes. I went over it with him for two days. I even had Akhan send three men to the town the day before. They checked all over.

All they saw was a bunch of drunk Serb police lounging around. It should've been easy."

"Then what happened, Terry?"

"I don't know for sure. What I think happened was one of Akhan's men was a mole and tipped off the Serbs. That's not my fault, you see? That's what the men in my team couldn't get through their heads. I didn't get Akhan killed. Whoever told the Serbs he was coming, he was the one who got Akhan killed."

"I understand," Morrow said. "What happened when Perrite and Machusco and Moore returned from Piluca?"

"What happened?" he said. "What happened was they all turned against me. None of them liked me much anyway."

"Was there a mutiny, Terry?"

He finally broke eye contact with Morrow. He looked over at Imelda and her girls as though he were seeing them for the first time. Then he started rubbing his legs with his hands, his palms wide-open. It seemed unconscious and mechanical.

"What happened was Persico took me off in the woods. He told me what the recon team found in Piluca. He spoke real quiet, but he was accusing me. He was staring at me like it was my fault."

He paused for a moment, but the leg rubbing continued.

"They all loved Akhan, you know? Something about him. I don't know what it was, but they worshipped him. I think they believed I deliberately set him up to die. Like maybe I was jealous. That's stupid, though, you know? He wasn't even a soldier. Besides, I liked him, too. I wouldn't have done that to him. When we came back out of the woods, they all started avoiding me."

Morrow said, "But there was no overt mutiny?"

"Not like you might see on a ship, maybe, but it was a mutiny. I knew they weren't going to do what I said anymore."

Morrow said, "Terry, at 1200 hours you reported to Colonel Smothers that Akhan's team was black. He then directed you to begin extraction. At the 1800 sitrep you reported that there was too much Serb activity in your vicinity to safely extricate your team. You reported the same thing at the 0600 sitrep the next morning and the 1800 sitrep that evening. Why did you report that?"

It took me a moment to realize the timely brilliance of Morrow's question. If it had been a mutiny, why had Sanchez conspired to keep the team in Kosovo? Had someone held a gun to his head?

"Persico told me to. He told me to buy us some time."

"Why, Terry? Time for what? What more was there to do?"

"You know," he said, avoiding her eyes. "Get Pajocovic."

"Pajocovic? Wasn't he the station commander in Piluca?"

"Yeah," he said. "Who else do you think we ambushed?"

Suddenly an avalanche of missing pieces came tumbling into place. The column they'd ambushed wasn't picked for its size—it was picked to punish the man who killed Akhan.

Morrow never stuttered or blinked an eye. "So you and Chief Persico kept the team in the base camp while Perrite and Machusco went back out and searched for Pajocovic?"

"That's right. Only I sent Moore out, too. They snuck into a few local villages, asking people if they knew where the Hammer was. Pajocovic was known by everyone in our zone. The Hammer, everybody called him. Finally some old man told Moore that the Hammer was in a little village named Ishatar. That was how Pajocovic operated. He'd sometimes go to local villages, spending a day or so terrorizing the citizens; then he'd go back to his station in Piluca. That's when I decided what we were going to do. We moved off, and I set up an ambush on the road between Piluca and Ishatar. We moved in the night before, and—"

"Terry," Morrow interrupted him.

He stopped and blinked a few times.

"Who was making all these decisions? It wasn't you, was it?"

"No," he said. "It was Persico and Perrite."

"Did you try to stop them or did you encourage them?"

This question went to the heart of who bore legal responsibility for the murder of the Serbs. I think that in a strange, remorseful way, Sanchez wished he had ordered the ambush, because that might have afforded him some residue of honor.

"I let them do what they wanted to do," he mumbled.

"What happened at the ambush?"

"Well, there was a lot of traffic on the road. We stayed there until nearly eight. Perrite was off on the flank. He had night-vision goggles. He was watching for the vehicles from Piluca. Pajocovic's vehicles had his station's name marked on the side. Around eight he gave Persico the signal they were coming. Persico waited till the lead vehicle got right over the two antitank mines planted in the road. The explosion sent this big truck catapulting in the air. Then we opened up. It lasted only seven or eight minutes; then we left."

I said, "Terry, someone went through after the ambush was over and shot the Serbs in the head. Was that you?"

He looked at me in shock. "No," he said. "I was shooting, just like everyone else. But as soon as Persico shot off the flare to order us to cease fire, we all stopped. Then we all left and started running for the rally point, a mile or so behind the ambush site."

"And were there still some Serb survivors?" I asked.

"Yeah. There were still a few down there firing back at us."

I was confused. If there were still survivors firing their weapons when the whole team was headed for the rally point, then who shot them in the head?

Morrow said, "Terry, when you all got back to Macedonia and were debriefed, why did you decide to lie?"

He looked pathetically uncomfortable, and he didn't seem willing to answer. He'd gone back to that odd leg-rubbing motion.

That's when I knew. I said, "Terry, did you make a deal with your team out there?"

He kept staring at the floor. "Yes, we made a deal."

I said, "Is that why you went along with the ambush, Terry? Why you bought them time with Smothers? You wanted them to do that ambush, didn't you? You knew it was a violation of orders, that if they killed Pajocovic and his men, they'd be facing court-martial when you all made it back. You knew that if they did that, they would have as much to hide as you. You knew, then, that the team would cover for you because they needed you to cover for them."

He kept staring at the floor, and that was an answer in itself. We now knew everything he knew. We knew everything except the most crucial thing. Who killed the last of the Serbs?

AFTER Imelda escorted Sanchez back to his cell, we all desperately needed to take a break. Imelda and her ladies went off in search of a coffee machine. I asked her to notify the air force warden that I wanted to see him.

Morrow and I were a little dazed. We both sat quietly at the table for a few minutes. Then Morrow pulled out her trusty pad of yellow legal paper and began making notes.

I watched her write for a few moments, then said, "I'm sorry about last night. I drank too much. I didn't do anything . . . uh, you know . . . too forward when we got to my bedroom, did I?"

What I hoped she'd say was, "Well, yes, actually you did. A very naughty thing, too, you animal, but the truth is, I enjoyed the hell out of it, and I sure hope you do it again."

Instead, she said, "Don't worry. You were snoring before you hit the bed."

I said, "Yeah. My ribs were hurting like hell."

"It wasn't your ribs," she said, still jotting notes. "It was your conscience."

"No it wasn't," I lied. "It was my ribs."

"You're not as absolute as you like to pretend," she said. "You like these men. They're just like you, and that bothers you. Admit it."

I thought about that a moment.

She put down her pen and turned to me. "You know, you're the right man to head this investigation, but you're also the wrong man. You've shared some experiences with them. No ordinary lawyer like me could ever hope to comprehend what happened out there. For the same reason, though, you can't look at them impartially."

I stared back at her. This sounded a little too much like psychoanalysis to me. That was Morrow's problem. The reason her eyes were so damned sympathetic-looking was because she was so sympathetic, and she was probing here for a fresh customer.

Imelda and her ladies walked back in at that moment, accompanied by the chubby air force warden. "You beckoned, sir?" he asked.

"Damn right!" I bellowed. "Is there a psychiatrist on this base?"

"Yes," he said. "There's one over at the base hospital."

"You get him over here today. I want him to spend time with Captain Sanchez." I bent forward. "Haven't you noticed that he's experienced a very severe weight loss?"

"Uh . . . no, I hadn't noticed."

"But surely you've noticed that he's very depressed?"

"No, I, uh—I hadn't noticed that, either."

"Then listen closely. If he manages to kill himself or loses even one more ounce, I'll see that you're charged with gross negligence. Do I make myself clear?"

"Uh, yes, sir." He scurried quickly away.

I'd just done the best I could for Terry Sanchez. I wasn't sure it was going to help, though. When a man walks all over his own image of himself the way he had, compromising nearly every principle he believes in, something dies inside.

I looked over at Imelda and asked her to get Chief Persico.

PERSICO sat down and casually hiked his right leg over his left. You couldn't help but notice the contrast between this gray-haired leathery self-assured man and the simmering, leg-rubbing wreck that was left of Terry Sanchez.

I said, "Chief, I want to be frank with you. You are facing possible charges of multiple counts of murder, failure to obey orders, inciting mutiny, and a long host of lesser charges. I advise you to have counsel present for these proceedings."

"I don't want counsel, Major. Mind if I start with a few points?"

"If you'd like."

He studied me carefully. "Major, I see you're wearing a Combat Infantryman's Badge. You were in combat, right?"

"Right. I was with the Eighty-second in Panama and the Gulf," I answered, which was technically true, since the 82nd Airborne Division was in both places while I was there with the outfit.

"Were you in leadership positions? Were you in the field?"

"Yes," I answered, which was also true.

"You get shot at any?"

"A fair amount," I admitted.

"I was in the Gulf, too. Didn't do Panama, though. Did Haiti, Mogadishu, Rwanda. Also spent years in Bosnia doing this and that. Me, Perrite, Machusco, Caldwell, Butler, the Moore brothers, we done nearly all those together."

He paused for a moment, and his gray eyes roved around the room. Then he faced me again. "Can't tell you how many refugee camps we've been through since the Gulf. I swear I've seen a hundred million miserable faces with those empty-looking eyes all those refugees got. Maimed kids, raped women, orphans, mothers who just lost their babies—you get tired of it. I mean, they call these things humanitarian operations, but a real humanitarian would go in and knock the crap out of the bad guys, wouldn't he? A real humanitarian wouldn't stand around putting Band-Aids on 'em after they got hurt. A real humanitarian would keep 'em from getting hurt in the first place."

"Chief," I said as kindly as I could, "we're not here to debate national policies. We're here to consider what happened in Kosovo between the fourteenth and eighteenth of June."

His voice was cool. "Any of the others tell you about Akhan?"

I nodded.

"Yeah, well, I doubt what they said did him justice. I seen some fine men in my time, but I never saw one who could touch him. Really had no business being there. The guy was a brilliant doctor." Persico looked me dead in the eye. "I wish I knew the words to describe Akhan. He was young—early thirties. A handsome guy, tall, thin, with this special calmness in his eyes. Thing is, Akhan never should've gone down to Piluca. Sanchez egged him into it. I knew Sanchez was jealous of Akhan. I mean, everyone just admired him, you know. You couldn't help yourself. And Sanchez? Well, he just couldn't get anyone to respect him. I think he wanted Akhan to try some hard things so he would fail. That make sense?"

"It makes sense," I said.

"Anyway, when Perrite and Machusco and Moore came back from Piluca, everything kinda came apart. I don't think Sanchez wanted that to happen. All of 'em getting killed that way—that was more than he bargained for. I took him off in the woods and told him about what Perrite and the guys saw, and he started crying like a little kid. The rest of the team didn't handle it real well, either."

"Did you tell Sanchez he couldn't lead the team? Was there an organized effort to keep him from doing his job?"

"No. But I didn't fix it, either. I knew what was happening. I just didn't want to fix it. Don't blame the men. They didn't have nothing to do with it. It was my fault. I saw that he lost his guts, and I just didn't make 'em follow his orders anymore. You wanta charge someone with mutiny, you charge me. I guess I mutinied."

I said, "When did you decide to ambush Pajocovic's unit?"

"That morning. Right away, really."

"Why? Why didn't you extricate when Colonel Smothers ordered you to?"

He reached into his breast pocket and pulled out the Camels. He withdrew one and tamped it down, staring at his palm. He lit it and inhaled heavily. Then he answered. "You gotta understand what it feels like to do all these humanitarian missions. It does get personal. Captain Akhan's head was on a stake like some kinda trophy. This guy Pajocovic was a real murderous bastard. He'd killed and tortured hundreds of people. However this Kosovo thing ends, he'd of just walked away from it."

"So you decided to execute him?"

He stared at the smoking tip of the cigarette. "Yes, sir, that's exactly what I decided to do. I don't regret it, either. The men just did what they were told to do. They didn't do nothing wrong."

I said, "Somebody did, though, Chief. Somebody went through and shot the Serbs in the head. Can you tell us who?"

He did not even blink. "Yeah," he said. "I did it."

These were the last words I expected or wanted to hear. "How, Chief? How did you do it?" I asked.

"Easy, really. Most of the Serbs were dead or wounded from the

316 | *Brian Haig*

ambush. I waited till there was only three or four still firing before I shot off the star cluster for everyone to cease fire. Then I ordered everyone to head for the rally point. They all got up and started running. I gave 'em a head start; then I went in a different direction. I ran up the hill on the other side of the road. The last of the Serbs were huddled behind their vehicles, still shooting at the hillside where our team had been. They had their backs turned to me. I shot 'em. Then I went down and put bullets through all their heads."

"Why, Chief? Why did you do it?"

"Ain't it obvious? One of those guys still firing back might've been Pajocovic. Besides, I guess I didn't want any witnesses left."

The room suddenly became very quiet. He calmly finished smoking his cigarette. He dropped it on the floor and ground it out, turning his heel four or five times to make sure it was completely extinguished. The physical metaphor was very powerful.

I said, "Okay, Chief, that will be all."

He stood up and actually saluted me. I saluted him back. Then he marched out and closed the door.

There were some very pent-up feelings inside this room, so I ordered everybody to take a twenty-minute break. Even Morrow got up and left. I sat in isolation at the small table we had set up.

Fifteen minutes passed before Morrow reentered. She fell into her chair and groaned. "This is awful."

Hard to argue with that. I said, "Only one more to go."

I got up and went out to find Imelda. I told her what I wanted her to do; then I returned to the interview room and quietly waited till Imelda's girls came filtering back in and took their seats.

Two minutes passed before the door opened. First Imelda came through, then Sergeant François Perrite.

"Have a seat," I told him.

He did, although more nervously this time. He broke out the cigarettes immediately and began tamping a fresh one.

I said, "You sure you don't want counsel, Sergeant? I would seriously advise you to have a lawyer present."

"Nope. There's enough lawyers in this room already."

"Nobody would argue with that," I admitted.

Then we looked into each other's eyes a moment, and he knew that I knew. I said, "Chief Persico just left. He took responsibility for everything. He said he was the one who made all the decisions, who led the quiet mutiny against Captain Sanchez, who decided to execute an ambush, who ignored the order to extricate."

Perrite was quietly nodding as I detailed this.

"Of course, Sergeant Perrite, you bear most of the responsibility. You were the one who came back and tried to incite the men against Sanchez. You knew they didn't like him anyway, and you stoked the fuel. It was your idea to kill Pajocovic, wasn't it? Yet Chief was in here trying to cover for you."

He didn't nod or acknowledge a word, only watched me.

I continued. "Then he confessed that he was the one who went around after the ambush and shot the Serbs in the head."

Perrite was now staring at the end of his lit cigarette, much as Chief Persico had sat and stared at his. It was uncanny. Perrite admired the man so much he even affected the same mannerisms.

I said, "The problem, Sergeant Perrite, is that you and I both know he didn't do that. Don't we? He was trying to save somebody he cares deeply about, and I only hope to God that man cares as much about him."

Perrite stayed frozen, still staring at that cigarette for what felt like eternity. "That's right," he finally mumbled. "I did it."

"Tell us what happened."

"You wouldn't understand," he said. "You're not really soldiers, you and that other lawyer up there," he said, waving dismissively at Morrow. "You got no idea what it's like out there."

Suddenly Imelda jumped out of her seat and walked over and stopped right in front of him. "I've heard enough, Sergeant. You don't know what you're talking about!" she yelled. "See that combat patch on the major's right arm? See that Combat Infantryman's Badge on his chest? What you don't see is the three Purple Hearts and two Silver Stars, and the Distinguished Service Cross he earned, too. Know why he's a lawyer? He spent six months in a hospital recovering after the last one. They wouldn't let him stay in the infantry after that. Now act like a soldier and answer that man."

Perrite glared up at Imelda. How she knew about all that was beyond me. My citations and awards were inside a musty drawer somewhere because they were given for operations that nobody knew happened and nobody was supposed to know happened.

Perrite looked at me. "That true?" he asked.

"I guess so," I admitted.

He pondered that a moment, then made up his mind. "Okay, Major. I was off on the flank, like I said. I heard the ambush go off, and I got curious. Bein' on security, you always wonder if your friends are gettin' killed. I knew I shouldn't, but I crossed the road and worked my way down till I was behind the Serbs. I got there just as Chief gave everyone the order to beat feet. There was still some Serbs down there, maybe three or four, still shooting. So I decided to . . . well, you know, I decided to . . . kill them."

"Why?" I asked.

"I dunno. Maybe because I wanted a piece of the action. And maybe because Chief should've made sure they were all dead so there was no witnesses."

I said, "And maybe you wanted a trophy?"

He looked at me in alarm.

I said, "When Captain Morrow and I viewed the corpses in Belgrade, one had no head left. Was that Captain Pajocovic's body?"

He turned his eyes away from mine. "I dunno. Mighta been."

"You cut his head off, didn't you, Sergeant?"

He began fidgeting and suddenly looked nervous. Pajocovic had decapitated Akhan, so Perrite returned the favor in kind.

"What did you do with it, Sergeant?"

He still refused to answer. But he didn't have to. I knew Perrite would've wanted his hero to be proud of him, just like a hunting dog brings its trophies back to its owner. "You brought it to Chief, didn't you? You wanted him to see what you did, right?"

He straightened up in his seat and dropped the cigarette on the floor. He stomped it out. "That's right. That's what I did."

"And what did he do?"

"He got real pissed. He tol' me not to say anything to the others, and he ordered me to bury the head."

"Thank you, Sergeant. You may return to your cell."

WE WERE back in Tuzla. It was the last time I ever planned to show those guards my orders, to grin stupidly into the camera, and to wait for Miss Smith to open the door. Only it wasn't Miss Smith who opened the door this time. It was General Clapper.

He thrust out his hand. "Sean, how are you?"

"Pretty crappy," I admitted.

He shook hands with Morrow, then led us down the stairs to the conference room in the lead-lined basement.

The long conference-room table had acquired an abundant audience. Tretorne was there, of course, and he was back to wearing that vest he seemed so fond of. Murphy was there. So was his boss, General Clive Partridge. None of them looked happy to be here.

Morrow and I had worked around the clock the past three days, dissecting the evidence and testimonies, considering every legal angle and alternative, until we built the packet we intended to present.

Clapper walked around the table and took the seat next to General Partridge. All of them were seated on one side. There were two empty chairs in the middle of the other side. These obviously were intended for Morrow and me.

I led Morrow over, and we both sat down. We spent a few moments digging through our legal cases and withdrawing our findings. We had made only ten copies, each numbered and stamped with the words TOP SECRET. Morrow got up and placed a copy in front of each of the men on the other side of the table.

I said, "Gentlemen, these are our findings. If you'd like, Captain Morrow will present our conclusions."

General Partridge made the call. "Tell us what you found."

Morrow swept her eyes across the line of faces on the other side of the table. Then she began. "On the morning of 18 June, at approximately 0800 hours, Captain Terry Sanchez's A Team did willfully execute an ambush that resulted in the deaths of . . ."

She spoke for nearly twenty minutes, skillfully unraveling layer upon layer of conspiracies, collusion, and connivance. The men across the table sat stone-faced and listened without interrupting. I watched their faces and tried to imagine what they were thinking.

Morrow finally finished. There was a moment of fretful silence.

General Partridge reached into his pocket, took out a pack of cigarettes, and I'll be damned if it wasn't a pack of Camels. He extracted one, tapped it on his palm a few times, then lit it. General Murphy got up, went over to a side table, and fetched a glass ashtray for his boss. Smoking is prohibited in all military and government facilities, but nobody in that room had the balls to remind the meanest, snarliest four-star general in the whole United States Army that this rule applied to him, too. I sure as hell didn't.

Partridge then stared at me. "So what do you recommend, Major? What do I charge, and who do I charge?"

I said, "Why don't we deal with the most serious charge first? The charge of murder." And in my most lawyerly tone I began. "Since Sanchez's team was actually in Kosovo for the express purpose of performing offensive combat operations, we concluded that the ambush conducted on the eighteenth of June was a tolerable act, not an act of mass murder. It was, however, a willful disobedience of orders, since Colonel Smothers ordered the team to extricate and since the orders the team were operating under strictly disallowed attacks on targets of opportunity."

Partridge said, "Noted." Nothing else, just that.

I continued. "Sergeant Perrite's initial attack on the remaining survivors was not murder, either. It was a case of willful disobedience of his orders. Also, he abandoned his post in combat, which you're aware is an added offense. He crossed the line from those infractions to murder when he purposely dispatched the wounded Serbs. He committed multiple acts of first-degree murder and one act of mutilating a corpse. We have included copies of the coroner's findings in your packet."

"Noted," Partridge said again.

I said, "The act of mutiny is a matter of complexity. The Uniform Code of Military Justice defines mutiny as a deliberate and organized attempt to usurp the authority of the designated leaders of the unit. Over the centuries there have been many test cases involving mutiny. Captain Morrow and I found no case in military law that precisely mirrors what happened inside Captain Sanchez's unit. However, our considered judgment is that Captain Terry Sanchez willfully abrogated his responsibility to lead the unit and that Chief Michael Persico took the commendable step of performing his duties. There seems a strong possibility that had Sanchez not voluntarily relinquished his leadership, there would have been a mutiny, but Sanchez's own passiveness preempted this offense."

Partridge flicked an ash in the ashtray. "Noted."

I said, "There are a host of lesser offenses, which are described and dealt with in your packet, but there are only two additional serious offenses left to be considered."

"And what are those?" Partridge grunted.

"Conspiracy to obstruct justice, and perjury. On these two charges we confront the most serious complications. The team's conspiracy passed through many evolutions, beginning with the agreement to make false reports to Colonel Smothers, to their failure to report the ambush, to their misleading of Colonel Smothers's debriefing officer. But then the army *and* the government became party to the conspiracy. The interests of the government to protect the cover of a secret war corresponded with the team's need to cover their crimes, and an overt bargain was reached."

I drew in a heavy breath. "General, were you party to or knowledgeable of this agreement?"

"I was," he frankly confessed.

"Then it is your duty to disqualify yourself from this case. You must cede your authority to decide on our recommendations."

I expected Partridge to leap across the table and rip out my throat when I said that. Morrow and I had discussed this issue for many hours. Quite possibly, no one on the far side of the table—or even in the existing chain of military command—could decide on this case.

A mass recusal was in order. It made for an interesting precedent.

Partridge merely smiled. He said, "You're right, Drummond. In front of these witnesses I hereby relinquish my responsibility for judging your recommendations. You've done a great job, son. You've shown real courage and character and intelligence. Your father would be proud of you. Hell, I'm proud of you. Now it's time for a little more off-the-record guidance. You ready to listen?"

"Yes, sir."

"How many counts of murder you recommending?"

"Maybe ten counts, sir. But only one man to be indicted."

"So, only one man. Sergeant First Class Perrite."

"That's right, sir."

"Then aside from this Perrite, none of the rest of the men in that team are guilty of any serious offenses. I mean, we could prosecute Sanchez for gross dereliction of duty, but what would that prove? He's crazy as a loon already. And we could hit some of the others for various misjudgments, but then we'd look vindictive. So all that leaves are these conspiracy charges, and if you're gonna make one charge of conspiracy to obstruct or perjure, then you're gonna have to make hundreds of charges that go in every which direction, all the way to the moon. I got all that straight, Counselor?"

"Yes, General. I'd say you have the whole picture."

He leaned back in his chair. "And Tretorne here, and Murphy, they told you that if you wanted to go public with this thing, then we won't stop you. That right also?"

"That was the deal, General."

"Well, a deal's a deal, son. So it's up to you to decide."

"Thank you, sir."

He chuckled. It was a humorless chuckle. "You thought about what's gonna happen if you go public?"

"I have, General. I think it will incite a considerable scandal."

"Drummond, if that was the worst of it, none of us woulda got in your way in the first place. Scandals come, and scandals go. Don't think Tretorne or Murphy or I did this 'cause we're afraid of some scandal. You been through any of the camps while you were here?"

"We have."

He nodded his approval. "Good for you. Right now we got nearly one and a half million Kosovars in our camps. One and a half million whose only hope is us. You go public, this whole operation to get them back their homeland's gonna fall apart. This thing's hanging together on a thin thread anyway. The Russians are accusing us of genocide. Our NATO allies hate us for making 'em do this. We shamed most of 'em into it. They find out we're running a secret ground war, they'll pull the plug faster than you can spit. The Italians won't let us fly off their soil anymore. The Brits might hang in, but there'll be nothing to hang on to. Think Congress will let us hang in? I don't. It might even cause NATO to fall apart."

I sat and listened to every word.

"It's up to you, Drummond. Do what *you* think is right. Milosevic's probably got thousands of murderers and rapists and every other assortment of criminal on his rolls. Most of 'em will never see the inside of a courtroom. But you go ahead and pit this one soldier, this Sergeant Perrite—you pit his fate against the fate of one and a half million Kosovars. You decide if going public's worth giving Milosevic a victory in this thing. You decide if you're willing to destroy the lives of millions of people so we can get a chance to punish one man for killing some bastards who probably deserved to die anyway. Think about how it would be for those millions of people to lose their country over some joker named the Hammer."

He got up and walked out of the room without saying another word. Until this moment Morrow and I had enjoyed our worm's-eye view of the world, thinking we were on a mighty crusade to right a terrible wrong. Now we were glued to our seats, too stunned to move. The other men stared at us.

I quickly blurted out, "If you gentlemen will please excuse us, Captain Morrow and I need some time together."

Before we left, I turned and looked at General Murphy. He could still look me dead in the eye, and without the slightest hint of guilt or shame. He and Tretorne had sucked me in one more time. I really had made a bargain with the devil.

ELEVEN

THERE are times in life when the wrong thing to do is actually the right thing to do. Maybe vice versa, too. I don't know. I haven't gotten around to testing that theory yet.

I looked across the courtroom and knew I had my hands full. The ten members of the court-martial board all had their eyes riveted on the defense counsel, who to my dismay was skillfully presenting an incredible opening argument. I turned around and looked at my senior legal assistant, Imelda Pepperfield. She merely shrugged and rearranged her gold-rimmed glasses. If I was looking for sympathy, I had turned to the wrong corner.

I had thought my case was fairly airtight. The facts were irresistibly simple. A sergeant assigned to one of the army's black units got caught making illegal use of his credit card.

Unfortunately for both him and the government, it was an army-issued Visa card. He'd used it to purchase a car, a camera with a zoom lens, some very expensive clothes, even a set of golf clubs. His unit commander discovered the fraud. My caseload had been staggering as a result of the month I'd spent working on that Kosovo thing, but the prosecution was assigned to me anyway.

Airtight, right? The very nature of the goods he'd purchased damned him. The only thing left was to explain all that to the board. As was always the case in this court, every board member was selected from a black unit. That was a defense counsel's nightmare because folks who go into "black" work tend to be pretty hard-nosed and unforgiving.

Unfortunately, the defense counsel wasn't going along with my scenario. She claimed her poor client suspected two officers in his unit of engaging in espionage. He made the purchases, she claimed, to complete a disguise he intended to use to prove their guilt. Once a month, she claimed, these two traitorous officers met with their for-eign contact on a local golf course, where they played as a trio. This was where the money and information changed hands. Her client, she claimed, bought the car so they wouldn't recognize his own car. He'd also purchased a false mustache and a wig to complete his dis-guise. And the camera with the 400X zoom lens? How else was he expected to record the money and envelopes changing hands?

I mean, you've got to be kidding. I never heard such a flimsy defense in my legal career. Unfortunately, the board members were all captivated by her sympathetic eyes, not to mention her other phys-ical charms. And the one thing she had going for her defense was that it was so dazzlingly unbelievable as to be completely plausible.

When she finished, Morrow flashed her most winsome smile at the board members, and you could almost hear their hearts flutter. Then she smiled at me. Only my smile wasn't like theirs. Mine was more like the way a lion might smile after a particularly delicious meal. Or maybe *before* a particularly tasty meal. Whichever.

She and I had obviously decided not to go public about Sanchez and the conspiracy. The truth is, you just can't trade the fate of one man against the fates of a couple million lost souls. At least that was the conclusion Morrow and I came to before we threw in our towels and enlisted in the conspiracy.

Clapper very generously gave us another three-day extension, during which we rewrote our report and completely absolved Sanchez and his men of all crimes. We threw ourselves into the whitewash whole hog. The Serbs convened a big press conference and complained about the fact that all their troops had been shot in the head. But Milosevic had spent so many years telling so many whoppers that he didn't have much credibility.

Chief Persico got another Silver Star, and a few of the other team members got Bronze Stars. Right on the White House lawn, too. I liked Persico anyway, so I didn't mind all that much. Terry Sanchez got moved to the psychiatric ward of a VA hospital somewhere in southern Virginia. And Sergeant Perrite? They pulled him out of the team and took away his green beret. That was one of the only two concessions I demanded before I began splashing whitewash at the government's behest. Perrite still had two years left on his current enlistment, and I talked them into reclassifying him into graves registration, where he'll spend the next couple of years digging holes and filling them with bodies. It might be a lot less than he deserves, but who knows? It might make him think.

What did I learn? I guess I learned that Murphy was right. Sometimes those principles of duty and honor and country clash against one another in ugly ways. You can't always make them fit together.

I went to Clapper and extracted one other tiny tribute in return for blemishing my previously pristine principles. My special legal unit had just lost one of our two defense counsels, and I made Clapper agree to give us Morrow.

Right at this moment, though, I felt a strong tinge of regret. I looked at the faces of the board members, all of whom still had their eyes glued on Morrow's shapely gams. How am I supposed to compete with that? I mean, give me a break. The guy bought a car and clothes and a fancy camera and a full set of golf clubs, all so he could expose some of his officers for selling secrets to the enemy? Morrow's been watching too many of those Oliver Stone movies.

But the last and final truth was that I kind of wanted to keep her around. I mean, she has those incredibly sympathetic eyes, and occasionally they come in handy.

In any case, by now you probably have figured this out about me: I don't give up easily. Someday soon, maybe right after I kick her ass in this trial, I'm going to prove to the lovely Miss Morrow that I'm not a Pudley. Maybe I'm no Humongo, but I'm no Pudley. Metaphysically speaking, of course.

BRIAN HAIG

Brian Haig's love affair with the U.S. Army got off to a rocky start. When the author was a teenager, his career army dad, Alexander Haig (later Secretary of State for President Reagan), could afford to send only one of his two sons to college at full tuition. The author's older brother got to pick Georgetown University, and Brian went to West Point, courtesy of Uncle Sam. It was a diffi-

"I stayed in love with the army— the whole 22 years I was in."

cult first year, Haig admits, but, he says, after serving with a unit in Germany during the summer of his sophomore year, he had a change of heart: "I absolutely fell in love with the army. Then you couldn't drag me out of West Point with a set of sharp calipers. I stayed in love with the army—the whole twenty-two years I was in."

A crack military strategist, the author started out as an infantry officer, eventually rising in the ranks to become a special assistant to the Chairman of the Joint Chiefs of Staff. Soon after he retired as a lieutenant colonel, he began plotting his first book. "I read all of the best-selling writers to see how they put together a good novel," he says. "The two that most impressed me were John Grisham and Nelson DeMille, both of whom bring a wry wit to their writing."

Haig remembers his childhood as fun, and the family remains close today. He says he would give his own four children the career advice his father gave him: "Look for something you love to do, that you're good at. Maybe not in that order."

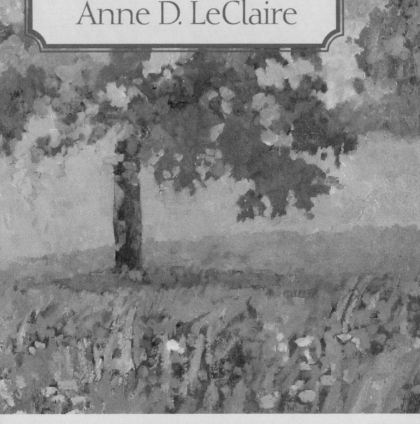

Entering
NORMAL

Anne D. LeClaire

A friend in need
is a flower
waiting
to open.

Prologue

THE sun has been in and out all day. Now it finds cracks in the clouds and threads through in ribbons, what Gram Gates used to call fingers of God.

Opal welcomes the fingers. They constitute a celestial hand beckoning her forward, and even though she will be the first to tell you she does not believe in any god and most certainly not the Presbyterian God of her grandma, she will gratefully take them as a sign of astral endorsement.

Opal lives by signs. She counts on them the way other people put their faith in heaven or weathermen or the possibility of everlasting love. She believes in them absolutely and holds tight to her conviction despite the number of people who offer the opinion that there is no sign by which one can foretell the future, no omen to warn of the disasters entire lives are hell-spent avoiding—or pursuing.

In two days she has covered stretches of six states and is now on the central section of the Massachusetts Turnpike, nerves high-wired from too many Hershey's bars and too much drive-through coffee in thin paper cups. Her eyelids sting from lack of sleep.

She hopes she is heading directly north, but she can't shake the feeling that she took a wrong turn somewhere back in New York. If Billy were along, sure thing he'd have picked up a road map somewhere along the line, but Opal can't be bothered. This is one way they differ along gender lines. He's a man but willing to be dependent; she's a girl and scorns it. If she has misjudged direction, it won't be the first time in her life. By the age of twenty she has made more than her share of wrong turns, and yet, for a fact, she does not regret a one. Certainly she doesn't regret the misstep that brought her Zack. Billy—now there was a big mistake. But not Zack. Never Zack. And so, perhaps, in some sense, not even Billy.

She glances in the rearview mirror, checks the back seat, lets her eyes rest too long for caution on her five-year-old son. Tucked in between the cartons that hold her doll makings and as many of their belongings as she'd dared pack, Zack is out cold, his pomegranate mouth slightly open. Watching him, she feels a familiar jolt in her stomach—the sharp, sweet terror of motherhood.

She returns her attention to the road, catches sight in the mirror of a car bearing down from the rear. She eyes the speedometer. She's below the legal limit; still, her breath doesn't come right until the vehicle is close enough to see it's not Billy's black Ram pickup. While she slows for the car to pass, she thinks again that there will be hell to pay when her parents hear what she's done.

"You've told them you're going?" Billy asked the night before she left.

"Yes."

"And they know where you're heading?"

Again she lied, said yes. Of course she hadn't said a word to them about her plans. Particularly to her mama. Melva's projected response comes to her with depressing predictability: the sniffy, self-righteous rant about how once again they are *so* disappointed in her, how once more Opal has been reckless, let them down. The echo of Melva's voice presses against her, cold and hollow as fog. She opens the window to bring in fresh air, to breathe.

The story she came up with for Billy is that she needs some time away to think. She's just taking Zack to Ohio to visit an aunt.

Actually, she hasn't a clue as to her destination.

The night before she left, she rolled one of the dice from Billy's

Monopoly game. It came up a three. A good sign. Six would be too many for Zack; one was nowhere near enough for her. So the plan is to keep going until she has used up three tanks of gas—exactly three tanks, no cheating, not even if she comes upon a place that looks promising after she has gone through two and a half.

She checks the fuel gauge. The needle edges toward empty, the final gallon of her third tank. She tries to collect her mind to see an exit or some other sign that will reveal to her what her next step should be. If her faith is to be repaid, she will see one soon.

Opal's belief in signs riles Billy. "Raylee," he said to her just before Zack was born, back before she changed her name from Raylee to Opal. "Raylee, you can't go living your life looking for signs. It's just about the dumbest thing I ever heard."

While she has given up trying to convince Billy that there are signs everywhere if you'll just open your eyes and look, her own belief in signs remains resolute. What else is there?

The sun beats on the Buick's hood. She cranks the window down another notch, checks the back seat again. Then, just as the needle on the gas gauge trembles into the red, just when she is praying she'll reach the next exit before she runs dry, at that moment she sees the sign: ENTERING NORMAL. She laughs right out loud, and the tiny nugget that has been caught in her chest ever since she left New Zion, North Carolina, that hard little pea, just melts away. As she flicks the right turn signal and veers into the exit lane, she feels the gambler's high, the wallop that comes when you've bet your stake against house odds and won. For two and a half days she's been thinking about the consequences of her actions, and now, as the old Buick rolls down the ramp toward a new life in a town named Normal, she doesn't care what Billy or her parents will say.

"Well now, haven't I just done it," Opal says aloud.

She is going toward something, and even though she doesn't know exactly what it is, she trusts it. The weight of the past six years shifts, then lifts, and although she can't recall the last time she experienced the sensation, she feels beneath her breastbone a combination of happiness and heartburn that might very well be hope.

FALL

Rose

NED is snoring, a thick thunder that rolls up from his chest. His arm is flung over Rose's ribs, and she takes a breath against the heft of it. He snores again, a long, rippling snort. Half asleep, she imagines herself picking up the pillow, holding it over his open mouth.

What on earth is the matter with her, thinking something crazy like that. Ned is a good man. Where she would be without him, she hates to think. She gives him a nudge, just enough to make him stop snoring, but not enough to wake him. The last thing in the world she needs right now is for him to wake and ask her what's wrong.

What's wrong? This is a question she doesn't want him to ask, not when all that is wrong swirls through the room, hangs above her face like smoke. The digital clock on the nightstand glows 1:40, red numerals that remind her of eyes, the alert eyes of some nocturnal animal. The time changes to 1:41. Very carefully she lifts Ned's arm from its hold across her ribs and scratches her stomach, hard.

It's still there. It's bigger. Maybe.

The itchy spot first appeared toward the end of September, the same week Opal Gates and her boy moved into the house next door. At first Rose figured it was an insect bite or dry skin. Yesterday she finally took a reluctant look at it, and even without her reading glasses she was able to see the small, raised welt right over the mole on her stomach. Definitely a bite she decided, pushing away darker possibilities conjured up by the Cancer Society leaflets she's read in Doc Blessing's waiting room, their bold letters enumerating the Seven Deadly Signs.

The itching is worse now. She edges out of bed, almost makes it.

"S'matter?" Ned asks.

"Bathroom. Go back to sleep." She freezes, willing his breathing to return to its heavy, half-snoring rhythm, then using the illumination from the night-light at the top of the stairs, she makes her way to the hall. Todd's door beckons in the dim light, and she almost allows herself to give in, to sit in his room and wait.

Months have passed since she sat there and hoped for a sign from Todd. Hoped, not prayed. She has long since lost her belief in the power of prayers or God; the most she can hold on to is hope, and even that has dimmed lately. Five years. If she is going to get some sign from him, feel some connection, wouldn't it have come by now? But even the dimming of active hope does not bring the resolution or the peace she might have expected, only more pain.

In the bathroom, she opens the cabinet and removes the bottle of Jergens, slathers it across her belly, easing the itch of the mole that woke her earlier. She returns the lotion to the cabinet.

On her way back to her room, she stops at the window and checks the street. Next door, at the Montgomery place, light spills from the dining room. *At this hour.* It is nearly two a.m. If Louise Montgomery still lived there, Rose would ring over, see if everything was all right, but she has no intention of getting involved with that girl. Rose supposes she should find comfort in the fact that Opal Gates is awake, that she is not the only one unable to sleep this night, but she feels no nocturnal bond with her new neighbor. In the few weeks since Opal moved in, it has become clear that there is nothing but tribulation in store for that one. All you need do is take one quick look, and you can see the whole story. Girls like Opal suck trouble to them.

Rose leaves the window and returns to bed. Ned snores on peacefully. She twists her head on the pillow and looks at her husband, studies his face in the slippery light of the moon. She doesn't need her glasses to see the deep lines that etch the skin between his eyes and make gutters from his nose to his chin. He is fifty-seven. We're getting old, she thinks. Her heart almost softens.

Sometimes she wonders why it is so easy for Ned. Isn't he angry about all the things that have been taken from them, simple things like Todd growing up, marrying, having a child of his own? For five years she has tracked all the things that will never happen, bitter anniversaries that keep grief alive and sharp but that she cannot stop her mind from recording: Todd's senior prom, his high school graduation, the fall he would have entered college. Doesn't Ned ever think of these things?

Once, three years ago, they were staring at some program on television, and she blurted, "He would be in college now."

"For God's sake!" Ned shouted. The green recliner snapped to an upright position, and he stalked from the room. As far as he is concerned, Todd is over, subject closed.

Men are different, she thinks.

ALTHOUGH she cannot remember falling asleep, she must have dozed off, for the next time she looks, the clock reads 6:30. Beside her, Ned moans softly; then he's awake.

"Time to get up," he says.

"Yes," she says.

She lifts the weight of his arm from her ribs and takes a little breath. In the morning light she can almost believe she has only imagined the itch, can almost believe that she has already experienced her lifetime's allotment of pain and grief.

They get through breakfast courtesy of the *Today* show. Ned switches on the set the second he walks into the kitchen, then folds the Springfield paper open to the sports section. Rose starts the eggs, gritting her teeth against the blare of the television, which seems to drill into her brain and settle there, buzzing on and on. Some days she wants to snatch the set right off the counter, cart it out behind the garage, and take an axe to it.

Calling the anchorman Bryant Gumball instead of Bryant Gumbel is Ned's morning joke. He says it every morning and then laughs as if this is the first time in his life he's ever said it. If he says it today, she thinks, I swear I'll hit him in the head with the skillet. She stays at the stove until the urge passes.

"What's on your agenda?" Ned asks.

As long as she can remember, he's asked this exact same question over breakfast. Years ago she made up the answers. *Oh, lunch with Rock Hudson and dancing with Fred Astaire. Just a quick trip to Bali, but I'll be back in time for dinner.* "Rose, you're a card," he would say, as if she were the funniest person on the planet.

"Nothing special," she answers, serving up his eggs.

"Can't imagine how you keep yourself busy all day," he says between a mouthful of eggs and a swig of coffee.

"I manage," she says.

After he leaves, Rose flicks off the TV, then does the dishes. She wipes the counters and replaces the quilted rooster over the toaster. Then she goes upstairs to strip their bed and put on new sheets.

Ned has been gone about an hour, and she is coming up the stairs from the basement with the laundry, when the phone rings. She just knows it is Anderson Jeffrey. He has been calling on and off all month, since she stopped going to writing class.

The class was Ned's idea. When he found the college catalogue on her dresser, he latched onto it, hung on to it the way he insisted on cleaving to hope. Dorothy Barnes, the checkout clerk at the Stop & Shop, had shoved the pamphlet into Rose's shopping bag along with the weekly sales circular. If Ned had handed it to her, or Doc Blessing, she would have thrown it away without taking a second look, but since it came to her by accident, she kept it, even gave it a quick glance, scanning the listing for the fall semester adult education courses at the local community college. As soon as Ned saw it, that awful expression of hope spread over his face. *She's finally going to return to normal.* That is his phrase: "Return to normal." As if a state of mind is easy to find, as if all you need is a road map. But things aren't as simple as men like to think.

"Well now, Rosie," he said when he picked up the catalogue, "aren't you full of surprises." He stood in their bedroom, looking over the brochure. There were about a dozen classes listed, including upholstering, personal computers, creative writing, conversational French, emergency first aid, and quilt making.

"It's nothing," she said. "Just junk." Still, she has to admit the quilt-making class caught her attention. All the sewing she has done, and she's never made a quilt. She could almost see herself taking the class. She'd use some of Todd's things. Maybe if she made a quilt with bits of her son's clothes, it would be a little like having something of Todd just for her, something that no one knew about and no one could take away.

She was getting ready to tell Ned that perhaps she'd like to take that quilt-making class, when he came home and announced that he'd enrolled her in creative writing, had paid the tuition. Right then she could just see that quilt she never made fading away.

The phone stops ringing. She wishes she could put the whole business of Anderson Jeffrey and the writing class out of her mind.

She takes the sheets out to the line. In a month the first snow will probably fall, but today is warm and sunny. It is the kind of Indian summer day that always fills Rose with sorrow.

A blast of noise from the Montgomery place startles her. She glances over and sees Opal Gates come out to the back porch carting a sleek black box that Rose identifies as the source of the noise—that horrid stuff young people mistake for music. Then the door opens again, and the child comes tumbling out of the house.

Initially, before Ned brought home the facts, she took the girl to be the boy's older sister. She certainly doesn't look a day over sixteen. She is scrawny, thin as a playing card, with red hair like nothing Rose has ever seen in captivity.

"She's the kid's mother," Ned reported one night, sharing the information he has picked up over coffee at Trudy's. Her name is Opal Gates; she is from the South—North Carolina, according to the plates on the Buick—and has rented the Montgomery place for a year. The husband has not been sighted.

Right then Rose understood the whole story. The girl has gone and gotten herself pregnant. Probably a high school dropout. Well, at least she didn't have an abortion. Give her credit for that.

The most interesting thing is that Opal Gates makes dolls. According to Maida Learned over at the Yellow Balloon toy store, the girl can take a photo of a child and produce a doll that's nearly a twin. Maida has already ordered several for the store, although Rose can't imagine this is the kind of thing you can make a living at.

Other bits of gossip have surfaced. The general opinion is that

Opal Gates is far too casual with her care of the boy. Gloria at the Cutting Edge said that when the pair turned up for the boy to get a haircut, he was allowed to run wild. And Gloria's daughter, Marcia, had seen them at the playground. When she tried to warn Opal about the jungle gym, the one the Levitt child broke her collarbone on, the girl laughed and then allowed her son to climb the bars. "Now don't you go worrying about that," she said to Marcia. "Boys bounce." *Boys bounce.* The audacity of it. The carelessness of it.

Boys *don't* bounce. They break.

In the yard next door, Opal fiddles with the radio while the boy runs around in circles, screeching like a little banshee. And here it is October and neither of them wearing shoes. You can't blame the boy—he's too young to know better—but the mother should use her head. Barefoot in October. A flea would have more sense. Rose isn't prejudiced and doesn't like to form judgments about people, but it looks to her that the girl is what you'd call southern trash.

Rose is pinning up the last pair of Ned's socks when she hears the girl's shouted "hello." Naturally, Rose ignores this. She has no intention of mixing in. Nothing but trouble there.

It galls her that someone has probably already told the girl about Todd. "That's poor Rose Nelson," they tell newcomers, as if that is her full name. *Poor Rose Nelson. The woman who lost her only son in that dreadful accident a few years back.* Spreading her business to anyone who will listen. Then she wonders, as she has all month, what brought Opal Gates and her boy to Normal.

NORMAL really is the name of their town, and there are plenty of jokes about it. Back when she used to care about things like that, Rose liked living in a place called Normal, thought it sounded like the name of a southern town. People in the South do have a sense of poetry about the naming of things that doesn't seem to exist in other parts of the country.

Their town is named after a Civil War hero who was born here, Colonel Percival Winfield Normal. Even though he was a lesser figure in the War Between the States, a statue of him stands in the square in front of their town hall. Percival Winfield Normal, now there is a southern name if ever there was one. When she walks by his statue, Rose often looks up at the colonel and wonders how he ended up in western Massachusetts.

But then, nobody really ends up where they think they are heading, do they? Look at her. Look at Ned. Look at Todd.

Opal

"DAMN," Opal says when the phone rings. The line has only been hooked up for two weeks, and already Melva has called eight times. Eight calls, eight arguments. Conversations Opal would rather not rehash this morning. Try as she might, she can't make her mama understand why she had to leave New Zion.

Four rings. Five. *Don't you bite; don't you grab the bait,* she counsels herself as she picks up the receiver. *No matter how much she provokes you, stay cool.* Staying cool is not one of Opal's strong points. Her fuse was born short.

"Raylee?"

"Raylee's not here." Her voice is perfectly calm.

Twice in the two years since she changed her name, Opal has sent Melva copies of the court order and the printed legal ad that appeared in the local newspaper, but her mama believes the whole name-change episode is just another phase Opal is going through.

"Raylee? Is that you?"

No winning this game. "Yes."

"Well, thank the Lord. I thought I misdialed. Are you all right?"

"I'm *fine.*"

"How's Zack? Does he miss his Melvama?" Melvama is the name Melva has coined for Zack to call her. She's much too young to be a grandmother.

"Zack's fine, Mama. We're both doing just fine."

Melva barely pauses for this response. "Billy drove on over and joined us for dinner last night," she says. "I swear, that boy looks just dreadful. He misses you both terribly."

Just when did her mama turn so soft on Billy? And why on earth would she invite him to dinner?

"He loves you, Raylee. I hope you know that. It just breaks my heart in two to see the way he misses his boy."

The same boy, Opal wants to tell her, he wanted me to abort; the same boy he can't even be bothered to call and check on. She holds her tongue. With her mama every conversation is a minefield, every word uttered something that will later be used against her.

"You know, Raylee, there are plenty of girls in New Zion who would jump at the chance to get a taste of Billy. Just jump. You can't expect him to sit around forever. You hear me, girl?"

Opal can't even sort out all the emotions this statement provokes.

"Raylee, why are you doing this to Billy? To your daddy and me? Is your heart made of stone, girl? When are you going to get all this foolishness out of your head and bring our grandbaby back here where he belongs?"

Opal considers all the answers she can give but takes the coward's way out. "I've got to get going," she says. "Zack needs me."

Zack does need her. But he certainly doesn't need Billy, whose idea of fatherhood is to teach his son how to pop the flip top on a can of Bud. She can't imagine why Billy is hangdogging around her parents. He doesn't really want Zack. Or her. He just wants what he can't have. Nothing new about that.

She goes to check on Zack. Three days ago he created a makeshift tent by draping a blanket between two ladder-back chairs. Since then, he regularly disappears inside for great lengths of time. A tepee? Cave? Space station? Opal doesn't dream of taking it down, although Melva would not have allowed something like this to remain in her living room.

Items vanish inside. Pillows. Toy trucks. Plastic bowls. Food. "Provisions," he tells her. *Provisions.* She truly can't imagine where in the world a five-year-old came up with a word like that. He's so bright it frightens her. She can't begin to figure out how she'll manage to raise him. There should be a class in that. She loves him. She knows that for certain. She hopes it's enough.

Sometimes she likes to think she just strayed into motherhood, like a character in a movie who drifts on-screen but doesn't have responsibility for the way the story turns out. But when she is looking real straight, trying to be honest, she has to ask herself if deep inside she wanted to get pregnant.

It's pure fact that that is one of the questions Emily asked her during their first counseling session. Therapy was part of the deal her mama made. Opal could keep the baby, but she had to see a psychologist. Of course this compromise about killed Melva, who still hasn't forgiven Opal for ruining the family's reputation.

Opal thought Emily Jackman would try to convince her to give the baby up, but she never did. She never judged her or made her feel ashamed. When Emily asked her if she had fallen for Billy because he was a star basketball player, she had to laugh. Opal and her friend Sujette were just about the only ones in school who didn't think the jocks were gods. They used to make fun of them, imitating the way they would walk through the cafeteria with total attitude like they were special messengers from heaven. Opal didn't see how anyone could be seriously interested in someone whose entire life ambition was to play guard for the Tar Heels.

She believes Billy first noticed her because she was just about the only girl in school who didn't faint when he walked by. He began sitting at her table at lunch and letting everyone know he was after her. Then, with all this attention focused on her, she began to taste what it was like to feel special. She liked the power his wanting gave her.

Of course, after they had sex, the power switched. Sex unhinged her. It was all she thought about. Kissing. Touching. Tasting. She totally understands how sex causes so much trouble in the world. For now, though, she has sworn off sex. Who needs it? She has absolutely no intention of getting caught again. Plus she is responsible for Zack. Having a child makes you old that way.

"Mama?" Zack reappears from the blanket tent. He runs to her, gives her a hug. She wants to kiss him, smother him, but she holds back so he will not be frightened by the ferocity of her feelings.

The first time she held Zack, she finally realized what love was, understood it in a way she never had with Billy. If anything ever happened to Zack, she would die. She would welcome death.

"I'm hungry," he announces. "But our cupboard is bare."

Where does he come up with these statements?

"Sounds like we need to take a safari to the store."

"Exactly," he says.

For a fact, she and Zack will be just fine. They don't need a man. Or anyone else.

AT THE checkout counter of the Stop & Shop, Opal stacks groceries on the conveyor while trying to keep Zack away from the candy display rack. Without Melva at her shoulder criticizing her every choice, she is free to put whatever she wants in her grocery cart. As she sets the items on the counter—Fruit Loops, Twinkies, white bread, hot dogs, a jar of marshmallow fluff, macaroni and cheese—it occurs to her that it looks as if Zack has done the shopping. She has to get serious about nutrition soon.

"Coupons?" The cashier's eyes catch hers, then slide away to take in her bare legs, her chipped and broken nails, her too long hair.

Opal recognizes disapproval on—her gaze falls to the green plastic badge—Dorothy B.'s face. What is it about her that elicits this tight-lipped disapproval from older women?

"No, ma'am," she says. "No coupons."

Dorothy B. rings up the Twinkies and hot dogs. "Don't think I've seen you before. Visiting?"

"No. We moved here."

"From the South, right?"

Opal nods.

"I knew it. The accent gave you away."

No kidding, Sherlock, Opal thinks. She just wants to get out of there, go home, convince Zack to take a nap so she can grab one herself. The last weeks have left her sleep-deprived. There was the trip from New Zion, the day traipsing around with the real estate agent looking for a rental, then the unpacking and settling in, finding a nursery school for Zack, all the while fielding Melva's calls. It has been a rough spell, made more difficult by the nagging apprehension that she is making a huge mistake.

How could something that seemed so right—so *fated*—back in New Zion now feel like a mistake?

The last Sunday in August, the day of the picnic, the one her mama had held every year as long as she could remember, was the day she decided to leave. Sitting on the porch while her daddy, his face all shut down, was grilling his special chicken, and Zack was wading in the kiddie pool, and Billy—Billy who didn't even *like* her mama—was flirting like Melva was his girlfriend or something, Opal felt a heaviness settle hard on her ribs. Then he called out for her to fetch him a beer. His old lady, he called her. She was *twenty*.

Her heart actually stopped beating—she felt her pulse cease—and in that icy moment she saw the rest of her life playing out in front of her, playing out in picnic after picnic after picnic.

That was when the extraordinary idea took hold. She could leave—just take Zack, pack up, and go. She hugged the thought close. If Melva looked over at her, for sure her mama would read this plan plain on her face. But her mama was busy with Billy.

Later, driving back to her apartment, at the intersection of County Road and Jefferson, Opal stared at the signal swaying overhead. Green light, go, she whispered. Red light, stay. Green light, go. Red light, stay. She sailed right through that go light. Sailed, eventually, all the way to Massachusetts.

"This is your son?" The cashier's question pulls her back.

Opal nods.

"I thought so," Dorothy B. says. "The red hair and all. But you don't look old enough to drive, let alone have a child."

"I'm twenty-two." Opal automatically tacks two years on to her age. She hates the way people look at her when they tally up the numbers and figure out she was pregnant at fifteen.

"I want a Twinkie," Zack says.

"Okay, sugah," she says. "You can have one when we get home."

"Where are you living?" the cashier asks.

"Chestnut Street."

"Big white house at the end of the block? Green shutters?"

"Mmmmmmm-hmmmm."

"You're in the Montgomery place. Next to poor Rose Nelson."

Well, isn't this the first interesting thing to come out of the woman's mouth? Zack starts pushing for a Twinkie, so Opal tears a wrapper off one and hands him the cake. "Poor Rose Nelson?"

"Tragic thing." Dorothy B. lowers her voice. "Tragic. The way she lost her boy. Only child, too."

Opal puts her hand on Zack's shoulder.

"He was sixteen. Let's see. Exactly five years ago this month. Course, after that, she's never been quite right."

Well, duh. How could you ever be all right again after you lost a child? How could you go on breathing in and breathing out?

BACK home, as Opal unloads the groceries from the Buick, she glances over at the neighboring house. Although the grass is kept up, the house has a vacant look. The shades are drawn; there is no car in the drive. She pictures her neighbor inside the house, surrounded by silence. After the accident she should have moved away. Opal knows she would have. There is a lot to be said for geographic cures.

She totes the grocery bags up the back steps and into the kitchen. The room is a study in avocado and gold, a decorating scheme Opal figures had its triumph before she was born.

The entire house is decorated out of a *Family Circle* of an earlier era, but it's bigger than she expected to find on her budget. Even with the luxury of Aunt May's check, she has to be careful.

Opal is unbagging the groceries when, through the window above the sink, she catches sight of someone in the yard next door. The cashier's words echo as she watches her neighbor make her way to the clothesline: *Poor Rose Nelson.*

She is surprised to see how ordinary the woman looks, how solid, standing there in a housecoat and sweater, carefully pinning up each sheet. Opal has envisioned Rose as someone thin, someone who looks like there is something broken about her, but Rose seems solid, close to plump. The words "pioneer stock" jump into Opal's head.

Watching Rose clip a sail of white linen to the line, she is reminded of square-shouldered prairie women and the Conestoga wagons she learned about in eighth-grade history, and then she envisions a figurehead carved on the bow of a ship, leading the way through storms. To Opal, Rose doesn't look "poor" at all. She imagines at that moment there is something Rose knows that she needs to know, although she cannot for the world imagine what it might be.

Rose

"MAMA?" the boy cries out in the neighboring yard.

Before Rose can steel herself against it, the memory comes full up, striking her breath away.

There is no guarding against memory. That's the devil of it. It slips in before you can catch yourself, closing your throat, startling your heart. Anything can trigger it—the unexpected convergence of a particular sight and sound, a specific smell, a song. Anything.

Now, the sun on her back, the clean smell of the laundry mingling with the crisp air of fall, the sound of the child next door shouting for his mother just as a transport from Westover flies over—all converge to flip her back five years. She was hanging the wash that day too, doing chores without one clue that her real life was about to end, that she was about to see her son and touch his warm body for the last time.

THE back door slams, and Todd comes out. He blinks against the sun. He takes the steps two at a time. Slow down, she wants to shout. Since he turned sixteen, everything he does is too fast, too loud. It seems to her he courts disaster. At the lake, he dives too close to hidden rocks, and none of her warnings can stop him.

Ned doesn't worry. Never has. She's the one who, since Todd's birth, has carried this vast helplessness inside. No one ever warns you about that. No one ever says that having a child is like having your heart walk around outside your body, bumping into things.

A C-130 heading back to Westover briefly shadows the yard.

"Mom?"

She watches as he lopes across the yard. All angles and joints. Gangly. Yet even in a body so suddenly large, there is an awkward grace. He will be a graceful man, she thinks, and feels a rush of pride.

"Jimmy and I are going out to the Quabbin. There's been a sighting of new eagles."

"What about work?" She hates for him to go to the reservoir. There have been at least two drownings there in the past few years.

"I already checked with Dad. He said as long as I'm back by noon."

That Ned has already given his okay irritates her. "I don't know," she begins as she clips an undershirt to the line.

"And I was wondering, Can I borrow the car? Dad said ask you."

So he's asked Ned first. Just this once why couldn't Ned say no? She looks over to the drive where the Pontiac is parked. As a surprise Ned registered it in her name. It is the first new car she has ever owned.

"Can I?"

She hesitates. He has only been driving for three months. "Why don't you take the pickup?"

"Dad might need it at the station. I'll be careful. Promise."

If he were going alone, on a short trip to the store, but to think of him driving out to the reservoir, the twisting roads, with Jimmy, in her new car, a car with not one single scratch or dent. No.

"Not today," she says. "I have some errands I need to do." Two words. Quickly said. Two words that change the universe.

"Okay," he says. "We'll take Jimmy's truck. Catch you later." He gives her a hug. Quick and casual.

Busy with laundry and still irritated that he is going to the reservoir, she doesn't return the embrace. "Be careful," she says.

THE thin voice of the child in the next yard brings Rose back. Her heart is beating with the familiar flutter of guilt and grief, heavy with a secret too shameful to bear. Boys *bounce*.

The pain of memory comes in spasms. Then the boy next door laughs, and Rose feels a contraction of longing as involuntary as a hiccup. She picks up the empty basket and flees to the house.

Ned

AFTER lunch Ned services the transmission on the Dowlings' '89 Olds. He drops the pan and lets the fluid out, then replaces the filter. As he slips the new gasket on, he feels the familiar band stretching across his temples. The headaches have been coming on more and more lately.

He's already had a bitch of a morning. Tyrone Miller, his part-time mechanic, hasn't shown, and now Ned is so far behind he's going to have to carry at least two jobs over to tomorrow.

At three thirty, head pounding so ugly it's an effort to keep his eyes open, he gives up and heads home.

THE house has an empty feel. "Rose?" he yells. "Rosie?"

He checks the kitchen and then upstairs. She isn't in their bedroom. Todd's door is closed, and as he approaches, he hopes to hell she isn't in there. He hasn't found her in there in months, and he clings to this as a sign she is getting better. He opens the door, smells stale air. Years ago the last traces of Todd's sweat and shaving lotion evaporated, but everything else is the same.

If Ned has his way, they would turn the room into a den—should have done it a long time ago. A place where he can do paperwork for the service station instead of the cramped space he now uses. Naturally, Rose won't hear of it. Where is she anyway? "Rose?" he calls again.

He goes out to the hall. From the upstairs window he takes in the reassuring sight of laundry on the line. Over in the yard at the Montgomery place, he sees two figures, hears the thump of rock music.

The Gates girl moved in last month. No husband on the scene, just her and the kid, although in Ned's eyes she isn't much more than a kid herself. Personally, he thinks she's a fruitcake. She runs around in bare feet and flashy skirts that either swing around her ankles or cut high across her thighs. No middle ground with her.

A couple of weeks ago she stopped by the station to fuel that old

Buick she drives, and it wasn't two minutes before she had Tyrone's tongue hanging near to his knees. The mechanic wasn't much good for the next half hour. It makes Ned nervous, her being next door, so close to Rose.

The boy seems nice enough, though. He says "sorry" when his ball rolls over to their yard. When Ned was out mowing the lawn the previous night, he saw the kid playing all alone, tossing an old Wiffle ball up in the air, tossing and missing, over and over until it made him dizzy to watch. It reminded him of all the nights he'd spent with Todd, teaching him to catch.

Ned had wanted more than the one child, but it hadn't worked out that way. Rose was thirty-three when Todd was born and had almost lost hope. If you have more than one kid, at least there are others if something happens to one. Not that he's blaming Rose.

Sometimes, when he allows himself to think about Todd, he is hit with an actual pain, a physical ache he can feel in his muscles and sinew and organs.

He notices the bathroom door is closed. "Rose," he says. "Rosie, you in there?"

"Go away."

He tries the knob, finds it locked. He sighs. "Rosie," he says, "open up. I need a couple of aspirin. I've got a hell of a headache."

The door opens enough for her to extend an arm, hand him a bottle of Excedrin. He takes it and waits—helplessly—while she withdraws her hand. He listens as the lock is turned.

He goes downstairs to the kitchen and takes the Excedrin. He would like to ask someone what to do about Rose. Doc Blessing hasn't been able to help. Oh, he gave her pills, but after a week she refused to take them. Reverend Wills has talked to them both, but that hasn't changed a thing. It's as if Ned married one woman—a woman who was a kind and good wife, a good mother, too—and then one day, an accident, and nothing was the same.

Rose closed. Just plain shut up. The first thing was, she refused to drive. "Sell the car," she told him. Sell the car? The Pontiac she was so crazy about she washed it nearly every day, like a teenager? He put it off, offering excuses, sure that she'd come around, until the day she told him if he didn't sell it, she would.

He keeps waiting for her to get over her grief. Nights, he sits in his recliner and tries to remember Rose. His Rose. Before. He goes back to the beginning, long before Todd. He was so in love with her then, it scared him.

Remembering never helps. It only makes the ache worse. In addition to losing a son, he's lost his wife, too.

Why can't she come back to him? Doesn't she think he misses Todd? Doesn't she know that when he put Todd in the ground, a lot of his dreams were buried there as well?

God knows, he loved his son. And he loves Rose; he really does. He loves Rose, but she is trying that love. Things happen to people. Accidents. Illness. But people get on with their lives. It isn't right—or normal—to act like the funeral was yesterday instead of five years ago.

Rose's grief, Ned thinks. Rose's grief will kill me, too.

Rose

"ROSE?"

She hears Ned calling her from the hall. "Rosie? You in there?"

She can't make herself answer. She sits on the toilet and rocks back and forth, her arms wrapped around her midsection. She hasn't had a spell like this for weeks. Months.

After a while the sound of laughter pulls her to the window, and she looks down on the neighbor's yard. That boy is still outside. Now he is kicking a ball around the grass. She yanks the shade to the sill, as if it were possible to shut out the unfairness of it. How is it possible that Opal Gates be given a child, blessed with a child, when she doesn't care enough to put shoes on her boy's feet?

Ned knocks again. "Rose, let me in. I need some aspirin. I've got a hell of a headache."

She goes to the medicine cabinet, takes out the Excedrin, unlocks the bathroom door. She catches a quick glimpse of him, his face pale, slack with pain, and feels a spasm of guilt. Recently he's been getting these headaches. She is truly sorry that she can't help him, can't come out of the bathroom. She hands the bottle to him, re-locks the door, shuts out the sight of his tired face. There is room in her heart for only so much pain.

She listens to his footsteps on the stairs; then kitchen sounds float up, reach her through the locked door. A cupboard door closing. A pan slapped down on the range. Sharp noises, each a messenger of Ned's anger and frustration. After a while the excited tones of a TV sports announcer rise up the stairs. Ned is done trying to reach her.

She raises the window shade and watches the sky turn pink. She knows that she can't stay here forever, that she'll have to unlock the door, return to life.

Eventually the ball game ends. She hears the distant sound of water running through the pipes as the toilet flushes in the down-stairs bath. Through the door she hears the sounds of familiar ritual as Ned readies himself for bed. His footsteps on the stairs. The rustling of clothes as he undresses. The click of the switch on the bedside lamp.

She opens the door, goes downstairs. In the kitchen, she flips on the overhead light. Ned has left his dishes in the sink, and she recon-structs his meal from the traces: toast, Campbell's Vegetable Beef Soup, cherry pie. There is one slice left, and she eats it standing at the counter. When she is finished, she fills the sink with water, squirts in detergent, submerges her hands to their chore.

After she has rinsed the last plate, she listens to the familiar creak-ing of the house as it settles into sleep. The deep hum of the furnace, the scratching of a rose briar against the kitchen window. They should be cut back, before the deep frost. Another chore for Ned.

"Foolish of us to keep this place," he told her over dinner last night. "It's too big for the two of us. Too much upkeep."

More and more he has been talking about a time in the near future—three to five years is his plan—when they will sell the house and the service station and buy a place in Florida. When he talks this way, Rose's heart congeals with something close to hatred.

Nothing on earth could make her move from this house. Doesn't Ned understand? This house is Todd's house. If Ned wants to get rid of the station, that is his business, but she isn't selling the house.

Lord knows, since Todd's death she has no illusion that she can control one single thing in this universe, but she can't help but cling to the nearly superstitious belief that if she can just freeze things, keep them the same, she and Ned will escape further harm and she will get a sign from Todd. In spite of all contrary evidence, she clings to this last belief.

Lately, in spite of her efforts, things are changing. Her balance is precarious, as if deep inside she is undergoing a tectonic plate shift, like the one she heard about on a *Nova* show. When the narrator explained that subtle movements occur within the earth's crust and that these alterations precede earthquakes, she felt a jolt of recognition. Since the accident this feeling has been growing, and she has especially felt it this fall, as if her interior world were oscillating in minute and dangerous movements.

She turns out the kitchen light and heads up the hall stairs to their bedroom. She undresses, slides into bed, careful not to disturb Ned. He is a good man. Honest and hardworking. She is lucky to have him. She repeats these words like a prayer.

After Todd died, Reverend Wills gave them a book written for couples who have experienced the loss of a child. The book said that the death of a child could bring a couple closer or drive them apart, that couples either turned to each other for comfort, or they divorced, the assault of a child's death too much for their marriage to withstand. Neither has happened to her and Ned. They just float, suspended in time, waiting for a life raft to find them.

Opal

DURING her first two months in Normal, Opal had prepared herself for a call from Billy, but the weeks have passed without so much as a single word. At first this lack of communication irritated her, but now she is reassured by it. It reinforces her belief that Billy is relieved to have them out of his life, that he won't make any fuss.

When he finally does call, she is so totally unprepared that his voice sends a jolt straight to her stomach.

"Hi, Billy," she manages, cool as you please. She slides down to the kitchen floor, her back against the cupboard, and cradles the phone base in her lap, unconsciously taking the same pose she held every night the fall of her junior year when, night after night, for hours, they would talk in whispers.

"I miss you, Opal." He speaks in a low voice. "How's Zack?"

As if he anything like cares. "Well, he's just fine." She lets her eyes roam around the kitchen and finally fix on the small yellow-and-blue spot stuck straight in the middle of a cupboard door.

The sticker—peeled from a banana—was there when she moved in. It was so startlingly out of place in the sterile avocado kitchen that Opal had taken it as a sign. She has not yet figured out the meaning. CHIQUITA. She pulls her attention from the decal.

"I miss you, Opal."

She pauses, knowing the prescribed response, the answer Billy waits for: *I miss you, too.* The wire hums with her silence.

"How're you doing? You okay?" he asks.

"I'm great," she says in a baton twirler's chirp. "Just great."

"Well, I'm glad," he says in a voice suddenly gone flat. "Me, I'm not doing so great. That story you fed me about going to visit a relative? Well, damn it all, Opal. You lied."

Ancient history, Opal thinks. "I'm sorry."

"Sorry doesn't count for much right now," he says.

"Let's don't fight," she says. "There's no point."

"There is a point, and the point is, I miss my boy, Opal."

Well, just how did Billy Steele grow himself a paternal streak? Here she's been away for more than two months, and he's just now getting around to calling her.

"Listen, Opal," he says with a voice so serious that an unexpected thrill of fear courses through her. "I want you back here. I want us to get married, be a family. I mean it, honey."

Fat to no chance of that, she thinks. Just because she made a mistake by getting pregnant, she isn't going to compound it by marrying him. Billy's last name should be He Always Wants What He Can't Have. The most popular kid in New Zion High, and the only reason he chose Opal was because she kept him dangling for weeks. Gave him only a little at a time.

"I mean it, Opal. We could get married. Give Zack a proper home. You can't just stay away like this."

"My being here has nothing to do with you, Billy."

"But Zack has something to do with me. He's my son, too."

"Like you really wanted him."

Billy's reply is muffled. He murmurs something on his end, then says, "When we're done, your mama wants to talk to you."

"You're calling from my mama's?"

"Yeah."

This news floors her. "What are you doing there?"

"I just stopped by for dinner."

Stopped by? It isn't like her parents' house is on his way home. There is another muffled exchange on his end, and then the phone is handed to Melva.

"This isn't easy for any of us," her mama begins. "I'm ashamed to think a child of mine could behave in such an irresponsible way."

"This isn't about you, Mama," Opal cuts in. Lordy, hasn't she heard all this before, but Melva is off and running.

"If you can't think of my feelings, or your daddy's or Billy's, you could at least consider your son. He needs a daddy."

Opal has spent many nights brooding over this very point. From day one she has been concerned about how the separation would affect Zack.

"For the life of me," Melva says, "I can't figure you out. Sometimes I think you deliberately set out to upset people's lives, to break people's hearts."

Damn. Doesn't her mama know she'd never deliberately set out to hurt people or break their hearts? How can she make Melva understand she is just trying the only way she knows to keep from drowning in the sea of other people's hopes and plans and expectations, from letting herself be talked into a marriage she knows in the deepest part of her heart would be a mistake?

"Are you listening to me, Raylee? I want you to realize that your actions have consequences."

Actions have consequences. "You gave me that lecture when I was a kid, Mama. I'm not fifteen."

Fifteen. Standing in the living room. Melva ranting on about how she won't be able to hold her head up around town and how she, Raylee, had her whole life still ahead of her, then getting down to the business at hand. *We know a doctor . . . this early on . . . a safe procedure.* Her mama couldn't bring herself to say "abortion," yet the word hung in the air like a sour smell. She was as surprised as her mama and daddy when she heard herself say no.

"Well, stop acting as if you were fifteen," Melva continues. "You're so gosh darn wrapped up in yourself you can't see we're heartbroken here. Absolutely heartbroken with missing our darling boy."

Opal can't traverse this territory one more time. "I have to go, Mama. I just got Zack to bed, and I think I hear him crying."

"Of course he's crying. He misses his daddy. He misses all of us. What you are doing to him is beyond irresponsible. It's criminal. Don't come back to me down the road and say I didn't warn you."

After Opal hangs up, the phone call reverberates in her head. She's wounded to think her mama believes she goes through life setting out to shatter people's hearts. Is Billy's heart broken? She has no idea. But she won't marry Billy just so Zack has a daddy, just so her mama can hold her head up. She doesn't love Billy enough, even if—she has to admit it—his voice still has power over her. Even if that night up in the old burial ground behind New Zion Baptist she had done things with Billy that even now make her blush.

The power of sex. And where does that get you? One of the hardest things about splitting from Billy is missing sex. Well, forget sex. She has no intention of getting caught in that trap again.

She climbs the stairs to check on Zack. In the dim light she negotiates her way through the twine Zack has strung across his floor, a cat's cradle that interlaces the legs of his bureau and bed. This web is a new creation, one he relies on to trap the werewolf, a monster that has come into his imagination—and bedroom—since the Halloween party at school.

Zack is bathed in the glow of his Batman night-light, already lost in the hard, serious sleep of childhood. She tucks the blanket around him, reluctant to leave. She could spend hours watching him sleep. As she tiptoes out of the room and goes downstairs, she replays the phone call, trying to pin down why she feels uneasy.

Months later, remembering this night, she will wonder how she could have ignored her mama's warnings, how she could have forgotten about the strength of Billy's resolve once he made up his mind to something. How could there not have been a *sign?*

The call has left Opal too edgy for sleep, and she heads into the dining room, where her current project lies on the cutting table.

The Montgomerys' maple drop leaf works just fine for cutting and sewing her dolls, and Opal has set up a card table for painting. Squares of fabric—tulle, cotton in a variety of prints, satin, organza, and denim—are piled in one corner of the room. Bags of kapok are stored beneath the table. Several plastic tackle boxes are stacked against one wall, their individual compartments filled with buttons, rhinestones, aglets, sequins, snaps, and hooks and eyes.

She picks up the order form and studies the girl in the photo attached. Dutch-cut brown hair and serious eyes that peer out through round-framed glasses. "Leave out the glasses," the grandmother has noted on the form. She wants a ballerina, the number one choice for girl dolls. Why can't people use their imagination? It's clear as warts on a toad's back that this child was not consulted about the decision. Opal sees intelligence in the girl's eyes, determination in her mouth. This child wants to walk on the moon, not pivot on knuckled-under toes. People can be so blind.

In the past few weeks word has spread about her dolls. Opal has picked up a half-dozen orders from some of the other mothers at Zack's preschool, and the local toy store has already reordered.

She sets the order form aside and goes into the kitchen. She has a serious case of the munchies. She combs the cupboards for something sweet and shakes out a handful of Fruit Loops. She would kill for a brownie—can almost feel the velvety weight on her tongue. Cereal just doesn't cut it.

The kitchen clock reads 10:40. The Stop & Shop is open for another twenty minutes. She climbs the stairs to Zack's room and picks her way through the web of twine leading to his bed.

"Zack?" she whispers. Then, a shade louder, "Zack?" He does not move. The trip out to the store and back won't take more than fifteen minutes. Twenty minutes tops. Round-trip. What could go wrong? What could happen to him asleep in a locked house?

"Zack." Louder this time. Then two more times before she picks her way back across the room.

Simple choices. A hunger for chocolate. Such an *ordinary* thing. How could she have foreseen that it is the beginning of all the hurt and sorrow that is to come?

OPAL drives along Main Street, passing the library, the town hall, the bank. She continues on past the police and fire stations, the Creamery, which is open, and a diner, which is not. At last she swings into the supermarket parking lot.

At this time of night Dorothy Barnes is the only cashier.

Opal heads directly for the bakery aisle and is debating between the brownies and eclairs when a voice breaks into her deliberation.

"Got a sweet tooth?"

The first thing she notices is the thick scar on his cheek. The second thing is that—scar or not—he's about the best-looking guy she's ever seen. She feels a jolt and for a moment is alive to *possibilities*.

"Me," he says, "I'd go for the brownies. I bet you're Opal."

She manages a nod. Merciful God, he *is* good-looking.

"Ty Miller," he says, holding out a hand. "I work for Ned over at the service station."

The moment their hands touch, Opal can feel her heart swell, can feel her pulse race. No mistaking the spiking of chemistry. She sees trouble coming, stretching ahead like ten miles of bad road.

"I've seen you when you've come by the garage," he says.

She wants the brownies, but because he has suggested them, she grabs the box of eclairs. "Gotta go," she says. "Nice to meet ya."

"You're out late," Dorothy says. "Where's that boy of yours?"

"Sleeping," Opal says. "With the sitter."

"Count your blessings." Dorothy nods toward the rack of tabloids at the end of the counter. "My heart goes out to her."

"Who?" Opal says. Her heart has still not returned to its regular beat. He must think she's an idiot, racing off like that. *Gotta go.*

Dorothy points to the headline above the photo of a young woman: DISTRAUGHT MOTHER BEGS: PLEASE RETURN MY SONS. "Kidnapped," she announces, dragging the box of eclairs over the scanner. "In Texas. By a Mexican. He jumped right into her car when she was stopped at a red light."

"God." *Zack.* Had she locked the door when she left?

Dorothy takes a ten from Opal, hands her her change. "The world's turned crazy. I blame it on drugs."

Would Zack even wake if someone broke in?

"We've started a collection." Dorothy indicates a coffee can. "For a reward. We're sending a check at the end of next week."

Opal stuffs her change through the slot.

HER hands are shaking by the time she pulls into the driveway. She has trouble with the house key; the door is locked after all.

Inside, she sets the pastries on the kitchen counter, checks the clock. It's 11:15. She hasn't been gone for more than half an hour. She heads for the stairs, and halfway up, she hears him.

He is at the top of the landing, his face puffy from tears.

"What happened, Zack? Sugah, what happened?"

"Where were you?" he accuses.

"Downstairs," she says, wrapping an arm around his shoulders.

"I called and called." He gives a shuddering breath that collapses into little ragged hiccups.

"I'm sorry, sugah." She will never, ever leave him alone again. *Ever.*

"I fell," he announces. The twine from the cat's cradle entangles his feet.

"It's okay, Zack. I'm here now." She tightens her embrace, and he yells. It's the pain yell, not the sad yell.

"What is it, Zack?"

"My arm," he says. Tears brim.

"Let me see," she says. In the glow from the downstairs light his arm looks fine, but when she runs her fingers over it, he cries out.

"Okay," she soothes. "Okay, sugah, I won't touch it."

She carries him to her room, careful not to touch the arm, and settles him in her bed, quiets him with two baby aspirin. Later, when she is sure he won't waken, she turns on the lamp. His arm *looks* okay. But when she strokes his forearm, he whimpers.

Months later, when everything begins to fall apart, she comes to believe it was not leaving New Zion that set the nightmare in motion. Not the string of lies she told, lies as tangled as the web of twine that tripped Zack that night. Not even Ty Miller. These things were just complications. The beginning was this night. It was the one grievous error of leaving Zack alone while she went out to satisfy her hunger.

Rose

AS SOON as Ned drives off, Rose gets out the Hoover. She is about to start vacuuming, an unnecessary chore since the house is spotless. She carries the Hoover into the dining room and is bending over to plug in the cord when a loud banging at the back door makes her jump. She's pretty sure who it is. Who else could it be, banging like a wild person? She stands perfectly still, but beneath her feet she can feel the floor tremble. The shifting of a continental plate.

"Mrs. Nelson. Mrs. Nelson."

If Rose knew a sign for warding off affliction, she would have made it. Instead, she opens the door. Opal Gates stands there. Her hair sparks out wild, and she carries the boy in her arms.

"Zack's hurt," the girl says. "His arm. I need to get him to the emergency room. Will you drive us?"

"I don't have a car. I—I don't drive," Rose manages.

"We'll take mine. I'll drive. You hold Zack and point the way."
The girl doesn't wait for more argument. Still carrying the boy, she
lopes across their yard to her car, sending the crows flying.

"Don't run," Rose says. "It will jar his arm."

The car floor is a mess, thick with Coke cans and fast-food wrappers. Rose uses her toe to nudge them aside. As Opal transfers the
boy to her, she braces herself. Even so, the weight of a small body
against her stomach catches her off guard. Before she can steel
herself, a knife blade of something akin to pleasure catches her.

The girl chatters nonstop, talking a blue streak, and Rose has to
bite her lip to keep from shushing her.

"Hold on, sugah," Opal keeps repeating. "We're almost there."
She pronounces it "thaya." Once or twice she takes a hand off the
wheel, reaches over, squeezes his knee. "It's gonna be okay, Zack."

As soon as they get to Mercy, Rose plans on calling a taxi.

OUTSIDE the doors of the emergency-wing entrance, Opal rolls
to a stop, switches off the engine, and runs ahead, calling for Rose
to follow. There is nothing for it but to carry the boy inside.

The nurse on duty takes their name and directs them to the waiting room. *The waiting room.* The room where she and Ned waited.

Everything is exactly the same, as if days have passed, not five
years. Gray industrial carpeting. Interlocking chairs with blue plastic
seats. Magazine rack affixed to the wall. A NO SMOKING sign. Five
years, and not one thing has been altered. Rose is faint with memory.

When they told her Todd was dead, she passed out in the middle
of the emergency room, the only time in her life she has ever
fainted. They swooped her off to a small room, made her lie down,
whisked the curtains closed. Such urgency. For what?

When they left the hospital—left Todd—she made Ned drive her
to the intersection at High and Church. He made a fuss about it,
but she wouldn't back down. The pavement was still wet from the
fire hoses. Near the curb, fragments of glass caught the sun.

A week later the fresh scar on the elm—a spot of bare bark
about the size of a dishpan—where Jimmy Sommers's pickup

had crashed, was the only evidence of what had occurred there.

Day after day she returned to the site, needing to stand at the last place her son had lived, had breathed. When Ned put his foot down and refused to take her there, she walked.

She was not surprised by the persistence of her grief. What surprised her was the idea that anyone *could* get over it. People thought grief was like the flu, something you got over. It wasn't. Oh, it ebbed for a moment—like a new moon tide flowing out—but then it rushed in and swept you away again.

THEY come for Zack. He is rolled off in a wheelchair by a nurse who is all efficiency. Opal goes with them, murmuring reassurances to her son. Rose watches them disappear behind swinging doors.

A nurse had handed Rose a plastic bag with Todd's clothes when they finally left the hospital. Ned assumed she threw them out, but she kept them. The blue jeans and plaid shirt, the navy T-shirt, his jockey shorts. Fingering each article, she would mentally recite the autopsy report. Fractures of wrists and arms and ribs, brain ripped—pons from medulla—aorta ripped. *Ripped.* The single word summing up all the violence done to her son.

Ned had wanted to cremate Todd's body, but she balked. It was unbearable to think of more damage done to him. Later she wished she had agreed. Then she would have his ashes.

"MRS. Nelson?" Opal plops down next to her.

"How is he?" Rose asks.

"Who the hell knows?" There is a hard edge to Opal's voice. She is near her limit. "They think it's a fracture, but they won't know until they've taken X rays."

Rose wants to tell the girl to lower her voice.

"God," Opal continues. "This is the most inefficient place I've ever been in. A vet could do a better job."

"Perhaps you should call someone?" Rose says. "Your husband?"

Opal looks straight at her. "Would if I could, but there ain't no such creature. I'm not married."

Lord, Rose thinks, what have I gotten myself into?

"Mrs. Gates?" A doctor approaches, looks from Rose to Opal.

"Miss Gates," Opal corrects.

"We've had a chance to read the X rays. Your son has a buckle fracture of the right wrist."

"Oh, God," Opal breathes. "Can I see him?"

"In a few minutes. Right now we're putting a cast on." The doctor looks down at his clipboard. "We need more information." He motions toward an alcove where vending machines are located.

Opal holds her ground. "I want to see Zack."

That's right, Rose thinks. Don't let them keep you apart.

"They're putting the cast on. While they're finishing up with that, I have a few questions."

"So ask."

"How did it happen?"

Opal's gaze shifts. "What?"

"Your son's injury. What caused it?"

There is a slight hesitation. "He slipped. In the tub."

"In the tub?"

"Yes," Opal says, her voice more confident.

"There is a rather significant bruise on his left thigh. Can you explain that?"

"Explain it?"

"Yes. How did it happen?"

"How the hell should I know? He's a boy. He plays at the playground. He falls down. Why are you asking me these things?"

"It's just routine. We have to fill out forms. Mandatory reports from the emergency physician, cases like this."

"Cases like this? What the hell does that mean?"

Rose can see from the doctor's expression that Opal's belligerence is not helping.

"You think I hurt my son?" Opal says. "You think I'd do anything to hurt Zack? Are you out of your mind?"

"Relax, Miss Gates. No one's accusing you of anything. We're required to ask these questions. Cases like this."

"Like what? Why do you keep saying that?"

"Were you alone with your son when he fell? Did anyone witness the accident?"

Opal doesn't speak.

"You have to answer these questions, Miss Gates. Were you alone when the accident occurred? Did anyone else witness it?"

"I did."

Both faces turn to Rose.

"And you are?"

Having uttered two words—words that still seem to hang, to echo in the air—Rose is incapable of further speech.

"Your name?" The doctor waits, pen poised over clipboard.

"Rose Nelson." Opal takes over. "Mrs. Nelson is my neighbor."

Rose could just bite her tongue. What had she been thinking?

"And you were there when it happened?"

"She just stopped by for coffee," Opal continues. "I had just finished giving Zack his bath, and while I was answering the door, he got back in to get his boat. He must have slipped."

Rose is appalled at how easily Opal lies.

"Is that true?" the doctor asks Rose.

She doesn't know how to retract the words. She nods.

He finishes jotting his notes, then closes the folder.

"I want to see him now," Opal says. "I want to see Zack."

Rose stares at her feet, unable to look anyone in the eye, as if she is the guilty one. Lord, she thinks, what have I gotten myself into?

Opal

THE total for the X rays, doctor's fee, and emergency-room fee comes to nearly four hundred dollars. Opal hands over her Visa. God knows how she'll pay it off. When she returns to the waiting room, Rose is nowhere to be seen. The ladies' room, Opal thinks. She could sure use Rose for moral support. The woman is as plain as a slice of bread, but there is something solid about her, something dependable that Opal needs right now.

"Mrs. Nelson called a taxi," the admitting nurse informs her.

Opal is disappointed. She wants to thank Rose for backing up her story with the doctor.

Opal knows for sure her own mama wouldn't have lied for her. Melva preaches honesty like it's her own special religion.

She doesn't want to be thinking of her mama just now. She can imagine what Melva will have to say about Zack's arm. Her mama would act like it was Opal's fault he fell. Like Opal isn't to be trusted with having a child. Just another thing she can't do right.

Right then, as she and Zack are leaving the hospital, Opal understands she can't go back to New Zion. Even if she wanted to, which she decidedly doesn't. In September, when she threw that Monopoly die and headed north, she was choosing something else for her and Zack, even if she wasn't exactly clear on what it was. And that changed everything. There are lines in life that once a person crosses over them, there's no going back to the other side. Trouble is, you don't always know there's a line you're stepping over until you're already halfway across. That's why keeping an eye out for signs is so important. It helps prepare you.

She surely does not have the least idea of what kind of life waits for her here in Normal or in the next place she lands. She only knows she can't go back to the way things were in New Zion. This lack of resolution could be depressing, but she tries to think of it as hopeful. Even today, with Zack's broken arm, she believes in the possible. Anything can happen. Any wonderful thing. Of course, this is another thing she and Billy disagree on. He expects the worst. As they cross the parking lot to the Buick, the sky darkens. "Looks like a storm coming on, bud," she says to Zack.

They barely drive two blocks when the rain begins to come down full strength, striking the windshield with the sharpness of hail.

Opal continues down Main and pulls into the Creamery's parking lot. "Want something to eat, bud?"

"Actually, the doctor said I'm not supposed to get my cast wet."

Lately he'd been starting every other sentence with that word: Actually, I'm not tired. Actually, I want a Coke. Opal doesn't know where he picked up the word, but she loves the way it makes him sound. Like a little professor.

She digs around the back seat until she retrieves a plastic grocery bag. "Here. We'll wrap your arm in this. Okay?"

"Okay," he says in a bitty voice.

Their waitress is dressed in just about the ugliest brown uniform on earth. The name badge identifies her as Tammy.

"Are you ready to order?" she asks.

Opal tucks the breakfast menu back behind the napkin holder. What is called for is some sugar. "Can we see the dessert menu?"

Tammy looks at Opal and then Zack. "Aren't we a little early for dessert?" she says, pushing the comment through a phony smile that doesn't fool Opal for one minute.

"No, *we* are not." Like she cares what this waitress thinks. She orders the biggest sundae the place offers. Zack gets a strawberry shake.

The waitress brings their order. Opal peels the paper sleeve from the straw and sticks it in his milk shake.

"Mama?"

"What, sugah?"

"I don't feel good."

"Come on, bud," she says. "Come sit by me." She moves over, making room for him in her side of the booth. "Here. Try some of mine." She scoops up some of the whipped cream.

"I don't feel good," Zack says again. "I want to go home."

He does look pale. Opal signals for the waitress and gets the check. Seven dollars, plus tax. Jeez.

"Mama," Zack whines.

"Okay, bud. We're going in a sec." She roots though her purse for her wallet. She *knows* she has a ten. Then she remembers. The box of eclairs, her impulsive donation to the fund for the mother.

"Is there a problem?" Tammy stands over the table.

This Opal doesn't need. "I'm a little short."

"I'll get the manager."

He comes right over. "There a problem here?"

"I'm a little short," Opal explains. "I was certain I had a ten."

"Mama?" Zack pulls on her arm.

"Just a minute, sugah."

"You can't pay?" The manager says this like, "You've murdered your husband?"

"I can pay. I'll bring the money back later. Promise."

The man looks like he's debating whether to call the police.

"Hi, Opal."

There, bigger than life, is Ty Miller. All duded up in tight jeans, suede jacket, and high-heeled cowboy boots.

"Need help?" he asks.

"No," Opal says.

"This woman can't pay her bill," the manager says.

"Well, shoot," Ty says. "No problem. Here. It's taken care of." He drops a ten-dollar bill on the table.

"Please," Opal protests, but before she can say another word, Zack pushes out of the booth and vomits all over Ty's boots.

Later Opal will play the whole day over and over. Zack's accident. The doctor's suspicions. Her lie about how he got hurt. Zack puking on Ty Miller. Each episode part of a larger, inevitable path that leads straight to a heart crushed flat.

Rose

ROSE looks up from measuring coffee to see Willard Scott sending off birthday wishes. A face flashes on the screen—an old dried apple face, all wrinkles, nose, and chin. A name—KATHERINE WAITE, 103, COURTLAND, KANSAS—scrolls beneath the withered face.

Ned sets aside the sports section. "It's best if you don't get mixed up with that one," he says, jerking his head to indicate the house next door. "I know her type. She's the kind who makes a mess of her life and then expects other people to clean it up."

"I guess," Rose says.

"You guess? I told you the minute I saw her that she was nothing but trouble. Dressing like a twelve-year-old. She's got Ty so turned around he doesn't know a wrench from a pair of pliers."

Rose would just as soon not get started in on Tyrone Miller. She can't figure out why, in spite of his background, Ned took him on as a mechanic, giving him a chance when no one else would.

"Going to the hospital with her was one thing," Ned continues, "but you have to stop it now, nip it in the bud. Next thing, she'll have you baby-sitting."

"You're right," Rose says. He doesn't have to lecture her. Despite yesterday's trip to Mercy Memorial, she has absolutely no intention of any further involvement with Opal Gates. The way lies just *tripped* off that girl's tongue. Rose wouldn't put anything past her.

She scrambles Ned's eggs. She cooks them until they are dry— the way he likes them—then spoons them onto a plate.

"I feel sorry for the poor bastard who married her," Ned says as he forks the eggs onto a slice of toast and folds it into a sandwich, a habit that drives Rose crazy. "Any fool can see why he left her."

How can Ned be so sure Opal isn't the one who wanted out of the relationship? And wouldn't he go right through the roof to hear she isn't even married? Rose can only imagine what he'd have to say if he knew how she lied for Opal at the hospital.

"More coffee?" she asks.

"Half a cup," he says, holding out his mug.

"You all right, Rosie?" he asks. There is unexpected concern in his voice, and he's looking right at her. Rose allows herself one weak moment when she nearly tells him all that she has locked inside. Not just about yesterday and how she'd told the doctor she was there when the boy got hurt, but about the mole on her stomach and most of all about how she had refused to let Todd use the car, sending him off with Jimmy to die in that accident. This weight lies so heavy in her heart she can't even imagine the relief of setting it free. She very nearly sets it out on the table right then and there, but she allows the moment to pass.

"I'm fine."

"What's on your agenda today?" he asks.

She imagines the day yawning ahead, but before she can manage a word, he has turned his attention back to the sports pages.

THROUGHOUT THE MORNING she half expects to hear from Opal, and when the phone finally rings, she picks it up without thinking.

"Hello, Rose. This is Anderson Jeffrey. From the college."

"Yes?" She is surprised to hear how normal her voice sounds.

"I need to talk with you," he says. "Can we talk, Rose?"

The thought of that first day of class cuts off all possibility of speech. Instead, she remembers how she laid out her paper and pencil, got set to write.

"We'll start with memory," professor Anderson Jeffrey had told the class. "Memory—this alluvial morass—is the territory of the writer."

Alluvial morass? Rose didn't have the slightest idea what he was talking about, but a shiver of unease rippled through her.

"Begin with this phrase: 'I remember.' And write a list of things."

"What?" She was so surprised by his directions that the question popped right out.

Anderson Jeffrey looked straight at her and smiled. "I remember," he repeated. "Make a list of all the things you remember."

A second ripple of anxiety took hold, but she carefully wrote, "I remember." The others in the room were scribbling noisily, but she thought a moment and finally put down "picking strawberries with Momma." This memory, surfacing out of nowhere, gave her courage. "Tootsie," she wrote next, thinking of the kitten she had as a child. And then, before her mind had even grasped what was happening or could catch up with her hand, she wrote, "Todd. I remember Todd."

Once her hand set that sentence to paper, it refused to stop. It was as if she had been waiting five years to get this down. She wrote all about Todd and how she missed him and how one minute a person could be in your life, laughing and smiling, and then the next, with no warning, they were gone.

She wrote about how, after the accident, people had consoled her. *It's not your fault. You mustn't blame yourself.* But the terrible thing was, it *was* her fault. She should have let Todd take her car, and then he wouldn't have been in the truck with Jimmy Sommers. She would have to live with the pain and guilt of that for the rest of her life. She wrote about Todd's birthday and how the first year after he died she waited all day for Ned to say something about it, to mention it, but he never did, and she realized then he had forgotten.

About this time in the writing, Rose became aware of Anderson Jeffrey standing by her. He had already collected the other papers and was reaching for hers. It never occurred to her he would want to take what they had written. Before she could object, she felt it gliding from her fingers to his.

In the cab, on the way home, she tried to figure a way to get that paper back. One more week, she vowed. She would go back to the writing class one more time so she could get that paper back.

The following week she planned on speaking to him after class. During the hour she was careful to write about safe things, things like the history of Normal. At the end of the session she was so grateful to escape that she forgot to ask for her paper back. The next day she telephoned the college and withdrew from the writing class, telling Ned that it had been canceled.

ROSE manages to pull herself together enough to tell Anderson Jeffrey that she can't talk now.

"Will you call me back?" he asks.

"Yes," she says, although she has no intention of doing this.

"Do you have a pencil handy? I'll give you my home number."

She'd rather strip naked on the town square in front of Colonel Normal's statue than take his phone number, but she writes it down.

After she hangs up, she looks out at the Montgomery place and sees Ty Miller pulling up the drive. Well, it seems as if that girl doesn't have to go looking for trouble. It will come looking for her.

Ned

NED burrows deep under the hood of Chuck Winski's Nova. Something is off with the timing, something he suspects Chuck tried fixing himself to save a trip to the garage. Nice enough guy, but he sure can squeeze a nickel until the buffalo farts.

Ned writes up the order sheet. In the service bay, Ty Miller is whistling, working out some new tune, his mind more on music than transmissions, as usual. Thinking about Ty, Ned shakes his head. The mechanic wears his hair in a ponytail and has a pierced ear. Still, except for not showing up every now and then, he isn't a bad kid. Understands engines. And in spite of his history, he stays out of trouble. Ned doesn't regret giving him a chance—not for a minute. Out front, someone pulls up to the pumps. Ned looks up and sees the gray Buick. It's his neighbor, the fruitcake.

As if operating on radar, Ty wheels his creeper out from beneath an Escort—leak somewhere in the exhaust—and crosses over to where Ned is standing. They watch Opal get out of the car, flashing legs naked up to there.

"Forget her," Ned says. He could have saved his breath. Ty is already out the door.

Ned tosses his grease rag on the counter and decides to break early for lunch. He goes into the john, scoops some Glo-Jo out of the jar, works most of the grease off his hands. When he comes out, damned if Ty isn't hanging all over the Buick. "I'm going over to Trudy's," Ned shouts, making a point of ignoring the girl. The boy is in the back seat. Cute little tyke.

The diner is near empty. He has beaten most of the lunch crowd. "You're early," Trudy says.

He takes his regular stool; she brings him a mug of high-test.

Although she isn't much older than he is, Ned can't remember a time when Trudy hasn't been behind this counter. The place belonged to her parents, and when they died, she took over.

"BLT, toasted," he says.

"Fries or slaw?"

He thinks about his persistent heartburn. What the hell. He orders the fries. He has the place to himself, and in spite of CNN on the tube, there is a peacefulness here that suits him. Through the opening in the wall above the counter, he watches Trudy work the grill. Ned's eyes fall on her hips, broad, the way he likes a woman's hips. No skinny-Minnie type for him. Give him something you can hold on to. Briefly he allows himself to contemplate what Trudy would be like between the sheets. Then he averts his eyes to the overhead television, stares at the stock market report.

He swigs the coffee and thinks about Rose. He feels like she is getting farther and farther from him. He's put up with a lot from her in the past couple of years. He's tried sympathy, tenderness, even anger. Nothing helps. He has always told himself that eventually things would get back to normal, but now he's starting to think that maybe Rose will always be this way, stuck in her grief.

Trudy brings the sandwich and fries, refills his coffee, and pours one for herself. She slides onto the stool next to his.

"How's Rose?" she asks.

"Doing fine," Ned says. "Just fine."

When he returns to the garage, Ty is gone. The Escort is still in the service bay. This day is turning into one long disappointment. He feels a headache coming on. Everything is spinning out beyond the reach of his hands.

Opal

OPAL swings into Nelson's service station and parks at the pumps. She barely has time to switch off the ignition and get out of the car before Ty Miller comes outside, like he's been sitting there waiting for her arrival. He moves across the lot with the liquid gait of a long-legged, loose-hipped man. She plans to get some gas and give him the money for her bill at the Creamery.

"Hello again," he says.

"Hi," she manages. A man walks like that, he's just got to know how to dance. Opal loves to dance. Billy hates it.

Tyrone takes the nozzle from her. "Fill it up?"

"Ten dollars. Regular."

She gets back into the car. Even sitting, her legs are all shaky.

Tyrone ducks down and looks in at Zack. "How you doing, buddy?"

Zack grins like they are old friends.

Ty strolls back to the pump as if he has all the time in the world and starts filling the tank. She could just die when he catches her watching him in the side mirror and winks. Then damned if he doesn't come around and start cleaning the windshield, staring straight through with the darkest eyes—eyes nearly black and so beautiful they make a person almost forget about the scar.

"Check the oil?"

"No," she says.

He's still working on the windshield, though it's so clean now you could let a baby eat off it. She looks at his hands—bold-looking, long-fingered hands that are separated from her by no more than ten inches and a sheet of glass—and knows the confusion of wanting something and not wanting it, both in the same breath.

After he's finished, he takes her money. With sense enough to feel the relief of a close call, Opal drives off. She's halfway home before she realizes she has still neglected to pay back his ten bucks. Well, no way she's going back now.

THE phone is ringing off the hook when she gets home. Three guesses who, and the first two don't count.

"Hello, Mama," she says.

"Where have you been? I've been calling for two days."

Six states and four months away, and she's still accountable to her mama. "Zack and I were out," she says. "Errands."

"I mean Tuesday night." Melva's voice is hard with suspicion. "You're not keeping Zack out late, are you?"

"No, Mama."

"What were you doing?"

Opal stalls for time. "I was here, Mama." Melva may have suspicions, but stuck in New Zion, there's no way she can dispute Opal's story. "What do you want, Mama?"

"I want to know when we can expect to see you again."

"I don't know."

"Raylee," Melva says in her bossy voice, "it's time you headed back here where you belong. We want Zack here for the holidays. I just can't abide the thought of him all alone up there at Christmas."

"He's not alone, Mama. He's with me."

"You know what I mean, Raylee. He should be with his kin."

"Opal," she says. "My name's Opal."

"Girl, you can call yourself any fool name you want, but our patience is wearing thin. It's time you brought Zack back home."

Before she can think of an answer, the doorbell chimes. "Listen, Mama," she says, "I can't talk now. There's someone at the door."

TY MILLER stands on the front steps. "Here," he says, handing her a box of brownies.

Zack runs in from the kitchen. "Hi," he says, not the least bit shy.

"Hey, scout," Ty says.

Zack giggles. "I'm not scout. I'm Zack."

"Well, Zack, this is for you." Ty hands him a bag.

Zack takes the bag. "Open it, Mama," he says.

Opal pulls out a bunch of bananas, of all things. "Why'd you come here?" she asks, though it's plain as day to her why he's there, and she's not interested. Well, okay. That's a flat-out lie. She is attracted, no denying *that,* but she's not about to get involved, not about to *lose* herself. She has Zack to think of now.

"I got a cractured arm," Zack says.

"That so?" Ty ignores Opal's question.

"Want to write on my cast? Can he, Mama? Can he write on it?"

Somehow, before she can muster up an answer, Ty Miller is standing in her front hall. Well, it'll take more than a box of pastries and a bunch of bananas for him to worm his way into her life. "I forgot to pay you at the garage," she says. "I'll get your money."

"No hurry," he says, but she's already halfway to the kitchen. When she returns, he's writing on Zack's cast. He's drawn musical notes with a black marker and is using a yellow one to make a little harmonica. Zack is leaning against his knee with a smile so big Opal's heart could just split because she's so jealous.

When Ty finishes the last flourish, she holds out a ten. She readies herself for his refusal, but he looks directly at her with those startling eyes and slips the bill in his jeans pocket.

"What's that?" Zack asks, pointing to the drawing on his cast.

"A harmonica," Ty answers. "You ever see one?"

"Nope."

"Wait right here."

It doesn't take Ty but two minutes to return. Ignoring Opal, he kneels down on the floor by Zack, cups his hands around the harmonica, and begins to play. He hasn't gone half a bar into the song when Opal recognizes an old blues number she's heard half her life: "Train Whistle Blues." In spite of herself, she closes her eyes.

"Well, that was nice," she says when he's finished, hearing in her voice the cool, extra-polite tone Melva uses whenever she doesn't like someone.

"Thanks."

Zack pulls on his arm. "Show me how to do it."

"Tell you what," Ty says. "How'd you like one of your own?"

"Zack," Opal says, "take these in the kitchen." She hands him the bananas. He starts to fuss. "Go on, sugah. Do as I say."

"You better go," she tells Ty as soon as Zack is out of sight.

"Did I do something wrong?"

"I just don't like people making promises to my boy. Promises they can't deliver on."

He looks her straight in the eyes. "I never say anything I can't deliver on, Opal."

In spite of all her best intentions, in spite of her vow to give up sex, she feels the arrow of desire shoot directly from her throat to her belly.

"I'm not a liar," he says. "Whatever else I am, I don't lie. A man should keep his word. Whatever it costs him." Reflexively his fingers trace the scar on his cheek. "And you, Opal Gates? What do you believe in?"

"Look here," she says. "I guess what I believe in is my business." Just because he comes marching into her house with a box of brownies, a bunch of bananas, and a harmonica sweet enough to make a dead goat weep, that doesn't give him any claim on her.

Instead of being insulted, he laughs. "You like blues? I play weekends over in Springfield. Maybe you could come hear us some night. You, too," he says to Zack, who has reappeared.

"Can we, Mama?" Zack asks. "Please."

"We'll see," Opal says, a phrase she's heard from Melva half her life and swore she'd never say to her son. "We'll see."

"Guess I better quit while I'm ahead," Ty says.

"What makes you think you're ahead?"

He laughs. "I'll call you with directions."

After he leaves, Opal returns to the kitchen. And isn't the very first thing her eyes land on the Chiquita sticker. Of everything on earth that Tyrone Miller might have chosen to show up at her door with, he's picked a bunch of bananas. Right then and there Opal knows she is in a heap of trouble.

"I'm getting a harmonica," Zack says. "Ty's getting me one."

"We'll see," Opal says. She gets him settled with a brownie and then digs out *1000 Names for Your New Baby*. She flips to the T's. "Tyrone," she reads. "(Celtic) of uncertain meaning. Dim., Ty."

She slams the book shut. The last thing she needs in her life is uncertainty. She marches straight over to the cupboard door and peels off the Chiquita sticker. She rolls it between her fingers until it forms a little ball and then throws it in the trash. The fact is, some signs need erasing before they can do much damage. The heat in her belly takes a little more concentration to make disappear.

Rose

ROSE opens the front door, takes the mail from the box and carries it into the kitchen. She puts the small pile of envelopes at Ned's place at the table. Bills and junk mail are about all they get, and she's happy to have him deal with it. She's turning away when the address on the top envelope catches her eye. "Raylee Gates," she reads. The *Ray* and *lee* are all scrunched together like one word. The boy's father? Didn't Opal say she wasn't married? Why the same last name?

Rose goes next door. It takes three rings before Opal answers the bell.

"Here," Rose says, thrusting the envelope at her. "This was mixed in with our mail." She can see beyond the girl's shoulder that the kitchen is a mess, with a sink full of dirty dishes. There is a spidery drawing held to the refrigerator by magnets: two stick figures with wide smiles. The big one has red bolts flaming out from the head. The small one has matching bolts. No sign of any father. No sign of any Raylee.

"Rose," Opal says, pleased, "come on in. Want a cup of coffee? A blueberry muffin? I made them myself."

Well, a person could tell that just by looking. Probably a mix.

"I think this letter's meant for you. Postman must have made a mistake," Rose says, ignoring the invitation. "The last name's the same and all, but it was addressed to a man, Raylee Gates."

"Oh." Opal smiles brightly. "That's me. Raylee was my name before I changed it to Opal."

"You *changed* your name?"

"Four years ago," Opal says. "Opals are my favorite stone. The way they look so soft and pretty but hold fire inside."

"Is it legal? Changing your name like that?"

"Well, I had to go before a judge and all. But it's important that your name fits you. I must've spent a hundred hours looking through my name book, trying to decide what to name Zack. Zackery means 'the Lord's remembrance.' "

Rose realizes she hasn't the slightest idea what the meaning of Todd is. She would like to ask Opal to look it up in her book.

"How did you land here in Normal?" she asks.

"It's where I was when I used up three tanks of gas," Opal says. "Listen, don't stay here standing. Come on in." Next thing, Rose is hearing all about the die from some Monopoly game and how this was Opal's sign of how far she should drive.

"I pay attention to signs," Opal says. "Don't you?"

"No," Rose says. She knows not to trust in such foolishness.

"Mama." The boy comes into the room. No shoes. A thin shirt. "I want a muffin," he says. He gives Rose a shy smile.

"Coming right up," Opal says. While she gets the boy a muffin,

Rose notices a ballerina doll sitting on the counter. "Is that one of the dolls you make?" she asks.

"Sure is," Opal says. She hands the doll to Rose.

"It looks real lifelike," Rose says.

"The trick is the face. You've got to put the features low."

Rose fingers the tulle skirt. "You make the outfits, too?"

"Yes."

The seams are double-stitched. Tiny stitches. "By hand?"

"Until I can afford a machine."

Rose thinks of the Singer standing idly in one corner of her dining room. Of course she keeps her mouth shut.

"Billy thinks my dolls're dumb," Opal continues.

"Billy?"

"Zack's daddy. He thinks making dolls is a pure waste of time."

Rose can see why Opal wouldn't marry the boy. If a person can't see the beauty in these dolls, they don't deserve marrying.

"Emily says I look for love in all the wrong places," Opal goes on.

Rose immediately thinks about Tyrone Miller. "Who's Emily?"

"Emily Jackman. My therapist."

Good heavens. For a young girl Opal has a complicated history. Name changes, therapists, boyfriends. Someone, she thinks, should warn her about Tyrone, especially with the boy in the house. She makes up her mind then and there to tell her.

"Rose," Opal says before she can say a word. "Rose, I'm real sorry about Todd."

Most people act like they would rather eat snake, would rather have their tongues pierced with a dinner fork than mention his name. Opal says his name like it's the most natural thing in the world. "Dorothy Barnes told me about the accident. Hell, I can't imagine what it'd be like to lose your child."

I can't imagine. You don't want to. You certainly don't want to.

The mole on her stomach, the spot that hasn't bothered her all the time she's been at Opal's, doesn't just begin to itch. It burns. All thoughts of warning Opal about Ty just vanish into thin air. She flees before Opal can say another word.

Opal

THE sun is shining—unseasonably hot for December—and Ty Miller has stripped off his jacket. From her perch on the back steps, Opal watches the muscles of his shoulders and arms move beneath his shirt. Today he's giving the Buick a tune-up, and she has that hard scratchy feeling in her chest she gets whenever someone does something nice for her.

He hasn't suggested a real date or even as much as touched her, but she's nervous about the way he's barreling into her life. And she's troubled by Zack's affection for him. The second time Ty stopped by, he brought the promised harmonica. Not a cheap plastic toy either, but a real chrome one. Opal doesn't want her son to become attached to this man who for dead certain will have no place in their lives.

"The timing's off," Ty tells Zack. "What we got to do here is adjust the idling; then we'll reset the points."

"We'll reset the points," Zack repeats. He is holding his body in exact imitation of Ty, who ruffles his hair before he bends over the fender of the Buick and disappears beneath the hood.

Opal's been jumpy all morning, and Ty is only partially to blame. For one thing, five days have passed since Melva has called, and as much as she'd like to believe her mama has given up the crusade to get her to return to New Zion for Christmas, past experience indicates Melva's silence means trouble is brewing.

A movement over at the Nelsons' draws her attention. A curtain shifts in an upstairs window. Rose is looking out the window.

Her neighbor is a mystery. After Rose lied for her at the hospital, Opal thought they might become friends, but it was soon clear as day that Rose was avoiding her. Then last week, when Opal had given up on any chance of friendship, didn't Rose appear with that letter from Aunt May and agree to stay for coffee, although she hardly spoke two words. Rose's silence made it easier to tell her things. Rose did not laugh or poke fun when Opal told her about her belief in signs and how you had to look for them.

"You want anything?" Opal calls to Ty. "Coke or something?"

"We're all set," he says. "Right, buddy?"

"Right," Zack says. "We're all set."

Opal decides she might as well use this time while Zack is occupied with Ty to catch up on her work. She's pushing a deadline on a birthday order for an astronaut doll. And she has less than three weeks to fill the Christmas orders.

She has been sewing for about an hour when she hears the sound of Ty's harmonica. The notes float in from the backyard. The tune is slow and sweet, with the right touch of loneliness every good blues song holds in its bones. It's dangerous music, music that could get inside her heart if she let it.

"Wailing blues," her aunt May calls it. She should know.

May's first and third husbands were guitar players, and from the time Opal was thirteen, her aunt advised her to stay away from musicians. "Might as well move directly on over to Heartache Hotel as lose your heart to a musician. They're born with nervous feet, feet that can't settle down."

Not that Opal is about to settle down with anyone. For dead certain not a part-time mechanic who plays in a second-rate band. No way. She has bigger things in mind for her and Zack.

Out in the yard, the song of the wailing blues plays on.

Rose

ROSE has come upstairs to put some ointment on her stomach. Several days ago, when the itch about drove her crazy, she got as far as picking up the phone to call Doc Blessing, but before her fingers even hit the first digit of his number, she replaced the receiver. She can't face the prospect of seeing him, being fussed over.

Through the window she hears noises from next door. Tyrone Miller is there again. She goes over to pull the blind. Tyrone's lower body extends from beneath the hood of the girl's car. The boy is at his side. Opal is sitting on the stoop watching them.

What was it the girl told her the therapist said? She went looking for love in all the wrong places? Well, it's clear as day she doesn't have to go about doing much looking. Trouble has found her. Tyrone Miller is as close to wrong as you can get and not break the law.

Ned is about the only soul in town who has much good to say about him, always telling people what a good mechanic he is, how well he's turned out considering he's been on his own since he turned fourteen and his stepfather kicked him out of the house.

She thinks someone should tell the girl about Tyrone's history. Not that she's about to take on that task. She can't imagine what got into her that she almost said something last week when she took the misdelivered piece of mail over there. It isn't her place to interfere.

Turning from the window, Rose loosens her waistline and adjusts her skirt so she can check the red-rimmed mole. The circle of inflammation looks larger to her. She takes the top off the tube of ointment and dabs some over the spot. When she is done, she tucks the tube safely away in her dresser drawer. She is overtaken with weariness. Just a nap, she thinks, and although it has been months since she slept in the afternoon, she stretches out on the bed and drifts off to the sound of a boy's laughter.

Opal

THERE'S a storm in the air, the temperature cold enough for snow. They'll need warmer clothes. The furnace rumbles on. Money literally burning up, going up in flames. The five thousand dollars Aunt May gave her seemed immense when she was living rent-free in New Zion in one of her daddy's apartments. Now she's amazed at how quickly the money goes, how it just *melts* away. One thing for dead sure, she isn't about to ask Melva for help.

Opal does not know what went wrong between her and her mama. She keeps hoping that Melva will change, that she'll say, "I love you, Opal. I'm so proud of you," and all the other things mamas are *supposed* to say, all the things Opal says to Zack. She wants to believe Melva feels them but just doesn't know how to show it.

One thing she knows right from the get-go is that her mama

wouldn't approve of any wannabe cowboy coming into her life.

As if her thoughts have conjured him up, Opal hears Ty's truck turning into her driveway. She presses her palms against her chest, trying to calm the flutter. She wishes she had washed her hair.

"Hi," she says.

"Hi."

"Zack's not here," she says, as if that's why he has come.

"I figured."

After a moment's hesitation she steps back and allows Ty in. She wishes she had shut the door to the dining room. Her dolls are spread out all over the place. She's used to her mama and Billy thinking she's the next best thing to retarded for spending her time sewing them, but she doesn't want Ty thinking that.

Of course, as if her thoughts have guaranteed he'll notice them, he looks over her shoulder straight at the table.

"Those the dolls I've been hearing about?"

"I guess." Who's he been talking to?

He crosses to the table, starts to reach for one, stops short, and takes a look at his hands. "Be right back," he says, and heads for the downstairs bathroom. She hears water running in the sink. It takes her a minute to realize he's washing up. He's *cleaning up* before touching her dolls. This simple act—the respect of it—threatens all of her defenses, all of her declarations to stay clear of him.

She's still working on the astronaut doll.

"You made this?" he says, picking it up.

"Uh-huh."

He takes his time looking at it. "It's amazing."

"Thanks." She works to keep her voice casual.

"No. I mean it. It's really something."

"You want a Coke or something?" *Distance. Resolve.*

"Nah," he says, setting the doll back on the table. "I just came by to give you this ticket. There's a blues night in Northampton in two weeks, and the band's going to be playing."

The price is printed right on the stub. Twenty dollars. "I'm not a charity case," she says.

Ty looks at her. "Never thought you were," he says. "Thing is, I like you. I'm just trying to show it in the only way I know how."

"I appreciate—" She swallows, tries again. "I appreciate all you've done for me. How you've fixed the car and all."

He runs a finger over the scar on his cheek. "Opal Gates," he says, "I've got to say you're different from most girls I know."

Opal gives a snort. "That's what Zack's daddy said. Told me he loved me because I was different, but as soon as he could, he started working to change everything about me that was different."

"Sounds like he doesn't know a good thing when he's got it."

"Something you should know, Tyrone Miller. Sweet talk doesn't go far with me."

"Never thought it would." He grins. "So are you going to take the ticket or not? It's New Year's Eve and all."

"New Years Eve? I'd have to get a sitter for Zack."

"You could ask the Nelsons if they'd watch him."

"You've got everything all figured out."

"If there's one thing I don't have, it's everything all figured out. So you'll come?"

"Maybe."

"There'll be dancing. Do you like to dance?"

"I used to." It's been a hundred years since she's gone dancing.

"It's not something a person forgets."

"No, I guess not."

He starts humming—a James Taylor song—and reaches for her hand. The charge jolts straight through her. She pulls her hand back. "I've got to go get Zack from school."

She watches Ty stride down the steps in his loose-hipped walk. She closes her eyes and recalls the heat of his hand on hers. She isn't sure what's ahead, but she feels a promise of something like joy hanging in the air, as sure as mist over May mountains.

This sense of pleasure stays with her all the way to the day care, and nothing, not even the teacher's disapproval, can spoil it.

"We need our parents to be prompt," Mrs. Lloyd says.

"I know. I'm sorry. It won't happen again."

"SHE WAS MAD," ZACK says as they get in the car.

"She's an old cow." *He washed his hands before he picked up her doll. He said it was great. Amazing. Really something.* "Let's forget about her. Hey, you know what? In seven days it's Christmas, and we haven't even bought a tree. What say we go get one right now?"

"A big one?"

"The biggest one we can find." It's Christmas. Their first totally on their own. *He likes her. That's what he said.*

Speeding through the winter twilight, caught in the magic of lights strung on trees in front yards, Opal allows herself to believe that at last everything is going to be all right. That the worst part of her life is behind her.

WINTER

Opal

AN END-OF-THE-YEAR storm has shut down half the state, and now Opal is marooned in Northampton with Ty. The concert canceled, the band has moved on to their own private New Year's party. Nothing about the evening is turning out like Opal expects.

"You sure we can't get back to Normal?" she asks. They are in the kitchen of the house two of the band members rent.

"Not with this storm," Ty says, brushing the hair off her forehead.

"I shouldn't have come. Zack will be worried."

"Zack will be fine. Rose is probably making him hot chocolate right now."

How can she expect Ty to understand? One of the few things her mama is right about is that you have to have a child to know what it's like. "I better give Rose a call."

"Okay." He smiles, trails his finger along her jaw. "The phone's upstairs. Tell her we'll be home in the morning."

Opal heads up the stairs just about torn in two. Of course she's worried foolish about Zack. He's never spent a single night apart from her. But a part of her—the part that always seems to be landing her in trouble in spite of her best intentions—that part is *excited* to be snowbound with Ty.

A Janet Jackson song drifts up the stairs. She picks up the phone, hears the hollow echo of a dead line.

"Everything okay?" Ty comes up behind her.

"Phone's dead." She crosses to the window. Below, trees are transformed into white sculpture. "When do you think it'll stop?"

"Probably sometime tomorrow morning."

"Is the snow always like this? So heavy?" she asks as Ty wraps his arms around her neck, holds her close. She has to remind herself to breathe. There is something about the storm that makes everything seem unreal. She is aware of the bed behind them.

"What? You don't have snow in North Carolina?"

"Not much. You sure we can't get back tonight?"

"Don't worry. Zack'll be fine."

Of course this isn't true. He'd be best off with her.

Ty pulls her to him, cups his hands over her ears.

Please, she thinks, don't let him be a good kisser.

But he is. His kiss is long and soft and deep, with just the right edge of insistence behind the gentleness.

"Well, damn," he says when he finally pulls back. "Come on, let's go down and dance."

Downstairs, Prince's "Purple Rain" is playing. Without a word Ty draws her to him. He waits an instant, just holds her still, his cheek resting on her head; then he begins to dance. She follows his lead, light-headed yet aware of everything. She wonders if it is possible for a life to change in such a short amount of time.

She wants to touch his scar, ask him how he got it, but she doesn't. Every girl he's ever been with must have asked that question. You're different, he had said. She wants that, wants to be different for him. It's a dangerous wanting. No future here. Aunt May's warning echoes somewhere in the depths of her brain.

Without letting her go, Ty picks her up, and carrying her as if she were no heavier than Zack, he heads back upstairs.

He carries her to the bed. "You okay?" he asks.

"Yes," she says. She's dizzy. From wanting him.

"Happy New Year," he says.

"You, too." She hasn't done a lot right in her life. It's important to do this right.

"You sure you're okay with this?"

"Yes."

Rose

IT'S been snowing since late afternoon, and a startling mantle of white covers the yard. The forecast was for four to six inches, but Rose can tell they're in for at least two or three feet.

Ned and the boy are watching TV. Rose is in the kitchen pouring her emotions into a piecrust. She hasn't heard one word from Opal. You'd think the girl would show some concern about Zack. About the storm. She mentioned this to Ned, but he immediately defended Opal, said the lines were probably down. If this keeps up, I wouldn't expect them back until morning, he said. Snowstorm or no snowstorm, Rose doesn't approve of the girl spending the night with Tyrone. She doesn't even want to think about what they're up to.

Earlier in the week, when Opal came over and asked if she'd baby-sit, Rose was caught off guard. Before she could even think straight enough to come up with an excuse, she found herself agreeing. She braced herself for Ned's disapproval, but he didn't say a word. Now he and the boy are curled up in the recliner—the boy in Ned's *lap*.

The sight of him sitting there with the boy was more than she could handle. She headed for the kitchen. She can't understand Ned. Whatever his feelings about Opal—which he's made pretty clear—he holds no grudge against the boy. Fine with Rose, but no need to go *overboard*. No need to sit with him on your *lap*.

She rolls out the dough, transfers it to a pie plate. New Year's Eve or not, it was a mistake to say they'd watch the boy. Now, with the storm, looks like they're stuck with him for the night.

Earlier, Rose went next door to get the boy's pajamas. Place was a mess, of course. Beds unmade. Clothes all over the floor. All she could find was a pair of summer pj's, so she'd grabbed one of the boy's sweatshirts and a pair of socks as well.

She opens a can of Comstock's blueberry filling, pours it into the pie shell. She crimps the crust, cuts vents in the center, slides the pie into the oven. Inside, Ned and the boy are laughing.

Rose wipes off the counter in a fury, her back stiff with protest. She tries to block out their laughter. How *could* he?

"All right," she says to the boy when she's cleaned up. "Time you were getting to bed."

Over his protests she takes him to the bathroom, strips off his clothes. He needs help putting on the pajamas.

"Actually, I don't wear that in bed," he says when she pulls on the sweatshirt.

"It'll keep you warm tonight," she says, in no mood to argue.

"When's my mama coming back?"

"She'll be here in the morning," Rose says.

Back in the living room, Ned watches while she makes up the couch. "Don't you think he'd be more comfortable upstairs?"

What is he suggesting? To think she'd even consider letting the boy sleep in Todd's bed. . . . What's *wrong* with him? He should know there's no way that will happen. No way in hell any other child is *ever* going to sleep in her son's bed.

"This will be just fine," she says. She settles the boy in, then flicks off the lamps. She goes to the kitchen to check on the pie.

"Zack," she hears Ned say, "you want me to leave a light on in the hall?"

"Yes, please," the boy says.

"Okay," Ned says. "You all set now?"

"My mama'll be here in the morning?"

"She'll be here."

"Night."

"Good night, son."

Son. The pain just takes her breath away.

Ned

NED wakes before five.

"Plowing?" Rose asks.

"Yup. Might as well get started. There'll be a full day of it."

"I'll make you breakfast."

"No need. I'll stop by Trudy's and grab something." He reaches over and pats Rose's shoulder. Last night she hadn't let him touch her. When he wished her Happy New Year, she nearly bit his head off. Course she'd been mad all evening. Taking it out on him. And the boy.

He heads downstairs, eager now to escape Rose's grief, her anger. He can't wait to start the plowing, to do something he can control.

"Lord." He jumps a foot when he sees the boy. "You near scared me to death."

Zack sits in the dim kitchen. He's already dressed. "I want to go home," he says. "When's my mama coming back?"

"Pretty soon," Ned says, hoping this is true. "Ever been in a snowplow?"

"No."

"Well, I'm heading out now. Got some driveways to plow. You interested in coming along?"

The boy shakes his head. "I'm waiting for my mama."

"You know, plowing's an important job. When my boy, Todd, was about your age, sometimes he'd come with me."

"He did?"

"Uh-huh. And I let him help push the lever that lets the plow go up and down. You think you could handle something like that?"

"I think so."

"Well, lets get you some working clothes." He finds an old wool sweater of his, Rose's windbreaker, gloves. "That should do it," he says. "You hungry?"

"Uh-huh."

"What say we stop by the diner and get ourselves some breakfast.

You like pancakes? My boy, he loved pancakes. With plenty of maple syrup. After we have breakfast, we'll go by the garage and pick up the plow, and you can give me a hand with a few driveways."

Before they go, he remembers to leave a note for Rose.

"Will she be mad?"

"Nah. Why'd she be mad?"

"She was mad last night."

Not much slides by this kid. "Don't you worry about Rose. She's not mad at you, just mad at the world."

"Because your son's dead?"

Ned pauses. "You know about Todd?"

"My mama told me."

Ned wonders if Rose can hear them upstairs. "Come on," he says. "Let's get ourselves some pancakes."

"Ned?" Zack says as Ned buckles the seat belt around him. "Todd was your little boy."

"He was, yes."

"Are you mad at the world, too?"

Rose

FROM the look of her it's clear as day what the girl's been doing all night. Circles under her eyes. Whisker burn all over her face. Rose purses her mouth in disapproval.

"I really appreciate your keeping Zack," Opal says.

"They should be back soon," Rose says, ignoring the thanks. Rose isn't a prude, but there are *standards*. She did not watch that boy all night so Tyrone could get in Opal's pants.

"How much longer will they be?"

"No telling," Rose says. "Might as well have a cup of coffee."

"Thanks." Opal plops herself at the table.

"Want some pancakes?" The words are out before she can stop them. What's gotten into her, inviting chaos into her home?

"Perfect," Opal says.

Todd liked pancakes. Rose is so close to saying this, she can feel the words in her mouth. She gets out the Bisquick, stirs in water, tests the skillet. When she's sure no treacherous words will slip through her lips, she says to Opal, "There's syrup in the refrigerator."

She spreads a thin sheet of butter on the griddle, spoons out the first pancake. Spoons out another.

"Rose, how did you and Ned meet?"

"Oh, I don't know. Seems like we've always known each other."

"You were childhood sweethearts?"

"No. We didn't start dating until I was in my junior year."

"How did you know that he was the one? That you wanted to spend the rest of your life with him?"

"I don't know. Just seemed natural." Rose's face softens as she pictures a young Ned, his full head of black hair, his wide grin. She recalls the urgency of their desire. Marriage couldn't come soon enough for them, but this is nothing she will share with Opal.

"How long have you been married?" Opal asks.

"Thirty-five years." That was 1955. Eisenhower was President. Hope was in the air. They had eloped, saving the wedding money to put down on their first house, a four-room place over on Easton.

"But how did you know you could trust him?"

Tyrone, Rose thinks. She's asking about Tyrone. "I felt safe with him." That was the truth, plain and simple. Back then she felt like nothing bad could ever happen as long as they were together. They were what? Nineteen and twenty-two. How could they have known there is nothing and no one that can keep a person safe?

"I never really felt that way with Billy."

"Is that why you didn't marry him?" One good thing about conversing with Opal, you can say whatever pops into your head.

"I didn't love him. At first I did, I guess. Emily—my therapist—"

Rose nods. She knows about the therapist.

"She says I was looking for love. She says I had a hungry heart."

Rose knows about the hunger of an empty heart.

"But it was mostly physical."

Rose certainly does not want to hear anymore. She flips pancakes onto two plates.

"And he bored me. With Billy there were no surprises."

This sounds good to Rose. A life with no surprises. She pours syrup onto her pancakes, cuts them into wedges.

"And we were always fighting."

"About what?" Rose takes a mouthful, chews.

"Any damn thing. And Billy's always making fun of me for believing in signs. He doesn't hold much truck with that stuff."

Opal and Rose are just finishing up when the phone rings.

"Hello," Rose says.

"Hello, Rose," Anderson Jeffrey says. "Happy New Year."

"Happy New Year," Rose responds.

"Have I called too early?"

"No," Rose says, "but I have company right now."

Opal makes a go-on-talking motion with her hands. She pours herself a second cup of coffee, sits back down.

"There's something I need to tell you," Anderson Jeffrey says. "It's about the piece you wrote in class."

The piece Rose wishes she had never written, the hot spilling of rage and loss and guilt.

"I've been teaching writing for twenty-five years," he tells her. "It's one of the most articulate essays about grief I have ever read."

Articulate? There is nothing articulate about grief. Grief takes your tongue, robs your brain, makes you mute.

"I submitted it to a magazine. A literary journal called the *Sun*. They've accepted it. They need your permission to print it."

Rose is truly horrified. "No," she says.

"Don't answer now. Think about it."

"No," she repeats, and hangs up the phone.

Anderson Jeffrey wants her to say yes to allowing strangers to look into her heart, to read things about Todd she hasn't even told Ned. Ned? He wants her to forget all about Todd, to return to herself, to move to Florida, to stay away from Opal Gates. And Opal, who is sitting there stirring sugar into her coffee, wants to be her friend.

Can't they all see they are asking more than she can give?

Opal

OPAL can't sit still.

"I'll talk to you later," Ty had told her earlier when he dropped her off. So she's spent all day watching the clock and waiting on the phone. She's tired as hell. They got—what?—two hours of sleep last night. Just the memory is enough to start her blood heating. And now it's nearly ten p.m., and he hasn't called.

What had Rose said? If a person's right for you, you feel safe with him. Does she feel safe with Ty? Last night she had.

Damn him. Pouring sweet words into her ear, and now, one night of sex, and he can't be bothered to pick up the phone.

She's just put Zack to bed—no school this week—and the silence grates on her nerves. She's in the kitchen when she hears a truck pull up. She pads across the floor and reaches the front door just as she hears the heavy fall of his feet on the porch. She swings open the door before he can even knock.

"Hey, Raylee," Billy says.

Her smile freezes, fades. "Hi, Billy," she says. He looks *almost* the same, but he's wearing his hair shorter. That must please her mama. "What are you doing here?"

"I drove all day and half the night, and that's all you got to say? Ain't you even going to let me in?"

She steps back, shuts the door behind him.

He looks around. "Where's Zack?"

"Asleep." He checks out the living room. He rubs his hands together. "Cold as a witch's tit," he says. "How do you stand it?"

"You get used to it. So why'd you come?"

He smiles, the same smile he used to get out of trouble in home-room or with the coach. The smile he used to get her *into* trouble.

"Figure you wouldn't come to me, I'd come to you. Figure that's what you're waiting on. So you win. Here I am."

"It's not about winning," she says.

"Well, what's it about, Raylee? *Opal.* Why'd you run away?"

392 | *Anne D. LeClaire*

What *is* it about? Nothing Billy would understand. It's about *choices*. It's about life and daring to go looking for it.

"You want to go messing up your life, that's your business, but you got to think of Zack."

What she's hearing here is Melva's voice. Blah, blah, blah.

"You got no right to take Zack away from me, from his kin."

"When did you get so all-fired hot on being a daddy?"

"Dammit, Opal, no woman walks away from me. No woman takes my child."

"No man gives me orders. Is that what this is about? Male pride?"

"You think you're smarter than everyone, Opal. You think you've got the answers, but you're wrong. As wrong as you can be."

"Well, what if I am? It ain't no concern of yours."

"But Zack is my concern. And you can't keep a boy from seeing his daddy."

"You ain't his daddy. A daddy does his share. You're just a mistake that planted the seed."

"Yeah? Well, this *mistake* is coming back here tomorrow. I drove for two days to see my boy, and I'm not going home until I do. No way you're going to stop me, Raylee. You got that? No way."

HE'S been gone a half hour when the phone rings. The usual pattern. He's calling to continue the fight.

"Listen—" she begins.

"Opal?"

She falls silent.

"You okay?" Ty asks.

"Yeah, I'm just dandy."

"I came over earlier, but there was a truck in the drive."

"Billy," she says. "Zack's daddy."

"Oh," he says. "Well, I won't keep you, then."

"He's gone."

"Well, I suppose it's too late for me to be coming over."

She's leaping straight from the pan into the fire here. "No," she says, "it's not too late at all. In fact, it's high time."

Ned

STU Weston's Mercury has broken down over in Pellington, a setback Ned doesn't need on the schedule. From Stu's description it sounds like a dead battery. Probably all that's called for is a set of cables. How a man can live to be in his fifties, run a business, and still not know enough to carry a set of cables is beyond Ned. Naturally, Ty has taken the afternoon off again. Probably over at Opal's. Dogs in heat, those two. Nothing for it but to close the shop early and head over to Pellington.

Ned backs the tow truck out onto the street. This time of year he's called out half a dozen times a week. If it's not dead batteries, it's someone stuck in a snowbank. He has never been that fond of winter, and now he's sick to death of it. It's hanging on like a disease, dragging him down, making him tired. He can't wait for spring.

That's another appealing thing about Florida: no snow. Ned pictures a new life down there, somewhere on the west coast, by the Gulf. Away from winter. Away from a house that holds grief.

The Sox have a training camp down there. He could catch some games, go fishing every day, maybe buy a little outboard—something with a little zip. He can almost *taste* this life. The salt breeze. A cool beer. Marlin on the grill. A man can dream, can't he?

He pulls up next to Stu's Mercury. It doesn't take him more than ten minutes to get the car started and send Stu on his way. It's almost five, and Ned decides to grab a cup of coffee at Trudy's.

He gets there just as she is locking the front door.

"I was just about to close up," she says.

Ned nods and turns back to the truck.

"Oh, for heaven's sake, come on in," she says. "I still have half a pot of coffee left. It'd be a shame to throw it out."

Inside, it's quiet. Trudy slips behind the counter. "You want anything with this?" she asks as she pours his coffee.

He's got a headache, but he doesn't want her to fuss. There's a doughnut left under the plastic dome. "I'll take that," he says.

She puts it on a plate. "If you sit in that booth where I can put my feet up, I'll join you."

He carries their mugs over, slides onto the bench. She sits down with a sigh. "We're not getting any younger," she says. "Not that I'd want to," she adds.

"You wouldn't?"

"Hell, no. Once around is enough. What about you?"

If it would turn out differently, he wants to say. If Todd doesn't die. If Rose doesn't turn into this stranger.

"If we lived our lives again, I think we'd just go on making the same mistakes," Trudy says. "I don't think we'd be any smarter."

Is this true? Or would a person choose a different route, marry someone else? And what would have happened if he had married someone else instead of Rose? Someone like Trudy.

"You know," she says, "I've always been a little jealous of Rose."

"Of Rose?"

"But if I did it all over again, I still don't think I'd be smart enough to latch onto someone steady. Someone good. Someone like you."

Trudy's words leave him completely tongue-tied.

SPRING

Opal

"WHAT'S the bravest thing you ever did?" Ty asks her.

She loves this, lying in his arms after they make love. Just lying and talking lazylike, saying the first thing that pops into your brain.

"Bravest? I don't know." Having Zack? She thinks of how scared she was toward the end when her belly was swollen out hard, knowing that in just weeks she was going to be giving birth to a baby.

"What about you? What's the bravest thing you ever did?"

"Easy one," he says. "Bravest thing was coming back here after you were so cold to me."

"I was not."

"Were, too. You were pure ice, lady." He reaches over and gets a potato chip from the bag on the nightstand, feeds it to her, then licks the salt from her lips. "I love you, Opal," he says.

"Mmmmmmm." She cuddles closer. Before she says a thing like this again, she is going to be *sure*.

He checks his watch. "What time do you get Zack?"

"Two thirty."

"Want me to get him?"

"What? You don't work anymore?"

"I'm taking a few days off, going down to Cambridge. There's an open mike at a coffeehouse there. We might do a taping."

"Oh," she says, drawing away. *Musicians have traveling feet.*

He pulls her back. "You could come."

"Can't," she says. "Zack's got school."

The doorbell cuts off the conversation.

She can't imagine who'd be ringing her bell. Rose? She gets up, pulls on her shorts, Ty's shirt. On the way downstairs it hits her that Billy might have come back. Would he dare show his face again? Except for the checks he's been sending since February, he hasn't been in contact. She peeks out the window to see if there's a black Ram pickup. What she sees is a police cruiser pulled up to the curb.

"OPAL Gates?" the officer says.

"Yes." Her tongue turns to cotton.

He holds out an envelope. "Here," he says. "I have to give you this." He thrusts the envelope into her hands.

"What is it?"

"Court order. Sign here," he says, pushing a pen into her fingers.

"I don't understand."

"Look," he says, not unkindly, "these papers have been filed in the district court, and I'm serving you with copies. There will be a hearing. You have twenty days to file an answer with the court."

"The court?"

The officer shuffles through the papers. "The hearing is March twenty-eighth. At the district court. Do you have a lawyer?"

"A lawyer," she parrots. Her mind brays, *A lawyer, a lawyer.*

"An attorney. You'll need one for the custody hearing."

Custody. The word strikes Opal with the swiftness of a snake. "Get off my porch!" she screams. "You get the hell out of here!"

"Opal," Ty calls from inside, "something wrong?"

"No sense getting upset, Miss Gates," the cop says. He's delivered papers like these before. "As soon as you sign, I'll leave."

Opal's hand shakes as she scrawls her name.

"What's the matter?" Ty is by her side.

"It's Billy. He's serving me with papers. He's trying to get Zack."

"You sure?"

"That's what the cop said. Well, here's what he can do with his papers." She tears the first sheet in half.

"Hey, take it easy." Ty kneels and picks up the papers.

"Just leave," she says.

"What?"

"Leave. Just go. Get out."

"You sure you want me to leave? I love you, Opal."

"I'm sure."

He looks at her sadly, then bends and kisses her. "I'll call later," he says. "You want me, just call. I'll be here."

Which is a lie. He won't be here. He'll be in Cambridge.

Later, after she's got Zack to bed, Ty calls.

"I've got a name for you. A lawyer. She's good. She's over in Springfield. Works alone." He gives her the lawyer's name and number, tells her he loves her.

Words are cheap, she thinks.

Rose

TODAY'S the day. She can't postpone it any longer. Much as she'd like to ignore the mole, no ointment she's bought to date has done one thing to relieve it. She's going to have to see someone. Doc Blessing is out of the question. He'd feel bound to tell Ned.

Rose gets the phone book, flips to the yellow pages. Lord, but there's a lot of doctors and clinics. Who would believe six pages of listings? She scans the pages, finds the Women's Health Services of Springfield. This sounds like what she wants, and Springfield is far enough away so she shouldn't run into anyone she knows.

She copies the number. She'll call after lunch.

Opal

OPAL checks the address scribbled on her paper, hoping there's a mistake. The lawyer's building is run-down, a dump, sandwiched between a storefront tax service and a shoe repair shop.

A shoe repair shop. Not a good sign. You don't need to be an Einstein to see that. She slows, scans the street for a parking spot, finds a place on the next block.

Lucky for Billy he's in New Zion, out of range. If he were here, no telling what she would do. When she thinks of him back in January, standing in her front hall and giving her all that sweet talk about wanting them to be a family, saying he loves her, when all the time he's been planning to take Zack from her . . . Well, when she thinks about this, she could spit bricks. No way it's going to happen. No way she's going to lose Zack.

Inside the tiny entryway, Opal finds a door marked VIVIAN CUMMINGS, ESQ., and knocks. A woman opens the door. She's overweight, gray-haired, and wears a shabby suit.

"Opal Gates? I'm Vivian Cummings."

Well, duh. She shakes hands and follows the lawyer into the inner office, where Vivian lowers herself into the desk chair. "You said on the phone you were served with a summons?"

"Yes."

"Got it with you?"

Opal opens her tote, takes out the papers, hands them over. Vivian takes up the papers and scans them, frowning when she's done. "I'll need some background," she says. "You're not married to this"— she refers to the papers—"William Steele. Correct?"

That is one mistake she's avoided. "No."

"Let's start with the paternity issue. Is there any question that William Steele is the father?"

"No."

"Do you have any formal arrangements with him?"

"Arrangements?"

"Visitation rights. Things like that."

"No."

"And he's never denied he's Zack's father?"

"No. That's why this doesn't make sense. Everyone knows he's Zack's daddy. Why is he making such a big deal about it?"

"Well, one reason is that establishing paternity is the first step in requesting custody, and it looks like he wants to gain custody."

"But he can't do that, can he? I mean, there's no way he can get Zack, is there? I'm Zack's mama."

Vivian studies Opal. "Let's back up a little before we get to that question. First thing. House rules: I need you to tell me everything. No secrets. No lies."

Opal nods.

"Okay. Let's start with your move to Massachusetts. When did you relocate here?"

"Last September."

"And why did you leave North Carolina?"

She might as well be talking to Melva. "It's a free country."

The lawyer leans back in the swivel chair. "Two pieces of advice: Get used to answering questions because, believe me, it's just beginning. And get the chip off your shoulder. It won't help you here, and it won't help you in front of a judge. Understand?"

"Okay."

"So how did you land here?"

Opal doesn't mention the three tanks of gas or the importance of signs. This woman has as much imagination as a basket of chips. "I've always wanted to live in Massachusetts," she says, making her voice soft and sweet. "Since I was a little girl. I thought there would be more opportunities for Zack. Down the road. College and things like that. I like to think ahead."

The lawyer squints at her. "No question, the fact that you left North Carolina complicates things. By moving here, Billy can make a case that he's being denied his paternal rights."

"But he didn't even *want* Zack. He wanted me to have an abortion."

"Well, he wants him now. He's asking for full custody, not shared. That means he's prepared to fight."

"Billy always wants what he can't have."

"To get sole custody, he will have to prove Zack would be better off with him, that he is the more fit parent. Is there any reason a judge would rule that Zack would be better off with him?"

"That's flat-out ridiculous." No one could take better care of Zack than she does. Certainly not Billy. Opal can't imagine Billy making meals, doing laundry, tucking Zack in every night.

"Here's the picture. The system is set up to protect the non-custodial parent—in this case Billy—from changes like a move out of state. Like it or not, Billy, as Zack's legal father, has rights. Now, it's not as cut and dried as it seems. They'll take into consideration things like Zack's current relationships with both you and Billy. Does Billy have an ongoing relationship with Zack?"

"He's seen him once in the past six months."

Vivian scribbles a note on her pad.

"What about before you left North Carolina? Were you and Zack living with Billy then?"

"Hell, no."

"And did Billy have a relationship with Zack then? Did he see him regularly? Share the care of him? Have him visit overnight?"

"Occasionally. If it didn't interfere with his life." She's tired of the questions. She wants this woman to tell her there is no way she's going to lose Zack, no way Billy is going to get custody.

"What about support? Does Billy give you money toward Zack's expenses?"

"Only for the past two months. I thought he was feeling guilty." Now Opal understands.

Vivian adds another note to the pad. "Was Billy ever abusive?"

"No."

"Drink heavily? Take drugs?"

"No."

She scribbles a few more notes. "Anything you want to add? Anything you think might help? Anything we haven't covered?"

"What will happen at the hearing?"

"The judge will listen to the petitions. He'll appoint a guardian ad litem."

"A guardian." Opal's heart actually stops. "For Zack?"

"That's the name, but try and think of it as an advocate. Someone who will investigate; talk to you and Zack and Billy, maybe friends and co-workers; try and get a picture of Zack's life; and then report the findings back to the court. Hold on. Let me check something."

She flips through a calendar, runs a finger along the page. "One piece of good news. Judge Carlyle is sitting that week. She's fair."

This is the best thing Vivian Cummings has said so far. Anyone who's trying to be fair, who's concerned about Zack's best interest, that person would *never* take Zack away from her.

"One thing," Vivian says as Opal prepares to leave, "from here on in, assume you're being watched. Billy's probably hired an investigator. That's what I'd do if he were my client. Custody cases have a way of turning nasty. What about you? Do you drink?"

"No. Only a beer every now and then."

"Do drugs?"

"No."

"And Zack's healthy? No illnesses. No accidents?"

Opal sinks back into the chair. "He did break his arm."

"How?"

House rules: No secrets. No lies. "He fell," she says. "In the tub."

"Were you alone with him?"

"No. My neighbor was there. Rose Nelson."

"Lucky for you. We'll have a witness if they try and make a case for neglect." Busy writing down Rose's name, Vivian does not see the fear on Opal's face.

Rose

"NAME?" The receptionist at the Women's Health Services has yellow hair straight from a bottle.

"Rose Nelson." She waits while the woman hands her a clipboard. "Have a seat and fill out this form. Front and back."

Rose scans the form. *Personal medical history. Reason for appointment.* Inflamed mole? Rash? She settles on "skin irritation."

She returns the form to the receptionist. Twenty minutes later she is called. She follows the nurse down the hall to a small examining room. She's handed a smock. "The doctor will be right in."

Rose slips the smock on, then sits on the examining table.

Several minutes later there is a brief rap on the door. A woman enters, extends her hand. "Hello," she says. "I'm Dr. Nutt. Two T's."

The doctor looks over her chart. "You've come about an itch?"

"Yes. On my stomach."

"Well, let's take a look." Dr. Nutt pats the table. "Lie back."

The paper makes a crinkling sound when Rose lies down. Her pulse pounds. Dr. Nutt takes a minute to wash her hands, then runs a fingertip over the mole. "How long has this been bothering you?"

Rose counts back to the fall. To September. "Seven months."

Dr. Nutt palpates the area. "Is this sensitive?"

"No."

She checks Rose's entire abdomen and chest. "Okay. You can sit up now." She helps her up. "Something's going on around that mole. I'd like to have you see a dermatologist, get a biopsy. Just to be safe."

Biopsy.

"Do you know someone you'd like to use? Or if you prefer, we can make a recommendation."

Rose feels faint. "A recommendation, I guess."

"I'd suggest Dr. Murphy. He's the best in the area. I'll have the desk call over and make an appointment before you leave."

Rose wants Ned. He'd know what to do. She could lean on him. It was a mistake to have come alone.

Opal

THE probate court is new, a brick building, soulless as a shoe box. Opal is late and so sweaty her blouse sticks to her skin. She is dressed according to her lawyer's directives: white blouse, navy skirt, black flats. Her hair is held back in one thick braid.

Inside, the corridors are crowded. Opal gets directions to the courtroom where the hearing will be held and spots Vivian.

The lawyer, dressed in a pantsuit that looks like it was born wrinkled, nods her approval at Opal's appearance. "How you doing?" she says. "You okay?"

"Just tell me there's no way he's going to get Zack," Opal says. "That's when I'll be okay."

Vivian takes her arm, leads her to a vacant corner. "Let's run over it one more time before we go in. I'll do most of the talking. If the judge asks you a direct question, you respond, but keep it short. Answer just what she asks. That's where people get in trouble. If you're not sure, keep quiet. And remember, keep your temper."

"Okay."

"Need to use the bathroom before we go in?"

"Oh, God."

"What? What's wrong?"

"It's them," she says. Of course she should have been prepared, but she isn't. There are five of them: Billy, her parents, and two others—a man and a woman, both well dressed. Attorneys.

Before she can even think, her daddy is there, holding her. "Hi, Opal," he says.

"Hi, Daddy," she says. She inhales his Old Spice, is comforted by the familiarity.

"Raylee," Melva says. One word that says it all as far as Opal is concerned.

Billy and the lawyers don't approach.

"It's time to go in," Melva says.

The courtroom is cavernous, with blond veneer walls. The judge's bench, flanked by two flags, occupies the front of the room. In front of the oak benches—pews, Opal thinks, like church—there are two long tables. Two officers in uniforms stand at one side laughing.

There are already more than two dozen people in the room. She had not realized the hearing would be open, that strangers would be there, listening.

The clerk, a balding man in a worn gray suit, enters and takes his place at a small table directly beneath the judge's bench. He leafs through a pile of papers.

"All stand," one of the officers says as a man in a black robe strides in through a door behind the bench.

"Damn," Vivian mutters.

"What's the matter?" Opal asks.

"They've shifted schedules. Judge Bowles is sitting today."

"Is that bad?"

"It isn't great."

The judge has black hair and a trim beard. He looks impatient. Opal wonders if being a man will prejudice him in Billy's favor.

The clerk checks through his stack of papers. "Docket number 5P754," he says. "*Steele and Gates* versus *Gates*. Appearances?"

"Come on," Vivian says, taking Opal's hand and leading her to one of the tables. She sets her briefcase on the table, motions for Opal to take a seat. Four feet away, her parents and Billy and their two lawyers stand at the other table. Billy stares straight ahead, ignoring her completely.

"Vivian Cummings here," Vivian says. "Appearing on behalf of Opal May Gates. Miss Gates is present."

At the other table a female attorney does the talking. "Appearing are William Steele, Melva Gates, and Warren Gates, and on their behalf, attorneys Steven Lodge and Carla Olsen."

Opal takes in the smooth voice, the shiny shoes, the woman's perfect helmet of blond hair. She's damn sure Lodge and Olsen don't operate out of a run-down storefront office. These people mean business. A cold nugget of fear lodges directly beneath her breastbone.

"Let's begin," the judge says. "This is the mother?" he asks, looking at Opal.

"Yes, Your Honor," Vivian says.

"And the father? And"—he checks his notes—"the boy's grandparents?"

"That's correct, Your Honor." Again Carla Olsen answers.

The side door opens, and a wiry woman in a pantsuit enters.

The judge speaks. "All the parties involved are aware that this is not a trial. It is a hearing to determine the matter of paternity and to appoint a guardian ad litem for the child in question."

"Your Honor," Carla Olsen begins, "Mr. Steele seeks full custody of his son."

"I am fully aware of what Mr. Steele is seeking," the judge says. "Let's not put the cart before the horse. The first motion is the matter of paternity. Mr. Steele," he says directly to Billy, "you maintain you are the father of Zackery, the son of Opal Gates?"

"Yes, Your Honor," Billy says.

"Miss Cummings, does your client deny Mr. Steele's claim of paternity?"

"No, Your Honor."

"Everyone agrees?"

Billy *is* Zack's father, but Opal feels she is giving away something important. Until now it has been her and Zack. Now Billy will be a legal part of their life.

"Paternity is granted," Judge Bowles says. "The next order of business is to appoint a guardian ad litem. Mrs. Rogers?"

The wiry woman crosses to a table by the recorder.

"Yes, Your Honor?"

"You've agreed to take the case?"

"Yes, Your Honor."

"Miss Gates, Mr. Steele," the judge says to her and Billy, "Mrs. Sarah Rogers will be, in effect, the voice of your son in the proceedings. She will conduct an investigation and report her findings back to the court. Is that clear?"

"Yes, sir."

"Yes, Your Honor."

"I'm going to set a hearing for ninety days from today. At that time Mrs. Rogers will have completed her investigation and will make her recommendations to the court. I will then hear testimony from all concerned parties and deliver my decision. Any questions?"

"Your Honor," Carla Olsen says, "the father wishes an emergency custody order. We have serious concerns about the boy's well-being while he is in his mother's care."

Opal is on her feet. "He can't do that. He didn't even want Zack. He wanted me to have an abortion."

"Miss Cummings, please tell your client to sit down."

Opal sinks back.

"Your Honor, this is outrageous," Vivian says. "On what basis is Mr. Steele seeking temporary custody?"

"A good question, Miss Cummings. Miss Olsen?"

"It is in the child's best interest, Your Honor. Mr. Steele is better suited financially to care for the boy. And he will have the additional support of the boy's maternal grandparents."

Melva taking care of Zack? The thought kills Opal. Kills her.

"We oppose the petition, Your Honor," Vivian says.

"Your Honor"—Carla Olsen again—"there is also the question of ensuring that the boy will still be here in Massachusetts in ninety days. Last September, with no advance warning, Miss Gates removed the boy from his home, from his grandparents and his father, and left town, thereby depriving them of their rights. Who can say she won't get it into her head to move to California next?"

"Miss Gates, are you planning another move?"

"No, sir."

"Miss Cummings, can you guarantee your client will remain where she is for the next ninety days?"

"Yes, Judge."

"I'm going to deny Mr. Steele's request. But I am going to order a two-week period of visitation for Zackery to visit his father between now and the hearing."

"Thank you, Your Honor," Carla Olsen says. She smiles widely.

Zack gone for two weeks. Opal's stomach feels hollow.

"One more thing," Carla Olsen says. "We are seeking an injunction preventing Mr. Tyrone Miller from having anything to do with the boy."

Opal's mouth drops wide-open. She looks over at Billy.

"Who is Mr. Miller?" the judge asks.

"Miss Gates's current boyfriend."

Opal's knees turn buttery. What has Ty got to do with anything?

"Relevance, Your Honor?" Vivian asks.

"Miss Olsen?" the judge asks. "On what grounds?"

"We are concerned, Your Honor. In the past, drug charges have been filed against Mr. Miller. Possession and intent to distribute."

"What?" Opal turns to Vivian, who is on her feet.

"Your Honor," Vivian is shouting, "this is outrageous. I am personally acquainted with Mr. Miller. Those charges are ancient history. They have no relevance whatsoever. This is an obvious attempt to discredit my client and to prejudice the court."

"Approach."

Opal, sickened, watches while Vivian and the other attorneys cluster at the bench. The judge calls over the guardian.

Melva looks over at Opal, her face smug as a cat full of cream.

OUTSIDE, in the corridor, Vivian says, "Judge Bowles's denying their injunction is a good sign. He isn't going to be swayed by anything that they can't substantiate by fact."

"Why the hell didn't you tell me about Tyrone? Why didn't you warn me? God, he's watching Zack right now."

Vivian grasps Opal's arm, faces her. "One, you didn't tell me you were dating him. Two, as the judge ruled, it doesn't pertain. As far as the court is concerned, he's clear and clean."

"Well, I can guarantee that's not what my mama's thinking. How did they learn about Ty anyway?"

"Probably hired a detective. It definitely looks like they're ready to play hardball. Here's my advice: For the next ninety days behave as if everything you do will be reported to the court. And start thinking about who you want us to call as character witnesses."

"The judge won't really give Billy custody, will he? He can't do that. I'm Zack's mama."

"That's what we're hoping for." Vivian gives Opal a quick hug.

WHEN Opal pulls onto Chestnut Street, she can't believe her eyes. Ty has Zack out in the street—in the *street*—playing hockey.

"Zack," she says as she gets out of the car. "In the house."

He looks up at Ty, his smile fading.

"Don't look at him!" she screams. "I said, get in the house."

"Hey, Opal. Calm down."

"What the hell were you doing in the street? He could have been hit."

"Hey, baby. Lighten up. It's a dead end here."

She turns away and heads toward the house. "Just go home, Ty. Go home and leave me and Zack alone."

"What's going on, Opal? What happened at the hearing?"

"What happened? I'll tell you what happened. Billy and my parents sat there looking concerned as their lawyer asked the judge for a restraining order. A restraining order to prevent you from having anything to do with Zack."

"Me?"

"You. Tyrone Miller. The drug pusher."

"Lord. What did the judge say? What happened?"

"Oh, he denied the request."

"So there's no problem. Right?"

"Wrong. You're the problem."

"The whole thing with the drugs happened a long time ago. It was a mistake. Okay?"

"Why didn't you tell me about being arrested?" she asks.

"I was a kid. It was a mistake. Haven't you ever made a mistake?"

"I can't afford a mistake, Ty. I can't afford your mistakes. I can't afford you."

"Wait. Listen to me, Opal. Let me explain."

"Explain nothing. I can lose you. I can't lose Zack."

[SUMMER]

Ned

JUST after four Ned lowers the lift. Officially, there's another hour before closing, but as he has every day for the past three weeks, he crosses to the door, switches the sign from OPEN to CLOSED, and heads over to Trudy's. Without knowing exactly how it came about, he has gotten in the habit of going over and sitting at the counter for a mug of coffee while she closes up. He looks forward to this time, but he can't shake the feeling that he's doing something wrong.

Today she sets out a slice of apple pie. "One slice left. You might as well finish it up." She makes it sound like he's doing her a favor.

Yesterday it was Boston cream. He knows he shouldn't be eating this stuff. It spoils his appetite for dinner. Not that Rose notices.

Trudy joins him at the counter. "How's Rose?" she asks.

"The same," Ned says, which is as close as he can come to telling anyone about how bad things are at home.

Rose has reverted to that vague, floaty state he remembers from the year after Todd's death. He might as well be living alone.

What the hell is going on? he wants to say. He wants to talk. He wants to tell her that he opened the letter Anderson Jeffrey mailed to her. He knows all about the piece she wrote for the writing class. All that stuff about Todd dying and Rose's guilt about not letting him use the car. Her anger at everyone. He had no idea.

He is ashamed he's read her mail. He's hidden the envelope in the back of the desk. He'd like there to be an opportunity to tell her he's read it, that he doesn't blame her for Todd's death and she shouldn't blame herself. He wants to tell her he loves her.

Well, now he has these afternoons with Trudy. His own secret. And two people who have spent most of their lives sharing everything, now drift like dandelion fluff in a field of secrets. Is that the way it is with secrets? One leads to another. And another.

Opal

"AUNT May? It's me, Opal."

"Opal, darling, how are you?"

Opal chokes back tears. "I'm sinking here, Aunt May."

"What's going on, darling? Tell your aunt May."

Instantly Opal is catapulted back to her childhood, to the number of times she would ride her bike over to May's for consolation.

"Have you talked to Mama?" Opal says. "Has she told you Billy is trying to get custody of Zack?"

"She told me. I laughed out loud. I mean, the whole idea of Billy getting Zack is a joke."

"Well, I'm not laughing. I'm sitting on my last nerve here. The woman the court appointed is due here in an hour."

"Well, anyone would be nervous about that, sugah, but any fool with two eyes can see that Zack's place is with you. Just look her straight in the face like you've nothing to hide. Be friendly."

How can you act friendly when a person is prying into your life, deciding whether or not to let you keep your son? "Do you know Mama and Daddy are on Billy's side?" she asked.

"Melva made that clear. She's turned pure crazy on this subject."

"Why does she hate me so, Aunt May? Why?"

"You remind her of too much, honey. She sees herself in you."

"I'm nothing like Mama."

"But she *was* like you. That's why she's so hard on you. Opal, I'm going to tell you something I've got no right telling you. It's something that may help you understand. When Melva was fifteen and just about the prettiest girl in New Zion, there was a boy we were all crazy about. Henry Munford. Lordy, was he good-looking. And smart. He went up north to one of those Ivy League schools. Anyway, he came home for the summer and swept your mama off her feet. He brought her flowers and wrote her poems. By September your mama was in love. Of course Henry headed back up north. About two weeks after he'd gone, she learned she was pregnant."

"Mama?"

"A week or two later, when she couldn't figure out what to do, she told me. Course, she couldn't tell our mama. One night after dinner we went to the phone booth down at Calley's Drug Store and called up Henry Munford. Told him the story. He surely didn't send flowers or poetry then. No. All that boy sent was money. To take care of it, he said." May stops to take a breath. "There wasn't even a note in the envelope. That about broke Melva's heart."

Is she supposed to feel sorry for her mama now? Is she supposed to understand? Well, she doesn't. More than ever she doesn't understand how her mama could want to take Zack away from her.

"Don't you see, Opal? Your mama couldn't keep her baby, and you got to keep Zack. She's always been bitter about losing her child, but now she's jealous, too. You're stronger than she is, child. You fought to keep your son. She can't forgive you for that."

SARAH Rogers takes a seat in the living room and gets right down to business. "As the judge explained, I'm Zackery's advocate. I'll organize and present all relevant information to the judge so that he can make an informed decision." She gives Opal a wide, fakey smile. "We all want what's best for Zackery."

Right, Opal thinks. As if I want what's worst for him.

"After I talk with you, I'll be talking with Zackery's teachers. Your neighbors. And of course, I'll want to talk with Zackery."

"Zack. I call him Zack."

Sarah digs out a notebook. "Zack goes to school. Is that right?"

Opal nods. "Half a day."

"Does he ever stay overnight anywhere else?"

"He's kind of young for sleepovers." Opal picks at her chipped nail polish. What does this have to do with Billy suing for custody?

Sarah Rogers makes a notation. "When was his last checkup?"

"Checkup?"

"Seen a doctor? Had a physical?"

Opal deflects the question. "Are you going to be asking Billy questions, too? He doesn't know the first thing about raising a child."

"Of course we'll be talking to Zack's father," Sarah says smoothly. "But right now I am interested in you. Let's see, where were we? Oh, yes, Zack's last checkup? Who is his pediatrician?"

"He hasn't needed one," Opal finally says.

Sarah checks her notes. "I see that he had a broken arm last fall."

Opal shivers, draws her arms tight. Who has Sarah Rogers been talking with? "That wasn't an illness. An accident."

"There was a notation about bruises on the hospital records. I gather there was some concern expressed by the covering physician. Have there been any other accidents?"

"No." Opal struggles to keep her temper from flipping on.

"Miss Gates, how would you characterize Zack's relationship with his father?"

Easy answer. "He doesn't have one."

"And before you left New Zion?"

"Zack hardly ever saw him. Billy didn't have the least interest in seeing him. I don't know why the hell he wants him now."

"And your parents? How was their relationship with Billy?"

"All right, I guess."

"How is it now?"

"Better than mine."

Rose

"JUST relax, Mrs. Nelson," the dermatologist's nurse says.

Rose is prone on the examining table, stripped to her panties.

The doctor presses a finger against the mole. "Hurt?"

"No. Just itches."

He turns to the nurse, who hands him a small instrument. His hands move over her stomach. "We'll take a biopsy. Then go from there," he tells Rose.

Rose—never a fainter—feels dizzy. "Now?" she says.

"It's a simple procedure," the doctor explains. "I'm going to give you a local. You'll just feel a pinch." He wipes her abdomen with an alcohol swab. She feels a pinch.

He pats her arm. "I'm going to let that take hold. Shouldn't be more than a minute or two."

He drops the hypodermic on a tray and leaves the cubicle.

A few minutes later he is back. "All set?" he says. He washes up, pulls on a mask. She hears the slap as he pulls on latex gloves. She stares at the ceiling, feels a sensation of pressure on her belly.

"All done," he says sometime later. He puts a block of gauze on her stomach and secures it with tape. Strips off his gloves. "We'll have the results in a week. I'll have the office give you a call."

"And then you might have to remove it?"

He looks at her and then laughs. "I just did."

"You did?" Rose had expected a big procedure. Hospital. Pain.

"Try not to worry," the doctor says. "From the look of it right now, everything will be fine."

WHEN Rose gets home, there is a car parked in the driveway. As she nears, a woman steps out of the car. "Mrs. Nelson?"

"Yes."

"I'm Sarah Rogers. I called you earlier."

Lord, she has completely forgotten about the appointment. "Yes," she says without apologizing for being late.

"As you know, I have been appointed by the court to evaluate and make a recommendation."

Evaluate. Sticking her nose in where it doesn't belong. The woman follows her inside.

"You're friends with Miss Gates," Sarah Rogers begins.

Rose hesitates. A land mine here. "Hmmmm," she says, noncommittally. She doesn't want to get involved, but she doesn't want to say anything to hurt Opal either. The girl may not be the best mother in the world, but the truth is, Opal loves her boy.

Sarah Rogers opens her briefcase and takes out some papers. "I'd like to know about Zack's relationship with his mother."

"I don't really know them that well," Rose says.

"According to Opal, you baby-sit for Zack."

"Once," Rose says. "New Year's Eve."

"Did she happen to talk to you about how she came to Normal?"

Rose tells Sarah about how Opal threw a die and drove that many tanks of gas. She tells her that Opal believes in signs.

Sarah checks her notes. "And she said you were there when Zack broke his arm. Can you tell me about that?"

Rose hesitates. "I need a glass of water. I'm parched. Can I get you one?" She doesn't want to lie. Buy time, she thinks. If she tells the truth, what will happen to Zack? She knows what Ned would tell her to do. But what does her heart tell her?

"Mrs. Nelson?" Sarah prompts.

Opal

OPAL stretches awake, glances over at the clock. It's after ten. It's been years since she has had the luxury of sleeping late. Except this doesn't feel like a luxury. It feels like a bunk in hell.

Zack has been in New Zion for one week now, with one more week stretching ahead. The loss feels physical, a hollowness Opal can feel in her stomach, her chest, her throat. Her heart.

She'd feel better if she could hear Zack's voice. She reaches for the phone and dials Billy's number. No answer. Where the hell are they? She feels the rumble of panic. She wants Zack.

Ned

THEY have finished their coffee and the last of a lemon meringue pie. While Trudy clears the dishes, Ned opens the register. He counts the bills, notes the amount on a slip, pulls an elastic band around the money, and shoves it into the canvas night-deposit bag. He has taken to helping Trudy close up. By the time he's done, she returns from the kitchen. "Can you give me a ride home?" she asks. "Phyllis needed my car." Her daughter is shopping for an apartment, the first step to leaving her husband.

"Sure."

Trudy waits while he makes room on the passenger side of the pickup. Then, in the confines of the cab, she lights a cigarette. "Mind?"

"No," he says, although he does. Rose will smell it on him. Although he has done nothing wrong, he feels guilty.

"You're quiet," Trudy says.

"Just tired." More and more lately, exhaustion takes him by surprise. He could use a vacation. He pulls up to Trudy's house.

"Come on in."

"I should be getting along."

"Oh, come on in for a minute. I don't bite. I'll give you a beer before you head home."

She's lonely, he thinks. Living alone like that. What the hell. He steps out of the truck and follows her up the walk.

The house smells stale, but it's neat. There is a woven blanket hanging on the living-room wall like some kind of painting.

"Miller do?" Trudy calls from the kitchen.

"Fine," Ned says. He looks around. A row of framed snapshots lines the mantel. He is crossing the room for a better look when the first pain hits. It radiates down his arm, up into his jaw. God, it's like the worst toothache he's ever had.

"Can or glass?" Trudy asks from the door.

He sinks into an armchair, struggles to get his breath.

"Ned? You all right? What's wrong?"

"Nothing," he says, relieved he can speak.

"You're sweating. You sure you're all right?"

"Fine. Just gas." He attempts a grin. "Too much pie."

She crosses to him, searches for a pulse with her fingers. "I'm calling the rescue," she says.

"No. It's nothing. Like I said. Gas."

"Listen, I watched my father go from a heart attack. I'm not watching you. Better safe than sorry."

What is she talking about, heart attack? The worst of it had been in his jaw. Who has a heart attack in his jaw? He corrals enough strength to argue. "I'm telling you, I'm fine. It's already gone."

But she is making the call. He listens, embarrassed.

He loses track of time. The next thing, Bud Flynn is walking in the door. He's carrying a green duffel bag. "Ned, what's happening?" There is a young kid with him, the new paramedic.

"Nothing. Indigestion."

Bud takes his pulse. "Maybe so," he says, "but let me examine you anyway." He opens the bag, takes out a cylinder of oxygen. Over Ned's protests he places the mask over his mouth.

The kid sets up another machine, a computer of some kind.

"I tell you, I'm fine," Ned says through the mask. He is embarrassed by the fuss, embarrassed to be found here at Trudy's house.

The kid wraps the blood pressure cuff around his arm and attaches the machine.

Bud checks the printout. "Your EKG is showing some arrhythmia," he says.

"What the hell does that mean?"

"It means you get to take a ride with us to Mercy Memorial."

"No," he says. "No way I'm going to the hospital."

But they make him lie on a stretcher. The kid—Dave—drives the rescue truck. Bud gets in back with Ned. As soon as they are under way, he inserts an IV.

When the IV is secured, Bud says, "How about I give Rose a call? Let her know what's going on?"

"No," Ned says. He can't see any sense in worrying Rose. He'll get checked out and head home before she even realizes he's late.

"You sure? I won't alarm her." Neither of them mentions the fact that he had been at Trudy's house.

Lord, how in hell is he going to explain this to Rose?

Rose

OPAL is out working in the garden. She's been at it all day, weeding and watering, fussing over her tomato plants. That girl is hurting, taking badly the separation from Zack. Plus there's that woman from the court asking questions all over town. Rose considers offering Opal an iced tea, but before she can do anything, the phone rings.

It has been more than a week since the biopsy. The doctor's nurse said they would be calling her in a week with the results, and today is the ninth day. She picks up the phone.

"Mrs. Nelson?"

"Yes."

"Dr. Murphy asked me to give you a call. We've gotten the results of your lab test. They're negative."

"Negative?"

"Yes. Absolutely. This is one problem you can forget, okay?"

Rose exhales one long sigh, thanks the nurse, hangs up. People say things like, a cloud lifted when they get good news, a weight off their shoulders, a new lease on life. Rose feels the surprising truth of these old saws. Does she want a new lease on life? She does. The fact, the *amazing* fact—the *startling* fact—is that she does.

Suddenly she wishes she hadn't kept so many secrets from Ned. How she lied for Opal at the hospital. How in that class she wrote all the things she felt about Todd's death. How a magazine wanted to publish her piece. How a mole on her stomach had been itching since last fall and she had gone to a doctor in Springfield to have it biopsied. And now the news that the biopsy proved negative. All these secrets built on the biggest one of all: She refused to let Todd take her car the day of the accident, and if she hadn't, he would probably be alive today. Some mistakes are both simple and huge.

Right then she decides that she'll let the magazine publish her essay after all. She wishes she had told Ned about the biopsy so she could share the news that the mole was benign. But it's too late to tell him. He would be angry that she hadn't told him earlier. Still, she'll make him a special dinner. Swiss steak with mashed potatoes.

When the phone rings again, she answers at once, sure it is Ned.

"Mrs. Nelson?" an unfamiliar voice says.

"Yes," she says guardedly.

"Mrs. Nelson, this is Helen Blake. I work in admissions over at Mercy Memorial. Your husband, Edward, has been brought into emergency. We're in the process of admitting him now."

An accident, Rose thinks. *The lift.* She has never trusted that thing.

She pictures Ned crushed beneath it. "Is he badly hurt?" she asks.

"I don't know, Mrs. Nelson. I just want to tell you he's being admitted. The doctors are with him. You can see him when you arrive. Get a friend to drive you, okay?"

Rose grabs her purse and heads over to get Opal.

The girl doesn't even take time to wash her hands.

"I've never trusted that lift," Rose tells her over and over, all the way to Mercy. "Never."

"MRS. Rose Nelson," she tells the woman at admissions. "Someone phoned me. My husband has been admitted."

"His name?"

"Nelson. Ned Nelson."

"We have an Edward Nelson."

"That's him."

"He's in north three, coronary care unit."

Rose is so unprepared for this information the woman might as well have been speaking Swahili. Coronary care? For an accident? "There's some mistake," she says.

"How do we get there?" Opal says.

"Take the elevator to the third floor and follow the arrows."

Opal takes Rose's arm, leads her to the elevators.

"He's just been brought in," a nurse tells them when they get to the third floor. "Give us five minutes to get him stabilized." She points to a room at the end of the corridor. "Have a seat in the visitors lounge, and a doctor will be with you shortly."

The lounge is empty. As they sit there, Rose is grateful for Opal, for the soil-stained fingers that are now interlaced with her own.

Another nurse approaches.

"Can I see him now? Why is he here, in coronary care?"

"Your husband has had a coronary episode. Right now he's stable. The doctor will explain everything."

"When can I see him?"

"Soon. In the meantime, I have a few questions." She holds her pen over a clipboard. "How old is your husband?"

"Fifty-seven."

"Do you have children?"

She falls silent. Opal takes over. "One. A son."

"And where does he live?"

"In her heart," Opal says. "He lives in her heart."

The nurse, for the moment, is silenced.

In her heart. Rose tightens her fingers around Opal's.

"When can she see her husband?" Opal says. "They told us five minutes, and it's been fifteen. What's going on?"

"And you are?"

"Her niece," Opal says without hesitation.

"Mrs. Nelson? I'm Dr. Richards."

This doctor looks too young to have finished college, let alone medical school. He holds out a hand that Rose ignores.

"What's wrong with my husband?"

"He's had a myocardiac arrest, but he's stabilized now."

"You mean a heart attack?" Dear God. An episode, the nurse had said. Myocardiac arrest is no episode. "Will he be all right?"

"It looks good. Would you like to see him?"

"Yes." Suddenly she is scared.

"It'll be all right," Opal whispers. "I'll wait right here."

Rose follows the doctor to Ned's room.

He is sitting up in bed, plastic tubes running from his nose. An IV tube drips fluid into the vein in his right arm. "Hi, Rose," he says.

"Oh, Ned." She starts to cry.

"Hey," he says. "Hey, Rosie. Don't cry."

"I can't help it."

"I'm fine," he says. "Look." He lifts his left arm and flexes it, making a muscle with his biceps and pointing his finger out, mimicking a bodybuilder.

She pulls her chair close to his bed, rests her head in the crook of his shoulder. He pulls her head back. "That's nice," he says.

She stays there, quiet, listening to his heart, his lovely steady heartbeat. "I love you," she says.

"I love you too, Rosie. I always have."

When she returns to the lounge, Opal has ordered a sandwich for her. Coffee. She is surprised to find she is hungry, amazed to find it is after eight.

The shifts change. A new nurse tends to Ned. "Go home," she tells Rose. "We'll call you if there is any change."

She decides to stay. Opal stays with her. Around eleven she finally believes it will be safe to leave Ned for the night. "Can I go in to say good-bye?" she asks the nurse.

"Five minutes. Sleep is the best thing for him now."

"Ned? Honey? It's Rose."

"I know that, Rosie. I had a heart attack, not amnesia."

She kisses his cheek, rough with a day's growth of whiskers.

"I'm going home now. I'll be back in the morning."

"Okay. That's good."

"Oh, Ned," she says. "Are you scared?"

"No."

"Honest?" She can't believe this. "I am."

"Rosie," he says, "there's nothing to be scared of."

She forces herself to say the word. "Death. I'm afraid you're going to die."

"Death is just the next big adventure."

"Don't you say that," Rose says. "Don't you say that. It's not." Don't you leave me, she wants to say.

She is shouting, and the nurse comes in, makes her leave.

Outside in the corridor, she apologizes. "Let me go back. I won't get upset."

"You're tired. Go home. Get some sleep. He'll need you to be rested. Come back in the morning. He'll be here. I promise."

As if anyone can ever promise anything like that.

AS THEY cross the lobby, a woman rises from a chair set in the shadows. "Rose?" she says.

It takes her a moment to recognize Trudy.

"Yes." What is Trudy doing here?

"How is Ned? They wouldn't let me come up. Only family."

"He's sleeping. He's had a heart attack."

"I know."

"You know?"

"He was at my house. He gave me a ride home."

A ride home? Ned gave Trudy a ride home?

"It all happened so quick. At first he thought it was indigestion from the pie. You know how he stops by every afternoon after work for a cup of coffee and piece of pie."

No, she doesn't know. At Trudy's. Without her knowing.

"His truck is at my place. I've taken the keys. I can drive it over to the station in the morning."

"No need," Rose says. "I'll get it tonight. Opal can drop me off."

The truck is pulled halfway up Trudy's drive. Rose hoists herself into the cab. She jams the keys into the ignition, turns the engine. She has forgotten to depress the clutch, and the truck lurches forward and stalls. Rose tightens her jaw, stomps on the clutch, and tries again. Slowly she edges down the drive. It is the first time in five years she has driven. Beneath the tires she feels the shift of the earth. A tectonic shifting.

Opal

THE phone wakes Opal, and even half caught in slumber, she thinks, Zack. She rolls over and grabs the receiver.

"Opal?"

It's Ty. Before her mind can fully waken, her body softens, opens to desire.

"Hi." She sits up, tents the sheet around her nude body.

"How are you? How's Zack?"

"I'm fine. We're fine." She doesn't tell him that Zack is visiting Billy. That she misses her son so much she can barely eat.

"I've been thinking of you."

She catches her breath, releases it in a long exhale. No sense following that line of conversation. It's a dead end. Over. Done. "How did the taping go in Cambridge?"

"Not bad." He pauses. "Opal, can I see you?"

She closes her eyes. Just once—*once*—she wishes something wonderful could happen to her without cost. Something perfect she doesn't have to pay for. "Not possible."

"Why? Because I was arrested years ago? Even the judge didn't take that seriously. I mean, he denied the restraining order, right? *He* wasn't the one who said I can't see you. Ask Ned—he'll tell you I'm dependable."

Damn. Ned. The hospital. "Have you heard about Ned?"

"Ned? No. What about him?"

"He's in the hospital. Heart attack."

"Is he all right?"

"He's stable."

"How's Rose?"

"Rose is okay."

"Tell her not to worry about the garage. I'll go down and open up. I'll take care of things."

"I'll tell her."

"And Opal? Will you call me sometimes? Let me know how things are going?"

"What's the point?"

"The point is, I care. The point is, after everything is settled, maybe there'll still be a chance for us. So will you? Call me?"

Will she? Can she? "I don't know. Maybe."

SHE is stepping out of the shower when she hears the phone. This time it's Zack. "Guess what?" he says.

"What?"

"Daddy's taking me to Disney World tomorrow."

Daddy. "Well, that's a big surprise," she says. So why is she not surprised? "Listen, bud, is Billy there? Let me talk to him."

"Hi, Raylee." He's using his cocky "I won" tone of voice.

"What's going on?"

"Like Zack told you. We're taking a trip."

"You can't do that."

"Yes, I can, Raylee. Check with that lawyer of yours. It's perfectly within my rights to take a vacation with my son."

"We'll see. I'm calling my lawyer as soon as we hang up."

"You go ahead and do that. I know my rights, Raylee."

"It's Opal, you idiot. My name is Opal." She slams down the phone and turns to see Rose at the screen door.

"What's wrong?" Rose asks.

What's wrong? What isn't? Opal stands in her towel, dripping water on the kitchen floor. "It's Billy," she says. "He's taking Zack to Disney World. For five years he's a no-show daddy, and now he's trying out for Father of the Year."

What happens next absolutely amazes Opal. Rose crosses to her and takes hold of both her hands. "Don't worry," she says. "He won't get Zack. We won't let him take Zack away from you."

Rose

"I CAN stay," Opal says as she drops Rose at the hospital.

"No. You go ahead. There's no use in both of us sitting."

"You sure?"

"Thanks anyway."

"You'll call me later? Let me know how Ned is?"

"I'll call," Rose promises. What can anyone do? Least of all Opal. Once on the unit, she stops and checks in with one of the nurses on the morning shift. She has to talk to someone, someone with experience in this kind of thing. "Last night," she begins, "when I saw him, he said he wasn't afraid of dying. He said something about death being 'the next big adventure.' " She pauses. "Is that normal? Does it mean he thinks he's going to die?" She has read somewhere that a person's will to live is a decisive factor in recovery. She needs for Ned to have this will. To not give up.

"Mrs. Nelson"—the nurse's voice is reassuring—"you'd be surprised at the things we hear. The truth is that when someone says he's ready to accept death, it's usually because he doesn't really believe he's going to die." She reaches over and pats Rose's hand.

"Why don't you go on in and see him? He's been asking for you."

"Hey, Rosie," he says when she enters his room. He looks good.

"Hi, Ned." He's wearing one of those dreadful gowns that tie in back. She makes a note to bring him pajamas. She kisses his cheek. "The Sox won last night," she says. "I brought you the paper."

"Who pitched?"

"Clemens," she says, pleased with herself that she remembers. She straightens out the blanket, adjusts the pillow.

"For God's sake, Rosie. Stop fussing."

She pulls her hand back, hurt.

"Rosie," he says. He averts his eyes, and she wonders what's coming. She doesn't think she can stand it if he starts up again with that foolishness about "the next great adventure."

"The pickup. It's over at Trudy's."

She cuts in before he can continue. She doesn't need to hear about Trudy. "I know. I picked it up last night. Opal dropped me off there."

"You drove it home?"

"Yes."

"By yourself?"

"Of course, by myself," she says, irritated.

He grins. "If I'd known this is what it would take to get you driving again, I'd have had a heart attack years ago."

"Don't you even joke about such a thing."

"Mrs. Nelson?" The nurse beckons to her. "We like to keep the visits under fifteen minutes the first day. Why don't you go down to the cafeteria, get yourself some coffee."

In the cafeteria, she slides a tray along the counter. A short-order cook stands ready to take her order. "A bagel," she decides.

"Toasted or grilled."

"Toasted." Less fat. Already she is beginning to think this way.

When she returns to the unit, Dr. Cassidy, the cardiologist, is waiting for her. "Your husband is recovering nicely," he tells her. "He's filled in some history, but I have a few questions."

"All right."

"How has his health been in general?"

"Good. He's hardly ever sick."

"Has he had any complaints lately?"

"Sometimes he has indigestion. A few headaches. Nothing else."

"How about his emotional health? Would you say your husband was worried? Is he an angry person?"

Anger. If anger caused a heart attack, she would be the one lying on that bed. Not Ned. "No," she says, "Ned isn't an angry man."

Dr. Cassidy finishes up with his questions.

"When can he come home?" Rose asks.

"We'd like to keep him here for another day or two. As soon as possible we'll get him out of CCU, move him to the west wing."

"What's to prevent him from having another attack?"

"Prevention is the best way to prevent," the doctor says, smiling. "Low-fat, low-sodium diet, lots of fruits and vegetables. Avoid alcohol. Get regular exercise. Your husband can live a full life. In every way," he adds, giving her a meaningful look.

She stares at him blankly.

"A lot of people worry about sex after a heart attack. There's absolutely no reason that he can't return to a normal sex life."

She doesn't care about sex. All she wants is Ned back. She wants to be given a second chance.

Ned

VISITING hours are over, and Ned is relieved. Rose's fussing drives him crazy. It's his third day in CCU, and he wants to go home, back to his own bed. He can't wait to get a good night's sleep.

This is his last day in the unit; tomorrow he's being transferred to medical west, which will be an improvement. According to Cassidy, he can expect to be discharged after a day or two.

He hasn't talked to Trudy. He wants to thank her for taking care of him, but he doesn't have a phone here. Of course he can't ask Rose to call her. He's tried to tell Rose that he was only giving Trudy a ride home, but she hasn't let him talk about it. He wonders what she thinks. Why can't they just talk? Get things straight.

He hasn't mentioned it to Rose, but he wonders about the garage. Even if they tell him it's all right, he's not so sure he wants to go back to work. And retirement isn't impossible. Although Rose doesn't know it, he has been approached by one of the big chains. Mostly they are interested in the location, and they'll pay big for it. He wants to grab what's left of life. Maybe now Rose will agree to a move to Florida. He feels funny thinking this—like his heart attack is a weapon he can use to bend her. But it has changed things. Like Rose driving again after all these years. There are so many things he wants to tell her. That he will tell her.

For one thing he would like to tell her how he opened the letter from that professor and read the whole thing. He wants her to know Todd's death wasn't her fault. He doesn't blame her for it.

He would like to tell her he loves her and that he has always been faithful. That he thinks he's a lucky man to have had her love. There are a million things he has never done. He knows his life has a huge blistering wound at its heart, but it hasn't been defined only by Todd's death. His life has been filled with ordinary joys.

He listens to his heartbeat, marvels at the steady, unremarkable pace of it. Even now, he can rely on his heart.

He has been lying there for some time—musing about his life—when he is suddenly seized with dread. Like a premonition. Beneath his ribs, his heart quickens.

The nurse, Nancy, reappears. "How we doing?"

It's the nurses he has come to trust. Not the doctors. "If anything happens to me, will you tell my wife that I love her?"

She takes his pronouncement calmly. She checks the IV. Then she slides her hand in his, leaves it there for a moment.

"Here's a funny story," he tells the nurse. "Coming here, in the rescue truck, I saw a long tunnel." He attempts a laugh. "You know people who say they have those experiences where they die and come back?"

"Near-death experiences?"

"Right. You know how they say they see a long tunnel? Well, I saw one." He chuckles. "Turns out it was a real tunnel, the one the ambulance goes through to reach the emergency entrance."

The nurse smiles. "They should warn people about that."

"Do you believe in that stuff? Life after death? Tunnels?"

"Yes," she says, "I do."

"I wasn't frightened." Just like he told Rose. Another adventure is ahead. Not that he's in any way near ready yet to leave this one. "I want Rose to know it wasn't her fault."

The nurse smiles, misunderstanding, and pats his arm.

"My son never had a chance to say anything," Ned tells her. "He died. Accident. When he was sixteen."

"That's got to be the worst."

"He was a good kid. Kind. He could make a stone laugh."

"You sure you don't want something to help you drop off?"

"No. I'm fine now."

She adjusts his pillow. He dozes off, wakes, dozes again.

When he wakes, he sees someone sitting in the shadows. A doctor? He squints. The form rises and comes closer. Trick of the light and the damned medication, no doubt. The boy needs a haircut—as usual—but he is whole, unharmed. And not the little boy Ned always remembers, but big, lean, almost a man. Ned struggles to sit up. Tears are smarting at the corners of his eyes, and he is aware of a loud, bright tone to his left somewhere. He opens his mouth to greet his son. "Todd," he says, and laughs aloud. Todd's shy smile widens. God, what a handsome kid; he'll give the girls some sleepless nights. He's a sight for sore eyes. Whole, unharmed, strong.

It's all right after all. Ned can't wait to tell Rose.

Rose

ROSE had done the strangest thing. She'd worn a pair of Ned's pajamas to bed. They were oddly comforting; still she spent a restless night. Even when she managed to drop off, she woke on edge, breathless with the knowledge that something was wrong; then the full awakening: *Oh, yes, Ned's had a heart attack.*

She has been up since before dawn, getting the house ready for his return, which, according to Dr. Cassidy, should be within the next two days.

Late last night when Rose phoned in, the nurse said Ned was sleeping. His signs are good, she reported, then added something about having him back on meds until he's stabilized. Stabilized? They had told her he *was* stabilized. The nurse had explained that around midnight the monitor had picked up some irregular beats—ventricular fibrillation, she said.

Ventricular fibrillation. Meds. Suddenly Rose considers the stairs. Will Ned be able to manage them? She wonders if she'll have to hire home-care people to help out. Will insurance take care of it? These questions can't be left until Ned is well enough to take over.

He keeps the desk in order. Their checkbook and savings passbook are in the top drawer on top of a manila folder. She picks up the folder, opens the flap, and withdraws several envelopes. The first one holds a life insurance policy. Suddenly superstitious, she pushes it back into the folder. She flips through the other envelopes. Appliance warranties. No health insurance papers.

In the next drawer she finds the recorded deed for their house. She remembers the day Ned made the final mortgage payment and they owned the house free and clear. She folds the deed and slips it back in the drawer. All the things he had worked so hard for. All the things they thought were so important.

She is about to close the drawer when a long white envelope catches her eye. She pulls it out, startled to see her name on the front. In the upper-left corner she reads Anderson Jeffrey's name and address. So he had sent her a copy of the piece she had written in his class. And Ned had opened it. Her stomach clutches at the thought of him reading it. Too upset to continue her search for their HMO papers, she shuts the drawer and escapes to the back porch.

So Ned knows everything. How she refused to let Todd take the car that day. He knows it's her fault their son is dead. How will she ever face him?

She stares out at the sun rising on the horizon. She thinks about

Ned. Does he believe there is something beyond this life? Is that why it was so easy—so simple—for him to go on after Todd's death? *The next great adventure.* She remembers how he looked when he said that. Denial, the nurse told her. But Ned's face was calm, as if he knew something, had already seen a place she hasn't.

At that moment, bathed by the dawning sun, she feels a stirring in her chest. Ned survived his attack. She doesn't have cancer. They are being given a new chance. This is the thought she tucks in her mind's pocket as she calls for the taxi to come pick her up.

SHE has barely stepped through the doors into the CCU when she sees the day nurse startle, rise, and head for her at top speed.

She knows immediately. Even as she keeps walking—her feet on automatic—she knows. *No!* her mind, her heart cries out. *No.*

The nurse reaches out and takes her hand. "Mrs. Nelson," she says, "I'm sorry."

She allows herself to be led to the visitors lounge. "I'm sorry," the nurse says again.

"He's gone?" Rose says as calm as if she is inquiring about the price of beef.

"I'm sorry." The nurse spills out the details: a massive attack. He had a good evening. A little restless. No pain.

As if these details would help. "Where is he now?"

"In his room. Would you like to see him?"

The nurse's words ring hollow, as if she is speaking from a distance. Rose reaches a hand out to steady herself.

"Here," the nurse says. "Sit. Let me get you some water."

THEY have cleaned him up. All the tubes are gone. The IV feeds. The monitor hookups. If you didn't know better, you would think he is sleeping. A slight smile on his lips. Yes, he could be asleep. Except it is too quiet. No snoring. No breath.

She thinks, shocking herself, How dare you? How dare you smile, as if you're happy to leave me alone? Later she will track down the night nurses, seek details. Listen to everything they tell her about his last night, every word he said to them. But now, at this instant, her first thoughts are for herself. How could Ned leave her like this? How could he leave her alone?

THE following days are one gray haze. She must have met with Ralph Evans down at Evans Funeral Home, must have made all the necessary choices one is called upon to make, choices she and Ned—mainly Ned—had to make after Todd died, but she can't remember a single thing about any of it or the funeral itself.

She finds herself reading the sports pages, turning on ball games, memorizing final scores, as if to report to Ned. It fools her mind, keeps her feeling tied to him. She still expects him to come in the back door. Nights are hard. She can't face sleeping in their bed. Instead, she stretches out on the sofa and waits for morning.

If it weren't for Opal, she wouldn't eat.

The girl has taken over, managing everything, practically moving in. Who would have thought that Opal would prove so competent? Who would have thought Rose could feel such gratitude? With all the troubles that child has on her plate—the custody battle and all—she's just pushed it all aside. She refuses to be denied.

From where Rose is sitting on the couch, she can see a paper with Opal's handwriting lying on the desk: a list of those who sent floral arrangements. When Rose feels up to it, Opal says they will write notes together.

She thinks of all the things she and Ned never did: trips never taken, words never spoken. Why hadn't she agreed to sell the house and move to Florida when Ned suggested it? It would have meant so much to him. Now he is gone. Life isn't a thing, a—what's the word?—a noun. It's an act. A verb. It's something you do. Or don't.

"Can I get you anything?" Opal stands at the door. She looks tired. The boy is hanging on her legs. Ever since he returned from North Carolina, they haven't left each other's side.

"No, thanks," Rose says. "You don't have to stay here."

"I know." Opal comes in, the boy with her. "I just thought I'd keep you company. I brought over some work."

Rose is used to spending time alone in the house, whole days when Ned was at the garage, but with him gone, the emptiness echoes. Soon she will have to get used to this. But not yet.

She watches as Opal threads a needle. Zack has brought a coloring book and crayons. He stretches out on the floor and starts coloring.

Opal lifts a doll from its protective tissue.

"What's this one?" Rose asks.

"A pioneer. A pioneer woman."

Opal's dolls are amazing. Such attention to detail. The girl has explained how she makes them. Simplicity is the secret, she's told Rose, showing her how she uses a thin wooden dowel in the neck to keep the head from tipping, how she paints the faces with a fine-pointed sable brush. And all the sewing by hand. Right then Rose gets the idea. She will give Opal her Singer. She should have given it to her months ago.

Pleased, she lets her head fall back onto the sofa cushion and closes her eyes. She hears the boy humming, hears Opal shush him. It's okay, she thinks, let him sing. It doesn't bother me. But she is too tired to manage the effort of speech. At last sleep overtakes her.

When she wakes, it is nearly dark. She must have slept for hours. For an instant—one heart-swelling instant—she thinks Ned is there. But it's Zack. The boy is nestled next to her on the couch.

"You had a nap," he says.

"I did," she says. "I had a lovely nap."

He pats her cheek with a damp hand. "That's good."

She hugs him to her. She has to hug *someone,* has to touch someone. She has to, or her heart will dry up and blow away.

Opal

OPAL uncoils the hose and snakes it to the garden. She adjusts the spigot so water will trickle into the soil beneath the tomatoes, which now reach her shoulders. As she moves among them, leaves brush her skin, releasing their pungent scent. Keep the tomatoes watered, Rose has told her, and they'll thrive.

Opal adjusts the hose. Her feet sink into the wet earth, and the water cools her down. Through a haze of wavy heat she looks across the lawn to where Rose sits with Zack. Rose is wearing a green macaroni necklace Zack made in nursery school. She hasn't taken it off since he gave it to her. She acts as if it's made of jade.

Zack has proclaimed that Rose is his new best friend. First thing every morning he asks, "Can I go over to RoseNelson's?" He always says it that way—her whole name, RoseNelson—like it is one word.

Although Opal worries that Zack may tire Rose, she also thinks her son is good company. Since Ned's death, her neighbor has spent most days sitting out under the maple staring into space, shaking awake only when Opal or Zack is with her.

"You send him home if he's a bother," Opal tells Rose every day.

"He's no bother," Rose always replies.

The other day Opal overheard a conversation between Rose and Zack. "You're a smart boy," Rose said. "I get smarter every day," Zack replied. "That's what my mama says." And then hadn't Rose leaned over and pressed her cheek to the top of his head.

Opal repositions the hose and looks up just as Rose and Zack, hand in hand, head toward Rose's house. Lemonade time. Rose walks with a measured pace, steps not just matched to Zack's small stride, but slowed by heat and grief.

Opal is on slo-mo herself these days. She inches toward the custody hearing, fluctuating between dread of it and eagerness to have it settled. To have Billy out of her hair.

To date, there have been two sessions with a mediator. The meetings were Sarah Rogers's idea, proposed in hopes of avoiding a hearing altogether.

During the second meeting Opal had agreed to a proposal allowing Billy visitation rights for *every* school vacation, as well as for six weeks in the summer and alternating holidays. Billy didn't give an inch. What more does he want? she had asked Vivian. As it turns out, he wants a lot more. He wants full custody of Zack. Well, now she knows plain. Billy's out for blood.

So far, in spite of keeping alert to the possibility, she has received no sign, nothing to relieve her fears, nothing to show her the way. All she has to count on is her lawyer's advice.

Their last meeting hadn't gone well. Vivian confronted Opal as soon as she walked into the office. "No lies," she said. "That was my ground rule from the beginning."

"What are you talking about?" Opal hedged. "I didn't lie."

"Can it." Vivian had picked up a pile of documents. "Sarah Rogers's report. It's all here. Everything."

"What does it say?"

"It says you're in trouble. Zack's broken arm?"

"I told you about that." She hadn't been able to meet Vivian's gaze.

"What you told me was that you had a witness to the accident. You didn't tell me the witness was lying."

"I was afraid of what it would look like. You know, 'cause I left Zack alone." How had the guardian found out? Rose, Opal had guessed. Rose must have changed her story and told Sarah Rogers the truth. "You think I'll lose Zack because of one little lie?"

"It's no one thing. It's a pile of a lot of things. They could add up to trouble. I want you to know the truth of what we're facing."

Opal had felt the blood drain from her face. "You think Billy could win?"

Vivian had relented then. "I'll tell you what. You've made mistakes, but Billy Steele will get full custody of your son over my bloody body."

Over my bloody body. Opal clings to the words. They are the closest thing to a guarantee she is going to get.

OPAL is waiting for Vivian. If she bites any more of her nails, she'll be chewing flesh. What she needs here is a sign.

It's raining for the first time in weeks. But if that's a sign, how should she interpret it? Are the drops tears? Meaning sorrow? Loss? Or does it mean a cleansing? Washing Billy out of her life. Or does it mean a change in the weather? Her head aches from thinking about it. She needs something she can't misread. Something huge, like skywriting. She's keeping her eyes open.

Her mama and daddy, Billy, and their lawyers have already gone into the courtroom, Billy striding by her like she wasn't even there. Before he went in, her daddy stopped to hug her and tell her he loved her, nearly breaking her heart. And her mama? Well, Melva looked straight at her, then walked through the double doors to the courtroom, where the future will be decided.

Finally Vivian appears. "Sorry I'm late," she says, pushing Opal through the doors.

Their case is first on the docket. They move to the table and take their seats. Opal sneaks a look over at Billy. He looks cool, confident. She straightens up in her chair. She can pretend anyway.

The clerk hands a sheaf of papers to Judge Bowles. While he reads, Opal studies him, searching for kindness, understanding. She can't read a thing in his expression.

At last he sets the papers down. He takes a deep breath and looks out at them. "Do I understand that both parties have exhausted all attempts at arriving at an agreement?"

"They have, Your Honor," Vivian says.

"That's right, Your Honor." Again it is Carla Olsen who speaks for that side.

"It's perfectly clear," she goes on, "that because of the geographic separation caused by Miss Gates's relocation to this state, Mr. Steele is being denied his rights as a father. While Miss Gates has agreed to grant visitation rights to Mr. Steele, having Zackery for a few weeks a year is not acceptable.

"As long as Miss Gates insists on living out of state," Olsen continues, "Mr. Steele has no alternative but to seek full custody. He wants his son returned to North Carolina, where the child can have daily contact with not only Mr. Steele but with both sets of grandparents as well."

"Am I to take it that if Miss Gates agrees to return to North Carolina, Mr. Steele would be flexible on the issue of custody?"

Opal nudges Vivian. Return to New Zion? She'd rather eat sand.

"Not necessarily, Your Honor," Carla Olsen says. "My client has other concerns that lead him to believe his son's best interests are not served by his remaining in his mother's care. In fact, Mr. Steele has grave concerns about Zackery's welfare."

"That's bull." Opal hops up, shaking off Vivian's hand. "Billy didn't even want him. Don't you get it?"

"Miss Gates, please sit down."

"I'm sorry, Your Honor," Opal says. "But how can Billy say he wants Zack when he didn't, not from the get-go?"

The judge peers down at her. "Miss Gates, Mr. Steele has demonstrated to the court's satisfaction that however he may have felt in the past, he is currently most definitely interested in playing a primary role in his son's life. That is, in fact, why we are here."

"Your Honor, may I continue?" Carla Olsen lifts a sheaf of papers. "Miss Gates likes to depict herself as a loving mother, but we have a list of serious concerns. Our documentation, backed up by depositions"—she shakes the papers—"paints a far different portrait." She ticks off the accusations, flicking a fingernail against the papers with each charge. "A good mother is not repeatedly late picking her child up from school. A good mother sees that her child gets routine medical and dental care. A good mother is not a runaway, lacking financial security." She pauses, takes a sip of water.

It's no one thing. It's a pile of a lot of things. Opal is afraid to look at the judge.

"Excuse me, Your Honor." Vivian rises. "What my colleague is describing is not unrepresentational of seventy percent of single mothers. It isn't grounds for the child's removal."

"I will be happy to address that issue in a minute, Your Honor," Carla Olsen says, then resumes her litany.

"A good mother attends to the nutritional needs of her son." She lowers her voice theatrically. "Judge Bowles, we have depositions here showing that not a half hour after her son's broken arm was set, at ten o'clock in the morning, Miss Gates took Zackery out for ice cream, causing him to vomit and indicating, at the very least, a remarkable lack of common sense. And on the subject of ordinary good sense, what kind of mother becomes involved with a drug dealer? What kind of mother leaves her five-year-old son alone? We believe Miss Gates is a negligent mother. At best."

Vivian leaps up before Opal can move. "Your Honor—"

Judge Bowles waves her down. "You'll have your opportunity."

"We agree with Miss Cummings that Miss Gates is operating under stress," Carla Olsen continues. Opal hates her. *Hates* her.

"Clearly the financial and physical, not to mention emotional stress, is too much for her. If Mr. Steele is awarded custody of his son, he has a support system in place. He has a job. He's financially secure." She pauses to place a hand on Billy's shoulder. "My client has the full support of not only his own parents but the boy's maternal grandparents as well, Miss Gates's own parents. In effect, four other people will help in raising the boy and seeing to his daily care." She pauses. What? Waiting for applause? Then she sits.

Death would be too good for her. Opal clenches her hands into fists. She will not cry.

"Mr. Steele, do you have anything you would like to say?"

Billy rises, like he's getting a prize. "No, Your Honor."

"Well then, Miss Cummings?"

"Your Honor, before I say anything, my client would like to address the court." Vivian nods at Opal. "You're on," she whispers.

Opal swallows, stands, locks her knees, which helps but doesn't totally stop the trembling. "Sir, I love Zack. He's my life. I may not be a perfect mother. Heck, I'm definitely not a perfect mother. I don't know if there is such a thing. But I love Zack. I love him so much, I didn't think it was possible to love something like I love him." She swallows. "Since he was born, it's only been him and me. No one else. Not my mama or my daddy. Not Billy. I know I've made some mistakes, but Zack's happy with me. I read to him. He's smart. It would kill Zack to be taken from me. And it would kill me, Your Honor. It surely would kill me."

Opal sits. Judge Bowles flips through the pile of documents, slips out a page, studies it.

"I'm trying to understand," he says. "Now, according to Mrs. Rogers's report, you told her that you moved to Normal because you rolled a three on a die?" His voice is incredulous. "Is that right?"

"It was a sign, Your Honor."

"A sign?"

From the other table Opal hears a snort. Her mama.

"Your Honor." Vivian stands. "Sometimes a well-intentioned person does the right things for the wrong reasons. Three tankfuls of gas may be the wrong reason for Opal to move from North Carolina to Massachusetts, but searching for independence from an overbearing family was a positive move, a step toward independence. If you check with the deposition taken from Dr. Emily Jackman, you will see that it is her opinion that Opal's move was a healthy choice. Opal was looking for a new start. In that context, rolling dice might be seen as a creative solution."

Opal could just hug Vivian.

The judge shuffles through the papers, chooses another. "According to the admitting doctor, Miss Gates brought her son to the emergency room with a broken arm and suspicious bruises."

"Bruise," Opal says. "There was only one."

"Your Honor," Vivian says, "Zackery Gates is an active, lively child. I would bet that you could walk into his nursery school and choose any of fifteen children and find a bruise or a Band-Aid or two. In Zack's case, the admitting doctor was satisfied there was no abuse involved."

"According to Mrs. Rogers, Miss Gates lied at the hospital."

"Your Honor, if I may. Miss Gates was traumatized by her son's injury. When the boy got hurt, Miss Gates had left him alone to run to the store. The boy was sound asleep when she left. Naturally, she knew what this would sound like if she admitted it to the doctor. She was being accused of abuse. She was terrified.

"With the court's permission," Vivian continues, "we would like to call a witness, someone who was with Opal at the hospital."

"Go ahead." One of the bailiffs opens the side door.

"Rose?" Opal whispers.

Rose moves slowly toward the front of the room. Her face is calm, strong. Opal is suddenly reminded of the first time she saw

Rose, the day Dorothy Barnes told her about Todd's death and then she'd seen Rose pinning clothes on the line. She had reminded her of a figurehead. A square-shouldered pioneer woman. Someone solid. Someone who could help her.

"Please state your name."

"Rose Nelson." Rose's face is red. She is wearing the macaroni necklace. A sweat-smudged line of green stains her neck.

"Your relationship to Miss Gates?"

"I'm Opal's neighbor, and I want to tell the court something. It wasn't Opal who lied at the hospital. It was me. It was me who told the doctor I was there when Zack broke his arm."

"Well, Mrs. Nelson, why would you lie for Miss Gates?"

"I had to."

"You *had* to? You've lost me, Mrs. Nelson."

"I could see what the doctor was thinking. It was the way he was talking to her. I'm not blaming him. He probably sees his share. But he was mistaken about Opal. She would never hurt that boy."

"Thank you, Mrs. Nelson, for clearing that up."

Rose is not done. "Your Honor, I know what it's like to lose your son. My Todd was killed. I lost him. I know what it's like. It isn't right that Opal should lose her boy. She loves Zack. You've got half a brain, you can see that. And that boy loves her. Opal may not have much money, but she can give that boy love. And that's something no money in the world can buy."

The judge stares at Rose.

"And she isn't alone, like they say." Rose glares over at Billy, at Melva. "She has me."

DURING the recess Opal doesn't trust her legs to hold her weight. She remains at the table, clutching Rose's hands.

"I'm pulling for you, Opal," Rose tells her.

Opal swallows, tightens her grip on Rose's hand. They sit like that until the judge returns.

"Making a decision in cases like these calls for a compromise," he begins. "Perhaps one neither of you would agree with. What the court seeks is a solution that serves the interest of your son: care, nurturing, love. Who best can provide that?

"Miss Gates, you have been careless, and you have made mistakes. You have lied. When you left your son alone, you exposed him to risk, and you were therefore negligent.

"In arriving at my decision, I have to take into consideration that not only does the boy's father want him back in North Carolina, but he is joined by both sets of grandparents."

She is going to be sick right there. She shrinks back, afraid to hear more, afraid to breathe. Rose's arm encircles her waist.

"According to Mrs. Rogers's report, Zack is a well-adjusted child. Remarkably well adjusted."

Opal allows the tiniest speck of hope.

"Mrs. Rogers, in her role as guardian ad litem, believes that it would be an erroneous wrenching of a nurturing bond between mother and son to grant Mr. Steele full custody." He pauses to smile down at Rose Nelson. "And I would like it noted that I do have at least half a brain. I can see that Miss Gates has a deep and unwavering love for her son, a love that outweighs lesser considerations. I concur with Mrs. Rogers. Miss Gates retains physical custody of Zackery."

"Yes," Vivian mutters.

Opal looks at her lawyer. Is that it? Is it over? She's won?

"However, this court—and Mrs. Rogers emphatically agrees on this point—cannot condone your removing the boy from his father. By doing so, you have deprived not only Mr. Steele of his rights, but you have deprived your son of a relationship with his father.

"Mr. Steele, I am going to deny your petition for full custody."

"Your Honor." Carla Olsen is on her feet.

The judge raises a hand, motions for her to sit down.

"Physical custody of the boy will remain with Miss Gates, but Mr. Steele will have full and unlimited visitation rights." He peers over his glasses at Opal. "Miss Gates, I cannot order that you return to North Carolina. That is not within my powers. What I can do is strongly encourage you to return, keeping in mind that it is in the best interests of your son. As far as I can determine, you have no pressing need to remain in Massachusetts.

"While it is certainly true that you have built a life here, made friends"—here he stops and glances over at Rose—"I believe that those considerations are overshadowed by other factors that are in the best interest of Zack, by which I mean, the need for a boy to have access to his father, a father who has clearly and forcefully established that—in spite of his past history—he now wants to be a part of his son's daily life. I must warn you that should you decide to stay here in primary concern for your own independence rather than in consideration of Zackery's needs, I would be inclined to rule differently if in the future Mr. Steele should reappear before me and reenter a petition for custody."

The judge raps his gavel. "Next case," he says to the clerk.

"You've won," Vivian says.

She's won. She has Zack.

And she's lost. She has to leave Normal. And Rose.

Rose

ROSE checks the window again. Tyrone is gone. A few minutes earlier she heard his pickup drive up—Ned's truck, actually, which she has given to Ty. What earthly use is it to her? She refused his offer of payment. The very last thing she needs is money. Between the sale of the garage and the astonishing amount of Ned's life insurance, money is the least of her worries.

When she looked out, she saw Tyrone hoisting Zack up in the air. Next he hugged Opal, holding the embrace longer than was decent to watch. Let them have their privacy, Rose told herself, turning away, although she wanted to stay glued to the window until the Buick pulled out and they were truly gone. The last thing she saw was Tyrone kissing Opal. They're not done yet, she thinks. Opal hasn't seen the last of that man. This is like those TV shows in May. A cliff-hanger. To be continued.

The boxes and bags stacked on the driveway since daybreak are nearly all loaded in the Buick. Rose would have liked to help, but Opal refused. She won't even let Rose come out to say good-bye.

"I don't like good-byes, Rose," Opal said last night when they met for dinner. Zack's choice: pizza and Coke. "Please don't come over tomorrow. Okay? Promise?"

Rose had turned away so Opal wouldn't see the way her face collapsed.

Why should she be surprised? Opal leaves things behind: Her name. Her family. The father of her son. She makes and breaks ties. It's what she does, and Rose won't judge her for that.

Left to say good-bye from a distance, Rose stands at the window, wishing she could hold them here. Opal will be all right, she tells herself. She's not totally alone. She has her aunt May. She wishes she could believe this.

The boy keeps looking over. When he sees her, his face splits into a grin, and he lifts a hand and waves. Rose's throat closes up. He turns to his mother, says something, pointing over toward Rose.

Opal nods, and the boy runs toward her.

She meets him at the door, hugs him hard.

"You're squishing me," he says.

She instructs her arms to release him. "Here," she says, handing him a brown bag. "These are for the trip. I baked them last night."

"Thank you, RoseNelson," he says.

"You be good for your mama, you hear me? She's a big lady, but she needs looking after, too. And tell her I said to drive carefully."

Outside, she hears Opal yelling for the boy.

"Your mama's calling," she says. "You better get going."

"Okay," he says.

"I love you, Zack," she says, too softly for him to hear.

But he has. "I love you too, RoseNelson."

She can't bear to return to the window. It will be easier after they've really gone. The doll Opal gave her last night—the pioneer girl—is on the counter. Even that hurts to look at. What had the girl said? *It reminds me of you.* Rose looks away. She pours herself coffee, picks up the newspaper, turns to the sports section.

For Ned. She'll go on. After all, that's what one does. Keeps going on. Regardless.

She settles herself at the table. Have the Red Sox won again? She checks the sports and then—then she can't believe her eyes. She reads the headline twice. A third time. What? Is Opal wearing off on her? But she laughs right out loud. Out in the drive, the Buick starts up.

She dashes for the door, paper still in hand. "Opal!" she yells. "Opal, wait. Wait."

The car heads down the drive. Rose runs behind it, so Opal has no choice but to stop. "Wait."

Opal brakes, rolls down the window. "Rose," she says, "I told you, no good-byes." She is crying, tears just streaming down her cheeks. "I can't. I just can't. It's way too hard."

"I have something to tell you. So turn off that engine. Listen."

"I'm listening." Opal tries to stop the tears.

"You want company?"

"Company? Where?"

"In that car."

"Huh?"

"You want me to come with you?"

"Come with me?"

"With you. And Zack. To New Zion."

"Rose, what are you talking about?

"Go with you. I'll help out. I'll baby-sit for Zack while you make your dolls."

Opal's so surprised she stops crying. "But how? Why?"

"I don't know why. I just know it's best. For you. And for me."

"Rose, no one has ever said anything so wonderful before."

This girl is overdue for wonderful things.

"Thanks, Rose. Thanks for even thinking of it. But I can't let you. I can't let you do that for me."

"It's not for you I'm doing it. It's for me."

Opal looks at her. "You're serious," she says.

"That I am. I most certainly am serious."

"But you can't leave here."

"Why not? What have I got to keep me here?"

"What about your house? Ned's here. And so is Todd."

"No. No, Opal, they're not." And that's God's honest truth. "They're not here. A house can't hold a person or even keep a memory alive. And the cemetery? It's just a piece of earth. Ned and Todd aren't really there." Someday she'll explain to Opal. For Ned and Todd to stay alive, she has to let them go. It isn't memories that keep us going. Being loved and needed is what keeps us from dying inside.

"Oh, Rose. Thanks, but I can't let you."

"You have to." Rose beams at her. "You have to, Opal, 'cause I got a sign."

"A sign?"

"A sign too big to ignore." She opens the paper and holds the headline up for Opal.

"Read it out loud," she says.

" 'Love Leads the Way: Davis Love III points the way home for his American teammates in the final day of the Ryder Cup play.' See? *Love leads the way.* It leads the way home, Opal. Sure as I'm standing here, it's a sign I'm supposed to go with you."

"A sign?" Zack pipes up from the rear seat. "That's exactly exactly what my mama says. She always says she sees signs."

"Are you sure, Rose?" Opal asks.

"And," Zack breaks in, "my mama's going to help me read my letters on the road signs going home."

"I know," Rose says. "We're all going to read the signs, Zack. All the way home."

Music is the inspiration behind LeClaire's fictional characters.

"Every parent lives in fear that her child will die," says Anne LeClaire of the loss experienced by Rose Nelson, the central figure in *Entering Normal,* the author's fifth novel. Midway through writing the story, she was surprised to learn of a grim family legacy from her mother. "For five generations the firstborn in my family had died, victims of accident or disease," LeClaire says. "That's something I didn't know when I sat down to write the book, but I think on some level it was a memory waiting to be released."

A deeply spiritual person, LeClaire, the mother of two adult children, is grateful for her own good fortune. One way she expresses this gratitude is by observing a day of silence twice each month, a practice she started nine years ago while walking on the beach near her home on Cape Cod.

The author began her career writing articles for the Boston *Globe,* but she was always "a closet fiction writer." She fell in love with Cape Cod—and her future husband, a commercial fisherman and former pilot—during a college summer in the 1960s and decided to stay. In addition to raising a family and becoming a licensed pilot (flying is a hobby), LeClaire attended writing workshops in nearby Truro, Massachusetts. One of her favorite recent fiction strategies is to pick theme music to help develop a character. To create *Entering Normal*'s feisty single mom, Opal Gates, LeClaire listened to Wynonna Judd.

A MULLIGAN FOR BOBBY JOBE

Bob Cullen

"He's got a million-dollar swing and a ten-cent head."

For rude, charming, sexy golf pro Bobby Jobe, winning at the game of life is about as easy as a hole in one.

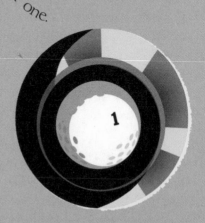

Chapter 1

WE WERE leading the PGA Championship by 2 strokes when he started seeing all the wrong stuff.

I read that sentence now, and I know it's a cliché. Caddies say "we" until the player messes up. Then it's "he."

I was a caddie. That's how I thought.

The fifteenth hole on the west course at the Oak Valley Country Club is a long, dogleg right, par 4, 463 yards, with a fairway that slopes from right to left. Palmer took a triple there one of the years he blew the PGA. It's got an elevated tee, and the grass was wet because of an earlier thunderstorm. I damn near slipped and fell as I humped Bobby's bag up the slope. He was five paces ahead and didn't notice.

What he did notice, unfortunately, was a blonde in a peach-colored shirt and shorts who was standing just the other side of the ropes along the right side of the tee. She was the kind of woman you often see around golf tournaments and golfers. Everything matches—the clothes, the lipstick, the shades, the shoes, the toenail polish. They're not teenyboppers anymore, maybe got a first marriage behind them, but they're fighting time in a gym, and they got the sleek little butt to prove it. This one did. Her name was Lane, or Blaine, or something—one of those family names that rich girls often get instead of Jane or Peggy. I think Bobby met her at one of the pre-tournament cocktail parties. I don't know if he'd gotten to her at that point, but her body language was saying she'd sure as hell give it up for a PGA champion.

I could've walked up behind him, plucked him on the sleeve, and said, "Bobby, you're in the last round of the PGA, and you're in the lead, and there's fifteen thousand people watching you—to say nothing of the guy from CBS with the Minicam and microphone right behind us—and you're technically still married, and so why don't you start thinking with your head and play some golf?"

But I didn't. Wouldn't've done any good.

He'd've just said something like, "Greyhound, why don't you shut up and go clean the grooves on my seven-iron?"

So I wiped the sweat off my forehead and took a little POWERade from the big canister by the side of the tee and cut it with water. Stuff tastes terrible, but it was a hot day.

"I don't know how you manage in this humidity with that big bag," said the lady who was walking with us, keeping score. She was an older woman, name of Florence.

"I treat my body like a temple," I said.

She had the grace to laugh. She could probably smell the beer and the hamburger grease coming out my pores. I was twenty-eight years old at that time, but my insides felt like fifty-eight.

Finally, ahead of us, Faxon hit up toward the green, turned the corner of the dogleg, and disappeared. Bobby strolled back to the bag. I looked down the fairway—a tight little ribbon of emerald flanked by thick forest-green rough. Spectators and oak trees lined the hole on both sides, and the low gray-black clouds overhead completed the frame. I was looking at the two bunkers 280 yards out and thinking, Let's stay out of those, and let's stay out of the rough.

I fingered Bobby's three-wood and pulled it halfway out of the bag. He had a nice little cut shot with the three-wood that went about 260 yards, and that's what I wanted him to hit—short of the bunkers, out of the rough.

But Bobby said, "Gimme the driver."

It was Blaine or Lane or whoever she was. The long drive is the mating display of golf, and Bobby wanted to show her his.

I almost argued with him, but I didn't. Bobby would've taken the driver anyway. Then he'd've stood up to the ball and thought, Greyhound doesn't think I can hit this club. That's not what you want your player thinking on his backswing.

So I handed him the driver.

And damned if he didn't just kill it. It rose straight up against those gray-black clouds, up over the oaks, and just stayed there.

"Serve dinner and show a movie before that one lands," I murmured to him, just loud enough for him to hear me, in that moment before the screams of the crowd washed over us. The ball soared out over the bunkers, faded just a little, and bounced to a stop in the middle of the fairway, maybe 320 yards from the tee.

Bobby half turned and flipped the driver toward the bag. "Don't show me a club till I tell you what I want to hit," he said. He turned his back on me and strolled off toward the fairway.

He was arrogant. But when you hit the ball 300-plus yards down the middle in the final round of a major, not too many people are going to begrudge you a little ego.

After I put the driver back in the bag, I had to kind of jog a little to try to catch up. No one looks good moving fast with a touring pro's bag on his back. You're like one of those wretched native bearers in a Tarzan movie. And my legs are short and a little bowed. A few people laughed as I hustled after Bobby.

Most people think that was why my nickname out on the tour was Greyhound—because my legs were short and I moved slow. That wasn't the reason, but I never bothered to correct people who thought it was. I didn't like the name no matter how I got it.

Montgomerie, who did hit three-wood, was seventy yards back of us, so we had some time while we waited for our next shot. I set the bag down and paced off the distance to the closest sprinkler head. I pulled out my yardage book and the pin sheet and did the arithmetic, going over it twice to make sure I had it right. We had 116 yards to the front edge, 142 to the pin, and another 4 to the back edge.

Bobby was standing there with his hands on his hips, and before I could give him the numbers, he kind of leered at me. "Nice set, huh?" he asked me, so quiet only I could hear it. "You figure they're real?"

It's a good thing Ken Venturi's never learned to read lips. I've watched the tape of the tournament, and at that moment Bobby was on camera and Kenny was telling people he was talking to his caddie about where he wanted to place his approach shot.

I wanted to chew Bobby out, but I didn't. For one, he wasn't paying me to chew him out. For another, who can say what's the right thing to think about in Bobby's situation? So I just said to him, "Okay, you got Joe Montana to the front and Walter Payton to the middle."

Bobby was a big football fan. Sometimes, just to try to loosen him up a little bit, I'd use old football players' numbers to indicate yardage: Joe Montana wore number 16 and Walter Payton was 34. I hoped that if I got him thinking about what number Walter Payton wore, he'd forget to ask me why I was giving him the yardage to the middle of the green instead of to the pin.

He didn't. "Gale Sayers to the pin?" he asked.

"Ronnie Lott," I told him.

He had no business thinking about the pin. It was set toward the back of the green, way back. Shooting for the pin brought a pot bunker into range. We didn't want to go there. But maybe in the back of his primitive little brain he was thinking of what Blaine or Lane might do for another birdie. "Gimme the nine," Bobby said.

Again, I didn't want to argue with him, didn't want to mess up his confidence. So I handed him the club. "Hit it close," I said.

Bobby hit it close all right—close to an old guy who was sitting in one of those little folding chairs behind the green. The ball took a big hop and half buried in the little bunker.

Bobby cursed, and you could hear it all over the golf course. He turned to me, his face red underneath his Callaway visor. "Wrong yardage, Greyhound," he snarled at me, like it was my fault.

I didn't say anything—just put my head down and walked up to the green. A caddie's got to take some abuse. It's part of the job.

Bobby made a pretty good shot from the bunker, but he had a downhill lie. He was lucky to get down in two putts and make a bogey.

I got next to him as we walked to the sixteenth tee. "No big deal," I said. "We're still one up."

He didn't say anything. Bobby had some history to get around. He'd played four years on the tour. He'd made a lot of money. But he hadn't won. Now every writer in the media center was thinking that he was going to blow it again.

He stepped out on the tee at number 16, par 5, 570 yards, with a creek running all the way down the left side and curling around the green. We had to wait because Faxon was in the fairway about 300 yards out, getting ready to go for the green in two. Bobby pulled a seven-iron out of the bag and started doing something I've never seen anyone else do—bouncing a ball off the club face without looking at it. You've seen Tiger do it in the commercials, but Tiger uses a wedge, and he looks. Bobby has always had remarkable hands.

THE first time I ever saw Bobby, he was winning money with those hands in a beer joint outside of Orlando, where we were both playing on a class D circuit called the Walter Hagen Tour. The Hagen Tour was for the most marginal of professional tournament golfers, mostly guys like me who were never going to get inside the ropes on the tour unless we became cops—or caddies. Once in a while some kid who was waiting for the Tour Qualifying School would spend a few weeks on the Hagen Tour before moving on. That was Bobby Jobe. He was out of the University of Georgia. He was supposed to be the next Fran Tarkenton, but he hurt his knees. Never played golf seriously till he was nearly through with college.

But he could play. First round he played on the Hagen Tour, he shot something like 63. That night I was sitting around with a couple of other Hagen Tour lifers, trying to forget the fact that we'd never shot 63 and never would and here he'd done it in maybe his second year of serious golf. He walks in and takes a seat at the bar, and the next thing I see, he's betting some guy a hundred dollars that he can drain six shot glasses full of Scotch and then juggle the glasses through the jukebox rendition of "Margaritaville" without dropping any. And of course, he did, grinning that arrogant grin of his the whole time. He was never movie-star handsome. But he had a mess of hair the color of the prairie, clear brown eyes, and a swagger in everything he did. He made an impression.

Before the night was out, I told him if he was looking for a caddie at Q School, I was available. We made it through Q School easy, and his first tournament was out in Palm Springs, the Bob Hope. I didn't have enough money to fly out. I had to take a Greyhound bus, and when I got into Indio, I had to call him to pick me up in his courtesy car. That's why he started calling me Greyhound and why I've always hated the name. It reminds me of being poor.

FAXON hit his shot toward the green. We couldn't see it land, but the gallery's roar told us it was on, maybe close. We knew Faxon was just a shot back. If he made birdie, we'd be tied.

Bobby didn't react. He just kept bouncing that ball off his iron and staring at a pot bunker in the middle of the fairway.

That bunker, 275 yards out from the tee box, was the defining characteristic of number 16. If you wanted to, you could hit short of the bunker, but then you couldn't hope to reach the green in two shots. Or you could try to hit over it. If you hit the bunker, though, you might need both hands to count your strokes on.

The breeze kicked up the way it often does before a thunderstorm, turning up the leaves on the trees around the tee.

Montgomerie hit his usual dead-straight three-wood, and it stopped about twenty yards short of the sand, right in the middle. But he was 3 strokes behind, and what he did didn't matter to us. It was Bobby and Faxon.

Bobby stepped back to the bag and laid a hand over the top of it. Just to kind of hint at what I was thinking, I reached down and snatched a handful of grass off the tee and let it flutter from my fingers. It blew back against the PGA logo across my caddie bib.

"Whattaya think?" he asked. It was a bad sign. Bobby only asked me for club advice when his instincts shrugged their shoulders and told him, "Don't look at us."

"Three-wood," I said. "Put it in the fairway, hit a two-iron, knock the wedge stiff. We'll get a birdie with your putter."

Bobby sighed. "Gotta try for the birdie, 'Hound. I think I can carry it." He pulled the driver out of the bag.

I wanted to say, "Bobby, you can't think you can carry it. You gotta know you're gonna carry it." I wanted to ask him if he wanted to blow it, if he was afraid to win. I didn't. I just watched.

Bobby made a pretty good swing, but a little quick. The wind seemed to freshen just as he hit the ball. It headed for that bunker like a laser-guided bomb, caught the lip, and disappeared. The crowd let out a soft little "ooh."

Bobby glared at me. "You had to tell me to hit three-wood," he snapped. "You knew I'd wind up hitting driver!"

I suddenly didn't want to take any more crap from him. "If you don't want to know what I think, don't ask," I snapped. "Why don't you quit being such an ass and play some golf?"

I still couldn't tell you exactly why I lost it like that. I mean, obviously, the guy's in the process of pissing away a win that would've been worth about sixty grand to me, since the caddie generally gets ten percent of a winner's purse. But it wasn't the money—or, at least, it wasn't only the money. I was just fed up with working so hard to help get Bobby into a position to win and then seeing him blow it.

A few guys out on the tour might've responded positively to hearing that, the way some kids will stop whining if you give them a little smack. Not Bobby. For a minute he looked surprised. Then his face kind of twisted. I knew then that I'd crossed a line.

As we walked down the fairway, Jello McKay sidled over toward me, looking almost as upset as Bobby. Jello was an old black guy, a freelancer. He was caddying for Montgomerie that week because Montgomerie's regular guy was sick. He looked at me pretty sternly. "Calm down, young man. This ain't the time for arguing," he said.

I should've listened to him. I just nodded.

The bunker was a nasty one, a little pit with walls about six feet high and barely enough room inside to take a club back. It was going to take a damn good shot just to get the ball out of there, let alone advance it far enough to reach the green in three. Just then another roar came from around the green.

"I think Faxon made birdie," Bobby said.

"Probably," I said. I could barely look at him, I was so angry.

"I think I can get the sand wedge out of here," Bobby said.

"Go for it," I said. I handed him the club.

He almost pulled the shot off. He caught it clean, and he got it up in the air. But the ball caught the lip and rolled right back toward his feet. He had to hop out of the way to avoid a penalty stroke.

Bobby turned pale for a moment, then purple. I don't think he was as mad about seeing his lead slip away as he was embarrassed to look like a Sunday hacker on national television.

And of course, he took it out on me. "Yeah, Bobby, you can get a sand wedge out of there. Go for it," he snarled. "Greyhound, you're the biggest waste of white skin I've seen in my damn life."

I didn't have any trouble hearing him. On the other side of the bunker, out of the corner of my eye, I could see that Peter Kostis from CBS had heard it, too. His mouth was open.

But I asked him anyway. "What'd you say?"

Bobby didn't even have the guts to own up to it. "I said gimme the lob wedge."

At that point I wanted him to leave a few more shots in the bunker. I try not to be a racist. I try to treat everyone the same, and I try not to say anything that'll offend someone. But where I come from, what Bobby said to me was cause for a fistfight. I couldn't tolerate it. For the moment I just handed him the club. But I knew I was going to have to quit when the tournament was over.

Bobby took a couple of deep breaths, tried to compose himself. And he managed to hit the lob wedge out of the bunker, pushing the ball maybe fifty yards closer to the green.

Then he started singing under his breath. *"They're writing winner's checks,"* he sang, *"but not for me."*

Only I could hear it. It was part of his routine when he choked. He liked to sing something to irritate me, to rub my nose in the fact that he was going to choke away a lot of money, a piece of which would've been mine. Most times he sang "I Fall to Pieces." He knew that got to me because I revered Patsy Cline. He was just mean when things went wrong.

I said, "Can't you pretend you're trying to win this thing?"

"Shut up, Greyhound," he said. "Get the yardage."

I paced off the distance from the nearest sprinkler head. "Two twenty-seven front, two forty-three pin," I told him. "Gotta be the two-iron." He just nodded.

I gave him the club. He couldn't seem to get his feet settled when he addressed the ball. He backed off once, then squirmed into position again. He waggled. He waggled again. He looked up one more time, and I could tell that what he was seeing wasn't the pin. It was the creek. And he swung.

It was an ugly swing, one I'd seen before. When Bobby choked, he usually swung too hard, snapped the ball left. He hit a duck hook that practically quacked. It dived into the creek about thirty yards shy of the green.

The crowd let out a punched-in-the-gut moan.

Bobby watched the ball sink out of sight and tossed the club toward the bag. "Nice clubbing, 'Hound," he said. "You're fired."

I didn't think. I just reacted.

"Fine, Bobby," I said mildly. "Carry your own bag in."

And I dropped the bag on the ground. I pulled the caddie bib off, dropped it on top of the bag, and walked toward the ropes.

Jello McKay intercepted me. He grabbed my elbow. "Don't do this, young man," he said quietly. "Don't matter what he said. You stay with the bag. Wanna quit, quit later."

It was good advice. But Jello seemed to me then a sorry figure with curly gray hair matted down under a cap, his shirt and his big belly wet with sweat. "Thanks, Jello," I said. "But I don't care."

I walked off. When I ducked under the ropes, people parted for me like I had the measles. When I looked back, Bobby was staring at me. Our eyes caught. He looked more forlorn than mad, like maybe he'd like to do the last twenty minutes over.

But I lived by the code that there are no do-overs in golf or anything else. People sometimes pretended there were. They'd take mulligans on the first tee till they'd be happy with a shot. But I knew that first ball is the only one that counts.

I know what happened to Bobby on the last few holes only by what I read in the papers and saw on tape. He drafted some kid out of the gallery to carry his bag. He dropped next to the creek, hit a sloppy pitch, and wound up taking 9 on the hole. And he bogeyed one of the last two. He finished tied for tenth.

I RETREATED to the little sideless tent that the PGA so generously provides to shelter caddies from the sun and rain. They had a few folding chairs there, and I sat awhile, got myself a beer from one of the concessions, and sat some more. A few of the guys patted me on the back and told me they'd have done the same thing, but they were obviously lying. Most of them stayed away from me.

My head was down, and I saw a pair of beat-up running shoes coming my way and smelled smoke from a cheap cigar. I looked up and saw Ken Alyda from the AP.

"Got a minute, Greyhound?" he asked me.

I usually didn't talk to reporters. No smart caddie does. But I knew Alyda a little. He was a gangly, ugly old guy, but he was one of the reporters who got out of the media center and its free buffet and actually walked around the golf course to see what was going on. Besides, I wasn't caddying anymore. So I said, yeah, I had a minute. He asked me what happened out there. I told him the truth. He took some notes.

When I was finished, Alyda shook his head. "That Jobe," he said. "A million-dollar swing and a ten-cent head."

I didn't argue with him.

"So what're you going to do now?" Alyda asked.

I'd been thinking about that. I had a little condo in Orlando, but I'd sublet it to a guy who was trying his luck on the Hagen Tour.

"I might go home for a little while," I said to Alyda. "My mother runs a little nine-hole course. She could use some help."

Alyda nodded. "Your home's in Virginia, right?"

I nodded, surprised he knew. "Allegheny Gap," I said.

"That's the course your father built?"

Alyda couldn't have surprised me more if he'd told me about the tiger tattoo I had on my butt for a while when I was in the army.

"How'd you know that?"

Alyda put the cigar back in his mouth and chewed a little. "I been out here a long time, Greyhound," he said. "I knew your father back when he was on the tour. How is he?"

I was still a little flustered, so I told Alyda the truth. "I don't know," I said. "He took off when I was thirteen. Haven't heard from him since."

Alyda stuffed his notebook into his back pocket and exhaled a cloud of smoke. "Sorry to hear that," he said. He shifted on his feet, uncomfortable. Then he told me he had to file his story, and left.

A rumble of thunder got me out of my chair. I stepped outside the tent and looked around. Nearly everyone was gone.

It was getting very dark. The clouds I'd seen earlier had massed and thickened. Off in the distance I could see the line of rain. Judging by the wind, it would be over the golf course in five minutes.

I had to catch the shuttle bus to a shopping center five miles away where the caddies assembled to ride to work. I headed for the bus stop, which was over by the practice range. The leaves were starting to rustle. I picked up my pace.

But above that rustling sound, I heard something else—the solid thwack you hear when a good player makes contact with a ball.

I was in the drive, heading for the parking lot. A grass berm separated me from the practice tee. I climbed it.

There was only one player out there, standing next to a loose pile of fresh Titleists. It was Bobby. He was swinging his two-iron, checking his backswing. It was getting black around the edges of the encroaching storm cell, but I could make out a white towel set about 250 yards from the tee. I knew immediately what he was doing. He was hitting the shot he'd butchered on the sixteenth hole.

More thunder rumbled, and then lightning flashed. The first few fat, warm drops of rain started to fall. A guy in a blue PGA blazer trotted out of the clubhouse to the practice tee just as Bobby launched another shot. I couldn't hear what the man was saying, but I could see him pointing to the sky. It was clear that he was telling Bobby it was dangerous to stay out there.

It was also clear Bobby wasn't in a mood to listen. Bobby didn't practice all that much. But there were times, generally right after he'd lost a lead, when he'd get obsessed with working some kink out of his swing. This was one of them. Of course, he should've been thinking of ways to work the kink out of his brain.

He took a practice swing that nearly clipped the ear off the PGA guy. The guy shrugged elaborately and trotted away.

The rain started to come down harder. I wanted to head for the bus, but I also had half a notion to say good-bye to Bobby. He had a ten-cent head, just like Ken Alyda had said. He was nasty mean. But he'd given me the chance to hang around the best golfers in the world for four years and get paid for doing it. That was something.

He swung again, taking the club back nice and slow and lazy-looking. Then the power uncoiled, and before you could even see what happened, his body unwound and the club came down and he was standing there in his follow-through position. The ball screamed off the range like an arrow, took one skippy bounce, and landed smack on the towel. I didn't know whether to clap or to cry. Bobby raised both arms toward that black, lowering sky in triumph, the club held high above him.

I didn't see the lightning bolt. You see lightning bolts, the jagged kind, from a distance. When it comes down nearly on top of you, all you see is a quick, general flash, like a strobe popping in your face. But I do remember seeing Bobby's club light up first, just for an instant, before everything disappeared in the general glare.

I felt a concussive kind of blast. It knocked me flat on my back. I may have been unconscious for a minute or two. I know that when I got up, Bobby was on the ground, writhing. It was raining harder, really pouring. The PGA guy was sprinting toward Bobby.

I ran toward him, too, but I couldn't move very fast. I was dizzy. I smelled a strange kind of electrical stench. When I got there, the PGA guy was crouched over Bobby, holding his head up, keeping his mouth open. The skin on his face was all red and swollen and blistered. The hair at the top of his head—the hair where his eyebrows used to be—was gone. His eyes were nearly swollen shut; they were just slits. He was moaning.

I stood over him, and that blistered, swollen face turned straight toward mine.

"Bobby, you okay?" the PGA guy yelled.

"Who's that?" Bobby croaked out.

Without answering, the PGA guy turned around and called for someone to send the ambulance.

Bobby's head rotated around, trying to locate the source of the voice. He couldn't. There was nothing behind those scorched eyelids but ashes.

Chapter 2

I VISITED him once in the hospital. The top half of his head was wrapped in bandages, like a mummy's, and I guess he was under pretty heavy sedation. I managed to say that I was sorry for what had happened to him and I was sorry I'd walked off and left his bag. I had a wan hope that he would say he was sorry for what he'd said and done, too, but he didn't.

He sat halfway up, propping himself on his elbows. His voice, when he started to talk, was raspy and low. This is what he said: "Greyhound, if it weren't for you, this wouldn't've happened to me. Go straight to hell and rot there."

He started to yell, his voice cracking under the strain. "Go to hell! Go to hell!"

The ruckus he raised caused the nurses to come running into the room. They shoved me out the door, and I left.

Bobby never paid me for my last week's work, but I figured he had enough problems, and he was out of my life, anyway. I didn't forget what he'd said to me, though. That sort of thing stays with you.

Jello McKay, it turned out, had been right about one thing. No one wanted to hire a caddie who'd walk off, even if he'd walked off from a certified jerk. So my temporary stay at home started to look ominously longer.

Eight long months passed. Spring came. It was time for the Masters, and I was watching it on the television set that hangs over the little snack bar at the Eadon Branch Golf Course, the one my father had built and my mother, Eudora, owned. I didn't like to watch much golf on TV. It made me miss the tour too much, and it made me feel like maybe I never would get out of Allegheny Gap.

Allegheny Gap is a good place for making you restless. It isn't much, just a mining town on the eastern side of the mountains in southwest Virginia, hugging both sides of the bottomland around the Gaulor River. It's big enough for a McDonald's and a Wal-Mart and a courthouse. When coal prices are good, there's a little money around. When coal prices fall, when miners get laid off, half the town goes to the hills to hunt small game. The rest go to bed hungry.

Eadon Branch G.C. is in a cramped little valley a mile outside of town, tucked in between Eadon Mountain and the county airstrip. The course was as important in the world of golf as Allegheny Gap was in the world—not very. My father had drawn up plans for eighteen holes, but he built only nine. The rest were just fading orange ribbons wrapped around trees my father would've had logged to make room for his fairways if he hadn't gone away. Still, even with just nine holes, it was a layout that was better than it looked. Clayton Mote had put the holes in unpredictable places. He'd laid out a reachable par 5 to start you off, but then he had doglegs left and doglegs right, a long par 4 with the water of Eadon Branch down the left side, and a par 3 over a little pond. Par 36 was a fine score. He'd set the course record the spring he left—31. The best I'd ever done was 35. We charged nine dollars for nine holes and fifteen dollars to go around twice, so it was a bargain, too.

We had a one-room clubhouse built of cinder blocks, with a peaked tin roof. It sat on a knoll a couple of hundred yards from the road and looked down on number 1, going away, and number 9, coming in. The clubhouse had a few racks of shirts and hats, a Formica lunch counter, a cash register, and three tables where some of the retired miners spent their time playing gin rummy. The walls had some posters my mother got years ago from a Wilson rep—Sam Snead promoting a line of clubs. The only thing new in the place was the television and satellite dish that my mother bought so she could watch the soaps. Eudora handled the cash and the lunch counter. I handled everything else.

This was a Saturday afternoon, and the early morning guys had all gone off and finished. I was sitting at the counter, working through a can of Miller and talking to a couple of regulars, Conrad Williams and J. R. Neill. The third round of the tournament was about half over, but we weren't paying close attention.

"Henry, you're on TV!" Eudora said. She grabbed the remote and raised the volume.

It was a tape of last year's PGA, the sixteenth hole in the final round, and I watched Bobby hit into that pot bunker and then stay in it. It was damned unpleasant to see again.

On the TV the scene switched to a shot of Bobby Jobe in a hospital in Nashville, wearing golf clothes and big Oakley sunglasses. It was a little strange seeing him on TV without his Callaway hat. The company had always paid him a bonus if he got interviewed with that hat on. I figured it meant that his Callaway contract had expired. He looked a little thinner, I thought, but strong. The swagger was still in his walk, even though he was walking a step behind a pretty girl with a frizzy mane of flame-red hair and fair skin. He had his hand on her elbow. She was his rehab instructor, Jim Nantz said.

I'll bet, I thought. Even blind, Bobby Jobe would have a good-looking woman at his side.

Now Bobby was sitting somewhere and the camera was full in his face—you could see the camera and the spotlight reflected in his Oakleys—and he was telling Nantz how much he appreciated all the cards and letters from golf fans all over the world.

"You've had a rough year in many ways," Nantz was saying. "You've had a divorce."

Bobby nodded. I was sorry to hear that he and Paula had gone ahead and made their separation final.

"That was in the works long before the accident, and it was all my fault," Bobby said.

Well, I thought, at least he told the truth about that.

Nantz asked him what he intended to do after his rehab was over. Bobby said he hoped to start a career as a motivational speaker.

I snorted. There were only two things I'd ever seen motivate Bobby: One was money, and the other was women.

The camera cut back to Nantz and Ken Venturi in the booth at number 18, and it was back to golf coverage.

The door burst open just then, and Raymond Vickers stuck his head inside just long enough to yell, "Incoming!"

"Hot damn," J.R. said. He and Conrad hustled outside, looking for their drivers.

"Henry, you've got to stop letting them do this," Eudora said. "The insurance man said we're not covered for it."

I turned and looked at her, and I was suddenly struck by how old she was getting. Eudora was only eighteen when she had me—six months after the wedding—and I'd always known she was the prettiest mother in all the classes I was in, right through high school. Whatever good features I have—thick brown hair, blue eyes, a good strong chin—came from her.

"It's all right, Eudora," I said. I patted her hand. "You know we can't hit anything." I picked up a demo driver, a discontinued TaylorMade, and hustled out the door behind them.

Eadon Branch didn't have a real practice range, but it did have a wide strip of weedy grass next to the first hole, with a lesson tee at the top. My father, I guess, had figured he'd be doing some teaching, so he'd built it there. We used it mainly for the junior clinics we held on Fridays in the summertime—and for shooting at airplanes.

Shooting at airplanes was a tradition at Eadon Branch. The way the wind blows most of the time in the Gaulor Valley, small planes coming into the county airstrip fly right over the golf course.

This plane was a little single-engine Cessna, and by the time I got up the hill to the practice tee, J.R., Conrad, Raymond, and a couple of other guys were already teed up.

J.R. has a bad left arm, permanently bent from an old mine accident, and he always hits too soon. His ball could only have hit the Cessna if it was parked on the ground 150 yards off the tee.

"Damn, that was close," J.R. yelled, which is what he's been yelling since Eadon Branch golfers started shooting at planes.

Conrad and Raymond and the others fired away before I could get set up properly. Their shots were about as good as J.R.'s. The plane was just about right in front of me when I drew the club back.

I knew that I wasn't going to hit it. No one ever had. You'd have to hit a drive that was 100 feet up in the air nearly 300 yards off the tee just to have a chance. But I liked to hit a good shot when I fired at planes. I was too rushed. Instead of a line drive over the wall in left center, I hit a pop-up behind third base.

"Oh, you scared him with that one, Henry," J.R. said. He was being sarcastic. "I think you missed by the most."

That meant I had to go down the hill off the lesson tee and pick up the golf balls, a house rule. So I picked up the milk crate and walked down the knoll to shag the balls.

I was sweating pretty good by the time I came back up the slope. The guys had all gone back inside to watch the Masters, and there was a lone figure standing there, waiting—a woman. She could've been twenty-five or thirty-five. It was hard to tell. She was wearing a New York Mets hat that barely stayed on the curly red hair that blasted out of her head in thick, shiny bunches. She was thin, pale, kind of tall, maybe two inches taller than me, almost gawky. She had a little pink lipstick on a wide mouth that seemed like it would hold a good smile. She had freckles, faded jeans, a red plaid shirt with no sleeves, and some kind of sandals on her feet. I couldn't see her eyes because of her sunglasses, but I thought she might've been pretty. Look at her from one angle, and she looked like a Raggedy Ann doll. From just a slightly different angle, she looked like Angie Everhart.

As I climbed up onto the lesson tee, she took a step toward me and said, "Are you Greyhound?"

And then I recognized her. She was the girl I'd just seen on television with Bobby Jobe—the rehab instructor.

I didn't know why, but I felt irritated. "No," I said, "I'm not."

That kind of brought her up short. "This is the Eadon Branch Golf Course?" She pronounced it ee-don.

"Nope," I told her. "It's pronounced ay-don."

She flushed a little. "And did I mispronounce Greyhound, too?" she asked, letting some irritation show.

"No," I told her, "but my name's Henry. Henry Mote."

I stuck out my hand. She took it. She had long, thin fingers. She told me her name: Angela Murphy.

"I work with Bobby Jobe, Mr. Mote," she said. I could tell by the way she said "Mr. Mote" that she was frosted.

"I know. I just saw you on TV."

She just nodded and then looked over my shoulder toward the golf course. It was a good time to look at it. The sun was getting a little lower behind Eadon Mountain, and the shadows cast by the hickory trees and the pines were sharp and cool. Eadon Branch glistened in the light, and the pond looked clear and blue.

"It's a beautiful course," she said.

"Just a country goat track," I said.

She looked at me. "And you're just like Bobby described you."

"And how's that?"

"Ornery," she said, but she smiled, and she had a smile that could take the sting out of anything.

"Bobby'll make you ornery if you're with him very long," I said.

"So I've noticed," she said, and she smiled again.

I put the milk crate down and pointed to a little bench we have under an elm tree by the first tee, and we sat down. She pushed her sunglasses off her nose and propped them on the bill of her cap.

She had blue eyes and soft, fine eyebrows. They were almost a kid's eyes, kind of wide and trusting, except that behind them there was something tough.

"So how is Bobby?" I asked her. "He looked all right on TV."

"Physically, he's doing well," she said. "His injuries have healed, except for his eyes. He's working out in a gym a couple of hours every day. But he's depressed. He needs golf," she said. She gestured with her hand. "He needs all this."

"So take him out to a course," I said. "Let him smell it. Let him hear the birds chirp."

"He needs more than that," she explained. "He needs to get back to doing what he used to do. When an adult is blinded, his future usually depends on getting back to his old job. Bobby needs to play golf."

"He sent you here to get me to help him get back to playing golf? Blind?"

She shook her head. "No. He doesn't know I've come here."

I saw her then in a new way. She was all zeal, all afire to transform at least something in the world. And she loved Bobby. She just happened to know nothing about what she was talking about.

"Miss Murphy," I said, "have you ever played golf?"

She shook her head. She was so frosted. "I'm not very coordinated physically, and I can't play golf," she said. "Bobby can, Mr. Mote."

"Bobby could," I corrected her.

Her jaw set. "You don't know what blind people are capable of. Blind people can play golf!" She was adamant. "There's even a blind golf championship! There's a blind golfer in New Orleans named Pat Browne. He shoots in the seventies."

Even if that was true, shooting somewhere in the 70s will make your wallet real thin real fast in professional golf. "Look, Miss Murphy," I said, "suppose you were one of the best piano players in the world. And you got in a wreck, and they had to amputate your hands. And then someone told you it was still possible to play 'Chopsticks' with your toes. Would you be interested?"

"But you don't play golf with your eyes," she said.

"You can't play without them," I answered.

"You'd be his eyes," she said.

I shook my head. "I might be able to line him up. But there are dozens of little shots that are all touch and judgment. You gotta see the hole. You gotta see the slope. He'll never be able to do it."

"Won't you come to Nashville and help me talk him into it?"

I didn't want to go. I didn't want to be tangled up with Bobby if some guy called from the tour, looking for me to caddie for him. I damn sure didn't want to watch another woman waste her time on Bobby Jobe. And besides, he'd flat out told me to go to hell.

So I said no. I told her I couldn't leave my responsibilities at Eadon Branch, which was true enough.

She drew in a breath. "Mr. Mote, I'll level with you," she said. "I'm not just thinking of Bobby. I'm thinking of all blind people. They need heroes, Mr. Mote. They need people to inspire them. Bobby can be one of those people."

I knew for sure then that she wasn't lying. Who'd make up that kind of drivel? She was an honest do-gooder, a crusader.

I said no again.

"All right," she said. "I'm sorry to have troubled you."

She extended her hand coolly, and I shook it.

I felt sorry she was going. But I couldn't think of anything to say that might make her want to stay. So I just walked quietly with her to the other side of the clubhouse, where she'd parked a beat-up old green Toyota. I told her to say hello to Bobby, though I was pretty sure she wouldn't, since she'd come to see me without telling him. And I watched the dust kick up as she started to drive off toward the highway.

Ornery was one thing, but I didn't like feeling nasty. You had to try to help a blind man. Even if blind golf was a dumb idea.

"Wait!" I yelled.

She stopped the car. "I can't leave Eadon Branch right now," I said, "but if you can get him here, I'll do what I can."

She gave me a smile that was all teeth and joy and promise.

"Thank you, Mr. Mote," she said. And that's all. She drove off.

A FEW DAYS LATER EUDORA told me to find someone to cover for us on Sunday afternoon. We were having Jimmy Edmisten and his family to lunch. Jimmy Edmisten, a tough, tightly wired little guy with wavy gray hair, was the cornerstone of the economy in Allegheny Gap. He owned the Chevy-GMC dealership, he was president of the Kiwanis, and he owned pieces of several mines. His son, Jimmy junior, was in my class.

I knew that Eudora had been seeing Jimmy a little. Jimmy was a widower. And two people can't keep company in Allegheny Gap without everyone knowing about it.

But since I'd been back, I'd been trying hard to keep some distance between myself and Eudora. I was way too old to be living with my mother. So I didn't move back into my room at home, which was a one-story brick house across the highway. I lived in the superintendent's quarters that Clayton Mote had put in over the barn where he kept the mowers and the tractor. Eudora and I saw each other during the day at the golf course, and we had dinner together a couple of nights a week. That was it.

So when she told me Jimmy Edmisten and his family were coming to Sunday lunch, it was a shock. A Sunday meal with families invited is a serious matter. It suggests commitment. I knew Eudora was eligible. She'd written me three or four years ago to tell me she'd finally gotten a divorce from Clayton Mote.

"You serious about Jimmy?" I asked her.

"You put on your coat and tie," she told me.

That was serious.

Jimmy arrived promptly at three o'clock, driving up in a gray Cadillac that looked big enough to hold a basketball game between the windshield and the hood ornament.

Peeking out the front window while Eudora attended to something in the kitchen, I could see he had Junior and Junior's wife, Kellee, with him. Junior was working by that time as the general manager of the GMC dealership. Kellee was busy being good-looking. They were dressed like they'd just come out of church at Easter.

They came in, and we said our awkward hellos, as if Junior and I were dear old friends who each hadn't known the other was in town for the past eight months.

The lunch was tense, brittle. Throughout, Eudora looked uncomfortable. Finally she mumbled something about clearing the table. She got up and went into the kitchen. Jimmy roused himself and cleared his own plate. I grabbed Kellee's, mine, and Junior's and followed him into the kitchen. Jimmy was standing, hands on hips, behind Eudora. Eudora was piling dishes in the sink and running water over them.

"Would you excuse us for a moment?" Eudora asked me.

I left.

Junior, Kellee, and I sat at the dining-room table, trying not to look as if we were eavesdropping on the conversation in the kitchen.

Moments later Jimmy Edmisten came out of the kitchen. He looked mad. Eudora trailed behind him. Her eyes were glittering.

"Thank you, Eudora. I don't think we'll stay for dessert."

Kellee looked baffled. Junior didn't bother to hide his relief.

"Henry." Jimmy nodded to me as they walked out.

Eudora closed the door behind them, walked back to the table, and started clearing the other dishes. A tear rolled out of her eye and down one cheek. I gave her a hug, and she clung to me in a way she hadn't ever done before, sobbing. She separated from me and took a deep breath.

"That didn't exactly go according to plan," she said.

"What was the plan?"

She sat down at the table, and I sat next to her. "The plan was that Jimmy and I were going to announce our engagement," she said. "I told him in the kitchen I couldn't go through with it."

I thought about how relieved I was not to face the prospect of Christmas with the Edmistens every year. And then I thought of Eudora, alone all these years, and of the likelihood that anyone else half as well off or respectable would ask her to marry him.

"I'm sorry, Eudora," I said, and I meant it.

She looked very weary. "There's something you need to know,

Henry," she said. "In a year or so I don't think there's going to be a golf course anymore."

"Why? What do you mean?"

"There's a loan." Eudora sighed. "I took it out a few years ago. I needed it to buy new carts, rebuild the greens, remember? There's a balloon payment due July first next year. I can't pay it. The course is still losing money."

"How much is it?"

"Two hundred fifty thousand dollars."

That was about $225,000 more than I'd managed to save.

"The thing is," Eudora went on, "that Jimmy thinks the land is worth a lot more if you sell it to a mine company and let 'em strip it. He's had geologists in. There's coal under there."

"So if you got married, you were going to sell it for a coal mine."

"He was going to buy it."

"How much?"

"Five hundred thousand."

"Probably worth twice that."

She nodded. "But Henry, you see, I need to have something in the bank. I'm not getting any younger."

"Can't you get the bank to reschedule the loan? They do it all the time for Russia and Mexico."

"Jimmy's chairman of the loan committee. I don't think he'll be too sympathetic. I'll have to declare bankruptcy. The course'll be auctioned off."

I could imagine what Jimmy would have to pay for it under those circumstances. I stood up, walked to the window, and looked out toward Eadon Branch. Suddenly the course seemed different to me, like a girl who starts looking a whole lot better when you see her out with someone else.

A Wal-Mart truck rolled slowly up the hill from the course, heading out of town. When it passed, I saw the beat-up green Toyota making its way toward us. It neared the house, stopped in the road, then turned into our driveway. There were two people in the car, and the man in the passenger seat was wearing Oakleys.

470 | *Bob Cullen*

"We've got company, Eudora," I said.

"Jimmy?"

"No. I believe it's Bobby Jobe."

I WENT to the front door and opened it. Angela was leading him up the walk. She was wearing shorts, a pink gingham top, and that same New York Mets hat.

"Steps," she said softly to Bobby. "Three steps."

"Hello, Bobby," I said. "Hello, Miss Murphy."

He stood, kind of disoriented, turning his head a little.

"Greyhound?"

"That's right," I said. "How are you, Bobby?"

"Geez, Angela," he said. "You brought me all this way to see Greyhound?" He was wearing a sport shirt with a button-down collar. The swagger I'd seen in his TV appearance must've been an act, because he looked tentative. His tone was weary and sad.

"You're just as charming as ever, Bobby," I said.

Bobby shrugged. "Angela has this idea that I should play golf again and you can help me," he said. "I've told her it wasn't gonna work and I didn't want to do it. So today she puts me in the car and just says we're going for a drive. I didn't know where."

Eudora came out of the door behind me to invite everyone in. I managed to make the introductions that had to be made. We stepped inside.

"How'd you know Angela?" Bobby asked.

"I was here last week," Angela interjected.

"Angela, how many times do I have to explain to you that this is just not going to happen?"

Angela's jaw set a little. "You hired me to help you with your rehabilitation. If you want to be rehabilitated, you have to play golf. You're a golfer."

"I told her I thought it was a bad idea, Bobby," I said.

"You got that right, Greyhound," Bobby said.

"And you can call me Henry," I said to Bobby. "Now that you're not paying me."

"Isn't it neat," Angela said, "the way warmth and love overflow when old friends are reunited?"

I looked at her, just making sure she was being sarcastic. Sometimes with women it's hard to tell. Angela had such an innocent face: porcelain skin and faint freckles. It dawned on me that if I didn't get Bobby out to hit some golf balls, she'd leave, and I didn't want her to leave. "Sorry," I told her. "Bobby, what do you say we go over to the course, make Miss Murphy happy."

"Sorry, Greyhound," Bobby said. "Not gonna happen."

"Bobby," Angela said, "either you go over to that golf course with us or I drive off and you can take the bus back to Nashville."

"You wouldn't do that," he said, but I could tell that just the suggestion that she might leave him terrified Bobby.

"Try me," she said.

He gave in, but not gracefully. "All right," he said. "We'll go take a look at Greyhound's golf course."

"Why don't you use Mr. Mote's arm?" Angela suggested.

"Think you can handle it, Greyhound?" Bobby said. Angela put his hand on my right elbow.

I guided him right into the doorjamb.

"Ouch," he said, rubbing his nose.

"The name's Henry," I said.

I looked at Angela. She didn't seem to mind what I'd done. I guess rehabilitation is a complex process.

So we drove off in Angela's car. We pulled into the gravel parking lot at the course, and Bobby started sniffing, almost like a dog trying to pick up a scent.

Seeing him do it made me sniff a little, too. I was aware, suddenly, of things I'd long ago stopped noticing—the smell of the wind filtering through the pines, the smell of grass clippings.

And I could hear things, too, hear them the way Bobby might hear them. I could hear someone teeing off on number 1, on the other side of the clubhouse. Whoever it was hadn't hit a very good shot, because a second later the word "mullicant" drifted over the clubhouse and into our ears.

"What's mullicant?" Bobby asked me.

"It's just what people here've always called mulligans," I said. "There's a sign by the first tee: 'No mullicants.' I guess whoever put it up couldn't spell."

"Maybe it means you can't take a mulligan," Bobby said.

"People do anyway," I told him.

Bobby smiled for the first time since he'd got to Allegheny Gap.

I got my golf bag, then walked him around the clubhouse to the lesson tee—only I didn't call it that, because I figured Bobby would only mock the idea that someone might actually pay me to give him a lesson. I told him we were on the practice range.

He listened. "Where're the other people practicing?" he asked.

"Not many customers this time Sunday afternoon," I said.

It was already close to five o'clock. The sun was getting low enough to start casting shadows over the fairways. The sky was pure blue and big. Someone in a group of six missed a putt on the fifth green, and hoots and whistles drifted up to the tee.

"Someone made a birdie," Bobby said. He'd been listening.

"Or missed a bogey putt, more likely," I said. "Big money game down there. Six-pack a hole."

Then something truly amazing happened. A tear trickled down from behind those Oakleys. I'd never seen Bobby cry before, not even when he blew a 4-stroke lead with two holes to go at the Heritage one year. It made me feel terrible, made me feel for the first time how much he'd lost.

Angela, I could see, understood very well what was going on. I guess she'd seen this grief with other blind people.

She patted him on the shoulder and stroked his arm. "You want to hit a few balls now?" she asked softly.

He nodded. But his shoulders were drooping, and his head was down. He was moving like a whipped dog.

Angela told me how she'd seen blind golfers hitting balls in a film. My job would be to make sure Bobby was lined up properly, to help him grip the club right, and then set the club head directly behind the ball. Then I was to step away.

I pulled the seven-iron from my bag and poked the handle into Bobby's hand; he grabbed it. He kept the grip in his left hand and ran his right hand slowly up the shaft and over the hosel to the club face, feeling with his fingers.

I teed a practice ball the way Bobby had teed them. I took the club face and set it down behind the ball.

"Now take your stance," I told him. I held the club face steady while he arranged himself. I could tell he wasn't into it. "Straighten up a little," I said.

"I am straight," he replied.

All right, I thought. Let him hit it this way.

I took a couple of steps back. "Okay," I said. "You're aimed downrange. Your club head is on the ball. Feel it?"

He pressed forward with his hands, nudging at the ball ever so gently. He took his usual two waggles and swung.

He shanked it. The ball hit the hosel of the club and skittered off to the right, banging against the bench at the first tee.

"Shanked it, didn't I? I could feel it in my hands."

"Yeah," I said, "but it was about the purest shank I ever saw."

He scowled, flipped the club in my general direction, and turned toward the last place he'd heard Angela's voice.

"Okay?" he asked. "Satisfied?"

Before she could answer, a ball came down in the vicinity of the ninth green—then another and a third. Each one made a light thump as it hit the ground.

Bobby, of course, heard them. "What's going on?"

I looked down the ninth fairway. I saw J.R., Conrad, Raymond, Joe Dill, Mel Lang, and a couple of other guys thrashing through the woods that separate the ninth from the fifth.

"It's just some guys playing cross-country golf," I explained to Bobby. "Cross-country's a two-hole course—down to the fifth green and from the sixth tee back to the ninth hole. Gotta go over a lot of trees. They're not supposed to, but we generally let 'em late in the day if it's not busy."

"Try that shot again, Bobby," Angela said.

Bobby shook his head. "Not with those guys watching."

"Boy, this'll make a helluva story for your motivational speech—if at first you don't succeed, give up," I said, goading him.

We stood there as the guys came up. Two of them were in a cart, and the others were walking. They were all drinking beer and having a fine time. We heard the distant sound of an airplane.

"Incoming!" J.R. yelled.

"Incoming!" Conrad whooped. "Two of 'em!"

"Two of what incoming?" Bobby asked.

So I told him about shooting golf balls at planes. As I explained it, J.R. and Conrad and Raymond and Joe and Mel were scrambling up the slope to the lesson tee, getting ready to fire.

Bobby stood there listening to the drone of the airplane propellers and the sound of the clubs striking balls.

"Shoot at the next plane, Bobby," Angela said.

Bobby hesitated for a moment. I remembered how he used to love to play games on the practice tee with the other pros. They used to fire at the little tractors that collect range balls, each betting fifty bucks the other couldn't hit it.

"Just like hitting a range tractor, Bobby," I said.

He said, "All right."

I gave him my TaylorMade driver. This time, after I teed the ball, I grabbed Bobby by the shoulders and put him into position, making sure his feet were aligned and his shoulders and hips were where they needed to be. Then I set the club head.

"Don't waggle," I said. "You'll lose the club-head position."

"Well, I always waggle," Bobby objected.

"You mean you used to always waggle," I told him.

I looked over to the east. The second plane was getting larger now. "I hear it," Bobby said. "When do I swing?"

"I'll tell you," I replied. "We're going to hit a little power fade and cut it right into the fuselage, okay?"

"Okay." Bobby's posture looked good.

I stepped back. I looked at the plane. "Count of three take it back. One. Two. Three."

Bobby drew the club back low and slow, nice and relaxed. He coiled, hesitated for a microsecond at the top, and then the magic happened. All that power and energy somehow flowed into his downswing, and again it was so fast you couldn't see it happen. But I heard his whoosh and his thwack, and I knew he'd pured it. The ball zipped out of there.

It would be a neat story, I guess, to say that Bobby became the first man ever to hit a plane at Eadon Branch.

He didn't.

He hit it over the plane. The ball kept rising, rising, and the timing was perfect. It was like watching one of those submarine movies where the torpedo and the ship are on the sonar screen, getting closer and closer, and you know they're going to converge.

But this ball kept rising, and the plane dropped down a touch. The ball passed directly over the cockpit.

"Holy smoke," J.R. said.

"Holy smoke," Conrad repeated.

"Sorry, Bobby," I said. "I overclubbed you."

Chapter 3

THAT near miss changed Bobby Jobe. It showed him the power and the promise he still had. As Angela said, "It's still inside you, Bobby. You just have to let it out."

Of course, I knew one shot didn't mean that much. I sure didn't think it meant Bobby could play tournament golf again. But I was willing to work with Bobby because I'd also had a little vision after I saw him hit that ball. I figured that even if he couldn't play tournament golf again, there was a good chance he could make some money doing exhibitions. I could get a piece of that. Plus I figured that once Bobby started making money again, I could suggest a little investment for him: Eadon Branch. That would save the place for Eudora and keep her occupied. At the same time, it would free me to get out of Allegheny Gap.

I knew it wouldn't be easy. Angela thought he just had to let it out. Angela didn't know golf. Golf is hard. It's hard even if you've got your eyes.

WHEN Bobby and I got together on the lesson tee at eight o'clock the next morning, I started to feel like I'd been too optimistic. He had on a yellow golf shirt I'd given him with EADON BRANCH G.C. embroidered on the left side, and an Eadon Branch cap.

I heard the sound of clubs clattering and turned around. Angela was coming down from the parking lot, and she had a surprise with her—Bobby's clubs, in his big pro bag with his name imprinted right above the ball pocket.

I hustled up to her and shouldered the bag. I'd forgotten how heavy it was. It didn't feel good to be hefting it again, but I was enough caught up in the moment not to mind. That's one of the things about golf. No matter how often it's smacked you in the face, golf on every new day dares you to hope. I set the bag down in front of Bobby and told him to put his hands on it.

"Clubs," he said, a little dubiously, as he fingered the club heads.

Then he touched the bulldog club-head cover, for the University of Georgia, that he used on his driver. "My clubs!" he yelped.

"I think he's glad to see them, Mr. Mote," Angela said.

"How'd you get them?" Bobby asked her.

"Asked Paula for them," she said.

"You knew I'd do this, didn't you?"

"Yes," she said. Nothing more. I believed she had known.

Bobby turned his head toward me. "Henry, what kind of shoes is she wearing?"

She was wearing sandals, same as the day before. Same shorts, same Mets hat, but a T-shirt this time that said she was a friend of the Bronx Zoo. Her toenails were painted pink. "Hippie shoes," I said.

"Well, you go in there and tell Eudora I'm buying you some golf shoes," Bobby told her. "You can't be hanging around a golf course in hippie shoes."

I half expected her to tell him where to stick his golf shoes. She didn't. She just smiled and went into the clubhouse. I still couldn't figure out women and Bobby Jobe.

Bobby and I now got down to practice. "We've got to get you lined up," I said. That meant putting his feet into the right position. So I squatted down and grabbed his shinbones just below the knee and half prodded, half pulled him into line.

I must've pushed Bobby when he expected to be pulled, because he nearly fell over on top of me.

"Uh, Henry, I'm not sure this is going to work," he said.

"I think you may be right."

I tried standing behind him and adjusting his shoulders, but that left his feet misaligned. I tried telling him to move his feet a few inches forward or backward, but it was like teaching an elephant to dance. You couldn't get precision. And we needed precision. If a golfer's body isn't aligned right, a good swing isn't going to help him. Finally I had an idea. I pulled his wedge and pointed it out in front of me, about thigh-high, along a line parallel to the line I wanted the ball to take. I told Bobby to step forward until he could feel the shaft snug against both thighs. He did. And there it was. He was aligned.

Angela walked out of the pro shop with Eudora. They watched us for a moment, Angela in her new golf shoes.

"Henry, I'm going to the Seven-Eleven to buy some tickets," Eudora said. "Angela's going to keep an eye on the shop." Powerball was one of Eudora's gambling vices. She knew the odds were like a jillion to one, but she liked the action.

I rolled my eyes. "What's it up to now?" I said.

"Four million," she said.

"Great," I said. "Our money problems are over."

"You're so cynical, Mr. Mote," Angela said. "Eudora, let me get a dollar. Buy one for me."

"With pleasure, Angela," Eudora said, looking at me triumphantly, as if to say, "See?" They went inside together.

Bobby and I now had to figure out how to put the club in his hands right. We worked out a compromise. I set the club head behind the ball while Bobby kept the shaft loosely in his hands. When I told him it was right, he tightened his grip. That helped. But his shots flew left and right; they never flew straight.

"Damn," he'd say when I told him a shot had strayed. But he didn't complain and he didn't give up.

After a couple of hours he suggested we go to work on putting, which I had figured was going to be the downfall of any attempt to play serious golf. I found a flat spot on the practice green and gave him a straight two-footer, a little uphill. We lined it up, and I got the club into his hands, squatting down behind and peering over the alignment stripe on top of the blade. He missed the cup by a few inches and rolled it three feet past.

"Close," I said.

Bobby got annoyed. "Damn it, Henry, if you're going to be my eyes, you've got to be my eyes. Now what happened?"

"You missed by three inches on the right side and pushed it three feet past."

"Thank you," he said. "Try it again."

And we did. He made the third and the fourth. He wanted to make ten in a row before he moved back to three feet. He'd get up to six or seven. Then he'd miss.

Angela came out with a couple of cups of lemonade. Then she spelled me for a while. My knees were aching.

Angela was a lot more descriptive than I had been. "Okay, Bobby, it's a beautiful little strip of green turf Mr. Mote's grown for us here, smooth and satiny," she said. "The hole's got some kind of white sleeve inside it. It's nice and big. Your ball says 'Titleist,' with a little number two on it. The cup's two feet away. Just needs a nice smooth swing."

He rolled it in. I could hear the rattle of the ball at the bottom of the hole.

"Hear that, Bobby? Sound of success. Make it for me again."

Bobby made his first five putts with Angela. I could see what she'd done. She'd given him a picture for his mind. He'd responded to it.

So we backed it up to three feet, and I took over. I did my best to make a picture for Bobby. And he got better at putting.

We spent hours on that green. I made marks in the grass with chalk, and then I'd pace off a distance from the mark—say, twenty feet. Bobby would putt from there. Angela would stand beside the mark and call out the distance. If he got it within a foot of the mark, she'd hoot and holler. If he ran it by, she'd tell him how much. "Twenty-three feet!" "Twenty-four feet." After about twenty hours of that, Bobby had a pretty good touch.

We did something similar with the irons. I got one of those new distance-measuring binoculars down at Wal-Mart, and we set flags out from the lesson tee at twenty-five-yard intervals. Bobby would hit his irons, and he'd try to say how far the ball was going to travel before it hit the ground. He might, for instance, be hitting an eight-iron, and he'd say, "One fifty-five," if he thought he'd caught it right. Angela was down on the range shagging the balls, and she'd call back the actual distance.

I could see that Angela had been right. Bobby needed golf. Once he got clubs in his hands, Bobby started to work harder than I'd ever seen him work at anything. He'd show up at eight in the morning, and they'd already have been to the gym, stretching and lifting weights. He'd hit balls or practice putting until dark.

When I wasn't available, Angela and Bobby would go somewhere and work on "facial vision." He'd shuffle slowly around the parking lot or the shop, trying to make sound from his feet bounce off the cars or the stock shelves, trying to use the sound to avoid the obstacles. Then it would be back to the range and hitting more balls. At night they'd head back to the Econo Lodge, where they were staying, and work on his other rehab program—I didn't want to ask what all else they did back there. It wasn't my business, and I didn't like thinking about it.

Over the next weeks we changed his routine. We started having him run his hand down along my arm to the grass and put his fingers just behind the ball so he could have a better idea of the lie he had. I tried to do better at filling in Bobby's picture. I gave him not just the yardage I wanted him to hit but also the trajectory, the flight path. Most important, Bobby tried to loosen up. I started to see his lips move a little before he swung, and I tried to figure out what he was saying to himself. I think it was, Let it happen. I couldn't help but think that if he'd had this attitude back when he was a touring pro, things might've happened differently.

He got pretty good at the little games we played, like the pitching drill with Angela calling out the distances. We had a putting drill where we dropped four balls on the practice green and then putted each to a different hole. Bobby got to where he could do it on the first try most of the time.

But it still wasn't working on the golf course. Bobby could feel the difference in his mind when we tried to play the first hole. "I can't free it up and let it go," he told me. "Once I know we're actually playing, my mind changes."

Then something happened—J. R. Neill got us into cross-country golf. He and Conrad and Raymond and some of their friends from the Pittston mine came out late on a Friday afternoon. We'd had rain earlier that day, so the course was pretty much empty. Bobby and I were working on the putting green when J.R. walked up.

"You and Bobby like to play a little cross-country?" he asked.

I looked at Bobby. "How about it?"

"What's cross-country?" He'd forgotten that J.R. and the boys were playing it that first Sunday at Eadon Branch.

"Well," J.R. explained, "it's sorta like ordinary golf, only you play, say, from the first tee to the seventh hole as fast as you can. That's what we're starting with today. And you drink a lotta beer."

We were both sick to death of putting drills. "Sounds good," Bobby said. "What are the stakes?"

"More beer," J.R. said.

"Sounds better," Bobby said, grinning.

There were six of us when we teed off. The first five all hit the standard tee shot for this particular cross-country golf route, which was a five- or six-iron over the pond to the front of the fourth tee.

A couple of them hit into the pond; J.R. and two others made it over. But when Bobby's turn came, I handed him the driver, and I pointed him toward the ninth fairway. He was going to have to hit it high and carry it about 250 yards, because there was a row of sycamore and ash trees lining the ninth fairway that J.R. and his crowd had no chance of driving over. But I didn't tell Bobby about the trees. I just told him to hit a high, smooth draw.

"See it and let it happen," were the last words I said to him.

He did. He found a swing somewhere in the vault of his brain that I hadn't seen in a long time. He hit himself a comet, a thing of beauty. It cleared the row of trees by about twenty feet and disappeared down the middle of the ninth fairway.

Bobby knew it was launched from the feeling in his hands, but he wasn't sure about the direction. "On target?" he asked.

"Piped it," I said, grinning. I wished he could've seen it.

"Hey," J.R. said in a fake whine. "You guys been sandbagging?"

"Nah," I said, "but playing for your beer is a powerful incentive."

We grabbed a cart, advanced ourselves a couple of Millers from J.R.'s cooler, and took off after the others. The ones that'd cleared the pond had to hit six- and seven-irons over the trees to the front of the ninth green, so we were a stroke to the good.

The next shot was a toughy. A big swath of woods separated the ninth fairway from the sixth, which was in turn separated by towering trees from the seventh. Bobby bent over and checked the lie with his fingertips. I gave him the five-iron, and he ripped it, clearing the trees and landing on the sixth fairway just a wedge from home. Bobby's third shot, a wedge, wound up thirty feet past the hole. J.R. and Billy, the only ones left alive, reached the green in 5, but they were inside Bobby's ball, each maybe fifteen feet away.

I guess J.R. was feeling a little irritated with himself for underestimating Bobby and not getting a handicap stroke or two. And J.R. always was the type to say anything he could think of to rattle an opponent. He hated to give beers away.

"Okay, blind boy, let's see if you can putt," he said.

Bobby raised the beer to his lips and poured it down his throat.

Then he belched loudly. "Care to press?" he invited J.R. That would double the beers at stake and make things more interesting.

"You got it, blind boy," J.R. said.

I could sense something in Bobby that I hadn't sensed in a long time. His juices were flowing, but he was still patient and calm, enjoying himself. It's the kind of confidence only someone with a gift like Bobby's can feel. I walked him carefully along a line parallel to his putt's. It was a downhill, left-to-right breaker, about as fast as they come at Eadon Branch. I lined Bobby up with the blade of the putter aimed about four feet left of the hole. "Twenty-footer," I told him. "Feel it and go."

He drew the putter back short and made a long, smooth, accelerating stroke. I thought for a moment he hadn't put enough pace on it, but the ball picked up speed down the slope and damn near went into the hole, missing by a couple of inches on the high side. It rolled about two feet past.

"Whoo," I said as the ball missed.

"What happened?" Bobby demanded.

"I should've told you nineteen and a half feet," I said. "Went by about a ball and a half on the high side. Got a two-footer."

"Damn," Bobby said. "I thought I'd made it."

J.R. and Billy putted, almost on the same line. Billy sank his, putting him in at 6. Bobby needed to sink his putt to win.

"Short putts," J.R. said, needling Bobby, "must be tough if you can't see the hole."

"Judging by you, J.R., I'd say they're tougher when you *can* see it," Bobby said. Hoots arose from the other golfers.

We lined up the next putt. It was a delicate one, the kind that causes putter shafts to get wrapped around tree trunks.

"Three feet," I said, adding one foot to the distance. "Straight in." I lined him up center-left, aimed at a bit of brown grass on the edge of the hole. Bobby rolled it right in.

"We're drinking," I said.

The two six-packs we won meant almost as much to me as the biggest check I ever got on the tour, which was five thousand dollars after Bobby finished second at Doral. I'd say they meant more, but I'm not that sentimental. One thing, though: I'd worked harder for them than I ever had for money.

J.R., Conrad, Raymond, and the guys looked a little like they'd been fleeced by some woman.

"What's the next hole?" Bobby asked. He was juiced.

"Well, we usually play to the ninth green from here," J.R. said.

"Let the beers ride?" Bobby asked.

"You got it, blind boy," J.R. said.

Bobby hit another great tee shot off the eighth tee, and we drove off. Birds were chirping, and the late afternoon sun was warm on our faces. Bobby was smiling.

"God," he said. "You know I never appreciated the way a golf course smelled."

I'd been wanting to ask him how he perceived things. "What's your sense of the place? Is it like being in a dark room?"

"Not really," Bobby said. He reached down, groping, till he found his Miller in the can holder on the dashboard of the cart. He took a sip. "It's more like being in a submarine. I can't see out. But I got other ways of knowing what's around me, just like the submarine guys do. Like I can hear wind in the trees, and I can hear a woodpecker from a mile away. I can tell you from my feet how firm the greens are. I can feel the sun on my face. I just can't see the light."

I nodded. He seemed very mellow, and I figured it was as good a time as I was likely to have to talk to him about investing.

"I think you're starting to like it around here," I started in.

"Great place." Bobby nodded. "You're lucky to have it, Coach."

"Well, as a matter of fact, we could use a partner," I said. "We got a quarter-million-dollar loan coming due. We could sell you a big piece of the place for a quarter million."

Bobby whistled. Then he clacked his tongue against the roof of his mouth. "Coach, I'd like to help you," he said.

I could sense the turndown coming, but I didn't stop him, partly because I was surprised he'd called me Coach. Angela had been telling Bobby to think of me not as a caddie, but as a coach—the

484 | *Bob Cullen*

term blind golfers used. But this was the first time he'd used that word.

"But I don't have that much money," he said.

I stopped the cart and looked at him. His face was hard to read behind those Oakleys, but I thought he must be lying. Bobby's official earnings on the tour were $2,733,457.67. I figured he'd made about that much more from endorsement deals.

"If you don't want to invest, you don't have to, Bobby," I said.

He put his hand on my shoulder. "Coach, I'm telling you the truth. I haven't got it."

I was confounded. "Where'd it go?"

He shrugged. "Paula and Robby got most of it. I agreed to that before the accident." Robby was his little boy.

"Couldn't you change it after—"

He shook his head violently. "Didn't want to," he said. "She deserves it. He deserves it. Hospital got a lot of what was left. Few bad investments. Prosperous agent. That sort of thing."

"You're broke?"

He smiled. "Not quite. Got enough to pay Angela till the end of the year. By then I'd better be rehabbed."

Bobby was feeling apologetic. "Coach, I'm sorrier than I can be about it. You've been working hard, and I know I haven't been paying you. I'm going to make it good for you. I just don't know how yet."

I felt sorry for him, so I said, "I know you will, Bobby, but you don't have to worry about it. I'm glad to help." And I realized, somewhat to my surprise, that it was the truth.

Bobby smacked a three-wood through the opening over the seventh tee and on down the ninth fairway. Then he hit a two-iron a little shy of 250 yards to the ninth green. He was on the green 2 strokes ahead of the nearest competitor, Conrad. Another two putts, and we'd won again.

"We got ourselves a case, Coach," Bobby said. A couple of the guys slapped him on the back, and J.R. said the payoff could be collected that night at Gully's.

"What's Gully's?" Bobby asked.

"Gully's is the entertainment capital of Warmerdam County," I said. "It's where the beautiful people in Allegheny Gap go to drink, stomp around, and call it dancing. And it's where beer bets at Eadon Branch normally get paid off."

"Well, I can't do it tonight," Bobby said. "Why don't you take Angela, Coach? She can have my beers."

I PULLED up at the Econo Lodge at about nine o'clock. Angela was ready. She had on a loose, flowery skirt, mainly black, and a severe, plain white blouse. It was as if she hadn't been able to decide whether to dress up or not and finally compromised in the middle.

"Been a while since I took a beautiful woman into Gully's," I said. I was feeling a little full of myself for some reason. I think it must've been the way Bobby had finally put it together on the course that afternoon.

When we got to Gully's, the parking lot was filling up and the little mobile sign outside said MIDNIGHT RODEO, FRI–SAT.

"They're going to have a rodeo here tonight?" Angela asked.

"No," I told her. "I believe that's the name of the band."

It was. They were starting to play the "Watermelon Crawl" when we walked in. Gully's was a big old cavernous place with a couple of pool tables, a couple of bars, and a central dance floor. There was a painting of the Western desert—cactuses and such—on the cinder-block wall behind the bandstand, and the whole place kind of glowed from the neon beer signs hanging on the walls.

J. R. Neill had seats set aside for us at a big table in the corner. "Pour from the pitcher," J.R. shouted as he gestured from the dance floor. "There's lots more."

I poured us each a beer. Angela watched what was going on on the dance floor, watching the way the line moved and slowed and moved again in unison. "They really dance," she said. "They're not faking it."

"You can't fake this dancing," I said. "I've had a few lessons."

Angela was different somehow in this place, or I was seeing her different. It was probably the way she was dressed. The women in Gully's tend to go all out in their own fashion. A lot of them wear special dancing outfits with boots or something. Their makeup is just so. But Angela looked a little lost in this atmosphere, with no makeup and clothes that seemed like she hadn't been sure if she'd be dancing or teaching school. When I'd seen her with Bobby, she'd been the guide—helping the blind, wise and competent. Now she seemed a little blind herself.

"Like to try a dance?" I said.

She shook her head. "I can't dance."

"I bet you could learn."

She just shook her head and sipped her beer, peering into the glass. "I'm a klutz. And I'm not very good at drinking beer, Mr. Mote," she said. "Can't hold it too well. Gotta learn."

"Why would you want to learn, Miss Murphy?" I asked her.

"You shouldn't call me Miss Murphy. I've been married."

That surprised me. Not that she'd been married. But that she'd get divorced. "What happened?" I asked.

"He ran around," she said.

"Some guys are idiots," I said, thinking of Bobby.

She gave me that smile, real quick. "Thanks, Henry," she said.

"You're welcome, Angela," I replied.

She swallowed some more beer, nearly gagged on it, and I started to worry about how much she was drinking.

"I seem to have a knack for picking inappropriate men, don't I?"

I figured she was talking about Bobby. I nodded. "You're not the first person that Bobby's done that to."

She shook her head. "Bobby didn't do anything," she said, then looked at me. "I never slept with him, you know."

I damn near spit up some beer when she said that. "Excuse me," I said. "Are we talking about Bobby Jobe here?"

"Well, he made a couple of passes at me early on. He was drinking, and it was professionally inappropriate, so I made him stop."

"How'd you do that?"

"I slapped him," she said.

"That'd work," I told her.

She smiled, not happily. "Then, after a while, I started to feel differently. But Bobby didn't do anything, and I'm, um, not too good at figuring out how to get that sort of thing started, you know?"

You could with me, I thought. But I just nodded.

"I think he wants Paula back. He sure doesn't want me."

"Give yourself a break," I said. "After all, he *is* blind."

She laughed and leaned my way. Then she smiled at herself, hung her head for a second, then raised it. "I'm a helluva woman, huh? Can't dance, can't drink, can't . . ."

I didn't want her to go on. I reached out and took her hand and moved it toward her lips to close them. Behind us, Midnight Rodeo started playing "Crazy." They liked Patsy Cline.

I stood up, still holding her hand. "Come on," I said. "I'll teach you to dance." And I did. She felt so light in my arms, like those filmy white curtains Eudora has that blow in the slightest breeze. She was hesitant and gawky at first, but she started to pick up the basic shuffle, and then we began to move around the floor. "You're doing great," I told her. "How come you said you couldn't dance?"

"I didn't think I could," she said.

We shuffled a little more and then attempted a twirl. She pulled it off and grinned like she'd just been hired to dance in the movies.

"How come you decided to teach blind people?" I asked her.

"I believe in second chances," she said. "I believe in third chances."

I was beguiled. "That's what golf does," I said. "It gives you a new chance every day. Every swing."

She smiled. "And is that why you became a caddie, Henry?"

There were a lot of things I could've told her, but the one that came to mind was this: "Listen to the music. Hear the piano?"

She listened, nodded. The piano accompaniment in "Crazy" is great—understated, melodic. Midnight Rodeo had an electric keyboard. The guy playing it was doing a passable job of imitating the arrangement on Patsy's recording.

"Most people don't notice the piano," I said. "They just hear

Patsy. But if I could do anything in music, I'd like to be playing piano for Patsy Cline. When she was alive, I mean."

The song ended, and the tune changed. "It's a sixteen-stepper," I told Angela. "Want to try it?"

Angela smiled and shook her head. "I don't think so. I think I'd better call it a night. Too many steps. Too much beer."

I took her back to the motel. She sat properly on the other side of the seat, close to the open window, letting the air flow over her face. I was very conscious of the expanse of vinyl between us.

We pulled into the lot at the Econo Lodge, and she directed me toward her room. When I stopped the truck, she opened her door before I could get out and open it for her.

"Don't get out, Henry," she said. She walked around the front of the truck and up to the window on my side.

"Thanks for teaching me to dance," she said. And she leaned in the window, kissed me on the left cheek. Before I could do anything, she was out of the window and gone.

BOBBY showed up at Eadon Branch before eight the next morning. Angela came with him, looking a little peaked.

I walked toward him and said hello. Bobby homed in on my voice. He stepped right to my side.

"I want to play, Coach. Dreamed about it all night. I'm ready."

It was a fine Saturday morning. The sky was a cloudless blue, the leaves were out on the trees, and wildflowers were blooming.

"I can't get you off right now, Bobby. I got foursomes out on the course and people lined up waiting."

Bobby frowned. He reached for his wallet, opened it, and held it out to me. "Take nine dollars," he said.

"What do you mean, 'Take nine dollars'?"

"I'm just a regular customer. Put me on line and tell me when you can caddie for me, Coach."

"You're really up for it, aren't you?"

Bobby nodded. "Coach, I had a dream. I was playing, playing good. I think I can play even better than I used to."

That set me back a bit. "How you figure that?"

"Well, when I used to screw up, it was usually because I'd see a bunker or a pond and I'd think, Don't hit it there. I'd get tense. Now you tell me, 'Hit this eight-iron a hundred and fifty-five with a little fade,' and I can just click on a picture in my mind—a nice big green, pin in the middle, no trouble anywhere. Then I relax, and the good swing comes out. I can be better 'cause I *can't* see."

"Okay, Bobby, I got a threesome coming up next," I said. "I'll see if we can go off with them, if you don't mind company."

"No problem," Bobby said. "Glad to do it."

The threesome was a group of guys who worked the night shift at Wal-Mart—Leo Grabowski, Jimmy Settles, and a guy named Peter. They were easy guys to play with, quiet and amiable.

So that was the foursome—Leo, Jimmy, and Peter humping their own bags, and me carrying Bobby's. Angela was our gallery.

The other three hit their usual fades and foozles off the tee, and then it was Bobby's turn. "Point me down the sprinkler heads, Coach," he said. I did, and we went through the routine of getting the club face lined up and getting his grip on it. It was habit by then. I took a step back; then he swung, taking the club back low and slow.

The ball soared over the horizon line, hung there for a while, and then blew on down the fairway. Then he hit a four-iron and wound up six feet away from the flag. He sank the putt for an eagle 3.

"Feels good, Coach," he said, grinning a little.

Leo Grabowski, finishing up his 7 after Bobby's putt went in, said, "So, that's the secret. Where can I get me a blindfold?"

I don't think Bobby heard him. Bobby was off somewhere in his own mind, like a horse ready to run, but calmer, more serene.

We played the next seven holes in a trance. He birdied number 4 with a seven-iron over the pond. He birdied number 8. He parred the rest, hitting every green. Bobby was 4 under on the ninth tee. And I started thinking of Clayton Mote's record of 5 under. I'd been there when he set it, caddying for him.

But I didn't tell Bobby about it. For one thing, that's not the sort of thing you want to tell a player when he's going good. For another, I didn't want Bobby to tie Clayton Mote's record.

I know. I was working for Bobby. And my father deserted me when I was thirteen. But for some reason, I didn't want Bobby to have that record. It was one of the last threads connecting me to my father, and I didn't want to cut it.

By the time we were on the bridge crossing the stream that led to the ninth green, I had a film of sweat on my forehead. There's a sense of anticipation when you're walking toward an eagle putt, a sense that you're stepping onto the dance floor and it's party time. You just know in this situation something good is going to happen, that the worst outcome is a birdie and that there could be an eagle that'll set everyone yelling. It's the jauntiest feeling I know.

I was still not sure I wanted Bobby to sink the putt and make eagle. But I'd had the putt myself before, and I gave him the line.

Sometimes there are putts, long putts even, that you can tell are going in from the minute they hit the putter blade. This was one of them. I knew it as soon as Bobby hit it. I had time to think, Damn, Clayton Mote's record is gone, before I saw it dive right into the center of the hole for the eagle.

Angela and Leo and Jimmy and Peter all swarmed around, pumping our hands and applauding, and I guess when Angela saw the tear in my eye and saw me wipe it away, she thought it was a tear of joy.

No one knew what the course record was except me and Eudora.

Chapter 4

IN GOLF, right when you think you've got every reason to be confident is when you have to be your most careful. Of course, Bobby loved being confident. When he was hitting it good, he saw no reason why he couldn't keep hitting it that way. So I wasn't surprised when Bobby decided he just had to rush off and play a real tournament.

The Monday after Bobby broke the course record, he and Angela came out to the fifth fairway to find me. Some pythium fungus had broken out, and I was trying to fix the spray attachment on the tractor so Hayden Pritchett, my so-called assistant, could lay down the fungicide. I wasn't exactly in my sunniest mood. I kept thinking about Clayton Mote. I had this idea that wherever he was, if he was alive, he'd want to know that someone had broken his record and that I'd been the caddie.

"What do you think of the Captain Dick Grand Strand Classic?" Bobby asked me.

"Is it a rum punch, or what?" I replied.

"It's a tournament, Coach," Bobby said. "It's on the Cooters Tour, down in Myrtle Beach. This week."

The Cooters Tour is somewhere between the Masters and a driving range in the world of professional golf. It has real tournaments, with real golfers, but they are about as far from the PGA Tour as Eadon Branch is from Pebble Beach. The sponsors throw in a little money, but most of the purse comes from the players' entry fees. The title sponsor is the Cooters restaurant chain, which gives the whole thing a raunchy aura.

"What the hell," I said. "If I can get this applicator fixed and get Hayden to work, let's go."

A DAY later we were in the air, flying from Roanoke to Myrtle Beach via Charlotte. Bobby had insisted on the window seat, which I thought was ironic, then dropped off immediately to sleep. That was one of the ways he had of coping with nerves. Angela was in the middle, and I had the aisle.

I was thinking of being in competition again and how strange it would feel. We were going to be the only ones in the field playing by our own set of rules—the U.S.G.A. rules for blind golfers. Basically they're the same as for everyone else, except that the caddie for a blind golfer is allowed to stay behind the ball throughout the shot, and he's allowed to place the golfer's club in the sand or a hazard so the player has a chance to size up the lie.

The beverage cart came down the aisle, and I got Angela and me a couple of Cokes and bags of peanuts.

"When did you learn to be a caddie, Mr. Mote?" she asked me.

"My father taught me. Clayton Mote." She nodded, and I felt like she wanted to know more. "Clayton came home for a year or so just before he took off for good," I explained. "I was about twelve years old. He hadn't been playing good. Lost his card, I guess, though he didn't tell me about it. But he was not playing the tour."

"And that's when you started caddying for him?"

I nodded. "He'd be playing in little tournaments around Virginia, trying to win some money and get his game back. And he said I was old enough to be his caddie and save him a few bucks."

"Did you like it?"

I thought about that. At first I liked it. I thought it was great just to be doing something with him. But it wasn't long before his moods got to me. Mostly it was his silence. He'd go through weekend tournaments, two full rounds, where he'd never say a word to me. He developed hand signals to show what club he wanted, and they were a little confusing. If I got it wrong, he wouldn't say anything, either. He'd just glower at me. If the truth be told, when he disappeared the summer I was thirteen, I was relieved that I wouldn't have to caddie for him for a while.

"It was okay," I said to Angela. "He taught me the job."

For half a second I was tempted to tell her all about me and Clayton Mote, but I didn't. When your father disappears from your life, it's not something you like to talk about, especially if after he never came back, you started to think maybe it was partly your fault.

"Well," Angela said, "now the job's getting bigger. Bobby needs you to think for him out there."

"I normally have trouble just thinking for myself," I said, "but I'll do my best."

She smiled at me. "I know you will."

The plane banked out over the ocean and the strip of hotels along the shore just before it landed. You could see a dozen golf courses between the water and the airport. During the spring and fall Myrtle Beach fills up with guys on golf vacations. But it's too hot for normal people to play golf at Myrtle Beach in the summer, and the course owners need some revenue. This particular tournament was being held at a course called Egret Landing Plantation, which is ten miles inland.

We were staying at a Holiday Inn across the highway. Angela went with Bobby to find some supper. But I figured I'd better take a look at the golf course and start making a game plan for the pro-am round the next morning. I walked across the highway.

THE next morning the Cooters Tour people had a table set up outside the pro shop where players were supposed to register. It was already a warm day. Sitting behind the table was a heavyset guy who jumped up with a big smile and extended a hand. I introduced myself to the guy first and then let Bobby shake his hand. His name was Clifton Jackson, and he was the executive director of the Cooters Tour.

Jackson pumped Bobby's hand and smiled. "I didn't think you all were really coming," he said. "I figured it might be a joke."

"No joke," Bobby said. "I'm here to play, pal."

Jackson looked like he'd just found a hundred dollars in a coat pocket. "Great," he said. "You all ready to play in the pro-am?"

"Countin' on it." Bobby smiled. "Need a practice round to learn the course, Cliff. Pro-am'll be fine for that, won't it?"

"Sure! We'll fix you up," Cliff said.

I gave him the check for Bobby's entry fee, and after Bobby changed shoes, we went to the practice range to hit some balls.

After he'd hit a few, I started to notice a crowd forming. First the players on the tee stopped their own practice and quietly watched. Then Clifton Jackson came over, and then a bunch of the amateurs who'd been warming up. Then a few Cooters girls, dressed in their tight purple short shorts and little white halter tops. Bobby started to hear a buzz of whispering voices every time he hit.

"How many watching us, Coach?" he asked. I could tell from the way he was swaggering that he was feeling better than good.

I gave a quick glance around. "Maybe fifty," I said.

"Well, let's give 'em a show."

And he did. Bobby rose to the occasion. He hit five crisp seven-irons right at the 175-yard marker, fading the fourth and drawing the fifth in. All I had to do was set him up. Pretty soon we walked over to the putting green and started getting a feel for the speed. When Bobby curled a twenty-footer into the hole on his second try, a kind of collective gasp came out of the crowd.

Then there was a loud voice calling Bobby, and I saw Clifton Jackson coming over with a group of people trailing behind him. The first of them was a big, beefy man in a hat that looked like the one the Skipper wore on *Gilligan's Island.* Jackson introduced him to us: Captain Dick Gootch, owner of Captain Dick's Marina and sponsor of the Captain Dick Classic.

He was one of those thick guys who seem intent on mashing your bones together when they shake your hand. He introduced the men behind him—Paul Ledbetter, Jamie Forrest, and Paul Birkin, distributors for Bud, Coors, and Miller, respectively, in the Myrtle Beach area. They were our team for the pro-am. And then he introduced Amy.

Amy was a Cooters girl. She had freckles and blue eyes and lightly frosted short hair. And of course, it was altogether evident that she was in superb physical condition.

"Amy's our drinks girl," Captain Dick explained. "When you sponsor the tournament, you get your own drink cart."

"Anything you want, you just ask," Amy said.

A horn sounded, and we took off—Captain Dick and the three beer guys and Amy in carts, Bobby and I on foot. We could have ridden, but we both wanted to do this the way it was done on the tour. That meant walking.

It was a shotgun start, and we were on the tenth tee. Bobby started with a birdie. Soon nearly everyone in the place who wasn't actually playing had joined our gallery, and there was a camera crew from a Myrtle Beach station making videotape for the evening news. It was damn hot, but after our thirteenth hole we were tied for the lead at 5 under. Amy, the Cooters girl, brought me a Gatorade on the next tee. "You guys are making it exciting out here."

I grinned back at her. "Yeah," I told her. "I'm gettin' a little pumped up myself."

She walked back to her cart. I turned around, and Bobby was facing in our direction, a little half grin on his face.

"What's she look like?" he asked in a low voice only I could hear.

"Normal," I said. "Two arms, two legs." I didn't like the look on his face or the interest he was showing.

"Amy," he called out, "could you find me a Coke, please?"

She jumped out of the cart and came bouncing back over to us with a cold can. "Cup of ice?" she asked.

"No thanks," Bobby said. "You're sweet."

She smiled, lapping it up.

"You know the worst thing about being blind?"

Her eyes widened. She opened her mouth, but no words came out. She hadn't ever been asked that question, I guess.

Bobby didn't wait. "It's knowing a woman is beautiful and not being able to see her," he said.

I almost gagged, but Amy bought it. Her eyes got shiny, and she reached up and kissed him on the cheek.

Bobby routined the next three holes, then bogeyed. As we approached the last tee, he suddenly got friendly with Captain Dick and the beer guys. "Any of you guys know a good place to go out and get some beers?" The beer guys lit up with that question.

"Best lookin' women are at the Toy Chest," one of them said.

They and Bobby set a time—six o'clock. They looked thrilled that an actual big-name professional athlete was going to let them take him to a girlie bar.

"I want everybody to come," Bobby said. "Amy, you free?"

"I'll need to make a couple of calls," she said, "but I can be."

"Good." Bobby grinned.

Bobby bogeyed the last hole, too, and knocked himself back to 3 under, which was where he finished. What surprised me was how disappointed I was. Looking back on it, I should've been ecstatic. Here was a blind man, playing his first competitive round in more than a year. That was good enough. To post a 69 was damn near miraculous.

Bobby said to the two reporters who pounced on us, "My swing's still a little rusty."

Cliff Jackson started pounding us on the back like we'd just won the Masters or something. "Great show, Bobby," he said.

Bobby just grunted. So I thanked Cliff and asked about our tee time tomorrow.

"We're going to have you going out late—around twelve thirty," Cliff said. "Reason is, I got to notify the media that you're here and playing so well. It's gonna be a big story."

"THE Toy Chest?" Angela said as soon as we were in the car we'd rented and were heading to the Holiday Inn. "The night before the tournament?"

"You'll like it, Angela," Bobby said.

"The hell I will," Angela replied. "I'm not going."

"You gotta come," Bobby said. "Coach might wander off with a dancer—then who'd take me home?"

"Let Miss Cooters do it," Angela groused.

"Whoo-ee," Bobby said. "What's got into you?"

"Nothing," Angela said. In the rearview mirror I could see her staring intently out the window, her arms folded in front of her.

"We need you in a good mood, Angela," Bobby persisted. "We need you happy."

Angela just stared out the window for a while. I started to wonder just what kind of relationship Bobby and Angela had. Then she spoke. "Henry, you have to go. Keep him out of trouble."

So I went.

THE Toy Chest had a pink neon silhouette of a showgirl over the front door. There was a GoKart track across the highway. As soon as Bobby got out of the car, the sound of the engines, high and flighty like hornets swarming, attracted his attention.

"We used to have one of those where I grew up in Dalton," he said. "Coach, you know I won my first trophy for racing GoKarts, not for golf?"

"No," I said, "but I'm sure NASCAR lost a great driver when you decided to play golf."

We went inside. It took a minute for my eyes to adjust to the dimness. Then I could see that Captain Dick, Amy, and the beer guys were already there, at a table up near the stage.

They cleared space between Amy and Captain Dick, and we sat down. Five minutes later Bobby was working on his second Scotch and starting in on Amy, telling her how impressed he'd been with her work on the golf course. "You had real panache," Bobby said.

Amy beamed.

"All these years we've been working together, and I didn't know you spoke French," I said to Bobby.

He didn't respond. He had only one thing on his mind, and that was Amy. I couldn't hear all of what was passing between them. For a while Bobby was apparently agog to hear about the time Amy finished second runner-up in the Miss Dillon County pageant. Then he was telling her how much more sensitive he'd gotten since his blindness, how he could hear and smell things much better, like the perfume she was wearing.

"Isn't anything I can't compensate for," Bobby was saying. "I bet I could even drive one of those GoKarts across the road."

"I'd pay to see that!" Captain Dick butted in.

"Me, too," Paul the beer man said. "Matter of fact, I got five hundred dollars says you can't do it."

"You're on," Bobby said.

"Wait a minute," I objected.

"Greyhound," he said, "you ever see me lose a bar bet? I know how to do this." He stood up and turned to Amy. "Sweetheart, let's take a stroll."

The beer guys and Captain Dick were getting up and grinning. I sat there a moment, wondering what I should do. Then I got up and went after them. When I got outside, Bobby's little group was already across the highway.

IT TOOK ABOUT FIVE MINUTES and a big wad of Captain Dick's cash for the manager to call all the karts off the track and announce a special exhibition. The kid drivers came off grumpy.

Bobby stood seemingly idle during all this, holding on to Amy with a long, snaky arm around her bare shoulder. He had somewhere picked up a three-iron, probably from the trunk of Captain Dick's car. He was rubbing the butt end of the iron along a wall.

I decided I had to make one final effort to talk Bobby out of it. I got there just as he and Captain Dick were going over the terms.

"One full lap," Captain Dick said. "No stopping. Gotta stay on the track."

Bobby agreed. The mechanic handed him a helmet.

"Bobby," I called to him. He turned in my direction. I walked up to where I could speak to him in a normal tone. "Angela and you and me haven't worked so hard to toss it all away on a stunt," I said. "Think of all that sweat."

"I am thinking about it, Coach," Bobby said. He grinned. Then he took Amy in his arms and gave her a kiss that lasted about as long as one of his best tee shots took to come down.

Bobby got into the kart, jammed the helmet on, and told the mechanic to roll him over to the inside lane. He still had the three-iron with him, and suddenly I understood what he was going to do. He told the mechanic to set the kart up within a foot of the inside curb. He grabbed the steering wheel in his right hand and got the butt of the club down on the curb, holding it in his left hand.

He let the clutch out real gradual, so the kart was barely moving. And he dragged the butt of the club along the curb as he moved, so he could feel the curves as they came. He drove that way through the first couple of curves and under the pedestrian overpass that got kids into the pit area.

"Yes, Bobby!" Amy shouted. "Whoo!"

Some of the kids got into it as they realized what was going on. "S curve ahead, man!" one of them yelled.

Bobby got through the S curve, through the backstretch.

"Whoo! Whoo! Whoo!" Amy sounded like a choo-choo train.

The kids were whooping it up big as Bobby rounded the final curve and headed for the finish line.

He didn't stop as he crossed the line and heard that he'd done it, just nodded his head, a big grin on his face.

"Okay, Bobby, you did it! Stop!" I yelled out. But I could see he wasn't satisfied. He punched it up to ten or fifteen miles an hour.

He got through that lap, and he started a third. Captain Dick turned to me. "Why doesn't he stop? He's won the damn bet."

"If he had sense enough to stop, he wouldn't've made the bet," I said.

Coming around the third time, he slowed down, and I thought he might've had enough. Instead, he got to the finish line, slowed to a crawl, and waved the three-iron in the air. His grin was huge.

"Watch this," he yelled. He threw the three-iron away. It clattered to the asphalt. Slowly Bobby started driving a fourth lap.

"Oh, no," I said.

He must've had a pretty good memory for the turns, because he moved left at about the right time going into the first one. But he went wide.

"Look out!" I yelled, which may be the absolute stupidest thing you can yell to a blind man.

He hit the overpass abutment almost head-on.

The front end of the GoKart bent in half, and Bobby sat, motionless, behind the wheel. I started running toward him.

As I ran, I could see him move, try to get up. When I got there, he was half out of the seat. He was like a fighter who's grabbed the ring rope, trying to get back on his feet. I grabbed him under the arms and pulled him up.

"Ouch," he said. He shook his head to clear it, got a little steadier on his feet, and pulled away from me, standing straight up.

"You okay?" I asked him.

"I'm fine," he said curtly, like it wasn't worth discussing.

But then he tried to pull his shoulders back and throw his chest forward. I saw him wince. I could see he'd banged himself pretty good on the steering wheel.

"Too bad you hit your chest and not your head," I said. "If it'd been the head, you wouldn't've hurt anything important."

"So, HOW'D it go last night?" Angela asked.

We were having the continental breakfast in the motel.

"Umgh," Bobby grunted. He was wearing his full Callaway outfit, all the patches and logos in the right places. He looked ready to play tournament golf. I knew he wasn't. I could see by the way he was carrying himself that his chest hurt him.

Angela waited for a second. Then she turned to me. "I assume you had a marvelous time, too, Henry," she said.

"Smashing," I said.

Bobby changed the subject. "I got a call from the tour just before I came down for breakfast."

"The tour?"

Bobby nodded. "Said they'd have someone watching us today."

Damn, I thought. Just what we needed. A distraction. "Let's not think about that," I said. "We got enough to think about."

Of course, that was like not thinking about presents on Christmas Eve.

WE PARKED near the back of the lot. I pulled the clubs from the trunk, and Angela spoke softly to Bobby, helping him get oriented for the walk to the locker room.

A squad of reporters and technicians spotted us and started moving at a sloppy double time toward us. The questions started flying.

"Bobby, is it true you're trying to get back on the tour?"

"What's the secret to playing golf blind?"

The cameras and mikes followed us into the locker room. Cliff Jackson came up at that moment. "Please, step back, fellas," he said. "Bobby'll be having a press conference later."

A few media people stepped back as Bobby changed his shoes, but the crush remained, and it followed us, like a swarm of angry bees, out to the practice range.

Fortunately, there was at least a rope to hold folks back at the practice range. But there must've been five hundred people stretched out behind it by the time Bobby started warming up.

I smelled cigar smoke and took a quick look around. Off to one side, I spotted two familiar faces. One of them was Ken Alyda, the AP golf reporter. And next to him was Cade Benton, a leathery-faced public relations official from the tour. They both caught my eye, and they both nodded.

The whirring of the cameras intensified as Bobby started hitting lob wedges. He hit a few of them, and his swing was fine. Of course, wedges don't take a full swing. He told me to give him the two-iron.

I gave it to him and lined him up. He took the club back normally, but he didn't quite finish the swing. I was watching the ball, and not him, so I couldn't see if he grimaced or not. But the ball flight told me he was flinching instead of following through.

"Hurt?" I asked quietly.

"No," he snapped. "I feel fine."

I looked at my watch. We had only a few minutes left, so I prodded Bobby to hit a few drivers and a few putts before we had to go to the first hole. I hoped his chest was loosening up.

I was sweating piggishly by the time we got to the tee. So was Bobby.

Our playing partner was already there—a big, broad-shouldered kid named DeWayne Elston, out of the University of Texas. He shook hands kind of stiffly. So did his caddie, who also happened to be his wife, Christie.

The first pin was set toward the right edge of the green, behind a big, deep sand bunker. That meant that if you wanted to go for the pin, you'd have to either flirt with that bunker or approach from the left edge of the fairway. A marsh ran down the left side of the hole nearly all the way to the green. We were going to play down the right side, stay away from the bunker and the pin, and make par, bogey at the worst. No point in risking a bad start.

Elston won the toss, and he wasn't playing safe. He drove the ball about 300 yards, left center. It was Bobby's turn.

Quietly I set up the situation for him. "Okay, Bobby. Nice, easy starting hole. Four eighteen. No wind. We're going to drive the ball down the right side. Just swing nice and easy."

I lined him up and set the club face behind the ball. As I stepped back, I saw his lips move. "Let it happen," he whispered to himself.

But he swung stiffly and awkwardly. It was his choke swing, paying a visit at the worst possible moment. The ball took off down the left side instead of the right side, and then a gust of wind capriciously blew it farther left. It disappeared in the direction of the marsh. The crowd moaned.

Bobby knew it was a bad shot. "Where'd we wind up?"

"In a swamp," I told him.

"Swamp?" he hissed. "There's a swamp on the left?"

"Maybe marsh is a better word," I said. "Sorry." I hadn't told him there was a swamp because I didn't figure he needed to think about it.

Bobby took a deep breath and visibly tried to compose himself. "Biggest round of my life, and he doesn't tell me about the swamp," he muttered to himself.

I started to say something about how if I'd been about to play the biggest damn round of my poor life, I'd've been in bed last night instead of trying that fool stunt in the GoKart. But I didn't.

"Might be playable," I said as mildly as I could.

"Let's go," he said. He listened for the sound of clubs rattling as I shouldered the bag and backed the butt end up toward his hand. He latched on. "From now on," he said, "don't leave anything out when you tell me what we're looking at."

"You got it," I said.

It was a long walk up the first fairway. Angela walked along with a slightly sick expression. Ken Alyda and Cade Benton looked grim, like they were walking into a funeral.

A bad tee shot on the first hole can give you that feeling. You'd like to yell "Do over" and hit again. But in real golf, like the sign said at Eadon Branch, there are no mulligans.

The fairways at Egret Landing turned to light rough and then sloped gradually into the marshes. Bobby's Titleist was sitting in a little three-foot-wide strip of gray-brown mud between the edge of the rough and the dank, murky water.

I told Bobby the situation. He wanted to feel it all with his hands and feet. So, gingerly, I walked him down the grassy slope to the mud strip. Our shoes sank several inches deep, but Bobby wanted to take a stance by the ball and see how it felt. He could barely do it. Pond scum was squishing up around his shoes.

"I think we should take a drop," I said. "It's just a stroke penalty. The worst that'll happen is a bogey. We go on."

But Bobby was not having it. "How far are we from the green?"

"About one sixty," I estimated.

He wiggled his feet in the muck and sank in a couple of more inches. "I think I can get a seven-iron onto the green," he said.

I wasn't going to argue with him. "Make it smooth," I said.

There was no way for me to get behind him except to squat in the marsh, so I did. I could feel my sneakers getting sucked into the ooze. I gave him the club and lined him up. I put the club head down behind the ball and stepped back farther into the marsh to get away from his backswing. Only I fell back into the water.

I came up sputtering, and when I opened my eyes, I saw that people in the gallery were laughing. Bobby was stopped in mid-backswing, his head swiveled back toward me.

"Sorry," I said. "Slipped." I sloshed to my feet, dripping. "Needed to cool off, anyway," I said, trying to make light of it. But it didn't work, at least not with Bobby. I saw his jaw jut. Then he shocked me. Rather than wait for me to reset him, he turned his head back in the direction of the ball and swung.

He missed. Missed the ball, that is. The club sent a big brown splash of muck up the slope of the bank. The ball ascended like a bad bottle rocket, weakly, about two feet in the air. It hit the bank, then rolled back and curled to a stop against Bobby's left foot.

I thrashed toward Bobby to try to get him away from the ball before he stepped on it. I grabbed him like a child who'd stepped into traffic.

"Did the ball hit my foot?" he asked me.

"Yeah," I said. " 'Fraid so."

He didn't get mad. He seemed more shocked than anything else. "When I heard you fall in, I got flustered," he said.

"It's all right," I said. "My fault. The good news is that you don't look as stupid as I do."

Bobby did not laugh.

I glanced over his shoulder and caught a glimpse of Alyda and Benton standing above us. They looked like what they had seen was both too ugly to watch and too fascinating to turn away from.

I felt ashamed, and I cast my eyes to the ground. "I think we better take our drop up on the grass and get out of here," I said.

He nodded, and I pushed him up the slope until someone in the gallery took him by the hand and helped him up the rest of the way. I picked up the bag and scrambled up the embankment.

A funereal silence had descended upon our gallery.

Bobby clamped a hand down on my shoulder. He leaned close to my head. "Well, Coach," he said, "worst thing can happen to me is I look like a guy trying to play golf with his eyes closed."

"We can afford to spot these guys a few," I said. "Golf tournament starts now."

He shrugged and held out his hand for a new ball.

I helped him get oriented two club lengths from the edge of the hazard. Bobby did a good imitation of someone trying his best to knock an eight-iron onto the green, but I could tell he didn't believe in the shot. The ball headed straight for that big, deep bunker like a sand crab going home. It dived in.

It didn't get much better after that. Bobby followed our routine on every shot, and I suppose he tried his best. But he just couldn't put the disaster of that opening hole out of his mind.

We made the turn in 46 strokes. Half the gallery, including Ken Alyda, dropped away. But Cade Benton stayed, taking everything in for his report to the PGA. So did Angela.

The back nine was like walking through a coal mine barefoot. It was a tough slog. We got to the eighteenth tee hot, sweating, heads hanging. Nearly all the spectators had gone.

"Where do we stand?" Bobby asked me. I knew exactly what our score was—87 to this point. I wouldn't tell him.

"No scoreboards out here," I said. "It's hard to tell."

Elston was up first, of course. He'd had the honor all day. He banged the ball down the middle, but not his usual 300 or so. "Didn't catch it," he said to his wife.

I aimed Bobby down the left side, figuring that the bunker down that side was a better alternative than the marsh that ran all the way down the right side and curled behind the green.

He hit it pretty hard. It was almost a good shot. But he hooked it, and he wound up in that bunker, maybe 180 from the pin. It was the first time all day we'd been past Elston off the tee.

Elston hit first, and he tried to cut a four-iron into the pin, but he overcooked it. The ball came down smack in the water.

Bobby, of course, didn't see this. He was busy tromping around in the back of the bunker, trying to get a feel for it. I had a sudden desire to finish with some style. I think Bobby did, too. "Okay," I said. "Elston's in the water. Our turn."

I looked at the lip of the bunker, maybe eight yards in front of our ball. The lie was pretty good. I figured it would take a five-iron to get to the green.

"Let's do this one right," Bobby said as I set him up.

"Okay," I said. "Wind's in our face, but no problem. Bunker's got a two-foot lip, but you got room to clear it."

Bobby flexed his hands on the five-iron and nodded.

"See the shot," I said. "Trust it."

I stepped back, and he swung.

It wasn't the greatest swing he ever made, but he put a lot into it. I stepped outside the bunker to get a better look.

The ball hit on the front edge of the green and started to roll. I could see that it was going to roll right off the green and into the marsh. Then, with a muted clank, it hit the flagstick, caromed about six inches into the air, and dived into the hole.

"Damn," I said.

"What happened?" Bobby asked me. "Where is it?"

I guess one of the worst parts of being a blind golfer is not being able to see your occasional miracle. "It went in," I told him.

He dropped his head and shook it. His grin was a little embarrassed. "Funny game, isn't it?" he said. "At least I didn't shoot in the nineties."

He'd known all along what the score was.

AS WE walked down the last fairway to the green, I was thinking hard. You might think that an eagle would make me eager for another chance the next day. You'd be wrong. That last shot was just a teaser, a final way of the golf gods smirking and saying, "See, look what talent we put at the disposal of a ten-cent head."

"Sorry I made you go through this, Greyhound," Bobby said. "It'll go better tomorrow."

I didn't snap at him or anything. I just shook my head before I remembered that he couldn't see that.

"No, Bobby," I said, "it won't."

"I'll play better tomorrow," he said.

The television guys were on their way. I had about a minute to talk to Bobby. "You're not going to play better tomorrow," I said. "You're gonna withdraw. We're not ready for tournament golf."

He shook his head. "I don't wanna withdraw," he said.

"You don't have a choice," I said. "You can't play without me, and I'm not doing it. I quit. I've had it."

His mouth dropped open, and then his face got red.

"You think *this* was my game?" he yelped.

"Yeah," I said, "looked very much like you playing out there."

He whined a little. "But tomorrow my ribs'll be better. I just need another chance," he said.

"You've run out," I replied.

He scowled. "It's 'cause I'm blind," he accused. "You think—"

I cut him off. "Don't tell me what I think," I said. "It has nothing to do with your being blind. It has to do with you."

He stiffened, but before he could say anything, the reporters were on us, pointing their cameras at Bobby.

"How do you feel?" the ESPN guy asked.

Bobby grimaced. "Hot. Thirsty. Humiliated," he answered.

"Do you still think it's possible for a blind man to play tournament golf?" the guy asked.

Bobby paused for a long time before he answered. "Yes," he said, "I do. But I'm not sure if I'm the blind guy to do it. I mean, I guess I'm not. I'm withdrawing from the tournament."

I caught a glimpse of Angela out of the corner of my eye. She was starting to cry.

"It took courage to come out here," the ESPN guy said. "You've won a lot of fans."

Bobby shook his head. "I just hope I haven't discouraged any blind people," he said.

I figured that was about enough. I picked up the bag and stepped in between Bobby and the cameras. "Gotta get to the locker room and cool off," I said. I shoved the butt end of the bag into Bobby's belly button and waited till I felt him latch on; then I plowed straight ahead, forcing the reporters to make way.

Bobby sat down on a bench in front of his locker, sagging like a three-day-old balloon. The little bit of charm he'd managed to muster for the TV people was gone.

"Do me a favor," he said. "Get outta here."

I got. I left the locker room and went looking for the bar. It wasn't hard to find. The bar was one of those new places that tries to look old, with forest-green wallpaper and prints of Scottish guys hitting golf balls at St. Andrews or someplace. I ordered two Coors and finished the first in about four seconds. I was starting on the second when Angela walked in.

She was composed, but barely. She sat down next to me, took off her hat, and pushed that thick red hair off her temples.

"Buy me a beer?" she asked.

I gestured to the bartender.

She turned to me. "How can he quit after that last shot?"

"That last shot was just a chain yanker," I said. "Golf is a game that likes to yank your chain. Just when you think you've got it, you hit one sideways. And just when you think you'll never get it, you hole one out of a fairway bunker like Bobby did. It's like a joke."

Her eyes widened. "But it shows what he's capable of!"

"Sure," I said, "but not what he can do when he has to."

"Can't you talk him out of it?" she asked me.

"I don't want to," I said. "I don't want to do this anymore."

She looked sad. "Why not?"

I thought about telling her about what Bobby had done the previous evening. I thought about telling her that I was tired of working in a boy's role for a person who wasn't yet a man himself.

"Bag gets heavy," I said.

She looked like she wanted to argue with me, then decided against it. She just took a long swallow of her beer.

So I sat there a moment, feeling awkward. Then Ken Alyda walked in and headed my way. He sat down on my left, and I introduced him to Angela.

"Tough day out there, Greyhound," he said. "Amazing he made that eagle on the last," he said.

"Yeah," I agreed. "Too bad it wasn't on the first."

Alyda nodded sympathetically and shifted on his stool a little bit. "Uh, Greyhound, I'm glad I ran into you, because I've been meaning to call you. It's about something kind of personal."

"I'll excuse myself," Angela offered.

"No, stay," I told her. I put a hand on her forearm. "She's a good friend," I told Alyda. I sipped on the beer.

He nodded. "Well, it's about your father."

I didn't gag on the beer or anything else you might expect.

"I know where he is," Alyda said.

"Well, you're ahead of me, then," I said. "Like I told you, I haven't seen him since I was thirteen."

"Maybe I shouldn't have looked into it," Alyda said. "But I kind of liked your father. He was a little grouchy, but so am I." Alyda looked sad, like he was telling me about a death. "He's at the VA Hospital in Staunton, Virginia. Has been for fifteen years."

"A hospital?"

I couldn't quite figure this out. "Is he sick?"

Alyda looked me straight in the eyes. He was being kindly, I could see, and truthful. He was too old to jerk people around.

"It's a psychiatric hospital, Greyhound," he said.

Chapter 5

A GOLF course is maybe the most fragile thing I know outside of a woman's feelings. If you don't tend to it every day, you start to lose it. When I got back to Eadon Branch, late on a Friday afternoon, I could see the signs of neglect. I walked into the clubhouse. There were no customers around. Eudora had the television and her apron both on. She was watching *Oprah* while cleaning up the grill.

"How'd it go in Myrtle Beach?" she asked. "Miss the cut?"

"We shot a bunch over and withdrew," I said.

Eudora wiped her hands on her apron and said she was sorry.

"Where'd Bobby and Angela go, back to Nashville?"

"Yes," I said. They'd dropped me off and headed to the interstate.

Eudora took a rag and wiped off the three little tables in the lunch area. I started stacking the chairs.

"Had an interesting talk with a sportswriter down in Myrtle Beach," I finally said. "Fellow that knows where Clayton Mote is. He says he's in a VA hospital up in Staunton."

She nodded, tight-lipped. "That's right."

"Why didn't you tell me?" I asked.

She stopped wiping, put down the rag, and faced me. "I thought about it. I kept thinking I would. But I didn't want you to think— Well, Henry, to be honest, I didn't want people around here to think we had insanity in the family. This is a small town."

I could see how she'd thought that about the town. But I couldn't see why she'd never told me. "What's wrong with him?" I asked her.

She shook her head. "He's schizophrenic, or so they say. Violent and delusional."

"Violent?" I asked her.

She spoke very quietly, as if afraid that someone out on the road might hear her. "He attacked Sam Snead in the locker room at Greensboro fifteen years ago. The tour kept it quiet, but if your father hadn't been hospitalized, he was going to be arrested and tried for assault with a deadly weapon."

"A deadly weapon?"

"I think it was a four-iron," she said.

I tried to imagine Clayton Mote attacking Sam Snead with a four-iron. The idea was painful and screwy, and I wouldn't have believed it possible, except that Eudora had no reason to be making it up.

I spent the next couple of days thinking about when and how I might go to see Clayton Mote, all the while trying to do something to save the greens that were burning up. And then a very odd thing happened. A storm called hurricane Gabe came out of the Caribbean, up through the Florida Panhandle and Georgia.

By the second day Eadon Branch was two feet over its banks and the ninth, third, and fifth fairways were partly underwater. That day I went up to the pro shop, which was deserted. I found Eudora's remote, turned on the TV, and flipped around till I found the Weather Channel.

I watched some guy point to swirling masses of blue and green color that were superimposed on the map of the eastern United States. That was hurricane Gabe. And then the scene cut to a picture of a golf course. I recognized it. It was Horsehoe Bend Golf Club, outside Cincinnati, where that summer's PGA Championship was scheduled. The tape showed half the twelfth green washing away into a swollen brown creek.

"The PGA Championship has been postponed," the weatherman said. "The storm is probably going to stay just about where it is until Thursday, when it will gradually move north and break up."

If he was right, that meant another full day of rain.

The phone in the pro shop rang.

"Eadon Branch Golf Course and Swim Club," I said.

"Oh, may I speak to the cabana boy, Mr. Mote?"

It was Angela.

"Angela, is that you?"

"Anyone else call you Mr. Mote except a state trooper?"

"No," I said.

"Then it must be me, huh? So, how's your father? I've been wondering about him."

"Well, I don't know," I said. "I'm going to see him as soon as this rain lets up and Eadon Branch goes down."

"You saw what happened at Horseshoe Bend?" she asked.

I told her I had.

"I heard they're not going to find a new course for the PGA for at least a month," she told me. "You know what that means?"

"It means they'll have it no earlier than September," I said.

"It means Bobby can still play."

So that was what this was about. "I guess he could," I said as coldly as I was able. "He finished in the top fifteen last year."

"He'd need you," she said.

"No," I told her. "He can get someone else."

Her sigh sounded raspy over the phone line, like she'd blown into the mouthpiece.

Two days later she showed up.

It was midmorning, a Thursday. When I saw her, I got out from under the tractor I was trying to start and walked over.

"I figured that with the rain stopped, you'd be ready to go visit your father," she said. "I'd like to go with you."

"Why?" I said, like she'd asked to look at my tax return.

"I don't know," she replied. "I just do."

"What about Bobby?" I asked.

"He's taking a few days off," she said. "Licking his wounds."

I wanted Angela to think that there'd never been any doubt in my mind about going to see Clayton Mote. So I told her I was ready to go as soon as I could change my shirt.

We took the old blue Ford truck. I'm not sure why, since her car would've been more comfortable. But the Ford was running all right, and I guess I had this notion that maybe we'd take Clayton for a ride and maybe he'd be glad to see his old truck.

It was a long drive to Staunton, and I was relieved when I saw a sign along the road saying the VA hospital was the next exit. We got off the interstate onto a two-lane state road that carried us through a couple of miles of apple orchards and dairy farms.

Then there was a fence—an ordinary chain-link fence that seemed to enclose a large piece of property—and a gate with a little guardhouse that said STAUNTON HOSPITAL, U.S. VETERANS ADMINISTRATION. Several flags flapped lazily on poles right behind it.

We parked in the visitors lot. There was hardly anyone there.

Someone directed us to the psychiatric division, which you could see through a grove of trees. There was no big lobby, just a little entry cubicle, with a thick, locked door behind it.

The receptionist was a guy named Martinez, in a white orderly's uniform. When we told him why we were there, he replied immediately, "You're not on the visitor list for today."

"I know. But he's my father, and we've come a long way."

"You'll have to see Dr. Mehta," Martinez said.

He picked up the phone and spoke briefly into it.

"Okay," he said. "Through that door, third office on the right." He pressed some kind of button, and we heard a buzzer.

I tried the door, and it opened onto a corridor with green walls, linoleum floors, and doors on either side. It could've been a school.

The sign on the third door said DR. MEHTA. I knocked. After a second a voice said, "Come in."

Dr. Mehta didn't look like I'd expected. He wasn't wearing a white coat. He was a dark-skinned Indian from India, with a big head on a skinny neck and glasses that made him look goggle-eyed. He was a cheerful guy. He smiled at us, asking us to sit down, telling us this was an unexpected pleasure.

Mehta had a thick file folder on the desk in front of him, and I could see from the name on the tab that it was Clayton Mote's. "So you're the pro's son," he said, leaning back and looking at me.

"Yeah," I said. "I only recently learned my father was here. My mother didn't tell me. That's why I've never been to visit him."

I don't know why I felt like I had to justify myself to this guy. He didn't look like he was blaming me for anything. I glanced at Angela, who was seated in the chair beside me. She looked quiet and composed.

Mehta waved his hand. I got the sense he wasn't too concerned about why I'd never been there.

"You call him the pro?" I asked.

Mehta smiled. "Yes, well, that was the name everyone used when I got here two years ago," he said. "Your father seems to like it."

"You're his doctor," I said.

Mehta nodded. "That's right. His psychiatrist. Your father has been here a long time." He tapped the file with his open palm, emphasizing its thickness. "Perhaps I should tell you something about schizophrenia," he said. "Do you know what it is?"

"Like a split personality?" I asked.

Mehta smiled a little. "That is the way Hollywood used to describe it," he said, "but schizophrenia is a disease of the brain. The symptoms usually include delusions, perhaps paranoia, hallucinations, thinking disorders. We know it's a physical disease. The usual treatment is drugs: chlorpromazine, haloperidol, fluphenazine."

"And you tried them?"

"We've tried them all," he said, "in varying combinations, varying doses. They all had some effect, generally for the better. The main problem was that he refused to take them once he was on his own. We made several attempts to move your father to a halfway house we have in Staunton. But the first thing he always did was stop taking the medication. One of the side effects is stiffness of the muscles. Your father claimed that it interfered with his golf."

"He still cares about his golf, still thinks he can play?" I asked.

Mehta chuckled out loud. His Adam's apple jiggled in his neck. "Oh, my, yes," he said. "I should say so."

Angela looked a little impatient for the first time. She leaned forward in her chair. "Can we see him?" she asked.

Mehta grew serious again. "Of course," he said. "But, Mr. Mote, I should warn you. He may respond well to you. He may not. He may simply be unable to recognize you. The disease won't let him."

"All right," I said. "I'll introduce myself."

"I am not sure I would do that either," Mehta said. "Just tell him you have come to talk about golf. Do you have a nickname he does not know about?"

"Greyhound," Angela said. "Some people call him Greyhound."

"That will do," the doctor said.

"Let's go then," I said. I actually didn't much feel like going through with it. If Angela hadn't been there, I might've told Mehta to forget it. But she was there.

Mehta nodded. But instead of taking us into the bowels of the psychiatric building, which I expected, he led us outside.

"Your father will be over by our golf area," Mehta said.

"You have a golf course?" I asked.

"Well, we have some grass and a couple of flags in the ground," Mehta said, "but some of the patients like it."

The hospital had a big sports field with a couple of softball diamonds. Back in the outfield area, against a backdrop grove of pine trees, I could see a couple of droopy flags.

I could see no sign of Clayton Mote. Then I heard one. It was the sound of a club shaft hissing through the air, followed by the thwack of a golf ball being crisply struck. It was the sound of a good player.

"He's over there," Dr. Mehta said, pointing into the pine grove, "at his practice ground."

We walked through the pines toward him. He was smaller than I remembered. He'd had a thick head of wiry black hair that he'd been forever unable to stuff neatly underneath a golf cap. But the hair was almost gone. The hospital barbers had shaved his head like a boot-camp recruit's, and the stubble had more gray in it than black. His eyebrows were still bushy, but they, too, had gone gray.

But it wasn't just that. He was thinner than I remembered. He was not quite an old man, but he was getting there.

His clothes suggested how much he'd changed. He'd always

taken clothing seriously, but he wasn't dressing well anymore. He had a plain white T-shirt on, soaked with sweat under his arms. And he had on some kind of floppy khaki shorts, black socks, and white sneakers that were old and scuffed.

One thing that hadn't seemed to change was his hands. They looked the same, thick and powerful and delicately clean. The other constant was his equipment. He was swinging the same Hogan driver I remembered, a sorrel-colored persimmon head with a steel shaft, the kind of driver that you don't see anymore.

He had an old, scuffed ball teed up in front of him. He was standing with his head cocked a little to the right, as if he was listening for something. He seemed to nod. Then he addressed the ball, his head still cocked. He waggled three times, just like he always had. He swung. His swing had changed, I thought. It was simpler, more compact. It was, to my surprise, better. He swung powerfully, and the contact with the ball produced a loud crack. The sound echoed off the pine trees, amplified.

We walked carefully closer to him, the way you might approach a skittish foal. I could see then that he was hitting down a narrow little alley in the woods, a cut maybe 15 feet wide and at least 250 yards long. If Clayton Mote practiced by hitting balls down that tight little chute, then it was no wonder his swing had got better. If you gave me a driver and a full bucket, I doubt I'd hit two balls out of fifty down that chute without touching wood.

"Hello, Pro," Mehta said. "How are you?"

My father didn't answer. Instead, he went through the same pre-shot ritual and produced nearly the same shot.

"Two," Clayton Mote said. "That's two."

He teed another ball up and swung again. But this time he pulled it just a bit. It was still a good shot, but about 200 yards out, it hit a pine with a tight, faint little thwock.

Clayton Mote's expression did not change. "Zero," he said. "Back to zero."

I didn't know what to do. I thought that maybe I should just step forward and hug him, but I couldn't.

Mehta intervened. "Pro, you have some guests," he said. He walked up to Clayton and gently put a hand on the golf club.

My father looked up in what seemed to be mild surprise.

"Gotta hit a hundred," he said, sounding a little annoyed. "Hogan says, gotta hit a hundred."

I couldn't just stand there anymore, so I stood right in front of him and reached out. His hand was lying loosely on top of the shaft. I took it. "Hi," I said. "I'm Greyhound. This is Angela."

I looked back. Angela smiled and nodded at him.

Clayton Mote looked at me. "Hey, Henry," he said, like I'd been coming to see him every day for the past fifteen years.

I started to hug him. But he shied away like my hands had shocked him. Mehta laid a hand on my elbow, telling me to go easy. So I stepped back.

"Been a long time," I said to Clayton.

He just looked at me and blinked. Then he went right back to what he'd been doing. He picked up another ball—he had maybe two dozen of them in an old black shag bag—teed it, and hit it straight down the chute.

"Nice swing," I said.

He perked up. "Not flat? Didn't lay it off?"

I shook my head. "On plane," I told him.

For the first time he smiled. "Good," he said.

I looked at Angela. She was standing there, taking everything in, but not showing what she thought about a father and a son separated for fifteen years whose first conversation is about swing plane.

"Your swing's fine," I said. "Hey, I'm sorry I haven't been here to see you. I only found out where you were a couple of days ago."

He shrugged. " 'S okay," he said. He was looking at his grip, flexing his fingers, getting ready to hit another shot.

"Stand behind me," he said.

We all moved. We watched him hit another ball, another pipe job. "Two," he said. "On plane?"

I just nodded. I didn't want to talk about his swing anymore.

Clayton grunted. "Good. Plane was Hogan's big problem."

Mehta took my elbow and prodded me back a little farther. "Do you know," he asked me in a whisper, "if your father knows anyone, or knew anyone, named Hogan?"

I thought everyone knew Hogan, but I guess I hadn't counted on Indian psychiatrists. "Sure," I said. "I don't know as he knew him personally, but Hogan would be Ben Hogan. A great golfer. Maybe the greatest. He died a few years ago."

"I see. And is—was—this Hogan known for having a secret?"

This was sounding goofier and goofier. "Yeah," I said, "Hogan liked to say he had a secret. Something about the way he cocked his hands at the top of his swing. He was a great ball striker. People think he must've known something no one else did."

Mehta nodded like he even knew what the top of the swing was.

"Why?" I asked. "Does he talk about Hogan's secret?"

The doctor's eyes widened. "Quite," he said.

Clayton swung and hit yet another pure tee shot.

"Three," he said. "Gotta hit a hundred."

"What's this 'gotta hit a hundred'?" I asked Mehta.

"It's a part of an obsessive behavior that your father's been exhibiting for many years," he said. "The file notes indicate that your father believes that if he can hit a hundred golf balls down the alley in the trees without hitting a single tree, he'll be cured and he can leave the hospital. But your father has not confided this to me."

Angela asked, "Is that possible?"

"What? Hit a hundred drives down that chute?"

She nodded.

No, I thought, it wasn't possible. Hogan in his best year, in 1953 when he won three legs of the grand slam, couldn't do that.

"It's not very likely," I said.

Clayton Mote, seemingly oblivious, swung again and piped another one. "Four," he said to the air and the trees.

"What's going to happen with him?" I asked Mehta. "Is there any chance he'll get better?"

"With a patient like your father, you never know," Mehta replied. "It's not uncommon to find that schizophrenic symptoms ease as a patient ages. We review his medication history every few months and try something different with him—a changed dosage, a new combination. And there are new drugs coming onto the market all the time. Perhaps something will have a more positive impact. I do not want you to give up hope."

It was about five o'clock, and an orderly in white pants was walking toward us. They eat early in hospitals. Dr. Mehta put a hand on Clayton's shoulder. "Sorry, Pro. Recreation is over. Time to eat."

I thought he'd protest, but he just nodded. Clayton and the orderly escorting him then turned toward the psychiatric building and walked ahead of us.

For some reason, at that moment I saw my father in a detached sort of way. He was just a rapidly aging hillbilly from the mountains of Virginia who'd had a few years on the tour, never won anything. He'd borne the brunt of things in Vietnam. And somewhere along the way, his brains got scrambled. Maybe the only thing of permanence he'd left behind was a half-finished golf course, and I was about to lose that for him.

It was Angela who broke the silence. "Pro, wait," she called. And she jogged ahead and got right in Clayton Mote's face and smiled.

"Pro, do you give lessons?"

Clayton Mote smiled back at her like she'd just asked him to run off with her for the weekend. "Yeah," he said in that raspy voice, "I give lessons."

THE next few days after Angela left, I worked on the latest problem we were having with the turf, a bout of gray leaf disease that was killing the ryegrass. I was thinking about money when Eudora came out of the shop and called me to the phone, saying Bobby Jobe was on the line.

"Coach, I need a ride," he said. No preliminaries, no how-are-yous. It irritated me.

"They got taxis in Nashville?" I said.

"I'm not in Nashville. I'm at the bus stop in Allegheny Gap."

"You took the bus?"

"Yeah. Why d'you sound so surprised? Don't underestimate me, Coach," he said. "So you gonna come and get me, or do I have to hitchhike out to Eadon Branch?"

I took the Ford down to get him.

Allegheny Gap didn't have much of a bus stop. It was just a brick shed down by the railroad yard in the most tired part of town. When I got there, Bobby was sitting on the bench outside.

Once I saw the golf clubs, of course, I thought I had a pretty good idea what he came for. And I still wasn't buying it. But I shook his hand and got his stuff into the back and him into the passenger seat, and headed back to Eadon Branch.

"Bobby, you're welcome to visit," I warned him. "But if you want to try to play golf again, you're wasting your time here. You gotta find yourself another caddie."

"Don't want to play golf exactly," he said. "Angela says I should take a lesson from Clayton Mote. I figure you must know him. You're the only Mote I know."

THE next morning Bobby and I headed north in the truck.

This time Dr. Mehta was expecting us. I'd called ahead. I introduced him to Bobby.

"How's the pro?" I asked him as we walked out of the hospital building toward the playing fields.

"It's been interesting to observe," the doctor replied. "He has not said anything, but I sense that he has been agitated by your visit. Change is almost always positive in a patient with Mr. Mote's history. If change is possible, progress is possible."

I started to sweat before we got halfway to Clayton's little practice area. The strap of Bobby's golf bag felt sharp on my shoulder. A hundred yards away we heard the first sound of ball striking club.

"What's he got there? Wooden clubs?" Bobby asked.

"Hogan persimmons," I said. "Classics."

We walked closer, and Clayton Mote's voice became audible to us. "Two," he said. "That's two."

I could see him about then, and what struck me was how absolutely identical everything was to the way it had been a few days ago. Same clubs, same sweaty T-shirt and black socks, same wide, unseeing look in his eyes. Same stubbly head of gray hair. He looked at us, then looked back down at the golf ball teed at his feet.

Before he could swing again, I walked up to him. "Hi. We're here for that lesson we talked about the last time. Remember?"

"Lesson?" he asked. Then, "Where's the girl?"

"She couldn't make it this time," I said.

"You want a lesson?" Clayton Mote asked.

"No, Pro," I said. "I've got a player here named Bobby Jobe wants a lesson."

Clayton looked at me for a long second. His eyes focused on mine, and I thought there was some contact there, some glimpse of the man he used to be. But he didn't say anything to me.

"Let's not hit here," I said. "I want Bobby to have some room. Let's go over to your first hole there."

THE little tee box was just a patch in the grass mowed about half an inch lower than the rest of the field, with two pieces of wood, cut from an old two-by-four and painted blue, as tee markers. The grass was clumpy and weedy, and there was a bare spot of dirt and brown grass where most of the players stood when they teed off.

"Warm up, and I'll watch you swing," Clayton suggested.

He sounded so normal suddenly. I was starting to understand a little more about Clayton's disease. He could engage with someone about golf. Other than that, the disease had control of his mind.

So Bobby stretched for a minute, then hit a few wedges, then some seven-irons.

As the sixth or seventh shot took off, Clayton Mote said to Bobby, "You know, your caddie's not allowed to stay behind you when you swing like that."

"Pro, he has to. The rules make an exception for the blind."

Clayton looked at him like he'd stuck a third arm out of an extra hole in his shirt. "You're blind?"

"Uh, yeah," Bobby said.

Clayton took a step toward Bobby and threw a left jab at his face, a punch that stopped shy of his nose. Bobby, of course, didn't flinch.

"Well, I'll be damned," Clayton said. "Hit some more."

Bobby worked his way down to a driver and even crushed a few toward the distant flag, which I figured was about 350 yards away.

"Let's see your position at the top," Clayton said.

Bobby drew the club back till its shaft was parallel to the ground.

"You got a tendency sometimes to close the face and snap it, don't you?" Clayton said.

Bobby reddened. "Sometimes," he acknowledged.

I thought about that first tee shot down in Myrtle Beach.

"Once in a while," I confirmed.

Clayton had figured out in a few minutes what some of the tour's swing doctors took half an hour to see.

"Let me show you what to do," Clayton said. And he took Bobby's hands and placed them in the proper position at the top. He tapped Bobby's left shoulder. "Feel that stretching?" he asked.

"Yeah," Bobby said.

"Go for that feeling. Try to feel like you're going to tear the sleeve of your shirt, you're stretching so much."

Bobby nodded. I could tell he was as impressed as I was.

"Other than that, your swing's perfect," Clayton said. "Don't change anything."

Dr. Mehta was beaming, so I guess he was impressed by the way Clayton was handling himself.

But then Clayton slipped away from us, from reality. "Learned that from Hogan," he said vaguely. "Hogan knows. Hogan hates Snead. Snead screwed me."

I felt mortified, somehow. You can't help but be embarrassed when your father starts raving.

"Is that Hogan's secret?" Bobby asked. "Stretching like that in the shoulder? I thought Hogan's secret was cupping the left wrist at the top. I try to do that, you know."

Clayton didn't respond directly. "Hogan hates Snead!" he said, emphatically. "Hogan knows. Snead screwed me."

I didn't like the way the conversation was going.

"We've still got a little time left," I said. "How about a playing lesson? Watch Bobby play. Show him how it's done."

"Playing lesson?" Clayton started to shift from one foot to the other like he was getting ready to run off. He was wavering between being with us and being with the voices in his head.

"I'll hit first," Bobby volunteered.

Casually as I could, I picked up Clayton's bag and placed it over my other shoulder, so I was carrying both. I squatted down to line Bobby's driver up. Ahead of us, I could see the flag, just a little bit past Bobby's range.

When Bobby was lined up, I stepped back. "Let it go," I said.

And he did. It was a titanic drive. You could tell by the sound that he'd caught it dead flush. It set off a little to the left of the flag.

"Not bad," I told Bobby.

Clayton hung back on the edge of the tee box. I walked up next to him and let his bag drop off my shoulder. I propped it in front of him, the way he'd trained me to do.

For a long time he just stood there. Then he turned slowly toward the target in the distance. And as if someone else were controlling his arm, he reached toward the bag and extended his right index finger. I understood. He wanted the one-wood, the driver.

Wordlessly I gave it to him. I thought he had to be remembering the summer I caddied for him, but if he was, he said nothing about it. He bent over and teed up.

Clayton hit a fine shot, left center of the fairway, not as long as Bobby's but not bad for a fifty-year-old guy who's spent the last fifteen years in an institution.

"Nice drive, Pro," I said.

I humped the bags up onto my shoulders and took a couple of steps toward the distant green. I reached for his driver, figuring I'd stick it back in the bag. But he held on. He didn't move.

"Wait," he said. "Mullicant."

It stopped me like he'd driven the club head into my gut. I remembered then who'd posted the NO MULLICANTS sign at Eadon

Branch. It was Clayton Mote, of course. There were no mulligans, he taught me, no do-overs. That's why he called them mullicants.

"Gotta have a mullicant," he said. He was talking to himself. "Gotta be down the middle. Gotta be straight."

I opened the pocket on Bobby's golf bag and handed Clayton a fresh ball. He swung again. And he hit another good shot. This one, to me, was perfect.

The sweat shone on his forehead. "Mullicant," he said, scowling.

"But why, Pro?" I asked him. "You've hit two good drives. Let's go pick one and play." I reached for the club.

He yanked it away from me and held it over his head. "Gotta be down the middle!" he said. He was almost yelling.

I backed off, afraid he was going to swing at me.

Bobby ambled toward the sound of Clayton's voice. Dr. Mehta, looking concerned, put a guiding hand on his elbow.

"Look, Pro," Bobby said. "I know you want to hit it perfect. So do I. But you can't. That's not golf. In golf you gotta take your best shot and live with what happens. Sometimes you hit it great. Sometimes you don't. Doesn't matter, y' know? That's golf."

"Down the middle!" Clayton insisted, as if he was about to boil over. "Down the middle!"

"But that's not golf, Pro," Bobby said softly, more sympathetic than he'd ever been with me.

I figured this was maybe what Angela wanted Bobby to learn from Clayton. Course, with Bobby, sometimes you had to beat him over the head with it a few times.

But this time Bobby looked like he'd figured it out. "We don't need to finish this hole, Pro," he said. "It's been a good lesson."

"Down the middle," Clayton said, his own voice softer and lower now. "Gotta be straight down the middle. Snead . . ."

He looked like he might start crying. I handed him a gift box of Titleists I'd brought. I'd had this fantasy that he'd bubble over with gratitude, embrace me.

He didn't. He stripped the wrapping off them and dropped them into his shag bag without a word. He never even looked at me.

"YOU HEARD THE ONE ABOUT Jack Nicklaus and Stevie Wonder?" Bobby asked.

He sipped at his beer, a Coors. We were sitting in Gully's, and the place was as quiet as it ever gets. It was Thursday, close to midnight.

"Haven't heard that one, but it sounds like category four."

A voice came from behind us. "Category four?"

It was Angela. She was wearing jeans and her Eadon Branch shirt. Bobby recognized the voice and turned on his stool. She kissed Bobby on the cheek.

"When'd you get here?" he asked her.

"Just drove in," Angela said. "Thought I'd find you here." She took the barstool next to mine.

"Category four," I said, sounding authoritative, "is blind golfer jokes. They all end with something about playing at night."

Angela looked bemused. "What do you mean, category?"

"There are only a handful of basic golf jokes," I explained. "Category one is your basic God-plays-golf joke. Category two is the golf-not-interrupted-by-death joke. Category three is your anti-wife joke. Category four is blind golfers. Category five is sex-on-the-golf-course jokes."

"I didn't think blind golfer jokes were that common," Bobby said sadly. He sucked down the last of his beer, smacked the bottle on the bar, and ordered another.

"What's your least favorite religion?" I asked him.

"Holy Rollers," he said.

"Okay. A priest, a rabbi, and a Holy Roller preacher were playing golf one day. The group ahead of them was terribly slow. It took six hours to play. They finally finished the round and went to the pro to complain. And the pro said, 'Didn't you know? Those players ahead of you were blind.'

" 'God forgive us our impatience,' the rabbi said.

" 'I'll say a rosary of repentance,' the priest said.

"The Holy Roller preacher thought for a minute. Then he says, 'Couldn't they play at night?' "

Angela smiled.

Bobby's face sagged a little behind his Oakleys. "Mine ended with Stevie telling Jack he could play him any night that week."

"It's a category," I said, shrugging in my most worldly way.

We were all feeling good, for reasons as divorced from reality as the swing tips Clayton Mote heard from Ben Hogan. Bobby was still blind, functionally broke, and a very short distance away from selling pencils. I was still lonely, quietly in love with Angela, and about to lose Eadon Branch. Angela was still pining for Bobby, I guess.

On the TV set, the first Thursday night college football game of the season on ESPN ended, and they switched to *SportsCenter*. A guy named Duke gave the baseball scores.

"And in golf," Duke said, "the PGA Championship has a new home. You remember that the tournament was washed out by hurricane Gabe last month. Horseshoe Bend couldn't repair its greens in time to hold the event this season. So tycoon F. Rockwell Peddy stepped up with an offer the PGA couldn't refuse. Peddy's putting up three million dollars, and the PGA is putting on its championship two weeks from now at the exclusive Sand Valley Golf Club, in the New Jersey hinterlands between Philadelphia and Atlantic City, where Peddy owns several casinos. Sand Valley is perennially ranked as the best, toughest, and most intimidating course in the world, but it has never hosted a professional championship."

I grabbed the remote from the bar and turned the television off. No one said anything for a moment.

"Sand Valley," Bobby said. "Wow."

I knew what he was thinking. But the way I saw it, if he couldn't handle a Myrtle Beach course in a Cooters Tour event, how could he even think about playing Sand Valley?

"You could play, Bobby," Angela said, ever the cheerleader.

Bobby made like he really wasn't interested. "Ah, I didn't enter the first time," he said. "They'd probably say the field was set when the entries first closed."

He turned his head my way. He wanted me to tell him that wasn't a problem, that the change in the schedule meant that there'd be some dropouts, so he could claim his place. I didn't.

"It'll be a tougher course than the one in Myrtle Beach," I said. "I hear they have some bunkers there; you can hear people speaking Chinese down toward the bottom of 'em."

Now Bobby could play the picked-on role. "You're trying to discourage me," Bobby said. "Haven't you ever heard people are supposed to encourage the blind?"

"I'll encourage you not to drive GoKarts anymore."

"I'm sorry about that stuff," he said. "It's in the past."

"Right," I said, sarcastic as hell. "Bobby, it's in you."

Bobby looked pained. "Don't you believe a person can change?"

I thought of Clayton Mote. "Yeah," I said, "but only for the worse." Angela looked wounded when I said that, and I suddenly felt sorry I'd hurt her feelings.

Bobby sipped at his beer. He was thinking so hard I could almost hear gears grinding in his skull.

I was thinking, too. "You want to play in it, don't you?"

He nodded. "What the hell else am I going to do for a living? Photography?"

The words came out of my mouth before I had a chance to think much about them. "Hell, Bobby," I said. "Go ahead and enter. I'll caddie for you."

I couldn't believe I'd said it, though I knew right away why I had. It was because I thought it was what Angela wanted to hear. I wanted her to think of me as magnanimous and generous.

She grinned. Bobby looked shocked.

"You sure you want to do that, Coach?" he asked me.

"Go ahead and enter," I said. "Before I change my mind."

"All right!" Angela exclaimed. And she threw her arms around me and hugged me, she was so delighted.

I couldn't help myself. I kissed her.

And then she kissed me back.

THE next morning Bobby faxed his entry down to the PGA headquarters in Florida. That was Friday, the beginning of the Labor Day weekend. We practiced each day. Bobby was hitting the ball well, but by Monday afternoon we couldn't concentrate anymore. We had to know. Bobby said the PGA office had a weekend crew, and he would call them. He placed the call from the pay phone by the men's room door. I went back behind the counter with Eudora and Angela to wait for the news.

We didn't have any chance to brood about what might happen. Labor Day was the day of the annual Allegheny Gap Headlight Tournament, which J. R. Neill organized. The rule was you had to have a miner's hard hat with a headlight on it to play. We had a couple of dozen miners in the shop, drinking beer, scarfing down hot dogs, adding up scores, and arguing about handicaps. It was one of our busiest days of the year.

"Eudora, where do you keep the hot dogs?" Angela called out.

"Should be another box in the back of the freezer," Eudora replied. "I bought extra."

I was grabbing a fresh six-pack from the refrigerator, so I opened the top side and got the hot dogs. I gave them to Angela without making eye contact. It wasn't just that we were busy. I was afraid if I talked to her very much she'd say something to let me know that that kiss in Gully's was just something caused by the beer.

"Thanks, Henry," she said.

"You're welcome," I replied.

That's the way we were being—polite.

Bobby came back from the pay phone, trailing a hand lightly over the corners of the tables and the backs of the chairs to orient himself. J.R., who was sitting there having his lunch, guided him to a stool. It was hard to tell exactly what Bobby had heard.

"What'd they say?" I asked him.

"Well, Coach," he said, "it's not good news."

"They won't let you play?"

He shook his head. "They say it's because I entered late, although they have had some cancellations. And they say they don't think the rules changes I need are fair to the rest of the field."

"Not fair?" Angela said. "What do they mean, not fair? Henry doesn't swing for you. He just helps you get set up."

Bobby shrugged. "They don't see it that way."

"Bastards," J. R. Neill said.

"Did they say anything about your playing ability?" I asked.

He shook his head. "Nope. But I'm sure they know about that damn eighty-nine."

"You got a lawyer?" I asked Bobby.

"You should sue!" J.R. said, excited.

Bobby shook his head again. "Nope. I do have a lawyer. But it would cost me thousands of dollars just to get started on a suit, file papers, and whatnot. Maybe fifteen grand."

"So?" I asked him.

He shook his head. "That's a lot just to try to get into a tournament where I might not win any money."

"You said you thought you could play."

He smiled, but weakly. "I do, Coach," he began, "but—"

I cut him off. "Shut up," I told him.

I went to the drawer under the register where Eudora kept the checkbook we used to pay the Eadon Branch bills. I found a pen. I wrote a check and put it in his hand.

"What's this?" he asked.

"It's a check for my half of fifteen thou," I said. "If we're in this, we're in it fifty-fifty."

Eudora looked like she was going to burst—and not with pride.

"My money, Eudora," I said to her. "I'll cover it."

Covering it would take about two thirds of the Henry Mote personal fortune, but somehow it seemed to me to be worth it. I didn't have a wife or kids to worry about. Besides, the only way I could think of to come up with a quarter million dollars to pay off the note on Eadon Branch was to get half the eight-hundred-thousand-dollar winner's purse.

Bobby just held the check in his hands, running a finger up and down its edge, not saying anything.

"I want a piece of that," J. R. Neill said. He pulled out his wallet, opened it up, and fished a couple of hundred-dollar bills out. He stuffed them into Bobby's hand.

"I wanna be able to tell people that I got hustled by a future PGA champ," he said. "Pay me back out of your winnings."

"I can't let you—" Bobby started to object.

But Conrad was, as usual, right next to J.R. And, as usual, Conrad followed J.R.'s example. He pulled a couple of hundred from his wallet—in tens and twenties.

"Pay me back from your winnings," he repeated.

I was amazed at the money J.R. and Conrad were carrying. Maybe we hadn't been charging a high enough greens fee.

Bobby didn't say anything for a moment, just kept running his fingers up and down over the check and the cash like he was trying to read the print on them with his fingers. "You guys shouldn't do this, and I can't accept it," he said, proffering the money.

No one took any. Eudora, in fact, reached into the cash register and pulled out the day's greens fees, a short stack of tens and twenties. She pressed the money into Bobby's hand.

"You're the playing pro out of Eadon Branch Golf Club," she said. "We're sponsoring you."

The room had gotten quiet as the rest of the miners heard what was going on. Then Conrad took his hard hat off and dropped another twenty into it. He passed it around the room.

Angela's eyes were glistening. She leaned over to Bobby and whispered in his ear, explaining, I guess, what was happening.

The hard hat came back. There must've been another thousand dollars in it, wrinkled old green bills nestled inside the gray plastic lining, worn shiny from use. I just took Bobby's hand and pressed it inside, let him feel the money.

"Well . . ." he said. His voice was cracking a little.

"Bobby, shut up and go practice," J.R. growled.

"Kick some butt, Bobby," Conrad said.

We did practice, till dark that day. But only after we made two phone calls. Bobby called his lawyer in Georgia and instructed him to file a suit to force the PGA to let him play.

And I called the AP and had them patch me through to Ken Alyda. I figured a little publicity mightn't hurt our chances.

WHAT I HADN'T COUNTED ON was a whole lot of publicity. But once Alyda's story hit the wires, our phone started ringing, and it didn't let up. Bobby talked to CNN, ESPN, MSNBC, NBC, CBS, ABC, and UPI. The only abbreviation that didn't call was NASA. I fielded calls from *The New York Times* and the Atlanta *Constitution*.

Finally, at around ten thirty, with the phone still ringing, Bobby said, "Let it ring. You think they can find us at Gully's?"

"Let's go," Angela said. "Film on TV at eleven."

So we got a vantage point in the bar at Gully's and watched TV. First there was some tape from the previous year's PGA and the disastrous sixteenth hole. Then there was some footage of Bobby playing in the Cooters tournament. Neither one was flattering.

The news stories themselves tended to emphasize Bobby's rights under the Americans with Disabilities Act, but that wasn't flattering either. The underlying message was "Here's a guy who can't really play golf anymore, but he's got a legal right to try, except that those bozos who run golf are too bigoted to let him."

ESPN, at least, tried to be balanced. They'd managed to track down Little Dickie Reynolds, and they put him on to make the case for barring Bobby from the tournament.

Little Dickie Reynolds was one of those pro golfers who just can't seem to understand how privileged he is. He was always one of the first to whine if something was wrong with the greens. He'd made a well-publicized move from California, where he was from, to Florida. Said he couldn't stand paying all that tax money to a liberal, big-spending state government. When he was on the Ryder Cup team, he refused to meet with the President at the White House on the grounds that the President had dodged the draft during Vietnam.

Despite, or maybe because of, those things, Little Dickie was a revered figure in the golf world. For one thing, he was a traditionalist. He still used wooden clubs. And he was good. He'd won a Masters and a British Open.

"It's not that I wouldn't like to see Bobby Jobe have a chance," Little Dickie was saying, "but there are some larger issues involved than just the misfortunes of one individual."

"And what," the reporter asked, "might those be?"

"The integrity of the game," Little Dickie said. "Golf competitions have always been about a single individual. A blind golfer needs his caddie to set up his club, pick out his line, and do all the things that a sighted golfer is expected to do. He's playing a different game, and it's not golf."

Surely, the reporter asked, Little Dickie didn't think blindness was an advantage.

"Of course not," Little Dickie said, clearly miffed by the question. "But golf has rules. Anyone who wants to play has to play by the rules. Bobby Jobe, unfortunately, can't play by them."

Did Little Dickie think he could still play at all?

"Well, to be honest—and I admire Bobby for trying to make a comeback after his accident—from what I hear, he can't. He has trouble breaking ninety. Now, the PGA Championship is about the best professional golfers in the world competing against one another. If we were to let Bobby enter, he'd be taking a spot away from someone who *is* one of the best professional golfers in the world."

I looked at Bobby. He couldn't see the bland, innocent look on Little Dickie's face, but the words were coming through clearly. Bobby's shoulders were drooping.

"Turn the damn thing off," I said to the bartender. After taking a glance at Bobby, he did.

Chapter 6

It would be nice if I could tell you common sense, justice, and kindness persuaded the PGA to let Bobby play.

It would be nice if I could tell you that Bobby's lawyer won a landmark lawsuit helping to establish the rights of the blind.

What happened was the bottom line persuaded the PGA to change its mind. Before Bobby's lawyer could even type up the papers for our case, CBS Sports and F. Rockwell Peddy were both leaning hard on the PGA to reverse itself. They had leverage.

We heard all this from Ken Alyda, the AP golf writer. He told me Tuesday morning that it would take about twenty-four hours for the PGA to knuckle under. And he was right, almost to the minute.

At ten o'clock Wednesday morning Eudora hustled out of the shop and down to the practice green, where Bobby and I were working on long sand shots.

Eudora looked like she'd just gotten a call from the lottery telling her there'd been a mistake in last week's Powerball drawing. She had hold of the folds of her skirt to help her move faster. "Telephone for you, Bobby," she said. "It's the PGA."

Bobby walked up out of the bunker and stretched out his hand. Eudora took it, smiling a little, and led him up the hill to the shop, just like he was her boyfriend.

By the time I finished raking the bunker and followed them in, Bobby was saying, "Thank you. Bye." He hung up the phone slowly. "I'm in," he said. He didn't look jubilant. He looked worried. I could relate to that. But he drew himself up a little and said, "Well, I guess we better do some more practicing, Coach. Got six days before we have to be in Jersey."

"Lot of time," I told him. "We should go tell Angela."

"All right," he said. "And I want your father to go with us."

"What?" I'd heard him. I just didn't like what I'd heard.

"He figured out my swing faster'n anybody I ever worked with," Bobby said. "I want him around."

BOBBY rented a car, a big Oldsmobile, for the trip to Atlantic City. It was just like the courtesy cars we used to get on the tour, a nearly new, plain-vanilla piece of Detroit iron. Our bags and the clubs fit easily in the trunk. It was early Sunday morning, chilly. Just before we pulled out, J.R. and Conrad drove into the lot in J.R.'s GMC. J.R. was carrying an envelope I recognized. It was the one I'd used to send back the money he'd collected from the miners to help pay for Bobby's lawyer. They got out and shook hands with Bobby, and told him Allegheny Gap would be watching and rooting for him.

Then he gave me the money.

"Thanks, but we didn't need it," I said. "We didn't have to sue."

J.R. put a big, callused hand over the one I was using to proffer the money. "They got betting in Atlantic City, right?"

"I believe so," I told him.

"Put it on Bobby's nose. We figure you'll get good odds."

The envelope felt worn and wrinkled and warm in my hands. "I will," I said. "We'll get good odds."

Eudora hugged Angela and Bobby and wished him luck. She gave me a bag of sandwiches and a kiss on the cheek.

DR. MEHTA had made a halfway successful effort to clean up Clayton Mote. He'd bought him some new clothes—a couple of pairs of khakis, some polo shirts, a pair of walking shoes.

I drove, with Bobby riding shotgun and Angela in the back seat with Clayton. I mostly passed the time watching them in the rearview mirror and listening to Angela talk to him. Clayton didn't respond to anything. As we drove into Atlantic City, he was mumbling to himself, staring out the window at a billboard that told him Harrah's was where serious slot players go. If he was thinking about being in a strange place, he didn't let it show.

Il Palazzo wasn't hard to find. The hotel was just a plain glass-and-steel box, but it was overlaid with a lot of plastic intended to suggest it was in Italy. When you drove up, there was actually a canal that led from the valet parking station to the door of the casino, and white gondolas, trimmed in gold paint, would carry you the last 200 yards if you wanted. There was a big sign over the door that said F. ROCKWELL PEDDY PRESENTS IL PALAZZO.

We checked in and got our small rooms without ocean views at the special tournament rate. I hadn't had a chance to unpack before the phone rang. It was Bobby.

"Let's go, Coach. I figure we can get out there and walk the course before dark."

I looked at my watch. It was five thirty. Bobby had never gone with me on a course inspection walk before. He'd never wanted to go out to a course this close to happy hour before.

"You know what time it is?" I asked him.

"I know we don't have enough of it," Bobby said. "Get the pro and Angela. Tell 'em they can come. We can eat late."

SAND Valley Golf Club is hidden away in a little town with a couple of pizza parlors, a Core States Bank, and a Mobil station. I might've driven right by the entrance if I hadn't had a map.

Years ago, when the course was built, there was nothing in that part of New Jersey but sandy, hilly land that was no good for farming. A few guys from Philadelphia recognized the land's potential, though. They bought it cheap, put together a club from among the best golfers they knew, and designed a course to test them—severely.

I started to get a feel for the place about a quarter mile after the turn from the little town. It's a private road. There's a guardhouse where you show your pass. You see a little clearing by the side of the road where, I suspected, the caddies had to park. TV trucks were in it. Then you go left around a curve, and you're right below the eighteenth green. You can see a fairway of crosshatched green, surrounded by sand and scrub. The whole thing is lined by woods. You get just that glimpse, and then you're in the players parking lot. Beyond it you can see the clubhouse and a dormitory for out-of-town members. They're just plain little frame buildings.

It was around six by then, and the late sunlight was coming in bright white shafts through the chinks in the pines that soared all around us. The sky above was a bright, clear blue.

Bobby got out of the car, sniffed, and turned slowly as if he could see it. "Some golf course, eh, Pro?" he said to Clayton. Clayton didn't reply, but he was looking, taking it all in.

"Let's go to eighteen green," Bobby said. I blinked. I hadn't known he knew I walked courses backward when I was checking them out. We headed across the lot toward the final hole.

"Young man!" a voice called out.

I turned and looked. It was Jello McKay.

We hadn't been close when I was on the tour. But I greeted him then like my best friend come back from the dead. I was really glad to see him. Jello was looking a little older, a little heavier. But he was looking good to me.

Bobby stuck out his hand. Jello looked at him coolly, then took it. "Nice to have you back," Jello said. "Guess you won't be making any more remarks about skin color."

Bobby reddened. Angela looked curious.

But Bobby had the grace to apologize, which I had almost never heard him do. "Lot of things I won't be making remarks about anymore, Jello," he said. "Sorry I said it."

Jello looked as surprised as I did to hear it. There was a moment of awkward silence.

"Who you with?" I asked Jello.

"Some lucky unknown," he said.

"Who?"

"Don't know yet," he said. "That's why he's unknown."

Jello was looking for work.

"But he will be lucky, that unknown man," Jello said. "See, I've caddied here before. Sand Valley is a track you gotta know. Greens here're very subtle—quick in most places, not so quick in a few. Harder to read than a blue-eyed woman."

"Help us out, then, Jello," Bobby said.

Jello, I guess, was feeling benevolent about Bobby's apology. He agreed. So we all walked together. I introduced Clayton and Angela as friends of Bobby's and let it go at that.

"Make you a bet," Jello said. He walked us onto the eighteenth green and took a golf ball out of his pocket. He squatted down by the pin and flipped the ball to me. "Bet you five you can't roll it to the hole and tell me which way it's going to break," he said. It looked like the ball would break about one cup to the right.

"Bet it goes left," I said. I rolled the ball to him. It broke a little left at the end, away from the hole. I got the break right, but not the speed. The ball drifted about four feet past the hole, like it was scudding on ice. Quick.

"Not many guys see that," Jello said.

I laughed. "I didn't either. Just figured you wouldn't bet me on a putt that broke the way it looked like it would."

Jello laughed. "Main thing," he said, "is not to get greedy here. Hit the fairway, play maybe a seven-iron to the middle, and be happy to make four."

That was standard advice for almost any hard par 4. But as we walked down the fairway, I could see why it wasn't easy to follow.

What Sand Valley did was try to intimidate a golfer. When you stood on the tee, you saw acres and acres of sand and brush. The fairway looked like a distant oasis. Not only that, but the trees pinched in just where the fairway began, making it look tighter than it really was. If you could ignore all this and hit a decent tee shot, you found that the fairway was actually quite generous. But standing on the tee, you thought you had to hit the best shot of your life just to keep it in play.

It was the same thing with the second shot. You couldn't see the green—just a bit of the flag flapping over enormous bunkers. You saw all the trouble very clearly, from the pond to the sand. You didn't see your target. You had to have faith to hit the ball where it needed to go.

The pattern repeated itself as we walked along, Jello explaining, and I making little notes on a scorecard. In front of every tee box Sand Valley had a couple of hundred yards of sand and scrub. Every green looked like it was an island in a heaving sea of trouble.

Sand Valley was a nasty, brutal, beautiful golf course. And it occurred to me that a lot of players would look at it and be intimidated. Bobby might play it better because he couldn't see it.

INSPIRATION can be dangerous, especially in a gambling town. It certainly was that night. The sense I had that Bobby Jobe was going to play well at Sand Valley overwhelmed my other senses—especially my common sense.

That night, after dinner, when everyone else was in their rooms, I used the TV remote and connected to Peddy's Internet sports book operation. I punched a couple of YES buttons, and the next thing I know the screen said, "Bobby Jobe 800–1."

I never was too good at math, so I used a little HBO booklet to write the multiplication on. If Bobby won, J.R. and the boys would be collecting $320,000 in return for the $400 they'd given me.

And that started me thinking. If I kicked in another $500 off my Visa card, the payoff to me would be $400,000. That'd be enough to get the course back in the black and buy my ticket out of Allegheny Gap in a new car.

I clicked the buttons. The screen asked me how much I wanted to bet. I clicked till it read $1000 and let it go.

THE next morning Angela said she'd like to stay at the hotel and wouldn't mind looking after Clayton. So Bobby and I drove out to Sand Valley. Bobby didn't say much on the way. It was like we were going to a funeral instead of a golf course. That wasn't good. The pressure of a tournament is a cumulative thing. The ideal attitude is loose and casual right up to the starting bell.

What Bobby needed was a good, relaxed practice session. It wasn't. After we found a spot on the practice range, he hit a couple of decent wedges, then asked for the two-iron. He took the club, and we addressed the ball, and I knew what he was thinking. He was thinking of the long two-iron on the sixteenth at Oak Valley in the last PGA, the one he'd duck-hooked into the creek.

Sure enough, he snapped it.

"Damn," he cursed. "The hook!" He slammed the club into the turf. Then he started trying to fix his hook.

It just got worse and worse. His rhythm and timing got all screwed up. He hit snap hooks. He hit high cuts. And with every bad swing he got more self-conscious. He couldn't see the way guys were looking at him, shaking their heads about the shots he hit. But he could hear the murmurs of the spectators behind the ropes.

I had to stop it before he forgot how to swing entirely.

I looked at my watch. It was a quarter to ten.

"Lunchtime," I said.

Bobby stuck the two-iron in the ground like a cane and leaned on it. "What time is it?" he asked me.

"Time to eat," I said.

He got it. He knew that if he kept hitting balls the way he was going, he wouldn't be able to hit the course with his hat.

"Okay," he said. "Might as well."

I EXPECTED to find the pro and Angela in his room, watching television—Dr. Mehta had told us that my father liked soaps—but they weren't there. We went looking for them. Or, rather, I did, and Bobby came along, his hand on my shoulder.

We found them at a five-dollar blackjack table.

"The pro is doing great!" Angela whispered as we approached.

I watched with her. Clayton stood with a 15 and then watched the dealer turn over a jack and a queen.

"Looks to me like he's losing," I whispered back.

"The point is he's playing," she said.

"Can you ask him to cash his chips so he can watch me practice?" Bobby asked, impatient.

"Wait a minute, Bobby," I said. "I think we ought to give it a rest." The last thing Bobby needed was a lesson. He just needed to relax and start trusting his swing again.

"Can't," he said. "Only got a couple of days till the tournament."

"Yeah, but . . ." I started.

Bobby wasn't listening. "Pro," he said, "I want to hit balls on the beach. I want you to help me stop hooking the ball."

The teacher part of Clayton Mote's sick brain switched on. He nodded. "Lesson on the beach," he said. He nodded again. "Stop hooking. Hogan knows."

I couldn't stand it anymore. I pulled Bobby aside and whispered in his ear. "Bobby, you can't go taking a lesson from him two days before the PGA! He could mess you up."

Bobby put a hand out and found my shoulder. "He can't mess me up much worse than I am now," he said. "And besides, I think he knows what he's talking about."

"What?" I snorted. "What Hogan's ghost tells him?"

He squeezed my shoulder softly. "I just have a feeling this is what I need, Coach," he said. "Let's do it."

WE DID it Bobby's way. We drove up the coast past Brigantine to a wildlife refuge. Apart from seagulls and sandpipers, it was deserted.

Bobby latched on, and we walked to a level spot on the beach. He hit a few wedges. The first one was fat. So was the second. The third he clipped. Each swing got uglier, until finally he hit a nasty, hooked top that veered about twenty yards left into the surf. The club went in after it, turning like a helicopter rotor.

"I can't hit the damn ball!" Bobby yelled to the sky.

I got the club, walking slow so he'd have time to compose himself. When I got back, I patted him on the shoulders.

"Tempo, Bobby. Slow tempo," I said.

But Bobby wasn't buying. He turned and said, "Pro?"

Clayton didn't say anything.

"Pro, whattaya think?" Bobby asked again.

"Hogan," Clayton said. "Hogan knows the secret."

Bobby stepped toward the voice and got in Clayton's face. "What secret? What is it?"

Clayton's eyes widened, and he stepped backward, but the teacher in him was engaged again. "Legs," he mumbled.

"What?" Bobby was nearly panting.

Clayton looked at him and smiled like he was getting ready for the Miss America contest. It was the biggest, kindest smile I'd ever seen from him. "Right knee," he said. "Drive the right knee."

Bobby took a stance and pantomimed hitting a ball, but on the downswing he pushed off hard from his right foot and drove his right knee toward his left.

"That's it?" Bobby demanded. "That's Hogan's secret?"

Clayton nodded, almost shyly. "Hogan's secret," he said.

"Wait a minute," I butted in. "You want quiet legs hitting off sand. Besides, Hogan believed in starting the downswing with the left hip. That couldn't be Hogan's secret."

I looked around for someone to agree with me. But Bobby was ready to do anything. "Couldn't hurt to try it," he said.

I gave in. I put another ball in the sand, expecting Bobby either to hit it fat or to hook it damn near to England. Of course, he didn't. Golf swings are peculiar that way. Sometimes making a change that shouldn't help does help, just because it changes the attitude of the player from pessimistic to optimistic. I think that's what happened. Bobby hit a sweet, crisp wedge off the sand that took off right where it was aimed and faded about three inches before it fell gently to the beach like it knew where it was going.

"How was that?" Bobby asked. But he knew.

"That was a useful shot," I said. "Try it again."

Bobby tried it again. Another perfect shot.

"Hogan's secret, Pro!" Bobby yelped. "Hogan's secret!"

Clayton looked at the sand. "Hogan." He nodded.

Bobby's confidence, nonexistent a few minutes earlier, soared like a rocket. He hit a few more wedges, then seven-irons, then three-irons, and finally a couple of three-woods off the sand, a shot that I'd've never even thought of trying. They were all near perfect.

"Good-bye, quacker!" Bobby shouted. "I know Hogan's secret."

He sounded giddy to me. You want a player to be confident, but Bobby's mood was like a balloon that was pumped up too much. I thought about telling him, "Look, Bobby, you know there's no way Clayton Mote knows Ben Hogan's secret. He's a lunatic. You're hitting it good because you've got your confidence back." And when we were finished and heading for the car, I started to do it.

"Bobby," I said, "you know that there's no way—"

I never finished the sentence, because Clayton Mote started glaring at me like he knew what I was going to say.

"No way what, Coach?" Bobby finally said.

"No way you're not going to play great," I said.

We drove back to the hotel. A couple of hours later Bobby suggested we go back to Sand Valley. So we went back out there and walked around the course in the twilight, putting dozens of balls. We got a feel for the speed and figured out some of the breaks.

We repeated that schedule the next day: out on the beach at the wildlife refuge, then out to Sand Valley to putt in the twilight. When Bobby was resting, I walked the course, planning shots. On the beach Bobby's ball striking kept getting sharper. By Wednesday night, the night before the tournament, I was half ready to believe that Clayton Mote actually knew Ben Hogan's secret.

RAIN moved in just after dawn Thursday. It wasn't supposed to last long—an hour or two, they kept saying. But at nine that morning, the sky over Sand Valley was still heavy and gray and it was still raining. Once in a while some lightning would glimmer over the horizon and thunder would roll overhead, and that was enough to keep the players off the course. I was worried. I didn't know how a thunderstorm would affect Bobby, but that wasn't all I was worried about. Bobby'd drawn an early starting time—7:12. He was in with a couple of club pros, Doug Hurt and Mike Kitay.

There was a message in that tee time. The tour didn't give stars such early times. It didn't pair established players with club pros. The tour was telling Bobby he belonged with the nobodies.

Finally, when the rain had diminished to a few spritzes, the word came down. Play would start at 9:45. They were going to start half the field on the tenth tee. That's a way of getting a few more groups around the course than by starting everyone off on number 1. We were going off number 10.

"Damn," Bobby said. "I liked number one for starters."

He was right. Number 1 was a good opening hole for him.

But it did him no good to think that way.

"Nope," I said. "Ten is best. We got a chance for a fast start."

"Chance to go in the Devil's Gullet, too," Bobby said.

I was surprised. I hadn't told him about the Devil's Gullet. I'd just told him that number 10 had a pit bunker front right. He must've heard about it in the locker room. The Devil's Gullet was maybe the meanest, most unfair pit bunker in America.

"It wasn't built there," Jello had told me. "The ground just caved in and filled with sand years ago. Like the devil did it." He'd grinned, but then he'd said, "Lots of time, you get into that bunker, the best thing to do is go back to the tee and hit your third."

We took a few practice putts and headed for the tenth tee. There weren't many spectators. The rain had held the crowd down, and the big names weren't scheduled to go off until later in the day. There might've been a couple of hundred people gathered at the tee. Angela and Clayton were near the front.

Then, of course, there was the television crew from ESPN, which was doing the early rounds. And half a dozen print reporters, including Ken Alyda. I nodded to him, and he clenched his fist and gave me a "Let's go" sign.

We drew lots for the honor, and Bobby finished third. Kitay, a stocky, gray-haired pro from a club in upstate New York, took an iron and got the ball in the center of the green, twenty-five feet from the hole. Hurt, a redheaded kid from Maryland, hit much the same shot. I checked in his bag to see what was missing. He'd hit a nine-iron.

"Now on the tee," the announcer said, and he paused. "From Dalton, Georgia." Someone whooped. "Bobby Jobe."

The applause came, and it was more than the polite applause that always greets a player on his first tee. It went on for a while. Bobby stepped forward and tipped his cap. I pulled his nine-iron and stepped up close to his right ear.

"Okay," I said to him. "You know this hole. Pin's back right a little. Eric Dickerson front. Richard Petty to the hole."

"Coach," he hissed. "I don't know squadoosh about stock-car racing! What the hell number is Richard Petty?"

Live and learn. I figured everyone from Georgia loved racing. "Forty-three," I said. "You've got one forty-three to the hole."

"How much to clear the Devil's Gullet?"

I looked at my pin sheet. "One thirty-five to be safe," I said.

"Whattaya think?"

"Solid nine," I said.

"And drive the legs," he said with a grin. "Hogan's secret."

I didn't want to argue with him about it. So I just clapped him on the back and squatted down behind the ball to line him up.

The shaft flashed before me. The click was pure and so was the shot. It rose high over the trees, headed straight for the flag. As it reached its high point, a pillar of sunlight broke through the clouds and lit up the green. I'm not making that up. Bobby's ball landed three feet beyond the pin and lay there, gleaming in the brightness.

Of course, the place erupted.

Bobby knew he'd hit it good. "Where?" was all he said.

"You're putting," I told him.

He nodded and then put his hand out and waited for me to butt the bottom end of the bag against his fingers. We took off.

Since the green was built like a pedestal, I could read it pretty well as we walked up toward it. Fortunately for us, Kitay had to make a four-footer for par on almost the same line as Bobby's putt. He played for about two balls of break and didn't get it.

So I aimed Bobby inside the right edge and told him four feet, firm. He hit it exactly that way, and the ball dived right into the hole. We'd birdied the first hole. The crowd erupted again.

We got a nice, steady par at number 11: drive in the fairway, wedge below the hole, lag putt, tap-in. We jazzed the crowd up on number 12, which was the softest hole on the course, a short par 4. Bobby hit a four-iron and sand wedge to ten feet, and the putt went down like it was on tracks to the hole. We were 2 under par.

There's a spot golfers try to get their minds to. Sometimes you hear people call it the zone. What it means is you're playing so well and so confidently that you don't need to think about how to do it. It's like being detached, except that you're completely engrossed in the game. It's hard to explain, but finding that spot is one of the big reasons people keep playing golf. It feels so good.

And that's where Bobby had got himself to—or fallen into.

I started to feel it myself on number 13, which is where the back nine at Sand Valley starts getting truly difficult. It's a long hole in two segments that looks like it ought to be a par 5 because it's a double dogleg. But it's a par 4. Bobby hit a great three-wood off the tee and then drew a three-iron into the green. He caught a bad break, and his ball ended up forty feet from the hole.

The putt went uphill and downhill, broke left and right and left again, and finally, about four feet from the cup, started to look like it was magnetized. I knew it was going in a split second before the crowd did, and I yelled, "Yes!"

All Bobby could hear was the "Ye—" because of the roar that went up. I looked around. Our gallery had grown to a couple of thousand or more, and they were clapping and whistling like we'd just outlawed downturns in the stock market.

And that's the way the round went. Nothing miraculous happened. Bobby didn't hit any 400-yard drives or hole out from any fairways. He just played golf the way it can be played. Fairway. Green. Hole. I sometimes had the feeling he was a ball-hitting machine and all I had to do was aim it right to get the shot we needed.

It wasn't until he lagged up to a foot on number 9, our last hole, that I looked at a scoreboard and realized what was happening. Bobby was still 3 under par. If he sank his last putt, he'd shoot 67 and he'd be leading the tournament, at least temporarily. I looked around a little, trying to catch sight of Angela. I couldn't see her, but I started to notice the thickening horde of spectators. People were literally hanging out of pine trees to see Bobby putt out.

I could sense that Bobby was breaking the surface somehow, because he was looking around, listening to the crowd as Kitay and Hurt putted out. When we lined up for the last putt, our rhythm was gone, and the putt slid by the left side of the hole. Bogey.

The crowd gave a quiet, perfunctory sort of moan. It was like the people were disappointed that they couldn't begin an ovation.

The ovation started a moment later after Bobby tapped in the bogey putt. It was a long, sustained applause. Bobby responded to it by tipping his cap and then turning around to high-five me. That was the picture the papers all carried the next day.

Bobby seemed more surprised than I was by what had happened.

"That was the best round of golf I ever played," he said, shaking his head. "Who'd've thought—Hogan's secret from your father?"

They needed three marshals to help us squeeze through the crowd pressing against the ropes that defined the path to the scorer's tent. I looked for Angela and Clayton. I couldn't see them.

Inside the tent, it was suddenly cool, dim, and oddly quiet. I added up the numbers again and put Bobby's hand in the right spot on the scorecard. He signed. We were official.

Cade Benton, the PR official, walked in. Last seen looking grim-faced at the Captain Dick Classic, he was now acting as though having us enter the tournament and be put on front pages around the world was his idea all along. "Well done, gentlemen," he said. "The press is rather anxious to speak with you, Bobby."

Bobby nodded like this was some kind of burden he'd take only because he had to. But I knew better.

IT TOOK a long time to get away that day. Bobby wanted to practice at Sand Valley instead of out at the beach. I understood. He wanted to wallow in it a little more, to stand out on the range and hear his peers tell him how well he played. He deserved that. And he enjoyed it. Hell, I enjoyed it, too. It was five o'clock before Bobby finally said he'd had enough, and we got into the car for the drive back to Atlantic City.

The celebrity treatment continued when we got to the hotel. A couple of photographers took our picture at the front door.

"Congratulations, Mr. Jobe, Mr. Mote," the doorman said. "Great round. Welcome back to Il Palazzo."

And it was like that all the way through the lobby and into the elevator. People were tripping over themselves to open doors for us and congratulate us. I looked around for any sign of Angela or Clayton, but I didn't see them. I was supposed to have driven them back to the hotel. I forgot.

When I got to my room, there were flowers and a basket of fruit on the desk, compliments of F. Rockwell Peddy—and there was an envelope. Mr. Peddy requested the pleasure of Mr. Jobe's and Mr. Mote's company at a dinner that night honoring past PGA champions. I put that aside.

I picked up the phone and dialed Angela's room. No answer. I tried Clayton Mote's. She picked up the phone.

"It's all right," she said after I'd apologized for leaving them behind. "We rode back in the caddie bus."

"You're sure you didn't mind?" I asked.

"Not at all," she replied. The way she said it, it was hard to tell whether she meant it.

"Uh, good," I said. Then I fell silent. Sometimes my own eloquence astounded me. "Well, hey, I'm sorry you had to look after the pro for so long," I said. "I'll come down and take over. And what do you say we go out somewhere for dinner tonight, celebrate? Bobby and I are invited to this past champions dinner, but I was thinking I didn't want to go."

I scowled at my reflection in the mirror. That was a stupid thing to say. Why hadn't I told her I wanted to be with her?

"No place fancy," she said. "I haven't got the clothes for it, and neither does the pro."

"That makes three of us," I said. I was ridiculously relieved she was willing to have dinner with me.

So I changed clothes and went down the hall to Clayton's room and knocked on the door. She opened it. Her hair was frizzy from the rain that day. We agreed to meet in an hour, and she left.

Clayton sat docile in front of the television, watching someone giving a golf lesson, until we went down to meet Angela in the hotel restaurant. At dinner, Clayton didn't say anything. He seemed to shrink within himself, like he was reacting to a cold wind.

WHEN Bobby came back from the dinner, he called me. Clayton and I were in my room, watching the Golf Channel.

"Hey, Coach," he said. "Come on up. I need you to tell me about these clothes they gave me."

"The pro's with me," I said.

"Bring him, too," Bobby told me.

So I got Clayton by the elbow and went to Bobby's new room—he had been moved to the ocean side of the hotel. Bobby opened the door before I could knock a second time. He was wearing a blue blazer with a yellow tie—silk, I think. He seemed keyed up.

"So whattaya think of these clothes?" he asked me when I was three steps inside the door. "They gave 'em to me for the dinner tonight. Should I keep 'em?"

I pulled Clayton into the room, sat him down in front of the TV, and handed him the remote. He started clicking until he'd found the Golf Channel again.

"They look fine to me," I told him. "But what do I know? I buy my good clothes at Wal-Mart."

"Guess I'll keep 'em, then," he said. "Guess who I sat with at dinner tonight?"

I shrugged. Then I remembered he didn't see shrugs. "Damned if I know," I said. I lowered my voice so Clayton wouldn't hear. "Hogan?" I was needling him.

But Bobby grinned like a pleased little boy. "Better than him," he said. "Jack Nicklaus."

I was impressed. "Fast company," I said.

"I was at a table with F. Rockwell Peddy, some babe named Marina he's dating, Nicklaus, Barbara Nicklaus, and Paul Runyan," Bobby reported. "Runyan— God, he must be nearly a hundred."

"Sounds great," I said.

"Trouble was, I was too nervous to eat. Wished you or Angela was there."

He started telling me a story about Runyan at the first Masters, back in 1934. I was only half listening, feeling restless.

Bobby's room had a sliding glass door that led to a balcony, and from the balcony, you could see the ocean, dark and endless. I opened the door a foot or two and let the sea air wash over me.

Down on the beach, I saw a woman walking. I looked harder. She had a mess of wild hair under a baseball cap. When she passed through a band of moonlight reflecting off the ocean, I could see her profile. It was Angela.

I stopped Bobby. "Bobby, there's something I gotta do," I said. "Tell me the rest tomorrow."

And I bolted out the door.

I ran down the hallway to catch the elevator. After I mashed the

DOWN button, I waited for about ten seconds, then ran down the stairs five flights to the casino. And I jogged through that, out the door of the casino and onto the boardwalk.

I ran past a pier with a ride called the Wild Mouse. I thought I saw her up ahead, ducking through the support pilings for another pier. I called out to her, "Hey, Angela!"

She stopped and turned. I stopped running. She waved at me.

The neon from the casinos were bathing her face in garish colors—blue and hot red. She had rolled up the legs of her jeans so she could walk in the surf, and she was standing a little splayfooted as I walked up. "What brings you out here, Henry?" she asked.

"Oh, just taking a walk," I told her.

Her eyebrows twitched when she heard that, and I realized how stupid it sounded, since I was still puffing from running after her.

"Okay, well, I saw you out here, and I thought I'd like to take a walk with you," I acknowledged.

"Where's the pro?" she asked.

"Bobby's watching him," I said. "Or, at least, Bobby's with him."

That made her smile. We started walking along the beach. The water broke over my sneakers, but I pretended I didn't notice.

"You remember that day you came to Eadon Branch the first time to ask me to work with Bobby?" I asked her.

"Very well," she said.

"You were right, you know. I never thought it was possible for Bobby to come back and shoot sixty-eight in the PGA."

"You and Bobby have done the work," she said.

"Yeah, but we wouldn't've without you," I told her.

She turned toward me. Her eyes were wide-open, and I thought they were glistening. "Thank you, Henry," she said.

I kissed her.

She put her arms around me and pressed me close.

I could have kissed her forever like that, but after a moment she pressed against my shoulders and separated us a little. She didn't pull away, though. She stayed there, in my arms.

"You know," I said. "This round changes everything."

"How do you mean?" she asked.

"Bobby's gonna be big," I said. "We're going to be back on tour. There's going to be money, finally."

"Um," she said. I should've listened to her more carefully. It wasn't an encouraging "um."

I pulled her a little closer to me. "So, anyway, what I want to say is that I don't want you to go back to Nashville. I want you to come out on tour." I was afraid to look at her when I said that.

"As what?" she said.

"Well, you could still help Bobby, of course," I said, "but mainly, uh, with me."

And then I did look at her. She was smiling one of those smiles that's very close to tears. But then she pulled away.

"No, Henry," she said, "it's not for me."

"But why?"

"It's not you," she said. She looked pained. "Let's not get into this now, okay? You guys have a tournament to play. After it's over . . ."

Now I felt she was telling me I wasn't man enough to handle being shot down and carrying a golf bag in the same week.

"Yeah, sure," I said.

She looked like she was struggling to not cry. She drew herself up and said she was going back to the hotel. I just stood there, watching her walk away.

"Why not?" I yelled after her. "Why not?"

Angela turned around. "It just wouldn't work," she said.

That was all. I couldn't figure out what she meant. Couldn't think of anything to say. All I could think of was how embarrassed I felt. I watched as she climbed the stairs to the boardwalk and disappeared into the hotel.

I went in then, up to my room. I flicked the remote control till I had the sports book at Peddy's Internet casino.

The odds on Bobby, I saw, had dropped from 800–1 to 100–1.

THE next day, in the second round, Bobby shot 76 and fell five places back. We were still in it. Barely.

At number 10 we had hit the Devil's Gullet, took a penalty, and returned to the tee—something Bobby had never done. The walk back seemed to take forever. Kitay and Hurt waited alongside the green.

At the tee Bobby started checking his wrists and his legs and his swing plane. I grabbed the club and stopped him.

"Forget that crap," I whispered. "Just see the pin and fire at it."

Bobby kind of snorted. His mouth wrinkled into a sneer.

"Try to remember, Greyhound, you idiot. I used to see. I can't see anymore. I can't see the damn pin!" He was halfway between screaming at me and crying.

"Bobby, you used to see, but you didn't have vision," I said, my voice low. "You used to be able to spot the difference between a C-cup and a D-cup from two hundred yards, but you couldn't see what you were doing to your life. Now you can't see, but you can have vision. True vision. And you can see that pin and see the shot you can hit to it."

He looked at me like I'd just puked up a toad.

"True vision," I said again, weaker.

Then he laughed, and I started to grin, too.

"Okay," he said. "Let's do it."

And we did.

THAT night I dreamed that Bobby was leading the tournament by 2 strokes going into the last hole. The dream was so vivid that I could see the scoreboard in my mind, and I remember who was in second place: Sam Snead.

In the dream I lined Bobby up perfectly for the second shot on the hole, and he hit it perfectly. It took off like a rifle shot, then dropped gently to the green, ten feet away from the hole. And then Clayton—but the younger Clayton, the bushy-haired father I remembered—ran onto the green and stole the ball.

The bell in the cupola over the clubhouse—I know, there isn't one at Sand Valley—started ringing. *Bong. Bong.*

I woke up. The phone was ringing. I picked it up. It was Dr. Mehta. "I am in the casino at Il Palazzo," he said.

He couldn't have surprised me more if he'd said he was calling from the moon. "Why?"

"I was watching television yesterday, and I saw a report on you and Mr. Jobe," he said in that odd accent of his. "It was very exciting. To think that one of our patients is involved in such a deed! So I decided to drive up here and see if I could be of service to you."

I looked at the clock. It was six thirty. "You drove all night?"

"Most of it," he said.

I invited him up to the room, and inside of five minutes he knocked on the door. He looked like he'd driven all night—his hair was rumpled, and his shirt was wrinkled.

I gave him my key to Clayton's room. To tell the truth, I was relieved he was taking over again.

Chapter 7

WHEN we got to Sand Valley that morning, you'd've thought Bobby was leading the tournament. People were on him from the time we got out of the car. They wanted more than autographs. They wanted to touch him. People even patted me on the back.

"Bobby," someone asked, "what did you mean by true vision?"

Bobby was even less prepared than I was for the question.

"How'd you know about that?" he asked.

"ESPN's got good microphones, Bobby," someone called out.

"What did you mean by true vision?" the first guy persisted.

Bobby gave 'em that bashful good ole boy smile. "Oh, Greyhound and I were just kidding around. Didn't mean anything."

We were paired with Jay Delsing, a guy pushing forty, with a long time on the tour but no wins. His caddie was a guy named Lizard Ziomecki, a name he got because of a habit he had of sitting in bars, tossing peanuts in the air, and then sticking out his tongue to catch them. We started off toward the practice green, but it was slow going because of the way the people surged closer to Bobby.

"Amazing," Lizard said to me, "how many fans Jay and I have around here."

I just grunted. Despite the ropes that were supposed to hold them back, people had crowded around Bobby. Before I could help, Delsing saw the situation and figured out what to do.

He got Bobby's hand on his shoulder and ran a sort of interference for him as they moved along. It was only a moment's kindness, but I respected Delsing for it. He'd never been this close to the lead this late in a major championship. He could've been totally absorbed in his putting stroke. He wasn't. When we'd finished putting and were ready to go to the first tee, he told Bobby to play well, and you could tell that he meant it.

Applause erupted from the bleachers alongside the first tee when we came inside the ropes. It was a strange kind of applause that came in two waves. One was from the people who could see, and then there was a second group that started a few seconds later. I glanced over that way and saw that several hundred blind people had found seats there. You could tell they were blind, because a lot of them had those long white sticks.

Out in the fairway Jose Maria Olazabal and Billy Mayfair were walking out of sight around the corner of the dogleg. It was time to play. The low murmur of the crowd died away, and I could hear a lark singing in one of the trees by the tee. But then all that fell away, and I saw only the hole. It lay before us like a winding road, and I felt as if all I had to do was drive. I pointed Bobby, he swung, and the ball went where we wanted it to go—down the fairway, onto the green.

He parred the first seven holes just like that. Bobby was giving me that feeling of being deep in the game, in the zone. I stopped noticing the sandy wastes in front of every tee. I was locked onto the targets we were aiming at. Bobby was hitting them.

The only distraction came between the seventh green and the eighth tee, where the guys from Allegheny Gap were lined up. Like Dr. Mehta, they must've driven half the night to get there. "Eadon Branch!" J. R. Neill called out. "Eadon Branch!" Conrad repeated.

Bobby stopped and grabbed the bag so I had to stop, too. He turned in the direction of the voices. "Hey, guys, how are you?" he said. "Nice of you to come up. 'Preciate it."

They beamed, and Bobby nudged the bag, telling me to move on.

I liked the way he handled it. He didn't lose his focus, and he made them happy at the same time.

Number 8 at Sand Valley is a tricky little par 4. I'd given Bobby the three-iron on the tee and set up a wedge second. It was a downhill lie—that was unavoidable. But he handled it, stiffing the wedge and nearly holing it. I aimed Bobby's putt a ball to the right of dead center, and it curled in. We were 1 under for the round.

From the way the crowd was yelling, you'd have thought we'd won the Ryder Cup or something. People screamed and yelled. I could only understand fragments. "All the way," I heard. "True vision." And the inevitable "You da man."

"Whatever you're doing, keep doing it," I whispered to Bobby.

He knocked his wedge to three feet and birdied nine. He parred ten, birdied eleven, and parred twelve. He parred thirteen, then birdied fourteen. The odd thing was, at first it didn't feel like he was hot, playing over his head. It felt like he was playing golf the way he should always play it.

No one else saw it that way. In fact, it started to look like the entire population of southern New Jersey was squeezed around the Sand Valley golf course, hanging from trees to get a glimpse of us.

I sneaked a look at the leaderboard as we waited to hit Bobby's tee shot on the fifteenth hole. He was 4 under for the day, even for the tournament. The only player ahead of him was Little Dickie Reynolds at 2 under. Everyone else except Jay Delsing had fallen back; he stood tied for fourth at 3 over.

Bobby's golf game had gotten to a new plane. It was effortless. It was joyful. But it wasn't something you could turn on like a television set and leave on. It was as delicate as a spider's web, as fleeting as water in your hands. The wait on the fifteenth tee was enough to cause it to leak away.

When it was finally cleared ahead of us, Bobby tried to do all the right things, but he wasn't where he'd been. He just started playing average golf on a harder-than-average golf course.

Bobby managed to par the next three, but it wasn't easy. He got up and down from a bunker on sixteen and chipped up close from the right side of the green on seventeen.

On the eighteenth tee Bobby hit his sloppiest drive of the day, a push into the rough on the right side. Then he hit an ugly little shot that was lucky to clear the pond near the green. It settled into the rough between two of the bunkers guarding the green.

"Sorry, Coach," he said. "Didn't put a good swing on that one."

Bobby grabbed the bag, and we started walking toward the little footbridge that spans the water that guards the green. The crowd was thick on both sides of the hole.

Suddenly a huge roar went up from the gallery. I followed the eyes of the sighted spectators to the scoreboard behind the green. The board showed that Little Dickie Reynolds had taken a 6 on the fifteenth hole.

"What is it?" Bobby asked. "Someone make birdie?"

"No, it's Little Dickie," I told him. "Bogeyed number fifteen."

"So where does that put us?" he wanted to know.

"Second," I said. "Stroke back."

"So if I par this one, I play with Little Dickie tomorrow?"

"Looks like it."

"All right," he said. "Let's go to work."

We found the ball, and he took the only stance available to him, with his rear foot in the bunker and his left foot in the grass. He choked down on his lob wedge, took a couple of practice strokes, and swung. Somehow he caught it just right. The ball popped up light as a balloon and floated up to the green, headed right for the flag. I could hear a thunk when it landed, but I couldn't see it. The green was above my head.

The swelling noise from the crowd told me it was a good shot. It got louder and louder as the ball rolled toward the hole. Then there was a moan. When I saw it on *SportsCenter* that night, I saw how the ball stopped on the edge of the hole and refused to fall in.

I stood up, grabbed Bobby's arm, and helped him out of the bunker. The crowd noise picked up as we came onto the green.

"Let's tap it in," I said, right in his ear. We did.

That touched off a new wave of cheering. I stepped away from Bobby, leaving him alone by the hole. The applause was coming in thunderous waves. Delsing tucked his putter under his arm and started clapping. Lizard joined in. Finally I did, too.

I GOT Bobby back into his suite. He said he wanted to lie down before dinner, so I left him alone. I had an urge to call Angela's room. No answer. As I hung up the phone, I decided I was lucky she hadn't been there. I'd had no idea what I would do or say if I actually saw her, and the odds were in that situation that I'd wind up saying something stupid. I decided to go for a walk.

J. R. Neill and Conrad Williams intercepted me by a row of quarter slots. They were wearing Eadon Branch golf hats. "Glad Bobby had a good round," J.R. said. "You bet our four hundred bucks?"

"Got eight hundred to one," I told them.

"Hot damn!" J.R. said.

"Don't go spending that money at the crap tables," I told Conrad. "We're a stroke down, and Little Dickie's a tough player. Lot of tough players out there."

"Doesn't matter," J.R. said. "I got a feeling about true vision."

"True vision!" Conrad chimed in. He was all but rubbing his hands together like a miser.

I tried to change the subject.

"So you drove straight through?" I asked.

"Damn straight," J.R. said. "And we brought your mother, too."

"Eudora?"

"You got another mother?" J.R. asked.

She was in the casino, playing blackjack with a couple of geezers at a five-dollar table. The dealer had a nine showing. Eudora had three hands going—a six, a four, and a three up. It was her play.

"Stick," I said, walking up behind her. "On all of 'em."

She recognized my voice, turned.

"I'm on a roll," I told Eudora. "Stick."

She just nodded and waved her hand over the cards. "I stick."

The dealer's expression never changed. She flipped over a five, dealt herself a queen, and paid Eudora three rose-colored chips.

"Told you," I said. I kissed her on the top of the head.

Eudora tossed one of her chips to the dealer and put the rest in the purse she was carrying, a white, woven purse that matched the white shoes she was wearing. She had on a pale green print dress.

"How d'you look so fresh after eight hours in a car?" I asked her.

"Well, we checked into a motel over by the golf course," she said. "Didn't think we could get a room here."

She closed her purse. "And of course, I didn't want to check in here if it'd upset your father. How're you two getting along?"

"You know how he is," I said. "Frustrating. Most of the time he sits and talks to himself or listens to voices in his head."

I think she was both sad and relieved. It would've hurt her to hear that I'd established a rapport with him. I put my arm around her shoulder. "I'm glad you're here," I said. "How about dinner tonight with me and Bobby?"

She brightened for just an instant. "Would your father be there?"

I nodded. "Dr. Mehta would be there, too."

She looked frightened. "I think I'd rather play blackjack, Henry," she said. "They'll probably comp me for a meal."

IT TURNED out to be just me and Bobby for dinner. Dr. Mehta decided that Clayton needed a quiet meal and an early bed. We still didn't know where Angela was.

The next morning, Sunday, I went back up to Bobby's suite for breakfast, but neither of us felt like eating much. When it was time to go, I pulled a hat from his Callaway collection and gave it to him.

"No," he said. "There's a hat in the closet I want to wear."

I went into the closet. On the shelf I found a beat-up old Eadon Branch hat he'd worn for practice that summer.

Neither one of us seemed to know what to say next. We just stood there like dopes.

"Well, I guess we better go," Bobby said. "We can't have the touring pro from Eadon Branch missing his tee time."

WHEN we got to the course, we were immediately surrounded. There were the state troopers walking around us, fending people off. There was the CBS crew. There were people from the PGA Tour. But it was a lonely cocoon. On the practice range nobody talked to us. I polished the clubs till you could've eaten with them.

Little Dickie Reynolds, our partner for the round, stayed on his end of the range. We stayed on ours. I knew his caddie, Albie Miller, a little bit. Albie nodded to me as they passed by. Little Dickie acted like he was the blind guy and couldn't see us.

Maybe Little Dickie wasn't thinking only about what he'd said about Bobby not deserving a chance. Maybe it was just his way.

On top of everything else, a weather front from the south had pushed up into New Jersey, and the air was muggy and close.

Bobby's game face softened for the first time when we got to the tee and the blind people in the gallery heard he was there. They went crazy, whooping and whistling and screaming.

Only when he saw the CBS camera crew move into position did Little Dickie walk up to Bobby with a broad smile on his face, grab him by the elbow so he'd know he was there, and say, "Bobby, best of luck today. Play well."

Bobby shook his hand. "Thanks, Dickie," he said. "I appreciate your kind thoughts. Same to you."

Our official for the day was Cade Benton. He tossed a coin, and Dickie called heads and won.

"Ladies and gentlemen, our two-o'clock pairing, please welcome, from Orlando, Florida, Dickie Reynolds." The crowd applauded politely, but underneath that sound I was sure I heard a few hisses from the blind section. So did Little Dickie.

But Dickie settled over the ball and hit a good, crisp three-wood into the neck of the dogleg.

I glanced to the right, and in the midst of a crowd of people with white canes, I saw Angela, wearing her Eadon Branch shirt. She smiled and held up a clenched fist. I'd been pumped up before I saw her. Now I was like the Pillsbury Doughboy.

"And from Dalton, Georgia, please welcome . . ."

The announcer didn't get Bobby's name out before the roar of the spectators drowned him out.

Bobby tipped his Eadon Branch hat, and I started forward toward the tee markers, but the noise was still coming. We had to wait an extra five or ten seconds before the last cheers and whistles faded.

I squatted, took hold of the club head, and laid it down behind the ball. For a moment I found it hard to breathe.

"Smooth three-wood," I told Bobby. "You know the shot. See it and hit it." Bobby swung smoothly, and the ball went where it was supposed to go. I exhaled.

Little Dickie's ball was five yards behind us, and he hit a seven-iron. It caught the bank on the edge of the green and tumbled down into the surrounding sand. From there he hit into a bunker on the other side of the green, then 3-putted after he chipped up.

Bobby parred the hole. Little Dickie started off with a 7. We didn't get close to the place we were at in the previous round, when the game seemed effortless. I felt every creak when I squatted down behind Bobby, and he was fidgety over the ball. But we managed to par the next five holes. So did Little Dickie.

Up ahead we heard a tremendous roar.

"Sounds like an eagle," Bobby said. "Duval?"

"I'm not looking at scoreboards," I said. And it was true.

Bobby had his three-wood out. He twirled it around in his hands. Ahead of us the fairway cleared.

"You're up, Mr. Jobe," Cade Benton said.

"Three-wood, Coach?"

The wind kicked up some—not much, maybe a club's worth.

"Two-iron," I said. I explained why.

I pulled the club, and we started getting set. As he held the shaft against his thighs to align himself, the wind died down. He lifted his head. "Still want two-iron?" he asked.

I told him yes. I figured wrong. He tried to hit the two-iron too hard, to make up for the loss of the wind. The ball faded right, then lit in the rough, bounced once, and disappeared in grass.

Little Dickie hit his own tee shot, a three-wood, straight down the middle. We trekked to the ball. Our lie was terrible. The ball had all but disappeared in the rough.

I guided Bobby's hand to the grass a foot behind the ball.

"Think I can get a four-iron on it?" he asked.

"Nah. Five-iron, wedge it close, and make par," I suggested.

I waited for him to argue with me, but he didn't. He bent down again and ran his fingers through the rough. "Okay, Coach," he said mildly. "Whatever you say."

He took the wedge and hacked the ball out into the fairway. The applause after the shot was scattered and hesitant. I could almost hear what was going through people's minds. The bad tee shot, the cautious recover—the gallery figured this was where Bobby Jobe started to lose it. I think Little Dickie thought that way. He drilled a two-iron down the fairway for his second shot, stiffed a wedge, and made birdie. Bobby missed a twenty-five-foot par putt and made bogey. As best I could figure it going off the seventh green, we were tied.

We had a new rhythm, though. The routine probably looked the same. But it felt like Bobby and I had merged, somehow. In a sense, we started playing better, even, than we had on Saturday. The crowd seemed to fall away. I can't tell you whether people kept yelling as we played the next seven or eight holes. I assume they did. But I didn't hear them.

We got to the sixteenth tee, and Bobby changed our focus.

"Coach, I think we need to know where we stand," he said.

He was right. The sixteenth is a hole you can play different ways, depending on the situation. So I looked at the scoreboard behind the tee. "You're still tied for the lead with Reynolds," I said quietly.

We heard a roar from down below, at the sixteenth green. The numbers on the board changed, clicking.

"Delsing's in third, a shot back," I reported. "He just birdied."

Bobby shook his head. "Guess he's hot."

I felt that unity between us start to crack. "Don't start thinking about Delsing," I said. "Let's think about this hole."

"Doesn't matter what he does," Bobby said. "We need a birdie here if we're gonna win this thing."

"Let's play it aggressive," I said.

Little Dickie still had the honor, and when he lined up his shot, I could see that he was thinking the same way we were. He aimed down the right side, swung, and hit a tremendous drive that landed a long way down the fairway.

I had an idea. "Let's hit a three-wood," I said to Bobby.

"I thought you wanted to be aggressive."

"It is, the way you're hitting it," I said.

I lined him up. It was one of those times when I thought not seeing was an advantage. The view from the tee was a long stretch of desert. The fairway was only a distant stubble of green.

"Straight out there, Bobby, nice and smooth."

That's the way he hit it.

"Radar-guided," I whispered to him. "Homing in on the target." The ball landed. "And we have a confirmed hit."

Suddenly I was aware of the crowd. It just roared all around us.

Neither of us said anything more as we walked up the fairway to the ball. There was no need to. We both knew what had to be done.

By the time we putted in, the noise from the people echoed off the pines. Little Dickie's approach shot had reached the green, but he had missed his first putt, and we were a stroke in front.

We walked to the seventeenth through a narrow gap in the mob. I tried not to think of the $800,000. I tried not to think about what I'd say to Angela if we won, or paying off Eudora's loan and telling Jimmy Edmisten where to stuff his coal mine, or of calling in experts, Nobel Prize chemists, to come up with a drug to bring back Clayton Mote. I tried not to think of any of that stuff, and of course, I failed.

Ahead of us I could see that Delsing was getting ready to hit.

He swung. The ball got airborne, headed for the flag, dropping toward the green.

The earth moved.

An instant later Delsing's ball rolled into the hole for an eagle.

I KNOW. A lot of people don't believe there was an earthquake at Sand Valley that day. But I know what I felt. And I know what five thousand other people around the seventeenth hole did. They yelled and screeched, startled, the way you might be if you came upon a snake in your bare feet.

No sooner did the startled, frightened yelling hit my ear than it was replaced by an astonished, appreciative roar that came from the seventeenth green and spread down the fairway toward us on the tee. I've seen what happened on television replays. Delsing had hit a nine-iron into the green. It lit ten feet past the hole and started drawing back. Then it broke sharply right and fell into the hole. He'd made a deuce and jumped past Bobby into first place. When Delsing figured it out, Lizard Ziomecki jumped into his arms, and they both fell to their knees on the grass.

Did the earthquake cause the ball to fall in? I don't know.

I do know that Bobby nearly fell over when the ground billowed.

"What's happening?" he demanded.

"I'm not sure," I said. "But I think we just had an earthquake, and I think Delsing just holed out from the fairway."

The scene in front of us was chaotic. A lot of people ran into the fairway. I guess they were trying to get away from the tremors. It took ten minutes for the security cops to get everyone back behind the ropes. By that time the scoreboard had changed, showing Delsing in the lead.

When the fairway ahead was clear, Cade Benton turned to Bobby. "Mr. Jobe, you're up," he said.

Bobby straightened his back and turned his head toward the fairway, almost as if he could see the hole.

"I think four," I said. "Same as yesterday."

I pulled the club, put it in his hands, and we got set up. He set, swung, and the click was solid and pure. The shot took off toward the horizon, hung there, and then fell gently toward the right, just as we'd envisioned. When it landed, I was surprised. It looked ten or twenty yards closer to the end of the fairway than it should have. Bobby was that pumped up. The crowd cheered.

"If I was any more juiced," he said, "I could get an endorsement deal from Tropicana."

It was Little Dickie's turn. He had not one but two strokes to make up on Delsing, so he absolutely had to have a birdie here.

When the spectators saw a driver in his hand, they cheered and whistled. It didn't help. Little Dickie yanked it. He was way left, and the ball settled on the downslope of a bunker.

We had 110 to the hole, a sand wedge. Bobby hit it straight at the flag. The ball flew at the pin and seemed to disappear.

The sound of the crowd told me and Bobby that something odd had happened. I couldn't see it.

"What?" Bobby demanded.

"I don't know," I said. "Sounds like it might be close."

I saw David Feherty from CBS fifteen feet away. He was looking into his cameraman's monitor and jumping up and down.

"You hit the flag!" Feherty shouted. "You're two feet!"

"My God," Bobby said.

He was standing there, numb. I took the club out of his hands and stuffed it into the bag, then grabbed him by the elbow. He stayed abreast of me, and we walked to the green together.

The crowd was frenzied now. I saw people crying. That's how intense it was.

"It's going to happen," Bobby said to me. "We're going to birdie this hole and birdie the next and win the PGA."

"Don't get ahead of yourself," I warned him.

We came up the little rise in front of the green, and I saw the ball for the first time. It was just below the hole, a straight putt, two feet away. I marked the ball, and then Little Dickie started focusing on his bunker shot. He looked at it up, down, and sideways.

In the mass of spectators pressing against the ropes, my eyes fell on Angela, Clayton, and Dr. Mehta. They had somehow gotten themselves into the front row.

Little Dickie was grinding his feet into the sand, trying to get firmly planted over his ball. It wasn't easy; the slope he was on was about as steep as a bunker can be. He hacked at the ball. It took off low and hot, skipped once on the green, and settled into a bunker on the other side. The crowd oohed sympathetically.

Little Dickie had one chance left to win the tournament, and it depended on holing his next bunker shot. He came close. I'll give him credit for that. But the ball missed the hole by an inch or two. He knocked that one in. Finally it was our turn.

I squatted behind the ball. It was dead straight. I got Bobby lined up and told him what to do. "Two feet, straight, firm."

I put the blade down behind the ball, and he started shifting his feet. Then I saw that his hands were trembling. "Nice and smooth," I said. "Back of the cup."

"My hands are shaking," he whispered.

"You've made putts with shaking hands before," I whispered.

Finally the club moved. He didn't put the worst stroke on the ball I'd ever seen. But he yipped it. The ball headed for the left corner of the hole, caught the left edge, spun around and then spun back out and hung on the lip. A horseshoe.

The sounds told Bobby what'd happened. There was no plunk as the ball dropped in. There was a gasp from the gallery.

"Oh, no," Bobby said. He slumped forward. "Oh, no."

He stayed like that a moment. Then he straightened up, turned his head toward the sky. A sound rumbled from his throat, then burst out. It was a single word: "No!"

I stood up then, too, and grabbed him around the shoulders.

"I choked, Greyhound," he said in a low, strained voice.

"You hit a good putt," I told him. "I misread it."

He didn't buy it. "I choked like a dog," he said. "I always find ways to lose."

"We haven't lost yet," I said. "There's one hole still to play."

EVERYONE on the golf course was around the eighteenth hole. They were ten and twenty deep all along both sides of the fairway.

I looked for Angela or Eudora or Clayton, but they'd submerged in the crowd. It was just faces, thousands of faces.

"Lot of people out there." I described it to Bobby.

He didn't say anything. I checked the pin sheet. "The hole's right where Jello McKay said it would be," I told him. "Right front. We gotta drive down the left side to get at it."

Bobby shook his head. "I can't believe I missed that damn putt."

"Forget that putt," I told him. "It's done."

"That was it! The tournament, handed to me. And I blew it."

"It's not over yet," I said. "We can still birdie this hole."

I looked at the leaderboard. It hadn't changed. I looked back at Bobby. Drops of sweat were dripping off the bill of his cap now. I reached up with my towel and wiped them.

Ahead of us Duval hit his shot to the green.

"We're up," I said.

Whispering, I laid out the fairway for Bobby one more time and told him where I was aiming him. "Let it out on this one," I said. I gave him the driver and set him up. He took it back slowly, very slowly, then crushed the ball. It blasted out against the sky. It was straight and true, a beautiful sight.

"Dinner and a movie," I said to him before the noise from the crowd rolled over us.

I picked up the bag, stuffed the driver back in, and waited for Bobby to latch on. Dickie hit, and we set off through the sand.

I didn't know, obviously, what it felt like to walk down the last fairway as the winner of a major championship. I couldn't imagine the cheers and applause being any louder.

"Stop a second," I heard Bobby say. So I stopped, and I felt his hand work its way up the bag toward my shoulder, and in a second he was abreast of me, his arm around me.

"Okay, Coach," he said. "Let's go."

So we walked that way, together, down the wide green fairway. I closed my eyes for a couple of seconds and just listened and smelled, taking it in the way Bobby was taking it in.

"It ain't winning," Bobby murmured, "but I don't feel too bad."

"Beats the hell out of the Cooters Tour," I agreed, "and you can still win."

I left Bobby by the bag and paced off the yardage as Little Dickie got ready to hit. He looked angry. He needed to hole his shot to tie Delsing, but he hit to the safe, left side of the green. I think he'd given up on the tournament, and he just wanted to beat Bobby.

It was our turn. I told Bobby what happened.

"Fifty-eight to the front. Sixty-three to the hole," I said.

"Seven?"

"Eight, I think. Tropicana."

He nodded. "Sounds good."

He seemed like a smoothly running machine again as he took the club. I set him up, aimed him straight at the pin. Bobby made his best swing of the day. From takeaway to follow-through it was like the drawings in Hogan's book—precise, powerful, graceful.

It was, of course, a little too good. He hit it ten yards farther than he ever hit an eight-iron. It flew thirty feet past the hole, right over the flag, hit the green, and stopped dead.

"Long?" he asked me.

"Some," I said. "Sorry. I misclubbed you. Let's make the putt."

We walked the same way, his arm around my shoulder, up the last bit of fairway and over the footbridge that spanned the creek in front of the green. "Something I want to tell you," I said to Bobby.

"What's that?"

"The way you pulled yourself together after you missed that putt. The way you hit these last two shots—you did good, Bobby."

He smiled, half chuckled. "I think that's the first time you've ever told me that, Greyhound."

When we got to the green, Dickie lagged his putt to a foot. He tapped in. I hunkered down to study Bobby's putt. It looked familiar, and then I remembered why. It was the putt Jello McKay had shown me that first evening when we walked the course together.

We walked the line of the putt, and I got Bobby set up. "Thirty-two feet," I said to him. "A touch uphill. Putt for thirty-five."

I looked at Bobby's hands. They were trembling again.

He stroked the putt. I heard a solid click as the blade met the ball. Trembling hands or no, this one looked good.

Halfway to the hole, we were in a playoff. Ten feet away, the ball was still hugging the line I'd planned. And then I could see the spike mark in its path. "Roll over it," I breathed.

"In the hole!" people were screeching.

The ball hit the spike mark. It hopped. It wobbled ever so slightly to the right, then resumed its roll. And then it was at the hole, rolling over the right lip, and coming to a stop two inches past the cup, straight behind it. The moan from the crowd let Bobby know. He dropped the putter and stood stock-still.

I fell from a squat to my knees. I've seen the pictures of that moment, including the one the next week spread over two pages of *Sports Illustrated*. The picture makes it look like I'd been praying for the putt to go in, and that's what the caption said. "Unanswered prayer: Caddie Greyhound Mote's anguished face reflects the fate of Bobby Jobe's last putt at the PGA."

That's a crock. I was just so shocked when the putt missed that I lost my balance. But I don't deny I was upset. I wanted to stand up and yell, "Wait! Let's do it over!" But you can't do it over, of course. What I did was stand up and put a hand on Bobby's shoulder.

"Sorry, Henry," Bobby said.

"No, I'm sorry," I told him. "You hit it just right."

I told him about the spike mark.

He grinned. "I thought I hit it good. Thanks for telling me."

I couldn't believe he was smiling. "You okay?" I asked him.

"Well," he said, "I intend to do some serious damage to the mini-bar tonight. But yeah, I'm okay."

I put my arm around his shoulders. He drew back a little.

"Don't hug me, Henry," he said. "If you do, I might lose it."

I turned the hug into a slap on the back. "Can't do that. Got a tap-in left," I said. He nodded, and I set him up. The putt hit the bottom of the cup with a clunk.

The next ten minutes are a blur. I remember the crowd, standing and cheering. I remember quick handshakes from Little Dickie and Albie. I remember Delsing coming out onto the green and embracing Bobby so hard that their hats got knocked off. Delsing was crying, and in a strange way I was glad to see that. It reminded me to feel good for him and Lizard. They'd been plugging away on the tour for a long time, and this win meant a lot to them. Feeling good for them took some of the sting out of finishing second.

Only after all that had happened did I realize I'd just lost my bet and the $800,000 that would have changed my life.

I TOOK Bobby to the scorer's tent and then to the media center. But I didn't go in with him. I didn't want to waste any time locating the people I wanted to see. So I turned Bobby over to one of Cade Benton's girls and told him I'd meet him at the car.

I found Angela, Dr. Mehta, and Clayton Mote standing in the players parking lot. They were a strange trio—the redheaded woman in the Mets hat and the Eadon Branch golf shirt, the Indian doctor with a body like a bowling pin, and the old man, his head cocked to one side, talking to himself.

Angela gave me a hug.

"Well done, Henry," she whispered. "I'm proud of you."

"What?" I said. I stepped back from her arms. "We lost the tournament." She didn't bother to argue with me. We both knew I was only pretending not to know what she meant.

"No gimmes," Clayton said loudly.

"I know, Dad," I said. I stepped toward him, wanting a hug, a touch, some kind of physical contact. He shrank away.

"No gimmes," he said, a little panicky. "No gimmes."

Dr. Mehta stepped up and put a reassuring hand on his elbow. Clayton calmed down.

"So," I said, "where would you all like to eat dinner? I think Bobby ought to be done with the media in fifteen minutes or so."

Mehta shook his head. "We cannot. I promised the hospital we would return tonight, and we must drop Angela at the airport."

I looked at Angela. "You're leaving right away?"

"I have to be at work tomorrow," she said.

I thought fleetingly about telling her I needed her to stay, but I couldn't quite believe it would do any good. She kissed me on the cheek. "Have a good celebration, Henry," she said.

Somewhere in my mind I was thinking that I had to take her in my arms and tell her I loved her and that whatever it took, I would do. But that was in the back of my mind. In the front of my mind I was still taking rejection with class. "We'll miss you," I said.

She blinked a couple of times, and I flattered myself into thinking she might be trying to hold back tears.

"I appreciate that, Henry," she said. "More than you know."

I shook Dr. Mehta's hand and thanked him very quickly. And I gave Angela one last brief hug.

I then turned to Clayton. He looked like he was trying to say something but couldn't. "D-d-d" was the sound he made.

It was painful to watch him. So I pulled him toward me and hugged him. I could feel his body stiffen and try to pull away. Then, for just a few seconds, he changed. He pulled closer to me, and his head was against my shoulder. His lips were very close to my ear.

"Don't," he whispered, and I thought he was saying he didn't want to be hugged. I let him go. But he clung to me, his fingers digging hard into my shoulders.

"Don't let her go," he said, looking at the ground.

His voice had been so low only I could hear it.

I blinked, unsure I'd actually heard him say those words. He couldn't have shocked me more if he'd cut down a power line and stuck it in my ear. I couldn't think, couldn't respond. I just moved on autopilot, took his arm, and opened the back door of the car. I made sure he fastened his seat belt. I waved as they drove away.

I HEADED back to the media center to find Bobby. I remember thinking that I shouldn't have been feeling so good. I'd lost the tournament. I'd lost Angela. I'd lost the bet that would have saved Eadon Branch for Eudora. Not only that, but I was very tired. It had been a long week.

Truth be told, I was feeling very good.

Bobby came out of the media center before I could get there, hanging on to the arm of one of Cade Benton's helpers, a woman named Debbie. Debbie, I noticed, was a good-looking blonde, maybe twenty-eight, with a short skirt and a helluva body.

"Mr. Mote!" Debbie called out. Then she turned to Bobby. "He's right over there," she said.

We met halfway across the parking lot.

"Uh, Henry, I got something for you," Bobby said. He thrust a piece of paper toward me, and I took it. I didn't unfold it. I almost didn't want to know what he'd written on it. Was it the usual seven percent caddie fee for a top ten finish? Or was it maybe the fifty percent I'd mentioned when I gave him the check to pay for the lawyer to sue the PGA? I was afraid it was the seven percent. I might've stood there, hesitating, for a long time. But Bobby was waiting, and Debbie was watching. I unfolded it.

It was a check made out to Henry Mote, drawn on the PGA Championship's prize account, for $400,000.

"That's second-place money," Bobby said. "I'm not much good at saying thanks. But thanks."

I blinked. "Uh, Bobby, that's too much," I said.

"No, it isn't," Bobby replied. "They made it out the way I told 'em." Bobby was smiling.

"But you need the money," I said.

"Nah," Bobby said. "Callaway's already talking about a new contract. My agent's left messages. Only money problems I'm going to have are tax problems. I want you to have that."

"Well, thanks," I said. "It's a helluva lot for caddying."

"You're welcome. You did a lot more than caddy for me."

I nodded, but I couldn't say anything. I was suddenly overcome with the knowledge that I would not be doing it for him much longer. Bobby, I guess, found the silence awkward, but it was the awkwardness of the moment, too. We weren't used to being nice to one another.

"Well, don't spend it all in one place."

"Sorry, Bobby," I said. "But that's exactly what I'm going to do."

Chapter 8

It was April again at Eadon Branch. The magnolia by the fourth fairway had bloomed. The stream was running high, and the grass was lush and fragrant. I was watching the third round of the Masters on television in the clubhouse. I was drinking a beer. Things change, though. This was draft beer, in a cup.

On the screen above the counter Bobby Jobe stood over a birdie putt on the eighteenth green. Jello McKay squatted behind him in his white Augusta National coveralls, aligning the putter.

"Too low, Jello," I whispered.

Bobby stroked the putt; his action looked smooth and buttery. The ball rolled toward the hole without the slightest bump or twitch, hugging that gorgeous Augusta grass.

"Get in the jar!" J. R. Neill yelled.

"In the jar!" Conrad urged.

Halfway there the ball seemed to have a chance. But it slowed, and died a foot away on the low side. The crowd at Augusta moaned. So did the crowd at Eadon Branch, maybe fifty people packed into the clubhouse, all dirty, tired, and sweating.

"Jobe will have a tap-in for a round of seventy, three strokes off the pace going into tomorrow's final round," Jim Nantz said.

"You were right. Too low. If you'd been there, he'd've made it," J.R. said.

"I don't know," I said, but I was pleased by the compliment. "Hard to tell on TV. Jello knows how to read greens."

"Don't be modest, Henry," Eudora said.

"You think he'll win?" Conrad asked me.

I shrugged. "I hope so. He's bound to win one of these times."

Out by the first tee the amplified sound of guitars tuning up drowned out the sound of a commercial. I grabbed Eudora's remote and turned off the set. "Okay," I announced. "Clubhouse is closed. Kegs are open. Band's starting up. Party time!"

The crowd streamed outside. The sun was getting low behind Eadon Mountain, and shadows were lengthening on the ninth and first fairways. The air might've smelled like honeysuckle and grass clippings except for the overpowering scent of roasting pork from the barbecue pit we'd fashioned.

On a little wooden bandstand we'd built for the evening by the lesson tee, Midnight Rodeo was ready to play. The lead guitar started in, and then the drummer and the harmonica. It was a song called "Eadon Mountain Hoedown," which never got famous because no one like Patsy Cline ever recorded it. But folks around Allegheny Gap played it all the time:

> *Moonlight gleams on a whiskey still*
> *Way up top of a green-tree'd hill . . .*

When they got to the chorus, I stepped up to the mike and spoke. The music kept going behind me, like an engine idling.

"I'd like to welcome you all to the First Annual Eadon Branch Golf Club Stump Pull and Pig Pickin'," I said. "And I'd like to thank all of you who helped out today clearing the land for the tenth hole. I hope you'll be back tomorrow to help with number eleven."

"We're all gonna be hung over!" Raymond yelled.

"That's all right, Raymond," I said. "We weren't going to let you operate any machinery anyway."

People laughed. I felt somehow taller and better-looking.

"Anyway," I concluded, "Eudora and I thought this was the best way to thank everyone. We want you to know that if things go according to plan, by the time we have the Fifth Annual Stump Pull and Pig Pickin', we expect to be clearing land for the eighteenth hole. In the meantime we ought to have the best damn eleven-hole golf course in the country by this time next year! So drink up and eat up, 'cause we have lots to celebrate!"

There was a cheer then, and the band picked it up. I hung around on the bandstand and sang the chorus with them.

> *"Grab that girl with the blue dress on.*
> *She looks like she could dance till dawn.*
> *Knows how to step and knows how to twirl.*
> *Don't you know she's an Eadon Mountain girl."*

Something strange happened to me right at that moment. The music, the urge to sing, just blew right out of me like the air going out of a punctured tire. I stepped off the stage and walked alone back into the clubhouse, sipping a beer.

I went to the pay phone and dug around in my wallet till I found the folded scrap of paper that had Angela's phone number on it. It wasn't the first time I'd thought about calling her. I'd thought about it lots of times. But this time I dialed her number. It rang four times. Then I knew I was going to get her machine.

I was sort of relieved, actually. The machine couldn't say no.

"Um, hi, Angela. It's Henry. Henry Mote. We were having a party here at Eadon Branch, and I was thinking about you. Kind of wish you were here. So, anyway . . ." I stopped. I wasn't quite sure what I wanted to say. "I wish you were here is all," I finished. I hung up.

I felt kind of stupid, waiting all that time to call her and then not having anything smart to say when I finally did. I went over to the lunch counter, pulled myself another beer, and turned the TV back on. Ken Venturi was talking about who still had a chance to win the Masters. Bobby was on his list.

When the Masters was over, I got up to walk outside and rejoin the party. The phone rang. "Eadon Branch Golf Club," I said.

"So you wish I was there, huh?"

"Angela?" I knew who it was, but I asked anyway.

"Look out the window, Henry," she said.

I almost yanked the phone out of the wall getting to the window. She was standing in our parking lot, holding a cell phone to her ear, in the middle of a row of pickup trucks. She was wearing her Eadon Branch hat, with her red hair spilling out under it, and a plaid shirt and jeans. She looked prettier than on that first April afternoon when I saw her a year ago. She waved at me.

"So," she said, "are you going to invite me to your party?"

I finally was able to say something. "How'd you know to call?"

"This phone tells me when I have messages," she said. "I was driving up here and talking to Bobby in Augusta. When I hung up, I saw you'd called."

I went outside. "Spring has officially arrived at Eadon Branch," I said, smiling at her. "You look beautiful, Angela."

She blushed enough that it was visible against the fire of the lowering sun. "Why, thank you, Henry," she said.

Without saying anything more, I took a step toward her, and she opened her arms and I hugged her. She felt small and light and very good pressed against me. When I pulled back a little from her, I kept my arm around her. "What made you decide to come?"

"Partly Bobby. He told me that as a minority stockholder, he needed someone up here to make sure you did things right."

"Partly Bobby?" I asked her.

"Partly," she said. "Show me what you did today."

I took her hand and walked her over toward the other side of the clubhouse, where we'd spent the day cutting trees.

"You trained Jello well," she said.

"He didn't need much help."

We came around to where the tenth tee was going to be. It didn't look like much, of course. It was just a long brown gash in the woods, stakes with orange ribbons on them, piles of tree trunks.

"The green's going to be like number ten at Sand Valley."

"The Devil's Gullet bunker?" she asked.

"Like that." I nodded. "If I can get it to drain right."

"The pro will like it, I bet," she said.

"I hope so," I told her. "I hope he can get here in the fall."

"Any word on the new medication?"

"Dr. Mehta says he's hopeful, but it's too soon to tell."

We'd been talking all around the main thing that was on my mind, and finally I asked her.

"Why else did you come here, besides Bobby?"

"To see you," she said a little shyly. She didn't exactly look at me when she said it. She was looking toward Eadon Mountain, and the sun was full in her eyes, making her skin pale.

"I should've invited you," I said. "I'm sorry."

She turned her face and looked straight at me. "Don't apologize," she said. "I didn't treat you very well back in Atlantic City."

"Oh, no, you were fine," I told her.

"I've been thinking a lot since then," she said.

"What about?"

"About appropriate men." She just let that hang there.

I smiled. "I've been thinking a lot, too."

"What about?"

"I've been thinking how much more appropriate I'm feeling."

"Seems like every time I see you, you look more appropriate to me, too," she said. She smiled, and I took that as an invitation. I kissed her, and it felt like that time we kissed at Gully's, except more deliberate, more confident. Happier. Like we were younger and older at the same time.

She took my hand. We strolled down by the pond. The top of the willow tree was still touched by the last rays of the sun, but down by the ground it was all in shadow. The pond was still and dark.

Up by the clubhouse, Midnight Rodeo started playing "Crazy," just the way they had that night at Gully's.

Angela came into my arms, and we pretended to dance, our feet scraping the dirt back and forth. She hummed a few bars along with the song; then I sang a few, about crazy for trying and crazy for crying. Angela cocked her head back sideways a little and looked at me.

"Why, Henry," she said. "I didn't know you could sing."

Neither, I told her, had I.

BOB CULLEN

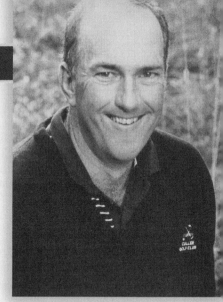

*Cullen finds references to golf
even in flying pumpkins.*

"People tend to become what they think about themselves," says Bob Cullen, the author of four nonfiction books with Bob Rotella on the mental side of golf. "It sounds simplistic, but it's very powerful advice." This is the core sentiment that propels golf pro Bobby Jobe to become a true winner in Cullen's witty novel, *A Mulligan for Bobby Jobe*. A sense of humor, of course, is another essential ingredient for success—in golf as well as in life. In a philosophical book about his favorite sport—*Why Golf?*—Cullen delights in drawing parallels between a 300-yard drive and the arc a pumpkin makes when it is shot through the air from a homemade compressed-air cannon, something he once saw at a "Punkin' Chunkin'" contest in Sussex County, Delaware. The inspiration for Bobby Jobe was far more grounded. "He was based on all the boys I knew and envied growing up who had natural ability at whatever sport they tried," the author says.

While serving as *Newsweek*'s Moscow correspondent during the collapse of the Soviet Union—"the best assignment a journalist could hope for"—Cullen was once interrogated by the KGB. This became not just a good dinner-party anecdote but the germ of a story idea that led to his popular Colin Burke thriller series in the 1990s.

Bob Cullen resides in Chevy Chase, Maryland, where he sometimes plays "twilight golf" with his two children.

The volumes in this series are issued
every two to three months. A typical volume
contains four outstanding books in condensed
form. None of the selections in any volume has
appeared in *Reader's Digest* magazine. Any reader
may receive this service by writing to
The Reader's Digest Association (Canada) Ltd.,
1125 Stanley Street, Montreal, Quebec H3B 5H5.

Some of the titles in this volume are also
available in a large-print format. For information about
Select Editions Large Type, call 1-800-877-5293.

ACKNOWLEDGMENTS

Pages 6–7, 8: illustrations by Jeff Wack
Page 157: photo by Patrick Demarchelier, Inc.
Pages 158–159, 160: illustrations by Janine Megna
Page 327: photo by John Apai/M Photography
Pages 328–329, 330: illustrations by Peter Fiore
Page 443: photo by Sarah Fernbaker
Pages 444–445, 446: illustrations by Craig White
Page 575: photo © Catherine Cullen

The original editions of the books in this volume are published and copyrighted as follows:
Envy, published by Warner Books, Inc.,
distributed by H.B. Fenn and Company Ltd at $36.95
© 2001 by Sandra Brown Management, Ltd.
Secret Sanction, published by Warner Books, Inc.,
distributed by H.B. Fenn and Company Ltd. at $34.95
© 2001 by Brian Haig
Entering Normal, published by The Ballantine Publishing Group,
a division of Random House, Inc.,
distributed by Random House of Canada Limited at $36.00
© 2001 by Anne D. LeClaire
A Mulligan for Bobby Jobe, published by HarperCollins Publishers, Inc.,
distributed by Harper Collins Canada Ltd. at $39.50
© 2001 by Bob Cullen

BOB CULLEN

"People tend to become what they think about themselves," says Bob Cullen, the author of four nonfiction books with Bob Rotella on the mental side of golf. "It sounds simplistic, but it's very powerful advice." This is the core sentiment that propels golf pro Bobby Jobe to become a true winner in Cullen's witty novel, *A Mulligan for Bobby Jobe*. A sense of humor, of course, is

Cullen finds references to golf even in flying pumpkins.

another essential ingredient for success—in golf as well as in life. In a philosophical book about his favorite sport—*Why Golf?*—Cullen delights in drawing parallels between a 300-yard drive and the arc a pumpkin makes when it is shot through the air from a homemade compressed-air cannon, something he once saw at a "Punkin' Chunkin' " contest in Sussex County, Delaware. The inspiration for Bobby Jobe was far more grounded. "He was based on all the boys I knew and envied growing up who had natural ability at whatever sport they tried," the author says.

While serving as *Newsweek*'s Moscow correspondent during the collapse of the Soviet Union—"the best assignment a journalist could hope for"—Cullen was once interrogated by the KGB. This became not just a good dinner-party anecdote but the germ of a story idea that led to his popular Colin Burke thriller series in the 1990s.

Bob Cullen resides in Chevy Chase, Maryland, where he sometimes plays "twilight golf" with his two children.

The volumes in this series are issued
every two to three months. A typical volume
contains four outstanding books in condensed
form. None of the selections in any volume has
appeared in *Reader's Digest* magazine. Any reader
may receive this service by writing to
The Reader's Digest Association (Canada) Ltd.,
1125 Stanley Street, Montreal, Quebec H3B 5H5.

Some of the titles in this volume are also
available in a large-print format. For information about
Select Editions Large Type, call 1-800-877-5293.

ACKNOWLEDGMENTS

Pages 6–7, 8: illustrations by Jeff Wack
Page 157: photo by Patrick Demarchelier, Inc.
Pages 158–159, 160: illustrations by Janine Megna
Page 327: photo by John Apai/M Photography
Pages 328–329, 330: illustrations by Peter Fiore
Page 443: photo by Sarah Fernbaker
Pages 444–445, 446: illustrations by Craig White
Page 575: photo © Catherine Cullen

The original editions of the books in this volume are published and copyrighted as follows:
Envy, published by Warner Books, Inc.,
distributed by H.B. Fenn and Company Ltd at $36.95
© 2001 by Sandra Brown Management, Ltd.
Secret Sanction, published by Warner Books, Inc.,
distributed by H.B. Fenn and Company Ltd. at $34.95
© 2001 by Brian Haig
Entering Normal, published by The Ballantine Publishing Group,
a division of Random House, Inc.,
distributed by Random House of Canada Limited at $36.00
© 2001 by Anne D. LeClaire
A Mulligan for Bobby Jobe, published by HarperCollins Publishers, Inc.,
distributed by Harper Collins Canada Ltd. at $39.50
© 2001 by Bob Cullen